ISBN 978-1-330-79327-5
PIBN 10106147

This book is a reproduction of an important historical work. Forgotten Books uses
state-of-the-art technology to digitally reconstruct the work, preserving the original format
whilst repairing imperfections present in the aged copy. In rare cases, an imperfection in
the original, such as a blemish or missing page, may be replicated in our edition. We do,
however, repair the vast majority of imperfections successfully; any imperfections that
remain are intentionally left to preserve the state of such historical works.

1 MONTH OF
FREE
READING

at
www.ForgottenBooks.com

By purchasing this book you are eligible for one month membership to ForgottenBooks.com, giving you unlimited access to our entire collection of over 700,000 titles via our web site and mobile apps.

To claim your free month visit:

www.forgottenbooks.com/free106147

Similar Books Are Available from
www.forgottenbooks.com

Trial of

Sedd

EDITED BY

Filson Young

EDINBURGH AND LONDON

AM HODGE & CO

SR

PRINTED BY
WILLIAM HODGE AND COMPANY
GLASGOW AND EDINBURGH
1914

TO

EDWARD MARSHALL HALL, K.C., M.P.

PREFACE.

VERY few people can hear an important criminal trial. The ordinary Court of law has accommodation for only a small audience, and few even of those whose interest is professional have the time to devote nine or ten consecutive days to the hearing of a single case. Yet the things that take place in these Courts are done in the name of every citizen, and when the judge and jury deprive a man of liberty or life, they do it on our behalf and with our authority. It is therefore of moment that the public should have the means of studying at leisure, in such carefully prepared records as those of the series in which this volume appears, the working of this immensely important machine to which people's lives and liberties are entrusted. And I cannot imagine any more interesting exercise in the judicial faculties for a thoughtful and reflective person than to read the evidence carefully and attentively, away from the personal distractions of the Court, where he can concentrate his mind on its significance sentence by sentence, and attempt to come to a calm judgment. One sees, in such a record, human nature laid bare; one follows, link by link, the chain composed of causes followed by their surprising effects; and one observes, far from the emotional storm that inspired the crime, the cold and durable nature of a man's acts when all the passion has died out of them and the tale is told and the reckoning to be paid. But the study must be made with patience and restraint. The tendency of the ordinary amateur in these matters is to make up his mind quite early in the case (it is what I am convinced nearly all jurymen do), and to throw down the book when the evidence has been half read, saying, " I am sure he did it " or " I am sure he is innocent," as the case may be. I need not say that a record like that which I am presenting in the following pages will be both useless and uninteresting if it is treated in this manner, but that if it be patiently read to the end it will not only engage the reader's curiosity and afford him a very considerable mental exercise, but inspire some sober reflections on the present-day administration of the criminal law.

I wish to record my thanks to the Lord Chief-Justice, who, as Attorney-General at the time of the trial, kindly placed at my disposal certain official records which would not otherwise have been available to me; to Sir Charles Darling for courtesies which he extended to me in regard to the proceedings in the Court of Criminal Appeal; to Mr. E. Marshall Hall, K.C., M.P , for not only giving me access to the whole material of the case in his possession, but for much friendly assistance and advice; and to Mr. T. Walter Saint, Seddon's solicitor, who spared time out of some very busy days to come and give me the benefit of his personal knowledge and information, and who also afforded me the use of many valuable documents.   FILSON YOUNG.

CONTENTS.

LIST OF ILLUSTRATIONS.

TRIAL OF THE SEDDONS.

INTRODUCTION.

THE great importance of the Seddon case lies in the fact that it focusses in itself a number of changes which have gradually been developing in the administration of the criminal law; and it is likely to be epoch-marking for this and various other reasons. First of all it will stand as a classical example of the working of the Prisoners' Evidence Act in capital cases. If Seddon had not given evidence himself the Crown would have failed to prove a case sufficient to secure a verdict of wilful murder against him, and without his evidence few jurymen would have dared to bring in a verdict of guilty. It was not that his evidence revealed any facts which really proved the case against him, but the prejudice, already large, was greatly increased by his cleverness and cool demeanour. No doubt if he had been confused and emotional, that also would have told against him. The case is remarkable for several other reasons. The evidence, entirely circumstantial, and concerned almost wholly with motive and opportunity, consisted of a chain of gossamer links joined together with immense ingenuity, and it was the length of this chain rather than its strength which enabled the prosecution to bind it round the prisoner. There is further no precedent capital case of comparable gravity in which two persons are indicted for the same offence, in which the same evidence is offered against either or both of them, and in which the jury are given their choice of four verdicts. All the evidence in the Seddon case was directed against both him and his wife; in fact, the evidence upon which Seddon was convicted pressed just as hardly, if not more hardly, upon her; but the jury convicted him and acquitted her. Further, the case illustrates a certain change which seems to have come over the administration of the English criminal law, a change relating to the ancient maxim that "the accused is presumed innocent until he is proved guilty." That has been a solid tradition of English criminal justice. The whole law has been framed on the assumption that this first principle will be observed in its administration; but nowadays, in the words of an eminent jurist commenting on this case at the time, "we hear judges talking of inferences, of presumptions, of the failure of the accused to account for his actions or omissions, while the necessity for the Crown establishing an indubitable chain of proof by testimony is ignored." And to one who heard the whole of this trial, it appeared as if in fact Seddon was convicted

Trial of the Seddons.

not because the Crown succeeded in proving his guilt, but because he failed to prove his innocence.

Another point which makes the case remarkable is the absence of all evidence as to the handling by Seddon of arsenic at any time. It is usually regarded as necessary for conviction in a murder case either to trace the weapon to the prisoner's hand, or, in the case of poison, if the actual poison cannot be traced, at least to prove expert knowledge on the part of the accused as to the method of administration and effect of the poison employed. In this case it was not proved that Seddon administered or even handled any arsenic, that he had any knowledge or source of information as to its toxic effects, or that his occupation or education was of a kind likely to make the presumption that he had such information a reasonable one.

A further distinguishing feature of the case was the use made of the famous Marsh test, which is the classical method of discovering the presence of arsenic when it exists in a quantity too small to be revealed by a simple analysis. This has hitherto been used almost exclusively as a qualitative test, as the presence of arsenic is only revealed by the slightest deposit on a mirror. It has never before, I think, been sought to base on this almost invisible mark any calculations as to quantity. Yet in the Seddon case it was of such vital importance to the prosecution to prove that there must have been at least two grains in the body at the time of death that the Marsh mirrors were used as a quantitative test. On reference to the evidence, it will be seen that in certain portions of the viscera which were analysed it was necessary, in order to arrive at the quantity of arsenic which must have been present in the material to use a multiplying factor of as much as two thousand. The margin of possible error therefore was enormous, and it is typical of the difficulties to which the prosecution were put in this case that so much of their case was obliged to rest on induction and deduction. Dr. Willcox, who conducted these experiments, is a man not only of the highest ability in his profession, but also of the most exact and scrupulous fairness, and one may assume that in this case the results of his experiments were understated rather than overstated. Nevertheless, such a method of arriving at a small fact on which a man's life depends might easily in less expert hands, and conducted with less scrupulous conscientiousness, have produced errors of the most dangerous kind. It is not for me to say whether such methods should or should not be relied upon as a means of bringing criminals to justice, but merely to draw attention to this further peculiarity which distinguishes the Seddon case from other famous poison cases.

Again, comments were made upon the way in which the police conducted the preliminary investigations, more especially with regard to the

Introduction.

identification of Maggie Seddon by the chemist Thorley (which was a vital point in their case), and of the manner, happily more characteristic of French than of English procedure, in which they took her by herself into the gaoler's room at the Police Court, and entrapped her into making a false statement in order that her evidence for the defence, when she came to give it, should be discredited. Finally, it was felt pretty widely at the time of the trial that the Attorney-General had pressed the case against Seddon with great severity, while dealing rather leniently with his wife. Scrupulously fair as was Sir Rufus Isaacs's conduct of the case, it differed more in omission than in commission from what hitherto has been regarded as the best tradition of his office. In his cold and remorseless methods there was more of the vengeance of a destroying angel than the scrupulous moderation of a high officer of the Crown laying before a jury facts on the interpretation of which two lives depended. There is, of course, a reply to this criticism in the fact that the Attorney-General had to bring home the crime to a cool and clever man, and in circumstances of great mystery and obscurity; and his remorselessly logical treatment of facts and inferences would no doubt have excited less comment if it had not proved so deadly. Seddon himself was a person who excited no sympathy whatsoever. He was as cold and hard as a paving stone, and had such a jaunty and overweening confidence in his sharpness and cleverness that, had the issue been less grave, it would have been only human to wish to triumph over him at any cost. He was obviously capable of the crime with which he was charged. But it is one thing to feel morally convinced that a man is a scoundrel and a murderer and another to bring it home to him by a strict and scrupulous use of the means which the law permits. The feeling excited in the legal world by the trial as a whole was a mixture of admiration and misgiving—admiration for the ability and dignity with which it was conducted, and misgiving lest the margin of judicial safety implied in the presumption of innocence might not have been dangerously narrowed.

But if this trial has a profound and far-reaching legal significance which makes it worthy of the study and consideration of the professional lawyer, it is also rich in that human interest which makes an appeal to every citizen who is intelligent enough to care for exact knowledge of the social conditions which surround him. For here the curtain is abruptly drawn up on a scene of life in the crowded London of our day; strong limelight shines upon the characters; people of a kind who would be obscure and totally unknown to the ordinary public are suddenly revealed in their habits as they lived; and the most intimate details of their life are made known to us. Their dealings with each other, their attitude towards

Trial of the Seddons.

life, their method and conduct of daily existence both among themselves and as between themselves and the world, are revealed with a fulness of detail and an exactness of circumstance unknown in any other kind of historical record. And to read the trial, not merely as a legal problem, but as a piece of human history of our own place and time, it is necessary to form a mental picture of the characters, not as they appear in the false proportions of a legal inquiry, but as that inquiry reveals them in the conditions of their daily life. Imagine, then, a household living in one of those prosperous and seemingly limitless residential districts that extend far to the north of London proper. Tollington Park is a road having pretensions to more than mere respectability. Its houses suggest not what houses of similar capacity in other districts so often suggest, a decayed and fallen gentility, but rather a crescent and gratified prosperity. You feel that the people who live there have come not from a better neighbourhood, but from one not so good, and that they are proud to live in Tollington Park. In one of these houses, No. 63, lived, in the year 1910, Frederick Henry Seddon, an insurance superintendent of forty years of age; his wife, Margaret, aged thirty-seven; his father, and a family of five children. The house has a bow window in the basement and the ground floor, three windows in each of the two upper floors, a strip of greenery called a garden, and a conservatory behind. At the time that Seddon moved into it he was a man obviously on the up grade. In his business as district superintendent of an insurance company he had moved from one position to another, and his moves were always marked with an increase of responsibility and income. As I read him, he was a hard-headed Lancashire man, who had early, in that industrial battlefield of the north, learned the value of money in the fight for existence; he was exact and exacting, thrifty, hard, and saving. He was conceited, but had no false sense of dignity, and seemed to be singularly free from the snobbish pursuit of appearance which is so often a weakness of his class. He was not ashamed of turning his hand to anything in the way of business by which money could be made. Whether it took the form of petty commission on this and that, or the owning and management of humble house property, or his own legitimate business, superintending a large number of petty insurance transactions, he applied himself with zeal to the business in hand. He appears to have been a man who wished to turn if possible every transaction of his daily life into a means of making money; pleasure meant singularly little to him; so far as one knows, his chief passion was the passion to be the possessor of property. In the strong light in which he stood throughout his trial this trait invariably came out. Of all the things that he said, the only phrases that can be called characteristic, that belong to and illuminate his individuality, were utterances about business and property. Echoes of these utterances remain

xvi

Introduction.

in one's memory, giving the character of the man—" I am always open to buy property at a price," "With this money and other money that I am possessed of (tapping a bag of gold) I can pay for this house," "This house I live in, fourteen rooms, is my own, and I have seventeen other properties." The only joke that is attributed to him is a joke about money when, putting a bag of gold on the table in the presence of one of his assistants, he said, "Here, Smith, here's your wages," and the assistant answered, "I wish you meant it, Mr. Seddon." He was one of those people for whom the word business has an almost sacred significance, and there can be no doubt that money was his god. No transaction was too great or too small for him, provided there was profit in it—whether it was buying £1600 worth of property, or (although he was a very prosperous man for his walk in life) exacting the sum of 6s. each from his two young sons for their weekly board, or buying and selling old clothes, or going and making a row at a music hall where he alleged, but of course could not prove, that he had been given change for a florin instead of half a crown   At the time the curtain rises on this drama, then, Seddon was living in this house with his wife and family of five children. It was a better house than he thought necessary for his habitation, but he had purchased it as a speculation, and rather than let it stand vacant lived in it himself, trusting, according to his habit, to turn this seeming extravagance to some financial profit. Thus he got from the insurance company that employed him a sum of 5s. a week as rent for the room which he used as an office, and he let the top floor unfurnished as a lodging for 12s. 6d. a week. By putting up a partition in one of the rooms he crowded six of his household, including his old father and the servant, into it, and thus had the use of the house while taking in money within half a crown a week of its rental value.

It is said of him that, with regard to women, he abused his position as an insurance superintendent with constant access to houses during the absence of the husband; also that during the year 1911 he had, although formerly a teetotaler, acquired the habit of drinking; but these accusations did not come out in the course of the trial. He had formerly been a local preacher, and a prop of chapel communities; but how much that may have had to do with his business interests it is impossible to say.

By merely confining one's self to the facts of the life of this household as revealed in this trial, it is possible to form a very definite picture of them; and, although so ordinary in its circumstances, it was really no ordinary household. There can be no question that the woman Miss Barrow, who came to lodge with them, was a very strange person indeed. She was ignorant with the dense ignorance of her class, suspicious, selfish, and, in a squalid sort of way, self-indulgent. At the time of this story she was forty-nine years old, and, having quarrelled with all her other friends,

Trial of the Seddons.

lodged with the Seddons alone, save for the companionship of a little orphan boy named Ernie Grant. She had quarrelled with and spat at her former landlords. She dressed badly, and was parsimonious in her habits. She had formerly been given to alcoholic indulgence, and, although there is no evidence that at the time under consideration this habit had continued, the probability is that she was not free from it. And it was a strange circumstance which brought together by mere chance these two people who had one passion in common—the passion for gold. Miss Barrow, when she came to the Seddons, was alleged to have in her possession a considerable sum in gold; there is no trustworthy evidence what the amount was. She was also the owner of £1600 invested in India stock, and of the lease of a public-house called the Buck's Head, and a barber's shop adjoining. She paid 12s. 6d. a week to Seddon for her rooms, and 7s. to Seddon's daughter Maggie for attending upon her, and bought her own food; her income was thus far in excess of her expenditure. As I have said, she had a passion for gold, not merely for money, but for gold coin. She mistrusted bank notes, and when she received one would generally get it changed into gold. When, as a result of her having parted with her leasehold property and stock to Seddon in return for an annuity to be paid by him, she was in the habit of receiving £10 monthly from him, she took it in sovereigns. And, further, when in an accession of mistrust of savings banks she drew a sum of £216 which she had on deposit at the Finsbury and City of London Savings Bank, she took the remarkable course of having it paid in gold— two bags of £100 each and £16 in loose sovereigns. Further, when remonstrated with by Seddon for having so much gold in the house, she was angry, and uttered the curious remark, " I know what to do with it." For the rest, although she had the run of the Seddon's house, she seemed to have chosen as a recreation to spend her time chatting in the kitchen with the charwoman and the general servant. When she became ill, and her illness was accompanied by circumstances of an offensive nature, she insisted on having the little boy Ernie Grant to sleep with her in her bed; and altogether seems to have been a woman of unpleasing, not to say squalid, habits.

Seddon also, as I have said, had his passion for gold. He had two safes in his house, one in his bedroom and one in the office in the basement, and seems to have been for ever carrying about gold from one to the other, and casting up his accounts, and taking loose sovereigns out of one bag to make up a sum in another, and generally fingering his money in the accepted manner of the miser. His wife, as she appeared to those who saw her at the trial, is a somewhat more inscrutable character. A woman with some pretensions to good looks, dressed with some taste, apparently gentle, and rather weak in character, she had been doing practically the whole of

Introduction.

the lighter household work of this fourteen-roomed residence, living, in short, the life of a domestic drudge. It was obvious from the evidence, and as a matter of knowledge outside the case, that she and Seddon were not on particularly good terms; it was obvious that every one in his household was frightened of him, and that he was a hard and tyrannous man. Business, and especially Mr. Seddon's business, came first in that house, and every one had to make way for it. Looking at his wife as she gave evidence, it seemed humanly incredible that he would trust her with any matter of importance outside the kitchen, and, in fact, I am convinced that he did not. They stood by one another loyally throughout the trial, however, and only once did Mrs. Seddon unconsciously reveal the attitude in which they stood to one another, when to the question as to why she did not tell him something, she answered, " He never used to take any notice when I said anything to him; he always had other things to think of." And, again, " I did not tell my husband everything I done; he never told me everything."

I do not propose to tell here the story which will be found unfolded both in the opening speeches of counsel and in the trial itself. It is enough to say that Miss Barrow lived for fourteen months, from July, 1910, to September, 1911, at 63 Tollington Park with the Seddons; that in the course of that year she made over to Seddon £1600 of India stock in return for an annuity of £103 4s. per annum, and the leasehold of a public-house known as the Buck's Head in Camden Town, with a barber's shop adjoining it, in return for a further annuity of £52 per annum. During the same period thirty-three £5 notes, known to have been paid to Miss Barrow, were traced to the possession of either Mr. or Mrs. Seddon. On the 1st of September, 1911, Miss Barrow was taken ill with what was regarded as epidemic diarrhœa, and died about six in the morning of the 14th of September, having been attended throughout by Dr. Sworn, of Highbury Crescent, who certified the death to be due to epidemic diarrhœa and exhaustion. The body of Miss Barrow, owing to the surrounding conditions, was removed to the undertaker's mortuary, and was buried at Islington Cemetery, East Finchley, on the following Saturday.

A few streets away from the Seddons lived a Mr. and Mrs. Vonderahe, cousins of Miss Barrow's, with whom she had lived before she went to lodge with the Seddons. They did not hear of the death till after the funeral, and naturally felt surprised at not having been advised of it before. When they went to see Seddon he told them that he had written them a letter on the day of Miss Barrow's death, of which he had kept a carbon copy; but they had never received any such letter. They naturally wanted to know what had become of Miss Barrow's property, and of the sum in gold and notes which she was known to have had in her possession;

Trial of the Seddons.

but Seddon explained that she had parted with her property for an annuity, and that, although they had searched everywhere, they had found nothing in her possession except a sum of about £10 in loose gold. From this fact, and a host of other small facts which will appear in the narrative, suspicion was gradually aroused. On the 15th of November Miss Barrow's body was exhumed by a coroner's order, and examined by Dr. Spilsbury in the presence of Dr. Willcox at the Finchley mortuary. Certain organs were removed for further examination and analysis. Dr. Spilsbury in his evidence said, "I found no disease in any of the organs sufficient to account for death, except in the stomach and intestines. In the intestines I found a little reddening of the inner surface in the upper part. . . . The body was remarkably well preserved, both externally and internally. This would suggest that death was due to some poison having a preservative effect, or to the presence of some preserving agent. I think the arsenic that Dr. Willcox says he found would account for the preservation of the body. . . . The reddening . . . was evidence of inflammation. I don't think there is anything to distinguish this from natural gastro-enteritis. The healthy appearance of all the organs, except the stomach and intestines, would be consistent with death from natural gastro-enteritis."

On the 23rd of November an inquest on the body was held, at which Mr. and Mrs. Seddon both gave evidence. The inquest was adjourned. On the 29th of November Dr. Willcox made a further examination of the body, and found arsenic present in all the organs and parts examined. At the adjourned inquest Dr. Willcox gave it as his opinion that there must have been more than two grains of arsenic present in the body at the time of death; that death was due to acute arsenical poisoning; and that a moderately large fatal dose must have been taken less than three, and probably less than $_{t}$two, days before death. On the 4th of December Seddon was arrested. On the 14th of December the hearing of the inquest was resumed. Seddon attended in custody, and reserved his evidence. At this inquest the jury returned a verdict which was recorded as follows :—

"That the said Eliza Mary Barrow died on the 14th of September, 1911, of arsenical poisoning at 63 Tollington Park, the arsenic having been administered to her by some person or persons unknown. And so the jurors aforesaid do further say that the said person or persons unknown on the 13th or 14th or 13th and 14th days of September, 1911, did feloniously, wilfully, and of malice aforethought murder and slay against the peace of our Lord the King, his Crown and Dignity, the said Eliza Mary Barrow."

On the 19th, 22nd, and 29th of December, and the 2nd, 9th, 16th, 19th, and 26th of January, 1912, the police proceedings took place. On the 15th of January Mrs. Seddon was arrested and charged with being concerned with her husband in the murder of Miss Barrow, and on the 2nd of February both prisoners were committed for trial.

Something had occurred in the meantime, however, which may suitably be noted here. On the 6th of December Maggie Seddon was sent, at the suggestion of her father, to buy some Mather's fly-papers. He had made this suggestion to his solicitor because, as he said, when puzzling over the problem of how Miss Barrow could have got the arsenic into her system he remembered that at the time of her illness there had been fly-papers in the room, and he had the idea of purchasing fly-papers now so that they might be analysed and the quantity of poison in them ascertained. On presenting herself at the shop of Mr. Price, 103 Tollington Park, and asking for a packet of fly-papers, Maggie Seddon was told that she could not be supplied. The chemist had heard about the case, and for some reason or other did not wish to be mixed up in it. Now the case for the prosecution rested on the hypothesis that Seddon had poisoned Miss Barrow by arsenic extracted from fly-papers, and although Mrs. Seddon admitted having bought them and put them in the room, another large purchase, from a chemist named Thorley, was alleged against Maggie Seddon, her daughter, in the month of August, 1911. This purchase was denied by Maggie Seddon. Later, when they were preparing the case, the police examined her on the subject of the purchase of fly-papers, and so framed their questions that she made a statement, which she signed, that she had never been to Price's shop to purchase fly-papers. This was not the case; but it is at least possible that what was in her confused mind was the importance of being accurate, and of not making any false admission which might be damaging to her father, and that what she meant was that she had never purchased fly-papers at Price's shop. If the form of the statement be altered from, "I have never been to purchase fly-papers at Price's shop," to "I have never been and purchased fly-papers at Price's shop," the mistake on her part is easily accounted for. But the fact that she had signed a denial of having been at Price's shop was used by the prosecution to discredit her sworn statement that she had never purchased fly-papers at Thorley's shop. Her identification by Thorley, however, was a still more doubtful point in the case for the prosecution. The common ground between both sides was that Maggie Seddon knew Thorley's daughter, had twice been to the house, and on one occasion had been admitted by Thorley himself. It was obvious therefore that he had seen her. On being questioned by the police who were making inquiries everywhere in getting up the case, Thorley said he remembered selling fly-papers to a fair-haired girl on the 26th of August, 1911. The police then asked him if he could identify her. He said he could not, and several times protested his

Trial of the Seddons.

inability to do so. By this time, however, the Seddon case had attracted a great deal of attention, and portraits of all the family had been in the newspapers. On the 2nd of February, 1912, Thorley was taken in a motor car to the Police Court and shown a company of twenty women, including two girls with their hair down their backs, and asked if he could identify the girl who had purchased the fly-papers. He identified Maggie Seddon. He had admitted he had seen her when she had been twice to his house. He had also seen her portrait in the newspapers. Hers was the only face in the whole company which he had ever seen before, and there were only two girls of an age which could possibly correspond with that of the purchaser of the fly-papers. Much adverse comment was aroused both by the method with which this identification was obtained, and by the admission of it into the trial as damning evidence against the prisoner. Mr. Marshall Hall referred to it in very strong terms in his address to the jury.

The trial was opened at the Central Criminal Court in the Sessions House, Old Bailey, on Monday, the 4th March, 1912, and occupied ten days. It was in every sense of the word a full-dress trial. The eminence of the counsel engaged, the many mysteries involved in the case, and the prosperous, middle-class position of the prisoners combined to excite in the public a very high degree of interest. The Attorney-General himself prosecuted; and in Mr. Muir, Mr. Rowlatt, and Mr. Travers Humphreys, he was supported by three of the most able of the counsel who are associated with the Treasury. In Mr. Marshall Hall Seddon had an advocate of established eminence in his profession and of proved brilliance and ability. He was assisted by Mr. Dunstan and Mr. Orr, while Mr. Gervaise Rentoul defended Mrs. Seddon. The trial was presided over by Mr. Justice Bucknill.

The Court was crowded from the first day, as the case attracted intense interest, both among the members of the bar and the general public. Seddon and his wife were accommodated with chairs in the dock; and my remembrance of them throughout the ten days of the trial is of two singularly calm and attentive figures, more like those of people assisting at an academic discussion than prisoners on trial for their lives. As the case was unfolded it became evident that there was matter for immense prejudice against them both. A great part of the trial was taken up with the financial transactions between Seddon and the deceased, with the identification of the bank notes, and with the medical evidence of Dr. Willcox and Dr. Spilsbury. It was not until Seddon himself was put into the witness-box that the dramatic interest became at all acute; but then, indeed, the full force of the prejudice against him came out.

Introduction.

In his long duel with the Attorney-General he remained unshaken and unperturbed. He appeared to be as calm and collected as if he had been in his own office. It was quite evident that his demeanour and coldness told against him with the jury—one could almost see it happening before one's eyes. He had an explanation for everything; he could account for every penny of money in his possession from long before he had ever met Miss Barrow until after her death; and things which his own solicitor and counsel had racked their brains to find an explanation for, he explained with plausibility and exactness. Only one or two things made him indignant. One was the police version of his words when arrested. According to Inspector Ward, Seddon's words when arrested were as follows:—He was told that he would be arrested for the wilful murder of Eliza Mary Barrow; for administering poison—arsenic. According to the police, his answer was "Absurd. What a terrible charge—wilful murder. It is the first of our family that has ever been charged with such a crime. Are you going to arrest my wife as well? If not, I would like you to give her a message for me. Have they found arsenic in her body? She has not done this herself. It was not carbolic acid was it, as there was some in her room, and Sanitas is not poison, is it?" He denied that he had asked the question about his wife, and denied it with great indignation. Indeed, a little knowledge of the way in which human beings speak would convince one that the words taken down by the police inspector could not have been the exact words used by Seddon, or, at any rate, they were not uttered in the order in which they appeared in his evidence. They read much more like an extract from a policeman's note-book than the recorded speech of a human being. But the suggestion that Seddon was seeking to bring his wife into it was bitterly resented by him. He was also quite shocked by the suggestion that he had counted Miss Barrow's money in the presence of his two assistants on the day of her death. It is curious to notice the kind of thing which he thought disgraceful. He was quite unmoved by the fact that he had bargained for a cheap funeral for Miss Barrow and accepted 12s. 6d. commission on it, and other instances of his mean and grasping nature left him quite unperturbed. But it seemed quite to shock him that any one should suggest that he was (in his own words) such an inhuman, degenerate monster as to count out the money he was supposed to have stolen in the presence of his two assistants. He undoubtedly was counting money, but it was not satisfactorily established that it was Miss Barrow's money.

The speeches at the end of the trial produced a great impression on the audience, though it is to be doubted if they made much impression on the jury, who appeared to be bewildered by the mass of technical evidence that had been presented to them, and to have either made up their minds already, or to be waiting for the summing up of the judge.

Trial of the Seddons.

The speeches of Mr. Marshall Hall and Sir Rufus Isaacs occupied nearly five hours each. They were admirable examples of two different methods. Mr. Marshall Hall's speech was an appeal to the heart, clothed in the subtlest intellectual disguise; Sir Rufus Isaacs's was an appeal to the head, solemnised rather than softened by an acknowledgment of the human emotions. The defence was eager and pleading, and had soaring moments of great eloquence, of which the music and manner alike were memorable. The speech for the prosecution was criticised by some who heard it as a "hanging speech," but it was certainly admirable in its clarity and in the force and weight of its cold reasoning.

The summing up was the least satisfactory thing in the trial. Mr. Justice Bucknill seemed to be feeling the effects of this very long and intricate inquiry, and perhaps a younger and stronger judge, with more experience of criminal law and less affected by the emotional aspects of the case, would have put its issues more satisfactorily before the jury. It is possible that Mr. Justice Bucknill, the most humane and kind-hearted of men, knowing that he was harrowed by the whole thing, forced himself on that account to be more severe; it is often the way with humane persons. At any rate, although throughout the trial he had seemed to incline now to this side and now to that, the whole tendency of his summing up was dead against the prisoner and all in favour of his wife. The usual direction about the benefit of the doubt he laboured at great length, but he chiefly laboured it to impress upon the jury that it was impossible for doubt not to exist, and he attempted to differentiate elaborately between reasonable doubt and unreasonable doubt. This seemed to me at the time, and seems still, a dangerous proceeding. There are two ways of uttering this warning. The traditional way is to say, in short, "If you have no doubt as to the prisoner's guilt you must declare him guilty, but if you have any doubt, any reasonable doubt, he is entitled to the benefit of it, and you must give effect to it in a verdict of not guilty." What Mr. Justice Bucknill said in effect was, "Of course, if you are convinced that there is a doubt in the matter, your verdict must be one of not guilty. But you must remember that there is an element of doubt in all human affairs, and what you must ask yourselves in this case is, is there any reasonable doubt judged by the standard which I should apply to the ordinary business affairs of my life? If there is not, then you must bring in a verdict of 'Guilty,' and not shrink from the consequences, strong in the sense that you have performed the duty required of you in your oath." There is no doubt as to the effect of this kind of charge; humanly speaking, it amounts to a direction to find the prisoner guilty. And that is what the jury did in this case.

The real drama in this trial came at the end of the long and anxious

Introduction.

address of Mr. Justice Bucknill to the jury. When they retired, and the Judge and Sheriff went to their apartments to have tea, the buzz in the Court reminded one of nothing so much as the *entr'acte* in a theatre at a matinee performance. I noticed that Seddon had been growing paler and more worn and strained-looking all through the day, and though he never lost his self-command, it was obvious that the strain of attention which he had given to the trial, to say nothing of the suspense, was telling on him terribly. Mrs. Seddon seemed less affected. They retired also; to what ordeal of suspense no man can measure. And the *entr'acte* of an hour began.

And then, suddenly, when the return of the jury was announced, the feeling in the Court was tuned up, like the rising pitch of violin strings, to an almost excruciating note. The jury returned and answered to their names. The Judge, with the Lord Mayor, the Sheriff, and Aldermen, came slowly back to the bench. Every one looked towards the dock; the wardresses and the warders and the prisoners came climbing back into it. This time there was a doctor with them, who also sat in the dock, and an officer stood close behind Seddon. You could have heard a pin fall.

The Deputy-Clerk of the Court, in pleasant, easy tones, asked the jury the fateful question, and asked it first as relating to Seddon. I looked away from them to him while I listened. His eyes were turned on them with a hungry, questioning look such as I have never seen before. I heard the word "Guilty." He never moved or changed his expression; and the question was again asked with relation to his wife. The answer came, "Not Guilty," and his expression relaxed a little. While the Clerk of the Court was entering the verdict in his book Seddon quickly went up to his wife and gave her one sounding kiss, the loudness of which echoed incongruously through the death-like silence of the Court; and then he turned to the front of the dock and took some papers from his pocket. She was half-supported, half-carried out, and we heard her sobs sound from below in the tense silence of the moment.

The Clerk of the Court asked Seddon if he had anything to say why sentence should not be passed, and he then went to the front of the dock and made that extraordinarily clear and explicit statement which will be found in its place at the end of the trial. Quite calm in his manner, swallowing a little as he spoke, but otherwise in perfect command of himself, he went through an intricate yet lucid array of facts and figures, and, finally, with his hand lifted up to take the Mason's oath, he swore by the Great Architect of the Universe that he was innocent of the crime. The moment was excruciating for any one who, if he was not assured of Seddon's innocence, was certainly not assured that his guilt had been satisfactorily proved, and there was more than one such person in the Court.

Trial of the Seddons.

The Judge's secretary, who sat beside him, had lifted a square of black cloth, and held it in his hand. A figure in a black gown had glided in at a side door and stood behind the Judge's chair; it was the chaplain. The secretary arranged the black square on the Judge's wig. Then the high tones of the usher sounded through the Court, crying the proclamation for silence while sentence of death is passing. The doors of the Court were locked. Seddon listened attentively, scrupulously, as though every word were vital.

And the quiet, gentlemanly tones of the Judge began again, admonishing the prisoner. But every now and then his voice dropped to a whisper. He reminded Seddon that they were members of the same brotherhood, but that it was a brotherhood that did not encourage crime, which condemned crime. He spoke gently of the wife, saying that, if it was any comfort to the prisoner to know it, he could tell him that he believed the verdict of the jury with regard to her was a right one. Seddon nodded in acquiescence at this, as he did again when the Judge spoke of his having had a fair trial. Twice only he interrupted the Judge, but in quiet and civil tones. Once, when the Judge spoke about his terrible position, he said quietly, " It doesn't affect me, sir—I've a clear conscience," and once again when the gentlemanly faltering voice implored him to make his peace with God, Seddon said, " I am at peace."

And I do believe he was the most peaceful man in the Court. The Judge was all but sobbing, and had to pause and brace himself before he could begin to utter the sentence, which he finished in tears, while the black-gowned figure behind him murmured " Amen." But Seddon was calm, and when it was all over, and while the Judge, wiping his eyes, was excusing the jury from attending for ten years, he hitched his overcoat about him with his old gesture and took a drink of water, and made ready to descend the stairs that would take him away from the world of men for ever. As he turned to go down he looked through the glass at the people at the back of the Court, where his own friends were, and where his own little girl had been sitting earlier in the afternoon—a bleak, wintry look—and then he was gone.

It cannot be said that Seddon suffered from any want of skill or resource in his defence. Everything was done that could be done; by himself, by his solicitor, Mr. Walter Saint, who brought great intelligence and unwearying energy to bear upon it; by Mr. Wellesley Orr, whose preparation of the brief and analysis of the evidence were masterly; and by Mr. Marshall Hall, whose eminent gifts as an advocate were never

xxvi

Introduction.

seen to greater advantage than in his whole conduct of the case in Court,
where his patience, his watchfulness, his tenacity, and his eloquence won
a generous and well-deserved tribute of admiration from the Attorney-
General. But doubts which in the case of a Madeleine Smith or a Florence
Maybrick would have been sufficient to procure either an acquittal on the
grounds of insufficient evidence, or at any rate a revocation of the sentence,
were unavailing in the case of Seddon. The hearing of the inevitable
appeal attracted almost as much interest in the Law Courts as the trial
itself had excited at the Old Bailey. For two days Mr. Marshall Hall
argued before an interested but unsympathetic tribunal; and Mr. Justice
Darling's clear-cut judgment put an end to any hopes there might have
been of help from that quarter. There remained only the appeal to
the Home Secretary, Mr. M'Kenna; an appeal which was supported by
upwards of three hundred thousand signatures. This also was unavailing;
and, although Seddon himself had placed high hopes upon it and was bitterly
disappointed by its failure, he received the dread news with something of
the philosophic stoicism which had marked his demeanour throughout.

Seddon never made any confession of any kind, and asserted his
innocence until the end. Many things about the case remain wrapped in
mystery. No one has any idea as to how Miss Barrow got arsenic into her
system. Dr. Willcox, who believed in Seddon's guilt, does not believe that
he used any decoction of fly-papers. It is possible that the idea of fly-
papers, introduced by Seddon himself, was a blind, and that he used arsenic
in the form of rat poison or weed killer. It was he himself who purposely
put the police on the fly-paper line, and it may have been a very deeply con-
ceived scheme to throw them off the true scent; whatever it was, it hanged
him. It served as a reasonable theory; but none of the counsel engaged
nor Seddon's own solicitor have any reasonable theory as to how or when
the poison was taken or administered. Mrs. Seddon's acquittal makes any
speculation as to her knowledge or share in it impossible here, but a
most deplorable act on her part falls to be recorded. A few months after
Seddon's death she married again, and has since, I believe, emigrated with
all her family to California. But the *Weekly Dispatch* of 17th November,
1912, published a signed declaration by Mrs. Seddon to the effect that
she saw her husband give the poison to Miss Barrow, that he administered
it on the night of her death, and that he terrorised her into silence with a
revolver. This produced a painful enough impression about Mrs. Seddon,
but the impression was heightened when a fortnight later *John Bull*,
which had sent a commissioner to Liverpool to inquire into the matter,
published an affidavit sworn before a Commissioner for Oaths to the effect
that the alleged confession was untrue; that she had done it for payment,

and in order to put an end to the gossip of neighbours who pointed her out as a murderess. No further comment on this incident is necessary.

Seddon remained interested in money until the end, and on the afternoon before he was executed sent for his solicitor for no other purpose than to ascertain what certain articles of his furniture had fetched at auction. He was roused to indignation when he heard the smallness of the amount, and, striking the table at which he sat in the warder's room, said in tones of scorn and resignation, "That's done it!" He was really anxious that his wife should get all that was possible out of the wreck of his fortune, but displayed no emotion whatever with regard to his own impending fate. His insensibility and steadiness of demeanour kept him company, I understand, to the threshold of death. There were seven thousand people— an unprecedented crowd—outside the gate of Pentonville on the morning of his execution—a circumstance which, could he have known it, would have flattered his vanity. But he could not know it; and it was in silence that he walked out through that square portal at Pentonville, through which so many others have passed, never to return. He lies beneath the quiet little plot of grass which in final mercy covers so many cruelties, agonies, and infamies; only a square stone inscribed with his initials and a date serving to remind the few who ever see it of the end to which so much industry, so much calculation, and so much coveteousness brought him.

Leading Dates in the Seddon Case.

1901.—Seddon appointed district superintendent for Islington under the London and Manchester Industrial Assurance Company.

Nov. 1909. Seddon comes to live at 63 Tollington Park, Islington.

June 20, 1910. Seddon instructs house agents to obtain a tenant for his top floor.

July 25, 1910. Miss Barrow and the Hooks come as tenants to Tollington Park.

Aug. 11, 1910. The Hooks leave.

Oct. 14, 1910. Miss Barrow transfers £1600 India stock to Seddon in purchase of an annuity.

Jan. 9, 1911. The Buck's Head property is assigned by Miss Barrow to Seddon in purchase of an annuity.

June 19, 1911. Miss Barrow draws £216 in gold from the London and Finsbury Savings Bank.

Aug. 5, 1911. The Seddons and Miss Barrow go to Southend.

Aug. 8, 1911. They return.

Aug. 26, 1911. Alleged purchase by Maggie Seddon of Mather's fly-papers at Thorley's.

Sept. 1, 1911. Miss Barrow taken ill with bilious attack.

Sept. 2, 1911. Dr. Sworn finds her to be suffering from acute diarrhœa and sickness.

Sept. 4, 1911. Diarrhœa better, sickness worse. Miss Barrow refuses to go to hospital when spoken to by Dr. Sworn.

Sept. 5-9, 1911. Miss Barrow visited daily by Dr. Sworn. Condition much the same.

Sept. 11, 1911. Seddon's sister and niece come to him on a visit.

Sept. 13, 1911. Miss Barrow worse. Incident of the midnight cry, " I am dying ! " (11.30 p.m.).

Sept. 14, 1911. Miss Barrow dies (6.20 a.m.). Dr. Sworn, without seeing her, gives Seddon a certificate. Ernie Grant and the young Seddons sent to Southend.

Trial of the Seddons.

Sept.   16, 1911.   Miss Barrow buried at Finchley.

Sept. 20-21, 1911.   The Vonderahes call at Tollington Park.

Sept.   22, 1911.   The Seddons go for a fortnight to the seaside.

Oct.   9, 1911.   Mr. Vonderahe's interview with Seddon.

Nov.   15, 1911.   Miss Barrow's body exhumed.

Nov.   23, 1911.   Inquest.

Dec.   4, 1911.   Seddon arrested.

Dec.   14, 1911.   Adjourned inquest and verdict.

Jan.   15, 1912.   Mrs. Seddon arrested.

Feb.   12, 1912.   Magisterial hearing concluded. Both prisoners committed for trial.

March   4, 1912.   Trial of the Seddons at the Old Bailey begins.

March   14, 1912.   Mrs. Seddon acquitted and released. Seddon condemned to death.

April   1, 1912.   Seddon appeals against his conviction.

April   2, 1912.   Appeal dismissed.

April   18, 1912.   Seddon executed at Pentonville.

THE TRIAL.

CENTRAL CRIMINAL COURT, OLD BAILEY.

MONDAY, 4TH MARCH, 1912.

Judge—
Mr. JUSTICE BUCKNILL.

Counsel for the Crown—
The ATTORNEY-GENERAL (The Right Hon. SIR RUFUS D. ISAACS, K.C., M.P.).
Mr. R. D. MUIR.
Mr. S. A. T. ROWLATT.
Mr. TRAVERS HUMPHREYS.

Counsel for the Prisoner, Frederick Henry Seddon—
Mr. MARSHALL HALL, K.C., M.P.
Mr. DUNSTAN.
Mr. ORR.

Counsel for the Prisoner, Margaret Ann Seddon—
Mr. GERVAIS RENTOUL.

Trial of the Seddons.

An Usher of the Court—If any one can inform my Lords, the King's Justices, the King's Serjeant, or the King's Attorney-General, ere this inquest be taken between our Sovereign Lord the King and the prisoners at the bar, of any treasons, murders, felonies, or misdemeanours, done or committed by the prisoners at the bar, let him come forth, and he shall be heard; for the prisoners now stand at the bar on their deliverance. And all persons who are bound by recognisance to prosecute or give evidence against the prisoners at the bar, let them come forth, prosecute, and give evidence, or they shall forfeit their recognisances. God save the King.

The Deputy-clerk of the Court—Frederick Henry Seddon and Margaret Ann Seddon. You are charged on indictment for that you on the 14th day of September in last year feloniously and wilfully and of your malice aforethought did kill and murder one Eliza Mary Barrow. Frederick Henry Seddon are you guilty or not?

Frederick Henry Seddon—Not guilty.

The Deputy-clerk of the Court—Margaret Ann Seddon are you guilty or not?

Margaret Ann Seddon—Not guilty.

The Deputy-clerk of the Court—Gentlemen of the jury, prisoners at the bar, Frederick Henry Seddon and Margaret Ann Seddon, are charged on indictment for that they on the 14th of September of last year did feloniously and wilfully kill and murder Eliza Mary Barrow. To this indictment they have severally put not guilty, and it is your charge to say whether they or either of them are guilty or not.

Opening Speech for the Prosecution.

The Attorney-General—May it please you, my lord. Gentlemen of the jury—The male prisoner, Frederick Henry Seddon, and his wife stand charged before you with the wilful murder of a Miss Eliza Mary Barrow at their house at 63 Tollington Park, in the north of London, on the 14th September, 1911, by administering arsenic to her. The case is one which demands your very close attention, not only because it is a charge of the gravest character known to the law, but also because it is a case which is placed before you by the Crown upon circumstantial evidence, and not upon direct evidence, of the administering of the poison. It will involve your inquiring in some little detail into the events during some months before the decease of this Miss Barrow, during which time she was living with the prisoners as a lodger in rooms which she had rented from them, and which she continued to occupy until this fateful 14th September. Gentlemen, I will only make one passing observation to you before I proceed to deal with the facts of this case, to remind you that this case must be tried, and will be tried, upon the evidence which is given in this Court, and in this Court only, and if you have by any possibility read accounts of inquiries into this case, or any comment upon it in the daily press, you will not pay any attention to that, but you will discard it entirely from your minds, and attend only to the evidence that is given before you, and to what takes place during the trial in this Court.

Now, gentlemen, may I point out to you, before I proceed to tell you the story, that in a case of this character the inquiry must necessarily depend upon three main points. Wherever you have a trial of this character

2

Opening Speech for Prosecution.

The Attorney-General

in which there is no direct evidence of the administering of the poison, you must necessarily look closely into all the facts leading up to the 14th September, the important date, and also you will have to consider what happened thereafter; and, as I shall submit to you, you will have to consider what the interest of these two persons was in the immediate death of this woman, what motive they had or could have for doing her to death. You will also have to consider what opportunities they had of administering this poison to her; and then you will also direct your attention to what happened after the death, what the conduct was of these persons both immediately before and immediately after and for some little time after the murder of this woman.

The male prisoner Seddon is a superintendent of canvassers for the Industrial Assurance Company. He had been in their employment for a number of years, had been superintendent of canvassers since 1901, and at the time in question, the material date, he was occupying a house at 63 Tollington Park, in the north of London, where he lived with his wife and family, consisting of five children, and where at any rate the upper floor, the second floor of the house, was let eventually during the important dates to which I shall call your attention directly, to Miss Barrow. The male prisoner's office was in the basement of his house, where there was a large room with a bay window out to the front, and where he did most of his business, and, as you will hear later on, it was the habit of those in the employ of this Industrial Assurance Company, whose duty it was to collect the moneys for him, to hand them over to him; the canvassers in his particular district handed their moneys over to him generally on a Thursday.

Eliza Mary Barrow, the woman who, according to the case which we submit to you, was murdered by poison on the 14th September of last year, was a spinster of just about forty-nine years of age. She appears to have been a woman of somewhat curious temperament. She is described by one or two witnesses as a somewhat eccentric person. She appears to have been deaf; according, again, to some of the evidence which will be called before you, very deaf; and she had one small boy who lived with her from 1909, now about ten or eleven years of age, to whom she was devotedly attached, who was an orphan, the son of a Mr. and Mrs. Grant, with whom she had lived from about 1902 till 1908, Mr. Grant having been some kind of a relative of hers, Mrs. Grant being a woman with whom she was on the friendliest terms; and after the death of Mrs. Grant, certainly some short time afterwards, Miss Barrow seems to have taken this boy to live with her, and adopted him as her own. There was a girl also, Hilda, but of her you will hear little in this case, and there is nothing of any importance that I need refer to in that connection.

In 1909 Miss Barrow went to live with some relative of hers, a Mrs. Vonderahe, who lived in North London, in Evershot Road. She went there to live, taking with her this small boy, Ernie Grant. She lived with Mr. and Mrs. Vonderahe, paying for her board and lodging, and continued to live there until she moved on the 26th July of 1910 to 63 Tollington Park, the house occupied by the prisoners. She left the Vonderahes in consequence of some disagreement. She had been living with them for some considerable time, something like eighteen months, but whatever the cause of it was there is no doubt that they did not agree in

Trial of the Seddons.

the end, and in consequence of this Miss Barrow looked out for other apartments, and lighted upon this floor, which was to be let by the Seddons, the prisoners. During this time and up to the time when she moved into this house on the 26th July of 1910, Miss Barrow was the possessor of a considerable amount of money, amounting to something like £4000 capital value. She had £1600 in India 3½ per cent. She was also the owner of a leasehold property which brought her in at least £120 a year profit, and that lease continues till 1929, when it expires. She appears to have had one very curious characteristic, that of hoarding gold and bank notes. She did not place them in a bank, but she appears to have kept them in a cash box, and kept gold and notes to a very large amount. According to the evidence that will be placed before you, she had during a considerable time some £400 in gold in a cash box, and a considerable number of notes, the exact number I am not able to tell you; but, as you will hear during the course of the case, there must have been at least 33 £5 notes in that cash box, because we shall trace every one of those notes and their subsequent history into the possession of either the male or the female prisoner. Besides that, she had a sum of £200 odd in a savings bank, the Finsbury and City of London Savings Bank. So that, as you will observe, when she went into the prisoners' house at 63 Tollington Park in this July, 1910, she had this considerable amount of property which I have explained to you. She appears, as you will hear a little later in more detail, to have been in the habit of cashing the cheque which she received from the leasehold property across the counter, an open cheque, each quarter, and receiving the notes for it, and then putting these notes into the cash box. It will be proved before you that some notes which were eventually traced to the possession of the prisoners are notes which were received by her from the bank across the counter for the cheques which she had received in respect of the property for a period ranging over some ten years, from 1901 till 1910, and as she got the notes, so it appears that she placed these notes into the cash box; they never seem to have gone into any bank at all. Either receiving gold or notes, she accumulated them and kept them in this box, and that box was moved with her to 63 Tollington Park in this July, 1910.

Gentlemen, I would like to direct your attention for the moment to the particular point to which I am now going to address you, so that you may follow it in all its bearings. It will be shown to you that all this property disappears by the 14th September of 1911, and that on that date there was no cash in her possession except a sum of £4 10s., according to one statement, and £10 according to another statement of the male prisoner; and that that was the total amount of property of which she died possessed, except for some personal belongings, trinkets, furniture, and clothing, which were valued at something like £15, so that she had come into the house on the 26th of July, 1910, with all this property, and on her death on the 14th September, 1911, she had nothing except these small amounts to which I have called your attention. You will hear that in the meanwhile all this property found its way into the possession of the Seddons, more particularly as regards the male prisoner. So far as we have been able to trace it, it all gets into his possession. I make that observation for this reason, that, according to the evidence which we shall place before you, we do not actually trace what becomes of the gold which was in the box according to the evidence when she moved into the house

4

Opening Speech for Prosecution.

The Attorney-General

in July of 1910, but as to the notes, which, of course, are much more easily traceable, there will be evidence before you which I shall submit to you placing beyond all question that these notes had got out of the cash box into the possession of these prisoners. The £1600 3½ per cent. stock disappeared at an early date from her possession, being transferred in October, 1910, to the male prisoner. The leasehold property was transferred also to the male prisoner; and, although I do not suggest to you that we trace the actual coins, upon the evidence I shall submit to you that the gold which was drawn out of the Finsbury and City of London Savings Bank in June of 1911, as it was consisting of £216, which represented the money which had accumulated there since 1887 for her account, and was drawn out by her in the company of the female prisoner in June, 1911, that something like that sum of money in gold was seen in the possession of the male prisoner on the afternoon of the 14th September, after Miss Barrow had died from this arsenic poisoning between 6 and 7 o'clock of that morning.

In some little detail I will show you later how all that happened. For the moment I want to direct your attention to this, that the money had passed therefore from her to the Seddons' possession, and I want to place before you the explanation, so far as there is an explanation, of what had happened with regard to that money. You will see that upon the male prisoner's own story with regard to this, if you accept it as true—I shall have some criticism to pass upon it for your consideration—but if you accept it as true, he had every interest in getting rid of this woman, Miss Barrow, on the 14th September of 1911.

In July, when she came to the house, she brought with her not only the boy, Ernest Grant, but a Mr. and Mrs. Hook, who were friends of hers. Mr. Hook was the brother of the Mrs. Grant, to whom I have referred, and they came to live there; but, as you will hear, they remained there for a very short time, because on the Sunday, within eight or ten days of their arrival at this house and their residence there, there was trouble caused in some way by their having gone out with the boy, and, as a consequence, as you will hear, they left the premises on the Tuesday, 10th August. So that from 10th August of 1910 until 14th September of 1911 she was residing in the house with Ernest Grant alone. She does not appear to have had any relatives calling upon her, so far as we know from the evidence, which you will hear, neither, apparently, had she friends. But at an early period, this period of October to which I have called your attention, when this money begins to disappear from Miss Barrow's possession, and when it passed from her to them, you will find that both the male prisoner and the female prisoner are dealing with the £5 notes which undoubtedly belonged to Miss Barrow, had belonged to her, which had been in this cash box; and you will find also that the female prisoner, in this month of October of 1910, at this important date when the India 3½ per cent. and the leasehold property were being transferred to the male prisoner, the female prisoner changed these £5 notes, endorsing them with a false name, M. Scott, and with a false address, 18 Evershot Road. No such person lived at Evershot Road; the female prisoner had nothing to do with 18 Evershot Road; it was a false name and a false address. The rest of the notes are traced, and show this, that between that period, the first date, 14th October, 1910, and the date of the death of Miss Barrow, thirty-three

5

Trial of the Seddons.

£5 notes had been dealt with, of which six went into the male prisoner's bank—he had a banking account, as you will hear—and the rest of them were dealt with by the female prisoner. There were altogether nine dealt with by her with a false name and address. Two of them as I have described to you already; six of them were dealt with, endorsed by her, and changed at tradesmen's, and endorsed "Mrs. Scott, 18 Evershot Road"; one of them was endorsed "Mrs. Scott, 12 Evershot Road"; nine of them therefore, according to the particulars I have already given you, were endorsed by her with a false name and a false address. You will have to ask yourselves during the course of this inquiry not only why that was done, but, of course, what bearing that has upon this trial? The rest of them are dealt with by her at various times during the same period; none of them is endorsed by her in her name, but they are exchanged on different dates, generally for small purchases which had been made.

Gentlemen, I am anxious that you should bear in mind this, that, of course, the charge made against these two persons is not that of abstracting her money; it is not a charge either of stealing or a charge of defrauding Miss Barrow of her money. But the reason why it is important to inquire into it in this case is that you will see, as I shall submit to you on behalf of the Crown, and you will consider it, that they are the only persons who at this time in September, 1911, had any interest in the immediate death of Miss Barrow. The explanation which has been given, and which will be read to you in due course, by the male prisoner with reference to the assignment leasehold interest, is that he agreed to give her an annuity of £1 a week for her life in exchange for the interest which she had in this leasehold property, which was of the value of some £120 a year, but which would expire in about nineteen years. I am not concerned, nor are you, with inquiring into whether what he gave her was the precise and proper amount that should be given under the circumstances as an annuity for a property of this character. It does not matter, and this case does not depend upon any minute arithmetical calculations as to whether he was dealing with her fairly or not. What does happen is that here you find this man, who is (so far as we know as the result of the inquiries that we have been able to make) in possession of a small amount of money, as his banking account will show, arranging to give this annuity of £1 a week to Miss Barrow for the rest of her life. It is right that I should tell you that the security for this is the property itself—so long as the property lasted, so long as the leasehold interest continued, the leasehold interest being of a public-house known as the Buck's Head and a barber's shop adjoining; the public-house bringing in £105 a year, and the barber's shop bringing in £50 a year, and subject to a rental which she had to pay of £20, and producing, it has been said, £120—it is said by the male prisoner himself a profit rental of £120, and I will accept it as that; it is not necessary to inquire more closely. For the £1600 of India 3½ per cent. there is no document of any sort in existence to explain what it was that the male prisoner gave her in exchange for that. There is neither any agreement in writing nor any note in any book or any entry of any kind or sort as to what he was to give her for that £1600; but, as you will hear, within two months of Miss Barrow being in that house with them, and after the Hooks, who had come with her had left, this property was transferred over to the male prisoner, and, as I

6

Opening Speech for Prosecution.

The Attorney-General

say, so far as any document shows, for nothing. The story which he has given with regard to it, which it is, of course, right that you should have before you early in the case, is this. He says there was a verbal agreement by which he bound himself to pay her an annuity of £72, besides allowing her to have the rooms in this house without paying any rent for them. The rent that she had been paying for the rooms was 12s. a week. That would amount to an annuity, according to him, or the equivalent of it, of about £3 a week. You will, of course, observe this, that, according to that story, there was absolutely nothing in writing, no record which bound the male prisoner to pay that annuity in respect of the India $3\frac{1}{2}$ per cent. Whether that is the true story or not, of course, you will have to make up your minds, or, at least, you will have to consider during the course of the case. Whether he ever did agree to give her an annuity for the India $3\frac{1}{2}$ per cent. is a question upon which I shall submit you will exercise your judgment during the course of this case;* or whether it was that this £1600 India $3\frac{1}{2}$ per cent. was transferred to him in consequence of the hold which he had managed to acquire over her, and the confidence which he had undoubtedly managed to instil into her, and as a result she entrusted it to him for safe keeping, as I suggest to you she had done with the notes which were being dealt with subsequently by these prisoners. These are all matters which, of course, you will consider during the course of the case; but I want to point this out to you, that even if you can bring yourselves to accept the story which the male prisoner puts to you, then if it is true, and if he had agreed to give her this annuity for the properties which had come into his possession, he had, of course, the highest interest in getting rid of her at as early a date as possible; the result of which would be that the annuities would cease, the capital would be his without any charge upon it to do as he liked with. My submission will be to you on behalf of the Crown that he is the only person, with his wife, who had a common interest with him in this—the only person who would really gain by the death of Miss Barrow. If those facts are correct, then, at least, it will have been established that there was every reason why they should desire her death.

Now, just let me tell you what happened afterwards. During the whole time that she is ill, which lasts from 1st September of 1911 until the morning of 14th September, you will find that the female prisoner is attending her, and in attending to her there is every opportunity for the male prisoner to go to her room; he does go on several occasions, and eventually on 11th September she makes a will by which he is appointed sole executor and trustee, and his father, who was living in the house at the time, is called in as a witness. By that will of 11th September there is no disposition of cash or other property, except furniture, jewellery, and personal belongings. The will will be read to you in due course. That is left to the children, the orphans, Hilda and Ernest Grant, when they come of age, and the property meanwhile is to be kept by the male prisoner as trustee. It is very little account, as you may imagine, but that is all the disposition of her property to this man.

My submission to you is that during the whole of this eventful period

---

* There is evidence that Seddon did actually pay to Miss Barrow the amount represented by this annuity until the week before her death.—Ed.

Trial of the Seddons.

the male and the female prisoners are those who have access to this woman's room. There was a kitchen next door to the bedroom which was inhabited by Miss Barrow; a kitchen in which apparently all her food, with one or two solitary exceptions, was cooked during the time that she was ill. She was in the habit in the ordinary course of things of having her meals served upstairs. She had them there with the boy Ernie Grant, and during this period the female prisoner was attending to her, cooking her food and doing everything that was necessary for her, and serving her. There was a servant in the house, but she never attended those rooms at all; she had nothing whatever to do with them. The mother, that is, the female prisoner, and the daughter, Maggie Seddon, seem to have done all that was necessary in the household, in that part of the house at any rate.

When she was taken ill on 1st September she had symptoms from which the doctor diagnosed that she was suffering from epidemic diarrhœa. She vomited, and undoubtedly had considerable diarrhœa and pains in her stomach. These continued—I only want for the moment to give you quite shortly the story—these continued for at least eight or nine days, but she began to improve; from about the fifth to the ninth day she seemed to be improving, and was attended by a doctor, Dr. Sworn. She seemed to be getting better, but on the 11th, the day I have told you when she made this will, the doctor had seen her in the morning. She made the will in the evening between 6 and 7 o'clock, and on the 13th was again seen by the doctor in the morning. She became rapidly worse; she was very ill all the night of the 13th with great pain, and could not remain in bed. The boy Ernie Grant, who slept with her usually, was sent down by her to call up the prisoners because she was so ill; and, as you will hear, the boy went down, and the prisoners did come up. This went on during that night of the 13th; no doctor appears to have been sent for, and in the early morning, at about 6 o'clock or a little after, of 14th September she died. Thereupon the male prisoner saw the doctor, and obtained from the doctor a certificate of death due to epidemic diarrhœa. He then saw an undertaker at 11.30 in the morning, and, as you will hear, it was arranged eventually that the body should be removed, and it was removed in the evening of that same day, the 14th September, to the undertaker's, to a mortuary there, and the funeral took place two days afterwards, on the 16th, from the undertaker's.

Now, there are some very significant facts with regard to what happens after the death to which I desire to draw your attention. You will see, first, that no relative was present at the funeral, no relative knew of the death until 20th September; she was buried on the 16th. The Vonderahes, whose names I have mentioned to you before, with whom Miss Barrow was living from 1909 until July of 1910, lived in the immediate neighbourhood within a quarter of a mile of the house, yet no information was given to them. A question arises upon this to which your close attention should be given. It is said by the male prisoner, and was said on the 20th September—not till then—the 20th or 21st September—that when Mrs. Vonderahe saw him he then said that he had written a letter which he had posted on the 14th September to Mr. Vonderahe telling him of the death, and also when the funeral was to be. You will hear from the

8

Opening Speech for Prosecution.

The Attorney-General

Vonderahes that no such letter was ever received by them. A copy of this letter was produced by him, and your attention will be directed to it in the course of the case.

But now I want you to bear in mind this further important consideration. When the male prisoner goes to the undertaker's on this day and desires to arrange for the funeral, he says that there is only £4 10s. with which to pay for the funeral, and that out of that the doctor's fees must come. The undertaker said, well, for that amount of money there could only be the cheapest kind of funeral, and that if she was buried she would have to be buried in a public grave, which means a grave in which a number of other persons are also buried. It is a very curious circumstance that the male prisoner should have assented to that, and arranged it, knowing, as he did, not only of her property, but of the relatives that she had, who, at least, one would have thought in the ordinary course, if he had nothing to conceal, would have been consulted before it was decided to put this unfortunate woman into a public grave. And it turned out, as you will learn during the course of the case, that amongst the papers found after the arrest of the male prisoner, was a document which showed quite plainly that Miss Barrow was entitled to burial in a family vault at Highgate.

Now, just see what that means. Let me, first of all, make this observation to you, that in the comment which I am about to make upon the conduct of the male prisoner I am drawing your attention to the character of the man as disclosed by those incidents, and as throwing some light upon the events which culminated in the murder of Miss Barrow. According to his own statement, to put it no higher than that—not to travel for a moment into any disputed area—by the death of Miss Barrow he came into possession of all the property to which I have already called your attention which had been charged with a life annuity. If this was an innocent death of hers, if he was in no sense responsible, the result, nevertheless, follows that from the moment her life came to an end he had the enjoyment of all the property which he had of hers when she came into his house some nine months before. But, apparently, so great was the cupidity of this male prisoner, and so much did he desire money, and the whole of the money, that he seems to have objected even to paying whatever it might be, a sovereign or two extra which it would have cost, to have given her a decent burial notwithstanding all that happened—notwithstanding the enormous profit which, on his own statement, if you believe him, he was making by the payment of the annuity ceasing from that moment.

But that is not all. I do ask your attention to this. Can you conceive under these circumstances innocent people not communicating with the relatives who lived in the immediate neighbourhood, within a quarter of a mile? What is said by the male prisoner—and I want to do full justice to what he has said—is that he wrote a letter which informed the Vonderahes of the death. It is a letter of 14th September. (My lord, this is exhibit No. 1.) This is the letter which, as I have explained to you, was never received, but which he says was written and posted. It is addressed to "Mr. Frank Vonderahe, 14th September, 1911." "Dear sir,—I sincerely regret to have to inform you of the death of your cousin, Miss Eliza Mary Barrow, at 6 a.m. this morning from epidemic diarrhœa. The

Trial of the Seddons.

funeral will take place on Saturday next about 1 or 2 p.m. Please inform Albert Edward and Emma Marion Vonderahe" (that is the brother and sister of Mr. Frank Vonderahe) " of her decease, and let me know if you or they wish to attend the funeral. I wish also to inform you that she made a will on the 11th inst., leaving what she died possessed of to Hilda and Ernest Grant, and appointed myself as sole executor for the will.— Yours respectfully, F. H. Seddon." That is addressed to "Mr. Frank Vonderahe, 31 Evershot Road, Finsbury Park."

You will observe from that letter, which he says he wrote and posted on 14th September to these relatives, that there is not the faintest reference to this very important fact that she was to be buried in a public grave. I am quite sure that you will agree in this as certainly a characteristic of life in this country, of the poorest, and perhaps even strongest amongst those who are not rich and not very well endowed with worldly goods— there is always the desire for a proper funeral; and the one thing that one would have expected would be that when this man knew, as he did, that he was only going to pay for a public grave for her he would have gone to the relatives, and if he had posted a letter which did not contain a single reference to that, at least before she was buried, he would have taken care to have got the relatives' acquiescence—to have brought the state of things to their notice, so that they might, if they liked, have said, " Oh, we will supplement this money; we will pay this extra £2 or £3, or whatever it may be, sooner than that our relative should be buried in a public grave." It is a subject of much comment which I am submitting to you, because, if the man was guilty at the time, the last thing in the world that he would want to do is to call the attention of the relatives before she was buried to the fact of her death.

As I have indicated to you, according to the evidence which will be placed before you, not one word was known, not a suspicion held by the Vonderahes of the death of Miss Barrow until the 20th September, that is, four days after the funeral had taken place. Then, by a chance circumstance, an inquiry was made, and it was ascertained that she was dead, and on the 21st of September an interview takes place with the two Mrs. Vonderahes, the wives of Mr. Albert and Mr. Frank Vonderahe, and as the result of that interview Mr. Frank Vonderahe desires an interview with the male prisoner. He has it, but not until very much later, because, although he wanted it, the male prisoner said he desired to go away, and he could not stop at that time; he was rather sick of it, and he wished to go away for a holiday, as he did. But on 9th October Mr. Frank Vonderahe does see him, and the result of that interview was that Mr. Frank Vonderahe made further inquiries, and became suspicious. The consequence of that was that communication was made to the authorities, with the result that further inquiries were instituted, and on 15th November, two months after the date of death, an order was made to exhume this body. Thereupon a post-mortem examination was made. Then it was found that in the body of this woman, who was said to have died of epidemic diarrhœa, there was arsenic widely distributed. You will hear from the medical testimony that the arsenic which was found in her body was the cause of her death. So far as we have been able to discover from the evidence which we shall place before you, there is not the faintest ground for suggesting that she was

Opening Speech for Prosecution.

The Attorney-General

taking medicine that contained arsenic, as we have been able to trace the medicines which she was taking, and that arsenic found its way into her body, according to the evidence which will be placed before you, during the days of her illness, and she must have died of a fatal dose of arsenic, which must have been administered within some forty-eight hours of her death.

It is perhaps, as you will understand when you have heard what the medical gentlemen have to say about this, not very remarkable that the doctor did not discover that arsenic was being administered, because the symptoms during life would be very much the same, whether she was suffering really and truly from epidemic diarrhœa, or whether she was suffering from the consequences of arsenical poisoning, the symptoms which would be present to the medical man attending would be the same. But the fact remains that this woman died from arsenical poisoning. The question you have to ask yourselves, and which is of much importance in this case, is, who administered the poison? And in that connection you must ask yourselves another question, who could have administered it in that house but the prisoners? And, in the same way, that question naturally leads to the further one, whose interest was it to administer it? The answers to those questions must necessarily be of the utmost importance in determining what your verdict will be in this case.

Gentlemen, I am anxious, in putting this case before you, that you should have all such details in the opening of the case as will enable you to follow the evidence as to see its bearing at the time it is given. It is, of course, of importance that you should, not only for the Crown, but for the defence, and it is in the interests of justice that you should appreciate what actually were the facts, and what had taken place in some more detail than I have so far indicated the story to you.

The evidence will show you this with relation to the case and to what had happened shortly before Miss Barrow was taken ill on 1st September. You will find that during the whole period of her stay in this house, and certainly from 10th August, when she was alone with this boy, Ernie Grant, and the prisoners and their family, so far as it is possible to place the material before you, that she had placed herself completely in the hands of the prisoners. Apparently, until the moment that she got into the house at Tollington Park, she was a woman of nerve, who knew how to take care of her money, who was of penurious habits, who saved persistently, who accumulated the moneys which were coming in to her from this income which I have already directed attention to; so that there was more and more money, and there were more and more notes in the cash box; and certainly, according to some of her relatives, as you will hear, as one lady expressed it, " It must be a clever person who could have got her money away from her." During this period to which I have already referred, and which I think will make it unnecessary to go into further detail in opening the case to you—until the end of August she appears to have been able to go about; she was out; she was actually out on the 30th August, 1911, which is the last date we trace. During that month she went to see a Dr. Paul, who examined her. At first she appears to have been suffering from a bilious attack; that seems to have passed away, and during the last two or three visits she was calling upon him, because she was suffering from a slight attack of asthma. As he will tell you, it was quite a small matter; there was no reason whatever why she should stop with him, and he treated her by giving her medicine, which you will hear about, simply and solely for this slight asthma from which she was suffering. That was on the 30th of August, 1911.

Now, there is one fact to which I have not yet drawn your attention, and which is of considerable importance in the case. On 26th August, a few days before she was seized with this illness, which in the end, at any rate, was a fatal illness, the daughter, Maggie Seddon, goes to a chemist's shop in the neighbourhood and purchases a packet of Mather's fly-papers, which are known and described on the envelope which contains the fly-papers as "Arsenical fly-papers." They are also labelled "Poison." Caution is given to remove always the plate containing these papers from the reach of children, and care is taken to show that they are undoubtedly dangerous. A packet of these papers contains six fly-papers. Each fly-paper not only contains enough, but more than enough, to kill an adult person. I am speaking not only of what is actually in the paper, and which may be extracted scientifically from the paper, or which may be ascertained by careful and precise and exhaustive analysis, but also from what would result from any person taking one of these papers, or two or three, as the case might be, and simply boiling them in a small quantity of water; the result would be that the arsenic in that water would be enough, and more than enough, to kill any person who took it. Arsenic apparently is tasteless, and it has no smell; even when it is the result of the boiling of a paper in a small quantity of water, it has no taste and no smell. It can be administered without fear of detection in any liquid which has anything like the colour of the water which would be the result of the boiling up of the paper. It would not be colourless, because, as you will have explained to you more fully in further detail, if you boil one of these papers in water, or even if you soak it in cold water, the result will be that the arsenic which is extracted does not itself colour the water, but the colour of the paper is also abstracted into the water, and the consequence of it is that you get a coloured water which contains the arsenic. If it were not for the colour in the paper there would be no colour at all in the water, and you would have the water with the arsenic in it quite colourless, so that the colour that you get is, as I have explained to you, the result of the paper, and not of the arsenic.

Now, you will hear that her food was given to her by the female prisoner. It was cooked in the kitchen on this second floor. To make it quite clearly understood of what these rooms consisted, there were three windows on the second floor, two windows were in the bedroom which was occupied by Miss Barrow, the kitchen was in the room adjoining, and had the other window of these three which faced the front. At the back of the house on this floor was another bedroom, at the rear of Miss Barrow's bedroom, which had originally been occupied by Mr. and Mrs. Hook, but when they left it had not been occupied for a considerable time. Then there was a small bedroom, which was sometimes used by the boy, Ernie Grant, but mostly he slept with Miss Barrow.

Now, the food which was given to Miss Barrow contained, amongst other things, the ordinary kind of things which an invalid, or a person of

Opening Speech for Prosecution.

that character who is ill, would take, such as Valentine's meat juice; you may know how that is given—in the form of a liquid—and tea was taken. You could, without difficulty, place arsenic which was in this coloured water by pouring the coloured water either into the tea or into the Valentine's meat juice, or into any other food which was being given, so long as it was not sufficient to discolour the food—so long as it was not sufficient, at any rate, to call the attention of the sick person to the change of colour. Now, I am not going to delay you with any lengthy description of the scientific evidence which you will hear upon this; but in the result I shall submit to you the fact will be established according to the tests which have been made by the most skilled experts beyond all doubt that arsenic was widely distributed in the body, and that she therefore died from the administering of arsenic, and then you have to face the question of who administered it?

During the whole of this period—during this eventful time—no one else (except for the visit of the father on 11th September, when he merely came up to witness the will), no one else appears to have gone into this room at all,* and Miss Barrow herself, you will observe, never was out—never was well enough to go out—from 1st September to 14th September, and from the quantity of arsenic which was found in the stomach and in the intestines it will be made clear to you that this arsenic must have been taken—at least the last dose, the dose which proved fatal—within, as I have said, forty-eight hours of the death. You will also hear that so much arsenic was in the body that not only was it found in the organs to which I have called your attention, and in the other organs, but it was even found in the hair, it was found in the nails, and it was found wherever an expert would expect to find it, and wherever a man who is skilled in the effect of poison would look for it, and would naturally expect to find it if the poison had been administered. As to that, the evidence will be before you, and you will have the opportunity of hearing it tested by my learned friends, and you will have also the advantage of hearing it explained by the witnesses in the box.

Now, gentlemen, I want to call your attention a little more precisely to what happens immediately after the death. The 14th September is undoubtedly a day of very great importance—I mean the events of that day after the death of Miss Barrow, and I want your attention to what happened on that day. I have told you already about the male prisoner having gone to the doctor at 7 o'clock, and I have told you about his having gone to the undertaker. The afternoon was spent in this way. It was a Thursday, and, as I told you when I started my address to you, Thursday was usually the day the male prisoner settled up the week's takings and business with the insurance company in which he was employed. On that date a Mr. Taylor and a Mr. Smith came to his house and saw him in the basement, which was his office where they habitually saw him, and there they proceeded to the settlement of the week's business. Suffice it to say, that that represented a sum of between £50 and £60 which had been taken in gold or in silver during that week, which would be paid by the canvassers to him, the male prisoner, as the result of their takings during the week, and for which he would have to account, after deducting

---

* Dr. Sworn was attending her regularly.—ED.

Trial of the Seddons.

his commission, to his employers, who were represented by Mr. Taylor and Mr. Smith. That was the ordinary routine of the business. We are not in this case concerned with it, except upon this one date, because upon this date, in the afternoon of this day, the male prisoner was seen by Mr. Taylor and Mr. Smith in the possession of at least two hundred sovereigns in gold. His banking account does not enable you to ascertain whence those sovereigns had come; in fact, it is quite clear that they were not drawn from that banking account. There is no means, so far as we are aware, of explaining where those two hundred sovereigns came from, except that I shall make the suggestion to you for your consideration, that those two hundred sovereigns, or about that sum, was the money which, on the 19th June of the same year, 1911, Miss Barrow had drawn out of the savings bank where it had been deposited, and for which she was receiving interest for many years. Why she drew it out we are unable to say. I shall suggest again to you that she went there with the female prisoner, and that it was only part and parcel of the system apparently that was being pursued of getting into their hands the whole of the property of this deceased woman. There was the £216 at this savings bank which was drawn out on this 19th June, and it was paid out in gold apparently, it is suggested, because of some doubt or some anxiety which had been aroused in the public mind by the failure of a bank. At any rate, there is no doubt about this, it was paid out in sovereigns. What became of that money there is not the faintest evidence to show, unless it was this two hundred sovereigns and odd which were found in the possession of the male prisoner in the afternoon of the 14th September.

At the same period, on 15th September, immediately after her death— I will not say whilst her body is still lying in the house, because it had been removed on the night of the 14th to the mortuary, but before, at any rate, she was buried—he goes to a jeweller in the neighbourhood and takes with him a ring, which was a ring which had belonged to Miss Barrow, which he desires to have made larger; he also takes with him a watch which undoubtedly was in the possession of Miss Barrow, which had the name of her mother engraved on it, "Eliza Jane Barrow." He takes this to the jeweller to erase that name and put a gold dial or a coloured dial instead of the plain white dial which had been on the face of the watch. Neither of these articles appears in the inventory of the jewels which were left, and which eventually come into the possession of Hilda and Ernest Grant when they come of age under the will. It is right to say with reference to that, that the female prisoner when asked about this said that the watch was a present to her, and that that was the explanation of the husband taking it to the jewellers. Well, gentlemen, that fact is one which you will take into account. In itself certainly I should not desire to make too much of it; but, taken in conjunction with the other facts and circumstances to which I have called your attention, does it not seem a little odd, if it had been made a present to her and there was nothing to conceal, that before even the body had been consigned to the earth she was having it taken to the jewellers to have the name erased? Might you not ask yourselves also, why erase the name at all? Then, again, within a few days, within two or three days, of her death you will find the male prisoner paying for shares in a building society, with which,

Opening Speech for Prosecution.

The Attorney-General

somehow, he was connected, and paying for three shares a sum of £90 in sovereigns. Altogether, so far as we have been able to trace, payments are made of at least over £150 in gold during these very few days which elapsed immediately upon the death of Miss Barrow, for which we are wholly unable to account either from his bank book or from his savings bank book. He had apparently two accounts. He had an account at a local branch of the London and Provincial Bank, and he had also an account at a savings bank. None of this money appears to have come from there, and this money does not appear to have gone into there; but there it is dealt with by him. So far as we have been able to trace with all the careful inquiry that has been made, with the exception of a small amount which has been paid in with some business money on the 15th which, according to the view which we present to you, was some of the gold which he had got from Miss Barrow's money (this £200 odd), and also a sum of either £25 or £30, which is paid into the savings bank within a few days, and the £90 which was paid in gold for the shares for the building society, also within this very short period immediately after the death—with those exceptions we are unable to trace what has become of the money. But that will account for something like £150. I am not able to give you the exact amount, but it is very near £150.

Now, one question which will have suggested itself to you, I have no doubt, already is, if this was not the money which belonged to Miss Barrow, of which the male prisoner was found in possession that afternoon, what had become of it? She was in the habit, as you will hear, and as I have already told you, of keeping gold in a cash box. What had become of the £400 which was in the cash box when she went into the prisoner's house in July of 1910? As I have explained to you, we know that the notes had got into their possession; and I suggest—but I tell you that I am not able to trace it—that equally the gold had found its way into their possession too; and with regard to the £216 which had been drawn in June and brought home by her to the house there is not the faintest ground, so far as I am able to put before you from the inquiries which have been made on behalf of the Crown, for suggesting that that money had been dealt with in any other way; and, again, so far as we know, there is no other means of explaining how it was that the male prisoner found himself in possession of this large sum of gold in the afternoon of this busy day when he was arranging for the funeral of this woman who had died in his house on that very morning, except that it had come out of that cash box. According to his statement, and according to a statement which he handed to the relatives, there was no cash at home except, as I have pointed out to you, this sum of £4 10s.; according to another document (so that I may put everything before you that he had said with regard to it) it is put as a sum of £4 10s. found, either in the cash box or near there, and £5 10s. which was found in the drawer, that is, £10; and then there is an explanation given of how that £10 was spent. But except for those trifling sums—at the utmost therefore this sum of £10— there is not the faintest suggestion or explanation of what had become of all this money.

Now, gentlemen, in that state of things the inquest took place on the 23rd of November; it began on that day. At the inquest the male

Trial of the Seddons.

prisoner gave some evidence, which will be read to you. The substance of it I have dealt with when I have been explaining to you in dealing with these various dates and events what the explanation has been that the male prisoner has put forward. His evidence will be read to you in detail, and you will, of course, give it the most careful consideration. I shall refrain for the moment from making any further comment with regard to it. But I desire now to direct your attention to what happened as the result of the inquest and the post-mortem examination. The inquest, as I say, began on 23rd November; it was adjourned, and was not resumed till 14th December; but on 4th December the male prisoner was arrested, and this is what he said when he was arrested. I invite your attention to it. Inspector Ward told him that he arrested him for the murder of Miss Barrow by administering arsenic. He said, "Absurd! What a terrible charge, wilful murder! It is the first of our family that have ever been accused of such a crime. Are you going to arrest my wife as well? If not, I would like you to give her a message for me. Have they found arsenic in the body? She has not done this herself. It was not carbolic acid, was it? as there was some in her room, and Sanitas is not poison, is it?" Then he repeated the word "murder" several times on the way to the station. Now, that is a rather remarkable statement, even making every allowance for the state of mind of a man who is arrested. It is a little difficult to understand why he should ask, "Are you going to arrest my wife as well?" He says, "Have you found arsenic in the body?" then he goes on. When he is taken to the police station he is left in charge of the sergeant there, and he says this, "Poisoning by arsenic—what a charge! Of course, I have had all her money affairs through my hands, but this means Police Court proceedings and a trial before jury; but I think I can prove my innocence. I know Miss Barrow had carbolic in her room, but there is no arsenic in carbolic." That is his statement, and it is right that you should have before you the view that he gave, whatever it was, when the arrest took place.

On 15th January, the inquest having meanwhile proceeded further, the female prisoner was arrested. All she said when she was arrested was, "Very well."

Now, gentlemen, after that somewhat brief outline of the facts of this case into which you will have to inquire, I shall proceed, with the assistance of my learned friends, to call the evidence in order to prove before you in the proper and regular way in a Court of justice what I have opened to you as to what will be proved by the witnesses on behalf of the Crown. Gentlemen, I would ask you to bear this in mind throughout this inquiry. It is important in the interests of justice, and important in the interests of the defence, that you should keep clearly before you that the charge which is made is a charge made against both the prisoners; that at the end of this case, at the end of the evidence—subject to any explanation that may be put forward by my learned friends, and subject, of course, to the direction of law from my lord, and to the assistance which you will get from my lord in the consideration of the evidence, you will then have to determine whether you are satisfied that both of these prisoners committed this murder. I say to you at once, in accordance with the principles upon which the criminal law is administered in this

The Seddons in the dock at the Old Bailey.

Opening Speech for Prosecution.

country, that if, as the result of the evidence which is put forward to you on behalf of the Crown, you come to the conclusion that there is a reasonable doubt of the guilt either of one or of the other, or it may be both, why, gentlemen, if you have a reasonable doubt, the prisoners are entitled to the benefit of it. But, equally if, when you have considered the evidence in all its bearings, and heard everything that is to be said in their favour by my learned friends—if, as the result of it all, the conviction is forced upon your minds, from the consideration of the evidence, that either the two prisoners, or one of them, was responsible for the administering of the poison to Miss Barrow, it will be your duty to say so ; it will be your duty to give effect to the conviction of your minds. It is your duty to do justice in this case, bearing always in mind, as I have indicated to you, that the conviction must be brought home to your minds before you should find a verdict either against the one or the other of these prisoners.

Evidence for the Prosecution.

PERCY ATTERSAL, examined by Mr. TRAVERS HUMPHREYS—I am Police Constable 266 of the E Division. I am accustomed to making plans. I now produce exhibit 6, a plan made by me of the neighbourhood of 63 Tollington Park, North. That plan is correct and drawn to scale. Evershot Road is a turning out of Tollington Park. Upon the plan I show No. 63 Tollington Park and also No. 31 Evershot Road, the distance between the two places being 244 yards. I also show on the plan 160 Corbyn Street, which is 433 yards from 63 Tollington Park. I produce exhibit 43, which is a plan showing the interior of the house 63 Tollington Park. In the basement there is a large room in front, which can be approached from the street without going through the front door, going down the basement steps, and there is also a back kitchen. On the ground floor there are two rooms. On the first floor there are two bedrooms, one front and one back, and on the second floor there is a bedroom looking over the front and what is marked as a kitchen next to it ; at the back there are a bedroom and a small bedroom. I also produce exhibit 27, a plan on a larger scale of the front room in the basement of 63 Tollington Park. (Copies of exhibit 43 were handed to the jury.)

Cross-examined by Mr. MARSHALL HALL—Just take the plan of the basement for the moment. Where you have got "Table" marked in the extreme north at the top, as a matter of fact there is a shelf, is there not, over that table, and a cupboard—not a shelf—next to the safe ? You have marked "shelf" next to the safe ; as a matter of fact it is a cupboard ?—The shelf is in the cupboard.

It is an enclosed shelf ?—Yes.

The same answer applies here ; this lower shelf is an enclosed cupboard ?—That is so.

ROBERT ERNEST HOOK, examined by Mr. MUIR—I am an engine-driver, and I live near St. Austell, in Cornwall. I had known the late Miss Barrow since 1896. At that time she was living with my mother at Edmonton.

Trial of the Seddons.

Robert Ernest Hook

I could not say the exact date when she went, but she stayed with my mother until she died in 1902, and then she went to my sister, Mrs. Grant, at 43 Roderick Road, Hampstead. My sister's husband was alive at this time; he died in October, 1906. At that time I was living at my sister's house.

Did you ever see any money that Miss Barrow had in her possession while you were in your sister's house?—Yes. That was in October, 1906; I helped Miss Barrow then to count it.

Mr. Justice Bucknill—Please answer the question and do nothing else; you will get into trouble if you do not.

Examination continued—You said you did something with regard to that money; what was it you did?—I helped to count it.

Mr. Justice Bucknill—You see why I spoke. These people are being tried on a capital charge. It might possibly be, if you do more than answer the question or make any remark, you might be doing or saying something which would not be evidence, and then the trial might have to be begun all over again.

Examination continued—It was gold that we counted; it was all loose when we started to count it, and it was afterwards put into bags. All these bags were blue and white, as far as I can give the colour. There was £20 put in each of ten blue bags; there was £50 put in one white bag with two two-shilling pieces in it, £30 put in one with three pennies in it, £20 put in one with "£20" written in ink upon the bag, and then there were two bags containing £120. I could not say how much was put in each of these two bags. The total sum in these bags was £420 4s. 3d. Then, besides that coin there were bank notes, but we did not count these. The bags and the bank notes were put in the cash box, which I now recognise as exhibit No. 2. My sister, Mrs. Grant, died in 1908.

Up to the time of her death Miss Barrow was living with her at Walthamstow, 53 Wolseley Avenue. After my sister's death she lived with Mr. and Mrs. Kemp at 38 Woodsome Road. Just after I got married, on 7th February, 1909, she left Mr. and Mrs. Kemp and went to live with a cousin, Frank Vonderahe, at 31 Evershot Road. I saw Miss Barrow at the cousin's house and also at my house at Hampstead. She lived with the Vonderahes up to the time we removed to 63 Tollington Park, which was somewhere about 26th July, 1910. I moved my furniture into the house first, and Miss Barrow also moved with my assistance on the same day. My sister had two children, Hilda and Ernest, a girl and boy. After my sister's death Ernie was living with Miss Barrow, and Hilda was living with me. When Miss Barrow moved to 63 Tollington Park Ernie went in with her; he had been living with Miss Barrow since his mother's death in 1908. The girl Hilda was down at St. Margaret's, at an orphanage there. Ernie and Miss Barrow were on the best of terms. He was about seven, or he might have been eight, at the time they moved to 63 Tollington Park.

Had you and your wife made any arrangement with Miss Barrow as to what rent you were to pay when you moved into Tollington Park?—Yes, the arrangement was that we should live rent free, and my wife was to teach Miss Barrow housekeeping and cooking. That was the only arrangement that was made.

After the time when you counted the money, and it was put into that

Evidence for Prosecution.

Robert Ernest Hook

cash box, did you ever see the cash box or the money again?—Oh, yes, I saw it several times. The first time I saw it was at Walthamstow, an the next time I saw it was at 31 Evershot Road. I saw it on three differen occasions at 31 Evershot Road. I cannot say how many times I saw it a Walthamstow; I saw it a great many times. I also saw it at 63 Tollington Park. I saw it open in this manner twice (describing) with these lid open. That is where the blue bags were. I saw the blue bags with th £20 in them. I did not see anything else on that occasion; I do not think there was anything else I could see, because the bank notes were unde this tray. That is all I saw.

For what purpose do you know was the cash box opened on tha occasion?—It was through Miss Barrow going to get money out of it; bu it was a usual thing for me to see her go to this cash box.

But when you saw it at Tollington Park do you remember what th occasion was of her opening it then?—Yes, to put her money in. In thi end of the box under the tray Miss Barrow always had a bag there, whic she termed an odd bag; I asked her what she meant by an odd bag, and she said for everyday use; and she took money out of her purse and put it into this bag. I dare say I saw it half a dozen times at Tollington Park.

What did you see in it at Tollington Park?—I saw the money, the ordinary packages, and my late brother-in-law's watch and chain were in it.

Anything else?—And the notes. Miss Barrow had four rooms on the second floor or on the top floor at Tollington Park. They were used as two bedrooms and a kitchen, and one was not furnished at all. My wife and I had the big room. Ernie Grant slept with Miss Barrow. My wife and I stayed at 63 Tollington Park for fourteen days; we went in on the Tuesday before August Bank Holiday, and left on the Tuesday week following.

How was it you came to leave 63 Tollington Park?—Well, we got ordered out by Seddon. On the Saturday evening before we left Miss Barrow and I went out for a walk; we went to the laundry at Grove Road. Having my shirts to fetch, I asked her if she would like to go walking with me to fetch them. We stopped in Tollington Park in the road a long time talking about the conversation (sic) of her public-house. We were out about two hours, and then we returned to Tollington Park. I was always on good terms with Miss Barrow. Between 9 and 10 o'clock on the Sunday night I got a written notice from Miss Barrow. Maggie Seddon gave it to me.

What had you and your wife been up to on the Sunday?—We went to Barnet, my wife, Ernie, and myself, after dinner on Sunday afternoon, and we got back about 6 o'clock in the evening.

Did you have any conversation with Miss Barrow yourself when you came back?—Yes.

Friendly or not?—Yes. When I got the written notice handed to me by Miss Seddon, I wrote a reply on the back part of it, on the extra leaf, and sent it back to Miss Barrow. The next I heard about our going was Maggie Seddon came up and told me that her father—the male defendant—wanted to see me. I went down and saw him. He said to me, "So I see you do not mean to take any notice of Miss Barrow's notice ordering you

Trial of the Seddons.

Robert Ernest Hook

to leave?" and I said "No, not this time of night." He then gave me an order to clear out within twenty-four hours, and I said, "I would if I could, and, if I could not, I would take forty-eight hours." He said, "I do not know whether you know it or not, Miss Barrow has put all her affairs in my hands," and I said "Has she?" I asked him if she had put her money in his hands. That seemed to surprise him, and he said "No." I said, "I will defy you and a regiment like you to get her money in your hands," and he said that he did not want her money, that he was going to look after her interests. That was all that was said at that time. The next thing that happened was the tacking of the notice on the door for me to quit. That would be about half-past one on the Monday morning.

How did you know it was on the door?—Because I heard the rapping at the door, and had a light in the room. I shouted, "Who is that?" and he said, "All right, Hook, now you go out of here careful and quietly to-morrow." I did not just at that moment think there was anything tacked on the door; it was later in the night. My wife was not very well. She was very restless, and I had occasion to get up and go out and get some water, and I saw this notice tacked on the door. It was a notice ordering me to clear out within twenty-four hours, and signed, "F. Seddon, landlord and owner." I left the house about 10 o'clock on Tuesday morning. I went back to the house the next day along with my brother. That was the only visit I paid to 63 Tollington Park after I left.

Had you ever seen any will of Miss Barrow?—Yes. I saw it in Miss Barrow's box on a good many occasions, and also in her hand. The last time I saw it was at 31 Evershot Road. She kept it in her trunk. Miss Barrow was very close with regard to money. She was careful, very careful. She did not spend much.

Cross-examined by Mr. MARSHALL HALL—I think you never saw Miss Barrow again after you left?—No.

That was in August of 1910. The next time that you come on the scene you saw an account of the inquest in the paper, did you not?—Yes.

On the 25th November, 1911?—Yes.

And then you wrote to Chief Inspector Ward, and said you had something to say?—I did.

You have been in the army, have you not?—Yes.

Did you have fever very badly when you were in the army?—I had enteric fever in South Africa, but not very badly.

Where did your sister, Mrs. Grant, die?—She died at Walthamstow, 53 Wolseley Avenue, in 1908.

Miss Barrow had been living with her ever since your mother's death in 1902?—That is right.

When Miss Barrow lived at your mother's house had you lived there too?—Yes.

How old are you?—Forty.

So you were about ten years younger than Miss Barrow?—Yes, about that.

Was she any relation of yours?—No.

I think you said before the magistrate that you had been sweethearts?—Yes.

Do you mean by that you had proposed to marry her?—No.

20

Evidence for Prosecution.

Robert Ernest Hook

At the time that Miss Barrow lived at your mother's house did you ever see her in the possession of any large sum of money then?—Yes.

Had she still got that little cash box at your mother's house?—I never saw the cash box there.

When did you first see the cash box?—At my sister's, Mrs. Grant's, house, in Lady Somerset Road.

Who lived in the house at Lady Somerset Road when Mrs. Grant had it?—Her husband and two children, and her husband's mother, Miss Barrow, and myself; I do not think there was anybody else.

No servant?—No servant, no.

Miss Barrow at that time was an active person?—She always was active when I knew her.

And very careful about money?—She was very careful.

Do you represent that she kept £420 in gold, besides a large sum of notes, in a little cash box in a house of that description in Walthamstow?—Yes, in that little cash box.

What was the rent of the house at Walthamstow?—9s. a week.

It was quite a small tenement house?—There were five rooms.

No servant?—No servant.

Miss Barrow, I suppose, had the usual sort of trunk or box?—Yes, a trunk with a half-round top.

The sort of thing that anybody could burst open with a chisel in about a minute?—I don't know about a minute; it might take them a bit longer. I think the lock was too strong for that.

This woman who was so careful of money, and who, as you probably know, had not only a deposit account at a savings bank, but an investment account with the savings bank?—Well, I don't know if she had an investment account.

But you know that you cannot deposit more than £200 on deposit account at the savings bank?—I knew that.

Did she ever tell you about her money?—Yes, otherwise I should not have known.

She trusted you very implicitly and gave you all information about her money?—Yes.

Did she ever tell you that she had opened a deposit account at the savings bank?—Yes.

Did she ever tell you that she had opened an investment account?—I don't know what you mean.

That is a sort of overflow account; when you have got £200, and you cannot put any more in the savings bank, you cannot deposit any more unless you open what is called an investment account; she never told you that she had opened an investment account?—No.

I have not got the date in mind for the moment, but would you be surprised to hear that early in 1909 she opened an investment account?—Yes, I would.

What did your sister die of?—I could not tell you. Her husband died eighteen months before her.

Now, I have to ask this question, I am sorry to ask it, but did not your sister die of excessive drinking?—No.

Come!—You had better get the death certificate.

Trial of the Seddons.

Robert Ernest Hook

She took a great deal too much to drink?—She did.

Miss Barrow took a great interest in your sister's children when she died?—Yes, and my sister.

Do you think that Miss Barrow was the sort of person who would have left £420 in gold and a large sum of money in notes in a little cash box in her box in your sister's house?—I do, and I know she did do so, too.

One does not like to say anything that might reflect upon the dead, but your sister was a careless woman?—She was after her husband died, yes.

Now, just take that cash box for a moment (handed) and tell me on how many occasions did you say you counted the gold in this cash box?—Once.

Only once?—That is all.

In the year 1906?—That is right.

Was anything kept at the bottom except bank notes?—Bank notes and gold.

Gold at the bottom?—In white bags under that tray.

That is the £50 bag?—Yes.

Therefore the £50 bag was under the tray?—That is right, and the £30 and the £20.

Then was any gold kept inside these openings of the tray?—Not loose.

No gold was kept in there loose at all?—No.

There were three bags kept in the bottom?—That is right.

One £50, one £30, one £20?—That is right.

Then the tray on the top?—Then the tray on the top.

No gold in the tray?—No gold in the tray.

And then you say there was £120 in two bags and two bags containing £20 each?—Yes.

Do you really mean to say you could get bags containing gold on the top of that tray and then shut the box?—Yes.

Was it in bags when you first saw it?—No, it was on a dressing-table in an apron of hers; she had taken it all out of the old bags, and was going to put it into new bags. The £420 in gold was put into new bags.

Had you ever seen so much in gold before?—No.

Nor since?—No.

As far as you know she had had that gold some time, I suppose?—Yes.

Where did Miss Barrow go when Mrs. Grant died in 1908?—She went to 38 Woodsome Road.

Did you go with her there?—I helped to move her things there, and took the cash there. I carried the cash box in my bag.

She was with the Vonderahes for two years?—I could not say the exact time she was with them.

You called there several times?—Oh, yes, several times.

And you saw the cash box there and the bags just the same?—Yes.

No more?—No, I did not see any more.

And no less?—Yes, I saw less.

In the box?—Yes.

What was it reduced to at the Vonderahes' time?—It was at Tollington Park I found that out.

Evidence for Prosecution.

But before we get to Tollington Park?—I never saw the bottom, only the top bag in Vonderahe's house.

Now, you helped to move again, did you not, from the Vonderahes to 63 Tollington Park?—Yes.

Who carried the cash box?—I carried the cash box.

Was it left behind, and did you go back for it?—No, we brought it with us. Miss Barrow picked up the carpet to see if there was anything under there, I think, or the oilcloth.

What time do you say you took the cash box to Tollington Park?—It would be just after 5, as near as I can tell you.

What time of the day was it that the move took place?—It would be between 4 and 5.

Did the man named Creek help you to carry out the goods?—He did.

I think he helped you to unload?—He did—him and his man.

It was Creek's cart?—It was Creek's cart, yes.

Now, be careful—how do you say you carried this cash box?—In my hand.

Was it covered up with anything?—Yes, it was covered up in an old apron and put in my hand bag.

Then it was in a bag?—Yes.

What sort of a bag?—A brown bag, about 16 inches long.

I put it to you that you had no bag with you?—I put it to you I had.

When you went to Tollington Park?—Well, I put it to you I had.

I am putting it to you that when you went round and helped Creek you had no bag in your hand?—I took this bag from Tollington Park to Evershot Road, in the first place, to put the cash in.

Now, I will put something else to you—that the whole of this moving was done between 12 and 3 o'clock?—Oh, later than that.

And that it was completely finished by 3?—It was not.

Do you remember Miss Barrow's holding the horse's head while you and Creek went into a public-house?—I am certain she did not, because there is not a public-house between 31 Evershot Road and 63 Tollington Park.

Did the boy and Miss Barrow leave Evershot Road with you?—Yes.

I put it to you that Miss Barrow held the horse's head while you and Creek went into a house. If you object to " public-house," I will say " a house "?—I put it to you that she did not.

During the whole of that time you had no bag in your hand?—I had the bag in my hand the whole time from the time we left Evershot Road until we got to 63 Tollington Park. Creek brought the chest of drawers up, and the drawers were put in the chest, and then I put the hand bag in the bottom drawer, and Miss Barrow locked the drawer and put the key in her pocket.

Will you swear that it was 5 o'clock?—It was near 5 o'clock, as I can tell you. I am not going to guess to five or ten minutes.

I put it to you that it was within a few minutes of 3 o'clock when the moving had been absolutely finished by Creek?—No, it was not.

You are positive?—I am certain of it. There is no question of a mistake about that.

Did the cart and horse stop anywhere on the way between Evershot Road and Tollington Park?—No.

Trial of the Seddons.

Robert Ernest Hook

And you will swear that all that time you had the bag with you?—I had the bag in my hand.

Did you and Creek go into any house on the way?—No.

Do you think this woman was the sort of person who would keep gold to that amount in the house?—I am certain of it.

You are the only person—I know of nobody else—who deposes to this quantity of gold having been kept in the cash box by Miss Barrow?—Yes; that is why I interested myself in it so much.

Now, let us come to your going to Tollington Park. When did you marry—just before that?—I married on 7th February, 1909.

You had not seen anything of Miss Barrow except that you had called at the Vonderahes?—I had called upon Miss Barrow, and Miss Barrow called upon me.

Had you taken your wife to see Miss Barrow too?—Yes.

When you moved to Tollington Park you and your wife were to give Miss Barrow lessons in housekeeping?—Housekeeping and cookery.

And you were to have your rooms rent free?—That is right.

Had Miss Barrow been in the habit of lending you money?—No.

She never lent you money?—She lent me 30s. to move my furniture, I paying the expense of moving hers from Evershot Road to Tollington Park, and my own from 29 Churchill Road to Tollington Park.

She lent you 30s. then?—Yes.

And you gave her an I O U?—I have been told so, but I did not know it.

Did you ever sell Miss Barrow any furniture?—Yes—well, I exchanged furniture; she gave me £3 in exchange. I had the same pieces of furniture back from her. There was a double washstand with a marble top, and she gave me a single one in place of it, and she gave me a small chest of drawers.

Was she very particular about things of that kind?—She was very particular; she wanted them, and I was very hard up—I wanted the money.

Yes, and you sold her some furniture exactly the same in description as what she sold to you, but yours was better than hers, so she gave you £3 as the difference?—Yes.

Did you give her a receipt for it?—Yes.

When was that?—I could not tell you the date of it. About July, 1909, I should say it was.

You were very hard up all this time?—I was.

She was an old sweetheart of yours?—Yes.

You were very great friends?—We were.

She had been kind to you?—She had.

You and your wife were going to live there rent free?—Yes. She had taken my wife and myself down to East Grinstead also.

She was a rich woman?—I considered so.

She had got £420 in gold to your knowledge, and a lot of bank notes besides?—Yes.

Did you ever ask her to help you when you were hard up?—I did; that is why she took these rooms.

It was rather a matter of importance to you, was it not, that you should have these rooms rent free?—It was.

Evidence for Prosecution.

Robert Ernest Hook

So you went there with her?—Yes.

You say you and she were on the best of terms?—Yes.

Was she an eccentric person?—No.

Was she bad tempered?—No.

Was she quick tempered?—She might have been quick tempered, but she did not use to show her temper.

She was very amiable?—Yes.

Never cross with you?—No.

Always very friendly?—Yes.

In the notice that she gave you to go did she say that you had behaved very badly to her?—Treated her badly that day.

She said you treated her so badly?—Yes.

That was on the 8th August. I understood you to say to my learned friend that you suggested it was Mr. Seddon who got you out of the house?—He did.

You thought very badly of Mr. Seddon then, did you not?—I did not think very badly of Seddon. I told him if he interfered with her money he would be in a rough corner. I said, " If he got her money he would be very clever."

Did you warn Miss Barrow against Seddon?—Yes.

Did you warn her against letting any of her money go down into Mr. Seddon's safe?—Yes.

That was before you left?—That was before I left.

We will come back to that presently. When Miss Barrow gave you this notice, did you write an answer back?—Yes, on the back of it.

Is this the answer you wrote back, exhibit No. 24—" 63 Tollington Park, 8th August, 1910 "—this is to the woman who had been your friend?—Yes.

Who had been kind to you?—Yes.

And to your wife?—Yes.

And was finding a home for you?—Yes.

Who had got one of the children?—Yes.

Who had been living either at your mother's or sister's for years?—Yes.

And I suppose paying for her board and lodging?—Yes.

With no quarrel of any sort. She writes you a letter that you had treated her badly, and that therefore you must leave. Then in answer you write this—" Miss Barrow, as you are so impudent as to send the letter to hand, I wish to inform you that I shall require the return of my late mother's and sister's furniture and the expense of my moving here and away.—Yours, R. E. Hook "?—That is right.

Did you think that she was very fond of the boy Ernie?—I did.

Did you think she would suffer very much if he went away from her?—She would worry a lot.

Is that why you added this postscript?—No.

" I shall have to take Ernie with me, as it is not safe to leave him with you "?—Yes, I wrote that to save a lot of trouble. I knew this letter had been dictated by Seddon to her and told by Seddon.

She had only been in the house a week?—A fortnight.

Trial of the Seddons.

Robert Ernest Hook

Do you say a fortnight?—Very near it; it would be on the following day.

"I shall have to take Ernie with me, as it is not safe to leave him with you." What did you mean by that?—What I said—what is said in there. As Seddon had got her under his thumb, it was not safe; I did not know what would become of the boy.

Do you really suggest that Miss Barrow was under Mr. Seddon's thumb in less than ten days after having met him?—She was.

The Attorney-General—Thirteen days.

By Mr. Marshall Hall—Why was it not safe to leave Ernie with Miss Barrow?—Well, it was not safe until you knew what she was going to do.

Knew what she was going to do?—Because she was under Seddon's thumb—she was likely to do anything.

Do you know that Ernie Grant has said in the course of this case that he was happy with the Vonderahes, but was happier with the Seddons?—He might have been.

And yet you said it was unsafe to leave the boy with the Seddons?—Yes, I did.

I put it to you that that was a deliberate threat on your part to Miss Barrow, that if she insisted upon your leaving the house you would take Ernie, and so you would hurt her that way?—It would have hurt her if I had taken him away.

And was meant to hurt her?—That was meant for her to consider that notice.

"I shall have to take Ernie with me, as it is not safe to leave him with you, and he not to go out again to-night." I do not know what the latter part means. Perhaps you can explain it?—I did not know what she was going to do; she was down with the Seddons at this time.

I put it to you, from that moment, as that letter failed to provide you and your wife with free lodging and board, you had your knife into Mr. Seddon?—I never had my knife into Mr. Seddon at all; I had never spoken to Seddon until he sent for me after that letter.

Anyhow, it did not have that effect, whether it was desired or not?—No, I am very pleased it did not.

And you went away?—I did.

As far as you knew, this woman had in the house then something like £420 in gold?—No.

How much had she?—£380, she told me.

£40 in gold had been got rid of since 1906?—That is right.

And she had a large sum in bank notes?—That is right.

And she was under the thumb of this man Seddon?—She was.

And you told Mr. Seddon, did you not, "It is her money you are after"?—I did.

Did you ever take any step of any sort or shape during the thirteen months that elapsed between your going away in August, 1910, and Miss Barrow's death in September, 1911?—No, I did not; I went down to Cornwall instead.

You never took any steps whatever to warn the Vonderahes or anybody against his evil influence?—I told people about it.

What people?—Mr. Shephard and a Mr. Scarnell.

Evidence for Prosecution.

Robert Ernest Hook

But the people to tell about this would be the Vonderahes, who were relatives, living within a stone's throw?—I cannot say whether it would or not.

You never yourself thought that Miss Barrow would leave you any money?—I never expected any.

You knew the Vonderahes and their address?—Yes.

You knew they were the nearest relatives Miss Barrow had?—I knew it was no good seeing them after I could see she was under Seddon's thumb; as they were just as helpless as what I was.

And yet you never warned the Vonderahes at all?—No, I never spoke to them.

During the thirteen days that you were at Tollington Park you examined this cash box again, did you not?—I did not examine it; I saw it.

And you understand that it was £40 less then?—Yes.

Did you look after her at all?—Yes.

Therefore it was a pure delusion on her part that you had treated her badly?—She only wrote it from Seddon's dictation.

It was in her handwriting?—It was written in her handwriting, yes.

Was she the sort of person who usually wrote things at other people's dictation?—She was on that night.

Why that night?—She had been crying all that afternoon because we had taken Ernie to Barnet, and she had not gone.

How do you know she had been crying?—Because Seddon told me when I entered the door.

As regards the furniture that you sold to Miss Barrow, was not that the furniture that had belonged to your sister?—It was.

It was not yours at all?—No.

What right had you to sell that furniture to Miss Barrow?—To pay a quarter's money for Hilda at St. Margaret's Orphanage.

When you get a little drink you get very excited, do you not?—It would entirely depend on what I had been drinking.

Since you had this fever in South Africa a very little intoxicating liquor will make you very excited, will it not?—No.

Are you a man with a very quick temper?—I do not know whether I am or not.

Did you say before the magistrate that you did not go and see Miss Barrow again "as I was excitable and nervous, and I did not know what I might say if I started talking"?—Yes, I did.

And did you frighten Miss Barrow?—No, not frighten her—never.

Had you got very excited with her?—No, I had never got very excited with her; there was no occasion to.

I think you were shown some jewellery before the magistrate which you, first of all, identified as having belonged to Miss Barrow, and on the second occasion you said that you had made a mistake, did you not?—No, I did not.

I thought you said when you were shown a piece of jewellery that you thought it belonged to Hilda?—Yes, but I said I would not swear to it, and then afterwards I said it did not.

My recollection is that you said one had got a stone in it and the

27

Trial of the Seddons.

Robert Ernest Hook

other had not?—That jewellery was shown to me on two different occasions at that Court.

I think on the last occasion—I am speaking from memory—you said, " I am now certain it is not Hilda Grant's "?—That is the second time.

Look at that (watch handed). The moment that was shown to you you identified it as Miss Barrow's?—Yes.

And you saw no difference in it?—I did say that, yes.

That watch originally had a white face?—Yes.

Now it has a gold face?—It has a gold face now.

Yet you see no difference, although its face is totally changed. That is what you said, you know?—If I said it I must have said it.

You did say it. Now you can see, as we know, the watch has been entirely altered; it has had a white face changed into a gold face?—I never knew it had a white face.

On your oath, do you swear it is anything like it?—Yes, I say it a dozen times.

And this little piece which you have given us to-day, and never gave us before about " It would take you and a whole regiment of people like you "——?—I have given that somewhere before, I do not know where it was.

I may have missed it, but I thought I had read the papers rather carefully. I suggest that it appears in no paper that has ever been made an exhibit in this case. It was quite an angry interview with Mr. Seddon, was it not?—As far as he was concerned—because I was listening to him the whole time.

Mr. Dunstan has reminded me of the passage about that watch. " I identify the watch, No. 21, by seeing it so many times. I do not see any difference in it to-day "?—Yes.

It is totally different, is it not—I mean the gold face on it has been substituted for an ordinary white face?—Yes, but I did not turn the face up to have a look at it.

Do you mean to say when the watch was first handed to you face upwards you did not look at it?—Yes, I did look at it.

What did you mean just now by saying, " I did not turn the face up "?—(No answer.)

This interview with Seddon was a very angry interview, was it not?— No. I never spoke to Seddon—not until after I asked him if he was going to take charge of the money, or if she had put her money into his charge.

It was the same night as the notice that Miss Seddon gave you, that Seddon sent for you, was it not?—Yes.

And did he say, " I see you do not intend to take any notice of this notice Miss B. has sent you "?—Yes.

And you said, " No, not at this time of night "?—Yes.

Did he say he would give you a proper notice to get out in twenty-four hours?—No, he ordered me to get out in twenty-four hours.

Did he not say anything about landlord or occupier——?—He never mentioned the landlord or occupier.

" I asked if she had put her money into his hands, and he said ' No.' " Now, according to you to-day, you said, " I defy you and a whole regiment of people like you to get her money into your hands "?—Yes.

28

Evidence for Prosecution.

Did you also say this, " I suppose it is her money you are after "?—Yes.

That was the last thing you said to Mr. Seddon?—That was.

And then you left the house?—No, I went to bed.

You left the house the next day?—No, I left on the Tuesday.

Was it the next day that you went?—Yes, it was the next day I went; that is right.

Just one more question; if you thought that Mr. Seddon had got this woman under his thumb, and that she was in possession of a large sum of money, and it was your view, as expressed to Seddon, that it was her money that he was after, why did you not go to the police?—I did not see I had any grounds to go to the police.

Cross-examined by Mr. RENTOUL—You suggest that Mr. Seddon tried to influence Miss Barrow against you?—Yes.

You do not suggest, of course, that Mrs. Seddon ever took part in trying to influence her against you?—I have not done so.

You would not like to suggest that?—I would suggest it.

So you have changed your mind since you gave evidence at the Police Court?—I have not changed my mind; I never had that question put to me before.

Let me read you one sentence that I put to you at the Police Court—" I believe Mr. Seddon influenced Miss Barrow against me. I cannot say Mrs. Seddon did "?—No, but I will say it now. She did.

The ATTORNEY-GENERAL—You might read the continuation of that sentence—" I cannot say Mrs. Seddon did. She did a lot of watching and listening on the stairs on Friday night when I was talking with Miss Barrow."

Mr. RENTOUL—And another sentence.

The ATTORNEY-GENERAL—Certainly—" I sent my wife down to see Mrs. Seddon, who was washing her bedroom floors."

Re-examined by the ATTORNEY-GENERAL—During the time when you were living with Miss Barrow at this house were you living on good terms with her, or were you on bad terms?—Always on good terms.

Had she ever before she went to live at Tollington Park kept house?—No, she always lived in lodgings.

You mean by that that she had paid for board and lodging?—Yes.

You told us this time she was paying 12s. a week for unfurnished rooms?—Yes.

And would have to provide her own food?—Food and furniture and everything.

Up to the time that you returned—I think you said at 10 o'clock you received the notice which Miss Maggie Seddon handed to you—had you any idea that there was any quarrel between you and Miss Barrow?—No.

I want to ask you a question or two about the moving to 63 Tollington Park. Do you know what the distance is?—I do not know what the exact distance is; I do not suppose it would be more than 50 to 80 yards. It is quite close.

The ATTORNEY-GENERAL—About 240 yards, I think.

By Mr. JUSTICE BUCKNILL—And if I understand you, there was no public-house on the way you went?—Not between the two houses.

Trial of the Seddons.

Robert Ernest Hook

Not the way you went?—No, my lord, there is not any way which you go.

Or any other house at which you stopped?—No.

I suppose you went the shortest way?—Yes, we turned to the left; it was a few yards down, and we turned to the right, and it is only a short distance up to 63 Tollington Park.

Further cross-examined by Mr. MARSHALL HALL—After the cart was loaded, and before it began to move, did you and Creek go to a public-house?—No.

Never?—No.

Never whilst that moving was taking place did you or Creek go to a public-house?—I do not know about Creek. I did not; I was with Miss Barrow the whole time.

Nor was there any interval of time during which Miss Barrow held the horse's head?—No.

That you swear to?—I will swear to it.

FRANK ERNEST VONDERAHE, examined by the ATTORNEY-GENERAL—I reside at 160 Corbyn Street, Tollington Park, Islington. I went there in the June quarter of 1911 from 31 Evershot Road. Eliza Mary Barrow was my cousin. She was in her forty-ninth year at the time of her death. She came to reside with my wife and me at 31 Evershot Road in 1909. She lived with us about fifteen months before she went to 63 Tollington Park. Ernest Grant lived with Miss Barrow when she was living with us. Miss Barrow paid 35s. a week for board and lodging for herself and the boy. She was very kind to the boy.

What sort of person was Miss Barrow—how would you describe her?—Well, she had rather peculiar ways with her. For instance, she dressed rather poor, I should say, for her position. I knew about her property when she was with us. She had £1600 3½ India stock. She had a rental coming in from the Buck's Head public-house of £105 per year, and a barber's shop adjoining the public-house producing £50 a year, and she had, I believe, over £200 in her bank in Upper Street—the Finsbury Savings Bank.

Did you ever see a cash box of hers?—I did.

Have you seen it open?—Once. I saw in it what I took to be some bags of money, and I saw likewise a roll of bank notes at the bottom of the cash box. I noticed that there was a tray in the box. The notes were below the tray. As far as I recollect now, I should say the bags were the same sort of bag as you would receive from a bank with say £5 worth of silver in it. On 26th July Miss Barrow moved with the boy to 63 Tollington Park. She took furniture there from my house. I had nothing at all to do with the removal. I presume the cash box was removed—I had nothing to do with it.

How was it that she left?—Well, because she got dissatisfied. After she left our house I saw her several times in the street, and I spoke to her. We were on friendly terms when we met. I never went to see her at 63 Tollington Park. The last time I saw her alive was in August, 1911, in Tollington Park. I saw her dead body about the commencement of November, and identified it in the presence of Dr. Willcox, Dr. Spilsbury,

Evidence for Prosecution.

Frank Ernest Vonderahe

and my brother. When we moved from Evershot Road to Corbyn Street in June of last year I gave notice of change of address to the post office. I have had letters delivered to Corbyn Street which have been addressed to Evershot Road. I did not receive any letter from the male prisoner in or about September of last year. I never received a letter of which exhibit No. 1, which is now shown to me, is said to be a copy. I have never received a letter like that at any time. [Letter read by the deputy clerk of the Court. See Appendix.]

Examination continued—I had a son who attended the Montem Street School. Ernest Grant attended the same school. I had no notice at all of the burial of Miss Barrow. I first knew of her death on 20th September.

Where did you get the information from?—By inquiring at 63 Tollington Park.

Just tell me "Yes" or "No" to this. Had some information been given to you before you called on that day at 63 Tollington Park?—Yes. When I called I saw the servant; I took it to be a Miss Chater. I asked to see Miss Barrow, and she said, "Don't you know she is dead and buried?" I said "No; when did she die?" She said "Last Saturday; but if you call about 9 o'clock you will be able to see Mr. Seddon, and he will tell you all about it." My wife and I called the same evening about ten minutes past 9, but we did not see him. I first saw the male prisoner on 9th October at his house; my wife had seen him on the 21st, the day after our call. When I saw him there were present a friend of mine, Mr. Thomas Walker, and Mrs. Seddon; my wife was not present. I had never seen him before in my life, but he seemed to know me; he seemed to know who I was. He came straight up to me and said, "Mr. Frank Ernest Vonderahe?" I said, "Yes," and then, turning to my friend, he said, "Mr. Albert Edward Vonderahe?" I said, "No, a friend of mine, my brother not being well enough to come." He said, "What do you want?" I said, "I have called to see the will of my cousin, and also to see the policy." He said, "I do not know why I should give you any information. You are not the eldest of the family. You have another brother of the name of Percy." I said, "Yes; but he might be dead for aught I know." He said, "I do not think so; but, if so, you will have to swear an affidavit before a magistrate that he is dead." He said, "You have been making inquiries, and talked about consulting a solicitor."

That is what he said that you had been doing?—Yes, I am repeating his words. He said, "It is about the best thing you can do." I asked, "Who is the owner of the Buck's Head now?" He said, "I am, likewise the shop next door. I am always open to buy property. This house I live in—fourteen rooms—is my own, and I have seventeen other properties. I am always open to buy property at a price." I asked him how it was that my cousin was buried in a common grave when she had a family vault at Highgate? He said, "I thought it was full up." I asked, "Who bought the India stock?" He said, "You will have to write to the Governor of the Bank of England and ask him, but everything has been done in a perfectly legal manner through solicitors and stockbrokers. I have nothing to do with it."

Was anything said about how or where he had come to become possessed of the Buck's Head and the barber's shop?—He said, "It was

31

Trial of the Seddons.

Frank Ernest Vonderahe

in the open market," and that he bought it. As I was leaving I said, "How about this annuity? What did she pay for it?" The answer he gave me was, "Taking into consideration your cousin's age, if you will inquire at any post office you will find she paid at the rate of 17 for 1, and she had an annuity of £3 per week"—he did not tell me from whom. I only knew about the annuity through the letter that he showed to my wife, exhibit No. 3, dated 21st September, 1910. That letter is addressed from "63 Tollington Park, London, 21st September, 1910," and is signed "F. H. Seddon, executor." It is headed, "To the Relatives of the late Miss Eliza Emily Barrow, who died 14th September inst., at the above address, from epidemic diarrhœa, certified by Dr. Sworn, 5 Highbury Crescent, Highbury, N. She has simply left furniture, jewellery, and clothing." That had come to my knowledge through my wife, and it was in consequence of that that I went to see the male accused. After the receipt of that letter, and up to the time that I left him at that interview on 9th October, I had no knowledge as to who it was that was paying the annuity. I never saw the male accused again until after I saw him at the inquest. After this I communicated with the Director of Public Prosecutions. Exhibit No. 2, which is shown to me, is the box that I refer to as the cash box. I know about the family vault at Highgate Cemetery in which Miss Barrow's near relatives are buried. It is not full up.

I am not quite sure that I understood what you meant by saying that when you saw the male accused you said you had come about Miss Barrow's will and a policy. What were you referring to when you referred to the policy?—The policy which would insure her life—her life annuity, according to that letter which you have just read.

Cross-examined by Mr. MARSHALL HALL—Just a question about this vault. Had you and Miss Barrow ever spoken of this vault?—Not of late years. Of course, we knew it was there.

Do you know that Miss Barrow was under the impression that there was no room for any further interment in it?—She knew different.

You talked about it while she was alive?—No.

How do you know that she knew different if you had not talked about it?—She had the proof of the grave in her possession.

All the document says is that certain people are buried in a certain grave?—Well.

It does not say how many. Anyhow, she never talked about it with you?—No.

Do you know Hook at all?—Yes.

Did he come and visit Miss Barrow often while she was living with you?—Several times.

Hook, I suppose, was always rather needy—I mean he was short of money?—No, not always.

Do you know whether Miss Barrow was in the habit or did she ever give him money?—I dare say she did.

Did you know that Hook took the furniture from Mrs. Grant's when Mrs. Grant died?—No, I cannot say I knew that.

Did you know that he sold some furniture to Miss Barrow?—Yes.

What furniture was that—it was not his, was it?—I presume so, or he would not sell it.

Evidence for Prosecution.

Frank Ernest Vonderahe

You naturally presume, because he sold it, that it was his?—Yes.

You never inquired whether it belonged to his sister?—No, I did not ask him.

Would you mind just opening that cash box for a moment. (The witness did so.) I understand you to say, "I saw a tray in the cash box. Under the tray a space. There was a roll of notes in the lower part under the tray. The bags were in the two compartments of the tray." Would you mind letting me have the cash box? (Handed.) This is rather an important matter. You say, "The bags were in the two compartments of the tray." You mean these two compartments (indicating)?—Yes.

And, of course, the tray lids were shut, because obviously the box will not shut when the tray lids are open. You see that?—Yes.

Therefore the bags, whatever they contained, were sufficiently small to go within those trays?—Not necessarily.

Obviously—because you cannot shut the box?—You need not have the lids shut quite close down.

But if anything sticks up at all (counsel manipulated the lids)?—Yes, but not quite so high as that.

Yes, but not with a roll of notes underneath. I will just show you. You see anything above the level of that (indicating) would prevent the box closing. You see there is very little above anyhow. Do you say the two lids were sticking up or not?—They were slightly open.

Slightly up, about as they are now?—Yes, they might be something like that.

Practically shut, but slightly up?—Yes.

You are quite sure the bags were in them?—Yes, and there were some few bags underneath as well.

You did not see those?—Oh, yes, I did.

You did not mention that in your evidence?—No.

I am reading your evidence—"Under the tray there was a space. Under the tray there were some bank notes, but the bags were in the two compartments of the tray." You did not say anything about the bags being under the tray before?—I am quite aware of that.

Why do you say it now?—Because it was so.

Then why did you not say it before?—Because I was confused at the time.

You gave your evidence at the Police Court. You were the person who communicated with the Director of Public Prosecutions, were you not?—Yes.

You took great interest in this case, and you gave your evidence carefully. "That is the cash box which belonged to Miss Barrow. There was a tray in it. Under the tray a space. The bags were in the two compartments of the tray. The bank notes were in the lower part under the tray." Would not any man reading that or listening to that conclude that there were no bags under the tray?—Well, I say that there were, but not many.

Were there any, as a matter of fact?—Yes.

How many?—As far as I could gather—I did not take the cash box in my hand——

Did you ever see the tray out?—Yes, I did.

Trial of the Seddons.

Frank Ernest Vonderahe

For how long?—For a few seconds.

Was there a purse underneath it or anything of that kind?—There might have been that leather purse there, but I could not swear to that.

Is it possible to buy a commoner box than that?—I do not know.

Look at it. Look at the lock. (Box handed)?—It is a very old one, I believe.

I suppose it is worthy of the name of a cash box because it is in the shape of it, but it is a tin box, is it not, with the commonest of common locks upon it?—I am no judge of cash boxes or tin boxes of any description.

Your cousin was a very eccentric woman, was she not?—She had very peculiar ways.

She spat in your wife's face or your brother's?—She spat in my wife's face.

She was a peculiarly excitable person?—She had very peculiar ways.

After the last Budget, was she very much alarmed about the question of taxation and compensation fund affecting these licensed premises?—She was very much worried about the compensation clause.

Was she very much alarmed about what she called Mr. Lloyd George's Budget—was she very anxious about it? Did she not consult you upon the question of the liability she would be under to contribute to the compensation fund under the Buck's Head property to begin with?—Yes.

And did she not tell you she was afraid that in consequence of the taxation on land she would suffer a great deal over the Buck's Head?—No, she never put it like that to me.

Did she consult you about it?—Yes.

You went so far as actually to draft a letter for her, did you not?—Yes, I did.

That was on 24th March, 1910, when she was at your house?—Yes.

Was that written to the Inland Revenue, or to whom?—That was written to the brewery solicitor.

The brewery solicitor?—Yes.

Suggesting that she should be allowed to make certain deductions in respect of the Buck's Head property?—No, I did not put that in the letter.

Well, I will read you the letter. I will put it in. It is dated 24th March, 1910. (It is only a draft, Mr. Attorney)—" I beg to acknowledge the receipt of your letter of 14th March, 1910. My relative who advises me has referred to sub-section 3 of the Licensing Act, 1904, of which you speak, and informs me that, as my lease is of the same term within a few days as that of my tenant, I am entitled to deduct as follows :—1908, 11 per cent., £5 10s." &c., &c. (reading down to the words), " will more than licence any rent due for more than twelve months."* Look at it, No. 125. Is that your handwriting?—It looks similar to mine, but I do not recollect writing it.

If it is not yours, can you suggest anybody whose it is?—No.

Will you kindly take a pencil and write the first few words yourself, " I beg to acknowledge receipt of your letter "; that will be quite enough. (The witness did so, and the document was put in and marked No. 126.)

Just look for yourself having written this ; have you any doubt whatever that that is your handwriting?—Well, I cannot recollect writing it.

---

* See Appendix A1.

Evidence for Prosecution.

Frank Ernest Vonderahe

I see. You are quite sure she did consult you about the compensation fund?—Yes.

And there was a letter from a solicitor?—Yes.

And you yourself drafted a letter for her to write to the solicitor to the brewery?—Yes.

Did you and she have a little bit of a quarrel while she was staying with you?—No.

Nothing of the sort?—Not a quarrel, no.

You know Miss Barrow's handwriting, do you not?—Yes.

I do not want you to do anything more than just to tell me if that document (exhibit 7) is in her handwriting. Is it her handwriting?—Yes, it is very much like it.

You have seen that document before, have you not?—No.

This (exhibit 7) was put in at the Police Court. It is a document in Miss Barrow's handwriting, and is as follows:—" To Mr. F. H. Seddon, 63 Tollington Park, N., 27th March, 1911. Dear Mr. Seddon,—My only nearest relatives are first cousins," &c. (reading the letter down to the words) " Yours sincerely, Eliza Mary Barrow."* (To the witness)—Was that a delusion on Miss Barrow's part that you had not been kind to her?—I should say so.

There was no foundation for it at all?—No.

You had never expected that she would leave you any of her property?—I should not have been at all surprised.

I think you said before the magistrate, " I never gave it a thought, as such a peculiar woman might leave it to a perfect stranger "?—Yes.

Did she seem much worried about this increase in the licence duties?—She could not understand how it was increasing each year.

Did it worry her?—To that extent; she wanted to know the reason of it.

Did she not also consult you about the proposed land valuation and subsequent taxation, quite apart from compensation?—No.

Did she not mention that to you?—No, I have no recollection of that.

That in addition to the burden that the compensation contribution put upon her, she was in peril of a further contribution in regard to this Buck's Head by reason of a proposed tax upon land—did she say anything to you about it?—She might have mentioned it at the time it was going on.

Did she tell you a great friend of hers, a Mrs. Smith, had bought an annuity?—No.

Do you know the Mrs. Smith that I am referring to?—I have seen Mrs. Smith.

Do you know that Mrs. Smith, who is in somewhat similar circumstances, had bought an annuity about that time?—I knew she was in receipt of an annuity.

Mrs. Smith and Miss Barrow were great friends?—They were.

Do you remember the day of the removal?—Yes.

What time do you say it took place?—I could not tell you; I was not there.

Where did Miss Barrow keep the cash box when she was in your house?—In a trunk.

---

* See Appendix F.

Trial of the Seddons.

Frank Ernest Vonderahe

The trunk was removed, amongst other things, from your house?—Yes, I suppose so. I was not there.

Can you suggest any reason why the cash box should be taken out of the trunk?—I don't know.

You saw her frequently after she went to Tollington Park?—Yes.

And I suppose you occasionally met in the street or at Tollington Park or other places?—Yes.

In the park itself did you ever see her meet other people there?—Not that I know of.

Sometimes she would get offended and not speak to anybody for a week at a time?—Yes.

And all about nothing?—Yes.

Did you see Hook when he came to your house to see Miss Barrow?—Yes, I have seen him two or three times.

You had plenty of conversation with him?—I had a conversation with him, yes.

That would be, as we know, between August, 1910, and the time of her death—some time in the late end of 1910 or early in 1911?—When I saw Hook?

When he came to your house?—That was before Miss Barrow left me.

Did you not see Hook again after he left Tollington Park?—No.

Had you a communication from Hook by letter?—None.

Hook knew your address, of course?—Oh, yes, he knew 31 Evershot Road.

You did move from there in the June quarter, 1911?—Yes.

And you have never got any letter such as has been put to you—such a letter has never been received?—No.

The Attorney-General asked you this. You got some information prior to 20th September. How soon before 20th September was it that you got that information about the boy not attending school?—Three or four days.

I put it to you that it was a little more than three or four days. I put it to you that it was more than a week before?—It may have been.

And that the information was that Miss Barrow was ill?—Yes.

You say it may have been more than a week before, and you said the information was that Miss Barrow was ill. Do you appreciate that. I do not want to catch you in the slightest?—I understand.

Do you appreciate what an important answer you have given me, because I do not want to get an answer from you from which the value is to be taken away hereafter by your saying you did not understand. You say it may have been more than a week before, and you believe the message was that Miss Barrow was ill. Do you still——?—No, I withdraw that. Put it this way. The first information I had from the school, or from my boy going to the school, was that the boy was ill. Then afterwards we heard Miss Barrow was ill.

Now, I put it to you that you did not attach any importance to it. I am not endeavouring in any way to draw any inference against you of any kind or shape, but what I want to put to you is that you did know Miss Barrow was ill?—Only through hearsay.

And this is common ground; you went on 20th September and called,

Evidence for Prosecution.

Frank Ernest Vonderahe

and you saw the servant, who said to you, " Don't you know she is dead and buried ? " and were told that if you came at about 9 o'clock you would see Mr. Seddon. Then your wife went with you that night, or did you go alone that night ?—Both of us.

And then your wife and your sister-in-law went round the next day ?— I think so.

When your wife saw Seddon the next day did you know that Seddon told her that he was going away for a holiday ?—Yes.

And that he would see you when he came back ?—Yes ; he was going away for a fortnight.

Do you remember the little boy, Ernie Grant, coming round to you just before 9th October to say that Mr. Seddon was back and could see you—do you remember the message coming to you ?—Yes.

Then you had the interview. You said, " I have called round to know about Miss B.'s will and the policy " ?—Yes.

I suggest to you that what you said was, " I have called round to know about Miss B.'s will and the annuity " ?—No, I said " the policy."

Are you quite sure that Miss Barrow had not told you herself at one of these meetings you had had with her that she had bought an annuity ? Will you take your oath to that ?—Yes, I will ; I am quite sure.

Will you pledge your oath you never knew until you were told by Mr. Seddon that Miss Barrow had bought an annuity ?—Yes. I never knew it until then.

You said before the magistrate that Mr. Seddon said to you, " I am quite willing to meet any solicitor, and I can assure you everything has been perfectly legal and done solely through solicitors and stockbrokers." That is the evidence you gave at the Police Court ?—Yes.

Now, you have added something to that to-day which apparently you did not say before the magistrate, which is of importance. You say he added something to that ?—He said, " You have been consulting a solicitor."

That is not what I am complaining about. This morning you said in addition to saying, " I can assure you everything has been perfectly legal and done solely through solicitors and stockbrokers," he said, " I have nothing to do with it " ?—Yes.

Why did you not tell that to the magistrate ? It is somewhat an important statement ?—As I told you before, I have never been in a Court of law in my life, and I was very ill at the time, and I got confused.

You agree it is a very important part of that conversation, is it not, if it is a fact that he said it ?—It is a fact ; you say it is important.

Did you and he part on good terms ?—Yes.

Did you have an interview with the Public Prosecutor ?—No.

Did you mention the word " arsenic " by any chance ?—Who to ?

The Public Prosecutor ?—I never saw him.

Did you mention the word " arsenic " to anybody ?—I never knew anything about it till after the inquest.

The answer is " No " if it is no. Had you said anything about arsenic ?—No.

Nothing at all ?—Nothing whatever.

Was Miss Barrow at all careful about her personal appearance ?—Well, no ; she did not dress very smartly.

Trial of the Seddons.

Frank Ernest Vonderahe

How late did you see her—do you remember the last time you saw her yourself?—August Bank Holiday week.

That would be right towards the beginning of August?—Yes.

She was quite well then?—Yes, except that she complained of the heat.

She had consulted a good many doctors in her time, had she not?—I don't think so—not a great many.

How many?—There was Dr. Martin.

That is one. Then Dr. Ball?—I do not know about him.

Whom else besides Dr. Martin?—Dr. Francis.

That is two?—That is all I know of.

Did you know a Mr. Jarman, a cheesemonger, at Crouch Hill?—Yes.

Do you know whether he was in the habit of changing dividend warrants for Miss Barrow?—Yes.

And did Mrs. Vonderahe sometimes go with her there?—Always went with her.

Did your wife sometimes get bank notes changed for her?—Never changed a bank note in my life for her.

Nor did she that you know of?—No.

Do you remember one occasion on which Margaret Seddon came round with a message to your house, and the door was shut in her face?—No.

What was that?—She brought a message, but the door was not shut in her face.

Tell us what you know about it?—My wife told me in the evening that a girl had been round there and asked if there were any letters for Miss Barrow, and my wife said " No "; that was all.

Was she treated rather discourteously?—No.

Did you rather resent Miss Barrow having left you?—No.

Was there a funeral at your house at one time in March, 1911?—No, no funeral at my house.

Was there a funeral to which Miss Barrow went at any time?—No.

Do you know whether Miss Barrow lost a friend early in that year 1911?—No. There was a death at my house and an inquest, and the burial took place at Devonshire Road.

Miss Barrow knew of it, did she not?—Yes.

Re-examined by the ATTORNEY-GENERAL—You mentioned Dr. Martin and Dr. Francis who had attended her. When was it that Dr. Francis attended her?—When she was living at Lady Somerset Road, Kentish Town.

As we know, she came to live with you some time early in 1909, and stopped fifteen months. It was some time before that?—Yes.

You told me that you had had some information, in consequence of which you went to the house and inquired. Now I want you to tell us what the information was, and, as near as you can say, when it was that you got it. What was it led you to go to the house to make the inquiry?—It was my little boy going to the same school as Ernie Grant. Ernie Grant was away from school. The Board school sent round a boy to inquire the reason why, and the boy brought back a message, and he said Ernie Grant was not well, as far as I can understand now or remember. Two or three days after that the school sent round again to inquire about his absence, and they then said that his aunt was ill. On two nights previous to calling

38

Evidence for Prosecution.

on the Seddons my wife and I were passing Seddon's house, and we saw all the windows of her apartments wide open.

By Mr. JUSTICE BUCKNILL—Was that unusual?—It was unusual.

You passed the place before?—Yes.

And it was unusual to see all the windows open?—Yes.

By the ATTORNEY-GENERAL—Now I want to know was it after that that you went to make an inquiry?—Yes.

You cannot fix it nearer than a night or two nights before you actually went?—About two nights previous.

Mrs. JULIA HANNAH VONDERAHE, examined by Mr. TRAVERS HUMPHREYS—I am the wife of the last witness, Frank Ernest Vonderahe. After Miss Barrow left our house I used to meet her sometimes. I saw her in the street at various places—Tollington Park or Stroud Green Road. I was on friendly terms with her. The last time I saw her alive was in the street towards the end of August. I first heard of her death from my husband, and I went with him that same night to 63 Tollington Park. I did not see either Mr. or Mrs. Seddon at that time. I went again next morning along with my sister-in-law, Mrs. Albert Edward Vonderahe. On that occasion Miss Seddon, the daughter, opened the door. We were shown into a sitting room, where we waited some time, and then Mr. and Mrs. Seddon came in. Mr. Seddon asked who we were.

Mr. JUSTICE BUCKNILL—Gentlemen, let me warn you for a moment. As the Attorney-General said just now, it is well that you should understand how the evidence applies. Anything that Mrs. Seddon said would not be evidence against her husband. You must try and remember that as we go on, so that you will be able to divide the evidence up properly.

The ATTORNEY-GENERAL—Your lordship means, of course, unless she said it in his presence.

Mr. JUSTICE BUCKNILL—Of course, I am speaking of this particular occasion; but not always in his presence if not in his hearing, I am speaking as we go along. Gentlemen, not even in his presence if he did not hear it.

Examination continued—Mr. and Mrs. Seddon came into the room together. Mr. Seddon spoke first; he asked who we were. He turned to my sister-in-law and asked whether she was Mrs. Frank Vonderahe, and I said, "No, I am." He then handed me the letter, exhibit 1 (letter dated 14th September, 1911, from F. H. Seddon to Frank E. Vonderahe). I read that letter. He asked me why we did not come, and I said we had had no letter, or we should have come, and I added that I must go to the post office and see why I did not receive the letter. I never received any letter like that on 14th September. Shown letter and envelope marked No. 127—That is a business letter which I had redirected to me on Saturday, 16th September from 31 Evershot Road to my then house, 160 Corbyn Street.

Mr. JUSTICE BUCKNILL—We would like to see how it is re-addressed. (The letter and the envelope were handed to the learned judge.) This has been addressed to "Mrs. Vonderahe, 31 Evershot Road, Tollington Park," and across it is written in ink, "Not known," and at the top of it is written "160 Corbyn Street." The postal date I cannot see.

Trial of the Seddons.

Mr. MARSHALL HALL—It has gone, but the words " Not known " are written on the envelope.

Mr. JUSTICE BUCKNILL—I just wanted to see whether it was unduly delayed or anything of that sort. The post mark is off.

Examination continued—Besides the black-edged letter, exhibit 1, Mr. Seddon gave me the letter addressed " To the Relatives," exhibit 3, in an envelope. He also showed me a copy of a will, exhibit 4; he gave it to me to read. Besides that he gave me a memorial card, exhibit 5— " In loving memory of Eliza Mary Barrow, who departed this life 14th September, 1911, aged forty-nine years. Interred in Islington Cemetery, East Finchley, Grave No. 19453," and then there are some verses. He put all these documents in an envelope which he gave me.

Did you have any conversation with him about Miss Barrow?—I did not have much. You see whilst I was reading these papers he was talking to my sister-in-law.

Before you went away, did you have any more conversation?—Mr. Seddon spoke about a letter that—well, he sent Miss Seddon about a letter of Miss Barrow's, and said that I slammed the door in her face, and I contradicted Miss Seddon, and said I did not do so. That was when we were parting with Mr. Seddon.

Did you make an appointment before you left, or was anything said about your husband seeing Mr. Seddon?—Yes. I asked him if he would see my husband and my sister-in-law's husband in the evening, and he said " No," he could not, as he was going away next day, and he had wasted enough time, and he could not possibly see them. I said they would not detain him long, and he said he could not see them as he was going away for a fortnight.

Did he mention anything about the night Miss Barrow died?—He said what a trying time they had had with her—how she had called them up, and he went up and said she must not call them any more, as they wanted their rest, and she must be quiet.

Cross-examined by Mr. MARSHALL HALL—Were you at home when Miss Barrow left your house to go to Tollington Park?—Yes.

Do you remember Creek and Hook helping to move the things?—I could not say what name.

A man came with a cart and horse?—Yes, there was a cart and horse.

Was anything left behind—did anybody come back for anything, do you remember?—No.

Will you tell me what time it was in the day when the moving took place?—As far as I can remember, it was started about mid-day.

They started about 12 o'clock and finished at about 3?—Something like that, as near as I can remember.

Miss Barrow gave a week's notice before she left—she had put it on the table, I think?—Yes.

I think you said before the magistrate that you had not exactly had a quarrel, but she had had one of her eccentric moods—not speaking to anybody?—Yes.

There was no cause for her leaving at all, was there?—No.

You saw her at the end of August, 1911, did you not?—Yes.

Evidence for Prosecution.

During that fourteen months or so she was at the Seddons' house you had seen her pretty frequently out of doors?—Yes.

Had she had a bad cold when you saw her at the end of August?—Yes. Otherwise she seemed all right?—Oh, yes, in good health otherwise.

The last week in August—just before September—you saw her again? —Yes, right at the end of August.

Do you remember Margaret Seddon coming round to ask if there were any letters for Miss Barrow at your house?—Yes.

Was the door just opened a little bit—what happened?—I opened the door myself, and I answered Miss Seddon, and said there were no letters, and shut the door.

A little quickly?—Not quicker than usual that I can remember.

Anyhow, if she thought it was done a little quickly, might there have been some justification for her thinking it?—Well, I cannot remember shutting it any quicker, unless there was any wind might have blown it, or anything like that, but I did not shut it quicker than at any other time.

I think you went several times with Miss Barrow when she went to change dividend warrants at Jarman's at Crouch Hill?—Yes, several times.

You never took any serious notice of her movements. Once she spat in your face, or something of that kind, but you did not take any notice of it?—No.

She was very excitable and irritable?—Yes.

(Exhibit No. 127 handed.) Where did you find this letter?—I was looking in my drawer, and came across it, and, seeing 14th September, I noticed it. I cannot say exactly the date.

Are you quite sure that letter came in that envelope?—Yes.

There is nothing on the envelope to show that you received it on the Saturday; it is only your recollection?—Yes. The stamp is cut off; I might just say on account of the children; they tear the stamps off the envelopes; they were collecting them; that was the reason the stamp is gone.

As the document appears now there is no date appearing on the envelope at all?—No, but that is the reason why.

That is the letter dated Thursday, 14th September, and you received it on Saturday, 16th?—Yes.

So there was a delay of two days according to you?—Yes.

You notice that the envelope is marked " Not known "?—Yes.

Re-examined by the ATTORNEY-GENERAL—As I understand it, you found this letter since you were examined at the Police Court?—I found it since.

You remembered at the Police Court that a business letter was addressed to Evershot Road, but you did not remember any more details than that?— Yes, it was that letter that I referred to.

You have looked for it, and you found it, and that is the letter now. Is that right?—Yes.

Mrs. AMELIA BLANCHE VONDERAHE, examined by Mr. TRAVERS HUMPHREYS—I am the wife of Albert Edward Vonderahe, and I live with him at 82A Geldeston Road, Clapton. On 21st September I went with my sister-in-law at 63 Tollington Park, and I saw Mr. and Mrs. Seddon there. I saw Mr. Seddon give my sister-in-law several documents in an envelope.

Trial of the Seddons.

Besides those documents there was another document which he read to us. It was a document in the terms of exhibit 7, which is a letter dated 27th March, addressed by Miss Barrow to F. H. Seddon, speaking of her relatives. I noticed a copy of the will, which Mr. Seddon produced, and I said to him that I noticed that the will was signed with lead pencil. Mr. Seddon said that that was only a copy, that he would not give us the original, and I said, "Well, of course, the original will would be taken to Somerset House for probate." He replied that he had been to Somerset House, but there was no probate required on a will of that description. He said he had the original will in his bank for safety. I asked him if he wished us to understand that Miss Barrow had parted with all her investments, and that she had bought an annuity which had died with her. I mentioned the Buck's Head and the barber's shop to him. He said, "Yes, everything," and I remarked, "Well, whoever had persuaded Miss Barrow to do that was a remarkably clever person," that Miss Barrow was a very hard nut to crack if you mentioned money matters to her. He made no answer to that.

By Mr. JUSTICE BUCKNILL—Did he say who had granted the annuity?— No, I do not remember him saying that.

Examination continued—What did he tell you had happened the last night that Miss Barrow was alive—what did he tell you about the events of that night?—He said Miss Barrow was a very great trouble to them. She sent down once or twice; she sent Ernie Grant down, but Mr. Seddon said his wife was worn out with waiting so much on Miss Barrow that he went up himself to her.

By Mr. JUSTICE BUCKNILL—"As his wife was worn out," then what?— With waiting so much upon her during her illness.

"That he had to go to her himself"?—Yes, and he asked her what she wanted, and he gave her some brandy, and said they would be retiring to rest, and he hoped that she would not trouble them again.

By "again" you understand that he hoped that she would not trouble them again that night?—Yes.

Did he tell you at what time of the day, evening, or night it was when he went up instead of his wife?—No. He did not mention the time, but the boy came down again after that, and he. Mr. Seddon, went up again and gave her some brandy. He did not say what time that was. He said that he had left some brandy in the bottle, which was gone in the morning. I do not remember him saying the hour that she died.

Examination continued—I think that is all that he told me about that night as far as I can remember. He mentioned Hilda Grant's insurance, and he also spoke about the funeral. I said that I thought it was a great pity that she was buried in a common grave when she had a family vault at Highgate, but Mrs. Seddon said that they had a very nice funeral; they did everything very nicely.

Mr. JUSTICE BUCKNILL—Either Mr. or Mrs. Seddon, I do not remember which, said that Ernest Grant was at Southend then. Mr. Seddon said that he had no legal claim on the boy, but he should always look after him, and if he could find a suitable home for him to go to he should let him go.

Examination continued—That was all the conversation, as far as I can

Evidence for Prosecution.

Mrs. Amelia Blanche Vonderahe

remember now. My sister-in-law and I then went away. We did not see either Mr. or Mrs. Seddon after that time at all.

Apart from the one matter as to the funeral being a nice one, did Mrs. Seddon take any part in the conversation?—Only to say that she had felt very ill through waiting on Miss Barrow, and that she was going to the doctor that day. Miss Barrow showed me her jewellery in the early summer of 1910 when she was living in my brother-in-law's house at 31 Evershot Road. (Shown exhibit 122.) It was a gold watch I saw, but I do not know whether it was this one; I saw a gold watch attached to this chain. (Shown exhibit 121, gold ring with a diamond set in a claw.) I saw a ring like that in Miss Barrow's possession; the setting is exactly the same, because I remember remarking to her that it looked rather like a gentleman's ring, and she said it was her mother's. I could not say about the size, but the setting is precisely the same. (Shown exhibit 123, a gold chain with a blue enamelled pendant attached to it.) I saw that when Miss Barrow showed me her jewellery.

Cross-examined by Mr. MARSHALL HALL—I suggest to you that the first thing that Mr. Seddon said to you when you came was, "Why did you not answer the letter that I sent you"?—Yes; he said that to my sister-in-law.

It was said to both of you?—Yes.

Did you tell Mr. Seddon that Miss Barrow was not responsible at times?—Yes, I said she was strange at times.

Not responsible?—Strange at times.

What you said before the magistrate was this, "I said to Seddon that at times Miss Barrow was not responsible"?—Yes, that is right.

Then did he say you could never get her to do anything she did not want to do?—Yes, that is right.

You agree with that—it was pretty difficult to get her to do anything that she did not want to do?—Well, I adhere to what I say—that she was peculiar.

You agree, do you not, that it was very difficult to get her to do anything that she did not want to do?—Yes, it was.

And anything about money?—Anything about money?

I think you said that she was a hard nut to crack when you touched her money?—Yes.

That seems to have been the common opinion of the Vonderahes and of Mr. Hook?—Yes.

They all seemed to think that?—Yes.

'She was a difficult person to handle when it came to a question of money?—Yes.

There is one question which ought to have been put in chief. Was Miss Barrow deaf?—Very deaf.

The ATTORNEY-GENERAL—That is common ground, but we have not asked a witness here yet.

By Mr. MARSHALL HALL—Did you know that the boy Ernie was very useful to her, because he used to shout into her ear the messages which she could not hear otherwise?—No, but he had to shout to her.

By the ATTORNEY-GENERAL—I suppose everybody had to shout?—Everybody had to; she was very deaf.

43

Trial of the Seddons.

HENRY EDWARD GROVE, examined by the ATTORNEY-GENERAL—I am a member of the Royal College of Surgeons. I am a Divisional Surgeon of the Hornsey Police and on the staff of the Hornsey Cottage Hospital. Dr. Cohen (the coroner who took the depositions at the inquest) has been under my care until to-day, when he has gone to a convalescent home. I saw him yesterday. He is not able, either physically or mentally, to attend the Court to-day or for three months.

WILLIAM DELL, examined by Mr. TRAVERS HUMPHREYS—I live now at 31 Evershot Road, Tollington Park. I went there on 1st September of last year. Three days after going there I received a circular addressed to a Mr. Vonderahe. I did not know Mr. Vonderahe's address at that time. I re-posted the letter after writing on it, "Not known," at the pillar-box at the corner of Fonthill Road and Tollington Park. I did not myself receive any other letters after that date addressed to Mr. Vonderahe.

Cross-examined by Mr. MARSHALL HALL—Mr. and Mrs. Hughes came into my house on 16th September. My household consists of myself, my wife, and three children, and no servants.

Just look at the envelope of that. (Handed.) Are the words "Not known" on that written in your handwriting?—No, that is not my handwriting. I should say that it is my son's handwriting, but I could not swear to that.

Mrs. ELEANOR FRANCES DELL, examined by Mr. TRAVERS HUMPHREYS—I live with my husband at 31 Evershot Road. No letter addressed to the name of Vonderahe came to our house about 14th September which I saw.

Cross-examined by Mr. MARSHALL HALL—I understand "Not known" is written on the only letter there was?—Yes.

STANLEY GEORGE DELL, examined by Mr. TRAVERS HUMPHREYS—I live with my parents at 31 Evershot Road. I remember receiving a letter that came by post addressed to Mr. Vonderahe. I crossed it "Not known," and put it back in the letter-box. (Shown exhibit 127.) The words "Not known" on that envelope are in my handwriting. After writing that I re-posted the letter.

The Court adjourned.

Second Day—Tuesday, 5th March, 1912.

The Court met at 10.15 a.m.

[Several witnesses were called to prove the possession by Miss Barrow of certain bank notes, and the dealings with them by the two prisoners.]

The ATTORNEY-GENERAL—My lord, that finishes all this evidence with regard to the notes, and I will state now what the effect is from the documents which have been produced. It is established that there were in all thirty-three Bank of England notes of £5 each, which are the proceeds

Evidence for Prosecution.

The Attorney-General

of cheques of Truman, Hanbury & Co. in favour of Miss Barrow at various dates extending from 1901 to 1910; and that those thirty-three £5 notes have been traced as to each of them as the proceeds of one or other of the cheques received by Miss Barrow from Truman, Hanbury & Co. for the ren of the Buck's Head. Then, my lord, of those thirty-three, six of them are proved to have gone to the male prisoner's credit with his bank; one on the 14th October, 1910, the other five on the 13th January of 1911 As to the remaining twenty-seven of the thirty-three, nine of them ar notes with endorsements in the name of Scott, of Evershot Road. Thos nine appear in this way. The two of them are endorsed in the handwritin of the female prisoner on the 14th October of 1910, endorsed by her wit the name of M. Scott, of 18 Evershot Road; six are endorsed in the name of Mrs. Scott, of 18 Evershot Road; one in the name of Mrs. Scott, of 12 Evershot Road; the remaining eighteen of the thirty-three are traced to Mrs. Seddon. The whole period covered during the dealing with these thirty-three £5 notes is from the 14th October, 1910, when both th male and the female prisoners are dealing with the notes, until the 23r August, 1911; that is the last date traced. Therefore my learned frien quite rightly pointed out that all these thirty-three notes are dealt wit before the death of Miss Barrow. That, my lord, is the substance of what has been proved. Each note has been traced out, as your lordship has seen. elaborately, but that is really what all this evidence has been called to establish.

Mr. JUSTICE BUCKNILL—You understand that, gentlemen?

The FOREMAN—Perfectly, my lord.

CECIL VANE DUNSTAN, examined by the ATTORNEY-GENERAL—I am senio clerk in the chief accountant's office at the Bank of England. I produce the transfer book for India $3\frac{1}{2}$ per cent. stock, exhibit 8. There is an entry in that book under date 14th October, 1910, of the transfer of £1600 $3\frac{1}{2}$ per cent. India stock from the name of Miss Eliza Mary Barrow, of 63 Tollington Park, to the name of Frederick Henry Seddon, of 63 Tollington Park. In the ordinary course that entry would be necessary in order to transfer the stock out of her name into his name. There is nothing in the book to show the consideration. The entry purports to be signed, as it has to be signed, by the transferor of the stock. She would have to appear at the Bank of England and be identified by some person who accompanied her. She would sign the book, and that transfers the stock out of her name into the name of the transferee, Frederick Henry Seddon. In the ordinary course of events a ticket would be in the first instance put forward by a stockbroker. The ticket, exhibit 9, was put forward b W. W. Hale & Co., stockbrokers, and that showed that there was to be the transfer made in our books. These are instructions to prepare the transfer, and we then make the entry; the transferor comes, and being identified, signs the book. Miss Barrow did that.

Cross-examined by Mr. MARSHALL HALL—As far as I know, the letter of 5th October, 1910, from Miss Barrow is the first document in that transaction. It is addressed, "To the Secretary, Chief Accountant, Bank of England," and is as follows:—"Dear Sir, as I am disposing of the whole of the above stock, please transfer same to Frederick Henry Seddon,

Trial of the Seddons.

Cecil Vane Dunstan

of 63 Tollington Park, London, N., and kindly inform me when it will be convenient, and I will call and sign transfer book. Early attention will oblige.—Yours faithfully, Eliza Mary Barrow, stockholder." Our answer to that is, " 6th October, 1910.—Miss E. M. Barrow, 63 Tollington Park, N.—Madam, I beg to acknowledge receipt of your letter of the 5th inst., and in reply to say that in order to effect your purpose it will be necessary for you to attend here, accompanied by a stockbroker, for the purpose of identification, and execute a transfer in the bank books here, or to grant a power of attorney to some person to act on your behalf in like manner. See enclosed memorandum." That letter is signed by H. B. Orchard. Miss Barrow replied on 7th October, and that concluded the correspondence. Thereupon the lady having been given due notice that a stockbroker would have to be present, attended with somebody for the purpose of identification, and executed the transfer, and the stock was in due course transferred into the name of Seddon. (The letters were put in and marked No. 130.)

WILLIAM WEBB, examined by Mr. TRAVERS HUMPHREYS—I am a member of the Stock Exchange, and my office is at 18 Austin Friars. I received some instructions just before 14th October, 1910, and in consequence my clerk prepared the stockbroker's ticket. exhibit 9, with reference to the transfer of £1600 3½ per cent. India stock from Eliza Mary Barrow to Frederick Henry Seddon. I personally attended on 14th October at the Bank of England with the transferor, Miss Eliza Mary Barrow. I witnessed her signature.

Cross-examined by Mr. MARSHALL HALL—I had some correspondence with Miss Barrow—two or three letters—and everything was done perfectly regularly. I had no instructions otherwise than to prepare a transfer and attend for the purpose of identification, and I duly carried out my instructions.

Re-examined—Certain formalities have to be gone through before you can transfer stock. All those formalities were duly carried out in this case. What had happened or why it was transferred I do not know.

ARTHUR ASTLE, examined by the ATTORNEY-GENERAL—I am a member of the Stock Exchange and manager of the firm of Capel-Cure & Terry, who carry on business at Tokenhouse Buildings and on the Stock Exchange. The male prisoner was introduced to me on 25th January, 1911. He gave me instructions to sell £1600 India 3½ per cent. stock, which I did, realising £1519 16s. We paid him a cheque for that amount. I identify exhibit 10 as that cheque. It is a crossed cheque on the London County and Westminster Bank, dated 25th January, 1911, " Pay F. H. Seddon, Esq., or order "—" bearer " is scratched out—" £1519 16s." It is signed by " Capel-Cure & Terry, Arthur Astle," and it is endorsed " F. H. Seddon."

Cross-examined by Mr. MARSHALL HALL—Mr. Seddon was introduced to us. I believe that my firm occupies a very high position on the Stock Exchange. The word " order " on the cheque was unnecessary, as the striking out of " bearer " would have had the same effect. It is an endorsed cheque to F. H. Seddon, and it has been through a bank.

Evidence for Prosecution.

Arthur Douglas Laing

ARTHUR DOUGLAS LAING, examined by Mr. TRAVERS HUMPHREYS—I am a clerk with the London County and Westminster Bank, Limited, Lothbury. Messrs. Capel-Cure & Terry have an account at that bank. (Shown exhibit 10.) That is a cheque for £1519 16s. drawn upon our bank. That was paid in to our bank on the same day, 25th January, by the opening of a deposit account in the name of Frederick Henry Seddon. The first withdrawal from that account was on 1st February, when £119 16s. was withdrawn in cash. On 6th March, 1911, the remainder of the money was drawn out, and the account closed, the amount drawn out being £1403 10s. 2d., which included the interest that had accrued. That money was drawn out in cash, and the account was then closed.

Cross-examined by Mr. MARSHALL HALL—I cannot say that I know that on the completion of a purchase of property it is usual to pay in notes instead of cheques. The payment out was in the shape of one £1000 note, two hundreds, three fifties, three tens, and three fives, the numbers of all of which were entered in our waste book.

EDWIN RUSSELL, examined by Mr. TRAVERS HUMPHREYS—I am a solicitor and a member of the firm of Russell & Sons, 59 Coleman Street. I never saw the male defendant until I saw him at the Police Court. (Shown exhibit 11.) That is an assignment of certain property which was prepared in my office by our managing clerk, Mr. Keble, who is now dead. In the transaction mentioned in that document my firm acted solely on behalf of Mr. Seddon. It is an assignment, dated 11th January, 1911, between Eliza Mary Barrow, of 63 Tollington Park, spinster, and Frederick Henry Seddon, of the same address, insurance agent, and it recites a lease of certain property of 27th June, 1853, for seventy-six and a quarter years, expiring in 1929. It shows that property became vested in Eliza Jane Barrow, and it further recites that Eliza Jane Barrow by her will bequeathed all that estate to Eliza Mary Barrow. Then, whereas Eliza Jane Barrow died, and whereas Eliza Mary Barrow has agreed with Frederick Henry Seddon to assign to him all the property mentioned in that original lease for the residue of the terms in consideration of the payment by or on the part of the said Frederick Henry Seddon to the said Eliza Mary Barrow of an annuity of £52 secured to the said Eliza Mary Barrow during her life, secured on the rents and profits of the premises, Eliza Mary Barrow assigns to Frederick Henry Seddon the premises comprised in the lease being the Buck's Head public-house and No. 1 Buck Street, and Seddon covenants to pay the annuity or yearly sum of £52, payable by equal payments of £4 every lunar month, and the annuity is to be a charge on the premises, and Eliza Mary Barrow is empowered by distress to recover that annuity if it is in arrear for forty days. It is signed " Eliza Mary Barrow," and her signature is witnessed by Henry W. D. Knight, solicitor. As soon as we were satisfied that the title to the property was in order, we required Miss Barrow to be represented by a separate solicitor. The solicitor introduced for that purpose was Mr. Knight. It was on 6th January, 1911, that Mr. Knight was brought into the matter after the assignment had been prepared. We received our costs from the male prisoner, and we also received from

Trial of the Seddons.

him by a separate cheque the costs which would have to be paid to Mr. Knight.

Cross-examined by Mr. MARSHALL HALL—It was your late clerk, Mr. Keble, who insisted upon a separate solicitor appearing for Miss Barrow, and he introduced Mr. Knight?—Our firm insisted.

Mr. Knight was introduced by your firm, he was not nominated by Mr. Seddon?—I think not, but I do not know. Personally, I know very little of the transaction. Our account was agreed at a certain figure for which we received a cheque; the amount was £29 8s. Mr. Knight's costs were fixed at the sum of £3 3s. That was agreed to at an interview between the parties, and it was paid to us by a further cheque for £4 13s., which included 30s. for something else. We paid Mr. Knight's costs out of that cheque. Mr. Keble, our managing clerk, called on 6th January upon Miss Barrow at Tollington Park, and he called again on 11th January. The entry in our account is "Attending, completing purchase and attesting execution."

Do you know that there were some defects in this title, and they had to have three statutory declarations?—Yes. I should not care to say that Miss Barrow knew of these defects. I do not think that they were points that she would appreciate at all; they are rather technical.

Without knowing any of the technicalities, did she know the broad fact that there were said to be defects in the title?—I cannot say, but she would probably know that the declarations were to be made.

And these are the three statutory declarations?—Yes. Our firm did not have the Buck's Head property valued, but I take it that the value could easily be calculated from actuarial tables.

Do you know that the present value of the property is £706?—I have no knowledge of that. The question of value was no concern of ours. (Shown letter dated 30th November addressed to Mr. Keble.) That appears to be in the same handwriting as the other letters from Miss Barrow. It deals with the information which is desired to be obtained from Truman, Hanbury & Buxton enabling us to transfer the property to Seddon. Referring to our bill of costs under date 7th September I see this item, "Attending Mr. Brangham informing him you had decided to purchase, and that valuation was only required as a precautionary measure and giving him particulars."

Then, "Writing him," so that obviously on the face of your bill of costs there was some correspondence in reference to a valuation. Do you find that item there?—Yes, but I should like to show you this letter of 7th December from the male prisoner, which has some bearing upon that. (Reads letter.) I should say it is purely upon the question of getting the fees arranged before Mr. Brangham valued. (The letters were returned to the witness.) (Shown letter No. 133 addressed to Truman, Hanbury & Buxton from Miss Barrow, dated 30th November.) That carries out what Miss Barrow says she is going to do in the letter she wrote to Mr. Keble.

HENRY WILLIAM DENNY KNIGHT, examined by Mr. TRAVERS HUMPHREYS—I am a solicitor practising at 22 Surrey Street, Strand. The late Mr. Keble was my brother-in-law. On 9th January, 1911, Mr. Keble mentioned to me the matter of the assignment of the Buck's Head, and on the same

48

Evidence for Prosecution.

day I communicated with Miss Barrow by letter. After receiving a reply from her, I, on her behalf, approved the draft of the assignment of the Buck's Head and No. 1 Buck Street. I did not in any way advise Miss Barrow in the matter. I was only to carry out the arrangement that they had come to. I attended on the completion of the matter at 63 Tollington Park on 11th January. Miss Barrow was very deaf. I asked her to read the material part of the assignment, that is, the charging of the annuity, and she read it in my presence. I witnessed her signature to that document. My costs were paid me by Messrs. Russell & Son through Mr. Keble. Miss Barrow said she was glad of the assistance, but she would not pay anything.

Cross-examined by Mr. MARSHALL HALL—(Shown exhibit 13, being a letter from witness to Miss Barrow.) What is stated in that letter is accurate. I was introduced by Mr. Keble, my brother-in-law, not by Mr. Seddon. Miss Barrow replied by the letter, exhibit 14. I remember that the draft deed of conveyance sent to me contained the clause charging the property with the payment of the annuity.

JOHN CHARLES PEPPER, examined by the ATTORNEY-GENERAL—I am chief clerk in the Finsbury and City of London Savings Bank, 18½ Sekforde Street, Clerkenwell. Miss Eliza Mary Barrow had a deposit at our bank. On referring to our ledger I find that that account was opened on 17th October, 1887, and it was never closed until the last transaction on 19th June, 1911, when the whole amount standing to her credit at the time was withdrawn with interest, £216 9s. 7d. I find that the last payment in to her account was on 5th October, 1908, and the last withdrawal before the final one of 19th June, 1911, was on 31st July, 1907. It appears that there was no transaction on the account at all after that date until the full amount standing to her credit was withdrawn on 19th June, 1911. I remember the withdrawal of the money on 19th June, 1911. Miss Barrow came with another lady whom I did not know. The money was paid over to her all in coin ; only the odd money, 9s. 7d., was in silver and coppers, the rest, £216, was in gold. The notice given the week previous asked for half notes and half gold, but by the time Miss Barrow came to the bank she had apparently changed her mind, and she asked for it and had it all in gold. It was not at all unusual at that time to pay a large sum like that in gold. We were paying cash more than usual at that particular time. There was a run on the Birkbeck Bank. The gold was paid out in two bags containing £100 each, and the £16 loose.

Cross-examined by Mr. MARSHALL HALL—I suppose a great many people had a fear in consequence of the Birkbeck trouble about that time ? —We were not so much bothered with it. We had no run on our bank at all.

Is it the rule of your bank that no ordinary savings bank account can exceed £200?—That is the Government rule.

But you allow it to exceed it as long as it is only the interest that takes it over and above £200?—That is it—interest on £200 only—not in excess.

Therefore, after they have deposited £200 they do not get any interest

D   49

Trial of the Seddons.

on the excess, there is no compound interest?—No compound interest; it is interest on the £200 only. If anybody wants to deposit any further money with us they have to open an investment account. Miss Barrow opened an investment account with our bank by the payment of £10 on 30th September, 1909. There was no further payment into that account except the money which accrued due for interest. On 7th April, 1911, she drew it out, £10 7s. 9d. The amount of interest on that amount was 2¾ per cent. People must have £50 to their credit before they can open a special investment account, and that account is limited to £500.

ARTHUR DOUGLAS LAING, recalled, further examined by the ATTORNEY-GENERAL—(Shown exhibit 2.) I saw that box in the afternoon of Friday last, 1st March. I saw sovereigns placed in that box by the chief clerk of our bank. They were placed in the top of the box, above the tray, in two bags. There was nothing under the tray at the time. I saw £500 in two bags placed on the top of the tray in sovereigns.

By Mr. JUSTICE BUCKNILL—I think the box was empty when we tried those experiments.

Examination continued—There was still room for another £500 I should say. In each of the two outer receptacles in the tray were placed £150, one bag in each receptacle. With £150 in each of those receptacles we could close the lid of the receptacles firmly down. I think a little more could be placed in each receptacle.

Cross-examined by Mr. MARSHALL HALL—The £150 was just shovelled into the bag from the scale.

Except that possibly the bottom would tumble out you could get about £1500 to £1600 in that box?—I should think so; it would be rather heavy. That box is hardly the sort of box that I would choose myself; I should not trust to the lock. It is a very ordinary box.

ERNEST GRANT, examined by the ATTORNEY-GENERAL—I live at 49 Corrance Road, Brixton. I was ten last birthday. I remember Miss Barrow; I have known her as long as I can remember. I used to call her " Chickie." I remember going to live with her.

Mr. MARSHALL HALL—As far as the depositions in this case are concerned, my friend can, of course, lead this witness.

Examination continued—I also remember going to Mr. Seddon's house to live with her in the rooms on the second floor. When we first went there I slept with her and afterwards I slept in a room by myself, that room being the little room, not the room that Mr. and Mrs. Hook had had, but the little room by the side of that. I remember going away to Southend for a holiday in the year that Miss Barrow died. After I came back Miss Barrow was taken ill, and she had to stay in bed. I remember at first when she was ill that, I slept in my own bed in the little room at the back. When she got worse she asked me to sleep in her bed, and I did so. I remember the last night that I slept with Miss Barrow. On that night she kept waking up. She waked me up and I went downstairs to call Mrs. Seddon, because Miss Barrow asked me to do so. Mr. and Mrs. Seddon slept on the ground floor. Mr. Seddon came

Evidence for Prosecution.

Ernest Grant

upstairs and Mrs. Seddon also came up, and then I got into bed again
with Miss Barrow. Mr. Seddon wanted me to go to my own bed to get
some sleep, and I went to my own bed in the little back room. After
that Miss Barrow called out again, and I went back to her and found Mr.
and Mrs. Seddon in the room with her. I had left them in the room
when I went to my own room to sleep, and Miss Barrow had called me
back again directly I had left. I got into her bed, and Mr. Seddon again
told me to go back to my room, which I did. Miss Barrow called me
back again, and I went back to her room and found Mr. and Mrs. Seddon
there. That occurred several times during the night, Mr. Seddon telling
me to go back to my room and then Miss Barrow calling me back. Later
on in the night Mr. Seddon told me to go back to my own bed, and I
went; Miss Barrow did not call me back, and I never saw her again. I
stayed in my own bed and slept there during the whole of that night.
Miss Barrow was an affectionate and loving woman to me. I remember
the next morning, the morning after this night when I had been sent
backwards and forwards. I was sent by Mr. Seddon to Southend that
day. I went with two of Mr. Seddon's children. It was while I was
staying in Southend, at Mrs. Jeffrey's house, that Mr. Seddon told me
that Miss Barrow was dead. I remember the servant, Mary, in the
house at Mr. Seddon's in London. I know now that her name is Mary
Chater. She never waited on Miss Barrow. Miss Barrow and I had our
meals together in her room upstairs before she was ill. Maggie Seddon
used to cook the things in the kitchen next door to Miss Barrow's room
before she was ill, and after she was ill Mrs. Seddon attended her throughout. I saw Miss Barrow taking medicine. Mrs. Seddon used to give it
to her; I have never given it to her myself. I only saw her taking
medicine once herself; I do not know exactly when it was, but it was
while she was ill in bed. It was in the day time I think. The medicine
was left by the side of her bed for her so that she could reach out and take
it herself.

Used she to ask for it, or was it given to her by Mrs. Seddon when
she came in?—It used to be by the side of the bed, and if she wanted it
she used to get it.

Who is the "she" who used to get it?—Miss Barrow.

Have you seen her take her medicine herself more than once?—No.

Then what do you mean when you say that when Miss Barrow wanted
her medicine she used to get it?—She used to turn over and reach out and
get it.

Reach out and get it from the bottle, or from the glass where it was
poured out?—She used to pour it out herself.

Then you have seen her pour it out herself more than once. Is
that what you mean?—No, I have seen her pour it out once and take it.

But only once?—At other times Mrs. Seddon used to pour it out.

You told us you saw Miss Barrow once reach out and take it herself?
Can you tell us how long that was before the last night?—No, I cannot
remember that. I cannot remember seeing any medicine given to her
at all on this night before I went away for the last time from her. I
cannot tell how many times she sent me down for Mrs. Seddon. She
waked me up to send me down for Mrs. Seddon because she felt so ill,

Trial of the Seddons.

and I went down and told Mrs. Seddon, and she came up. Mr. Seddon was there several times when he sent me back to my own room.

Did Miss Barrow tell you what it was that you were to tell Mrs. Seddon?—No, she only used to tell me to go down to call her.

Mr. MARSHALL HALL—I am not objecting to this, because I am going to ask about some conversations, and they will be admissible in cross-examination.

Examination continued—Did she tell you to tell Mrs. Seddon that she had pains in her stomach?—Yes. I do not know whether that was the first time I was sent down to fetch Mrs. Seddon or not.

Do you remember when Mrs. Seddon came up whether she made a hot flannel and put it on Miss Barrow?—Yes. I cannot remember whether that was the first time she came up or not.

Can you remember whether Mr. Seddon was there then?—I do not think he was.

During that night did you see Miss Barrow being sick at all?—Yes.

More than once?—Yes. She was badly sick.

Was that only during part of the night, or did that continue whilst you were with her?—Only part of the night.

Do you remember her getting out of bed at all and sitting on the floor during that night?—Yes.

Can you remember whether that was before you had been sent down for Mrs. Seddon or after?—After.

Do you remember whether during the time you were with her that night she got out of bed more than once?—No, I do not remember.

Do you remember her saying " I am going "?—Yes.

What did she do then?—Sat down on the floor.

Did she seem in great pain then?—Yes. She remained on the floor till Mr. Seddon came up and put her in bed again.

You said "till Mr. Seddon came up." Did Mrs. Seddon come too?— Yes. (Shown exhibit 2.) I remember seeing that box. I used to see it in Miss Barrow's big black trunk. I have seen Miss Barrow taking money out of that box, but I never saw inside the box while she was alive. I saw her put the box on the bed and turn out on to the bed some of what was in the box. It was gold; sometimes she used to count it, and sometimes she used to take one out. I could not tell how much there was. I noticed one bag inside. I think I saw another one. I have seen Miss Barrow put money into a bag in the cash box. I have seen her come up from the dining-room with some pieces of gold. That was the dining-room on the ground floor to the left when you come in at the front door.

Have you seen how many pieces of gold she brought up from the dining-room?—Yes, three. I cannot tell how many times I saw that, but it was more than once. She put the three pieces of gold that I saw her bring up from the dining-room into the cash box. When I went to Southend for the holiday Miss Barrow took me. It was before she took me to Southend for the holiday that I last saw her count the money. It was when I came back from the holiday at Southend that she was taken ill.

Cross-examined by Mr. MARSHALL HALL—Mrs. Seddon and Mr. Seddon were very kind to Miss Barrow, were they not?—Yes.

And Miss Barrow was very fond of them both?—Yes.

Evidence for Prosecution.

Ernest Grant

I think you said you were very much happier at the Seddons than you were at the Vonderahes?—Yes.

They were very kind to you, were they not?—Yes.

And after Miss Barrow died you went on living with Mr. Seddon and his children?—Yes.

And you were very happy there?—Yes.

They were kind to you?—Yes.

And you went to school, did you not?—Yes.

Used to go to school every day?—Yes.

I want you to try and remember the time when you went to Southend before Miss Barrow was so ill, not the last time you went, but the time before that. Miss Barrow and you and Mr. and Mrs. Seddon all went down to Southend together, did you not?—Yes.

Do you know how long you stayed there, if at all?—A week-end.

Then did you all come back together?—Yes.

And then did you go back to school?—Yes.

Whilst Miss Barrow was ill you were still at school every day, were you not?—Yes.

What time in the morning did you get up to go to school?—I cannot remember.

But it was early, was it?—Yes.

You did not always sleep with Miss Barrow, did you—you sometimes slept in your own bed?—Yes.

But I understand when Miss Barrow was ill you slept with her nearly all the time?—Yes.

I do not know whether you remember on one day about ten days before that last night you told us you went to your own bed that night, did you not?—Yes.

You remember that?—Yes.

Did Miss Barrow have a cup of tea in the early morning brought to her bedroom?—(No answer.)

A cup of something, whether it was tea or not—when she was well?—Yes.

When she was ill did it go on or not?—I cannot remember.

Who used to bring the tea in the morning to her?—Maggie Seddon.

Was it Maggie Seddon or was it the girl Chater?—Maggie Seddon.

Not Mary?—No.

Did not Mary bring the tea sometimes?—No.

Did Miss Barrow before she was ill go out and buy things for her own food?—Yes.

You used to go with her sometimes, did you not?—Yes.

Did you not go messages?—No.

Did you go out walking with her?—Yes.

Did she take you to school in the morning, and come and fetch you back?—Yes.

How soon after she came back from Southend was it that she complained of pains?—I don't know how long after it was.

How soon after you came back from Southend did you sleep in her room?—I don't know.

Trial of the Seddons.

Ernest Grant

How many nights had you been sleeping in her room before the last night?—I don't know how many nights before.

Whilst Miss Barrow was ill, of course, you were not there in the day-time?—No.

When you came back at night did you find a very nasty smell in the room; do you remember that?—I did not notice any.

Do you remember the doctor putting up a sheet in front of the door?—Yes.

Do you know what carbolic smells like?—I remember smelling it.

You did not notice a nasty smell in the house, did you?—No.

Do you remember the doctor giving Miss Barrow first of all a thick white medicine, rather milky-looking?—Ye

Did you ever see that?—Yes.

She did not like that, did she?—No.

She would not take it?—No.

I think you said the only time you ever saw Mr. Seddon give her any medicine it was white stuff like water?—Yes.

It was not the thick milky stuff, was it?—No.

Do you remember the second medicine, which was a medicine which had to be done in two glasses?   Do you remember he put one in the one glass and one in the other, and poured the two together, and when you poured them together they began to fizz?—Yes.

That was the medicine she did like?—Yes.

Was that the medicine that you saw Mr. Seddon give her?—Yes.

That is the only time you saw him give her medicine.   Do you remember Miss Barrow had very bad breathing sometimes, she found it very difficult to breathe?—Yes.

Did you ever see her take anything for that—little lozenges, or things like little lozenges?—Yes.

Did you ever by chance see the bottle she used to take them out of?—No.

I have just roughly drawn it.   Did you ever see a little bottle that sort of shape? (Sketch handed.)—No.

Did you ever see her take things for her cough out of a little bottle like that?—No.

Did you ever see a little bottle like that in her possession?—No.

Dr. Willcox has given me this bottle—was it a bottle of that sort of shape?—No, I have not seen any.

Did she often take these things for her asthma—did she cough at the time she had it, or did she go like that? (Counsel took several short breaths)?—I cannot remember how she went.

But it was difficult for her to breathe?—Yes.

Do you remember if she ever took them when she was out of doors?—No, I don't remember.

When Mr. Seddon asked you to go into your own bedroom that night, that was because you were being woke up?—Yes.

He told you to go to your own room and get some sleep?—Yes.

And when you say "several times," it happened twice or three times, did it not?—Yes.   I don't know exactly how many times.

You remember Mary Chater?—Yes.

Evidence for Prosecution.

Ernest Grant

You say that you only saw her once in Miss Barrow's room?—Yes.

Was that once when she came to see Miss Barrow when Miss Barrow was ill?—Yes.

About what time was it that you went to school, do you remember? I cannot tell what time.

About what time did you come away from school?—Twelve o'clock i the morning and half-past four in the evening.

Miss Barrow took you in the morning, brought you back to dinner took you again after your dinner, and brought you back again?—Yes.

While Miss Barrow was ill who took you to school?—Nobody.

You went by yourself?—Yes.

Sometimes Miss Barrow got cross, did she not?—Yes.

She was very deaf, was she not?—Yes.

You had to shout into her ear to make her hear what you had t< say?—Yes.

And did you sometimes repeat what other people had said so that sh could hear it?—Yes.

She used to get annoyed, did she not, because you got up early an ran round the room like a child in the morning? I suppose that made he cross sometimes, didn't it?—I don't think so.

Did you not get up early while she was still in bed and run roun the room?—Yes.

And she complained about it?—Yes.

Once she said she would throw herself out of the window, did she not —Yes.

Because you annoyed her. Do you remember Miss Barrow sayin anything about her relations—did she tell you that her relations had no been kind to her?—Yes.

Sometimes you had meals with Miss Barrow and sometimes you ha them in the kitchen?—Yes.

When you say the kitchen, do you mean the little kitchen near Mis Barrow's room or the kitchen downstairs?—The little kitchen upstairs.

I want you to bring your mind to the night that Miss Barrow was so ill. Do you remember what time it was when you went to bed that night? —No.

Miss Barrow was in bed when you went to bed, of course?—Yes.

Did you notice anything in the room that night that you had not noticed before? The room was very nasty smelling—very nasty all night —did you not notice it?—No, I did not notice it.

Do you smell things easily, or do you not—do you smell things very easily, or do you find it very difficult to smell?—(No answer.)

(From the way he speaks, I should think he had adenoids.) Never mind. How long had you been in bed before Miss Barrow asked you to fetch Mrs. Seddon?—I don't know; I went to sleep, and then she woke me up again.

Was it dark when you woke?—Yes.

Was the weather very hot about this time?—Yes.

Very hot indeed?—Yes.

Had you been troubled very much with the flies?—(No answer.)

Trial of the Seddons.

Ernest Grant

Do you remember Miss Barrow saying anything to you about the flies?—No.

There were a great many flies, were there not?—Yes.

They were all over the place?—Yes.

So far as you are concerned, you cannot remember whether Miss Barrow ever said anything to you about the flies?—No.

Do you know whether she complained about the flies to anybody else?—Yes.

Did you hear the flies talked about?—Yes.

Were things like this lying about with a picture of a fly on it, and "House fly, kill it!" like that?—No.

You did not see one?—No.

You can read, can you not?—Not much.

Do you remember anything being got to kill the flies with?—No.

Perhaps you would not know whether there was or not?—No.

The first time you went down to fetch Mr. and Mrs. Seddon, Mrs. Seddon came up, and you think Mr. Seddon came with her?—Yes.

And the first thing that Mrs. Seddon did was to make a flannel hot and put it on Miss Barrow's stomach?—Yes.

Did that seem to give her some relief from the pain?—Yes.

Were you in the room at any time when Miss Barrow had to use something in the room when she had diarrhœa?—Yes.

Pretty often, was it not?—No, I don't think so.

Anyhow, she was very sick, too?—Yes.

And she got out of bed once that night?—Yes.

Was that after Mrs. Seddon had put the hot flannel on her stomach or not?—After, I think.

Do you remember?—I think it was after.

Then it was after the second time I suppose that you had been sent down for them that she got out of bed and got on to the floor?—I do not know which time it was.

Anyhow, you were very frightened then?—Yes.

And she said, "I am going"?—Yes.

And both Mr. and Mrs. Seddon lifted her up and put her back into the bed?—Yes.

You knew old Mr. Seddon?—Yes.

You used to call him "Grandfather"?—Yes.

On the last night that we have talked about were Mr. Seddon's boys sleeping upstairs with the grandfather?—Yes.

You do not remember, do you, a lady coming to stay with a little girl?—Yes.

You used to go to bed at all sorts of times—no regular time?—Yes.

Before Miss Barrow was ill did you go for walks with her in the park—Tollington Park?—Yes.

Did you meet a good many people there?—No.

Did you go to shops with her ever?—Yes.

You used to meet Mrs. Vonderahe sometimes?—Yes.

You knew her, of course, because you lived in the house there?—Yes.

I think you went away with Inspector Ward?—Yes.

And they have been looking after you. You told us about this time

Evidence for Prosecution.

Ernest Grant

when she went down and fetched three pieces of gold and brought them up and put them into the box. You cannot say how many times she did that?—No.

You say you saw one bag of money in it, and you thought there was another in the box?—Yes.

What sort of bag was it—was it a bag like either of these (produced)? —No.

Was it a paper bag?—Yes.

Was it a blue bag, or brown, or grey, or what?—Greyish colour, or green.

That sort of colour (bag produced)?—Yes.

Was it as big a bag as that?—Bigger, I think.

When it had money in it, how big did it look?—I don't know exactly how big it was.

Can you tell us whether the bag seemed to be full or half-full, or what?—Half-full, I believe.

Do you know why Miss Barrow left Mrs. Vonderahe's?—Because she did not like the way she cooked the food.

Anything else?—I cannot remember anything else.

She was rather particular about her food, was she net?—Yes.

You remember the time when Mr. and Mrs. Hook lived at Tollington Park? When you first went there?—Yes.

And you remember when Miss Barrow was very angry with him because they had taken you out for a walk and left her at home?—Yes.

And she told them to go?—Yes.

Re-examined by the ATTORNEY-GENERAL—Were you there when she told them to go?—Mr. Seddon told them to go.

Do you know what a fly-paper is?—I have seen one.

When did you see one?—When I was down at Southend at Mrs. Henderson's house.

Was that the first time you had seen one?—I don't know.

You were at Mrs. Henderson's after that night when you were sleeping with Miss Barrow when she was so ill?—Yes.

You were with Mrs. Henderson some little time?—Yes.

And then went to Mrs. Jeffreys; is that right?—Yes.

Did you ever see any fly-papers in Miss Barrow's room?—No.

Or anywhere in Miss Barrow's four rooms?—No.

Or in Seddon's rooms?—No.

Further cross-examined by Mr. MARSHALL HALL—When you say you saw that fly-paper down at Southend, what sort was it—was it one that flies stick to—a sticky thing?—Yes, a sticky thing that flies stick to.

By Mr. JUSTICE BUCKNILL—Did Maggie Seddon ever show you a fly-paper?—No.

Further re-examined by the ATTORNEY-GENERAL—Did you ever see a fly-paper like that? (Handed.)—No.

Mr. JUSTICE BUCKNILL—Is that one of Mather's?

The ATTORNEY-GENERAL—Yes, Mr. Thorley will produce the packets in which they are sold.

(The envelope containing this fly-paper was put in and marked No. 134.)

Trial of the Seddons.

Mrs. Annie Henderson

Mrs. ANNIE HENDERSON, examined by Mr. MUIR—I live at Riviera Drive, Southchurch, near Southend-on-Sea. The boy Ernie Grant stayed with me from 14th to 28th September of last year.

Cross-examined by Mr MARSHALL HALL—Mr. Seddon never came to the house while Ernie was there.

Mrs. LEAH JEFFREYS, examined by Mr. MUIR—I live at Briar Villa, Southend-on-Sea. I remember Mr. and Mrs. Seddon coming to my house. The first time Mr. Seddon came to me was on 5th August, and he stayed until the 8th. Miss Barrow came into my house several times. She only came in to meals, she had not rooms there. She came in to three or four meals, and went away on the 8th. She seemed to be very well at that time. I next saw Mr. Seddon on 22nd September, when he stayed with me until 2nd October. He had with him Mrs. Seddon and two daughters and a baby. Ernie Grant was not staying with me, but he came in several times to see them. Ernie Grant never stayed with me at any time.

Did you hear Mr. Seddon say anything to the boy, Ernie Grant, about Miss Barrow in September?—He asked him if he knew she was dead, and the boy said, " No," so Mr. Seddon said, " Oh, yes, she is dead." I think that was either 22nd or 23rd September. I am not sure whether it was the same day or the day after they came.

MARY ELIZABETH ELLEN CHATER, examined by Mr. TRAVERS HUMPHREYS —I am now living at Compton Terrace. I was general servant to Mr. and Mrs. Seddon at 63 Tollington Park. I was with them for nearly twelve months, and I left on 1st February. During the time I was there there was another servant employed in the house, a Mrs. Rudd, who came as charwoman, but did not live in the house. There was no other servant kept. I slept in the room where Miss Margaret Seddon and her youngest sister slept. My room was below Miss Barrow's floor. Mr. and Mrs. Seddon slept on the same floor as we were sleeping on. My room was at the back, and Mr. and Mrs. Seddon's room was in the front. The room which I slept in was one which had a partition in it. On the other side of the partition in that room there slept Mr. William Seddon, that is the eldest son, Freddie Seddon, and his grandfather, when I went there. Nobody slept on the top floor except Miss Barrow and Ernie Grant. Mrs. Seddon cooked the food for herself and her husband and children downstairs in our kitchen. She also cooked the food for Miss Barrow, and Miss Margaret cooked it, too. They cooked that food up in Miss Barrow's kitchen on the top floor. I never cooked any food for Miss Barrow, nor did I ever wait upon her. I had nothing to do with her at all. I remember her going away to Southend for a short time, and her being ill after she came back. I used to open the door to Dr. Sworn, who came to see her. From the time the doctor came I never saw Miss Barrow downstairs at all. I think she always kept to her room. I cannot remember the date the doctor came, but I remember him coming quite well. During Miss Barrow's last illness Mrs. Seddon cooked her food upstairs in Miss Barrow's room. I never saw any of the food prepared for Miss Barrow. I have never been into Miss Barrow's

Evidence for Prosecution.

Mary Elizabeth Ellen Chater

kitchen except once when Miss Barrow was out before her severe illness. During Miss Barrow's last illness I never saw any food prepared for her downstairs in the kitchen. I knew that some Liebig's extract came, but I did not see Mrs. Seddon prepare it. I did not see any Valentine's meat juice in the house, but I knew it came. I did not see any actually prepared. I never went into Miss Barrow's room where she slept.

Cross-examined by Mr. MARSHALL HALL—You have three times bee asked by my learned friend if you saw any food prepared downstair during Miss Barrow's last illness, and three times you have said " No "?— Yes.

Now, I ask you the fourth time, did you ever see any food prepare downstairs during Miss Barrow's illness?—No.

Did you say this before the magistrates, " She had light food durin her illness—Liebig's Extract, rice pudding, and sago, and Valentines.] saw them prepared downstairs "?

By Mr. JUSTICE BUCKNILL—First of all, do you remember saying that —I did not see Mrs. Seddon actually prepare it.

By Mr. MARSHALL HALL—Not only once did you say it, as I sugges to you, but you were recalled after Mrs. Seddon had been arrested, an this is what you then said, " I did not see Mrs. Seddon prepare any foo upstairs. Downstairs I have seen her prepare Liebig's and Valentine' meat juice, and gruel sometimes, and light puddings once or twice." Tha is a very specific statement. Why have you said four times to-day tha you never saw any food prepared downstairs?—I said it was done upstair in Miss Barrow's room.

You could not see it done upstairs, because you never went upstairs?— No, I never went upstairs.

You are shown in both those statements which have been taken do and which you have signed as saying that you had seen it prepare downstairs. Why have you altered that?—I have not seen her preparin it; I knew she was preparing it, but I was not there to see her preparing it

On two different occasions at intervals you said the same thing. Firs of all, early in the evidence you will see, " Mrs. Seddon and Maggi Seddon prepared Miss Barrow's food in Miss Barrow kitchen, except " you say the same thing again—" the Valentine's meat juice, Liebig's, an things like that." A little later on you say, " She had light food during her illness, Liebig's extract, rice puddings and sago, and Valentine's.] saw them prepared downstairs." These are the exact words, " I saw some light puddings prepared downstairs, and the meat juice "—it is a more specific statement than I thought it was—" and the meat juice was sent up in a cup and saucer," so there is no question of a mistake. Now, when you were recalled in consequence of Mrs. Seddon's arrest on the 19th January you said this, " I did not see Mrs. Seddon prepare any food upstairs. Downstairs I have seen her prepare Liebig's and Valentine's meat juice, and gruel sometimes, and light puddings once or twice." That is three specific statements made at different times in which you say that you have seen these things prepared downstairs. Now, you say you never saw them prepared. Why have you changed your story?—I did not see her doing it. I knew she was, because I heard her, but I did

Trial of the Seddons.

Mary Elizabeth Ellen Chater

not see her doing it. When she used to be taking them up they were for Miss Barrow.

Why do you wear nurse's uniform?—Well, I used to be a nurse years ago, but I was not engaged as a nurse at the time I went to Mrs. Seddon's.

Do you always wear a nurse's uniform?—Well, I have done since I have been in London, and before I came to London.

I think your father was an inspector of nuisances?—Yes, Thomas John Chater, of Rugby.

I think you have a cousin—Frederick?—Yes, a surgeon-dentist.

Where is he living now?—I do not know exactly. I had a letter from Nottingham the other week saying he had not lived there for five years.

Is he a man who is a confirmed invalid?—Well, he has not been in good health; so I understand from a letter I have had.

Mentally or physically?—Well, I do not know exactly whether it is mental or not.

Is he at the present moment in a house of detention?—Not that I know of.

In an asylum?—Not that I know of.

You are quite sure of that?—Certain.

Have you any immediate relative in an asylum at the present moment? —Not that I know of.

That you swear?—Yes.

I think your first employment was with a Miss Nicholson at Rugby?— Yes.

You took charge of a mental case?—Well, I used to be there with her, yes.

And you stayed with her until she died?—No, I was not with her until she died; I was there some time before she died.

Then I think you went to Leamington?—Oh, yes. I was at Leamington nearly all the time—a large incurable hospital at Keswick Road. Miss Armitage used to be the sister in charge there.

That was a private hospital for incurables?—Yes.

Then I think you went as a nurse in a large hospital near Liverpool?— Yes, Brownlow Hill.

And stayed there about two months?—Yes.

Then I think, in 1891, you went to Canada for four and half years?— Yes, I was in Quebec four and a half years.

Again as a nurse?—Yes.

In the hospital and for doctors at Quebec?—Yes.

You came back to England and went to a coffee tavern at Rugby, I think?—Yes, I was there boarding until Miss Nicholson engaged me.

Then I think you first took a situation as a general servant at Ferntower Road, where you stayed about four months?—Yes.

Then I think you went to a home for discharged servants at Mildmay Park?—Yes.

Then for another short time in Highbury Place?—Yes.

Did you subsequently go into service with a Dr. Day?—Yes.

And you were there twelve months?—Nearly twelve months, yes.

Evidence for Prosecution.

Mary Elizabeth Ellen Chater

Then you went to another place at Kelross Road, Highbury?—Yes, that was Colonel Cooper's.

Then I think you went back to nursing again?—Yes.

Then from the home did you go to a private hospital for mentally incurable cases?—Yes.

From Kelross Road you went to Turle Road, Tollington Park, for some sixteen months, as a nurse?—Yes.

Then I think you went to a registry office at Upper Street, Islington, and stayed there?—Yes.

And then as a general servant to Mrs. Page, a dressmaker?—Yes.

You stayed there ten months?—Seventeen months altogether.

Then did you go to 115 Queen's Road, Finsbury Park, and stay there for four months?—Yes.

And then you went back to Mrs. Page and stayed the other seven months?—Yes.

Then you were out of a situation for a time?—Yes.

Then in April, 1911, you went to Mrs. Seddon's?—Yes.

You have made a considerable study, have you not, of mental cases?—Yes.

And medical works?—Yes.

And you have taken a great interest in medical things altogether?—Well, I have taken a great interest.

Did Miss Barrow suffer greatly from asthma?—Well, I thought she was inclined to be asthmatical when I first saw her.

Did you see then that she suffered badly from asthma?—She used to sit down, and I used to notice when she was going upstairs that she had difficulty in breathing, and that she was asthmatical.

Did you know she had a great difficulty in getting her breath?—Yes, I used to notice that.

Did you ever tell her anything about what was good for asthma?—No.

You say no relative of yours is in a lunatic asylum?—Not that I am aware of.

Has not your brother been in Hatton Lunatic Asylum at Warwick for twenty years?—I do not know, I am sure.

Have you got a brother?—Well, I had one brother.

Do you not know your brother has been in a lunatic asylum for twenty years?—No.

You must know it surely?—I knew he used to go there, but I did not know he was there.

Confined in a lunatic asylum for twenty years?—(No answer.)

Have you any doubt whatever about it?—Well, I was not there at the time.

Hatton Lunatic Asylum, Warwick?—I was away from home if that is the case.

On more than one occasion have threats been made to inquire into your mental condition?—No.

Do you know Lord Leigh?—Yes. I do not know him personally; my father knew him because he used to be in the Warwickshire Battalion.

Were you constantly talking about Lord Leigh as a friend of yours?—He used to know my mother, but I never knew him myself personally.

Trial of the Seddons.

Mary Elizabeth Ellen Chater

But have you constantly talked about him as a personal friend of yours?—No.

Did you say that your cousin, F. Chater, had done you a great injury by taking some money away from you?—I never had any money taken from me by him.

Did you say so or anything of the kind?—No.

Do you know Miss Magner?—Yes.

Were you in her service?—Yes.

Did she complain of your mental capacity?—No.

Never—never suggested that?—No.

That you were not responsible for your actions?—No.

Why should you wear a nurse's uniform as a general servant?—Well, when I first went to Leamington, of course, I was engaged there as a nurse, and Lord Leigh, I believe, was the president of that home for incurables at Leamington, and I was engaged by a Miss Armitage, the matron.

You have left Tollington Park now?—Yes.

You left on 1st February?—Yes.

Did you begin to break the crockery?—No, there was a lot broken before I left.

Did you break all the crockery, and say, " I am going ; they will arrest me next "?—No, I made no such remark.

You were with Harrington for some time about six years ago?—Yes.

Were you engaged there as a nurse?—Yes, £2 a month.

Did she complain that you were very eccentric and incapable of doing your work?—No.

Do you remember occasions when she used to send you out to the iron-monger's and you went to the draper's?—No.

Did you insist upon wearing a uniform at that place?—Well, she always used to allow me to wear it.

Did she remonstrate with you for wearing it?—Oh, dear no ; I left there at the time she went to Scarborough on a visit.

When you were with Dr. Day did you suddenly break out into violent fits of shouting and say that people were after you?—No. Nothing of the kind. I had too much to do to shout about his place.

Never mind whether you had too much to do, did you shout at imaginary persons?—No.

Did Dr. Day represent to you that you were quite irresponsible?—No.

Do you know Mrs. George Chater, of Bridget Street, Rugby?—Yes.

Did you stay with her some little time?—I think I was with her about a month.

Where is Mrs. Chater's husband?—I do not know. I haven't one, that is certain.

Is her husband your brother?—Yes.

Yet you do not know where he is?—Yes.

Is that the brother I was asking you about just now who, I suggest, has been for twenty years in a lunatic asylum?—I suppose so.

Have you any other brother?—No, not that I know of ; I have one dead.

Yes, but have you any brother alive?—No.

Evidence for Prosecution.

Mary Elizabeth Ellen Chater

You see you have made a very important statement in this case, a statement that you have seen Valentine's meat juice and the gruel and the puddings prepared by Mrs. Seddon downstairs?—I knew that she did prepare them.

You have sworn three times that you have seen her do it, not that you knew that she did it. The Attorney-General, who opened this case, has suggested, you know, to the jury that it was in the preparation of these things, the gruel, or the Valentine's beef juice, that arsenic was added. What do you now say? Have you ever seen Mrs. Seddon prepare any of these things or not?—I knew she did prepare them.

Have you ever seen her?—No, sir, I would tell you if I had.

Then why did you swear three times before the magistrate that you did?—(No answer.)

What time did Miss Barrow get up in the morning?—She was always up in time to see Ernest to school.

Did she have an early cup of tea?—Not from me.

You say you never went into her room at all?—No.

Now, Ernie Grant has sworn that you went into her room to see her once when she was ill in the last illness?—Yes, but that was when Mrs. Seddon was there and the doctor—I had to go there. There was a lady came.

Why did you say you did not go into the room?—I did not go inside her room; I was outside the door.

Have you ever seen any fly-papers in this house?—No.

Never?—Never.

Were you very much plagued with flies in August, 1911?—Well, we had a great many in the kitchen, but we never had fly-papers in the kitchen that I know of; I never saw any.

Were you plagued all over the place with flies?—Well, we had a great many flies, but nothing so very extraordinary.

The medical officer of health sent round a circular telling people to be very careful to get the flies destroyed?—No.

You did not see that?—No.

Who washed up the things that came out of Miss Barrow's room?—Miss Margaret used to do it when she first did her work.

Was nothing sent downstairs to be washed?—The later part, of course; I used to sometimes; things that came down—glasses and little things, perhaps a cup and saucer.

You know a good deal about medicine?—Well, I do not know much about preparing medicine and all that kind of thing.

Did you tell Mr. Saint that arsenic was a very good thing for asthma?—I never heard of such a thing in my life.

You signed a written statement, did you not? Just look at that signature and tell me if that is your signature?—He asked me that question, but I said not that I knew of. I never used any of it. (Statement handed to witness.) That is my name.

Did you ever see Miss Barrow take any little pills?—No.

Did you ever see much of her?—No, except when she used to come in when I used to answer the door to her.

She would come into the kitchen?—No, go straight upstairs.

Trial of the Seddons.

Mary Elizabeth Ellen Chater

Did she come into the kitchen?—Not to sit with me.

Do you really mean she never came into the kitchen?—She used to come into the garden sometimes when I first went; that was before they went away to Southend-on-Sea.

Did you not think she was in bad health all the time?—Well, I thought so from the time I saw her.

She always appeared tired, did she not?—Yes, always resting when she came in.

And she had diarrhœa and sickness long before this illness?—Yes. Constantly?—Yes.

It was very warm weather at the time you knew her?—Yes.

Was there a very bad smell in the house during this last illness?—Yes. Dreadful, unbearable?—Yes.

You know they had to put up carbolic sheets?—Yes, they did.

You did not go into the bedroom to look after that?—No.

You remember the relatives coming up while Miss Barrow was so ill, do you not?—I think so; yes.

Did you say Miss Barrow did not come to your kitchen?—She used to go through the kitchen into the garden in the early part of the year when I first went there.

Let me read to you what you said before the magistrate, "Miss Barrow sometimes used to come down to the kitchen and sit awhile; and sometimes interfered with me, but I put that down to her illness. She was very irritable sometimes. I never quarrelled or had words with her. She was not a heavy woman. She had difficulty in getting her breath, especially after her going up and down stairs"?—Yes.

When you say that she was not a heavy woman, she was not a thin woman, was she?—No.

She would be a bigger woman than Mrs. Seddon is?—Well, I suppose so.

Did she complain of the way you did your work at Tollington Park?—They never did to me. I do not know what they did afterwards.

What wages did you get?—£12 a year.

And soon after you got there did Mrs. Seddon say she would not keep you any longer because you were no use at all?—Well, once she said something about making some alteration or something of the kind, and I had a letter that had been written to me about a fortnight or a week before——

Did you implore her to keep you on as you had nowhere to go to?—Oh, no. I said, "If you wish to finish with my services I will take the offer that is offered to me now," but she asked me to remain, so I did. That was Mrs. Barnett, of Stapleton Hall Road.

Did you ever talk to her about your friendship with Lord Leigh?—Never, because I never knew him myself personally.

You are quite sure you never saw any——?—Quite sure—certain.

What was I going to ask you?—(No answer.)

What were you quite sure about?—I said I never knew Lord Leigh personally.

No, I was asking you about something else altogether. Are you quite sure that you never saw any fly-papers of that sort in the house (a Mather fly-paper produced)?—Quite certain.

Not in saucers?—Positive.

Evidence for Prosecution.

Mary Elizabeth Ellen Chater

That you swear to?—I can swear that.

Have you ever seen one of those fly-papers before?—No.

Have you never heard of those fly-papers?—I have heard of them, but I have never bought them in my life.

And never seen them?—No.

You have never in your life seen fly-papers of that kind?—The only fly-papers I have seen is the ordinary fly-paper.

Have you not seen in hospitals or anywhere fly-papers of that sort?—No.

Never in your life?—No.

You have heard of them?—Yes.

You are quite sure you never saw any in Tollington Park?—Yes.

Did Mrs. Seddon complain to you that you were really not responsible for what you said?—No.

Nothing of the kind?—No.

Re-examined by Mr. MUIR—What is the longest time you have been in any one service?—Well, I think in Turle Road, Tollington Park.

What is the name?—Mrs. Roche used to live there.

When was that?—Three years ago.

How long were you in her service?—About sixteen months altogether.

You were with a Miss Magner?—Yes.

How long were you with her?—About four months.

Where did you go to from Miss Magner's?—I went to Mr. Fry's registry office, and boarded there.

Did Miss Magner give you a character?—I never went for one.

You went to the registry office and got a character there?—No, I stopped there until I had another situation offered me.

Now, as regards Mrs. Harrington——

Mr. JUSTICE BUCKNILL—I should like to know where we are. If her cross-examination as to her supposed mental condition and as to the places where she was supposed to have been in service, and where she says she was, is to credit, and to credit only, then her answers are to be taken, and if her answers are to be taken you need not re-examine, need you?

Mr. MUIR—I think, my lord, I can add something to the effect of her answers by eliciting how long she was in service.

How long were you with Dr. Day?—Nearly twelve months. When I left Dr. Day I was boarding at the Cambridge Institute, Holloway Road.

Did you get a character from him?—The lady that engaged me was Mrs. Barnett, and she went to Dr. Day for my character, and that was the lady that wanted to engage me when I stayed on with Mrs. Seddon.

So you referred the lady you went to after Dr. Day to Dr. Day for a character?—Yes.

Does that apply to your other situations—did you refer to the persons you had been with?—Yes, sir, yes.

Did you ever know that arsenic was good for asthma?—Never in my life.

Mr. JUSTICE BUCKNILL—If you do not ask this question, I shall. (To Witness)—Did you ever administer arsenic to Miss Barrow?—No.

Mr. MARSHALL HALL—I am not suggesting that she knowingly administered arsenic to Miss Barrow for a moment.

By Mr. JUSTICE BUCKNILL—Knowingly or unknowingly?—No, sir.

Trial of the Seddons.

Mary Elizabeth Ellen Chater

Mr. MARSHALL HALL—I am not suggesting for a moment that she did it knowingly.

Mr. JUSTICE BUCKNILL—I do not think for a moment you meant to do so.

(To Witness)—As a specific for asthma, did you ever administer arsenic to Miss Barrow—of course, I mean as a medicine?—No, sir, no.

Either for asthma or anything else?—No.

By Mr. MUIR—Did you make a statement to the solicitor for the defendants, Mr. Saint?—Yes. I cannot say exactly the date, but he saw me in Mr. Seddon's house.

Was that after the arrest of Mr. Seddon?—Yes.

Was that after the arrest of Mrs. Seddon?—Before.

Did you give him all the particulars of the situations that you had been in?—Yes.

WILLIAM SEDDON, examined by Mr. TRAVERS HUMPHREYS—I reside at 63 Tollington Park. I am the father of Frederick Henry Seddon. I went to live with him at 63 Tollington Park about the middle of February of last year. I slept in the back room on the second flat over the basement. I had nothing to do with Miss Barrow in the way of waiting upon her. I never prepared any food for her at all, nor did I ever give her any food or medicine. I was living in the house at the time of her last illness, and I saw her on two or three occasions then. I do not exactly know why I went to see her. I went on one or two occasions previous to her illness, and on about three occasions after she took ill. I remember on one occasion she made a will when I was there. (Shown exhibit 31.) I signed that at the bottom as a witness, and Miss Barrow signed that in my presence. My son, my daughter-in-law, and myself were present when she made that will. The date is 11th September. On the other occasions when I went to see her she was in bed. I went up to fetch some tools that I had left up on the top floor, and I saw the door open, and I went in to ask her how she was. She said she was poorly, and I hoped she would get better soon. That was the last time I saw her. I remember Mrs. Longley, a married daughter of mine, coming to stay at the house on 11th September. She stayed until after Miss Barrow's death. I went about with Mrs. Longley during the day to different places of amusement. She was up with her little girl just for a holiday. I went to the funeral of Miss Barrow along with my son and my daughter-in-law. The funeral started from Mr. Node's (the undertaker), Stroud Green Road.

Cross-examined by Mr. MARSHALL HALL—I think your son has been for twenty years in his present employment?—A matter of twenty-one years, I believe.

It is a big insurance office, the London and Manchester Industrial Assurance Company?—Yes.

He has been superintendent ten years?—Yes, about that; it might be eleven.

And is your son-in-law, Mr. Longley, in the same office?—Yes.

You did not see any writing of Miss Barrow's will itself—any making of the will?—No.

We know Miss Barrow was very deaf?—She was.

Evidence for Prosecution.

William Seddon

Did she take the will and read it for herself?—The will was read to her, but she could not thoroughly understand; she asked for it, and asked for her glasses to read it herself, and she read it.

Did she say anything?—She signed it, and she said, "Thank God, that will do."

What did she sign it with?—With a fountain pen.

Do you remember on that day having to go to the mantelpiece to get your pipe?—No, not my pipe. I went to get her glasses from the mantelpiece.

Did you see anything on the mantelpiece that you remember?—Well, I cannot positively remember whether there was anything; I did not look very minutely.

On the same day that she signed the will she seemed quite all right?—She seemed perfectly sane altogether.

Quite able to understand and to talk quite rationally?—Yes, quite able to understand every word that was said to her.

Did you go into her bedroom again after that?—Not that day, not until the Wednesday, when I went upstairs for a screwdriver and a hammer that I had left in the recess.

We have been told that she was very eccentric. Did you notice that too?—Very often.

Before this illness and before the night she died had you heard her complain of being ill?—I understood she had been under a doctor, and Mrs. Seddon advised her to go, and she hesitated on several occasions to go, and Mrs. Seddon had to take her down to a Dr. Sworn, and he attended her to her death.

The doctor was coming pretty constantly, as we know, during the last ten or twelve days?—Yes, Dr. Sworn.

Did you notice the dreadful smell that there was in the house?—Yes, there was a kind of peculiar smell at the time.

Do you remember the weather then—was it very hot about that time?—It was not excessively hot, but it was very, very warm indeed.

Did you know about the medical officer having sent a notice round about the flies? Did you see the notice?—No, I did not.

Did you notice whether there were many flies about at that time or not?—There was plenty of flies knocking about, both upstairs and downstairs.

As far as you know, did Miss Barrow ever complain of the flies?—Not that I am aware of; I could not say.

Just look at that thing which has been produced—that coloured fly-paper. (Handed.) Have you ever seen fly-papers of that sort in the house at any time—anything like that?—I cannot say; well, I have seen some in the house, I think, about the month of August.

Wet or dry?—I cannot say exactly whether they were wet or dry.

You think you saw some?—I think I saw some.

Were they in a saucer or in anything?—I could not exactly say.

Did you go to Node's (the undertaker) with Mrs. Longley when Mrs. Longley went?—Yes.

And was his son there at all?—No; there was me, Mrs. Seddon, and my daughter, Mrs. Longley, went and took a wreath on the Friday

Trial of the Seddons.

afternoon and placed it upon the coffin lid, and we got the woman in the shop to remove the coffin lid, and Mrs. Seddon stooped down and kissed the corpse.

Mrs. EMILY AMY LONGLEY, examined by Mr. TRAVERS HUMPHREYS—I am the wife of James Longley, who is a superintendent in the employment of the London and Manchester Industrial Assurance Company. I live at Wolverhampton. I came up to London on 11th September on a visit to my brother, the male defendant, at 63 Tollington Park. I was accompanied by my daughter, who was then fourteen years old. We stayed in the house till Friday, 15th September. Every day we went to places of amusement. It was always very late when I came back. My daughter was always with me, with the exception of Monday night, when I left her in the house and went to the Empire. On the other occasions she always accompanied me. My father went with me every day.

Did either your brother or your sister-in-law go with you on any of those occasions?—Only on the Monday evening; the first night they came out they took me to the Empire at Finsbury Park. I went out on the evening of the 14th, the last night I was there. I went with my daughter, Mrs. Seddon, and her son Willie. During the time I was in the house I prepared no food for Miss Barrow. I had nothing to do with her at all.

Cross-examined by Mr. MARSHALL HALL—I think on 14th September, that is the day after the night of the death, the blinds were all pulled down?—Yes.

I think you inadvertently on the morning of the 15th, without a thought, pulled up the blind?—On the morning after she had gone out of the house, on the Friday morning, yes.

And when Mrs. Seddon came in she instantly pulled it down?—Oh, yes, she was quite annoyed at my pulling it up.

Do you remember going to the undertaker's with your father and your sister-in-law, Mrs. Seddon?—Yes, Friday afternoon.

And you took a wreath with you?—Yes, she took the wreath with her.

An elderly lady was there in the shop?—The undertaker's wife was there.

And was there a young man there?—No, none whatever.

HARRY CARL TAYLOR, examined by Mr. MUIR—I am the assistant superintendent for the Holloway district of the London and Manchester Industrial Insurance Company. The male prisoner was the superintendent for that district. I used to go to his house every Thursday to make up the accounts of moneys received by the collectors. I went into the front room of the basement, which was used as an office, and the collectors came there also. On 14th September I arrived at the office about 12.30, but the prisoner was not in then. I saw him when he came in at about 1.30, and I continued working with him all that day. During the afternoon he complained that he felt very tired, that he had been up all night; I suggested that he should lie down for a couple of hours, and he did so. That would be sometime after 4 o'clock. He came back soon after 5. The amount of money received from the collectors in the industrial branch that day was £63 14s. 3d. The

Evidence for Prosecution.

Harry Carl Taylor

collectors used to pay in once a week. The money was generally in the form of gold and silver—about half and half, I should say. I saw gold there on the night of the 14th. There was some gold that the collectors had brought in.

Any other gold?—Yes. About a little after 9 o'clock, I should think, I was busy writing, and I heard the chink of money.

By Mr. JUSTICE BUCKNILL—A little after 9 o'clock on the 14th I saw some gold. The last collector was out of the place certainly before 7 o'clock.

Examination continued—As I said, I heard the chink of money, and I just turned my head where I had a side view of Mr. Seddon's desk, and I saw several piles of sovereigns and a good little heap besides. At the time I estimated that there was over £200 in gold. I should say that that was not part of the collectors' money. The collectors' money was put in the till which Mr. Seddon kept in the cupboard. (Shown exhibit 28.) That is the till I am talking of, and I recognise it as the one the prisoner used to put the collections into. On occasions I have seen him bring this till out of the cupboard, pull out the drawer in his desk, and put it across it so that he should not have to travel to and from his desk to the cupboard. At the time I saw this quantity of gold, which I estimated at £200, the till was in the cupboard. The prisoner packed this quantity of sovereigns into four bags. Then he took them up, and he held three in his hand, and, taking up the other one in his hand, turned round and faced myself and Mr. Smith, my fellow-assistant, and put the one bag in front of Mr. Smith, and said, "Here, Smith, here's your wages." He picked it up again, and then he put the four bags into the safe, which was alongside the fireplace, about two steps from the cupboard where the till was. (Shown exhibit 27.) That plan shows the cupboard where the cash till was kept. The chair marked with the letter "S" is where Mr. Seddon sat, the chair marked "H.C.T." is where I sat, and the chair marked "J.C.A.S." is where Mr. Smith sat. The safe is situated behind the chair where Mr. Seddon sat. The collectors came in at the door in front of Mr. Seddon's desk, and put their money in front of him when they came in. They would come in from Tollington Park, down the area steps into the passage, and then into that door.

Cross-examined by Mr. MARSHALL HALL—How long had you known Mr. Seddon—a good many years?—I have only known him personally since last April. I have been in the employ of the company nearly six years.

You know he has been there nearly twenty years?—That is quite so.

And had you come often on these Thursdays to make up accounts?—Since April.

You were there, I understand, from about half-past twelve till a little past one when you first saw Mr. Seddon?—That is so.

Then from 1 to 4 you worked with Mr. Seddon?—That is so.

And at 4 o'clock Mr. Seddon went away and did not come back again until 5. Was any more money brought in by the collectors while Mr. Seddon was away?—No.

It was all in before?—No, it was not all in; there was some left behind, but during the time he was away no collectors came in, as far as I remember.

Trial of the Seddons.

Harry Carl Taylor

Did you stay right away from 5 to 9?—Yes, we were there till midnight.

But did you not go out at all from 5 to 9?—No.

The till we have seen is kept in this cupboard facing the window?—Yes.

The safe, which we see upon the plan is a largish safe, is there (indicating on the plan)?—Yes.

About 9 o'clock did Mr. Seddon get up, fetch the till from the cupboard, put it on this desk, and proceed to count the contents?—No.

You are quite sure of that?—I am perfectly certain.

The first thing that attracted your attention to the money was the chink?—It was the chink.

And when you looked round did you find money on the desk?—On the desk.

That was the chink you heard?—That was the chink I heard.

Are you prepared really to say that some of it—not all of it—was not money that had been taken from the till?—I am quite prepared to say it was not the money from the till.   I feel positive about it.

As a matter of fact, I see the collection sheet for that week shows £80?—Yes, but then you had to deduct the men's commission, first of all, and then you had to deduct also the amount of salaries and bonuses paid to the men on new business, so the amount really was about £50 that he had in the till.

I am not suggesting that you did not see gold—nothing of the sort—but I suggest to you that you are wrong in the amount.   You say you estimated it at £200?—£200.

I suggest to you it was something at or about £100?—No.

You are quite positive?—I quite agree with you that I may be wrong as to the amount, because since I have made an experiment with the same kind of bags, and those four bags contained, according to my experiment, over £400.

I see.   Then you think he had £400 now?—Judging by the size of the bags I saw in his hands.

£400, and one of the bags he holds up to Smith and says, " Here is your salary "?—Yes.

He said that as a joke?—As a joke.

He was in a very good temper?—I never saw him the same as he was on that day.

Smith said, " Don't say that, I only wish it was "?—Yes, he said, " I wish it was true, Mr. Seddon."

You know the suggestion that is now made—that this £200 that you then said, or the £400 that you say now, is money that this man had stolen from a dead woman he had murdered?—Yes.

And he is joking while the dead body is lying in the house, according to your story?—Well, he did hand the money to Mr. Smith.

When you gave your evidence, which was some months after that, you had been told that there was an amount of money missing, had you not?—That is so ; I saw it in the papers.

Then, of course, your mind travelled back to this night, and you were sure.   Of course, he was handling gold, but I suggest to you that it was £100 in gold, and not £200?—No.

Evidence for Prosecution.

Harry Carl Taylor

Now you say you are wrong in saying £200, and say that it was £400?—Yes.

Mr. Smith must have been wrong, too?—I said £200, but I thought it was more than that that very night.

Curiously enough, Mr. Smith, who was with you, said what he saw was £100 and some more in the bags?—That is so, I believe.

Has he also come to the conclusion that it is now £400?—I could not say.

You have not talked it over with Mr. Smith?—Well, we tried the experiment together, as a matter of fact.

Did you know that Mr. Seddon was in the habit, and had been for years, of keeping a large sum of money in the house?—No, I never did.

Did you know he had a second safe up in the bedroom?—I did not know at that time.

You know now?—I know now.

That was a largish safe downstairs?—Yes, it was.

And the custom was that all the money was mixed together and then paid into his account, and then he would draw a cheque for the insurance office money out of the bank?—I believe it was so, but I am not quite certain about it.

Had there been a fuss about a little money that had been missing, had Mr. Seddon been making a fuss about some moneys short in collections? —He did say in the week that he was £2 out in his cash.

Did Mr. Seddon also say that the business was not as good as it used to be, and they would have to decrease the staff?—No, I do not think so. He told me that he expected that he should have to do with one assistant superintendent, and if that was so he would have to decrease the staff by getting rid of some of the men.

By getting rid of you?—No.

It does not follow that yours would be the vacancy?—No, it was not in his power to dismiss me.

No, but did he not tell you that he would have to report, and they would have to do with one officer less?—No, he did not tell me he would have to report it.

That he would have to reduce the staff?—He told me he would have to report it, and apply for an exchange.

Let us just get this once more. This took place on 14th September? —Yes.

You did not think anything of it at the time—you made no report to anybody?—No, but I had my thoughts about it.

But when you saw in the papers the account of the inquest and the statement that £200 was missing then your mind travelled back to this night?—No.

That is what I want to know?—I made up my mind that the money was over £200 that very night.

I am not dealing with that; I am dealing with the question of your mind going back to the occasion. The next thing that brought your mind back to it was what you saw in the paper about the inquest?—Yes, that would be so.

Trial of the Seddons.

Re-examined by Mr. MUIR—You said you had never seen Mr. Seddon like that on any other day before?—No.

What did you mean by that—like what?—He looked very tired, weary, and haggard. He was in a state that I had not seen him in before.

Did he tell you he had been up all night?—He told me he had been up all night.

The Court adjourned.

Third Day—Wednesday, 6th March, 1912.

The Court met at 10.15 a.m.

JOHN CHARLES ARTHUR SMITH, examined by Mr. TRAVERS HUMPHREYS—I am assistant superintendent of the Holloway district of the London and Manchester Industrial Insurance Company. On Thursday, 14th September last, I went to 63 Tollington Park in the ordinary course of my duties. I got there about 12.45, in the middle of the day, and I stayed there until 12 o'clock midnight.

In the course of the evening did you notice anything particular on the desk of the male prisoner?—I did. About 8.30, as far as I can remember, I noticed a large amount of gold, loose sovereigns and half-sovereigns. Two bags had already been filled when I noticed this.

Did you estimate at all how much gold you saw loose on the table?—I did at that time—about £100, because I have experimented since.

Mr. JUSTICE BUCKNILL—Oh, don't do that. You must answer the question, sir. These people are being tried on a capital charge. Any observation made by any witness over and above a clear and plain answer to the question put might be most disastrous. I might have to begin the whole thing again. You know perfectly well you must not make observations. Now, go on.

Examination continued—I estimated it at about £100. I did not see any silver or copper on the table. Mr. Seddon was placing the gold into bags when I saw it. Two bags were already filled, and I saw the prisoner fill other two. He placed the four bags in his safe. He handed one of the bags to me on my desk, and said, " Here's your wages." He said that jokingly. I turned round and smiled, and said, " I wish you meant it, Mr. Seddon." The safe in which I saw him put the bags was not the place in which he usually put the money which he received from the collectors. The money he received from the collectors he usually put in a till.

By Mr. JUSTICE BUCKNILL—I had seen the collectors' money being dealt with for very near twelve months, and the practice was to place the money in tills provided for that purpose. This accounting took place every week during the twelve months that I was there.

Cross-examined by Mr. MARSHALL HALL—When did you first come into connection with the police with a view of giving evidence? Some time in December?—Yes.

Evidence for Prosecution.

John Charles Arthur Smith

You have been at Mr. Seddon's house pretty frequently for the past twelve months?—Yes.

You are in the same employ?—Yes.

You are almost next in rank to him, are you not?—No, Mr. Taylor is the senior assistant.

Now, I think you said in the evidence that you have given that you saw about £100 worth of gold loose, and that two bags were already filled when you noticed that?—Yes.

You drew the conclusion that the other two bags also contained gold?—I did.

You do not suggest, and you have never suggested, have you, that you saw the other two bags actually filled with gold?—No.

They were the ordinary £5 silver bags?—The ordinary light brown bags which the bank will supply for the purpose of gold.

Five shillings in copper, £5 in silver, or £100 in gold?—I should say they were £100 in gold bags, a really large size.

Is there any difference in size between the £100 in gold bag and the £5 in silver bag?—Not much, I think.

Do you not know that the bags to hold £5 silver and the bags to hold £100 in gold are the same size?—Yes, they are.

Do you know Maggie Seddon?—Yes, I do.

Earlier in the afternoon did you see Maggie Seddon in the street and pat her on the back?—I did not.

I put it to you that earlier in the afternoon you had called Maggie Seddon who was outside the house, and you just patted her on the shoulder and said, "How are you"?—I did not.

You never saw Maggie Seddon that afternoon at all?—I may have seen her when she came to the office to see her father about something in the office, but not outside.

Your evidence before the magistrate was, "I make a rough estimate of the money I saw as £100"?—On the table.

After the inquest did you go to the house and see Seddon?—I went there in the ordinary course of business.

Did you say to Mr. Seddon, "I remember seeing £100 in gold on the night that I came in to check the receipts"?—No, certainly not.

Did you offer to come and give evidence at the inquest?—No.

Nothing of the kind occurred?—Nothing of the kind occurred.

Did you tell them that you remembered the letter being posted?—I told them that I thought—I had an idea of a certain letter being posted.

By Mr. Justice Bucknill—What was the idea?—That he had written a letter to the relations.

Was any particular letter spoken of?—It would want a slight explanation, my lord.

Re-examined by the Attorney-General—I want you to tell us what this statement was and how you came to make it, and what you were referring to when you did make it. Let us understand what it means?—On the night after Miss Barrow's death, which would be the Friday, Mr. Taylor and I went to the office as usual, and Mr. Seddon turned round to me and said, "Fancy, the relations have not been near, and the funeral is to-morrow." Then on 27th November Mr. Seddon sent me a post card to

73

Trial of the Seddons.

John Charles Arthur Smith

call upon him. When I arrived he was very busy with legal documents, and he had been showing me several of these referring to this case, and in the midst of looking at these papers I was rather taken off my guard. He said to me, " Oh, Smith, you remember me writing a letter to the relations." Well, my mind went back to the day——

Mr. JUSTICE BUCKNILL—Keep your witness in hand.

By the ATTORNEY-GENERAL—Do not tell us about your mind going back. Tell us what you said?—Well, I remember him saying to me in the office, " Fancy, the relations have not been near, and the funeral is to-morrow," and I felt that he had written this letter. I thought he had written this letter. I said I had a recollection of the letter being written.

Had you seen him writing a letter to the relations?—I had not. Mr. Seddon was always writing letters during the day.

Had you seen him writing letters at all during that day?—Yes.

In the office in the basement?—Yes.

Did you know to whom the letters were being written?—I do not.

Did he say to you anything at the time he was writing these letters?— He did not.

About the persons to whom they were addressed or anything of that kind?—No.

Will you tell us how you came to say that you thought you recollected, or some such expression of that kind?—From the fact that he told me, or said at the office, as I previously mentioned, " Fancy, the relations have not been near, and the funeral is to-morrow." I thought perhaps he had written it from the fact of him saying that.

ALFRED HARTWELL, examined by Mr. TRAVERS HUMPHREYS—I am one of the directors of the London and Manchester Industrial Assurance Company. The male prisoner has been employed by that company since 1891. Since 1901 he has been superintendent of collectors and canvassers for the North London district. Up to March, 1911, his salary was £5 3s. a week, and from 25th March it was £5 6s. a week. In addition to that salary, he was entitled to commission on the ordinary branch of the business. The majority of the business done by my company is industrial insurance, but the prisoner was not entitled to commission on that. During the year ending March, 1911, the average sum paid to him for salary and commission was £5 16s., and from March, 1911, to November, 1911, his earnings were £5 15s. 10d. a week, although his salary had been increased a little. As the superintendent of that district, it was his duty to receive money every Thursday from the various collectors. He would do that at his own house, where he had an office in the basement. He would receive the total amount collected by the collectors, less their commission—they would deduct the commission before they would pay him over the cash— and he would then pay to the collectors any salaries and procuration fees for new business. The balance would remain for him to pay into his own bank account. He used his own banking account for the purpose of the company's money as well as his own. It would be his duty to draw a cheque payable to the name of Mr. Dawes, our managing director, for the amount due to the company, that is to say, for the amount left to him

Evidence for Prosecution.

Alfred Hartwell

less his own salary and any commission due, which he would deduct. He had a small allowance of 8s. 9d. a week for stamps and office rent, and that he would be entitled to deduct from the amount he paid in and from the amount he drew the cheque for to Mr. Dawes. I find that the total amount of the collections before the commission was deducted for the week ending 14th September was £80 4s. 7½d. Eighteen shillings of that was collected, but was owing by the discrepancies on the part of previous agents, so that the total amount of cash paid by the collectors would be £79 6s. 7½d. Before that passed into the hands of the prisoner the collectors would deduct commission due to them, amounting to £15 12s. 3½d. Therefore the prisoner would actually have in his possession at one time £63 14s. 4d. for the industrial branch and £2 17s. 7d. for the ordinary that week. £66 11s. 11d. would go into the bank. He would pay back to the collectors £4 12s. 6d., the new business fees. The total of the salaries on that occasion was £9 16s. That included his own salary of £5 6s., so that £4 10s. is the amount which he would pay back to the collectors for their salaries, leaving £57 9s. 5d., which he would pay into the bank if he chose. Out of that there was due to the company £48 17s. 1d. for the industrial and £2 17s. 7d. for the ordinary. It was his duty to draw separate cheques for those amounts to Mr. Dawes, and he did so on that day. The discharging of either Mr. Smith or Mr. Taylor would not be in the hands of the prisoner at all. He would recommend the directors probably, or through his superintendent, to get rid of a certain man, but we would inquire into it first.

Cross-examined by Mr. Marshall Hall—Promotion in our office is like promotion in any other office; when there is room on the top somebody comes up from the bottom. The prisoner was for about twenty-one years in the employment of my company. He was allowed to pay in money he received into his own bank, and then he would draw a cheque for the proportion due to the company in favour of Mr. Dawes, our managing director.

And there was no question about irregularities. It was a perfectly regular thing for him to pay your money into his bank?—Yes.

There would be no objection to the wife of one of your men carrying on a separate business if she liked, nothing to do with insurance?—Yes, as long as he did not interfere with it. But we do not like them doing that, because we feel that part of their time is devoted to that. I heard quite accidentally from Mr. Seddon about three or four years ago that his wife was carrying on a business.

Re-examined by the Attorney-General—It was a wardrobe dealer's business. I made particular inquiries, because we did not want our business neglected for another business.

If his wife carried on a wardrobe business, would that have anything to do with your business?—Well, I mean that we did not want him to interfere.

Mrs. E. A. Longley, recalled, by Mr. Marshall Hall—My husband wrote and asked Mr. Seddon if he would put us up for a day or two before we came. Mr. Seddon wrote back that the old lady in the house was ill, but if we liked to take pot-luck we might come. I noticed a very bad

Trial of the Seddons.

smell in the house. My sister-in-law had a baby about twelve months old in the house. I saw Ernie Grant once in bed and once on the morning when he was sent to Southend. He looks very delicate.

Did you call attention to the fact as to whether it was healthy or not for Ernie Grant to sleep in the same room as Miss Barrow?—Yes. He was in bed with Miss Barrow when I saw him, and I thought it was not healthy for the boy, nor was it decent for him to be there.

ERNEST VICTOR ROWLAND, recalled, by Mr. TRAVERS HUMPHREYS—I produce exhibit 35, a certified extract from the books of my bank, the London and Provincial Bank, Finsbury Park branch, showing the payments in and out during the time which includes the month of September, 1911. It shows in what form the payments in to the account were made. On 15th September, 1911, there was a payment in to the account of £81 7s. 6d. in coin and in drafts £6 17s. 2d. On the same day there was a further payment in of £7 16s. in cash, making a total of £96 0s. 8d. for that day. On 16th September the account is debited with a cheque drawn to the order of Mr. Dawes of £48 17s. 1d. On the 19th there is another cheque drawn to the same person to the amount of £2 17s. 7d.

Cross-examined by Mr. MARSHALL HALL—There was a payment in on 15th September of £88 4s. 8d. and £7 16s. £88 4s. 8d. was made up of £81 7s. 6d. in cash and £6 17s. 2d. in drafts. £7 16s. was paid in in coin. Out of the £81 7s. 6d. in cash there was £15 17s. 6d. in silver.

£15 17s. 6d. in silver would be about three ordinary bags full of silver?—Just over three bags. The drafts were cheques and postal orders. There is a weekly sum paid in of somewhere approaching £7 or £7 10s., or something of that sort pretty regularly. I do not know whether that was the proceeds of rent. It is all cash.

Re-examined—Sometimes this sum is £6—it varies about £7.

CHARLES JAMES CRASFIELD, examined by Mr. TRAVERS HUMPHREYS— I am an assistant secretary to the National Freehold Land and Building Society, 25 Moorgate Street. My society advanced to the male prisoner on 27th November, 1909, a sum of £220 on a mortgage of the lease of his house, 63 Tollington Park. I received the letter, which is exhibit 15, dated 19th September:—" Dear sir,—Please let me know the exact amount required to date to pay off the mortgage on above premises, and oblige, per return." I replied the next day. The amount of the mortgage has not yet been paid off. On 18th September, 1911, I received from the prisoner an application (exhibit 16) for three completed shares in my society. The value of the three shares as there stated is £90, and there is an entrance fee of 3s. On that date the male prisoner purchased those shares and paid me £90 3s. in cash. He was given the pass book, exhibit 17, which shows that £90 3s. was paid in coin.

CLARA MAY COOPER, examined by Mr. TRAVERS HUMPHREYS—I am a counter clerk and telegraphist at the Finsbury Park Branch Post Office, 290 Seven Sisters Road. (Shown exhibit 37.) There is a post office savings bank book in the name of F. H. Seddon, 63 Tollington Park. On 15th September, 1911, a sum of £30 was paid into that account. I do not

Evidence for Prosecution.

remember how it was paid in or who paid it in, but I am able to say that at least £25 of that sum must have been in gold.

Mr. MARSHALL HALL—How can this be evidence against either of these prisoners—a payment in by somebody whom this witness cannot recognise?

Mr. JUSTICE BUCKNILL—It is only as a fact. By itself it is not evidence against them. Of course, it will occur to you at once in the absence of any evidence identifying the person paying it in, it is not evidence against him.

The ATTORNEY-GENERAL—According to this witness, on that day £30 was paid in to the credit of his account. At the present moment we are proceeding to ask her how that money was paid in. She is not able to identify the person paying it in, and I quite assent to what your lordship says upon that. But it would be evidence against the prisoner that money is paid in to his account; assuming she says £25 of it is gold, £25 in gold was paid into his account on that date to his credit.

Mr. JUSTICE BUCKNILL—That is evidence that on that day that was done, and his account had the benefit of that amount. Strictly speaking, if this lady cannot tell us who paid it in or how it was paid in, but only that somebody paid into this account that sum of money, it is a fact for the consideration of the jury. But taken by itself it is not evidence of guilt in this case.

The ATTORNEY-GENERAL—If I may say so, I quite assent; by itself it is not evidence of guilt.

Mr. MARSHALL HALL—I must take a formal objection in a case of this kind. There being no identification of the person who paid this money in, the details of the payment which was made are not evidence in this case, even as evidence of a fact. Before I had noticed it I had allowed the answer to be given, that on that day a credit of £30 was passed to the credit of F. H. Seddon, who I do not for a moment dispute is the prisoner. Beyond that, I submit this witness cannot go.

Mr. JUSTICE BUCKNILL—I shall tell the jury this—I will repeat it once more so that there will be no mistake—that with regard to this payment in, if it were the only question in the case I should rule that it was no evidence against him of guilt in this case, but I cannot reject as a fact that on 15th September, which is an important date, the day after the death of this lady, his banking account was increased by £30.

Mr. MARSHALL HALL—I do not object to that, but what I do object to now is any evidence being given as to the form in which that £30 was paid in.

The ATTORNEY-GENERAL—I submit we are entitled to get as evidence how that money came into his account.

Examination continued—On that day, 15th September, I went on duty at 2 o'clock in the afternoon. I was handed £10 in bank notes by the colleague whom I relieved. When I went off duty at 8 o'clock that night I had £15 in bank notes. Between 2 o'clock and 8 o'clock I did not receive more than £5 in bank notes from anybody. Between 2 o'clock and 8 o'clock on that day this sum of £30 was paid in to that account by somebody.

That being so, are you able to say how much of that £30 could have

Trial of the Seddons.

been in a form other than coin?—£5 might possibly have been by the bank note which I received that afternoon.

Cross-examined by Mr. MARSHALL HALL—The money that is paid in is not kept distinct from the payments out; we pay out of the same till as we pay in to.

Therefore do you know how much you paid out that afternoon?—Yes. I am quite sure that I did not pay out any notes at all that afternoon. As far as I know, the whole £30 may have been paid in in gold. I do not remember it being paid; I do not know who paid it in or how it was paid in. Looking at the savings bank book I find that £43 17s. 9d. was paid out of that account on 27th November, 1911. That left exactly £20 in the account.

THOMAS WRIGHT, examined by the ATTORNEY-GENERAL—I am a jeweller, carrying on business at 400 and 402 Holloway Road. I know the male prisoner as a customer. I remember his coming to my shop on 15th September, 1911, and bringing with him a small single stone diamond ring, exhibit 121. He said that he wanted it made very much larger. When it was brought to me it was a gentleman's single stone little finger ring, but it might be used by a lady. The ring was left with me. He returned later that same day, bringing with him a gold watch. exhibit 21. He said he wanted the name "E. J. Barrow, 1860," erased from the inside. That name was engraved right inside on the back plate which I indicate. It is not possible to get at that plate without opening the works of the watch. He also wished a gold dial to be put in in place of the old enamel one, which was very much cracked. He left the watch with me, and I did the two commissions which he gave me. The female prisoner was with him when he brought the watch. On 20th September Mr. and Mrs. Seddon came together, and I handed back the ring to him. It is now in the enlarged form in which I made it according to his order. I delivered the watch on 17th November. It took me a long time to get the gold dial. Mr. Seddon called several times for the watch between 15th September and 17th November. I had his address; I had known him for quite a year. He paid for the ring and the watch.

Cross-examined by Mr. MARSHALL HALL—I have known the male prisoner as a customer. I believe on a previous occasion he had had the diamond ring altered. I believe he took this particular diamond ring off his little finger, and I think he said he wanted it altered to fit his middle finger. There is no mystery about my having taken a couple of months to put the gold dial on to the watch, as it is a very difficult thing to do. At the same time that he brought the watch he did not bring a large locket of Mrs. Seddon's to have a stone put in. (Shown exhibit 21.) The enlarging of that diamond ring would not in any way destroy its identity. It is merely a question of hammering out the gold. The stone weighs under two grains, it is slightly yellow, and it might be worth £4 or £5.

Re-examined—I would give £4 for it—that is about its value.

WILLIAM NODES, examined by the ATTORNEY-GENERAL—I carry on business as an undertaker at 201 Holloway Road, and I have a branch

78

Evidence for Prosecution.

William Nodes

office at 78 Stroud Green Road. I have known the male prisoner since 1901. In April, 1902, I did a small funeral business for him. I used to see him occasionally. I remember him calling upon me at 78 Stroud Green Road about 11.30 a.m. on 14th September of last year. He said that a death had occurred in his house, and he wanted to make arrangements for the funeral, which must be an inexpensive one. He did not describe the person who had died; he merely said an " old lady " or an " old girl," I do not remember which it was, had died in his house, and that he wished to make arrangements for the funeral. He said that it must be an inexpensive funeral from the fact that he had found £4 10s. in the room, and that would have to defray the funeral expenses, and that there were also certain fees due to the doctor. I suggested an inclusive funeral of £4, but he said that 10s. would not cover the doctor's expenses, and then I told him I would do the funeral for him for £3 7s. 6d., an inclusive charge, to enable him to cover all expenses, including the doctor and that sort of thing. I explained to him what kind of funeral it would be for the price; it was a £4 funeral really, and it would mean a coffin, polished and ornamented with handles and inside lining, a composite carriage, the necessary bearers, and the fees at Islington Cemetery, Finchley, and it included the interment in the grave at Finchley. I do not know that I specified what kind of grave she would be buried in, but it would mean interment in a public grave, a grave dug by the cemetery people, who allow interments in it at a certain price, which includes the use of the clergyman. By a " public grave " I mean a grave which is not the particular property of any individual; it is used for more than one person. I think it was distinctly understood by Mr. Seddon that it would not be a private grave.

When you say it was distinctly understood, did you talk about it at all?—No, not emphasising the fact of its being a public grave. I only said that it would be a public grave; we went into no details. In about twenty minutes I drove Mr. Seddon in my trap to 63 Tollington Park, and I measured the body. I found a very bad smell in the room where the body was. When we got downstairs I said to Mr. Seddon that, as there was a very bad smell, if he liked we would remove the body at the same time as we brought the coffin, and he said that he would let me know later on when he let me know about the funeral. the day of the funeral, as he had others to consult on the matter. I then left to make the arrangements that were necessary. Between three and four o'clock in the afternoon of that same day I got a telephone message from Mr. Seddon saying that we might move the body when we brought the coffin, and settling the day of interment for Saturday. The body was removed to 78 Stroud Green Road that evening, Thursday, the 14th, about half-past nine as near as I can remember. The funeral took place about two o'clock in the afternoon of Saturday, 16th September, starting from 78 Stroud Green Road. I did rot attend. There were no instructions to send carriages for other mourners, and none were sent. No mourning carriage went to No. 63 Tollington Park, and nothing started from there in the shape of a funeral conveyance. I received £3 7s. 6d. for the funeral. I remember it being reported to me that some hair had been cut from the deceased's head at our place. I believe it was placed in

79

Trial of the Seddons.

one of our envelopes and handed to somebody, but I do not know to whom. I have never seen it since.

Cross-examined by Mr. MARSHALL HALL—There is no suggestion that this was a pauper's funeral. The number of bodies which are buried in a grave of this kind depends entirely upon the cemetery authorities; it depends upon the depth of the grave which is available, and the cemetery authorities decide how many bodies they will bury in one of these graves.

You have told us that there was a very, very bad smell in the room. Did you know that Mrs. Seddon had a little baby?—I did know that.

Did that affect your suggestion that the body had better be removed? —Yes, that was one thing that had to do with it, and then I thought by the body being removed it would give them an opportunity of cleansing the room. I am not suggesting that the room was not clean, but the smell was very pregnant, it suggested itself to me as being a smell of fæces, and therefore I suggested that the body should be removed at the same time with the coffin. There is nothing unusual in a body being removed in that way.

Even with people who are very much attached to the dead person?— When there are no unpleasant surroundings we are very often asked to do that. There was nothing unusual in the funeral being from our place. I should say that it was shortly after three o'clock when the telephone message came to me that Thursday afternoon. I have a reason for thinking that it was not as late as four or five. I did not suggest Saturday as the day for the funeral. I simply put the question to the prisoner. He said, "When can the funeral be?" and I said, "Whenever you like." He said, "Saturday"; and I replied, "If you wish it." If we did not bury on Saturday it would mean burying on Monday, and having regard to the state that the body was in and the diarrhœa that had taken place, the warmth of the weather, and the fact that there was no lead lining to the coffin, it seemed quite reasonable that the body should be buried on Saturday. There is nothing at all unusual in a person who died early on Thursday morning being buried under these conditions on the Saturday.

Re-examined by the ATTORNEY-GENERAL—(Shown envelope marked No. 135.) That is an envelope which comes from my establishment. I cannot recognise the handwriting either on the inside or on the outside.

WALTER THORLEY, examined by the ATTORNEY-GENERAL—I am a chemist and druggist carrying on business at 27 Crouch Hill. I remember a girl coming to my shop with reference to some fly-papers in the summer of 1911. I remember subsequently identifying that girl at the police office, the girl being Margaret Ann Seddon—I think her second name is Ann. She was about fifteen years old. I was present when she stood forward in the Police Court in the presence of the prisoners. She did not say anything, but I heard her addressed in the presence of the prisoners as Margaret Seddon. I remember the date on which she came to my shop; it was 26th August, 1911. She made a purchase at my shop.

Will you tell us what it was she purchased?—A threepenny packet of Ma——

Mr. MARSHALL HALL—I formally object to this evidence as evidence

Evidence for Prosecution.

Walter Thorley

against the prisoners, but if your lordship thinks it is evidence I shall not press it at this stage. I say, however, that this evidence cannot be evidence against the prisoners. For instance, if two persons, A and B, are charged with the wilful murder of D, how can it be evidence against either A or B to say that C bought papers containing arsenic?

The ATTORNEY-GENERAL—Your lordship will observe the question I put. I submit I am entitled to prove the fact that a purchase was made by the girl who, according to the evidence, lived and helped in the house.

Mr. JUSTICE BUCKNILL—When you have proved that Margaret Seddon lived in the house, then I think it is clearly evidence, but you are now rather putting the cart before the horse.

The ATTORNEY-GENERAL—It has been proved, my lord. Mary Chater, the servant, proved it, and so did Ernie Grant. Mary Chater said, " I slept in the room with Maggie and her youngest sister."

Mr. JUSTICE BUCKNILL—The mere fact that Margaret Seddon was the daughter of the accused people is not enough. On evidence being adduced that Margaret Seddon was living in the house on 26th August, 1911, with her parents I shall admit the evidence.

The ATTORNEY-GENERAL—I think I am right in saying that it has been proved, but it can be put beyond all question.

Mr. MARSHALL HALL—There is another objection, and that is that if there is evidence of this why does not the prosecution call Margaret Seddon?

Mr. JUSTICE BUCKNILL—That is an observation; it is not an objection at the present moment.

The ATTORNEY-GENERAL—That leads to the retort that it is open to my learned friend to call Margaret Seddon.

Mr. JUSTICE BUCKNILL—You had better call the girl Chater again.

M. E. E. CHATER, recalled, further examined by the ATTORNEY-GENERAL —During the time that I was a servant at Mr. and Mrs. Seddon's, Margaret or Maggie, the daughter, lived there. She slept in the house throughout the whole time, and took part in the household duties, cleaning the floors, doing the kitchen upstairs, and all that kind of thing.

Further cross-examined by Mr. MARSHALL HALL—Did Maggie Seddon sleep there every night?—Yes.

Was she never away?—No.

Did she not go to Southend?—Well, she went there once. I could not say the exact date, but she did go down there. I cannot give an idea of the exact date.

How soon after Miss Barrow was taken ill did she go down to Southend?—I could not say the date, but she went down I know. I do not know on what day it was that Miss Barrow came back from Southend.

WALTER THORLEY, recalled, examination continued—On 26th August, 1911, Margaret Seddon purchased from me a threepenny packet of Mather's fly-papers. There were six fly-papers in each packet, and they were similar to the packet of Mather's fly-papers now shown me, exhibit 136. Outside that packet I see " Mather's Chemical Fly-papers. To poison flies, wasps, ants, mosquitoes, &c. Prepared only by the sole

Trial of the Seddons.

proprietors, W. Mather, Limited, Dyer Street, Manchester. Poison. These arsenic fly-papers can only be sold by registered chemists, and in accordance with the provisions of the Pharmacy Act.'' The words, '' These arsenic fly-papers,'' are in larger print than the other portion of the sentence. Taking one of the papers out, I find that in the centre it contains the following :—'' Directions for use. For flies, wasps, ants, mosquitoes, &c., spread each paper on a dish or plate and keep moist with cold water. A little sugar, beer, or wine added two or three times a day makes them more attractive. Caution. Remove the tray or dish beyond the reach of children and out of the way of domestic animals.'' Then, at the bottom of it, there is '' Poison.''

(Fly-papers were handed to the jury, who examined them.)

I would not like to say definitely how many grains of arsenic there are in each of those fly-papers; there might be more in one than in another. I do not keep any note of my sales. I think there is a large sale for those fly-papers; I myself sold many of them last year. I was asked about this sale of Mather's fly-papers about a week before the day on which I gave evidence at the Police Court, which day I remember was 2nd February, 1912. I was asked to go into a room where there were about twenty women and girls to identify the girl I had sold the fly-papers to. Nobody went with me.

Did you identify her?—Yes.

Did you subsequently see her in Court?—Yes.

In the presence of the prisoners?—Yes.

And did you hear her addressed by name?—Yes.

As?—Margaret Seddon.

Cross-examined by Mr. MARSHALL HALL—Margaret Ann Seddon is the name of the prisoner?—I cannot tell for certain the second name, but it was Margaret Seddon.

Was there any second name at all?—I believe so.

On 26th August, 1911, you say a girl came and bought some fly-papers at your shop. Did you ever see the girl who came to your shop to buy those fly-papers until 2nd February, 1912, when you professed to identify her at the Police Court?—I may have done.

Did you?—I cannot say for certain.

Will you say that you did?—No, I cannot recollect.

What sort of a day was 26th August?—A Saturday.

Was it a hot day, or a cloudy day, or a fine day, or a wet day, or what?—It was a hot day.

It was a very hot summer?—Yes.

Was this a hot day like the rest of the hot summer?—Yes.

Do you know that there was only one hour's sunshine on that day?—No.

Saturday, 26th August, was the exceptional day of that year, with very little sunshine, but you remember it was a day with bright sunshine?

The ATTORNEY-GENERAL—He has not said that.

Mr. MARSHALL HALL—He said it was a bright hot day like the other days.

(To Witness)—Can you tell me who was the customer you served before or the customer you served after this girl?—No.

Evidence for Prosecution.

Walter Thorley

How many packets of these Mather's fly-papers did you sell this last season?—The last season or in August?

In August, if you like?—Sixteen.

Sixteen packets?—Yes.

And eight dozen during the season?—Eight dozen in August.

Mr. JUSTICE BUCKNILL—Where does the sixteen come in then?—

Mr. MARSHALL HALL—Sixteen packets is eight dozen papers.

(To Witness)—Did you keep a record of the papers or the persons they were sold to?—No.

Do you not know that under the Pharmacy Act you are required to keep a record of the persons to whom you sold the papers?—No.

Did you know that those papers contained two, three, or even four grains of arsenic a-piece?—I can realise it.

But can you sell two, three, or four grains of arsenic to a person?—No.

Yet you can sell the paper which contains it?—Yes.

Without registration?—Yes.

As a matter of fact, do Messrs. Mather, who make these papers, supply you with a book in which to record the persons who buy them?—Yes.

Do you use it?—No.

Do you know a Mr. Price, a chemist?—Yes.

He is a witness in this case?—Yes.

Does he carry on business somewhere near you?—Yes.

On 2nd February you were fetched in a motor car, were you not, by the police?—Yes.

To come to the Police Court. Did Mr. Price, the chemist, come down in the same motor car with you?—Yes.

Did you know that Mr. Price was coming down to the Police Court to prove that on 6th December (I want the jury to bear the date in mind very carefully, because, if your lordship will allow me to say, the prisoner was arrested on 4th December) Margaret Seddon had tried to buy some fly-papers from Mr. Price?—No.

Do you swear that?—Yes.

Did you ask Mr. Price what he was going down to the Police Court for?—No.

Did you not know?—I thought it would be something to do with poison.

On the 2nd February, when this had been in the paper for weeks, did you not know that you and Mr. Price were both going down to the Police Court to give evidence?—There was another person present.

Did you never have any conversation with Mr. Price?—Not about what we were going to do.

Not about the girl who had come to his shop for some fly-papers on 6th December?—No.

Do you swear that?—Yes.

You did not know Price was going to give evidence that Margaret Seddon (and it was not disputed) had been to his shop with some other young ladies on 6th December for the purpose of trying to buy some fly-papers?—No.

And that he had refused to sell them?—No.

You did not know that?—No.

Trial of the Seddons.

Walter Thorley

That you swear?—Yes.

Did you see an account of this inquest in the paper in November?— No; I did not read it at all.

Had you often seen Mr. Price?—No.

Have you ever talked this case over with Mr. Price?—No.

From 27th August, 1911, your attention was never called to it again until one week before 2nd February?—No, that is right.

How many customers do you think you serve a day?—(No answer.)

A good many?—Yes, a good many.

And a good many girls, do you not?—Yes.

Had the police been to you in December to ask you if you had sold any fly-papers to anybody about August or September?—Yes.

Do you know that the police were making inquiries at other chemists' shops in the neighbourhood early in December as to whether fly-papers had been purchased, and, if so, by whom, in August and September of 1911? —Yes.

Did you tell the police that you had no recollection of any purchase? —No. Of course, I had had purchases made.

Did they ask you if you had any record of the persons you had sold them to?—Yes.

And, of course, you told them you had no record?—Yes.

Did they ask you if you could identify anybody to whom you had sold fly-papers about that date?—Yes.

And did you tell them that it was a long while ago, and that you could not identify any one?—(No answer.)

Did you tell them you could not identify anybody?—I said I did not know whether I could or not.

How many times did the police come to you in all?—Oh, I do not know; a good many times, I think.

And you were not able to bring your memory sufficiently accurately back—I will not put it stronger than that—until February or the latter end of January, 1912?—(No answer.)

That is so; you were not able to give the police any information that you could identify any one who had bought fly papers in August, 1911, until February of 1912, could you?—They never asked me before.

But you said they had been to you a good many times to ask you if you could identify anybody at all. Do you really mean to tell me that you profess to be able in the month of January, 1912, to identify a casual girl who comes into your shop on the 26th August, 1911, and buys fly-papers?—Yes.

You do. Will you tell the jury how you profess to remember the date of 26th August? You have no note, have you—no memorandum of any sort or shape?—I have got my invoices. She had the last packet of a dozen that was ordered on one day.

Did you keep a record of the sale of the last packet?—No.

How do you know when the last packet was sold?—She asked for four packets.

Four packets or four papers?—Four packets.

Twenty-four papers?—Twenty-four papers.

Threepence a packet?—Threepence a packet. That was the last one

Evidence for Prosecution.

Walter Thorley

I had. I put them down to order in the book, and told her she should have some more on Monday.

Then you fix the date from the fact that you did sell your last packet on 26th August?—Yes.

Do you know the girl Margaret Seddon at all?—Yes.

She is a friend of your daughter Mabel, is she not?—She is known to her. I did not know her as Margaret Seddon until I saw her in the Police Court, although I have seen her about the neighbourhood.

The girl you identified in the Police Court as the person who came to your shop to buy these fly-papers is somebody who has been to your house to see your daughter Mabel?—Yes.

On two occasions she called to see Mabel, did she not, and you opened the door—a private door?—She did not come in.

You opened the door and said Mabel was not at home, and she went away?—Well, I could not identify anybody I did that to; I did that to many other girls.

That is the point I am on. The person you identified as having bought the papers after this lapse of time is the identification of somebody whom you had seen on your premises having come to see your daughter. That is the suggestion I make to you?—I have seen her in the shop.

I suggest to you that you have made a mistake. I am not suggesting that it is a wilful mistake, but I am suggesting to you that you have made a mistake, and that the girl you identified on the 2nd February, 1912, as the girl who had bought fly-papers at your establishment on 26th August, 1911, is not that girl, but the girl who had twice called at your place to see your daughter Mabel. Do you still say that she is the girl who bought the fly-papers?—Yes.

Let us come to the identity. You are fetched in a motor car on 2nd February. That is so, is it not?—Yes.

You are brought down to the Police Court with Mr. Price and somebody else in the car. Were you and Mr. Price taken in together to a room where there were about twenty people?—No, that was in the morning. I came down by myself in the morning.

You had been down to the Police Court before you came down in the motor car?—Yes.

Had you seen a picture of Margaret Seddon in the papers?—Yes.

Before you went to identify her?—Not that day, before it.

You were taken down by the police to identify a girl whose picture had been published in the illustrated papers, and which you had seen?—I refused to identify the girl from the pictures I had seen.

Of course, naturally you would, but the picture was shown to you for the purpose of identification?—It was not shown to me by the police.

Anyhow, you tell me you had seen it?—Yes.

You had seen the picture of a girl whom you knew to be Margaret Seddon, the daughter of the man who is charged with this murder, and you are taken down by the police to identify that particular girl among twenty others. That is so, is it not?—(No answer.)

Is that so?—I do not know whether they knew I had seen the picture.

Did they not happen to ask you?—No.

You knew you had seen the picture, did you not?—Yes.

85

Trial of the Seddons.

Walter Thorley

Unless I had asked you would you have told anybody that you had seen that picture?—Yes.

It is a very important factor in the case, is it not, on the question of identification? Out of those twenty people that you were taken to identify was the girl you identified the only girl who had got her hair down her back?—No.

That you swear?—Yes.

How many had?—At least one other.

Was there anybody approaching her in height?—Yes.

Of course, the moment you saw Margaret Seddon, that was a face that was familiar to you?—Yes.

Familiar to you for two reasons—first, because you had seen it in the illustrated papers; secondly, because you had seen her come to the house to meet your daughter. Anyhow, that would be a face familiar to you?—Yes.

Re-examined by the ATTORNEY-GENERAL—Do you know the Seddons at all—have you had any acquaintance or friendship with them?—No.

Nothing to do with them?—No.

I want you to be quite clear about the reason for your remembering this particular purchase. Will you tell us now what happened when the girl came into the shop? Tell us in your own way what took place?—She came in and asked for some fly-papers. I said, "Do you want the sticky ones?" She said, "No, the arsenic ones."

Have you any special reason for remembering this particular sale by you to the girl you identify as Margaret Seddon?—Yes.

Will you tell us what the special reason is?—She asked for four packets of fly-papers, and I had only one in stock.

Was any particular kind of fly-paper referred to?—Arsenic fly-papers.

Who used those words?—Margaret Seddon.

Then what did you say?—I said, "Will you take a packet?" She said, "I will take four." I said, "That is the only one I have. I shall have some more on Monday." She took the packet and left the shop.

Had you any more Mather's fly-papers in stock than that one packet when the girl came in?—No.

Did you make any note or entry in a book on that date?—Yes.

Did you order any more Mather's fly-papers?—Yes.

Further cross-examined by Mr. MARSHALL HALL—Was this last packet of fly-papers on the 26th August, 1911, a full one, or did it contain only four papers?—It contained six.

It was a full packet?—Yes.

Further re-examined by the ATTORNEY-GENERAL—Do you remember making a statement to the police which was taken down in writing?—Yes.

Had the police been to you before that, or was it the first time?—They had been before, I think.

Do you know how often before?—They called round in December, and then while the Police Court proceedings were on.

Will you just look at your statement? Is that your signature (handed)?—Yes.

Evidence for Prosecution.

Walter Thorley

Mr. MARSHALL HALL—I will take the date from my learned friend, 31st January, 1912.

The ATTORNEY-GENERAL—Yes.

(To Witness)—Did you go to the Police Court twice on the day tha you gave evidence?—Yes.

When did you go first?—In the morning.

That was, as I understand you, not in a motor car?—No.

Did you go alone or with anybody else?—By myself.

When was it that you saw the twenty girls and women in a room?—In the morning.

When you were by yourself?—Yes.

Was that the Police Court?—Yes.

Did you then go home?—Yes.

You did not remain at the Police Court?—No, I was there for perhap an hour afterwards, and then I was told I could go home.

Then later on you did go to the Police Court again?—Yes.

Was that the occasion when you went in the motor car with Mr. Price?—Yes.

Was there anybody else there?—Yes, a detective sergeant.

Were you fetched in the motor car?—Yes.

Did you know what for?—Yes, to prove the sale of the papers.

To go to the Police Court to give evidence?—Yes.

And you did go to the Police Court, and you were called that after noon, were you not?—Yes.

2nd February. There is one other matter with regard to the girl Did you know this girl, whom you subsequently identified and now know at Margaret Seddon, at all before she came into the shop?—No, sir.

By Mr. JUSTICE BUCKNILL—Before Margaret Seddon came into you shop on 26th August, did you know her as Margaret Seddon?—No.

By the ATTORNEY-GENERAL—When she came into your shop and mad this purchase on 26th August, did you recognise her as a person you ha seen before or not?—I had seen her before.

By Mr. JUSTICE BUCKNILL—That is not quite an answer. Did yo recognise her then as a person whom you had seen before?—Yes.

By the ATTORNEY-GENERAL—Did you know her name?—No.

Or who she was?—No.

ROBERT JOHN PRICE, examined by the ATTORNEY-GENERAL—I am a pharmaceutical chemist at 103 Tollington Park, Holloway. I went with Mr. Thorley in a motor car on 2nd February to the Police Court.

Cross-examined by Mr. MARSHALL HALL—I do not remember that I had any conversation with Mr. Thorley as to the object of our visit to the Police Court.

Dr. JOHN FREDERICK PAUL, examined by the ATTORNEY-GENERAL—I am a member of the Royal College of Surgeons, and I reside at 215 Isledon Road, Finsbury Park. I was called as a witness at the inquest on 23rd November, 1911. I attended Miss Barrow, who lived at 63 Tollington Park, as a patient. She came to me first in November, 1910. I think

Trial of the Seddons.

Dr. John Frederick Paul

she was suffering then from congestion of the liver, but it was nothing of any consequence. I think I only saw her once at that time. She came to me again with Mrs. Seddon on 1st August, 1911. I judged that she had congestion of the liver then, but it was nothing of any consequence, nothing to prevent her going out. I gave her a mixture containing rhubarb, bicarbonate of soda and carbonate of magnesia, which is quite harmless. She came to me again on 3rd August, I think, with the boy Ernie Grant, and I prescribed the same medicine, as she was suffering from the same thing. I dispensed the medicine. She had a bottle on each day. I think she came again on 17th August, and I gave her the same medicine, as she was suffering from the same thing. I think she had the boy Ernie Grant with her. I saw her again on 22nd August in my consulting-room, and, as far as I remember, the boy Grant was with her. She complained of asthma, and I prescribed bicarbonate of potash and some nux vomica.

By Mr. JUSTICE BUCKNILL—She had not said anything about asthma on the previous occasions.

Examination continued—The asthma of which she was complaining was very slight, and there was no necessity for her to keep indoors, or anything of that kind. I saw her again in my consulting-room on 27th August. The boy Grant was with her then. She was suffering from asthma, and did not complain of anything else. I gave her some chloral hydrate. There was no need for her to stay at home. I saw her again in my consulting-room on 30th August. The boy Grant was with her that time. She complained of asthma, and nothing else, and I gave her some extract of grindelia. The asthma was not of any consequence then, and there was no need for her to stay at home. I would not describe her as a person who was ill at all under those circumstances. I cannot say that I saw any attack of asthma. I treated her on the symptoms she told me she had in the night. She did not complain on any of these visits in August of diarrhœa, sickness, or pain. On 1st and 3rd August, when I found that she had congestion of the liver, she complained of constipation. She did not complain of any rash or of any running from the eyes. I never saw her again after 30th August. I was called on a Saturday, I think it was 2nd September, between half-past six and eight in the evening, by Margaret Seddon, who wanted me to go and see Miss Barrow, but I could not go as I was too busy.

Cross-examined by Mr. MARSHALL HALL—I think you say Miss Barrow when you first saw her was suffering from congestion of the liver?—Yes.

Congestion of the liver might produce a certain amount of colic pain, might it not?—Yes.

She was a well-nourished woman, was she not, and rather inclined to be stout than thin?—Yes, she was.

We have had some evidence that she was a woman who experienced considerable difficulty in her breathing after she had been up and down stairs. She was the sort of woman whose appearance would convey that to you as a medical man, would it not?—No, I do not think it would. I did not notice anything wrong with her breathing.

Would you say she was above or below the average weight?—If anything, I should say she was a little above.

Evidence for Prosecution.

Dr. John Frederick Paul

You say she complained of asthma, but you did not yourself hear any asthmatic attack?—No.

Of course, asthmatic attacks are intermittent?—Yes.

And it is a fact that very often they are very much worse at night when the person is lying down?—Yes.

I notice that you mention an American drug you gave her, grindelia. I see it is a specific "for reducing the frequency of convulsions and spasmodic attacks which occur in asthma"?—Yes.

So, although you did not see it, you accepted her story that she was suffering from asthma?—Yes.

On 2nd September, Saturday, Miss Margaret Seddon did come to fetch you?—Yes.

And you were very busy, and you advised that they should fetch another doctor?—Yes.

Cross-examined by Mr. RENTOUL—I think it was Mrs. Seddon who first brought Miss Barrow to your house?—Yes, it was.

Further cross-examined by Mr. MARSHALL HALL—Mr. Seddon, I think, when the inquest came on, asked you if you would attend the inquest?—Yes.

Dr. HENRY GEORGE SWORN, examined by Mr. TRAVERS HUMPHREYS—I am a doctor of medicine and licentiate of the Royal College of Physicians, 5 Highbury Crescent, Highbury. I am and I have been for over ten years the family doctor of the two prisoners. On 2nd September last I was telephoned for to attend Miss Barrow between ten and eleven o'clock at night, and I went to 63 Tollington Park and saw Miss Barrow in bed. Mrs. Seddon was in the room at the time. I do not remember any one else being there. I got the history of the case from Miss Barrow and from Mrs. Seddon, being told that on Friday, 1st September, she had diarrhœa and sickness. I mentioned the fact to Mrs. Seddon, that she appeared to be very ill, and asked how long she had been ill. She said she had been ill on and off for a long time, that she had had a liver attack, and that she had suffered from asthma.

By Mr. JUSTICE BUCKNILL—I asked if she had been attended to by any other doctor about that time, and they said that she had been attended by another doctor, that they had sent for him at twelve o'clock that day, and again at eight o'clock.

Examination continued—I examined Miss Barrow, and found that she had pain in her abdomen, sickness, and diarrhœa. I was told that she had been vomiting. I prescribed bismuth and morphia.

By Mr. JUSTICE BUCKNILL—The bismuth was to stop the sickness and the morphia to soothe the pain. I gave her ten-grain doses of bismuth and five-minim doses of morphia in the same mixture. She was to take a dose of that quantity every four hours.

Examination continued—I saw her again next morning between eleven and twelve, and found her to be still about the same as she was when I saw her the day before. Mrs. Seddon was present, and told me that Miss Barrow was no better. I prescribed the same medicine. I saw Miss Barrow again on Monday, the 4th, and found her to be the same.

By Mr. JUSTICE BUCKNILL—She was being sick two or three times a day, and being purged; it was not continuous. The diarrhœa and sickness

Trial of the Seddons.

Dr. Henry George Sworn

had not stopped; my prescription had been ineffective. She was not much weaker; she was about the same—she was no weaker. I was not satisfied with her condition upon that day. I mentioned the fact, and Mrs. Seddon told me that she would not take her medicine. She said that to me before I went up and also before Miss Barrow.

Examination continued—Miss Barrow was deaf, and I should say that she could not hear what was said if it was spoken in an ordinary tone of voice. I gave the patient an effervescing mixture of citrate of potash and bicarbonate of soda, which would be administered in two separate parts. On that day the diarrhœa was not so bad, and therefore I gave nothing for the diarrhœa. I told Miss Barrow that if she did not take her medicine I should have to send her into the hospital, and she said she would not go. I called again upon the next day, the 5th, and found her to be slightly better. Mrs. Seddon was there when I saw her, and she said the sickness was not so bad, and that the diarrhœa was a little better than the day before. I did not alter my prescription in any way on that day; I continued the effervescing mixture. On the 6th, 7th, and 8th I found the patient to be slightly improved, and I continued the same medicine.

By Mr. JUSTICE BUCKNILL—On the 4th I dropped the morphia, because the abdominal pain was less.

Examination continued—On the 9th I found her to be about the same, but on that day Mrs. Seddon mentioned to me that her motion was so very offensive that I gave the patient a blue pill which contained mercury. I told Mrs. Seddon that if the patient was any worse on the Sunday she could telephone for me, but I did not get any telephone message. I did not call again until Monday, the 11th, when I saw her, I think, between ten and twelve in the forenoon. She was about the same as when I saw her on the Saturday. I saw Mrs. Seddon that day, but she did not tell me whether the diarrhœa or the sickness had stopped, or anything about it. On that day Miss Barrow was suffering principally from weakness caused by the diarrhœa and sickness that she had had. She had not any pain; if she had had any I should have sent her something for it.

By Mr. JUSTICE BUCKNILL—I was keeping on with the effervescing mixtures at that time, and I ordered her to take Valentine's meat juice and also some brandy for the weaknes

Examination continued—With regard to the diet, I instructed Mrs. Seddon, while the sickness was on, to give soda water and milk, and then I advised her to give her some gruel, and then later on I told her she could give her some light puddings—milk puddings—in addition to the Valentine's meat juice. I do not think Miss Barrow's mental condition was ever very good; on the 11th it was not very good. Nothing was said to me by anybody that day about Miss Barrow making a will. I looked upon her as a woman to whom you would have to explain a thing like a will if she had to make one; she would not grasp the whole of the facts, but she would be quite capable of making a will if you explained it to her. Her mental condition did not improve at all from the first day I saw her on 2nd September; I did not consider it got any worse; it remained about the same. I think it was some time after the 4th that I first ordered Valentine's meat juice for her. I did not see her on Tuesday, the 12th.

Evidence for Prosecution.

Dr. Henry George Sworn

I saw her on Wednesday, the 13th, I think, between eleven and twelve in the forenoon. She was rather worse; she had diarrhœa on again, but she did not seem to be in much pain, and I gave her a mixture for it. She had a little return of sickness, but it was not much. I gave her a bismuth and chalk mixture that day.

By Mr. JUSTICE BUCKNILL—She was still about the same so far as her strength was concerned; in fact, she was a little weaker on account of the diarrhœa coming on again.

Examination continued—I saw Mrs. Seddon, and I simply told her that the patient was worse, and I would send her up a diarrhœa mixture that she would take after each motion. I do not remember giving any instructions as to diet on the 13th. I thought that she was then in a little danger, but I did not consider her to be in a critical condition.

Did you expect her to die that night?—I did not expect her to die any more than I should expect any patient to die in that condition. Any patient who had had an attack of diarrhœa and sickness, and got weak, would be likely to die—would stand a chance of dying. The patient might die from heart failure or anything like that.

By Mr. JUSTICE BUCKNILL—Her pulse was rather weak, it was weaker than on other days, and I put that down to the purging. It was not intermittent, it was weak.

Examination continued—The 13th was the last time I saw her. During the time I was attending her I took her temperature twice, as far as I can remember. On the one day the temperature was up to 101, and on other days it was fairly normal. I think it was on the 7th that the temperature was up to 101, and some days it was 99. It was not a continuous temperature. I never found it subnormal. I did not take the temperature on the 13th. The next I heard about Miss Barrow was at 7 o'clock on the morning of the 14th, when Mr. Seddon came to my house and said that Miss Barrow had died in the early morning, about 6 o'clock, I think he said. I asked him how she was, and he said that she seemed to have a lot of pain in her inside, and then she went off sort of insensible.

By Mr. JUSTICE BUCKNILL—He said that they had been up all night with her, and she had been in a considerable amount of pain, and then went off a sort of unconscious, insensible. Nothing else was said. I do not remember him telling me of having put a hot flannel over her stomach.

Examination continued—I do not remember whether he said that they had given her anything at all in the night; I did not ask him. I said to him, "I am going to give you the certificate."

You gave a certificate then?—Yes.

As I understand, you had not seen the body after death?—No. The last time I saw her was about 11 o'clock the day before. I certified the death as due to epidemic diarrhœa. Exhibit 41 is the certificate of death, and it states, "Cause of death, epidemic diarrhœa." All that I certified was the cause of death, and "duration of illness, ten days." That was a mistake in the duration; a miscalculation. I attended from the 2nd to the 14th, and I stated that at the coroner's Court. The information as to her rank or profession was not filled in by me.

Was there any arsenic in any of the medicines which you prescribed?—No, there was not any arsenic. There was no reason for giving it.

Trial of the Seddons.

Dr. Henry George Sworn

As a fact, there was not?—No. I have the prescription here.

Cross-examined by Mr. MARSHALL HALL—When you say "no arsenic" you cannot say, of course, that carbonate of bismuth does not contain minute quantities of arsenic?—No, without I tested it. Carbonate of bismuth has been known to contain arsenic.

I do not suggest that there would be sufficient arsenic to account for the death, but you cannot say that carbonate of bismuth does not contain arsenic—it is well known as an adulteration of carbonate of bismuth?—It has been known, but I should not think that what we have from our chemist would have it.

Do you make up your own medicines?—I have some one who makes up my medicines.

But you would get the best drugs you possibly could?—I do.

You had attended the Seddons for about ten years?—Yes.

You had not attended Miss Barrow before, because we know she had been attended by Dr. Paul?—Yes.

And you knew, or you know now, at any rate, that Dr. Paul had said he was too busy to attend her on that day, and therefore you were sent for?—Yes.

There was no question of professional etiquette, because Dr. Paul had refused to come?—I asked about that at the time, because I would not have taken the case.

Now, Dr. Paul has told us that Miss Barrow had been complaining on and off from about 3rd August of congestion of the liver. Dr. Paul told us—I do not know whether you will agree—that congestion of the liver would itself produce severe colic pains?—Yes, it would.

Is that due to the improper action of the bile?—Yes.

Bile is a very acid and a very irritant thing, and if it is not properly secreted it would cause a great deal of pain and intense pain?—You get it sometimes if you have too much bile secreted, and sometimes if you do not have any at all you have the same effect.

Dr. Paul had been giving her rhubarb and magnesia as early as the 1st August of that year. Did you notice any signs of asthma at all when you saw Miss Barrow?—Yes, I told Mrs. Seddon that she appeared to me to be a woman that suffered from asthma.

Did you infer that she was a woman rather above the average weight for her height? Do you agree with that?—Yes.

And a woman of a somewhat full temperament?—There were appearances about her as if there was a certain amount of arterial tension from attacks of asthma—in the blood vessels.

When you saw her for the first time on 2nd September was she in the condition of a woman who had been passing through the incipient stages of an attack of epidemic diarrhœa?—No.

You did not see, then, any evidence of acute diarrhœa at that time?—No, I saw no evidence of it being previous to that. She had diarrhœa at that time.

According to you, as far as you knew, it had commenced on that day?—Yes, the day before I saw her.

That would be on the 1st?—Yes.

Evidence for Prosecution.

Dr. Henry George Sworn

The condition of diarrhœa was fairly acute on that day, was it not?—Yes.

Was she in a condition to go to the lavatory on that day or any other day?—I should think she could go to the lavatory; she was not so bad as that.

But you would not have advised it?—I should not have advised it, but I have no doubt she could have gone. She might have had heart failure there.

I think, as a matter of fact, you inspected the stools and the vomit, did you not?—Yes. Mrs. Seddon showed me one of the motions.

Were they particularly offensive?—They were, very.

And I think you gave her a carbolic sheet to put up to counteract the smell?—I ordered her to put a carbolic sheet up.

Mrs. Seddon described the symptoms to you?—Yes.

Have you any doubt whatever that Miss Barrow seemed very ill when you first saw her?—Oh, she was, yes, very ill.

Did Mrs. Seddon tell you that she had been ill on and off for som little time?—Yes, but not with this attack.

And that the vomiting and diarrhœa started the previous day?—Yes.

Did what you saw of the case lead you to believe that that was a true statement on the part of Mrs. Seddon?—Yes.

The symptoms you found were consistent with that state of things?—Quite.

Mrs. Seddon was in attendance—there was no nurse?—No.

Later on, when you threatened to send Miss Barrow to the hospital if she would not take her medicine, did she say that the Seddons could manage for her very well?—She said that Mrs. Seddon could attend to her very well indeed, and she was very attentive.

As far as you could judge, during the whole time that you saw Mis Barrow, did she seem attached to Mrs. Seddon?—She did.

And as far as you could see was Mrs. Seddon very kind to her?—As fa as I could see she was very kind.

And attentive?—And attentive.

You called, then, on the 3rd, we have heard, and on the 4th, an on the 4th you thought she was getting better?—Not on the 4th; the 4th was when I changed the medicine.

The diarrhœa was not so bad?—The diarrhœa was not so bad, but the sickness was bad.

She was, of course, getting weaker naturally?—Yes.

I suppose the weather was very hot?—Yes, very hot.

And, of course, owing to the heat of the weather, with a woman with her asthmatic tendency, and this arterial tension about her, and things of that sort, she would very rapidly get weaker?—She would.

May I take it that one of the main dangers in an attack of this kind was the danger of heart failure?—It is.

I think you said that even if she went to the lavatory, although sh might have been able to do it, she might at any moment have failed from heart failure?—Yes.

Now, it was Mrs. Seddon who told you, was it not, that Miss Barrow would not take her medicine?—Yes.

Trial of the Seddons.

Dr. Henry George Sworn

She objected to this bismuth mixture, which would be chalk and milk?—No, Mrs. Seddon did not say that; Mrs. Seddon said that Miss Barrow would not take her medicine, and asked me to give her a good talking to, and I said, " I will go up and talk to her," and so I told her. I said, " If you will not take your medicine you will have to go to the hospital," and I gave her a dose of medicine.

That was the chalk mixture?—The chalk and bismuth, and I said, " She is very thirsty. She is fearfully thirsty. If I send her an effervescing mixture she will be only too pleased to take it." The patient herself said she was thirsty.

Thirst is the normal condition of that illness?—It is quite a normal condition.

And, if I may use the expression, an abnormal thirst is the normal condition of that?—That complaint, yes.

Of course, this first medicine you gave her, this carbonate of bismuth, would have to be suspended in some gummy solution?—It is suspended in mucilage—gum and sugar.

So you would have a thickish sort of medicine which would not be very thirst quenching?—No, it would not.

And you could quite understand the reluctance of a person who is thirsty to take this syruppy white milky stuff?—Yes.

You suggested a change by giving her citrate of potash and carbonate of soda, an effervescing drink made in two mixtures, each being non-effervescing by itself?—Yes. The little boy told me he did see Mr. Seddon give the mixture, that he had two glasses, and he poured the contents of the one into the other, and it effervesced.

That would be your effervescing mixture?—Yes.

And that would be white?—Quite clear, like water.

Did she give you any reason for disliking her medicine?—No.

Did you talk to Miss Barrow in the way you are talking to us?—Yes.

And you made her hear?—I could make her hear quite easily. She was not stone deaf.

When you said that you would send her to the hospital she heard clearly enough then?—She heard that. I never found any difficulty in speaking to her.

Did you hear on the next day that Miss Barrow had left her bed and had gone into the boy's bedroom on the night of the 4th?—No.

Did you hear it on the 5th?—No, I heard that she had been out of the bed.

Did you hear that she had gone to the boy's bed?—I did not hear that she had gone to the boy's bed. I know she could get out of the bed if she liked. I did not remonstrate with her. I told Mrs. Seddon that she was not to be allowed to get out of bed.

As a matter of fact, do you think it was a very good thing for a boy to be sleeping with her when she was in that condition?—No, I never knew the boy was sleeping with her. I do not remember seeing him in the bedroom.

Did Miss Barrow say anything to you about being plagued with the flies in the room?—No.

There was a very big epidemic of flies about that time?—I have never

Evidence for Prosecution.

Dr. Henry George Sworn

seen so many as I saw in that room.   I put it down to the smell of the motions which would attract them.

Do you happen to know that the medical officer of health for the district had circulated a bill about flies (No. 137)?—No, I did not know. It had not been sent to the medical men—it is sent to the people, I think.

On the 5th did you notice any fly-papers in the room?—No.

I suppose you would not go much near the mantelpiece?—No, I should not go near it.

The temperature on the 7th of 101 was the maximum, as far as you know?—Yes, as far as I know.

But you did not take her temperature on the 13th?—No.

I think you said that she might have some brandy?—Yes, I told them to give her brandy.

Did you find any blood in the vomit?—No.

Did you notice at all whether she had any signs of leaky eyes, or running eyes, or anything of that sort?—No, she had not.

Nothing of that sort, nor any rash?—No.

When you spoke just now about the will I think you also said this, if the things in the will were properly explained to her she was in a condition to understand it?—Yes, that is the view I took.

You never thought her mental condition was very strong?—I never thought she was very good mentally, but if you explained matters sufficiently she could understand them.

Now, on the 13th there was again difficulty about the medicine, was there not?—No, not on the 13th.   On the 13th I gave her diarrhœa mixture because she had a little diarrhœa come on again.

The diarrhœa having returned you were bound to revert to the bismuth mixture?—Well, I gave her a different mixture.

Bismuth and chalk?—It was aromatic chalk mixture containing some bismuth, and that was only to be given after each motion—not to be continued.

The dose of bismuth which you were giving to her on the 13th was a fairly stiff dose?—A ten-grain dose.   That is not a stiff dose.   You can give twenty-grain doses.

On the 13th did you realise that she was in danger?—Yes.

Although you did not expect her to die that night, were you surprised to hear that she was dead the next morning?—No.

Her pulse, you have said, was weak.   Was it fairly and easily compressible?—Yes, it was weak—compressible.

A weak, compressible pulse—fast?—Yes.

Thin and fast?—Yes, it was not very——

By Mr. Justice Bucknill—Fast—thin and weak?—The pulse was.

By Mr. Marshall Hall—What was it beating at as a matter of fact, do you remember?—I do not quite remember.

Valentine's meat juice you had ordered, as far as I remember, from the 4th?—Yes.

Valentine's meat juice is a concentrated essence of beef or meat of some kind?—It is the compressed juice, and it is diluted with water.

Now, the next morning, assuming that this poor lady had died at 6.30, 7 o'clock would be as early as you would reasonably expect anybody

Trial of the Seddons.

Dr. Henry George Sworn

to come and see you if he had been up all night?—Yes, I should not have thanked him to come before.

He told you Miss Barrow was dead?—Yes.

You then asked the questions. Did he ask for the certificate, or did you give it to him?—No, I gave it to him.

If you had wanted to see the body, or if you had in your discretion thought it necessary to see the body before granting the certificate, do you anticipate there would be the smallest difficulty about your doing so?—No, there would not. I should have gone and seen it.

Did you as a medical man, having regard to what you had previously seen, think it necessary to see the body before giving the certificate?—No, I did not.

Had you any doubt in your own mind at that time that what you stated on the certificate was correct—that she had died from exhaustion brought on by epidemic diarrhœa?—I stated what I believed to be true.

There was a great deal of epidemic diarrhœa about at that time, was there not?—Yes.

In epidemic diarrhœa, however carefully it is looked after, there is always a danger of a sudden relapse?—Yes.

And if there is a sudden relapse in epidemic diarrhœa which has been going on for ten or twelve days would you expect death to result from heart failure?—Yes.

It would, of course, be accompanied by a comatose or unconscious state?—Yes.

Re-examined by the ATTORNEY-GENERAL—When you left this lady on the morning of the 13th, did you anticipate that she would die within twenty-four hours?—Certainly not. I should have gone back later on in the day if I thought there was immediate danger, but heart failure is a thing that comes on suddenly in these cases. If I had gone the same evening I should not have expected it, but yet it might have happened.

What I was asking is this, having regard to the condition in which you found her with regard to the pulse, had you any reason to expect that she would die within twenty-four hours?—I had as much reason to expect that as in any other case that dies. She was not in what I should call a dangerous condition. There are many cases that die from heart failure. There are some cases in which you can say how long the person is going to live. I have known a person to be told there is no danger and to die an hour afterwards from heart failure. My own father died in that way.

I am not disputing that. What I want to get at is this. I really want to understand from you whether you thought that at that time she was in such a dangerous condition that she might die within the twenty-four hours?—She might have died five minutes after I left. She was in that condition that I should not have been surprised if they had come back ten minutes afterwards and said she was dead.

Surely there is no difficulty in answering a simple question?—No, I am telling you.

But apart altogether from what might happen, what I want to know is what your expectation was as a medical man attending a patient who had been under your observation from the 2nd to the 13th September

Evidence for Prosecution.

Dr. Henry George Sworn

when you left her on the morning of the 13th September?—My expectation was that she might recover—that she was in about the same condition, but I was not surprised that she died the next day from heart
failure.

Do you think she was in a critical condition?—I thought she was in
a critical condition all along.

I must ask you this. You have told us you thought she was in a
little danger, but not critical?—Yes.

Was that correct?—Yes.

On the 13th September?—She was in danger all along, that is what
I told you. She might have died from heart failure days before.

But is this correct—what you swore in answer to my friend this
morning? This is on the 13th, "I thought she was in a little danger,
but not critical"?—Yes, she was in a little danger, and she was no
critical. It depends upon what you call critical.

I am asking what you say?—I say she was in a little danger, but no
critical.

One last question upon this. I only want to know, as a medical man
if you found her in a little danger, and that her condition was not critical,
would you expect her to die within twenty-four hours?—How should I
expect her to die? I know that she is likely to die. I cannot expect
her to die unless I can say exactly how long the case is going to last. Her
case was not a hopeless case. You are asking me questions that are
impossible to answer in that way.

I am only asking you to give us what your view is?—I am giving my
view—that she was not in a critical condition—she might have died five
minutes after I left her, she might have been alive now. I cannot say
any more than that.

Have you any part of the carbonate of bismuth left which you had
then?—No.

Have you any carbonate of bismuth in stock?—Plenty.

Can you tell us when the stock was exhausted from which you gave
her the medicine in September?—I cannot. I have nothing to do with my
medicines. They are ordered by my partner, and they are arranged by the
dispenser. I never see the medicines.

Then you cannot help us?—I cannot tell you, but I know the stock
must be out by this time that was being used then.

By Mr. MARSHALL HALL—Is liability to heart failure a well-known
danger of epidemic diarrhœa?—Yes.

And therefore the liability is greater the longer the epidemic diarrhœa
has gone on?—Certainly.

And the longer it has gone on the less the probability of the patient
resisting the attack if it comes on?—Yes.

By Mr. JUSTICE BUCKNILL—Does vomiting generally attend epidemic
diarrhœa?—It does. Epidemic diarrhœa used to be called English
cholera years ago, and one of the most frequent symptoms is persistent
vomiting.

And you saw some of the vomit, did you?—Yes. It was a brownish
mucus—a yellowish mucus.

G   97

Trial of the Seddons.

Dr. JOHN FREDERICK PAUL, recalled, further examined by the ATTORNEY-GENERAL—There was no arsenic whatever in any of the medicines I gave to Miss Barrow.

ALFRED KING, examined by Mr. MUIR—I am superintendent and registrar of the Metropolitan Borough of Islington Cemetery. Eliza Mary Barrow, aged 49, was buried at that cemetery on 16th September, 1911. I produce certificate of her death. Her address was given as 63 Tollington Park, and the date of death 14th September, 1911. She was buried in grave No. 19,453, section Q—that is what we call a common grave. I produce the order for exhumation of the body signed and sealed by the coroner, Dr. George Cohen, and dated 11th November, 1911, exhibit 138. The body was exhumed on 14th November, 1911, and it was re-buried in another grave by order of the coroner on 22nd December, 1911.

WILLIAM ALEXANDER FRASER, examined by Mr. R. D. MUIR—I am the coroner's officer for Hornsey and Friern Barnet. I was present at the Coroner's Court at the inquest on the body of Eliza Mary Barrow. That Court was opened on 23rd November, and concluded on 14th December. I saw the coroner taking the depositions of the witnesses, including the two prisoners. I saw the prisoners sign their depositions taken on 23rd November. These depositions are as follows. (Depositions read.)

Chief Inspector ALFRED WARD, recalled, further examined by Mr. R. D. MUIR—I was present at the Police Court when Dr. Cohen gave evidence, first on 9th January, and afterwards on 26th January. On 9th January the male prisoner only was in custody; on 26th January both prisoners were in custody, and both had an opportunity of cross-examining the coroner. I saw the coroner sign his depositions. (Depositions read.)

Examination continued—About 7 p.m. on 4th December I saw the male prisoner out of doors at Tollington Park. I told him I was a police officer, and was to arrest him for the wilful murder of Eliza Mary Barrow by administering poison—arsenic. He said, " Absurd. What a terrible charge—wilful murder. It is the first of our family that has ever been accused of such a crime. Are you going to arrest my wife as well? If not, I would like you to give her a message for me. Have they found arsenic in her body? She has not done this herself? It was not carbolic acid, was it, as there was some in her room, and Sanitas is not poison, is it?" He repeated the word " Murder " several times on the way to the station. When at the station at Hornsey Road he was charged, and when the charge was read over he made no reply. I searched the house at 63 Tollington Park the same day, and in a trunk in the top bedroom that had been occupied by the dead woman I found the cash box, exhibit 2. The trunk was locked. I got the keys from a safe in the prisoner's bedroom. The female prisoner was present, and she told me that it was the late Miss Barrow's trunk and her belongings. I found the pass-book, exhibit 17, and also a paper bag, exhibit 20, which has " £20 gold " written in ink on the front, and " Gold £19 " in indelible pencil on the back. I should say that the pencil handwriting is the male prisoner's.

Evidence for Prosecution.

Alfred Ward

There were nineteen sovereigns in the bag. I found it in the safe in the prisoner's bedroom, which is on the first floor. I have the sovereigns in my custody, and can send for them if they are required. In the same safe I found a ring, exhibit 21; exhibit 22, a gold chain; and exhibit 23, another gold chain and pendant. Mrs. Seddon was present. The chain was attached to it as it is now. I asked Mrs. Seddon whose watch it was, and she said, " It is mine." I asked her where she got it, and she said, " It was a present to me." I said, " Is it not Miss Barrow's? " and she said, " Yes." In the safe in the office in the basement I found a Post Office Savings Bank book, exhibit 37, made out in the name of Mr. F. H. Seddon, 63 Tollington Park. Under date 15th September, 1911, I find an entry of £30 deposit paid in. I also found in the office safe the bank pass-book, exhibit 34. In the secretaire in the front room on the ground floor I found a copy of the will, exhibit 38. In the safe in the front bedroom I found an envelope containing some documents, of which exhibit 39 is one. The first entry on that document is " £10 cash found at Miss Barrow's death," then " Statement of how utilised,"* and it is signed " F. H. Seddon." The handwriting is all that of the male prisoner. In the same envelope I found a conveyance of a grave at Highgate Cemetery to Eliza Jane Barrow, exhibit 40, dated 9th February, 1874, and attached to that a slip of paper with the words, " Last interment, 16th December, 1876. Eliza Jane Barrow." In the same envelope there was a certificate of Miss Barrow's death, exhibit 41, and a copy of a letter dated 21st September, " To the relatives of the late Miss Eliza Mary Barrow," exhibit 42, being the same as exhibit 3. There were other documents in the same envelope, which included Miss Barrow's rent book and the lease of the Buck's Head. I also found an envelope containing some hair. It had writing on it when I found it—the male prisoner's handwriting, I should think—" Miss Barrow's hair, for Hilda and Ernest Grant," and then on the back, " Eliza Mary Barrow, died 14th September, 1911." I handed that envelope to Sergeant Cooper. I afterwards saw Dr. Wilcox produce it when he was giving evidence. I saw the female prisoner at 5 p.m. on 15th January at 63 Tollington Park. I asked her if she knew me, and she said " Yes." I then told her that I was going to arrest her for being concerned in the wilful murder of Miss Barrow by administering poison, and she said, " Very well." I took her to the police station, and she was then charged, but made no reply whatever. (Shown exhibit 121)—That is a gold ring which I found in the safe in the bedroom on the first floor on 4th December. (Shown exhibit 123)— That is a neck chain with a pendant which was found in the secretaire in the dining-room on the first floor. I have examined the inventory of Miss Barrow's effects, exhibit 32. Neither the chain and the pendant nor the chain attached to the watch was included in that inventory.

None of these things are in the inventory?—None of these articles are shown in the inventory. On 1st February I caused notice to be served upon Mr. Thorley to attend at the Police Court, and he attended next day at ten o'clock in the morning. I saw him myself.

Now, just tell us what happened with regard to the identification of

---

* See Appendix G.

Trial of the Seddons.

Alfred Ward

Maggie Seddon?—Maggie Seddon, with a large number of males and females, was sent into the waiting room, and upon the arrival of Mr. Thorley he was asked to go into the room to see if he could identify any one there, as the person who purchased from him certain fly-papers on 26th August last. He entered the room alone, walked round the room, came out, and pointed Maggie Seddon out to me as the girl who had purchased from him on that particular day.

Cross-examined by Mr. MARSHALL HALL—You have said that you had accused Seddon of causing the wilful murder of Miss Barrow by administering arsenic?—Certainly, sir.

Then he asked a question, "Have you found arsenic in the body"?—Yes.

Then was the next thing a question, "She has not done it herself," negatively or not?—No, he said them all one after another. I asked him no question. I did not speak to him until I got to the station.

Now, Mr. Thorley has told us that the police had been to him several times in December and January about this matter?—Yes.

I understand he went down on 2nd February in the morning, went into a room where there were about twenty people?—There were more than that.

And he then came out, and told you that he had identified a certain girl?—He pointed Maggie Seddon out to me.

After he had come out?—No, he came to the door and pointed the girl out. He said, "This is the girl who purchased the fly-papers from me."

You have been in Court—you have heard Mr. Thorley's evidence that there was one other girl there with her hair down her back?—There were several more—when I say several I will say two or three.

You know Miss Barrow's handwriting, do you not, by this time?—I only know what I have been told.

You have seen several specimens of her handwriting. There are certain things which are admitted to be in her handwriting—letters written to the solicitors and that sort of thing?—Yes.

Are these signatures, so far as you can say, the signatures of Miss Barrow? (Documents handed to witness)—Yes, they are similar, of course.

You cannot say more?—I do not know that any one has seen her sign.

Let me have them back—I will get them probably from some one. My lord, I understand from the Attorney-General that there is no dispute that there was, in fact, a payment in respect of both of these transfers, the transfer of the Buck's Head and the transfer of the Stock?

Mr. JUSTICE BUCKNILL—At the present time the evidence is that everything is in order, and the learned Attorney-General very candidly says, "I am not charging in this case a fraudulent transaction from a commercial point of view."

By Mr. MARSHALL HALL—Have you seen the rent book?—Yes.

I see that from 25th July to 26th December apparently there appears to be a payment of 12s. a week for rent?—Yes.

After that date all the entries of each week are entered up as clear?—Yes.

That is to say, no payment?—Yes.

Evidence for Prosecution.

Did you find that book at Tollington Park?—Yes, amongst the effects. That is the document you handed me—that is the Post Office book?—Yes.

The Court adjourned.

Fourth Day—Thursday, 7th March, 1912.

The Court met at 10.15 a.m.

CHARLES COOPER, examined by Mr. MUIR—I am a detective-sergeant in New Scotland Yard. I was present at the male prisoner's arrest. On 11th December I took an envelope, exhibit 135, containing some hair which I had received from Chief Inspector Ward to Dr. Willcox. On 30th December I went to 63 Tollington Park and took away the till, which is exhibit 28, from the place which is marked on the plan, exhibit 27.

Cross-examined Mr. MARSHALL HALL—At the station the male prisoner said, "My wife will be in a terrible state," or something of that sort, and he asked me to get Mrs. Bromwich to assist her.

WILLIAM HAYMAN, examined by Mr. MUIR—I am a detective-sergeant in New Scotland Yard. I assisted in the arrest of the male prisoner. I stopped him in Tollington Park, and said to him, "Mr. Seddon, Chief Inspector Ward wants to see you." He said, "May I go home first?" but I did not answer him. Mr. Ward came up almost immediately, and I heard what was said between him and the prisoner.

Cross-examined by Mr. MARSHALL HALL—He said "Murder" several times, and then "Poisoning by arsenic—what a charge." Mr. Ward spoke to him the moment he came up.

Re-examined by Mr. MUIR—On 8th December I purchased one packet containing six fly-papers from Mr. Price, chemist, 103 Tollington Road, and on 11th December I handed these over to Dr. Willcox at St. Mary's Hospital. I purchased a packet of fly-papers on 29th February from Messrs. Spinks, chemists, 27 Tottenham Court Road, and also from Dodds' Drug Stores, 70 Tottenham Court Road, and from Needhams, Limited, chemists, 297 Edgware Road. I took these packets to Dr. Willcox at St. Mary's Hospital. Last night I got from Dr. Sworn's surgery two ounces of bismuth carbonate, which I handed over to Dr. Willcox. I also got two ounces from Messrs. Willows, Francis, Butler & Thompson, druggists, 40 Aldersgate Street, which I handed over to Dr. Willcox. I was informed that these were the persons who supplied Dr. Sworn with his drugs.

By Mr. MARSHALL HALL—It was on 8th December that I first bought some fly-papers. The male prisoner was arrested on 4th December.

Dr. BERNARD HENRY SPILSBURY, examined by the ATTORNEY-GENERAL— I am a Bachelor of Medicine and a Bachelor of Surgery, and I am a pathologist at St. Mary's Hospital. In November of last year I made a post-mortem examination of the body of a woman who was identified as

Trial of the Seddons.

Dr. Bernard Henry Spilsbury

Eliza Mary Barrow. I was present when the body was identified by Albert Edward Vonderahe and Frank Ernest Vonderahe.

Mr. MARSHALL HALL—There is no suggestion here that the body is not the body, and there is no suggestion here that any arsenic came from any clothing, so all these details may be disposed of.

Examination continued—With the exception of the stomach and intestines, I found no disease in any of the organs sufficient to account for death. The stomach was a little dilated, and a black substance was present on its inner surface. In the upper part of the small intestine the inner surface was red. The body was very well preserved, internally and externally, apart from some post-mortem staining externally. Taking into account that the death took place in September, 1911, the state of preservation in which I found the body was very abnormal. I was not able to account for it at the time the post-mortem examination was made, but since the analysis which has been made by Dr. Willcox I think the preservation was due to the presence of arsenic in the body. I include the stomach with the rest of the body, and also the skin, bones, and the hair. On an external examination I found no evidence of shingles or pigmentation of the skin, but the skin had a green colour, which I thought was due to post-mortem discolouration. The skin of the face was brown and shrivelled. By "pigmentation" of the skin I mean that the skin is of an unusual colour, generally either brown or black, and that would be the result sometimes of chronic arsenical poisoning. There was no thickening of the skin on the palms of the hands or on the soles of the feet. There was no thickening in the nails of the fingers or of the toes, nor was there any other change in the nails of the fingers or the toes. There was nothing abnormal about the appearance of the hair. I was present during some of the tests made by Dr. Willcox for arsenic. From what I saw of the results of these tests my opinion is that the death was the result of acute arsenical poisoning—poisoning by one or more large doses of arsenic, as distinguished from poisoning by small doses of arsenic over a long period of time. By a "large dose" I mean a poisonous dose, which would certainly be two grains, and less than that would give rise to symptoms of poisoning. Two grains in one dose might be sufficient to kill an adult person. I think that two or three doses of two grains or upwards within a short period of time would be sufficient to kill an adult person.

Cross-examined by Mr. DUNSTAN—In making my post-mortem examination I found that the height of the body was 5 feet 4 inches. The body was well nourished. The average weight for a person aged forty-nine of a height of 5 feet 4 inches would be somewhere between 8½ and 10½ stones, and if she was a well-nourished and plump woman she might be well over the average weight. On examining the internal organs I found no evidence of disease at all, except in the stomach and intestines. I found a slight reddening of the lining of the bowel. We could not see the mucous membrane of the stomach as it was covered with the black substance I have already mentioned. The first part of the small intestine, the duodenum, was reddened throughout, and the next part, the jejunum, was slightly reddened. Beyond that the inner surface showed no reddening.

Evidence for Prosecution.

Dr. Bernard Henry Spilsbury

Apart from that reddening, there was no sign of any disease at all?—None at all.

And death might have been due to syncope or heart failure?—Certainly, apart from the reddening, so far as I could see.

The reddening would be equally consistent with death from epidemic diarrhœa of ordinary duration?—Yes, it would.

Would it be consistent with death from epidemic diarrhœa extending over some ten or twelve days?—Yes, it would.

The absence of any disease in the other organs would be equally consistent with death from epidemic diarrhœa?—Certainly.

Apart from Dr. Willcox's report there is nothing inconsistent with Dr. Sworn's death certificate in this case from what you saw at the post-mortem?—That is so, with the one exception of the condition of the preservation of the body.

The preservation of the body varies greatly?—Oh, yes.

I believe it is a fact that amongst the Styrian peasants arsenic is taken considerably?—Yes.

You know that as a scientific fact?—Yes.

And those arsenic eaters die of other diseases than arsenical poisoning?—That is so.

The preservation of the bodies of Styrians is well marked also?—Yes, I have heard that.

You have told us that there was no sign of any skin rash?—Yes.

You would have expected some skin rash had arsenic been given from 1st September?—Not necessarily.

By Mr. JUSTICE BUCKNILL—Where would you find the rash?—The rash might appear over any part of the body.

Suppose this woman took small doses of arsenic, for example—I am not suggesting it is the fact—from the 2nd September to the 11th, where would you expect to find the rash?—She might have the rash over the upper part of the body, and she might have the rash over the limbs; it might appear almost anywhere.

By Mr. DUNSTAN—Would it tend to disappear between the date of the death and your examination?—Yes.

Would the eyes become affected soon with the administration of arsenic in fairly large doses?—No, I think not—not in fairly large doses.

Would you give your opinion as to how soon the eyes would be affected with a largish dose?—I think probably not at all.

I think Dr. Willcox defined this dose as "a moderately large fatal dose"?—Yes.

Dr. Willcox defined it as five grains and upwards?—Yes.

It would be a large dose?—It would be a moderately large dose—a moderately large fatal dose.

At what time would a dose of that class prove fatal?—It would not be likely to prove fatal—a single dose, of course—in less than three days probably, and it might be longer.

By Mr. JUSTICE BUCKNILL—Now, would you give us a little history of what you would expect to take place in three days. First of all, what would happen on the first one, and then on the second one, and then on the third day, and the day of the death. What would you expect to find

103

Trial of the Seddons.

Dr. Bernard Henry Spilsbury

with such a dose on the third day?—The patient would develop symptoms probably between an hour or two hours.

That would be the first day?—That would be the first day.

Go on, please?—The symptoms would be nausea, followed by vomiting and a pain in the stomach.

Go on, please. Give us from the first day to the third?—In a few hours afterwards diarrhœa would develop. This would continue in a severe form almost up to the time of the death, and the patient would become collapsed, and would develop great thirst.

On the first day there would be symptoms in an hour or two?—Yes.

Nausea would then come, followed by vomiting, followed by pain in the stomach?—Together with pain in the stomach; the two would come at the same time.

A few hours afterwards diarrhœa would develop. This would continue in a severe form almost up to the time of death, and the patient would become collapsed, and would develop a great thirst?—Yes.

And then?—And then death would ensue.

" On the third day I should expect death might ensue "?—It might ensue on the third day.

By Mr. DUNSTAN—I believe epidemic diarrhœa is very prevalent in the summer?—Yes, that is so.

By Mr. JUSTICE BUCKNILL—And sometimes it is very painful?—Extremely.

Frequently?—Yes.

And ignorant people call it " English cholera "?—Yes.

By Mr. DUNSTAN—In fact, it was prevalent last summer?—That is so.

And the symptoms would be those described by Dr. Sworn?—Yes, they would.

And the final cause of death would be heart failure?—Yes.

Re-examined by the ATTORNEY-GENERAL—And those would also be the symptoms of acute arsenical poisoning?—That is so.

And in the result would death ensue from heart failure?—Yes, it would.

Just the same for acute arsenical poisoning as it would for epidemic diarrhœa?—Yes.

Are the symptoms which we have heard described by Dr. Sworn—the vomiting, the pain in the stomach, and diarrhœa, and so forth—all consistent with a case of arsenical poisoning from what you describe as " large doses "?—Yes.

And, assuming a doctor to be called in who neither knew nor suspected arsenical poisoning, how would he diagnose the illness?—In all probability as a case of epidemic diarrhœa.

In a case of acute arsenical poisoning, would there be any external indication that arsenic had been administered in fairly large doses?—No, I think none at all.

Supposing that you suspected arsenical poisoning in a case to which you were called in, with the symptoms which you have described, how would you then ascertain whether or not a large dose, or a fairly large

Evidence for Prosecution.

Dr. Bernard Henry Spilsbury

dose, of arsenic had been given?—Do you mean ascertain during life or after death?

I mean during life, what could you ascertain?—Only by an analysis of what was vomited or of the other excreta.

Then you would have to analyse some excreta in order to detect the arsenic?—Yes, that is so.

You were asked by my friend, Mr. Dunstan, whether the eyes became affected soon. When would you expect, and under what circumstances would you expect, the eyes to become affected by arsenical poisoning?—I should only expect them to be affected when the patient had been taking arsenic for some little time—a matter of weeks—several weeks or months.

Supposing a patient had been taking arsenic for several weeks or months, would that be a case of chronic arsenical poisoning?—Yes, it would.

And in those cases you would get a running from the eyes?—Yes, the symptoms of a cold.

Would those symptoms be regarded chronic arsenical poisoning, or would they also apply to the acute case?—They would be confined to the chronic type.

So you would distinguish a chronic case by the running of the eyes? —I think so, certainly.

In the case of chronic arsenical poisoning would you expect to find a rash such as you have described?—It is possible that a rash might develop, but I should hardly expect it.

In the case of chronic arsenical poisoning?—I understood you to say acute.

No, I said chronic?—I am afraid I misunderstood you.

By Mr. Justice Bucknill—In an acute case it is possible, but not likely, that the rash would appear?—Yes, it is possible, but not likely.

By the Attorney-General—Would you tell my lord as regards a chronic case?—In a chronic case it would be usual to see rashes in the skin.

What other indications would you expect in a case of chronic arsenical poisoning which you would not find in a case of acute arsenical poisoning? —There would be thickening of the skin in the palms of the hands and in the soles of the feet. There would be thickening of the nails and a skin eruption known as shingles. The hair would probably fall out also. Then the patient might develop symptoms of nervous disease, such as pains in the limbs and a muscular weakness.

Would there be anything on internal examination which would indicate chronic arsenical poisoning as distinguished from acute arsenical poisoning? —There might be. Of course, now you mean a post-mortem examination, do you not?

Certainly?—There might be extreme fatty degeneration of the liver or of the heart walls.

On your internal examination of this body did you find either of those?—No, I did not.

Assuming the symptoms which Dr. Sworn has told us, and the patient died during the heat of summer, about September, 1911, was the preserva-tion of the body which you saw more consistent with epidemic diarrhœa or with . acute arsenic poisoning?—It was more consistent with acute arsenical poisoning.

Trial of the Seddons.

Dr. Bernard Henry Spilsbury

What would you expect to find in the case of a patient who had died two months before, during that period of the heat, from epidemic diarrhœa?—I should expect to find advanced putrefaction.

By Mr. Justice Bucknill—Do we gather from that that arsenic is a preservative?—Yes, it is so; it frequently acts as a preservative of any part of the body to which it gains access.

By the Attorney-General—Will you tell us what quantity of arsenic was found in the stomach and intestines?—About three-quarters of a grain.

Leaving out all the other parts of the body, supposing you found three-quarters of a grain in the stomach and the intestines, would that indicate to you whether there had been that or more arsenic taken?—Yes, it would certainly indicate that more had been taken.

Why?—Because some of the poison would certainly have been vomited again.

By Mr. Justice Bucknill—Would none have passed off in the water?—Yes, I was going to say that; some might be in the urine, some certainly would be vomited, and, of course, in the excreta as well.

By the Attorney-General—Would it be a likely thing for it to pass in the excreta?—Not unless extremely large doses had been taken. I wish to add that I am leaving out of account the possible absorption into the body of the arsenic.

What I really want to get at is this. Suppose what we will call a moderately large dose of arsenic had been given to the patient, would the patient in the ordinary course retain the whole, or can you give us any idea what portion of it you would expect to remain in the body and what portion would pass into the urine or vomit or excreta; I only want a general idea?—It would have to be very general, because they vary very much in different cases.

Yes, quite?—But a large part might be rejected by vomiting.

Or?—Well, it is so general that it is very difficult to say.

You said that if an extremely large dose had been given some of it would pass in the excreta; is that right?—Yes, that is right.

Must it be an extremely large dose for it to pass in the excreta?—Yes, I should think so, to pass in any amount from the excreta. There might be traces after any case of arsenical poisoning.

Have you had very much experience in post-mortem examinations?—I have.

And have you had post-mortem cases of acute arsenical poisoning before this?—Yes, I have.

And, of course, you are familiar with the works upon this?—Oh, yes, of course.

In an ordinary case, speaking of a case of acute arsenical poisoning, would you expect to find more or less reddening than you find in this case of reddening in the intestines?—No, I think——

Taking into account, of course, the period which had elapsed?—No, quite so; taking that into account I should not.

Taking the two months which had elapsed into account, you would not expect to find more reddening than you did find in this in any case of arsenical poisoning?—That is so, yes.

Further cross-examined by Mr. Marshall Hall—The expression has

Evidence for Prosecution.

Dr. Bernard Henry Spilsbury

been used by my learned friend, the Attorney-General, "chronic arsenical poisoning." There is such a thing as chronic arsenical taking, which would not amount to chronic arsenical poisoning?—Yes, that might be so; we have had a case quoted, of course.

At the ordinary druggist's shop you can buy one-twentieth or one-fiftieth of a grain of arsenic in bottles prepared by Burroughs & Wellcome—you know that?—Yes.

Things put up in an ordinary tabloid form, containing one-twentieth or one-fiftieth of a grain?—Yes.

Taking one-twentieth or one-fiftieth of a grain of arsenic for a period of time would not lead necessarily to chronic arsenical poisoning?—No, not unless symptoms developed.

It would not develop any symptoms?—It might not develop any symptoms.

Not unless symptoms of poisoning developed?—That is so.

That is to say, the taking of what are known as medicinal doses for a long period of time would not necessarily develop symptoms of arsenical poisoning?—Yes, that is so.

The elimination of urine, of course, is considerable, is it not?—Yes, it is.

In the post-mortem examination that you made the bladder was naturally empty of urine?—Yes, it was.

But there was at the bottom of the bladder a deposit of some sort. Did you notice it?—I do not think I recall it. I am afraid my only note is that the bladder was empty.

You did not notice whether there was in the bladder a deposit—the result of the evaporation, of course, of the urine—there may have been?—No, I did not. I think if it had been considerable we should have noticed it.

By Mr. JUSTICE BUCKNILL—It will be fair to put, "that is all I noticed"?—Yes, that is all I noticed.

By Mr. MARSHALL HALL—Is it a scientific fact that if there is any poison in the body at the time of burial it does not matter how you bury the body, there is a tendency for that poison to gravitate to the left side organs?—I did not know that.

Especially arsenic?—No, I was not aware of that, I am afraid.

Supposing a person died of arsenical poisoning, is not there a tendency, however the body is buried and lain, for the arsenic to be found more on the left side than on the right side?—I was not aware of that.

You yourself did not make any of the tests; you were telling us what Dr. Willcox has told you?—They are Dr. Willcox's figures.

If a fatal dose is administered seventy-two hours before death, and death ensues from that dose, would you expect to find any improvement in the condition of the patient between the administration of the dose and the death of the patient?—No, I should not.

Re-examined by the ATTORNEY-GENERAL—You make the qualification, "From the dose only"?—From the dose only.

What my learned friend called the fatal dose?—Yes; I understood him to say a moderately large dose.

Trial of the Seddons.

Dr. Bernard Henry Spilsbury

My learned friend's question is based upon this, that it was the dose, whatever it was, that caused the death?—Yes.

Suppose a moderately large dose had been given a few days before the last dose—if such a dose had been given a few days before the seventy-two hours, or before the seventy-two hours, might there be an improvement in the condition of the patient after the first dose had been administered?—There might, yes.

Might that also apply if there had been another moderately large dose before the last dose?—Yes, there might.

Would the fact of one moderately large dose having been given before the last dose aggravate the condition when the second dose is given?—Yes, it would.

I will put it if I may in a plain, concrete form. Suppose a dose of a few grains to have been given on one date, and then a few days after another dose—a moderately large dose—had been given, would that second moderately large dose produce a greater effect upon the patient than if the last dose had been the first given?—Yes, it would.

It really means that the effect would be cumulative?—To that extent, yes.

MAVIS WILSON, examined by Mr. MUIR—I have a dress agency at 158 Stroud Green Road. I have known Miss Maggie Seddon for about fifteen months. On 26th August of last year I sold her in my shop a pair of shoes and a little writing case. I made a note of the purchase in my book. My shop is about two minutes' walk from 27 Crouch Hill.

Dr. HENRY GEORGE SWORN, recalled, further examined by Mr. MUIR—Last night my son handed to Sergeant Hayman a sample of carbonate of bismuth from the stock I had. What I had in use at the time I gave it to deceased was exhausted. I always get it from the same people, Willows, Francis & Butler. I was dispensing bismuth from the same stock to a great many other patients in September last, and there were no ill results so far as I know.

Further cross-examined by Mr. MARSHALL HALL—Is it not the fact that carbonate of bismuth is known to contain a slight adulteration of arsenic?—I always thought it was commercial bismuth that contained that.

Do you not know that in the pharmacopœia there is a minimum adulteration which is recognised?—I know there is a trace of arsenic.

As a matter of fact, do not your opponents, the homœopathists, claim that the sole merit of bismuth carbonate is due to the minute quantity of arsenic in it?—Yes, I know that is their idea.

Dr. WILLIAM HENRY WILLCOX, examined by the ATTORNEY-GENERAL—I am a doctor of medicine and a Fellow of the Royal College of Physicians. I am senior scientific analyst to the Home Office. On 15th November of last year I was present at the post-mortem examination of the body of Eliza Mary Barrow, made by Dr. Spilsbury. The liver, stomach, intestines, spleen, kidneys, lungs, heart, blood-stained fluid from chest, a portion of the brain, a muscle, and some bone were removed for analysis.

Evidence for Prosecution.

Dr. William Henry Willcox

The body was well preserved, especially the internal organs. On 29th November I made a further examination of the body and removed some of the hair of the head, some muscle, and nails from the hands and feet, and I weighed the body. All these organs and tissues have been care fully examined and analysed by me.

What did you find in all the organs and tissues?—Arsenic.

And in the blood-stained fluid?—Yes. I found the largest proportion of arsenic in the intestines, the stomach, the liver, and the muscles. I also found traces of arsenic in the skin, the hair, and the nails—I found arsenic distributed throughout the body. The fact of two months having passed would not in any way have destroyed the arsenic—a mineral —which was in the body when it was buried; it may be preserved for years. Arsenic is practically tasteless, and when dissolved in water it forms a colourless solution like water. I heard the evidence of Dr. Sworn at the inquest, and also here. I heard his description of the symptoms—vomiting, pain in the stomach, diarrhœa, and weakness.

Assuming a doctor called in to a patient, and that doctor had no suspicion of arsenical poisoning, would there be anything to indicate to him that it was a case of arsenical poisoning and not of epidemic diarrhœa? —No. As a result of the examination and the various analyses that I have made in this case, I am of opinion that the cause of death of Eliza Mary Barrow was acute arsenical poisoning. I have a large experience of such cases. In the analysis of an organ, say the liver, I took a certain portion of that organ; and weighing that portion, having previously weighed the whole organ, from that portion I estimated the amount of arsenic and calculated from this amount the quantity of arsenic present in the whole organ. In this case a quarter of the whole organ was taken in the case of the liver and a fifth in the case of the intestines. I always reserve a portion of the organs for further analysis, so that if I want to test or confirm what I have already done, I have something already undealt with in order that I may do it. I have the unanalysed portions. still, which could be analysed if desired. In the case of some of the other organs smaller aliquot portions were taken for analysis, so that the multiplying factor would be greater. I have applied all the well-known tests for arsenic, including "Marsh's test." As the result of those tests I would be able to detect that there was arsenic, and from the process I have described I would be able to ascertain the quantity of arsenic.

It is Marsh's test that gives the "mirror"; I have the mirrors from all the organs here, and I produce five specimens. Taking the stomach as an example—a portion of the stomach was treated so as to destroy the organic matter, and a solution of this portion was obtained. This was placed in the hydrogen apparatus used for the Marsh test. When arsenic is present it comes off as a gas, and if a tube, through which the gas is passing, be heated, the gaseous arsenic compound is decomposed so that the arsenic is deposited as a black deposit called a mirror. If there was no arsenic there would be no black deposit. That is a scientific test by which we detect whether there is arsenic present or not, and in my experience it is an infallible test if done with proper care and skill. I used the greatest care and precautions in all these tests. In this case.

Trial of the Seddons.

Dr. William Henry Willcox

I also used sheep's liver, and I did the analyses side by side, so that had any arsenic been present in the apparatus or in the chemicals used, it would have been detected. I did not get any mirror from the sheep's liver.

I produce a table which I have made containing the result of the various tests of the organs and parts of the body. The total weight of the stomach is given as 105 grammes, and it works out that by the calculations in the whole of the stomach there was found ·11 of a grain of arsenic. In the case of the liver and the intestines the quantity was estimated by weighing, and the result was that ·63 of a grain was found in the intestines. The weighing process which I adopted was a well-known process, not Marsh's test; in all the other cases I used Marsh's method. In the case of the stomach I took 20 grammes and made that into a solution, and then I took a portion of that solution which represented ·48 grammes, and my mirror is arrived at from that small portion which I have taken of the whole solution.

Leaving out what you found in the hair, the bone, and the skin, what was the total amount, according to your calculation, that you found in the body when you analysed it?—2·01 grains. More arsenic had been taken by the patient, because almost invariably, when arsenic is taken the body rejects it by vomiting, by purging, and by the passing of urine, which will contain arsenic. There must have been considerably more than two grains, but I cannot give the exact figure. There might have been up to about five grains taken within three days of death. I do not give any figure for the hair, skin, and bone. I have not given any figure in the case of the skin, because I did not know how to make the calculations; and then, in the case of the bone, there was scarcely any arsenic present—it was only the most minute trace.

By Mr. JUSTICE BUCKNILL—In the case of the hair there would have been difficulty because the arsenic lay chiefly in the part next the skin, near the roots, so that I could not really calculate it out very well. The passing of the arsenic into the hair would occupy more time than the passing of the arsenic to other parts of the body, the liver, say. It would take some little time, some few days, for the arsenic to deposit in the nails, a little longer than in any of the organs. As regards the bone, it is stated that in chronic cases of arsenical poisoning, where it has been taken for many weeks and months, there is a considerable amount in the bone, but I cannot speak from my own experience about the bone.

The ATTORNEY-GENERAL—I do not propose to read the table through, but I should say that it contains the result which can be shown to the jury if my lord thinks proper; it is the analysis which makes up the table of the 2·01 grains, and is the analysis of the stomach, kidneys, spleen, lungs, heart, brain, blood fluid, bones, nails, skin, muscles, hair, liver, and intestine, and the two grains is made up without taking into account the bone, skin, and hair; that is how it stands. (Copies of the table were handed to the jury.)

Examination continued—As the result of the various analyses and tests which I made, in my opinion the fatal dose of arsenic was taken within two or three days of death, probably within two days.

Did you find any other poison than arsenic in the body?—I found

Evidence for Prosecution.

Dr. William Henry Willcox

bismuth and traces of mercury corresponding to the proper administratio
of these drugs.   I have heard the evidence as to the medicines that wer
administered to the deceased, that mercury was administered in a blu
pill and carbonate of bismuth in another medicine.   The quantities
found in the body corresponded with what I would expect to find fro
these administrations.   I had two samples of carbonate of bismut
delivered to me last night.   I analysed these by the Marsh's test, an
I find that they are practically free from arsenic ; there is a very minute
trace only, about one part in a million, so that it would take abou
2 cwts. of carbonate of bismuth to give two grains of arsenic.   Th
relatively large amount of arsenic found in the stomach and in th
intestines leads me to the opinion that I have given as to the time whe
the fatal dose was administered.   The arsenic had been taken durin
the last two days ; I cannot say exactly how long it had been taken before
but it is likely that it might have been taken for some days before th
fatal dose, because of the presence of arsenic in the hair and nails an
skin, the decomposition of which would take probably some little time.
some few days.   In a case of acute arsenical poisoning the stools would
be offensive ; as compared with the stools from epidemic diarrhœa, I
do not think that any one would distinguish between them in that respect.
The body of a person dying from epidemic diarrhœa would decompose
rapidly in hot weather.   The body of a person who died from acute
arsenical poisoning would not decompose as rapidly as the body of a person
dying from epidemic diarrhœa, because the arsenic would probably exer
some preservative action on the organs in which it was deposited.   I hav
found that result in other cases of arsenical poisoning.

On 11th December I had a packet of Mather's fly-papers brought to
me, and I analysed them.   During the course of this case I have had a
number of packets brought to me, which I have also analysed for the
purpose of extracting the arsenic.   I analysed two of the papers that
I got on 11th December—these papers were obtained from Mr. Price—
and I found that one contained 3·8 grains of arsenic and the other
contained 4·17 grains.   I also obtained some Mather's fly-papers from
Mr. Thorley, and I found 4·8 grains in one paper.   In one of Needham's
papers I found 6 grains ; in Dodds', 3·8 grains ; and in Spink's, 4·1 grains.
The extraction which I have given is the result of a scientific process
which extracts the whole lot.   I have also made experiments to extract
arsenic by boiling a fly-paper in a little water.   If a paper is actually
boiled in water for some minutes nearly all the arsenic comes out.   I took
a fly-paper out of a packet which I got from Needham's, and I immersed
it in a quarter of a pint of water and boiled it for five minutes ; I then
left it standing over the night, and I poured the liquid off and found that
there was 6·6 grains of arsenic in solution in the liquid.   There was
another of Needham's papers which I boiled for five minutes, poured the
liquid off at once, and then found six grains of arsenic.   With one of
Dodds' papers I found three grains, that being the lowest I got in this
process of boiling.   Arsenic which is found in fly-papers is in combination
with soda, and is in a particularly soluble form.

You have told us that you found 2·01 grains as the result of these
tests.   Would that be sufficient to kill an adult person ?—Yes

Trial of the Seddons.

Dr. William Henry Willcox

You have told us that that, in your view, was part of a dose of some five grains?—Yes.

Would that be sufficient to kill an adult person?—It probably would. The fluid, as the result of this boiling process, would have a slightly bitter taste, and the water would be more or less coloured by the paper. (Two bottles of fly-paper solution put in, and marked exhibits 140-141. Bottle of Valentine's meat juice put in, and marked exhibit 142. The bottle, exhibit 140, was handed to the jury, who tasted the contents.) The more arsenic there is the more quassia, and so the more bitter it tastes. There is a grain of arsenic in solution in the bottle which the jury have.

Could arsenic in solution of the kind you exhibit be administered in Valentine's meat juice without detection by the patient?—I think so. ("Particulars of Analysis" put in, and marked exhibit 144.)

What are the symptoms of chronic arsenical poisoning as distinguished from acute arsenical poisoning?—The patient suffers from anæmia and general weakness, vomiting is usually not present, and abdominal pain is usually not present. The skin often becomes brown in colour, and rashes may appear on the skin. The eyes may become red and sore and inflamed. The patient often suffers from chronic cough and irritation in the throat, and after a few weeks signs of neuritis occur, which are pains in the limbs, numbness, and finally some paralysis. The finger nails are thickened and brittle, and lose their lustre, and the skin of the palms and soles often becomes thickened. The hair may become coarse and fall out. I have some of the nails here; they appear to be quite normal. The palms of the hands and the soles of the feet appear normal. I did not observe anything that would indicate chronic arsenical poisoning. By acute arsenical poisoning I mean the result of one or more fatal doses. The symptoms are of a very pronounced character; the patient is faint and collapsed, there is severe pain in the abdomen and severe vomiting and purging, and death is likely to result within a few days. Sometimes there are cramps in the ankles, but that is not a constant symptom. There would not be constipation in acute arsenical poisoning; in chronic arsenical poisoning it would be an unusual symptom. Usually there is looseness of the bowels even in chronic arsenical poisoning. There would be great thirst in acute arsenical poisoning, the thirst depending on the amount of vomiting and diarrhœa.

Now, taking the result of all your various analyses, tests, and examinations, what do you say was the cause of Miss Barrow's death?— Acute arsenical poisoning.

Cross-examined by Mr. MARSHALL HALL—You told us the result of your experiments upon the fly-papers procured promiscuously which produced a varying quantity of arsenic from three up to six grains?—That is boiling with water.

Now, have you tried at all how much can be eliminated from the paper by the application of cold water?—Yes, I have tested two papers. In one paper ·6 of a grain was obtained from the whole paper. That was tearing the paper up and soaking it in cold water for sixteen hours. In the other case 1·3 grains.

So that even in cold water you can get 1·3 grains?—Yes.

Evidence for Prosecution.

Dr. William Henry Willcox

In what quantity of water was that?—That would be about a quarter of a pint of cold water.

There is nothing on the face of the fly-paper itself or on the back to indicate even approximately the quantity of arsenic it contains?—No.

They merely say that it ought to be kept out of the way of children and animals because of that?—Yes.

Would the regular mode of employing these fly-papers be to put them in some hollow receptacle like a saucer or a soup plate, and then put water on them?—Yes.

The effect on the fly is that the fly drinks the water and dies elsewhere—it does not die in the saucer?—No.

So that the fluid that would remain in the saucer would remain clean and clear?—It might.

And with cold water you do not get the same amount of colouring that you do with hot water?—No, it is paler.

It is very much paler, is it not?—Yes.

But suppose the fly-paper were put in a soup plate or a deep saucer, and the cold water was poured on it and it was allowed to remain for twenty-four hours, thirty-six hours, or forty-eight hours, the water on the top of that would contain a very small portion of arsenic?—It might contain a couple of grains—from one to two grains.

On your theory of extracting the arsenic by means of boiling water you must get the colour?—Yes.

And as you concentrate the resulting solution you must equally heighten the colour, because you cannot extract the arsenic without extracting the colouring matter with it?—That is so.

Therefore, if we are going to get your full quantity of three grains or six grains—your poisonous dose—out of a fly-paper, the result of that is that unless you make a very dilute solution you will get relatively a highly-coloured solution?—Yes.

What is the dose of Valentine's meat juice—a teaspoonful in a tumbler full of water?—On the bottle it says, " One spoonful to be diluted with three tablespoonfuls of water."

If you are going to put the resultant extract from a fly-paper into that, you have got to put much more than three tablespoonfuls of water, have you not, if you are going to get the whole quantity out of your fly-paper? —It depends upon how much water.

I was going to say you have the alternative of two things, whether you are going to have the maximum colour or concentrate your solution?—Yes.

Or you have to have the maximum of the quantity by reducing the colour of the solution?—Yes.

Because if you reduce the quantity of fluid you increase the bitterness of the solution?—Yes.

Now, in order to get a full dose of arsenic from a fly-paper into approximately three tablespoonfuls of water you would have almost the maximum of colour, would you not?—You would have a great deal of colour.

And a correlative amount of bitterness?—Yes.

Now, I want to begin at the beginning of this other matter, where my

Trial of the Seddons.

Dr. William Henry Willcox

learned friend, the Attorney-General, left off for a moment, on the question of what he calls chronic arsenical poisoning as distinguished from acute. There is another stage, is there not—there is the chronic stage of arsenic taking which could not be said toxicologically to amount to poisoning?—Yes.

I mean the dose, say, of one-tenth of a grain is a recognised medical dose, is it not?—One-tenth of a grain is rather a big dose. One-tenth of a grain given during the day is a recognised dose

One-thirtieth of a grain three times a day is a recognised dose?—A common dose.

It was admitted by, I think, Dr. Smith, that a well-known firm, who are only wholesale, supply the retail chemists with arsenious acid in the form of twentieths of a grain and fiftieths of a grain in the tabloid form?—Yes, that is so.

And they are weighed with the utmost accuracy, and are probably reliable?—That is so.

Now, supposing a person was taking a large but safe medicinal dose continuously for a period extending over months, and even possibly over a year, that would not necessarily produce arsenical poisoning?—No, not necessarily. It depends on the patient.

We are coming to a very important matter, the question of individual tolerance?—Yes.

There is no doubt that the idiosyncrasy with regard to drugs is well-nigh inexplicable?—Yes.

For instance, belladonna may be taken in large doses by some, while others can only take minute doses?—That is so.

And morphia has the same feature?—Yes.

And the same idiosyncrasy prevails with regard to arsenic?—Yes.

We know there has been a very important Royal Commission on arsenical poisoning quite within the last few years owing to the poisoning that took place in Manchester by reason of the beer?—Yes.

And one of the chief features investigated there was the individual idiosyncrasies with regard to arsenic?—Yes.

And the absence of poisonous symptoms in people who had taken comparatively large doses of arsenic over a long time?—That is so.

In the report of that Commission I find that they gave one instance certainly where three-tenths of a grain two or three times a day had been taken, and it was quoted as an instance of tolerance of comparatively large doses?—Yes, page 11, section 29.

" Instances of tolerance of large medicinal doses such as," &c. (reading to the words), " three-tenths of a grain of arsenic two or three times a day have for some time been reported by Dr. Stephenson and Professor Darby." Of course, I am not going into the stereotyped question, because there is a question of time there, and there is a question of a long period of tolerance, because you may get up to twenty grains a day with impunity? —Yes. In these cases where large doses are given the patient has to be worked up to it. For instance, with regard to this dose mentioned here, the patient would be given one-tenth of a grain a day first, and then they would gradually increase so that he took three-tenths a day.

A little lower down the report goes on to say, " The epidemic of 1907 afforded many instances of tolerance. In fact, one of the most instructive

Evidence for Prosecution.

Dr. William Henry Willcox

facts of the epidemic was the large number of people who must have been drinking beer from which there must have been eliminated by arsenic," &c. (reading to the words), "without any apparent result"? Do you agree with that?—Yes.

You would not say that it was impossible that the patient could take medicinal doses of arsenic for more than twelve months without showing any signs of poisoning?—No.

And may I take it that in the case of a patient, whether by reason of peculiar idiosyncrasy as to tolerance, or for any other cause unexplained, they are able to take medicinal doses of arsenic for a long period of time? You would not expect to find any symptoms of arsenical poisoning?—They might be absent, but usually the skin gets browned.

I was just going to put it to you that probably the only one that would not be avoided would be the browning of the skin?—The browning of the skin. There might be some changes in the appearance of the nails, but that does not necessarily follow that it would be present.

I quite understand the position you take up, that upon the experiments which you have made, which I am going to deal with in detail in a moment —on the experiments you have made, and the results you have obtained, you have come to a considered opinion that this was a case of acute arsenical poisoning?—Yes.

Of course, that does not bring us any nearer as to whether it was wilful or accidental taking?—No.

In the case of acute arsenical poisoning you would expect to find, would you not, burning in the throat immediately following the administration of the fatal dose?—I should not expect necessarily to find it. It might be present.

Would you not expect to find cramp almost at once in a very marked form if the dose was large?—Not necessarily. In a good many cases cramp was absent.

I suggest to you that the cramp normally would follow very shortly, and in severity would be proportionate to the size of the fatal dose?— Frequently cramps are absent. It is not a constant symptom.

I take your answer. You would expect, however, in the case of the administration of a dose like four or five grains acute pain in the abdomen within thirty minutes at least?—Probably in about thirty minutes. It depends upon the state of the stomach.

And, of course, the more delicate the state of the stomach—and by delicate I mean the more irritated the membrane was—the quicker would be the pain caused by the arsenical administration?—Yes.

Except for the fact, if it is a fact, that you say that two grains of arsenic was present in its entirety in this body—that is your calculation— was there anything in the condition of this body that negatived the assumption of death from epidemic diarrhœa?—The only other condition present was the preservation of the internal organs.

I ought to have put that to you—that therefore it is the presence of arsenic in the quantity in which you found it, of course?—Yes.

The presence of a much smaller quantity of arsenic would not, of course, confirm your view so strongly, would it? I mean supposing the quantity of arsenic turned out to be something like half what you have

Trial of the Seddons.

Dr. William Henry Willcox

calculated. I mean upon your calculations that would modify your view as to its being a case of acute arsenical poisoning?—I do not know that it would.

Just one question on the question of preservation. It is a fact, of course, that arsenic is a preservative?—Yes.

It is not in any way a disinfectant, is it? How does it act as a preservative—by being a disinfectant?—By the term "disinfectant" you mean something which prevents the growth of microbes?

Yes?—Arsenic does do that to some extent.

Therefore to that extent it is a disinfectant?—To some extent.

Would you not expect to find, if that is so, that stools brought on by acute arsenical poisoning would be less offensive than stools of a normal character?—I know as a fact that there is practically no difference, and the preservative effect of arsenic is rather in this way. It is easier to prevent the growth of microbes than to kill microbes when they are in luxuriance. In the intestines there are millions and millions of microbes swarming which the arsenic would not be able to kill, but in the liver and kidneys the presence of a little arsenic there, where there are no microbes, will prevent them from growing.

But there are recorded cases, are there not, where in the case of confirmed arsenic eaters who have died, the bodies have been found in a very short time in a very advanced state of decomposition?—This condition of preservation is not constant.

You put it in this way, that the presence of it is in your opinion confirmatory of your arsenic theory, but you do not say it is universal?—It is not universal.

Now, so far as thirst is concerned, thirst is merely a natural effort to replace moisture that is wasted?—Exactly.

And so therefore if you are wasting your moisture by being sick and by constant purging, it does not matter what the cause be that excites those two symptoms, you naturally would expect thirst?—Quite so.

So therefore we may eliminate thirst, I mean as pointing either one way or the other. It would be a common factor either of epidemic diarrhœa or of arsenical poisoning?—Yes.

What do you say is the extreme period that could have elapsed between the fatal dose which you think caused death in this case being taken and death ensuing?—Three days.

That is the extreme. Now, would you also tell me what in your opinion is the minimum period? I think you said not less than six, and probably not more than twenty-four, hours. What is the minimum time?—A few hours.

Assuming the dose be what you call a moderately fatal dose, what would you say in your opinion would be the time, having regard to the condition of the body on which you have founded your observations, between the administration of the dose and death ensuing?—A few hours.

By a few what do you mean?—Probably five or six. It might conceivably be less.

But in that case the agony would be intense, of course; if the dose were so strong that death ensued within three or four hours?—There would

Evidence for Prosecution.

Dr. William Henry Willcox

be very intense agony at first, and then probably the patient would become faint and collapse, and then would not feel very much.

But the intense agony would be hardly bearable by any ordinary human being?—It would be the same pain as in severe cholera—choleraic pain or severe diarrhœa.

Your symptoms of chronic poisoning would be, of course, symptoms of a severe chronic poisoning which, if not arrested, would result in death? —Not necessarily.

When you get to a state of paralysis and irritation to the throat would you not expect to find chronic cough?—In chronic poisoning symptoms there is so much individual susceptibility—some patients may manifest some extreme symptoms and others only slight. These symptoms may last for months.

You said something about constipation. In the Manchester report they found, did they not, that constipation was quite usual?—They said it was present, yes.

In a very large number of cases?—Yes, in many cases.

Now, first of all, I will deal with the organs—the entire organ is removed from the body?—Yes.

Having got the entire organ, you then separate a portion from that for the purpose of preparing your experimental liquid?—Yes.

Or experimental substance, whatever you call it. Having got your sample quantity you proceed to test it for arsenic by what is known as the modified Marsh test?—Yes.

In order to control your experiments you test a piece of sheep's liver to see that it does not contain arsenic?—Yes.

And having found that it does not contain arsenic you use some portion of that sheep's liver in order to make a similar solution to what you want to test?—Yes.

So that you are then able to get a perfectly neutral liquid which contains no arsenic, and which under the Marsh test will produce no mirror?—Yes.

Now comes a matter of great skill, is it not, on the question of observation. As I understand it there is a hydrogen apparatus which, we will take it, is also free from arsenic—care is taken to see that the hydrogen gas is passed through a tube where the suspected arsenic is, and if arsenic is there the arsenic becomes arsenious hydrogen, and deposits in the tube in the form of a mirror? Is that correct?—No.

You have to heat the tube?—The substance to be tested is really in the hydrogen apparatus.

And if there is arsenic in the stuff to be tested you convert your hydrogen into arsenic salt, do you not?—Yes.

And that deposits on the side of the heated tube in a black substance on that which you call a mirror?—Yes.

Now the quantity of arsenic so deposited can only be estimated by comparison with known mirrors containing known quantities?—That is so.

You first make a mirror which contains a particular quantity, and it must be very minute, because if you do not have it minute you get an opaque mirror, and you cannot see?—It is too big a mirror to match.

Trial of the Seddons.

Dr. William Henry Willcox

You get a piece of this very sheep's liver, to which you add a known quantity of arsenic; you make a mirror from that, and from that you know that that mirror shows a certain percentage of arsenic, as you have added it to the neutral substance?—Yes.

Then having got that mirror you compare it with the mirror which is given by the suspected substance, and from the one you deduce the quantity of the other?—Yes.

By examination?—We have a series of mirrors. I have them here if you want to see them.

There must be, because the human eye could not trace the resemblance —it must have an actual resemblance in order to produce, to carry it out, so that you prepare a series of mirrors?—A series of standard mirrors.

So that you ascertain the mirror coming off from a known quantity of arsenic, and then you compare the mirrors produced by the suspected substance with the mirrors, the quantity of arsenic in which is known. Now, the actual quantity of arsenic that you, by comparison with the mirrors—take, for instance, the lungs—the mirror that you prepare from the lungs shows 1-50th part of a milligramme of arsenic?— Yes.

Of course, that is absolutely an unappreciable amount to the human eye?—I have the mirror here.

You could not get off that mirror the 1-50th of a milligramme, and weigh it even if you could get it off?—But you can see it.

It is a question of eyesight?—Yes.

That is to say, with your eyes you see it exactly corresponds with another mirror that has been made by a solution containing 1-50th of a milligramme of arsenic. Is that so?—Yes.

Is that the standard one?—No; that is the one from the lung—the 1-50th.

Now have you got a standard 1-50th?—Yes. (Same produced.)

I take it, of course, the standards were prepared by you?—Yes. They were all done by me.

Just let me look. Now, you say that this particular mirror I have in my hand approximates to a mirror which is marked here "1-50th"?—Yes.

There are two colours, the brown and the grey, are there not?—A brown and black.

Ought the brown to be the same tint?—You go by the whole mirror.

Just take those samples for a moment. (Same handed to witness.) On each side of the 1-50th is a 1-40th and a 1-60th?—Yes.

They both seem to give a metallic mirror, do they?—There is rather more of the brown in those two than in the 1-50th one. They vary a little.

(The witness shows the mirrors to the jury.)

Now, you would agree with me as to the importance of absolute accuracy—absolute accuracy, not relative accuracy—the importance of absolute accuracy with regard to whether it is 1-40th, or 1-50th, or 1-60th, is of vital importance in this matter?—It is most important to be as accurate as possible.

But a very minute difference makes a very great difference in the result of arsenic calculated as in the body, does it not?—I fully admit that.

Evidence for Prosecution.

Dr. William Henry Willcox

Take, for instance, the lungs. The mirror that you have got shows 1-50th part of a milligramme, which is equivalent to 1-3240th part of a grain?—Yes.

That is what you get from a sample which weighs six grammes. Is that not so?—Quite so; the multiplying factor is a big one.

I daresay you will tell me the multiplying factor in order to arrive at the amount of arsenic which that particular organ contained?—Roughly, it is fifty.

Therefore any error in the diagnosis of the mirror is multiplied fifty times in the calculation as to the quantity of arsenic?—Exactly.

Of course, it would be physically impossible to separate the quantity of arsenic in any other way as a mirror. You could not get it out in a chemical substance, could you?—No. You could; but it would be so small that you could not weigh it.

Could it from the mirror itself be reduced again into solution and then precipitated in any way?—Yes. It would be such a small amount that you could not weigh it properly.

Probably there is no machine known to the world that could weigh it, and I suppose it would want a very good microscope to see it?—It would not want a very good microscope, because you can see it with the naked eye.

I know, but I am talking of metallic arsenic—of arsenic itself?—It would be visible, but it would be very small.

Is what you see on the mirror metallic arsenic very finely subdivided and spread on the face of the mirror?—Yes.

Therefore if that is metallic arsenic it can be scraped off?—Yes.

And, of course, would be visible as you reduce it to fine subdivision?—It would be very small.

By Mr. JUSTICE BUCKNILL—You could not reduce it to a crystal?—You could have a crystal of another compound of arsenic.

Of the same weight?—Yes.

By Mr. MARSHALL HALL—A crystal which no machine known to science at the present day could weigh?—It could be weighed, but it would not be practicable to weigh it.

Would you mind telling me what the multiplying factor was in the case of the stomach?—The multiplying factor in the case of the stomach would be about 200.

In the kidneys how much?—60.

Would you mind telling me as I am passing which kidney you took?—I could not tell you that—portions of each, as far as I recollect.

If you tell me there is practically no difference between the organs on the left or right hand side or between the right hand lobe or left hand lobe I will leave it?—There is none.

What was the multiplying factor in the spleen?—13.

The multiplying factor in the lungs was 60, was it not?—Yes.

What is the multiplying factor in the hair?—50.

In the brain?—There is such a little there that I think we might leave that.

The blood fluid?—The multiplying factor there was $11\frac{1}{2}$.

The nails—there, again, there is so little?—4.

Trial of the Seddons.

Dr. William Henry Willcox

The skin?—Well, I did not add that up.

Obviously you did not attempt that, because it would be practically too small?—Yes.

Now comes the liver, which was done by another person. You have got ·17 of a grain?—Between one-fifth and one-sixth of a grain

In the intestines you got a little over half a grain?—Yes.

Two-thirds of a grain. You have given us the multiplying factors in the others, and I know that the quantities found practically are one-thirtieth, and one-thirtieth, and one-thirtieth of a milligramme, one-fiftieth and one-sixtieth of a milligramme. The quantities you found or rather estimated—the actual quantities I am going to show from these samples which you produced; one is 1-1944th of a grain; another the same; another is 1-3240th of a grain; another 1-3888th of a grain; and in the case of the brain it is 1-16000th part of a grain. Then it is 1-1944th of a grain in the nails; the same in the skin, and 1-5837. In the hair what?—1-5184th.

So that in every one of these cases a very minute error in the original measurement by the mirror would, of course, make a very great difference in the ultimate calculation?—That is so.

And it is only fair to ask you on that account, you have taken the very greatest possible care in your examination of the mirrors to examine them to the very greatest of your ability?—Yes, I have done my very best.

Now I come to what I think is a matter of more importance. You have taken the weight of the body here as given. The weight of the actual body as weighed on that day was 67 lbs. 2 ounces. Is that right?—That was the weight of the body.

When exhumed—the total body?—It was a fortnight after exhumation.

We have heard from what Dr. Spilsbury has told us that the probable average weight of a woman of this height, and nourished as we know she was nourished, rather inclined to be on the stout side than on the thin, would probably be about 10½ stone. Would you agree with that? From 9½ to 10½ stone, I think he said?—I think he said from 8 stone.

By the ATTORNEY-GENERAL—8½ stone?—It might be anything between 8½ and 10 stone.

By Mr. MARSHALL HALL—May we take 9 stone or 10 stone as the fairly average weight of the body in life?—I could not say what the weight of the body would be in life.

I think it is of great importance?—I think the body might have weighed 10 stone before the illness, but the illness would cause a great loss of weight.

I am told it can be proved that the body was 11 stone in weight, but you would not accept that?—I would not accept that it was 11 stone at the time of the death.

Would you, if I suggest 10 stone, accept that it may have been 10 stone at the time of death?—I should say that it was less than that.

The woman measured 5 feet 4 inches after death. That would probably mean some slight shrinkage?—It may be.

You would probably expect to find another inch?—Possibly—half an inch.

Evidence for Prosecution.

Dr. William Henry Willcox

And we know that she was above what you might call the medium build. I do not think 10 stone would be an unfair weight to take as a probable weight?—Not when she was in health.

In the case of muscle examination the sample that you took weighed six grammes?—Yes.

And you produce a mirror which you diagnose as one-thirtieth part of a milligramme?—Yes.

The multiplying factor in that case is something enormous, is it not?—It is very big.

It is nearly 2000 as I work it out?—It would be approaching that.

In the case of the muscles you have no absolute weight by which you multiply your sample, have you?—No.

Because it obviously would be impossible to extract from the body all the muscle so as to compare the amount of muscle in the body with the weight of a small portion of muscle which you had used as a sample for analysis. It would be impossible?—Yes.

Now in the case of the muscle I find that the result of your calculation that in the muscle was no less than 1·03 grain of arsenic?—Yes.

That is to say, slightly more—infinitesimally I agree, but slightly more than half the total calculated weight of arsenic in the body?—About half.

Now you have worked upon the assumption that the weight of the muscle in the body is equivalent to about two-fifths of the weight of the body. That is an accepted medical dictum, is it not?—That is accepted, yes.

But this is the relative calculated weight of muscle to body in the living body, is it not?—Yes, or in the dead body.

In the living or the dead body—when dead, immediately after death, or practically immediately after death. I will put it to you to make myself perfectly clear, the weight of the body is made up practically of bone, organs, blood, and muscle, is it not?—Yes.

And the weight of all the component parts of the body is to some extent dependent upon the weight of water in those parts?—Yes.

Now, then, if you have a part of the body which in life or immediately succeeding death has a known relative proportion to the total weight of the body, the weight of the water in the whole body and of the portion, including the weight of water, both in the portion and in the whole body, will be proportionate. It must be? That is sound, is it not?—Yes.

Now, in this case you have got a drying up of the whole body all over, have you?—Yes, some drying.

The ratio of the drying is quicker in the muscle than it is in the other portions of the body?—Not necessarily.

But I suggest to you that it is—the muscle contains ·77 of water?—Yes.

According to the medical books?—Yes.

Bone contains only 50 per cent., so that you see the muscle would lose water, assuming that they are all losing at the same rate, in a greater proportion; that is in the proportion of 77 to 50 over the loss in

Trial of the Seddons.

Dr. William Henry Willcox

the bone?—I agree with you as regards bone, but not as regards other organs.

But what preportion to the weight of the body does the bone have?—A considerable proportion.

I would sooner take it from you than make a guess. What do you say?—I forget the exact figure.

Anyhow, it is a very considerable proportion, and then, of course, there is the loss of water in the organs?—The organs would have less water as a result.

The proportion would not be altered in the case of the organs?—No.

But in the case of the bone you admit there ought to have been an allowance made?—I admit there is a difference as regards the water contained.

The bones dry very slowly, do they not?—They dry slowly, yes.

And I am sure it was an oversight, I mean, I may be wrong, but in making this calculation you have made no allowance whatever for the loss of water?—No, I have not.

Do you not think you ought to have made some allowance?—Well, the calculation of muscle must only be approximate.

Yes?—I have estimated it at one grain.

That is to say, taking the whole weight of the muscle in the body as two-fifths of the weight of the body?—Yes, but I admit that must only be approximate.

And, of course, as the water increased out of the muscle disproportionately to the bone, so the multiplying factor is unduly increased?—Making that allowance for the reduced quantity.

If you make the allowance that I suggest ought to be made, the effect of it would be to slightly reduce it?—To slightly reduce the amount.

To slightly reduce the quantity given?—Yes. I do not claim this one to be strictly accurate, because it must be approximate from the method which was used because of the multiplying factor being so great.

Whereas in the case of the skin you have appreciated the difficulty to such an extent that you do not profess to make a quantitative experiment?—No.

Using it honestly, to the best of your ability, it is only an approximate calculation that you have arrived at in regard to the amount of arsenic in the body?—That is so.

And, of course, that is most important from the point of view with regard to the mirror of the muscle, because as far as the mirror of the muscle goes, the multiplying factor is enormous—close upon 2000, and so far as the multiple is concerned it is practically 50 per cent. of the total calculation?—Oh, yes, the total quantity in the water.

It is important from both points of view. With the mirror used the multiplying factor is 2000. Do you think you arrive at that quantity?—Yes.

It has a most important effect, because the result of it is to bring out 50 per cent. of the total calculated arsenic in the body?—Yes, I agree.

Evidence for Prosecution.

Dr. William Henry Willcox

Now, I want to come to another matter altogether. You are con
vinced, Dr. Willcox, that this is a case of acute arsenical poisoning.
That is your honest opinion?—I have no doubt about it.

Did you examine the hair? I notice that in the table which you
prepared you give only an examination of ·4 of a gramme of what is
called proximal hair—that is the hair nearest the scalp?—Yes.

And the hair which grows at the extremity is called the distal end?—
Yes.

You did, as a matter of fact, examine the distal end of that?—Yes,
I did.

·In the proximal end the mirror showed one-eightieth out of ·4 of
a gramme, which is approximately slightly less than you found in the
heart. You found in the heart one-sixtieth of a milligramme, and in
the proximal end of the hair you found one-eightieth of a milligramme?
—Yes.

What did you find in the distal end of the hair?—One three-
thousandth—about a quarter as much.

You took a length of hair which was about 12 inches, I think?—
They varied. I should say the average would be about 10 inches.

And in order that you should have a proper examination you took
3 inches from the distal end and 3 inches from the other end. Is that
so—from the proximal end?—Yes.

In the proximal end you found one-eightieth of a milligramme, and
in the distal end one three-hundredth?—Yes.

Was this not one of the most important subjects of investigation
in the Royal Commission, arsenic in the hair?—Yes.

And especially the length of time during which the arsenic must
have been taken before you find it there. That was one of the great
subjects of the Commission, was it not?—That was one of them.

In the report they prepared exhaustive tables dealing with the question of hair only. If you look at the second volume of the report,
right at the end of page 377, you will find a very careful report prepared
of the experiments, dealing only with hair. Now, will you please check
me for a moment. Taking, as I understand you did, the quantity that
you did, I worked it out that the hair chips, we will call them, the
distal end contained one-eightieth of a grain of arsenious acid, and the
hair roots contained one-fifth of a grain of arsenious acid?—Between
one-fourth and one-fifth, yes.

Do you agree that in all cases of the finding of arsenic in the body
or the presence of arsenic in the system, you have to make allowance
for the possibility of small quantities of arsenic being received from more
than one source of food and drink. I am reading from the report of
the Royal Commission?—You have to bear in mind the possibility. That
possibility is very much less now than it was at the time that the report
was written, because so very much more care is taken over food stuffs.

But still these very minute quantities of arsenic are contained in
various kinds of food?—There may be very minute amounts, but the
amount is one one-hundredth of a grain to a gallon, and one one-hundredth
of a grain in 1 lb.

Trial of the Seddons.

Dr. William Henry Willcox

Now, I come to this question of the hair. That was made the subject of a very careful report, and there is an appendix to this report
which sets out all the experiments on hair. "Out of a total of 41 con-
trolled cases, principally hospital and infirmary, &c." (reading down to
the words) "male patients who had been taking 3 minims of arsenic
three times a day, about one-tenth of a grain of arsenic daily, at the
end of two months showed amounts of arsenic varying from one-twentieth
to one-fifth of a grain per 1 lb. of hair, which had grown during the
interval." That is obviously so, is it not? The position of arsenic in
the hair would not alter after death?—It would not alter after death.

The metabolic changes cease—you get no alteration in the amount
of arsenic?—No.

So when the arsenic goes to the hair it first goes to the piece of
hair nearest to the root as it grows?—Yes.

Then as time goes on it pushes further up?—I do not think we can
say that—that it is an exact limitation of the arsenic. The bulk of it
deposits in the hair at the time it is taken, but probably there is a little
may get up to the hair. The bulk of it remains.

Practically—roughly speaking—for practical purposes it only gets
in during the growth of the hair?—It gets in during the growth.

What I am putting to you is that the presence of that quantity of
arsenic in the distal portions of this hair, according to the Schedule of
Cases that was made upon this Arsenic Commission, demonstrate that
this arsenic in the case of Miss Barrow must have been taken for a
period exceeding two or three months?—No, I do not admit that.

I will give you the specific figure in a moment. "Male patients
taking smaller amounts of arsenic medicinally, &c." (reading to the
words) "which had grown before the demonstration of arsenic at the
time." That would, of course, make a difference for the purpose of
examination?—Yes.

Now, you took only 3 inches of the distal end?—Yes.

If the presence of arsenic in the distal end of the hair is evidence
of a lengthy period of arsenic-taking, the period is probably longer according to the quantity found in the distal end of the hair?—Yes, that would
be so.

Now, for the purpose of ascertaining the quantity in the distal end
of the hair you will get a much more concentrated result if you take the
last 3 inches than you would if you took the last 9 inches. Do you
follow what I mean?—I do not.

Because if you take 9 inches you may have arsenic in the whole of
it, whereas if you took only 3 inches it must be in the last 3 inches that
you find the arsenic. Do you follow what I mean?—I think it is rather
the other way round, is it not?

For the purpose of examination, if you found it in the last 3 inches
you would probably find more in the next 6 inches—the 6 inches near
the roots?—Yes.

That is what I mean. So that if you are taking 9 inches, your
probable average of the 9 inches would be a higher average than it would
be for the last 3 inches?—Yes.

Evidence for Prosecution

Dr. William Henry Willcox

I only wanted this for the purposes of comparison in the cases reported. They only deal, I think it is, with 6 inches, whereas in your case you take the 3 extreme inches?—Yes.

I see on page 349 of the Commission report you find a table in the appendix No 32, "Arsenic in the hair." You find there in the top column the amount of arsenic in grains of arsenious oxide per 1 lb. of hair, and I am dealing with the cases given here. There are three here, I see, where arsenic has been taken for more than five weeks. First of all there is "No arsenic taken." Then, "Arsenic taken in larger or smaller doses for five weeks or less." I am disregarding that. Now, "Arsenic taken for more than five weeks in the whole length." You find that in the middle?—Yes, I see.

I will try and put it generally as nearly as I can. Is this the result of it—that in the five cases who took arsenic for more than five weeks the tips were found free of arsenic in one of the three cases, and contained one two-hundred-and-fiftieth of a grain per 1 lb. in one case and below one two-hundred-and-fiftieth of a grain per 1 lb. in the other case?—Yes.

So that you see even in the case of people who have taken arsenic for more than five weeks, in three different cases you only have one two-hundred-and-fiftieth of a grain per 1 lb. from the distal end, and in the other case it is not even fully that. Now, what is the rate of growth per year of the hair—about 6 inches, is it not?—It would be about that.

Is there any evidence of any metabolic change in grown hair—hair when it is once grown?—There is very little evidence of what I call living change. It is disputed. You mean hair on the living body?

Yes, hair on the living body?—There is probably not a great change.

Dr. Mann is a great authority on it?—Yes.

He was giving his evidence on page 139, and I see his answer is, "I suppose when the arsenic gets into the arterial structures it would be likely to remain there," &c. That would be the case of hair, would it not?—Probably there is not much metabolic change.

I will take it at that—it is so small as to be practically negligible?—It is not much.

Now, look at case No. 63, where the patient has been taking arsenic for a longer period than five weeks. They tested the three samples of hair in the whole length in one case, in the roots in one case, and in the tips in one case. They found in that case, did they not, one-fiftieth of a grain per 1 lb.?—That is in the tips.

You will find that on page 358 of that report, case 63, where it is all set out absolutely in detail. It is a case taken from the Lambeth Infirmary, and they give the age and the name of the deceased, and this is what he had been taking—12 minims daily for five days, from the 23rd to the 28th of October. Then it is discontinued for ten days, from the 28th of October to the 7th of November. Then 12 minims daily for twenty days, from the 8th to 28th November. Then discontinued forty-nine days, from the 29th November to the 16th January.

Trial of the Seddons.

Dr. William Henry Willcox

So you see there had been a taking of arsenic for a period of nearly three months prior?—Yes.

Now, they found there one-eightieth of a grain in the roots—I am talking of the same relative weights—and one-fortieth of a grain in the tips, but the tips were of 9-inch length. From that do you not think that the conclusion is justified that you do not and never will find arsenic in the distal end of the hair unless the taking of the arsenic has been spread over some considerable period?—Generally, when arsenic has been found in the tips of the hair, there has been some taken for some period before.

Can you point to any recorded case in which arsenic has been found in the distal tips of the hair unless arsenic has been taken for a period exceeding ten weeks?—In this report it says that arsenic is found in the hair in people who have never had arsenic.

I am talking of the distal end of the hair right at the end?—That would certainly refer to the distal end.

I am talking of arsenic to this extent.—This is one-twenty-fifth of a grain in 1 lb.

I refer to page 13 of the final report. That is where they are taking no arsenic medicinally, but it did not follow that they had not been taking arsenic from a contaminated source?—As far as was known they were taking no arsenic.

No arsenic was being given medicinally, and in one case one-twenty fifth of a grain was the largest amount found per 1 lb.?—Yes.

There were three cases, one of one-hundredth of a grain, one of one-fiftieth of a grain, and one of one-twenty-fifth of a grain per 1 lb.?—Yes.

Was not that used as an argument, or rather as a proof that they had been taking arsenic over a long period of time, or else they would not have shown it in the distal end of the hair? The inference drawn from that in the report was that, although they had not been given medicinal doses of arsenic, they must have been having arsenic from contaminated beer?—Not necessarily from contaminated beer. Sometimes arsenic may be present in what is called normal hair in small amounts.

I put it to you that you cannot get what you admit there was in this case, that it is one-eighteenth of a grain in 1 lb. in the distal end of the hair, unless there has been the taking of arsenic over a long period?—That does not necessarily mean that arsenic had been taken over a long period. It is possible that some arsenic might have been taken at some previous period.

Is the finding of the arsenic in the hair corroborative of acute arsenical poisoning or of chronic arsenic-taking?—If arsenic is found in the hair it indicates that probably the arsenic had been taken for some period.

I am sure you will give me a fair answer. Apart from all other symptoms, or any other question, if you only find arsenic in the hair, you would take that as being a symptom of a prolonged course of arsenic? —Of a course of arsenic over some period.

And the minimum period would be something about three months?— I think that.

Evidence for Prosecution.

Dr. William Henry Willcox

Ten weeks to three months?—I think in less than that there would be arsenic in the proximal portion of the hair.

In the proximal portion, but not in the distal portion. You would not expect to find it in the distal end in three months, would you?—Not in large amounts.

Not in the amount you have got here—one-eighteenth of a grain per 1 lb. That is a comparatively large amount for the distal end?—This one-eighteenth of a grain in the distal end might possibly mean some arsenic might have been taken, perhaps a year or more ago. It does not mean that the taking of the arsenic had continued—had been going on continuously from that time.

That it meant it had been going on continuously or not continuously?—No.

That is to say, it might have been taken and left off possibly?—That there might possibly have been some taken, say, a year ago or more than a year ago.

A year ago or more?—More than a year ago.

The presence of arsenic in the distal end of the hair is indicative probably of the taking of arsenic more than twelve months ago?—Probably.

But it does not in any way affect your opinion as to the poisonous dose and the actual poison that you found in the other portions of the body?—Not in the least.

As the result of your information do you incline to the opinion that it was one fatal dose or more than one dose?—One fatal dose within the last three days.

But do you think, having regard to the fact that we know this woman had been suffering from epidemic diarrhœa for certainly eleven days, that the administration of a large dose of arsenic in the early part of those days would not have proved fatal?—It is possible that the symptoms may have been due to arsenic.

Do you suggest that it was possible that there was a series of doses?—It is possible.

But do you incline to that opinion as a result of a considered consideration of this case?—I think it is possible that the symptoms might have been due from arsenic throughout the illness.

You go as far as that, that this may have been a constant administration of arsenic?—There might have been.

That was not the opinion you expressed before the magistrate?—I said it might have been.

Therefore the doses would have had to have been very small or they would have proved fatal more quickly, would they not, than small doses?—If it had been taken.

If it be the result of a series of doses, the earlier doses must have been small, because, of course, it would not be cumulative except as an irritant, would it?—It would not be cumulative.

Because of the expulsion by the fæces and by the urine?—Yes.

So that a small dose of arsenic—not a fatal dose or approximating

Trial of the Seddons.

Dr. William Henry Willcox

to a fatal dose—would probably be expelled in one form or another either by the sickness or the diarrhœa?—Yes.

And would be non-efficient so far as the fatal result is concerned?—No.

It would be non-efficient. Would it prepare the system for a fatal effect from a similar dose. Do you mean that?—If a dose were given or were taken to produce symptoms of poisoning, then another dose would have a greater effect than if the patient had not had the previous dose.

Even the elimination would not counteract that?—No.

But as a cumulative poison arsenic is not known—as a cumulative poison?—No.

It is not like lead and those class of poisons which are known to be cumulative?—No.

The elimination of arsenic in the system by the natural means is very rapid?—Yes.

Taking all probabilities, which do you incline to—that it was a case of an administration of a small dose culminating in the larger dose, or that it was the taking—when I say administration I mean taking, I am not dealing with the question of administration by another person—was it the taking of a series of small doses or the taking of one large, fatal dose at the end? Which of the two opinions do you incline to?—I can only speak with certainty as to the taking of a large dose during the last two days.

But under no circumstances would you—if it had been administered for ten days, if arsenic had been taken for ten days—under no circumstances would you expect to find arsenic in the distal ends of the hair, that being the only administration of arsenic given?—I should not expect to find it in the distal part of the hair in the ten days, but it is possible that there might be some in the distal end, because it says in this report that sometimes arsenic is found in the hair.

Yes, but that is the point I have been dealing with. The growth takes place near the scalp. There is no metabolic change in the hair. It is an obscure theory?—We do not know all about the changes which go on in the hair.

Dr. Mann is a great authority upon it?—Yes, the greatest authority.

His view is that the arsenic does not move with the metabolic changes, and you agree with me that the metabolic changes in the top of the hair would be practically nothing?—Yes. There is one point which I have not mentioned, which I ought to mention here, which rather affects these results, and that is that when I took the hair for analysis it was at the second examination, and the hair had been lying in the coffin, and it was more or less soaked in the juice of the body.

Yes, but you washed it—you washed it carefully?—I washed it, and I washed off anything that was on the surface, but it is possible that some soakage may have occurred in spite of the washing, so that the results are a little higher than they would have been if the hair had been taken dry. That opinion is borne out by the analysis of the hair from the undertaker; the figure came lower.

Do you seriously suggest really that, with all the care you took,

Evidence for Prosecution.

Dr. William Henry Willcox

there may have been some arsenic from outside which had got into that hair before you examined it?—No, I mean in the coffin.

But surely in a case of this importance, and the examinations that have to be made, if there was any possibility that after washing any external arsenic could have been soaked into the hair why examine it at all?—There was no external arsenic, only some may possibly have soaked into the hair.

But if there was a possibility of a soakage otherwise than by natural means, why examine it at all? Why not disregard it at once? And then you have taken the trouble not only to examine, but you have made a report upon it, and you have actually calculated it out according to the ratio of weight in grains to the lb. of hair, and you evidently attach great importance to it. I do not think it is quite fair to put upon me now that that examination may be stultified by the fact that some portion of arsenic may have got into the hair from outside?—I mentioned that because I ought to give you the figures of the other specimen of hair.

Of course, you will give it to me. I have no other figures except your figures to work upon. I did not know that they had been separately examined?—The other was one-twenty-first of a grain to 1 lb. That was mixed hair.

That is hair that was taken, of course, just after death?—Yes.

Assuming that this lady had taken arsenic medicinally, would that make the effect of gastro enteritis more serious to her or not?—It depends upon the amount which had been taken. If it had been taken medicinally as a tonic it probably would not have any effect upon the gastro enteritis. If it had been taken in amounts to cause irritation of the stomach, then obviously the gastro enteritis would increase.

Just in the same way that, as arsenic would accentuate gastro enteritis, so gastro enteritis would accentuate the effect of arsenic?—Yes.

Now, you agree, do you not, that from all Dr. Sworn could see, his certificate was fully justified?—Yes.

I want to put a proposition to you. Of course, the theory of the prosecution is—it is a theory—that one or both of these persons was administering arsenic to the deceased person with the intention of killing her, and, in fact, killed her, during this period preceding her death. Do you not think it would be a highly dangerous thing for anybody having regard to his or her safety to be doing a thing like that, with a medical man coming in daily? Do you not think so?—Do you mean the possibility of detection?

I mean the possibility of detection?—There would be some risk.

Now, in the present day, when we have got the present advance of medicine, the examination, and the minute examination, of fæces or of urine is a common practice for the purpose of diagnosis?—It is a common practice, but not an analysis for arsenic. That is a very unusual thing.

I am not talking of an analysis for arsenic. Could they not detect it by any process short of analysis?—No.

Do you mean to say that that is known to the ordinary person, that you cannot detect arsenic either in the fæces or in the urine, or in the vomit, except by analysis?—No. Except by a special analysis. I cannot

Trial of the Seddons.

suggest what this meant to an ordinary person. That is the fact, that it cannot be detected except by a special analysis.

But supposing this arsenic had been given, if there had been an analysis of vomit, urine, or fæces, it would have clearly demonstrated the presence of arsenic in the system?—If there had been an analysis for arsenic. The ordinary examination of the urine would not deal with the question of whether arsenic was present or not.

Is it a matter of universal medical knowledge that the symptoms of arsenical poisoning and of chronic diarrhœa are identical. Is that a matter of common medical knowledge?—Yes.

Surely in these days of advanced medical science, if a doctor found a case of chronic diarrhœa did not yield to the proper treatment, he would immediately have the evacuation analysed with a view of testing for arsenic? —He would not do so unless he suspected arsenic.

The mere fact of these symptoms not yielding to ordinary treatment? —Certainly not. In many of these cases of diarrhœa they may go on for two or three weeks. It would not follow that the doctor would have the urine and the fæces examined for arsenic.

In a case of diarrhœa and sickness brought on by arsenical poisoning, would you expect to find that the medicines which were given, such as bismuth and chalk mixture, would have any beneficial effect upon the patient—I mean the illness being due to arsenical poisoning?—They would have a beneficial effect.

As great as if the illness were chronic diarrhœa?—I do not think one could possibly say. They would have a beneficial effect. Of course, if a large dose of arsenic were taken it would produce poisonous symptoms.

You know Dr. Sworn did see this woman at eleven o'clock on the morning of Wednesday, the 13th, and she died on the early morning of Thursday, at six o'clock—she died on the early morning of the 14th?— Yes.

He saw her at eleven o'clock, and he has told us what he found. Do you suggest it is possible that at that time, or within a short distance of that time, she had been given a fatal dose of arsenic?—I said within two days the dose was given.

Do you really ask the jury to accept the theory that at the time Dr. Sworn saw her on the morning of Wednesday, at eleven o'clock, she may then have had in her a fatal dose of arsenic?—She may have had some arsenic in her.

But surely, with the diarrhœa that was going on, it must have been a very large dose?—She may have had some arsenic after Dr. Sworn saw her.

In which case, if it had been a large dose before Dr. Sworn saw her, you would have expected Dr. Sworn to have found some of the effects of that dose?—He would have found diarrhœa and sickness.

Indistinguishable from epidemic diarrhœa and sickness?—Indistinguishable from epidemic diarrhœa.

Re-examined by the ATTORNEY-GENERAL—You have told us that a doctor, in your view, could not detect the presence of arsenic, having the fæces and urine, unless he made a special analysis. What kind of

Evidence for Prosecution.

Dr. William Henry Willcox

analysis do you mean by that?—A special analysis for arsenic, such as was made on these remains by a specialist using special tests for arsenic.

Which you made in the post-mortem examination?—Yes, a doctor in ordinary practice would not have the apparatus required for making such an examination. A specimen would have to be sent to an analyst.

Supposing a doctor were attending a patient thirteen days for epidemic diarrhœa, in the circumstances described by Dr. Sworn, without suspecting that there was any arsenic being administered, in your view would you expect him to make any such special analysis?—No.

Supposing arsenic had been given to Miss Barrow about the 1st or 2nd September and the treatment during the next few days had been carbonate and bismuth, and subsequently the effervescing mixture which was described, might that have a beneficial effect upon the patient?—Yes.

Assuming the dose was not too large, might the patient recover?—Certainly.

And if the patient was recovering would the symptoms of vomiting, diarrhœa, and pains gradually cease?—Yes.

I understand you to say, in answer to my friend, the last dose, which was described as the fatal dose, must in your view have been given within two days—that is what you said last?—Yes.

Are you able to fix the minimum time within the two days that the arsenic may have been administered?—I cannot fix it, but it might have been given within a few hours of death.

There is nothing which enables you to say more precisely than that?—No, I would not be more precise than to say within two days.

I just want to get it clear if I can what your view is about the hair. First of all, you told my friend you had made two analyses of hair?—Yes.

And one, you said, which was of mixed hair taken just after death, gave the one-twenty-first part of a grain?—Yes.

What do you mean by "mixed hair"?—I did not know whether it was at the tip or the root. Probably it would not be cut off very close to the skin. It was perhaps the middle of the hair and the end.

It was hair which had been cut off, and which had been given to you for the purposes of analysis?—Yes.

You did not see it cut?—No.

And then the other analysis which you made was of hair which you yourself took in the post-mortem examination?—Yes.

You have been asked a good many questions about what you found in the hair. Have you taken any quantity of arsenic from the hair in your calculation of 2·01 grains found in the body?—No, none at all.

I mean, whether it is from the proximal end or the distal end for the purposes of that figure is quite immaterial?—Yes.

Supposing you have a case of acute arsenical poisoning, and you examine the hair, would it be possible to find any trace of arsenic in the distal end as well as in the proximal end?—The bulk of the arsenic would be found in the proximinal end.

Clearly the bulk would, but would there be any trace found in the distal end?—Yes, there might be some trace of arsenic in the distal end, but that trace may very possibly have got in before the arsenic was taken.

I understand you did find some arsenic in the distal end?—Yes.

Trial of the Seddons.

Dr. William Henry Willcox

Does that in any way affect your view that this death was due to acute arsenical poisoning?—Not in the very slightest.

Why?—Because there was a considerable quantity of arsenic in the stomach—one-tenth of a grain; there was nearly two-thirds of a grain in the intestines, and that arsenic must have got in within two days of death; and the amount in the liver.

By Mr. JUSTICE BUCKNILL—Your reason, or one of your reasons, perhaps your chief reason, as I understand, for saying that this woman had had this fatal dose of arsenic administered within two days of her death is because of the amount of arsenic which you found in the stomach and the intestines?—Yes, that is the chief reason.

And your opinion is not altered at all because of arsenic found in the hair?—Not in the slightest.

By the ATTORNEY-GENERAL—Would the finding of that amount in the intestines and the stomach, in your view, show that it was acute arsenical poisoning or chronic arsenical poisoning?—There cannot be the slightest doubt as to this being a case of acute arsenical poisoning.

Can you tell me whether a gentleman skilled in medicine came to you from the defence during the course of this case?—Yes, Dr. Rosenheim, a physiological chemist.

And did you show him the mirrors which you had made?—Yes.

Did you show him the standard mirrors?—Yes.

Did you show him the results which you had got?—I showed him everything, yes. We went together through all the mirrors from every organ mentioned, and we matched together with the standard the mirrors obtained from the organs.

Had you any part of the organs left at that time?—Yes.

Was the apparatus set up?—Yes.

Was it in such a position that you could use it there and then if necessary?—Yes.

You have told us about the muscle and the result of your analysis with regard to that. You remember you said that that result was not strictly accurate, but approximate?—Yes.

You explained it that it must be approximate?—It must be approximate.

Would you just mind telling us why it cannot be strictly accurate, and must be in that case approximate?—Because it is impossible to weigh accurately all the muscles, and the amount of arsenic in them is such that it can only be determined by the method of making of mirrors, not by weighing.

Was the result which you arrived at with regard to that the best that you could obtain dealing fairly with it by these scientific tests?—Yes.

Is there any other known method than either this or the other method which you have used for the purpose of ascertaining the presence of arsenic and determining the quantity?—Neither was there in determining the amount. The muscle is not analysed, but the assumption is made as to the amount which would be present. The amount which I give as being present in the muscle is really a low one if one had not made an analysis, and had assumed what would be the amount.

Usually an assumption is made without ascertaining?—Yes.

E. Marshall Hall, Esq., K.C., M.P.

(Photograph by Swaine, New Bond Street.)

Evidence for Prosecution.

Dr. William Henry Willcox

Relatively to the other parts of the body?—Yes.

In this particular case you did not take the assumption, but you did the best you could to ascertain it?—Yes, that is so.

If you had taken the assumption which is usually taken for these purposes would you have got more or less than you actually did get?—Probably more.

So that you have taken the less quantity?—Yes.

By Mr. MARSHALL HALL—The sample you took from the intestines was not a very large amount, was it?—Yes, it was six ounces—about one-fifth of the total amount.

How was that prepared for analysis? Was it very closely mixed like with a mincing machine, or was it merely cut with a knife?—Do you mean where did I take the one-fifth from?

Yes?—I took it from different portions of the intestines so as it should be a representative part.

Each part?—Yes.

Some of the duodenum?—Yes.

And so on passing down?—Yes.

And did you mix up all those portions together very carefully?—Yes, and made them into a solution, and I weighed the arsenic which I got.

There are plenty of places to which urine can be sent for analysis for a fee of something like 5s., and an analysis can be made of it. There are plenty of places?—Yes.

The Court adjourned.

Fifth Day—Friday, 8th March, 1912.

The Court met at 11.15 a.m.

Dr. WILLIAM HENRY WILLCOX, recalled, further examined by the ATTORNEY-GENERAL—I have made experiments showing that arsenic extracted by soaking fly-papers can be administered with brandy.

Cross-examined by Mr. MARSHALL HALL—Were the standardised mirrors that were produced made expressly for this experiment, or are they kept?—I had some by me, but I made a fresh lot for this case.

You see the object of my question—because there might be a certain amount of fading?—Quite so.

Mr. MARSHALL HALL—My lord, my friend has said that he has now closed the case for the Crown, and it becomes my duty now to submit to your lordship that there is not sufficient evidence as against either of these defendants upon which they can be put in peril upon a charge of murder. I quite agree that if there is sufficient evidence the overlaying of it with prejudice does not affect the case; if there is not evidence, no amount of prejudice, put upon the top of it could create the evidence which is alone the factor upon which in our Courts persons are entitled to be tried. It would be idle to remind your lordship, with your lordship's great experience, of the presumption that nobody has ever questioned for one moment that

Trial of the Seddons.

every man accused of any offence is presumed to be innocent until the proof of his guilt is made manifest by the evidence for the prosecution.

Mr. JUSTICE BUCKNILL—What you say is that there is no such evidence here, or that there is such a small amount of evidence that I ought to tell the jury that they cannot convict?

Mr. MARSHALL HALL—That they ought not to convict.

Mr. JUSTICE BUCKNILL—That they cannot reasonably convict.

Mr. MARSHALL HALL—Exactly, my lord, that is my point. I will put it in this way. This is an absolutely unique case. In all other cases of poisoning—especially where two people have been joined together in the charge—there has always been some evidence called tracing into the possession of the persons charged the poison with which it was alleged the murder was committed. In the cases that are most familiar to us, cases tried in this Court—the case, for instance, of Lamson, and the case of Cream, and men of that sort, and in the famous case of Palmer—they were all cases where the accused had large medical knowledge, and it was possible to assume against them that they had an intimate knowledge of poisons and of their effects. In this case the position of the prosecution is greatly weakened by the fact that they have two persons in the dock. What might be strong circumstantial evidence against one of them ceases to be circumstantial evidence against one, if there are two people against whom it may apply. The Crown put two people in peril of their lives and say to the jury, "Here are two people, death resulted from poisoning" (I shall have a word to say about that in a moment). "Now, both these people had the opportunity of administering the poison during the period which our scientists say that it must have been administered; we cannot say which of them did it; we have not a particle of evidence to prove that either of them ever did it, or that there was any acting in concert, or that, indeed, any poison was actually found in the physical possession of either of these prisoners, but the motive we say in one case is so overwhelming (and we suggest in the other case that there is also a motive), that upon that evidence we ask you to convict either one or the other." Such a state of things has never been known in this country. The mere fact that they have arrested the wife after originally charging the husband is an evidence of weakness on the part of the Crown—an evidence that they had concluded that they could not bring the case home as against the man, and therefore they arrested the woman. The only object of arresting the wife— and the argument I use on behalf of the male defendant is, *a fortiori*, an argument to be used on the part of the wife—the only object of arresting the wife is to introduce mere prejudice; because, unless the wife is in the dock, the evidence of cashing bank notes which belonged to the dead woman would not be admissible evidence against the male prisoner. Therefore the only effect in this case of the introduction of the woman into the case is to get the opportunity of giving evidence of the cashing of twenty-seven bank notes by her under circumstances which the Crown say excited suspicion.

My lord, the case is weaker than that. That eccentric witness, if I may call her so, who appeared here on the first day dressed as a nurse,

Opening Speech for Defence.

Mr. Marshall Hall

and on the second day changed her dress, when before the magistrate and before the coroner swore that on three separate occasions she had seen Mrs. Seddon preparing the food, the Valentine's meat juice and the puddings and things of that kind, in the kitchen downstairs. She came into the witness-box on Tuesday and said that she had never seen anything of the sort, but "she must have done." That, I submit, is evidence of a class which a judge cannot allow to be relied upon by a jury. I submit that your lordship's duty is to say that people must not be put in peril of their lives upon such evidence. In an ordinary case, of course, the same rule would apply; there is no difference about the application of the rule in a murder case except that there is naturally greater care and caution on each side displayed in a capital case. If a man is charged with stealing sixpence, the rule of evidence is the same, but in the case of murder—the value of human life being inestimable and irreplaceable—naturally in a case of this kind one cannot but apply rules in the strictest possible sense.

My learned friend, the Attorney-General, cannot point to any particle of direct evidence that either of these people ever possessed arsenic in any shape or form, or that they ever administered it. That is a very strong proposition, and I submit that it is all the stronger because the prosecution have said in their opening of this case, and in their conduct of it, "We do not direct our evidence more against one prisoner than against the other; here are the two people who had the opportunity of administering the poison, against one of whom we prove a motive." My lord, if interest is to amount to motive, any person who is interested in the death of another person has a motive to kill that person if by the person's death the other person benefits. The mere fact that this man, having given an annuity for a term of years, would benefit if the annuity ceased immediately, as it would do upon her death, is put forward as a motive for committing the crime of murder. But my learned friend is not content with that. He drags into this case—I will not say he drags in, because my learned friend has conducted this case, as he always conducts any case, with perfect fairness—but he felt coerced—and I am sure he would not have done it unless he had felt coerced—to bring into the case this further motive. It is one that your lordship and the jury must examine most minutely and cautiously. The motive my learned friend puts forward is this, that this man deliberately murdered this woman in order to obtain possession of a large sum in gold and notes. It will not do if at the time the woman died he had in his possession money which was not his. That is not the charge. This man is not charged with dishonesty, as your lordship was careful to point out to the jury earlier in the case. Therefore the entirety of the motive has to be dealt with, and the entirety of the motive is that this man murdered the woman for the purpose of obtaining possession of her property. That is not supported by a particle of evidence. The only direct evidence of any sort or shape in this case is the evidence of the little boy, Ernie Grant, who says, "I on one occasion saw the prisoner Seddon administer a drink to Miss Barrow which was a clear drink like water." Then when he is cross-examined by me (of course, upon instruc-

Trial of the Seddons.

Mr. Marshall Hall

tions) he admits that it was the mixture together of the two solutions, so as to make it an effervescing draught—as clear as water, and *ex hypothesi*, it could not possibly have been water containing a fly-paper solution, because such water would be discoloured.

I pass to another point. Is there any proof here—any proper proof —and this, my lord, is peculiarly for your lordship—any proof upon which the jury can act, that this woman died of arsenic poisoning? All things are to be presumed to be rightly done. We have got the certificate here that she died of epidemic diarrhœa. Dr. Willcox and Dr. Spilsbury (who, I again say, gave their evidence with absolute fairness), Dr. Sworn and Dr. Paul all admit that unless there was evidence to satisfy them con- clusively that there is this large quantity of arsenic in the body, the certificate of death would have been thoroughly justified, and that all the symptoms of death from gastro enteritis are the same as the symptoms of death from arsenical poisoning. I say that the balance of evidence is such as to leave it so uncertain that your lordship ought not to leave the case to the jury. Dr. Willcox says that by a process of calculation he has arrived at the determination honestly arrived at—no one suggests for a moment anything against the honesty and fairness of his evidence— that there was present in this body practically two grains of arsenic. And he is borne out in that view by the fact that the body is in what he considers an abnormal state of preservation, having regard to the state in which he found it at the time the autopsy was made. That is the only point that goes to destroy the suggestion of death from gastro enteritis.

On the question of arsenical poisoning you cannot reject the evidence which was sifted most exhaustively before the Royal Commission that the presence of arsenic in the hair is strong evidence that there has been a course of arsenic-taking, and Dr. Willcox admitted that that would point to the taking of arsenic for a period of perhaps twelve months, and we know that arsenic is a remedy for asthma, from which this woman suffered. The whole of the evidence in this case is totally different from the evidence in any other case of which we have any record. It is entirely construc- tive evidence; it is entirely argumentative evidence, and your lordship will not fail to appreciate the minute quantity of arsenic which was alleged to have been deposited upon the mirrors which were produced as the evidence of arsenic in this case.

Now, my lord, there is one flaw in the Marsh test which I have often wanted to have an opportunity of referring to in these Courts. The Marsh test for arsenic is a splendid test to detect the presence of arsenic, that is to say, whether arsenic is or is not present in the tested solution. But if your lordship takes the evidence that has been given by Dr. Will- cox, there is a defect in that test for the purpose of measuring the quantity of arsenic. From the very nature of the experiment it is absolutely essential that the quantity of arsenic to be deposited upon that mirror tube must be infinitesimal, and unless it is infinitesimal you will find that it destroys itself, because it becomes so opaque that the purpose for which the experiment is being performed is not served. I have not in my mind what the range of standardised mirrors is. I do not know what is the smallest portion and what is the largest portion of a milligramme.

Opening Speech for Defence.

Mr. Marshall Hall

I think we have it that it is from the thirtieth to the fifth of a milligramme. Does your lordship realise what a milligramme is—the two-thousandth part of a grain, or, to be accurate, the 1944th part of a grain. How is that mirror prepared? It is prepared by the introduction of a known quantity of arsenic into a certain amount of matter for the purpose of testing. Nobody suggests for a moment that you can introduce the exact thirtieth of a milligramme of arsenic into the solution. You have to make a solution, and you have to put a certain quantity in and break it up, and assume that it is equally distributed, and then take a portion which represents the thirtieth part of a milligramme. The process is destructive of accurate quantities for this reason. There is the formation of a gas; arseniuretted hydrogen is formed, but, if arsenic is present, the hydrogen becomes converted. Dr. Willcox says, "If I put what I know to be the thirtieth part of a milligramme into the solution and test it by the Marsh test I get this mirror which is in that form," but there is no evidence whatever that the whole thirtieth of a milligramme of arsenic is deposited in the making of that mirror—none whatever. This being a gas which is passing off, you cannot analyse the gas which passes off in the form of hydrogen. How do we know that some portion of the arsenic has not passed off in the gas and not been deposited on the tube? If that is so, the quantity deposited on the tube may be much less than the 1944th part of a grain. If it is much less it will make an enormous difference in the calculation, because Dr. Willcox tells us that the most minute particle of arsenic will be reflected on the mirror. If you get the minutest fraction of error in your calculation it results in a most enormously magnified error, because the multiplying factor is nearly 2000. Not only that, but with the greatest skill in the world it comes to be a question of the most marvellous eyesight. You have to differentiate between different shades of colours, differing in so minute a way that the most clever observer cannot detect the difference.

Upon the question whether there is affirmative and indisputable evidence that this woman died of arsenic poisoning the calculation under which the total amount of arsenic present in the body is arrived at is a calculation which is dependent, first of all, upon this most minute experiment dealing with the 30th of a milligramme of arsenic. There is no evidence whatever that the total 30th of a milligramme is the test solution deposited on the mirror; and the slightest error will be multiplied by 2000 in arriving at your calculation. My lord, I say that that is evidence so fine, so nice, that where you have got a large amount of prejudice it becomes the duty of the judge to see that the prejudice is neutralised as much as possible.

Mr. Justice Bucknill—That is always done by the judge in his summing up.

Mr. Marshall Hall—I quite agree, my lord, but I submit that the evidence here is so infinitesimal—it is like the 30th part of a milligramme of arsenic—the evidence is so small that it would be dangerous—whatever the suspicion in this case may be it would be dangerous to submit this case to the determination of a jury whose minds are biased—of course, perfectly honestly—I do not mean to reflect in the slightest way upon

Trial of the Seddons.

the jury at all, but it is your lordship's province if you think that there is no sufficient evidence—that is the proper word—no sufficient evidence—upon which the prisoners should be put in peril—it is your lordship's province and your lordship's duty to say, in your judicial capacity, that there is not sufficient evidence to go to the jury, and your lordship should withdraw the case from them.

Mr. RENTOUL—My lord, I desire to identify myself, on behalf of Mrs. Seddon, with every word that my learned friend Mr. Marshall Hall has said, especially with regard to the medical evidence. Of course, everything that he has said on behalf of the male prisoner applies *a fortiori* to the female prisoner. But, speaking generally on the case for the prosecution that has been made out against Mrs. Seddon, however weak it may be against the male prisoner, it is immeasurably weaker against the female prisoner; in fact, so weak, my lord, that I do wish strongly to submit to your lordship that against her there is no evidence at all which your lordship could safely allow to go to the jury.

Mr. JUSTICE BUCKNILL—It has been submitted by the learned counsel on behalf of each of the prisoners, in the first place, that is to say, with regard to the man, there is not sufficient evidence to justify the jury in coming to a verdict hostile to the defendants, and so, on behalf of the woman, it has been argued that there is no evidence at all. In all capital cases which I have tried during the many years I have been on the bench when similar arguments have been addressed to the Court which I have not been able to accept, I have taken care to confine myself to one observation, so that it would be impossible for any one to think that I have formed any opinion in the matter, and I do that to-day. I confine my observation to saying that the case must proceed.

Mr. MARSHALL HALL—My lord, I shall call the male prisoner and witnesses as to facts.

Opening Speech for the Defence.

May it please your lordship. Gentlemen of the jury, a good deal of what I have to say to you, gentlemen, has been said to my lord in your hearing just now, and therefore I will not recapitulate it. A great deal of what I should have had to say to you I have said to my lord, and I dare say you will have noticed that I was watching to see whether you were giving it the same careful attention which you have paid to the whole of this case. Therefore, so far as that portion of my argument goes, I need not recapitulate it here. I shall have another opportunity at a later stage of addressing you, and after the patience you have shown through the whole of this case I am not going to take up your time unduly. The case is a strain upon all of us—I care not whether it be the learned judge who sits there, or my learned friend who sits here, whom I have known for so many years, and whom I admire and respect—it is not affectation on my part to say so—and, as to myself, after many years' experience of these Courts, I can say honestly that I trust this may be the last big capital case in which I shall ever be engaged. The strain upon counsel in these cases is a great deal more than you can possibly realise; but, gentlemen, do not think that I disguise from myself that the greatest

Opening Speech for Defence.

Mr. Marshall Hall

strain, after all, is upon you, and I am, to the last degree, grateful for the attention which you have given, and I know will give, to the end of this case, although it has involved, in your case, the giving up of your home life and the sacrifice of a great many other things. But, gentlemen, when you come to deal with the question of human life there is no one who is not prepared to make a sacrifice in order to come to a just and righteous conclusion. With those few prefatory remarks I will, if you will allow me, proceed with the few words I have to say in opening this case on behalf of the male prisoner, Seddon. The female prisoner is defended by my learned friend Mr. Rentoul. I am appearing for her husband, and, to some extent, my defence, of course, must cover her defence as well, but I am not going to encroach upon my learned friend's province. He will have an opportunity of addressing you, and, at the proper time, he will no doubt adopt such of my arguments as he may approve of, and he will advance such further arguments as he thinks fit in the interests of his own client.

Gentlemen, I will deal with the case very shortly, and I will, first of all, say just a few words upon the great responsibility which attaches to you in this case in consequence of the prejudice with which it is surrounded. The prejudice is really a real danger in this case, because you have to be more than ordinarily careful here to remember that the only charge that we are investigating, the only direct issue in this case (I know my lord will tell you so) is, did the male prisoner, Frederick Henry Seddon, or did his wife, Margaret Seddon, either acting singly or jointly administer a fatal dose of arsenic, or series of fatal doses of arsenic —because there is a certain variation now between the case as opened and the case as conducted at the Police Court—did he, or she, or both, administer either one dose or a series of fatal doses of arsenic between the 2nd September and the 14th? We need not go behind those dates, because there is no suggestion of any earlier date than that.

I have already pointed, and my lord, I know, will also point out, that you cannot deal with a case of this kind upon suspicion. It does not matter how great the suspicion may be, it does not matter how overwhelming you may think the motive is, it does not matter how mean and despicable you think the conduct may be of the man who is charged. That is not sufficient to convict him of the charge of murder. You must be satisfied in your own minds that the person whom you are going to find guilty, if it is one person, of this offence—either he or she—administered this arsenic with the intention of destroying the life of the person to whom it was administered. You can, of course, say, if you think there is any evidence upon which you can find it, that these two people acting together jointly and in concert determined to do away with this unfortunate woman —combined together to murder this woman by, perhaps, one preparing and the other administering the dose or doses of arsenic. Gentlemen, I say at the outset upon that that I submit to you that there is no evidence you can act upon as men of the world. You may have suspicion. You may feel that here there is a motive which is a strong motive as against the male prisoner; you may feel that he has behaved badly in the unfortunate matter of the funeral; you may feel many things which are to his prejudice; but I submit to you that there is no evidence whatever upon

Trial of the Seddons.

which you can find him guilty of the administration of this poison; and it is only by finding him guilty of the administration of this poison that you can find him guilty on the indictment upon which he is charged.   As an advocate, if I were dealing with this case as an ordinary case, where the case for the Crown is closed, I would suggest to you that the proper course for me to pursue would be to rest upon the contention I have made, and to say, so satisfied am I that my contention is sound that, although my lord cannot say that there is absolutely no evidence, and I can trust my lord to point out to you what a small amount of evidence there is—which I must presume now to exist because my lord has held that the case must go to you—I might trust to that and say I will call no witnesses, and will trust entirely to the weakness of the case for the Crown in order to defeat its own proposition.   But, gentlemen, this is a capital case; this is a case where there are no means of remedying a mistake if once made; there are no means of getting back that which may be, in consequence of your verdict, absolutely taken away.   Therefore, in my view—and I say it publicly—it is for the prisoner to elect what is the proper course for him to take; and in this case both prisoners (I am instructed that my learned friend will adopt the same course)— both prisoners desire to go into the box, and to take advantage of the privilege that has been given them of giving evidence in cases of this kind, and both of them promise to go into the box and tell you their own story.

I do not know—I have no means of knowing—whether or not my learned friend will think it necessary to pursue a line of cross-examination with regard to the male prisoner somewhat indicated by the line of his opening.   There will be a nice question for my lord to decide whether such a cross-examination is admissible in this case.   It is a rule of our Courts, laid down at the time when the law enacted that prisoners might give evidence on their own behalf, that they are not liable to be cross-examined as to the commission of any other offence unless the commission of such an offence is a material part of the question whether they are guilty or innocent of the crime with which they are charged.   Where a prisoner is charged with the most serious offence known to the law there is the danger that your judgments may be warped and your minds pre-judiced by a cross-examination designed to show that after this woman's death he took possession of money which he has denied strenuously he ever saw, and the existence of which, I submit, has never been satis-factorily proved.   Gentlemen, that is a matter which will be dealt with in cross-examination.   I shall be able to prove before you, fortunately by independent witnesses, that in 1909, long before the existence of Miss Barrow was ever known to him, this man was in the habit of keeping large sums of money, to the amount of £200 in gold, in his house—long before Miss Barrow was ever heard of.   Fortunately I am able to call inde-pendent witnesses who will prove that.   In addition to his insurance business, he had another little business from which some ready money came.   He had a sort of mania for keeping money.   He had two safes in the house.   The arguments upon this more properly belong to the final speech that I have to make; I am merely now indicating the line of evidence I shall call.   I shall call before you witnesses who are above any suspicion whatever, who will tell you that as early as 1909 this man

Opening Speech for Defence.

Mr. Marshall Hall

had two safes, one in his bedroom and one in his office downstairs, and that he kept as much as £200 in the house; you will hear that upon one occasion he had as much as £230 all in gold.

Gentlemen, the suggestion of the prosecution is that immediately before this woman died—that is, what the question really comes to—if you are going to deal with Hook's evidence—the most tainted evidence, I suggest, that you could possibly deal with—that there was some £400, or £500, or £600, in this box—I do not quite know whether the suggestion is that this man took possession of this money, and such a callous, hard-hearted brute was he that on the very day that he murdered the woman he took possession of the money—that when he murdered this woman on that very afternoon he did not wait, but took the gold from the room where the woman died down into the safe downstairs, and then paraded it before his fellow-employees—money which he had just obtained by the murder of the woman. One's own intelligence, I think, shudders and revolts at a suggestion of that kind. Is it credible that a man would do anything of that kind in that way at that moment, and under the circumstances which are alleged against him?

There is another point which my learned friend will have to grapple with when he comes to deal with this case. I pointed it out to my lord just now, and I need only just indicate it to you again. You will find in the history of these cases of murder by poisoning that the person convicted of poisoning has been generally a person who has an intimate medical knowledge of poisons. What evidence is there here that this man knew— did any of you know—ask yourselves—did any one of you gentlemen know that the symptoms of acute arsenical poisoning were identical with the symptoms of epidemic diarrhœa? Unless you do know it, it seems to me that it is incredible to suggest that this man should poison this woman with arsenic. For some reason, although there is a special Act of Parliament dealing with arsenic, as far as one can judge from what one knows of things in general, the facility with which arsenic can be purchased in the form of weed killers and things of that kind, is extraordinary; but I take it that that is because it is so improbable that anybody should administer a poison so agonisingly painful as arsenic when there are so many poisons that are painless and difficult of detection that it is hardly credible that anybody would administer arsenic. But is it credible that a man of his position in life, having this woman ill in his house—and there is no suggestion whatever that those visits of Dr. Paul were caused by anything but illness—she is complaining of congestion of the liver and pain up to the 22nd August—there is no suggestion that that was not genuine—should go to a strange doctor, and then, when on the 2nd September she is suddenly taken really ill, be so bold, such a hardened criminal, and so skilled that he knows that he can now safely administer arsenic in minute quantities, because she has now got epidemic diarrhœa, as to bounce the situation by calling in a medical man who will attend all through, and who does attend, and never has the smallest suspicions, and who at the end certifies that death is due to epidemic diarrhœa? Then I suggest to you another matter for your consideration. It is now admitted, having regard to all these public institutions which exist—you cannot have it both ways— that if this man's medical knowledge was such—and I suppose it will have

Trial of the Seddons.

to be suggested (although he will tell you on his oath that he never bought any arsenic in his life, and that he knows nothing about poisons, or the peculiar effect of arsenic)—it will have to be suggested that he knows so much about it as to know that it will not be possible to distinguish at all between the symptoms of arsenical poisoning and the symptoms of epidemic diarrhœa; and he has the audacity to adopt arsenic as his means of poison, when in these days there are hospitals and other institutions where upon payment of a small fee any doctor attending to a case may go and have the excreta, or anything else, analysed without troubling himself to do it. It is a very strong proposition.

Gentlemen, there is another matter that you will have to deal with, and in opening this case it is a matter that I should like to say a few words about. There is one witness whose evidence, speaking on behalf of the male prisoner, I resent. I refer to the evidence of Mr. Thorley. I was rather hampered at the moment in cross-examining him, because it was so unnecessary to call him at all. I suggest to you that his evidence is totally unreliable. It is a very fair instance, I suggest, of the danger of identification of this kind. The position Mr. Thorley takes up is this, "In the month of December I was approached by several policemen who asked me if I could identify a girl who bought fly-papers; I knew," says Thorley, "at that time that this North London case was going on." You can imagine what sensation was caused in this immediate neighbourhood where these people lived. He knew the name of Seddon, because Seddon was the person charged. It took place in September, and he knew that Seddon had given evidence, and it was all over London—"The North London Mystery." "The police came several times, and I told them that I could not identify anybody. It was a fact that I found on looking at the books that I had sold a packet of fly-papers on the 26th August, 1911, but I could not identify that girl." Now, what do we know? That several efforts were made by the police——

The ATTORNEY-GENERAL—He did not say that he could not identify anybody.

Mr. MARSHALL HALL—He said that the police called several times, and he told them that he could not identify the purchaser. However, I am in your hands, gentlemen; you are the judges of this. The impression that Mr. Thorley conveyed to me, and which I am trying to re-convey back to you, was that he led the police to understand when they called upon him early in December that he did not think he could identify the purchaser—I do not care whether he said he could not identify her, or did not think he could identify her; it amounts to the same thing. If this girl who bought these fly-papers on the 26th August was Margaret Seddon he must have known then that it was the same girl who had called to see his daughter Mabel on two occasions. Therefore all he had to do to elucidate the identity of the purchaser was to ask his daughter Mabel, "Who is the girl who calls for you?" the girl would at once have said, "Why, that's Margaret Seddon." Then he would at once say, "Well, of course, I cannot identify her personally, but I can tell you that she is the same girl who called to see my daughter, and my daughter tells me that her name is Margaret Seddon." Then on 2nd February this man is taken down in the motor to the Police Court; he is taken to

Opening Speech for Defence.

Mr. Marshall Hall

the Police Court first for the purpose of identifying—whom? For the purpose of identifying Margaret Seddon, whose portrait he has seen in the illustrated papers as connected with this particular case. And so when he goes down, and twenty people are put in a room before him, the first person he sees has a face that is familiar to him for two reasons—it is familiar to him because it is the face of the girl who has twice been in his shop and seen his daughter, and, secondly, he recognises her from her portrait; it is familiar to him because it is the face of the girl dressed identically as she is dressed in the picture published broadcast in the public press. So that with all the honest intention in the world—and I do not for one shadow of a second suggest against Mr. Thorley that he is doing anything deliberately dishonest or with any intention of deceiving the Court, but he has persuaded himself that the girl he identifies, and does really and properly identify, as the girl who had been to see his daughter, and as the girl whose photograph he had seen in the public press, he identifies her as the girl who bought the fly-papers in August, 1911. Gentlemen, upon that evidence of identity you would not, I was going to say, give effect to it supposing that this was a question of identifying a person upon the most simple charge, but certainly in the case of a person indicted upon the capital charge you would not treat it seriously at all.

I submit that the identity of the girl as the person who purchased fly-papers on that day there is absolutely valueless. But, gentlemen, it is valuable to me for this reason—and this reason only—that it shows the weakness of my learned friend's case. If the Crown, with all their resources, with the whole of Scotland Yard and the detective force at their command, with unlimited money to spend, with the facility of making any inquiries they choose—if that is the best evidence of the purchase of fly-papers that there is against these people, it shows how very weak their case must be; because if that is the link in the chain—and no chain is stronger than its weakest link—how weak that link is. I should be sorry to have to rest, if I were prosecuting a person upon any indictment, upon a chain of which that link formed a small component.

The prosecution are bound to formulate some definite theory with regard to this poisoning. Their case is not that arsenic was obtained from any other source, but that fly-papers were purchased, and that from fly-papers was extracted arsenic, and that arsenic in the form of a coloured solution was administered to this unfortunate woman until her death was caused. Gentlemen, that is a far-reaching proposition, and there are a great many premises which you will have to accept before you act upon it. First of all, you have got to presuppose that Seddon knew—did any of you know?—that these papers contained arsenic; I doubt it; I do not know what your knowledge is, but I doubt very much, whether, knowing as we do, the deadly nature of arsenic, we could conceive it credible that the Legislature would allow fly-papers containing such deadly poison to be sold haphazard to any child who went into a shop and asked for them. The very fact that these things can be obtained is of itself destructive of the proposition that the person who bought them knew the quantity of poison that they contained. That is the first proposition that has to be assumed against me before you come to the second part of the pro-

Trial of(the Seddons.

position. The second part of the proposition is that not only did Seddon know that these papers contained this arsenic, but that he knew that the arsenic could be abstracted from them. Did any of you know that? Ask yourselves. I cannot tell what your ranks in life are, but your own knowledge in these matters is important. I am never so astonished as I am every day of my life at my own ignorance when I find that I know so little about matters about which other people know so much. I dare say you will agree with me that it is very improbable that any of you twelve gentlemen would know either the quantity of arsenic which is now proved to be contained in these fly-papers, or that you knew that that arsenic could be extracted in a fluid form by treatment of the paper. It appears now that Dr. Willcox has made it public to the world that if you do it scientifically with boiling water you can get in some cases as much as six grains, and from another paper that was got from one particular shop—I do not know whether that shopkeeper has any special arrangement with Messrs. Mather, by which he gets a specially strong fly-paper—but still there is the fact that out of one fly-paper he got five or six grains by boiling for a certain number of hours; as you boil it it increases the colour, because you get out the colouring matter, and so you make it less useful for the purpose of its being given to a person without detection and without exciting suspicion. That is another premise that you have to assume. Then Dr. Willcox says with cold water you can get out a grain and a half—and you do not get such a strongly coloured decoction then. Again I ask you gentlemen, did you know that? Is everything to be assumed against this man that he knew all these scientific facts; is it to be assumed that he knew how to treat these fly-papers in the best possible way to get these poisonous matters? Gentlemen, I do not know where we are going in assumptions against this man. There is no evidence that he ever got a fly-paper in his life; there is no evidence that he ever had a fly-paper in his hands in his life, but it is all to be assumed against him because, forsooth, he benefits to the extent of about £2000 by the early death of this woman. Why are they troubling with the fly-papers at all? Because my learned friends have no other case which they could find to put before any jury; because a man cannot buy arsenic in the ordinary way except by signing a poisons book.

We know that in a case which excited the whole country a few months ago the purchase of a far more deadly poison than arsenic was entered in the poisons book and signed for by the man who purchased it. Here there is no question that arsenic was procured from anybody else, and so they are driven to the fly-papers. From whom does the suggestion as to the fly-papers arise? From the defence; it is in consequence of something that happened on 6th December, that Mr. Thorley told us about, that this fly-paper theory is put forward. What was it? On the 4th December—and never was there a more important factor in a case than the one statement of Inspector Ward in this case—one of the most cogent and important words—and, gentlemen, I warn you that a word may make all the difference in a case of this kind—one of the most important statements was this. The first thing Inspector Ward says to Seddon is, " I am arresting you on a charge of murdering Miss Barrow by arsenic."

Opening Speech for Defence.

Mr. Marshall Hall

"Arsenic? Murder? She could not have done it herself. Arsenic?" And on the 4th December this man is arrested. Of course, it is known that he is arrested on the charge of poisoning by arsenic. Although you know that legally you are not bound to prove your innocence, he had said, "I can prove my innocence of this"—but "arsenic—what on earth can I have had that contained arsenic; where is arsenic?" Then they remember that they have had some of Mather's fly-papers (which I will deal with in a moment) in the month of August; and in order to ascertain whether these fly-papers did, in fact, contain arsenic sufficient for a fatal dose, on the 6th December the girl, Margaret, on the instructions of the solicitor for the defence, goes into the shop of Mr. Price; he was the gentleman, you will remember, who wanted to give you a little exposition; you will remember the gentleman with the grey beard. On the 6th December she goes to that shop, watched by the police, or, anyhow, in the knowledge of the police; because the next day the police themselves go to the same shop and buy fly-papers; they either watched the girl or got information that she had gone to the shop; I do not care which; for all I know it may be that the solicitor told them, but we have the fact that the police go themselves the very next day to the same shop for the purpose of buying fly-papers from that shop. It is because Margaret Seddon went to buy some fly-papers for the purpose of experiment on the 6th December that this theory of poisoning by fly-papers is set up by the prosecution. On the part of the Crown there is not a tittle of evidence of the presence of fly-papers in this house. All the witnesses called for the prosecution I cross-examined as to whether they had seen fly-papers. It does not matter to me two straws, because I am going to prove that there were fly-papers, and I am going to put into the witness-box the person who bought them. Margaret Seddon did not buy them; she did go for one on the 6th December, and the chemist would not serve her; but she never bought any fly-papers herself. It is because on the 6th December fly-papers are bought for the purpose of seeing whether these Mather's fly-papers contain sufficient arsenic in them that the police go to the same shop to purchase fly-papers in order to experiment to see whether there is arsenic in those papers, and whether by any possibility the arsenic could have been got from the papers—it is through this that, on the instructions of the solicitor, who has displayed conspicuous ability in this case, young Mr. Saint, who instructs me—it was upon his instructions that Margaret Seddon was sent to buy fly-papers for the purpose of their testing them to see whether they did, in fact, contain a poisonous dose of arsenic. It is in consequence of that that the fly-paper theory is advanced.

But, again, what is the presumption? Assuming, and assuming effectively, the fly-papers were in this house. It is part of the case for the Crown—and for once I am at one with my learned friend; that is part of my case—that fly-papers were in this house. When I say fly-papers, I am dealing with arsenical fly-papers all along—Mather's fly-papers; whether they were Mather's I do not know, but arsenical fly-papers —papers that you wet and the flies drink it; those are the papers that I am talking of. They were in this house at this time; but what evidence is there that there was a poisonous dose? It is not for me to prove my

Trial of the Seddons.

Mr. Marshall Hall

defence, and I am merely making a suggestion. I am going to suggest that this woman, parched with thirst, a raging thirst, and not strong in her mind, with this clear fluid available—because I understand it does not show any colouring; I am only putting this forward as a mere possibility or suggestion; there is no evidence of it one way or the other, because, if it did take place, *ex hypothesi* she is alone and unattended. Why may she not, in her raging thirst, have drunk some of the water in which fly-papers had been soaked, or some of it may have got into whatever she was taking (that is assuming that you are satisfied that death resulted from arsenic); may not something of that sort have happened through the servant—that hare-brained woman—without intending for a moment to administer arsenic, leaving something of this sort about; might that not have happened with a slovenly 5s. a week servant, and so the whole thing have been brought about by mere accident? But it is said, no, everything of this kind is to be eliminated from the case; the possibility of accident is to be eliminated. Oh, no, they say, it could not possibly be an accidental death on the part of this woman, because there is such motive for Seddon doing it. There is no evidence of Seddon doing it, but you must eliminate the possibility of the woman's death being caused by accident because the motive for Seddon committing the crime is over-whelming, and therefore you must convict him of the murder.

Gentlemen, did you notice the evidence of Dr. Sworn? I asked him about flies. He said he never in his life saw so many flies in a sick-room as when he went there early in September. And he gave the reason: the flies were drawn there by the fœtid smell of the urine and excrement, and so forth, that was passing from this unfortunate woman in her acute diarrhœa. Mrs. Seddon will tell you when she goes into the witness-box that she bought some fly-papers, and she will tell you the shop, she will tell you the place of the chemist where she bought them early in September, and that she bought them in consequence of a request of Miss Barrow that something should be done to mitigate the nuisance of these flies. If you have ever been ill yourself in hot weather, you will know how deplorable a thing is the presence of flies in a sick-room. I suppose there is no source of irritation in a serious illness that is so trying as the constant buzzing and settling of flies upon the exposed parts of the skin; I suggest to you that there is nothing more terrible or irritating to the invalid except, of course, the agonising pain. Mrs. Seddon will tell you in her evidence that in consequence of the request of Miss Barrow that something should be done to mitigate this nuisance of flies, fly-papers, or something, should be bought, but she particularly requested that Mrs. Seddon should not buy those nasty, sticky things. You, gentlemen, probably know these sticky fly-papers—the flies with their little feet stick on to the paper, and they keep buzzing, buzzing, in their anxiety, until this gummy stuff which is holding them to death takes effect. I think you will agree that to introduce such fly-papers into a sick-room, the remedy is worse than the disease. That is why this other form of fly-paper is so popular—because it is absolutely non-irritating; the flies drink the liquid in which the paper is put, and they do not die in the liquid, but they go elsewhere and seek their place of death where they like, having been poisoned by the arsenic in the liquid.

Opening Speech for Defence.

Mr. Marshall Hall

Therefore gentlemen, for what it is worth, it is admitted that in this sick-room there were fly-papers put early in September. Mrs. Seddon, racking her brain to think of any possible explanation of any way in which this could have got accidentally into any portion of the food which Miss Barrow may have taken, can think of nothing except that upon one occasion the contents of four saucers were emptied into one plate, and she is not quite sure of what was done with the plate temporarily; whether it was put on the wash-stand she is not able to say definitely.

Do not forget that it is no part of my case here to prove my client's innocence. The presumption is that he is innocent until that presumption is displaced by evidence of guilt. It is not for the defence to prove the innocence of the person accused. Therefore, all I can do to assist you in coming to a right conclusion is to put two or three hypotheses before you upon which you can find a verdict not adverse to the client I represent.

Gentlemen, I will not deal with that in any further detail. At some further stage of this case after the evidence is concluded, I shall have, of course, to deal rather exhaustively with the evidence, and to put before you finally the position I take up on the part of my client. Of course, it is impossible for us to finish this case this week—quite impossible—and there will be some opportunity later on for me to prepare what I have to say when all the evidence is concluded and the cross-examination is over, and I shall have an opportunity of finally addressing you. My learned friend, the Attorney-General, whether I called evidence or not, would have the right of reply—the right inherent in his great office, but, of course, now there is no question of his having right in his official capacity. I am going to call evidence as to facts, and therefore he would be entitled in any event to reply. When the evidence is concluded I shall address you, and my learned friend, Mr. Rentoul, will address you on behalf of his client; then my learned friend will reply, and, finally, my lord will sum up. Gentlemen, all I press upon you is this—to keep your minds open. Do not let in prejudice, which must inevitably tend to warp your judgment in a case of this kind. Be men, and throw it away. Do not allow prejudice to enter your mind. If it does influence you, let it influence you in favour of this man; because it is more dangerous to deal with a man judicially against whom you are prejudiced than it is to deal with a man against whom you have no prejudice at all. Prejudice is a grave danger, and therefore, as prejudice has and will be excited in this case as against the male defendant—I know not whether it will be excited against the female defendant, but, as it will be excited against the male defendant, as you will, of course, feel that if there is a true case against him, it is a cruel, cowardly, and despicable murder—let this be in your mind, that taking all things together, the fact that this man has for twenty-one years been in honest and respectable employment without complaint of any sort or shape, with practically unlimited control of money for a time, with the actual power of paying the company's money into his own account and dealing with it as his own instead of as their agent; having regard to all this, is it credible that a man would have committed a murder such as this in the scientific way in which it is alleged that he did it?

Trial of the Seddons.

Mr. Marshall Hall

Do not forget one thing more. If this man is the clever poisoner that you must find him if you accept the theory of the prosecution, is it credible that he was not one little bit cleverer still? He had got a medical certificate of death. It is admitted that on the body as it lay there were no objective symptoms from which that certificate could have been questioned. He had only to get another medical man to view that body and give him a certificate, and, within a few yards from where he lived, that body could have been taken to the Golder's Green Crematorium and have been burnt to ashes. Is it credible that a man who is such a clever poisoner as this would have left undone that final piece of skilful work which he is supposed to have done? He had got one doctor's certificate; it is volunteered to him; he did not even ask for it; the symptoms are admitted to be identical with the symptoms of epidemic diarrhœa. There is not a shadow of suspicion against him. He could have had the body cremated merely upon the production of a second certificate; that is all the law requires. You have to have the certificate of two medical men as to the cause of death, and, upon the production of two certificates, the body could have been cremated, and every possible evidence of this crime would have disappeared.

I suggest, first of all, that the commission of such a crime by this man is incredible; that it showed a knowledge of poisons which this man never possessed, and which cannot be attributed to him. Therefore, it is incredible, and almost impossible, that he committed the murder. But I submit further that even if you think that he may have committed the murder, you must take the one thing with the other; if he knew so much, if he was so hardened a criminal that he could deliberately lay himself out to commit this crime for the purpose of gaining money, it is incredible that he should not have taken, as he could have taken, this one step further; he had only to call upon Dr. Paul, who lived in the neighbourhood, who had attended to this woman before, who had seen the body and knew of the smell in the room, and so forth—everything consistent with death from epidemic diarrhœa, and in all human probability that doctor would have granted a second certificate upon the certificate of Dr. Sworn, and then this man could have disposed for ever of all evidence of his crime. If he knew as much as is attributed to him by the prosecution in this case; if he had studied the question of arsenical poisoning, one of the first things he must have found out would have been that which has been brought to light time after time in the criminal records of this very Court, that arsenic has one very extraordinary effect; it preserves the body instead of destroying it; it preserves the evidence of the administration of the deadly poison, so that it is ready for postmortem examination and detection at a later date, whenever that postmortem examination takes place. I say that if a man has studied sufficiently to administer arsenic for the consideration suggested by the prosecution, it is an inference that you must draw that he would inevitably have reckoned that the danger of arsenical poisoning is that it preserves the body from any destructive change, and therefore it is incredible that a man who has the iron will necessary to commit a murder of this kind

Opening Speech for Defence.

Mr. Marshall Hall

should not go one step further and destroy the body of his victim, and destroy all evidence of his crime by having the body cremated.

Gentlemen, as I say, I do not profess to have dealt exhaustively with the case now, or to have dealt with it even in its general bearings; I have merely given you the outline of the line of defence which we shall adopt in this case. I will call my witnesses before you, and, having called them, I shall ask you to say when I address you again, whatever your suspicions may be, whatever the prejudice may be, that there is no evidence whatever upon which you can possibly convict, and therefore you must say that, as the evidence for the prosecution has fallen short of the quantum of proof which is necessary to prove the crime alleged against this man, you must say that he is entitled to acquittal at your hands. I do not ask that he shall have the benefit of the doubt, but he demands at your hands the acquittal which every man in this country is entitled to, unless the evidence for the prosecution is sufficient to justify his conviction.

Evidence for the Defence.

SYDNEY ARTHUR NAYLOR, examined by Mr. DUNSTAN—I am a member of the firm of Sydney Naylor & Co., auctioneers, 256 High Road, Tottenham. I have known Seddon for about six years or more. I remember meeting him in June or July, 1909, in connection with the Legion of Frontiersmen, of which he was a member. After the meeting, which was held in the Hornsey Wood Tavern, Seven Sisters Road, we went to his shop, which was also in the Seven Sisters Road; he had a wardrobe business there. He said he was doing very well there, and, as a matter of fact, he produced several costumes to me that he had purchased for a very low figure, and which he anticipated he would sell for very good sums. I think he mentioned that he would probably get 35s. for something that he had bought for 5s., or something like that. After supper we were discussing business generally, and Mr. Seddon spoke about his insurance business and his wardrobe business, saying how successful he was, and the profits he was making, and so forth. He left the room and returned with a bag of gold which he showed to me. He mentioned the amount was about £200; I formed the opinion that it was something between £150 and £200.

Cross-examined by the ATTORNEY-GENERAL—Mr. Seddon lived over the wardrobe shop in Seven Sisters Road. He mentioned that he had the money that I have told about by him in order to pick up any cheap stocks—that he would have to pay cash when they would not accept a cheque. I could not exactly say when he ceased to carry that business on, but I understand he was in the business for about twelve months. I believe he went from Seven Sisters Road to Tollington Park, where there was only his insurance business carried on.

WILLIAM JOHN WILSON, examined by Mr. MARSHALL HALL—I am a post office employee, and I live at 81 St. Stephen's Avenue. I was present on the occasion when Mr. Seddon and Mr. Naylor were together

Trial of the Seddons.

William John Wilson

in 1909. During the evening Mr. Seddon produced a bag of gold, but he did not say how much was in it. I estimated the amount at about £200.

Cross-examined by the ATTORNEY-GENERAL—About two months ago, or somewhere about that, I was asked if I knew anything about this case. The money was in a buff-coloured bag, a plain bag, with no name on it whatever. It looked to me to be a rather rough paper bag. Seddon told me that it was gold that was in it; he opened it, and put his hand in, and withdrew some of the coin and showed it to me.

SYDNEY ARTHUR NAYLOR, recalled, further examined by Mr. MARSHALL HALL—When I saw the account of this case in the papers at the Police Court I wrote to Mr. Seddon about the gold.

FREDERICK HENRY SEDDON (prisoner, on oath), examined by Mr. MARSHALL HALL—I am forty years of age. At the time of my arrest I was living at 63 Tollington Park. I had been in the employment of the London and Manchester Industrial Insurance Company since I was nineteen years of age. I have held the position of district superintendent since 1896, and district superintendent for the Islington district since 1901. I have had a constant progress in the way of my position in the business. The other prisoner is my wife. We have been married a great many years, and we have five children living, the eldest being William, who is seventeen; then Margaret, who is sixteen; Frederick, fifteen; Ada, eight; and Lily, who was born in the beginning of January of last year. About eight years ago I purchased 57 Isledon Road. Since that date I have purchased 63 Tollington Park and other property since I have resided in Tollington Park. I made a profit on Isledon Road. I invested £400 in Cardiff stock, which I still have. I have always been in the habit of keeping money in hand—never less than £50—since I have been in London.

Just prior to February, 1909, I lived at Southend for twelve months, coming up to town every day. I then took a house and shop at 267 Seven Sisters Road, where the business of a ladies' wardrobe dealer was carried on in my wife's name, Rowen. I found the money for stocking the shop. I think it was in September of the same year that I bought the second safe; I had had one for several years. The profits that came from the wardrobe business I kept on hand to replenish the shop should a bargain ever turn up. The profits were not banked, and until I had the safe I kept them in a roll-top desk; afterwards I kept them in the safe in the bedroom. My other safe was in the office in Seven Sisters Road.

I remember the evening that has been spoken of by Mr. Naylor when the money was produced. I could not say how much gold there was in the bag, but there might have been anything from £100 to £130 or £150. That would be the balance of some money I had after purchasing stock and profits accumulated up to that date. On the occasion that I showed it to these two men I took it from the pigeon-holes in my secretaire.

In August, 1909, I entered into negotiations with Messrs. Ramsay & Wainwright, 279 Seven Sisters Road, for the purchase of 63 Tollington

Frederick H. Seddon.

Evidence for Defence.

Frederick H. Seddon

Park. I believe I had sold £100 worth of Cardiff stock for the purpose of starting my wife in this business, and that left me with £300 worth of Cardiff stock. I forget exactly the price that was asked for the house, 63 Tollington Park, but I reduced the figure down to £320. I had somewhere about £200 in gold on hand at this date, and then I intended to sell a portion of the Cardiff stock to make up the £320. Somewhere about this time that the arrangement was made, I paid Mr. Wainwright a deposit of £15. I took my gold bag out of the secretaire and extracted £15 from it in cash, and he said, " Oh, a cheque will do for me, Seddon," and I gave him a cheque and put the gold back into the secretaire. Mr. Wainwright suggested I should get a mortgage, and when he explained to me the object I fell in with the suggestion. I eventually got £220 lent on mortgage, leaving a balance of £85 after taking into account the £15 deposit. I sold £100 worth of Cardiff stock, which realised something like £85.

About this time, the end of 1909, my wife and I had a little difference on family matters, and there was a separation for a short time. In consequence of that I had to shut down the wardrobe business, because it was not a business that I could engage in. I practically gave away the stock to Mr. Keegan for £30. I had previously opened a Post Office Savings Bank account, and I opened another account with this money on 17th January, 1910. That did not affect the £200 approximately which I had in gold. I had the idea at first of letting No. 63 Tollington Park in flats, but not having let it, I moved in there and lived in the house, somewhere about the end of January of 1910. My wife had then returned to me. I transferred my office to the basement of 63 Tollington Park, and I occupied the whole of the house except the top floor. The safe that I had in the office in Seven Sisters Road I removed into the basement office at Tollington Park, and the bedroom safe was already there with my household goods in the bedroom. I counted my cash before I left the shop, and I counted it again on my removal into Tollington Park. There was about £220 or £230, which was all my own. I kept it on hand to pay up the mortgage at any time desired. In case of burglary I kept £100 I believe in the lower safe and £100 in the bedroom safe, and the £20 I kept in loose cash in an ordinary £5 silver bag in the bedroom safe on the shelf. The £100 in the office safe was kept in one bag. A £5 silver bag should hold about £100 of gold—it did, at all events.

In the event of anything happening to you, there would have been the ready money to pay off the mortgage?—Yes.

So that your wife could pay it off and she would have the house?— Without any delay. My second floor had been occupied up to June, 1910, and then it was vacant, and I instructed Gilbert & Howe, house agents, Crouch Hill, to obtain a tenant. In July, 1910, Miss Barrow called at Tollington Park with Mrs. Hook, and saw my wife and inspected the rooms. Eventually she agreed to become my tenant at a weekly rent of 12s. for the four rooms on the top floor. The tenancy commenced about the end of July. Mr. and Mrs. Hook and Ernest Grant came with her to live in the house. Mr. and Mrs. Hook stayed something between

Trial of the Seddons.

Frederick H. Seddon

ten days and a fortnight. I was not at home when they arrived in the house.

Just tell us the details of how Mr. and Mrs. Hook came to leave?—They were creating a disturbance in the house which I was not used to; they proved undesirable tenants. There had been a quarrel on the Saturday, and I gave them all notice to quit—Miss Barrow and all. Miss Barrow said she did not want to leave, that the cause of the trouble was Mr. Hook. She was afraid of him, and I said, "Well, of course, this kind of thing cannot go on." She asked if I would speak to him, and I said, "Well, you had better speak to him yourself." This would be on the Saturday, I think. On the Sunday Hook and his wife went out all day, taking the boy with them, and left the old lady absolutely unattended, and she could not attend or wait on herself. My wife and daughter informed me that she was crying all day. I said, "Well, I will see what he means about it when he comes home," because I understood that Mr. and Mrs. Hook had come to occupy rooms with Miss Barrow on the express condition that they would look after her, and the wife was going to do the cooking and keep the rooms clean and show her how to look after herself. There was absolutely no arrangement when Mr. and Mrs. Hook and Miss Barrow came that my wife or any servant of mine should do any cooking. I should not have taken them on such a condition. Miss Barrow gave Hook notice to quit to satisfy me, because I said that they all had to go. Miss Barrow wrote to Mr. Hook, "Mr Hook, as you and your wife have treated me so badly," &c. (Reads.) The answer to that is exhibit 24, "Miss Barrow, as you are so impertinent to send the letter you have, I wish to inform you." (Reads.)* At that time Mr. Hook's conduct to Miss Barrow was very abrupt, rather cruel.

Did you in any way incite or suggest to Miss Barrow that she should get rid of the Hooks?—Absolutely no. Miss Barrow communicated to me the answer that she had received from Hook. She was distressed at the idea of Ernie going. She said to me, "As landlord, can you not tell him to go?" I told her she was my tenant, not Hook, but that I should certainly give him notice to go if she so desired it. I waited for him till late that night, and when he went into his room I knocked at the door, but he would not open the door, and I said, "Well, the notice is for you on the door." I gave a formal notice to quit—I think it was typewritten. After Hook found the notice on his door he came down to see me the next day in the drawing-room. I told him I was not used to this kind of conduct in my home, and I did not intend to tolerate it under any circumstances; that he must get out according to the notice I had left on his door; it was Miss Barrow's desire, and she claimed my protection.

While the Hooks were in the house I became aware of the fact that Miss Barrow had a cash box; I did not know it before. She was terribly upset at the bother that the Hooks had created, and she came down into the dining-room, where my wife and daughter were, and she asked me to shut the door. She asked if I would put her cash box in my safe, as she was afraid Hook might take it with him when he was leaving. I

---

* See Appendix A.

152

Evidence for Defence.

Frederick H. Seddon

asked her how much money she had in the box, and she said between £30 and £35. I said, " I should not like to take the responsibility of minding your cash box if you are not sure how much is in it, without you count it out in my presence, and I will give you a receipt for the bo and its contents." I thought she would agree to count it out there and then. She said she would take it upstairs and make sure how much was in it, and then she went upstairs. I naturally waited for her to come down with the box to tell me how much was in it, but she did not return. My wife or daughter said that she had locked herself in her bedroom. I had my own business to go out and attend to, and I did not trouble any further. I did not see that cash box again during Miss Barrow's life. I believe the cash box that has been produced in this case is the same one.

Hook left that day. I think his brother William paid for the removal. Miss Barrow gave it to him, of course. I told Miss Barrow she ought to get a servant in to look after her, and she asked if my daughter Maggie could not look after her, and she agreed to give her a shilling a day pocket money. Maggie was to look after her rooms, cook, and do everything, but she was not to do the washing.

In consequence of something my wife and daughter said to me, I had an interview with Miss Barrow in the month of August, 1910. I saw Miss Barrow about some property somewhere in the autumn of 1910. My wife and daughter told me that Miss Barrow was continually crying, and very despondent and greatly worried about her properties. When they told me that I had no knowledge as to what Miss Barrow's property consisted of. I said, " What has she got to worry about? I understand she has got plenty." They requested me to see Miss Barrow, but I did not see her then; I was approached on several occasions before I troubled about it. I told my wife that I would have a chat with Miss Barrow as soon as I had time. She came down one Sunday in the month of September into the dining-room, and had a chat with me about her property. I asked her what she was worrying about, what was her trouble that she was always crying, was she not satisfied with the wa Maggie was looking after her? and she said, " Yes, that she was perfectly happy, but it was her property that was worrying her." She said she had a public-house at Camden Town called the Buck's Head, and it was the principal source of her income; she had had a lot of trouble with the ground landlords, and she said that Lloyd George's Budget had upset licensed premises by increased taxation; that her tenants, Truman, Hanbury, Buxton & Co., had a lot of licensed houses, and she was afraid they might have to close some of them, and she said, " Whatever would I do if I lost them as tenants? I would not be able to let the premises again." She thought the barber's shop next door depended a lot upon the public-house for his customers, and if she lost them it would mean nearly £3 a week to her. I asked her how many years her lease had to run, and she said she thought it was about seventeen years. She said that Truman, Hanbury & Buxton were tenants throughout the term, but she had an idea that if they had to close the public-house they would give it up certainly because they had complained that customers were

Trial of the Seddons.

bad and that they could not renovate the place. I did not say to her that they would have to pay the rent whether they gave it up or not.

At a later stage she produced some correspondence that she had had about this. I asked her about what her other source of income was, and she told me that she had got some India stock that she had lost a lot of money on. She produced a paper showing that she had paid as much as 108 for it and at that time it was down at 94, and that worried her. She told me that she had £1600 stock which had cost her about £1780. I said that it was a gilt-edged security, and there did not seem very much to worry about; I said, "That will keep you out of the workhouse anyway." I asked her what she wanted, and she said she would like to purchase an annuity the same as a friend of hers. I did not know the name of the friend until I got it—Mrs. Smith—from Vonderahe at the interview after Miss Barrow's death. I told Miss Barrow that she must remember that an annuity died with her, and she said that she did not mind that, that she had only herself to consider as her friends—her relatives—had treated her badly. She said that if she could get an annuity of between £2 10s. and £3 a week she would be pleased. I asked her what was the value of her public-house and barber's shop; she said she did not know, and she was not sure whether her title was clear or whether she had power to sell. "Well," I said, "look here, the best thing you can do is to consult a solicitor." She said she had had quite enough of solicitors, that they had not been any good to her over the compensation dilemma, they charged too much. I said, "If you want an annuity, the best thing for you to do is to go to the Post Office." I think that ended the interview on that day. I never at any time got anything for her from the Post Office. She produced a prospectus—an annuity prospectus.

Mr. MARSHALL HALL—I call for that document, which was found by the police. (Document produced and handed to witness.)

That is exactly as it was produced by the police after your arrest and before you had any opportunity of dealing with the documents?— Yes, this is the very one she brought herself. First she told me that her age was forty-eight, and I marked it off. I asked her if she was sure that she was forty-eight, and she said, "No," she was forty-nine, and so I said, "You will get that for 7s. a year less." I put the mark on it. She asked me to explain this, and I told her she would have to pay £1700 to produce £100 or something over. Her objection was that she would have to part with that £1700 first, and wait six months before she would get any return, as the annuity was only paid half-yearly. She was not sure whether she could sell the property until the title was investigated, as I advised her to have it investigated. I will not swear that this is the document I handed to the coroner on 23rd November. I believe it passed out of my custody into the custody of the coroner then —anyhow it has never been in my custody until now. When Miss Barrow pointed out this difficulty with regard to the Post Office annuity she asked if I could not grant her an annuity—she said, "Could I not grant the annuity?" I calculated it on this basis—I took into consideration the Buck's Head and the barber's shop and the £1600 India $3\frac{1}{2}$ per cent. stock, and I calculated that with that I could grant her with safety an

Evidence for Defence.

Frederick H. Seddon

annuity of between £2 10s. and £3 a week. I took into consideration that if I paid her £10 a month and allowed her to live rent free, it was between £3 and £3 2s. a week. That is altogether £151 5s. per annum, and that is what I was prepared to do. At that time I did not know the actuarial value of the public-house property, but I was taking it on its yield at about £3 or £4 a week. On 14th October, 1910, the India stock was transferred to me. Before the bargain could be legally finally concluded it was necessary to get a valuation of the Buck's Head property, also to satisfy Miss Barrow as to her power to convey, and therefore there was no transfer of that at this period. The payment of the actual annuity was not begun until the New Year; she said she would be very pleased if I could commence at the New Year. With the proceeds of the India stock which I sold, I bought some houses, but that was not until three or four months afterwards. The whole of the proceeds of the East India stock and the Buck's Head property are intact and held under an order of the Court at the present time.

Mr. JUSTICE BUCKNILL—There must be no misapprehension about this at all, gentlemen. There was an order—perhaps by consent I ought to say—under which that property is at the present moment locked up, so to speak, in case of any possible question about any will. It has nothing to do with this man; it has been done by consent.

Examination continued—I think it was about the end of January, 1911, when I sold the India stock. I had begun making investigations with regard to the Camden Town property in October, but these investigations took a long time. (Shown letter dated 15th October, 1910, from Eliza Mary Barrow to F. H. Seddon, exhibit 150)—That is in Miss Barrow's handwriting, and it is as follows:—"Re the Buck's Head public-house, 202 High Street, N.W., also hairdresser's shop adjoining, i.e., 1 Buck Street, N.W. Dear sir,—You are at liberty to have my title to the above properties investigated to know that I have power to transfer my interests in the same to you. For this purpose, I place all my documents relating to same in your hands. (Of course, any legal expense that may be incurred to be paid by yourself when the transfer has been completed.) Please arrange for the completion of transfer as early as possible. I am writing to my tenants instructions to forward rents in future direct and payable to you."

I took the documents down personally to explain the situation to Mr. Keeble, clerk with Messrs. Russell & Sons, he being the gentleman who had the matter in hand. There was a correspondence between Messrs. Russell & Sons and myself and Miss Barrow with reference to the dealing with the Buck's Head property. I believe at this time Miss Barrow was attending Dr. Paul off and on. I asked Messrs. Robson & Perrin to make a valuation, and they sent me a valuation from Mr. Brangwin, auctioneer and valuer. The facts upon which that valuation is based are accurate. Negotiations went on till 4th January, 1911, when the following letter was written by Miss Barrow to Messrs. Russell:—"Re the Buck's Head public-house, 202 High Street, N.W., and the hairdresser's shop adjoining, No. 1 Buck Street, N.W. Mr. Keeble, Messrs. Russell & Sons, solicitors, 59 Coleman Street, E.C. Dear Sir,—I regret I was unable to call upon you to-day with Mr. Seddon as requested by your letter to

Trial of the Seddons.

him of the 3rd inst. However, I understand from him that you are preparing a deed of conveyance of these properties to Mr. Frederick Henry Seddon, entitling him to receive rents and take over liabilities and responsibilities connected with these properties from quarter day, 25th December last, in consideration of a life annuity of £52 per annum (one pound weekly) payable to me by him. These arrangements I am quite agreeable to, and will arrange to be at home between 3 and 4 p.m. on Friday next to meet you to sign deed of conveyance. Yours faithfully, Eliza Mary Barrow.''

Messrs. Russell advised that Miss Barrow should be separately represented, and I quite concurred. She was separately represented by Mr. Knight, but she would not pay any money for his fees. She said I might take all the legal steps I liked if I defrayed the expenses. I paid the whole of Messrs. Russell's fees and a separate cheque for £4 13s. for Mr. Knight. I explained to Miss Barrow that the fees were tremendously heavy—heavier than I anticipated, and I felt under the circumstances she ought to pay Mr. Knight's fee. She said she had no money to spare, and later on she brought me down a small diamond ring and made me a present of that. I wore that diamond ring on my little finger until after Miss Barrow's death, and then I had it made to fit this other finger (indicating). I have a diamond ring of my own, which is four times the value of that ring.

On 9th January Mr. Knight wrote to Miss Barrow saying that he would attend at her house on Wednesday, the 11th, to witness her execution of the assignment. Miss Barrow wrote to Messrs. Russell on 10th January, saying that she trusted there would be no further delay as she wished the matter to be completed. On 11th January the assignment, exhibit 11, took place. Mr. Knight was present and witnessed Miss Barrow's signature. There is a clause in the deed charging that portion of the annuity of £52 a year upon the property whilst it existed. The annuity was to be paid on the first of every month. I paid her £10 in advance in the first week in January, and I continued to pay £10 per month regularly in advance. I always got two receipts, £4 for the property and £6 for the stock. The letter, exhibit 82, is the letter she wrote to the Surveyor of Income Tax stating that she was in receipt of £124 per annum for value received. (Two series of receipts dating from 11th January, 1911, to 6th September, 1911, showing that £4 or £5 or £6 a month had been received from the prisoner by Miss Barrow in respect of the property and stock respectively every month, were put to the witness.) All these receipts are in Miss Barrow's handwriting. The first of the first series is as follows:—'' Life Annuity, 11th January, 1911. Received from Mr. Frederick Henry Seddon the sum of £5, being five weeks' annuity allowance as arranged on assignment of property situated at Buck's Head, Camden Town, N.W., and barber's shop adjoining, up to and including 30th January, 1911, from 25th December, 1910. Eliza Mary Barrow.'' The first of the other series is—'' 6th January, 1911. Received from Mr. Frederick Henry Seddon the sum of £6, being the monthly allowance as arranged in consideration of the transfer of £1600 India 3½ per cent. stock.'' I handed these receipts to Mr. Saint, my solicitor, after the first inquest and before I was arrested. In January,

Evidence for Defence.

Frederick H. Seddon

1911, I instructed Capel-Cure & Terry to sell £1600 of India stock, I having entered into negotiations to buy certain leasehold property in Coutts Road, Stepney. The stock was sold on 25th January, and realised £1519 16s. A cheque for that amount was handed to me, and I placed £1400 on deposit at the bank on which it was drawn (this was just sufficient to pay for the property), and I drew the remaining £119 16s.

At this time what had become of the £220 which you had in your safe?—I have still got it. I put the £119 16s. into the London and Provincial Bank as far as I can remember. Being shown my pass-book, exhibit 36—On 1st February, 1911, there is an entry of £50 to my credit in current account. I opened a deposit account with the other £70. On 6th March I drew the £1400 and paid for the fourteen leasehold houses in Coutts Road, Stepney, less £70, which I had already paid as a deposit by a cheque drawn by my solicitor on my current account. Under "2nd February" in my current account there is an item, "Hickman, Property £70." On 7th March I paid a further £30 into my deposit account at the London and Provincial Bank, bringing it up to £100. At that time I had the £100 deposit at my bank and I had the £220 in gold in my safe.

My father came to live with me about the end of February. Miss Barrow wrote me the letter dated 27th March, 1911, exhibit 7.* I think Miss Barrow was in a very despondent state when that letter was written. She had been out and had seen the funeral of somebody that she knew, and then she came in talking about funerals and death and one thing and another, and she said, "How would it be if anything happened to her now regarding the furniture and the jewellery that she had got which belonged to Ernest and Hilda Grant's parents?" I told her that she ought to make a will because she was afraid of either the Hooks coming into possession of it or that her relations should get it. I told her that her nearest relatives would come into possession unless she made a will. I suggested that she ought to have a solicitor, but whenever she heard the name of "solicitor" she got annoyed. I then went away, and when I came back at night I got that letter from my wife, it having been handed to her by Miss Barrow in my absence. I took it that she meant the letter to be a kind of will, and I put it away in my secretaire. On 30th May, 1911, I took the notice to the Surveyor of Income Tax and he said, "Oh, this is not necessary; you will be charged with it and you can deduct it off her."

About this time there was trouble with the Birkbeck Bank, in consequence of which Miss Barrow consulted me. She asked me—Could my missus go up with her to draw her money out of the bank in Upper Street, and I asked her why, and she said "It looks as if all the banks are going smash." There had previously been the Charing Cross Bank and then the Birkbeck Bank on top of it; she had been deeply interested in this, and I think it was the only occasion on which she had bought the newspaper. On 19th June Miss Barrow and my wife went to the bank and drew out £216 9s. 7d. I have never seen that money. My wife told me that she had brought it into the house in gold, and I did

---

* See Appendix F.

Trial of the Seddons.

Frederick H. Seddon

not like the idea. I told her I did not consider that her trunk was a very safe thing to keep such a sum of money as that, and especially in my house.

On 1st August Miss Barrow went to see Dr. Paul, accompanied, I believe, by my wife. From 5th to 8th August we were all at Southend. The last week in August and the first week in September were intensely hot. Miss Barrow and the boy Ernie often used to go into the garden. The boy was very friendly with my children—they were his only play-mates. I believe Miss Barrow and the boy had their meals in their own kitchen upstairs. I understand that she always bought her own food, and it was cooked by my little girl Maggie up in her own kitchen. I could not say whether on some occasions the food was cooked downstairs by my wife.

When the boy first came to the house he slept with Miss Barrow. I advised her to buy a small bed and to let him occupy the same room, which she did until she took ill on 2nd September. On 1st September my wife told me that Miss Barrow had a bilious attack and that I should not trouble her. I remember that because her annuity was due and I wanted to pay it to her. On Saturday, 2nd September, she sent a message down by my wife that she thought she could manage to sign for her annuity. About noon I paid her £10 in gold, as I always did— £9 in sovereigns and £1 in half-sovereigns, and she signed the two receipts for it. Although one is dated 17th August it was in fact signed on 2nd September. I cannot say whether she got better or worse after that. On 4th September I went up to remonstrate with her for leaving her bedroom and going into the back room. At that time the boy had left his own room and had started to sleep with her. On that day, 2nd September, my daughter Margaret was sent to fetch Dr. Paul, but as he could not come, I suggested sending for Dr. Sworn, who had been our family doctor for ten years. Dr. Sworn called about eleven o'clock. When I went into Miss Barrow's room on 4th September there was a lot of flies in the room. My wife told me that Miss Barrow had seriously complained about the flies, and that that was why she had left the room; she said the room was too hot and the flies annoyed her, and she had the boy constantly fanning her.

Do you know whether your wife got any fly-papers on that date?— She told me she did.

From first to last did you ever handle a fly-paper that came into the house?—Absolutely no. The first time I heard of Mather's fly-papers was at the Police Court. On the night of 11th September when the will was signed I saw a couple of fly-papers upon the chest of drawers, next to a mirror, and a couple in saucers on the mantelpiece. These four fly-papers were papers that you put some water on; I could not say whether they were Mather's or not. I did not know that they contained arsenic; I merely knew that the flies drank it and died.

Have you ever in your life boiled down a fly-paper and made a concoction of fly-paper?—Never.

Or have you ever made a concoction of fly-paper without boiling?— I have never known anybody to do it until I heard in this Court that it·

Evidence for Defence.

Frederick H. Seddon

had been done by experiment. Dr. Sworn continued to call every day except on Sunday, the 10th.

On 11th September my wife told me that Miss Barrow was worrying again about the furniture and the jewellery in the room for the boy Ernest and Hilda Grant. I said, "Why did she not do what I told her —have a solicitor," and my wife said, "She wants to see you about it." About three or four or five in the afternoon I went up to Miss Barrow and asked what she wanted. She said, "I do not feel well, and I would like to see if anything happened to me that Ernest and Hilda got wha belonged to their father and mother." She said there was some jewellery that had belonged to her parents, and there was a watch and chain that had belonged to the boy's father. I said, "Don't you think then I had better call in a solicitor and have a proper will made out?" She replied, "No, you can do it for me," and I agreed to do so. I was very busy at the time with my own business, and my sister and her daughter had only just arrived from Wolverhampton. I drafted a wil up hurriedly between five and six in the evening, including what she had mentioned, and between six and seven I asked my father and wife to com up and witness her signature to it. I told her I had drafted a will out, and that I would read it to her. I read it to her and asked her if it would do, and then she asked for her glasses to read it herself. I turned to my wife and said, "Where is her glasses?" She said to my father, "There they are on the mantelpiece, pass them." They were passed over to her, and she read the will over herself. She asked me where she should sign it. I had brought up her blotting pad for the will to rest on. I propped her back up with pillows, and she signed it somewhat half-reclining. I then took the blotting pad and the will and put it on the side table at the side of the bed and showed my wife where to sign. My father was standing at the foot of the bed, and I showed him where to sign. I explained to Miss Barrow that they were to witness it and it was all right now, and she said, "Thank you. Thank God, that will do." When I prepared that will I had no idea that it would ever be acted upon as a will. It was my intention to take it to Mr. Keeble, explain the circumstances to him, and get him to draft one up in a proper legal form and bring it up for her signature.

Did you know when you drafted that will that it did not carry any money with it?—I never gave it a thought. I had never drafted wills up before. When my wife told me about the will that Miss Barrow wanted making, or that she wanted to see me about the property, she had explained that she would not take the medicine that the doctor had given her—this chalk mixture as I have heard in the evidence—and the doctor had given her some effervescing mixture, and it had to be drunk during effervescence, but Miss Barrow would not take it while it was fizzing. I asked Miss Barrow, "Are you not aware that your mixture is no good to you without you drink it during effervescence?" and to emphasise it I said, "You must drink it while it fizzes." I asked my wife to give me a dose and see if I could not get her to take it during effervescence. I was not aware till then how it was mixed. My wife got me to hold one in each hand and she poured some out of both bottles into the separate glasses. She said, "When you put the two together

Trial of the Seddons.

Frederick H. Seddon

it fizzes, and it has got to be drunk quick." I said, "All right, I will practice on myself," and I put the two mixtures together and drank it. I told Miss Barrow that that was how she had to drink it, and I prepared it again and passed it to her, but she did not drink it during the effervescence. I said, "That is not a bit of good," and I told my wife she ought to tell the doctor about it. I told her that she ought to go to the hospital.

Did you ever on any other occasion during Miss Barrow's last illness give her anything to drink or to eat?—The night she was very ill, the last night, I gave her a drop of brandy. A day or two before the will was executed I had a letter from my sister, Mrs. Longley, asking if she might come up to stay with me, and I wrote back saying that I had got an old lady ill in the house, but if she liked to come up and take pot luck she could come. She arrived between three and four o'clock on the afternoon of the 11th, and we gave up our best bedroom to her, the room that my wife and I had hitherto occupied. We went into the first floor back room, where the boys had formerly slept, and we put up a large extra bed for my father and the boys in the back room, next to Miss Barrow's room, a room that was really one of Miss Barrow's rooms, but she had never occupied it since the Hooks left. The servant, Chater, remained in the room she always occupied with my daughter and my little girl, Ada. The night that Mrs. Longley arrived we all went to the Finsbury Park Empire except Maggie, who had to stop in to look after Miss Barrow. We got back about midnight. My father and Mrs. Longley and Miss Longley went out somewhere every day.

At 9.30 in the morning of the 13th the Longleys, my father, Frederick, and Ada went for the day to the White City. I believe I was in bed when Dr. Sworn called that morning between ten and eleven. I was not very well. I went out about two o'clock in the afternoon, I think, and then I came back for a bit of tea about half-past six or seven. I went up to the Marlborough Theatre between 7.30 and 7.45. Just to fix it, in case any question arises about it, I had a small dispute at the Marlborough Theatre about a two-shilling piece and a half-crown piece that night. When I returned home about 12.30 midnight, I heard from my wife that Miss Barrow had called out she was dying, "I am dying," or something like that. I said, "Is she?" and she said, "No," and smiled. Dr. Sworn lives about twenty-five minutes from us; I could do it in about fifteen or twenty minutes, but I am a quick walker. I had been in the house about half an hour when Ernie called out from upstairs, "Mrs. Seddon, Chickie wants you." My wife said that she had been calling like that, and that she had done all she could for her, and put hot flannel on her. She had been up several nights that week till the early hours of the morning with her. I might mention this was nothing unusual during that period for the boy to call out, "Mrs. Seddon, Chickie wants you," in the early hours of the morning. My wife was resting on the couch, and I said to her, "Never mind, I will go and see what she wants," and she said, "Never mind, I will go." I said I would go, and I asked my sister to come up with me. We both went up together, and my wife immediately followed us, so we three were

Evidence for Defence.

Frederick H. Seddon

in the room together. I said, "Now, Miss Barrow, this is a sister of mine that is down from Wolverhampton. You know Mrs. Seddon is tired out, and I would like you to try and let her have a little sleep. You know it would do you more good to rest." She said, "Oh, but I have had such pains." "Well," I said, "Mrs. Seddon says she has put hot flannels on you and done all she can for you." She did not take any interest in my sister, and my sister left the room. She asked for more hot flannels and she asked for a drop of brandy. I said, "My dear woman, do you not know that it is after one o'clock in the morning? We cannot get brandy now." My wife said, "There is a drop there in the bottle," So I said, "Oh well, give her a drop then." My wife passed me the bottle and I gave her the brandy. There was very little altogether; I only gave her half of what there was, and left the other drop in the bottle. I think there was a soda-water syphon there, and I put a drop of soda in the brandy.

Had you the slightest suspicion at that time that Miss Barrow was fatally or dangerously ill?—No; you see, every night had been alike, sending down and calling out, and my wife having to go up and down, up and down, all the time giving her hot flannels. My wife had been up and down nearly every night that week. After I gave Miss Barrow the brandy, I left my wife preparing hot flannels and I went down.

How long were you altogether in Miss Barrow's room at this time?— Not many minutes, a few minutes—four or five minutes. My sister had just got to the bottom of the stairs and she waited there for me, and I had a conversation with her. There was a shocking smell in Miss Barrow's room that night; I could not bear to be in the room, as I have a delicate stomach. Mrs. Longley had said that it was not proper for the boy to sleep there, and I said, "If we don't allow that we would get no sleep at all," meaning that Miss Barrow would not sleep unless he did sleep with her; she wanted either my wife or the boy with her. I went to bed about 2.30, and in a few minutes the boy called Mrs. Seddon again, and she went up without me. I said, "It looks as if she was going to have you up all night." My wife was called up twice within the space of half an hour, and then the third time she was called I went up with her to see if I could try to get Miss Barrow off to sleep, and explained to her that if she was going to have Mrs. Seddon up all night she would not have any one to attend to her or wait on her to-morrow. I said, "You know really we shall have to get a nurse, or you will have to go to hospital," and she said she could not help it. The boy Ernie said he was tired and could not get any sleep. I asked my wife what she was going to do, and she said, "I will sit up with her." I said, "Well, you had better go to your own bed, Ernie, and get a sleep." Miss Barrow closed her eyes, and we thought she was going to sleep. As my wife began to leave the room she opened her eyes and asked for Ernie; she did not like to ask my wife to stay with her. I told Ernie to get back to her bed again, and he did so. Later on I sent him to his own bed. Each time my wife went up that night she made hot flannels for Miss Barrow, getting the hot water from Miss Barrow's kitchen, where there was a gas stove. We went downstairs again, and in about

Trial of the Seddons.

Frederick H. Seddon

a quarter of an hour the boy shouted "Chickie is out of bed." We both rushed up and found her sitting on the floor at the foot of the bed in an upright position, and the boy was holding her up. I said, "Whatever are you doing out of bed?" and we lifted her up into bed. The boy looked terribly upset and worried.

Was Miss Barrow in pain?—No; she lay quiet. She did not suggest that there were any pains. I asked her what she was doing out of bed, but she did not say. She seemed to know what she was doing, but she gave no explanation. We got her into bed. I said to my wife that she had better stay with her, and she agreed to do so, and then I told the boy Ernie to get into his own bed—this was between three and four o'clock in the morning—and I said, "You need not go to school in the morning, as you have been up pretty well all the night." My wife told me to go to bed, but I said, "Never mind, I will put a pipe on and keep you company." I did not go to bed; I kept going up and down to see how the baby was, and I also stood at the door smoking my pipe. My wife sat in the easy chair by the bedside, and Miss Barrow went into a sleep. I said, "She seems to have gone into a nice sleep," and my wife said, "What's the good of going to bed, getting undressed, and being called and having to get up again?"

About 6 o'clock what happened?—We decided absolutely that she should go to the hospital the next day, so I said to the wife, "You can stop up with her, and you will be able to go to bed to-morrow, because when Dr. Sworn comes I am going to tell him to see she goes away to the hospital." She was snoring during the hour or hour and a half after that—a kind of breathing through her mouth like that (showing). I was smoking and reading, and my wife was dozing, when this snoring did not seem quite so heavy, and all of a sudden it stopped. I said, "Good God, she has stopped breathing."

She died quite peacefully and quietly so far as her death is concerned?—Yes, she died about 6.15 or 6.20 by her clock. I hurried off for Dr. Sworn; I was in a terrible state. He gave me a certificate; I did not expect it then. I got back about 8 o'clock I think, and I found the charwoman, Mrs. Rutt, and my wife either in Miss Barrow's room or in the dining-room, I am not sure which. Mrs. Rutt laid the body out. I helped to lift the body while the feather bed was being taken from under her. I asked my wife if she knew where the keys were, and she handed me a bunch of keys, with one of which I opened the trunk. In the top of the trunk I found the cash-box, and I put it on the bed and opened it with another of the keys in the presence of my wife and Mrs. Rutt. In it I found four sovereigns and a half-sovereign. Towards the afternoon I said there ought to be some more money than this, and we started to search the room. We had already turned the trunk right out in the presence of Mrs. Rutt. I felt there ought to be more money, because I had paid Miss Barrow £10 on 2nd September, and she had never been out of the room to my knowledge. In the same drawer as my wife said she had found the keys, I found three sovereigns wrapped up in separate pieces of tissue paper. I said to my wife, "Let us have a look at that handbag," and in the close-fitting pocket at the side of the bag we found two sovereigns and a half-sovereign. In a loose bag that

Evidence for Defence.

Frederick H. Seddon

was hanging at the foot of the bed we found a few coppers. These were placed with 5d. that Ernie had got in the money box, making 8d., and I gave him a shilling out of my own pocket for pocket money to go to Southend-on-Sea.

Ernie, Frederick, and Ada went to Southend and stayed with Mrs. Henderson. I thought I would not tell Ernie of Miss Barrow's death till he had recovered a little bit from the shock. I thought it would be better to tell him after he had had a little holiday; I had to consider the boy's feelings. At 11.30 I went to see Mr. Nodes, the undertaker. At that time I had only £4 10s.; we had not yet made a thorough search. The account given by Mr. Nodes of what occurred is practically correct, but I think there is a lot that he has forgotten. For instance, I did not say " old girl "; I said that an old lady had died in the house, and I wanted to arrange about the funeral. He asked me what kind of a funeral I wanted, and I said, " Well, I am rather surprised; I have only found £4 10s. in her cash box, and there are the doctor's fees to be paid." " Well," he said, " look here, old man, I can give you a very nice turnout for £4," and he explained the kind of funeral, a composite carriage. He asked me who was going to the funeral, and I said, " Well, I do not know yet; I am going to drop a line to the relatives. Though they have never been near her during the time she has lived in the house, and they parted very bad friends, I don't know whether they will come to the funeral or not. If they don't turn up there will only be me and the wife and my father to go." " Well," he said, " you can have a composite carriage," which he explained would hold three or four comfortably, and would carry the coffin under a pall under the seat. I said, " I do not want the coffin exhibited like that." He said, " It is not seen; it is covered with a pall, and I can assure you it is quite a respectable turnout." I said, " Where do you bury? " and he said " At Finchley." I said, " It will be all right at £4? " and he said, " Oh, yes—quite an ordinary funeral." I asked, " It can easily be altered, then, if the relatives turn up? " and he said, " Oh, yes, it will make no difference," meaning the arrangement could be altered or carriages added, or anything like that that was required. So he said, " just pop in the trap and I will come round and measure the body." I have known Mr. Nodes for over ten years, and I gave all my agents his business card to try and introduce business to him. Apart from his business as undertaker, I have met and chatted to him, but I have not made a personal friend of him. He drove me up to my house, and went in to measure the body. Miss Barrow had told me that there was a family vault, but when her mother was buried it was full up. She told me that it was in her mother's name. I forgot to mention that Mr. Nodes explained what kind of coffin it would be; what he explained to me was satisfactory. On the way to Tollington Park he said, " Look here, Seddon, between you and me—I would not do it for anybody else—I can do this funeral I mentioned to you for £3 7s. 6d., but, of course, I will give you a receipt for £4." I said, " A little bit of commission like? " When we got to the house we went up to the room where the body was. There was a very bad smell there, so much so that I had to leave the room. Mr. Nodes suggested that the body should go to the mortuary,

Trial of the Seddons.

Frederick H. Seddon

and he also suggested that the burial should be on the Saturday, but I could not decide at once. That would be about a quarter to 12. I don't think I had any regular dinner that day as I had been too much upset. I think I might have a cup of tea or something like that in the middle of the day. About 1 o'clock Taylor arrived, and then Smith— I could not say whether they came together or not, but anyhow I joined them both in the office. I telephoned to Nodes that afternoon, but I don't remember exactly when. I had a talk with my wife and father about Saturday being a satisfactory day for the funeral on account of the condition of the deceased, and it being a slack business day for me. I think I told Mr. Nodes in the bedroom that I would agree to the body being removed when the coffin came.

I should say that it was between 3 and 4 o'clock when I set to work with Smith and Taylor in the office. I was waiting about some details of the business, and I was complaining that I was tired and worn out and could do with a sleep. Mr. Smith suggested to me, "Why not go and have a rest? We can get on with the work." I said, "Yes, all right, I think I will, but I will have to send a letter off to the relatives of the deceased and let them know she is dead, as the funeral is for Saturday, and then I will go and have a rest." I have a typewriter in my office, and I do my own typewriting. I had some mourning paper in my pocket in the office at the side of the safe, and I got my typewriter over from the corner of the office and put it on the desk underneath the pendant, where I generally sit when I use the typewriter. My position is wrongly shown on the plan that has been exhibited. (The witness indicated the proper position on the plan.) I wrote on the typewriter that afternoon an intimation to the relatives that Miss Barrow had died. What is now shown me is a carbon copy done at the same time as the original. I had only two sheets of black-edged paper; one went to the Vonderahe's, and what is shown me is the other sheet. I addressed the letter to "Frank E. Vonderahe, 31 Evershot Road, Finsbury Park, N." I got that from the address Miss Barrow had given me on 27th March. After I had written the letter I put it in an envelope. I stood up and put it out of my way on Smith's desk, and then I carried the typewriter back to the position I got it from. I called my daughter Maggie in and said, "Take this letter and post it, and see you catch the 5 o'clock post; I want them to get it to-night." Smith, who was in the room all the time, said that I looked bad, and he had been bad himself, and he wanted to know could he go out and get a drop of brandy, and I said, "Certainly," and he followed Maggie out.

Later on, when this matter appeared in the papers, Smith came of his own accord and saw me, and said he had seen the case about the inquest in the paper. I asked him did he recollect that on that day Miss Barrow died, and I had mentioned I had been up all night, and he suggested to me going and having a rest, that they could get on with the business, and I said, "Yes, but I must first write a letter to the relatives?" He said, "Yes, I do, Mr. Seddon, perfectly well. You wrote it on mourning paper and put it on my desk in the envelope." I said, "Did you notice that?" and he said "Yes." I said, "That is good," and he said, "Yes, and I seen Maggie post the letter, and I

164

Evidence for Defence.

patted her on the shoulder as I passed her, and said ' Good afternoon.' "
He said it was quite clear to him.   My wife and Maggie were present
when he said this.   I think my father was also present, but I am not
sure, nor do I know whether there was not one of my sons present.   I
then said, " Do you think that Taylor would be able to remember the
incident?"   He said, " I don't know, but I will refresh his memory, as
you have refreshed mine, and perhaps he will."   He said he was quite
willing to come forward and give evidence.   I instructed Mr. Saint, my
solicitor, to secure his attendance as a witness at the Coroner's Court if
necessary.   I don't think Mr. Saint called him ; I don't know.   Mr.
Nodes took away the body from my house in the evening.   I got a lock
of the hair for the two children, Ernie and Hilda.

The Court then adjourned.

Sixth Day—Saturday, 9th March, 1912.

The Court met at 10.15 a.m.

FREDERICK HENRY SEDDON (prisoner), recalled, further examined by
Mr. MARSHALL HALL—In the early days of Miss Barrow's residence at
Tollington Park he took the boy to school every morning, and met him
again at noon, brought him home to dinner, took him back to school, and
went out in the afternoon.   I have no knowledge of what she did with
her time or where she went during these months.   She used to go out in
the evening with the boy.   So far as I could see she was not healthy and
strong.   From my observations as a superintendent of insurance regarding good and bad lives, she was not a life that I could recommend for
insurance.   She was able to walk and all that sort of thing, but her
complexion was very sallow.

On 14th September I went back to the office somewhere between
five and six o'clock, after I had been lying down, and I found Smith
and Taylor there.   On this occasion they had been taking the collectors'
money.   I always counted the money up into bags and put it into my
safe, and then, when I went to bed, I took it upstairs with me and put
it into my bedroom safe.   I never left any money in the office on the
Thursday nights.   On the Friday afternoon I paid the money into my
bank.   On the occasion in question the collections were over £80 for
the week, and after all the expenses had been paid I think I had to pay
into the bank on behalf of the company something like £57.   On this
night the silver was in three bags and the gold in one bag.   There was
over £60 of gold in the bag, that being made up of £29 of the company's
money and £35 that I was adding to my own current account.   That £35
came out of the sum of £80 of my own that I had on hand in the
office safe.   I still had the £100 in my safe upstairs.   The £100
downstairs had been reduced to £80 in this way.   On several occasions
Miss Barrow had given me £5 in payment for rent, and I had taken £5

165

Trial of the Seddons.

Frederick H. Seddon

in gold out of the bedroom safe to cash the note and I replaced the same by the note. This had been done to the tune of about £25 between October and January, so that there would be £75 in gold in the bedroom safe and £25 in notes. By January I had reduced my current account by the £34 that I had paid to Russell & Sons, solicitors. I took these £25 notes to the bank on 30th January to make up my balance. I subsequently reduced the amount in the office by £20, leaving £80 there, and with £5 that I had loose I brought up the amount I had in the bedroom safe to the original amount in gold to £100. On one occasion in October, 1910, Miss Barrow gave me a £5 note and £4 8s. in cash to pay the ground rent of the Buck's Head, and I sent a cheque through my own bank. (Shown pass-book)—I find there, on 13th October, 1910, a debit to my account, "Cholmley & Co., £8 4s. 4d." That was the first time I had ever sent the ground rent to Cholmley & Co. As far as I recollect that is the only time on which a bank note came into my possession from Miss Barrow.

To come back to the 14th September, and the showing of gold and the offering of the bag to Mr. Smith—it was my practice to count up the whole of the office money. This evening I had the cash to count, and I counted £15 7s. 6d. in silver and £29 in gold of the company's money. I took the £80 out of the safe for the purpose of counting out £35 from it to add to my account, and consequently I would have, with the £29 in gold of the company's money, £109 in gold altogether, and the three bags of silver containing £15. I returned the £45 balance to my safe. Taylor has said that I had the money on my arm—three bags—and another in my hand. That is absolutely false. I put the four bags in the slide till and passed them into my safe. Smith has said that I showed him a bag holding between fifty and sixty sovereigns— that would be about accurate. Taylor and Smith left the office about midnight.

On Friday, the 15th, I went to Mr. Wright, the jeweller, and also to the bank, where I paid £88 4s. 8d. into the credit of my current account, and also a sum of £7 16s. 10d. This was made up of £64 in gold, being £29 of the company's money and £35 of mine, and £15 17s. 6d. in silver, 30s. in copper in blue 5s. bags, and £6 17s. 2d. in cheques and postal orders. I also paid in £7 16s. into a separate account that I kept for the rents of the Coutts Road property, which were the proceeds of the India stock. On that same day my current account is debited with £100, which was the transfer of the profits on the Coutts Road property for the half year. From March to September I had made £100 on the Coutts Road property after paying all expenses. That is a leasehold property consisting of fourteen houses yielding £8 a week rent. The deposit account credit was thus brought up to £200. Out of the £45 that was in gold in the downstairs safe I put £30 into the Post Office Savings Bank on 15th September. On the afternoon of that day the Longleys returned to Wolverhampton.

On the Saturday the funeral took place, and my wife, my father, and I attended. It started from Stroud Green Road.

On Monday, 18th September, I applied for and obtained three shares in the National Freehold Land and Building Society of £30, and I paid

Evidence for Defence.

Frederick H. Seddon

for these in gold which I took from my bedroom safe. I went to put the £100 that I had in my safe in the Building Society, but I found I could only purchase £30 shares, and so I bought three for £90, and brought £10 home again, which was put in the upstairs safe. I had £15 in gold in the downstairs safe. (Being referred to the annuity receipts)—These receipts add up to £91, being nine for £10 plus the extra £1 on the first payment. That £91 was paid to Miss Barrow in gold. On occasions I wrote the cheque payable to "Self," drew the £10, and paid it to her, to save breaking into the money I had. To bear out this statement, I read from my counterfoil cheque-book four items dated 31st January, 1st March, 31st March, and 31st July, marked "F. H. S., £10." All these cheques were applied towards the payment of those £10. In two cases the counterfoils are marked "E. M. B., £10." As to the other five payments, I withheld £10 from the company's money I had to pay, and debited my own account with the sums.

On Wednesday, the 20th, at nine o'clock at night, Mr. Vonderahe and his wife called, but I was out with my wife and did not come in till midnight. They left a message that they were coming next day, and I stayed in to see them. On the 21st, about ten o'clock in the morning, I was informed by my daughter that the Vonderahes had come, so of course I went in knowing I was going to see them. My daughter had left a message on the table when we came in at night to say that the relatives of Miss Barrow had been wanting to see us, and that they would be back in the morning. I said, "Are you Mrs. Frank Vonderahe?" and the smaller woman said, "No, I am Mrs. Frank Vonderahe." I said, "How is it you did not answer my letter and come to the funeral?" She went quite flushed and seemed quite excited, and she said, "We never got no letter." So I pulled out of my pocket the copy of the letter. She read it, and then she said, "We never received a letter." I asked where they lived, and she said Corbyn Street. "Well," I says, "The letter was addressed to 31 Evershot Road. You had better make inquiries at the Post Office about it." She said she had heard that Miss Barrow was dead and they had come to interview me respecting it. Later she asked me about the investments, and I said that Miss Barrow had disposed of all her investments to purchase an annuity. I gave her a statement and said, "Here is a full statement of it. Give this to your husband." I also gave her a copy of the will and three mourning cards, one for each of the three relatives. The original will was in my safe upstairs at that time. I told them, on their asking, that she was buried at Finchley. She said, "In a public grave?" and I said "Yes." She said, "Fancy, and she had got a family vault," and I said, "It is full up." She said, "No, it is not," and I said, "Oh, well, it will be an easy matter for the relatives then to remove the body." Mrs. Vonderahe said whoever had persuaded her to part with her money must have been a very clever person. I said she was anxious to purchase an annuity as a friend of hers had an annuity, and that this friend of hers had no worry whatever, whereas she was constantly worrying about it. So the two Vonderahes spoke to one another, and they said, "It would be that Mrs. Smith." That

167

Trial of the Seddons.

Frederick H. Seddon

is how I came to know of the existence of Mrs. Smith. We spoke about the boy, and Mrs. Vonderahe said that Miss Barrow had been a bad, wicked woman all her life, and that it was good enough for her—that was to be buried in a public grave. She had spoken about quarrels that had taken place between her and the boy's mother, and they had thrown things at one another, and she said, "Really, it is a good job for the boy that she has passed away." She said, "She even spat at us before she left." I said, "She was a woman that wanted humouring; you ought to take into consideration her infirmities, and she was to be pitied." They did not display any affection whatever for Miss Barrow at that interview; they spoke of her as a vindictive woman, a bad-tempered woman. I said, "That is only part of her complaint," and she said, "Oh, you don't know her as well as we do." I said, "Well, we have had her here for fourteen months any way." I never found her a vindictive woman; the woman was all right, she had her fits of temper, but I used to tell the wife and children to take no notice. The Vonderahes then asked what was to come of the boy, and I said, "Well, unless the boy's relatives interfere there is a home here for him." As a matter of fact, I did keep and clothe the boy until he was taken away from us by the police in December. I bought him a new suit, and my wife made him some new flannel underclothing, which was shown to the Vonderahes. They said they could see that he had got a good home, and I said he was quite happy and contented with my children. They also added that they always told their husbands that Miss Barrow would never leave anything to them, and they were not surprised that she had left them nothing. They asked me if I would see their husbands, and I said that we were going away for a fortnight but I would gladly see them on my return.

On my return on 2nd October I sent Ernie round to say that I was back, and Mr. Vonderahe sent a message by the boy that he was coming. About 9th October he called, along with some one who I assumed to be his brother. He said, however, that his brother was ill, and I said, "What did you want to bring a stranger for? This only concerns the next-of-kin." He said, "Well, surely there is no reason why you should not speak in the presence of my friend?" I said, "Well, I don't know. I understand you have got the matter in the hands of a solicitor." He said, "My brother is not well, and he could not come." I said, "Very good. Well, what would you like to know, because I have placed all the information in the hands of your wife? I sent you a copy of the will, and I gave you a statement in writing as to what she had done with the properties and purchased an annuity. I also showed your wife a letter that she had written to me stating that you had treated her badly and that she did not wish you, her relations, to benefit. What else would you like to know?" He said, "Well, can I see the will, the original will?" I said, "No, you have got a copy." He said, "Well, I can see the original will, can't I?" I said, "If you are the next-of-kin you can." He said, "Well, I am," and then I said, "I understand that there is an elder brother." I had learned that from Miss Barrow, who explained that this elder brother and they were not friends—he was the black sheep of the family, or something of that

Evidence for Defence.

Frederick H. Seddon

kind, and they did not know where he was—he was missing. Mr.
Vonderahe said, "Supposing he is dead?" I said, "It is a very easy
matter to get a copy of the certificate of death, and to go to a Commissioner of Oaths and swear an affidavit that you are the legal next-of-kin,
and I will go into details with you." He said, "I don't want to be
bothered with solicitors, and all that sort of thing." I said, "You have
got all the information I can give you; I put it down in writing, and I
am prepared to stand by it. Everything has been done in perfect
order." He said, "Who is the landlord of the Buck's Head and the
barber's shop?" I said, "I am." He said, "How did you come by
it?" and I replied, "I have already told you that. If you will prove
to me that you are the legal next-of-kin I will go into further details
with you." Then he said, "What about the boy?" and I said, "The
boy has a comfortable home here unless the relations interfere with him.
Of course, I have no legal claim on him, no more than what Miss Barrow
had, but I should like to know he has got a good home, and if the uncles
can give him a better home than he has got here, and they wish to take
him, of course I cannot stop it." My wife was present, and showed him
some things she had made for the boy, some new flannel underclothing,
the same as she had made for her children, and he said, "Yes, I can
see the boy is well cared for." Although the interview—which lasted
about three-quarters of an hour—was a little stormy at the beginning,
it was very friendly at the end. I said, "I am going to have the girl down
for Christmas. I have never seen her in my life. Don't upset the girl by
letting her know of Miss Barrow's death; leave it to me to break the
news gently, as I have done to the boy." I added, "We could go to
the orphanage and try and arrange to bring her up for Christmas, and
she could spend Christmas with her brother." We parted quite friendly,
and shook hands. That was the last I saw of Mr. Vonderahe.

I heard that he had been making inquiries at the undertakers who
had advised him to see a solicitor, but he said he did not want to bother
with any solicitors. I first knew that an inquiry was going on into this
matter, so far as the public were concerned, on 22nd November, when the
coroner's officer called upon me while I was busy with correspondence in
my office. He started making inquiries about Miss Barrow's death, and
I answered them all, and gave evidence at the inquest on the following
day. The notice was very short, because it was between 9 and 10 o'clock
in the evening when the interview took place, and the inquest was for
the following morning. I was arrested by Ward on 4th December.

The first thing Ward told you was that you were charged with the
murder of Miss Barrow by poisoning her with arsenic?—He came up
afterwards and told me if I came round the corner he would let me know
why I was arrested. He took me into Fonthill Road.

There is only one other matter I want to ask you about. Just take
your Post Office Savings Bank book (handed). The bedroom safe £100
has been exhausted. In the downstairs safe there was £15 in gold. How
was that £15 in gold downstairs used?—I used it for my holiday at
Southend.

That disposes of all the money in the downstairs safe?—Yes.

I see by that book that on 27th November, 1911, you withdrew

Trial of the Seddons.

Frederick H. Seddon

£43 17s. 9d. from the Post Office Savings Bank?—Yes. Of that money £20 was in £5 notes. I put £20 of the gold in a bag, and wrote outside " £20." I drew £1, and then put " £19 " on the bag, that being the bag that has been produced, and was found by the police in my safe. This £43 17s. 9d. was drawn out so as to always have cash on hand, as I had always been in the habit of doing.

There is one final question I want to ask you. Did you ever administer or cause to be administered to Miss Barrow any arsenic in any shape or form whatever?—I never purchased arsenic in my life in any shape or form. I never administered arsenic. I never advised, directed, or instructed the purchase of arsenic in any shape or form. I never advised, directed, or instructed the administration of arsenic. That I swear.

Cross-examined by the ATTORNEY-GENERAL—Miss Barrow lived with you from 26th July, 1910, till the morning of 14th September, 1911?—Yes.

Did you like her?—Did I like her?

Yes, that is the question?—She was not a woman that you could be in love with, but I deeply sympathised with her.

Was she a woman about eight or nine years older than yourself?—She was nine years older than myself.

You talked of her as " an old lady " when you went to the under-taker?—I always addressed her as an " old lady."

During the time that she was living with you at your house did you advise her on her financial affairs?—Certainly, I advised her.

From quite an early period of her coming to your house did she, to use your words, place herself under your protection?—Only against Hook.

When she came to live with you on 26th July of 1910 she had, as you ascertained afterwards, £1600 India 3½ per cent. stock. Is that right?—I did not ascertain that till September.

But that is what she had when she came to you on 26th July, 1910, as you afterwards ascertained?—She must have possessed it.

And that would bring in?—A trifle over £1 a week.

Was she also the leaseholder of the premises, the Buck's Head and the barber's shop?—The superior leaseholder, yes.

And was she drawing an income from that of at least £120 per annum?—Something like that.

Was that a lease that would expire in 1929?—About eighteen years, or eighteen and a half, at the time she was speaking to me. That was another source of anxiety to her.

And were Truman, Hanbury & Co. the tenants of the public-house, the Buck's Head, for the period of her lease?—For the full period?

Yes?—I do not know. I was under the impression that they could give up the tenancy.

Do you mean when the assignment was made?—Up to the time I was advising her.

Do you mean that at the time the assignment was made?—To me?

Yes?—No, because Mr. Keeble had explained then.

At any rate, at the time the assignment was made you knew that

Evidence for Defence.

Frederick H. Seddon

Messrs. Truman, Hanbury & Co. were sub-lessees for the whole period of her term?—Yes.

She had to pay £20 rent to her lessor, and she would get from Truman, Hanbury & Co. £105 a year for the tenancy of the public-house, is that right?—Yes.

And £50 a year from the tenant of the barber's shop?—Yes.

Then she had the compensation fund to pay out of it. I will not forget that. That will be £155 without going into any detail; I will take your own figure; after paying out whatever sums there were to be paid from that £155 it left her an income of £128?—I believe so.

So that she had £120 a year until 1929, and she had £56 a year coming from the India 3½ per cent. stock, as you subsequently found out?—Yes.

What are you looking at?—Some figures.

You will do much better to listen to the questions I am putting to you. In your own interests it is better that you should not give me only half your attention to what I am asking. If there is anything you want to look at, say so, and I will wait until you have looked at it?—I want to make sure as to the returns from the property—what she got from her property—so much a year.

I thought we had agreed on that; I have put this question to you already. As I said to you, I will take it without going into too great detail. You said it was a little over £1 a week from the India stock?—Yes.

There is no doubt about that, and as to the rest I have taken your own figures. As you subsequently ascertained, she had also over £200 in the Finsbury and City of London Savings Bank?—Yes.

She also had a cash box with some money in it when she came to you?—Yes.

Some gold?—I do not know; I never saw the inside of the cash box.

There was some money in the cash box, according to a statement she made to you?—£30 or £35, she said.

And you did not know whether it was in notes or cash?—I only took her statement for it.

Are you representing to my lord and the jury that you never knew whether she had notes in the cash box or not?—At that date, yes.

At any date?—I knew she had notes in October, because she had given some to me.

From the cash box?—I do not know where she got them from.

Had she a banking account?—The Finsbury——

Any banking account except that?—I do not know.

Now, we will leave out of consideration for the moment altogether the cash box and the notes from that or elsewhere. She came to you, then, with India 3½ per cent. stock, bringing in £1 a week, the property bringing in £120 a year, and over £200 in the Finsbury Savings Bank; that is right?—Yes.

She remained in your house from that date, 26th July, 1910, till 14th September, 1911, when you examined all that there was to see of the property that was left?—Yes.

Trial of the Seddons.

Frederick H. Seddon

When she came to live with you did she bring this boy Ernie Grant with her?—Yes.

And did he live with her right up to the end?—Yes.

Did you know that he was an orphan?—Yes.

That she was deeply attached to him?—No.

That she was looking after him?—Yes.

That she cared for him?—Well, she found him very useful to her.

He lived with her entirely?—Yes.

She paid for him?—She could not very well do without him.

And she paid for him—she clothed and fed him?—Oh, yes, yes.

She had been very attached to his mother, had she not, you knew that?—Not that I have learnt; I have heard they quarrelled a lot.

But she certainly had some desire to leave property to the boy, had she not?—She was satisfied that the boy had a good home with me.

What do you mean by that?—Because I promised her he should have a home with me.

When did you promise her that?—I often told her that.

When did you tell it her first?—I could not say for certain.

About when, do you think?—I could not remember.

Was it about the time that you entered into these negotiations to grant her the annuity?—I think it was about March—about the time I got the letter from her when she was talking about the will, when she had been to a funeral, as far as I recollect—about that date.

On 14th September, 1911, when she died, was all the property that was found of hers a sum of £10 in gold, and furniture, jewellery, and other belongings to the value of £16 14s. 6d.?—According to the inventory ta en by Mr. Gregory, a reputed auctioneer and appraiser, it was £16 odd.

And the only cash that was left was, according to you, £10, of which £4 10s. was found in the box, £3 in the fold of a paper in the drawer, and £2 10s. in a bag which was hanging by the bed?—That, I swear, was all I found.

And during that time, and until you made the arrangements about the annuity, was the amount which she had to pay to you 12s. a week?—Rent, yes.

There was, besides that, as I have understood from what you have said, a shilling a day which she paid to your daughter Maggie?—For pocket money.

Which would make the total amount she had to pay 19s. a week. She lived upstairs in the bedroom with this little boy Ernie, did she not?—Yes, she had four rooms.

For the 12s. she had the four rooms?—Yes.

She lived very simply?—She did not live as simply as what we lived ourselves.

At any rate, as I understand it, so simply that your daughter cooked her food mostly?—My daughter never cooked chickens for her. Whatever plain food she had, my daughter cooked, but whenever she had anything else that needed my wife to cook my wife cooked it for her.

She was living well within the income I have just referred to, was she not?—I could not say.

Evidence for Defence.

Frederick H. Seddon

Have you any reason to doubt it?—I was the superintendent of an insurance company; I was not the housekeeper.

So far as you know, during the time that she lived in that house, was she living within her income, as far as you could judge?—I could not say; I had not any idea.

That means, at any rate, that you had not any idea—you did not know that she lived above it?—I knew when my wife was cooking chickens and anything like that for her. She had everything she fancied, as far as I knew.

Did you know that your wife had had a number of bank notes which had come from her?—I knew my wife had one.

You know now, do you not, from what has been proved and admitted in this case—proved by some forty witnesses altogether—that during this period thirty-three bank notes have been traced either to you or to your wife?—My wife tells me that she admits it, and I admit six.

That makes, at any rate, £165 in notes which somehow or other had come from her during the period in which she was living in your house?—Which she has apparently turned into cash.

Who is "she"?—Miss Barrow.

What do you mean by "apparently turned into cash"?—That she has had the notes turned into cash.

Who—Miss Barrow?—Yes.

Let us go by steps and see what you mean. Thirty-three £5 notes have been traced as coming from her to you or to your wife?—Yes.

What I am putting to you is that that, at any rate, shows that she had at least £165 in notes within the period that she was in your house? —I do not attempt to deny it.

And that she came with those notes to your house?—I could not say.

Where did you say the notes came from?—I could not say.

When did you first know that your wife had used a false name and address in cashing these notes?—When she was arrested.

Did she tell you—(What are you looking for?—Only a drink of water). Take it by all means (handed)?—I heard it in evidence at the Police Court, and I asked my wife about it in the dock. She said yes, she had given a wrong name and address at one or two where she was not known.

Any other explanation?—I have another explanation; she said she gave Miss Barrow the change, of course, when she cashed them; she explained that to me.

Did she explain that to you in the dock?—I certainly questioned her in the dock, because it was a big surprise to me. She said that Miss Barrow had always had the change; she was asked to cash them for her.

Was that why she was giving a false name and address?—I do not know why she gave the false name and address. She said she had only done it where she was not known. She did not want everybody to know who she was.

Why should not everybody know who she was when she was cashing a £5 note?—She explained to me if she went into a shop where she was

Trial of the Seddons.

not known to buy a small article she did not want everybody to know who she was.

Do you mean making purchases in the ordinary course of things?—Yes, I think so. That is what I understood from her.

Children's clothing?—I do not know what they were.

Is that the only explanation that has been given to you, according to you?—She has not had much time to give me much explanation. She has been in custody all the time. · She could only whisper this to me at the North London Police Court. I was naturally anxious and surprised, and I wanted an explanation.

Do you know that those notes have been traced as having been cashed during every single month of the year from October to the end of August, 1911?—No, I do not.

Was it about October that you began negotiations with her about an annuity?—About September, I think.

According to the documents we have, the first letter is 5th October?—Yes. Would that be the first letter to the Bank of England?

It is the first letter of which we have any trace?—Yes.

You, of course, were very familiar with annuity transactions?—I was not.

Your company did annuity business?—Yes, I believe so, but I never during the whole twenty years I was with the company once introduced an annuity.

You are familiar with your company's prospectuses?—Yes, they have an annuity.

Do you not know there is a table for immediate annuities, as they have for all kinds of policies?—Yes.

And I suppose you get a commission from your company for any special business you may introduce?—Yes; I do not know what the special commission is on that table.

It would not appear on the table, of course?—No, but I have never been informed what the commission on that table is.

According to your statement you arrived at an agreement with her that she was to transfer to you all her India stock and her property, the "Buck's Head" and the barber's shop, and you were to give her an annuity of £2 to £3 a week?—What she wanted.

That was her proposal?—Yes.

And you were advising her?—I was agreeing with her.

Had you ever done an annuity transaction before?—Never in my life.

This is the one solitary instance?—Yes; it has never entered my mind.

This has turned out a remarkably profitable investment from the monetary point of view?—Only from that point of view.

On your statement you had paid out altogether £91?—Yes.

And the whole of the property fell in to you?—I was already in possession of the whole of the property.

But you had no longer any money to pay out?—That did not yield me very much.

Evidence for Defence.

Frederick H. Seddon

What do you mean by saying that did not yield you very much?—I had only to pay out £2 8s. a week.

But it left you at any rate in possession of the property, without any payment to make at all?—But I was 7s. a week out that was paid to my daughter, and I had the boy to keep, which was nearly 13s. a week; that is £1 a week. It only left me 28s.

You had got the property on the condition that you were to pay out the annuity?—Yes, exactly, which I did.

You had sold the India 3½ per cent. stock for some £1516?—For a better investment.

You had bought the property in Coutts Road with that?—Yes.

The fourteen houses which we have heard of?—Which brought me £4 a week against her £1—£4 a week profit against her £1 a week.

You had got that property?—Yes, exactly; it was good security for her, too.

What I am putting to you is that when she died it is clear you had no longer to pay out money to her, whatever it was you had agreed to pay her?—Certainly not; that is the basis on which an annuity is granted.

That I agree. It is very important, of course, in the purchase of an annuity to have security that the money would be paid?—Yes.

Would you tell me what security you gave her for the payment of the annuity during the whole of the remainder of her life on the India 3½ per cent.?—Yes, she had 12s. a week saved in rent, which was entered in her rent book "rent free," as arranged, and I gave her an annuity certificate in payment of the amount of the annuity which would be paid to her by my heirs, executors, or administrators in the event of my decease.

You are speaking of an annuity certificate?—Yes.

You told the coroner at the inquest that this arrangement about the 3½ per cent. was a verbal one?—At that time it was a verbal arrangement. She got no annuity certificate from the date she transferred the stock from October until January.

What is the annuity certificate that you are speaking of?—It is a type-written certificate drawn up by myself and signed and witnessed over a sixpenny stamp.

Where is it?—I do not know where the original is; there is a copy of it in existence.

I should like to see the original?—The original is with the duplicate deed of the Buck's Head. Miss Barrow had charge of that, of course.

Whatever the document was, the security was the obligation on you to pay?—I am bound legally to pay.

Oh, I know, but do you mean to say you do not know the difference between security and a personal obligation on you to pay after your years' experience in business?—I had 5 to 1 on security.

I am not asking about you; I have no doubt you had sufficient security?—I intended to carry out my obligations. I have never been known to break them during the whole course of my life.

I put to you a very definite question, and I want your answer to it. You were dealing with this woman who was living in your house, and who had certainly, as regards this matter, no other advice?—That was

175

Trial of the Seddons.

Frederick H. Seddon

her fault; she was offered it; she was advised to have a solicitor. What more could a man do?   I bound myself by legal documents to pay her the annuity, and I carried out my obligations.

Till 14th September?—I would have carried them out during the whole course so long as she lived.   The funds were increasing year by year.   I was getting stronger financially all the time, and I gave her better value than the Post Office could give by over £460.

This is what you said, is it true—"I guaranteed to her another annuity from the 1st January on India stock of £72 a year, and she saved 12s. a week in rent.   She had no security"?—I do not think I said it in that form.

Is that not true?—I think it was a leading question put by the coroner.

But is it not true that she had no security?—Isn't legal documents security—isn't my financial strength security?

Did you realise she had the security in respect of the £1 a week from the Buck's Head charge?—She had.

Charged on the property?—Charged on the property.

That is security?—Yes, that is security.

Do you wish the jury to believe that you do not know the difference between making an obligation to pay the money and giving security for the payment of it?—But isn't a legally drawn up certificate security on my estate?

Do you not know that is only a personal obligation on you?—I understand it is recoverable by law.

Well, I have given you an opportunity of dealing with it.   "She transferred it to me in October on the verbal condition that I should allow her an annuity in all of between £2 10s. and £3 per week."   That is right?—That is right.

So that in October, when she transferred this to you, you were in complete possession of it?—I was in possession of the £1600 of India stock.   She was depending absolutely upon my verbal promise to grant her the annuity at that date.

You told us that all this as regards the Buck's Head and the barber's shop was done by solicitors, and that the stock was transferred by stockbrokers, and so forth?—Yes.

Did you try to do it first of all without solicitors and stockbrokers?—I believe I did.

Did you try to do it by a document which you drew up between yourself and her?—Yes.

Without any solicitors in the matter at all?—Yes.

Or stockbroker?—Yes; well, I did not try to do it, but I drafted up a document.

Did you have it witnessed?—Yes.

By whom?—My wife.

Anybody else?—Not to her signature.

To whose signature?—To my signature.

By whom was it witnessed?—It was a double document, you see.

By whom did you have your signature witnessed?—Mrs. Seddon's brother.

What is his name?—Arthur Jones.

176

Evidence for Defence.

Frederick H. Seddon

Anybody else?—I cannot recollect.

What has become of that document?—It was destroyed.

Why?—Because I intended to put the document in the hands of the solicitors, Russell & Sons, and have the whole property investigated.

Were you advised that a document drawn up in that way was of no account?—Yes.

And therefore you went to the solicitors?—Oh, no, no; it was the solicitor, Mr. Keeble, that advised me a document of that description would be of no account.

And that, therefore, it had to be drawn up in proper legal form? Exactly; that is how it is.

The solicitors came upon the scene?—I had gone to them.

But you had gone to them to advise you as to whether this document was good?—No; I decided myself that the document was not good.

Why?—Because I did not consider it would be sufficient.

What was the matter with it?—I cannot recollect now the terms of it exactly. It was a document that I drew up myself; it was not drawn up in a proper legal way.

It was what?—It was a document that was not drawn up in a proper legal way; it was in general terms—something to the effect that I would allow her so much a year, and she would transfer the stock and property.

The point of the question that I am putting to you is this, you have been laying stress on the fact that this was done through solicitors and brokers, and all done in regular form?—So it was.

Was not that because you were advised that having started to do it yourself it would not be a good and valid document?—No.

You were so advised?—I was so advised.

And you had drawn it up beforehand?—Yes.

And you had intended to carry it out?—I decided before I went to the solicitors. I studied it myself.

You studied what yourself?—The document. I considered myself it would be no good. One thought led to another in the transaction. I did not intend to grant her an annuity first myself. It was when she suggested that I should grant her an annuity the thought entered my head, and I started, of course, to study it; one thought led to another, and this is when I drafted the document up.

Not only had you drafted the document up, but you had had it witnessed by your wife, according to you, your wife's brother, and I suggest to you somebody else?—Yes.

A Mr. Robert?—Roberts.

John Roberts?—Some name like that.

So that was the document. It had been signed when you had it?— Well it had not been signed entirely; they witnessed my signature afterwards.

You signed it?—Yes.

And your wife witnessed your signature?—No.

I thought you told us that?—No, my wife witnessed Miss Barrow's signature.

Your wife witnessed Miss Barrow's signature, and your wife's brother and Mr. John Roberts witnessed your signature?—The next day.

Trial of the Seddons.

Frederick H. Seddon

So that the document was complete?—For what it was worth.

Who is Louie?—A sister of mine.

Were you anxious that this matter should not come out at the inquest about your having drawn the document first of all, and having had it witnessed before you went to the lawyers?—No.

Did you wish the assurance given to your brother-in-law, Arthur Jones, that he was not in it at all?—Yes.

And that he would not be called?—Yes.

And that nothing would come out about those original documents which have been drawn?—I did not say so.

Was not that the effect of it?—No.

Was not that what you meant?—No.

And everything had passed into the hands of the lawyers?—I told him that before he left London.

In point of fact, nothing has ever been said until the question I put to you just now had been answered about these documents having been drawn up and this document having been drawn up and witnessed before the lawyers came upon the scene at all?—Nothing had been said to anybody.

Nothing had been said either at the inquest or at the Police Court?—No.

Or here in this Court?—No; because they are non-existent.

I want to put one question to you to which I want your particular attention. By the death of Miss Barrow you benefited in money, at any rate, by not having to pay the annuity?—To the amount of 28s.

And the amount of 20s.—you arrive at——?—Weekly——

By taking into account the 12s. a week which you would have to pay, as I understand you——

Mr. MARSHALL HALL—He said he would have to pay 13s. for the boy, and he would lose the 7s. that the girl got.

By the ATTORNEY-GENERAL—Will you tell us, I am not sure how you make that up?—I paid her £2 8s. a week. Out of that my daughter received 7s. That makes £2 1s. Then I keep and clothe the boy, which I consider is equal to 13s. a week, so that is £1 out of £2 8s., which leaves 28s. And at that time I am in receipt of £14 14s. 3d. weekly.

Can you tell me whether you can suggest anybody else who would benefit, according to what you know, in money, by the death of Miss Barrow?—If Miss Barrow died intestate naturally the cousins would inherit.

Yes, but she did make a will?—But the relatives were not aware of that before she died.

The will was made on the 11th, and she died on the morning of the 14th?—Yes.

I am asking you about what the state of affairs was on the morning of the 14th, when she died. Was there anybody who would benefit by the death except yourself?—And the children.

To the extent you mean of the furniture and belongings?—Yes.

I will leave that out; that was a small matter of £16?—No; I cannot say that they would, but I had not taken that into consideration.

What?—I had not got that in my mind.

Evidence for Defence.

Frederick H. Seddon

But, I am right in saying, am I not, that there was nobody else would benefit except the children to that extent?—You put that in my mind.

That is right, is it not?—Yes, of course.

What do you mean by saying that I put that in your mind; do you mean that it had never occurred to you before?—I had not given it consideration before.

Do you mean you had not thought of this before?—Only by what the prosecution had suggested, that the fact of my benefiting may——

What?—From the fact of my benefiting they considered they were justified in arresting me.

Was Miss Barrow a person of ordinary mental capacity?—Yes, ordinary; I consider she was a very deep woman.

Was she very deaf?—She was not deaf that she could not hear; she could hear fairly well; you had to speak in her ear; she could hear me speaking in ordinary tones, if I was speaking close to her ear. She could hear music and singing well.

She wore glasses to read by, did she not?—Sometimes, not always. She could see without glasses.

And the room in which she lived, I suppose, was an ordinary bedroom?—Yes.

With the ordinary bedroom furniture?—Yes.

I mean, with a basin, jug, and water?—Yes.

Water bottle, and all that sort of thing, with a glass?—Yes.

A chest of drawers?—Yes.

And a bed, and the usual bedroom furniture?—Yes.

Where was the light in that room?—Over the mantelpiece.

What light was it?—Gas light.

During the whole time that she was with you, from 26th July, 1910, to 1st September, 1911, had you ever known her to be laid up?—Occasionally a day or two in bed, or anything like that, but never what you would call bedfast.

You said something just now to my learned friend about your not thinking she was a good life?—I did not; from my observations, I considered she was an indifferent life.

Did you form that opinion at the time you were negotiating with her for the annuity?—I might have done.

You would have done?—Yes, I might have done; I looked upon her as an indifferent life.

That is an element which you would take into account in determining whether or not you would enter into the annuity transaction?—Her average expectation of life in any case was only twenty or twenty-one years, and I calculated if she lived out that term how my financial position would be; it would increase year by year.

Your view was that she would not live over that term?—I did not feel she would.

And according to your view, as you have expressed it, you thought she would live less than that term?—Yes, I did not expect her to live her average expectation of life—a woman in her indifferent state of health.

Trial of the Seddons.

Frederick H. Seddon

And you have told us you would not expect her to live twenty-one years?—Yes; she would not be a life that I could recommend to an insurance company to accept.

I should like to understand, if the ordinary expectation of her life was twenty-one years—the life of a woman of that age—and you thought, as you told us, it was going to be less than that, what sort of a view did you form in your own mind about it?—I could not say; I could not tell how long the woman was going to live.

But some years less?—I have known people in consumption outlive healthy people; as the old saying is, "A creaky gate hangs a long time."

During the whole time that she was at your house, how often were you in her room? Take, first of all, the period before 1st September, when she was taken ill?—I never went up into Miss Barrow's room excepting I had occasion as the landlord of the house to go, whenever she had repairs she wanted to do—when she complained of whiting falling off the ceiling, and that sort of thing.

Did she used to come into your room at all?—Always into the dining-room; she had the free use of the house; she went where she liked.

From the time she was ill, 1st September, is it right that your wife was attending her?—Yes.

And looked after the food?—Yes, as far as I knew.

And looked after her generally from the time she was ill?—Yes, she wanted her; it was too much for Maggie.

You told us about the will you made on 11th September. Had you any idea that she wanted to make a will?—Not until my wife told me.

When was that?—I could not swear whether it was on the Sunday or the Monday, the day that it was made; I am not quite sure. It was mentioned to me twice before I attended to it.

There is no doubt that you did draw the will?—Oh, I did, yes; I do not deny it.

It is in your handwriting?—Yes.

You have told us about the instructions she gave you as to what she wanted?—Yes, but I knew what she wanted doing, she had often told me.

Did you think it was important that she should make a will that day?—I did not think it was important that she should make a will that day, I only drafted it up to satisfy her; it was my intention to go and see Mr. Keeble and get a proper one drafted up.

Drawn by a solicitor?—The one that had acted in respect to the property before. She would not have solicitors. Of course, I intended to take her to a solicitor.

What property did you think she had to leave on that date, 11th September?—I never gave it a thought.

When you were thinking of having a solicitor to come and draw it? —Yes.

Do you say, then, that according to your view you did not know that she had any property at all?—She was dealing with the children's property.

The furniture and the jewellery?—Yes, that is what she was con-

180

Evidence for Defence.

Frederick H. Seddon

cerned about; she did not want that to get into Hook's hands, because he was the next-of-km to the sister, Mrs. Grant.

The jewellery and her personal belongings?—She said that the watch was the boy's father's watch, and she wanted the boy to have that watch.

Who suggested you should be trustee and executor?—She decided I should be. She wanted me to look after everything; she had taken me into her confidence from the beginning, and, naturally, she wanted me to attend to everything in the end.

You were in her confidence—she looked to you for assistance and protection, did she not?—Yes, there was no particular claim regarding protection; I mentioned the word "protection" when the Hooks were living in the house.

What I mean by protection is that you were in her complete confidence?—I was the owner of the house, and I would naturally protect my tenant.

Never mind Hook for the moment. You were completely in her confidence?—Not completely in her confidence, no.

We will say you were in her confidence?—She had confidence in me, that is what I mean; I was not a confidant of hers; she never told me anything about herself, or affairs, or family.

Of course, you realised that she was, at any rate, trusting in you?—To see that the children got this, yes.

As far as I understand from what you have said, her whole anxiety about this will then was simply as to this furniture and the small amount of jewellery to the boy and girl, Hilda and Ernest Grant?—Yes; her principal anxiety was about the uncle of the boy.

What about her money?—She never mentioned it.

But you were making her will?—Yes, but I tell you I drew it up hurriedly. I never expected that that will would ever be used.

Is that why you made it?—I made it to satisfy her. She wanted a will, and I told her to have a solicitor.

Is that why you wanted it witnessed when it was made?—It had to be witnessed.

In order to be a legal document?—Yes, it would not satisfy her without.

You knew she was worse, did you not?—No, I did not.

Mr. MARSHALL HALL—I do not want my learned friend to mislead. I think the doctor's evidence is that she was better.

The WITNESS—I did not consider her any different to any other day that she had been in bed.

By the ATTORNEY-GENERAL—The doctor has told us that he came to see her in the morning, and he has told us what her condition was?—But I did not know then; I know now from what the doctor says.

Did you inquire at all as to what her condition was?—No.

At least, you knew then, did you not, that supposing she happened to die before her will was made——?—She was a woman who complained more than necessary with regard to her ailments.

She does not seem, according to her view, to have complained as much as was necessary?—I do not follow that.

Trial of the Seddons.

Frederick H. Seddon

On 11th September she was ill, was she not?—Yes.

She had been in bed from 1st September?—2nd September.

Taken ill on 1st September, and remained in bed?—She was in bed, at any rate, as far as I know, from 2nd September and got up on one occasion and went out of the room right along the landing into the boy's room.

Then on 11th September, when this will was made, how long consideration had you given to it?—I had not given a great amount of consideration to it at all.

You have told us that she asked you to do it once or twice before?—Yes; well, it passed my mind again after; I did not give it a great amount of consideration; I always felt in these matters she ought to have independent legal advice.

Had you some forms of wills in your possession?—I think I had a torn one. (After a pause.) No, not on that date.

When did you get it?—At a later date.

When?—Some time after the death.

How long after the death?—I could not say; I bought some for the purpose of having my own will drafted up.

Had you any experience in drawing wills?—No.

Had you anything to help you to draw this one—had you any form before you when you drew this one?—No, I do not think so; no, I had not a form before me. I have seen the printed form of wills.

This is a document, as you know, which is drawn up in a legal form?—I do not know that it is drawn up in legal form. For instance, I was informed at Somerset House that the attestation clause was wrong or something.

At any rate it uses legal language?—It uses legal terms that I am acquainted with.

That is what I want to get from you, legal terms that you are acquainted with?—Yes, I have seen on the printed will forms.

That is what I put to you; you had seen the printed will forms, and you had seen the kind of language, at any rate, that had to be in the will, and you draw up, " This is the last will and testament of me, Eliza Mary Barrow, 63 Tollington Park, Finsbury Park, N. I hereby revoke all former wills and codicils." That you knew?—Yes.

You knew the expression, did you not, " all she died possessed of "?—I used that expression.

Not in the will. Do you not know that you did not use it in the will? Look at the will. In the will you speak of " household furniture, jewellery, and other personal effects "?—Does it not say " inclusive of " something? I thought " all she died possessed of " was in the will.

Let me understand what you mean by that. Just think a moment. Are you suggesting that you thought that in the will the property that was to be passed upon her death would include cash?—I did not know; I never gave it consideration. It escaped my mind for the time being. It was done quite hurriedly. My sister had only just come from Wolverhampton, and I was busy with my office work at the time, and I did it quite hurriedly.

Evidence for Defence.

Frederick H. Seddon

Let me put to you the suggestion I am going to make quite plainly, so that you may understand it before I put the question to you. Now, I want you to follow it. I do not want you to fall into any trap, so that I am going to put the point of my question to you so that you may just follow?—Yes.

In the will again and again you speak of "all my personal effects," "all my personal belongings, furniture, clothing, and jewellery," "all my personal belongings comprising jewellery and furniture and clothing," "and articles of furniture and clothing," "any article of jewellery," and so forth. There is no reference to anything else but that. In your letter of 14th September, 1911 (the copy letter which is in question), you write to Mr. Vonderahe this—"I must also inform you that she made a will on the 11th instant leaving all she died possessed of to Hilda and Ernest Grant"?—At that time I knew what she had died possessed of. That is a later date after I had gone through her trunk and cash-box, and knew what she was possessed of.

This is written three days after the will—on 14th September?—Yes. Well, I was in the same position at this date. I had gone through the trunk then; that is what I say.

In the letter of 21st September you said—"As executor to the will of Miss Barrow, dated 11th September, 1911, I hereby certify that Miss Barrow has left all she died possessed of to Hilda and Ernest Grant"?—Yes.

That is the same expression which is used in the copy letter on the mourning paper on 14th September?—Yes.

Did you mean Mr. Vonderahe to understand by that expression that she died possessed of——?—All that I knew she was possessed of.

Including cash?—Anything, yes.

When you made that will on 11th September, did you think she had any cash at all?—I never gave it any thought. If I had known that will would be required shortly, perhaps I would have exercised more care in the drafting up of it, or if I had thought that she was going to die shortly I should have absolutely insisted upon a solicitor being called in. I never anticipated this.

Let me read the whole of the language of the will to you—"This is the last will and testament of me, Eliza Mary Barrow, of 63 Tollington Park, Finsbury Park, London North. I hereby revoke all former wills and codicils, and in the event of my decease I give and bequeath all my household furniture, jewellery, and other personal effects to Hilda Grant and Ernest Grant, and appoint Frederick Henry Seddon, of 63 Tollington Park, London North, my sole executor of this my will "—" sole executor of this my will "?—That is no benefit to me; the will is not in my favour. The will is for the boy and girl.

" To hold all my personal belongings, furniture, clothing, and jewellery, in trust until the aforesaid Hilda Grant and Ernest Grant become of age, as they are at this date minors. Then for him to dispose as equally as possible all my personal belongings, comprising jewellery, furniture, and clothing to them, or to sell for cash any article of furni-

Trial of the Seddons.

ture or clothing either of them do not desire, and equally distribute the cash so realised, and no article of jewellery must be sold. Signed this 11th day of September, 1911." That is witnessed by your wife and signed by Miss Barrow, and witnessed by your father. That is the document?—Yes.

How long did it take you to write out that document?—A very few minutes.

Do you mean you wrote it off just as it is here, out of your head?—Yes.

Without looking into any book?—Yes.

Without looking at any form?—Otherwise I should have had the attestation clause in.

Using the language that is there merely from memory?—Yes.

Memory of what you have read in other forms?—Yes.

Had you studied them at all?—No; but I had often seen them. You read them in the Encyclopædia and Post Office books.

What?—I have seen them in a book.

What book?—I could not say what kind of book.

I heard you say something about an Encyclopædia?—Something like that—some kind of a book like that.

Like the Encyclopædia?—Yes—how to draw up a will.

Have you looked into the Encyclopædia at all?—I think I have in days gone by.

Do you possess one?—I do not know whether I did or not. I forget. I think I have got something like that in the office.

Let me come back to the letter which I am putting to you, dated 14th September, 1911. "I must inform you that she made a will on the 11th instant leaving what she died posesssed of to Hilda and Ernest Grant." As I understand from the answer you have given, what you meant was that you knew then what money there was, and when you said, "What she died possessed of," you meant to include everything?—I used terms that I had not given sufficient thought to.

You see, you are writing to her relatives. It is rather important, is it not, to tell the relatives how she left her property?—Yes, but I gave them an exact copy.

That is not an answer?—I am not perfect; I could not make a perfect will; I could not make a perfect document.

I am not criticising the language of the document?—If we could then we would not want solicitors to draw up a will. It is a home-made will. It was never intended to have been acted upon, not that one.

What do you mean by repeating that?—It was my intention to have taken it down to Mr. Keeble and to have a proper will drafted up.

This was on the 11th?—Yes; I did not know she was going to die in a day or two after.

And you did not think she was in danger?—I did not. There is always danger where there is illness, certainly.

Was that present to your mind?—It was not present at the time; no, I did not give sufficient consideration to it.

Evidence for Defence.

Frederick H. Seddon

Did you think that this patient was in danger at all during any time of her illness?—The doctor never gave me any idea.

That is not an answer to the question?—Well, I had no idea she was likely to die.

That is not an answer to the question I am putting to you. Any time during that illness did you think she was in any danger?—I did not think she would die; I thought she had exaggerated her ailment.

Then do you mean that you never thought there was any danger in her illness?—I have said there is always a danger in illness.

Any danger of that illness terminating fatally?—I did not consider it would.

You never gave a thought to it; is that what you mean?—No, I am a busy man when I am out; I had other things to occupy my attention.

You told us what went on during the time from 2nd September to the night of the 13th, which I will come to directly. During all that time this patient had been rather trying, as I understood you?—To the wife. She always preferred the wife to attend to her instead of Maggie.

Except for one day during this period the doctor had been coming every day?—Yes.

You were finding her so troublesome that you were talking of having her sent to a hospital?—I wanted her to go to the hospital, or I wanted her to have a nurse. I suggested calling a relative in, Mrs. Cognoni, who had written to her.

At the time you saw Mrs. Vonderahe, on 21st September, when you gave her the letter, exhibit 3, in which you said, "She has simply left furniture, jewellery, and clothing," you knew she had drawn out £216 on 19th June, 1911?—Yes.

That is not three months before her death?—No.

What has become of that?—I do not know.

Your wife was with her when it was drawn out?—Yes.

It was drawn out in gold?—My wife said so.

It was brought to your house?—Yes, and she said she knew what to do with it. She never spoke to me for nearly a week after, because I said she had no right to bring so much gold to put into her trunk.

So did you offer to take care of it for her and lock it into your safe?—No, I said there were plenty of good banks if she was not satisfied with that small one up in Upper Street.

Why should you not offer to lock it up in your safe for her?—Because I did not want to have anything at all to do with it.

Why not?—There was no necessity.

Why should you not take charge of her money, and lock it up in your safe for her?—I did not want the responsibility, I did not want such a responsibility.

You had offered to do that long before?—Only temporarily, while Hook was in the house. I said if she would count it out in my presence she could hold the key, and I would give her a receipt for the amount in the box.

Mr. Justice Bucknill—In that connection would you ask him whether he expected on 14th September to find the money?

Trial of the Seddons.

Frederick H. Seddon

By the ATTORNEY-GENERAL—When you went to look on 14th September, after her death, did you expect to find that £200 odd?—I did not know.

Did you expect, was the question I put to you?—Well, I thought it might be there, but I had no idea as to what she had done with it. She said she knew what to do with it. I did not mention the money to her again, because she did not speak to me for over a week because I spoke to her about bringing it into the house, because it was only a frail trunk, and she had workmen there doing repairs, and the window cleaners, and it was not safe with people going in and out of her rooms like that.

Did you ever say one word to either Mrs. Vonderahe or Mr. Vonderahe, when you saw him, about this £216 having been withdrawn?—No, I did not.

So far as they were concerned, until it was given in evidence that this had been drawn out from the bank after it was traced by the police, they knew nothing whatever of it?—Not from me. I knew nothing of it myself.

Had not your wife told you on the very day it was drawn out?—Yes, I am referring to what had become of it.

During the whole time of that illness did you think that money was in existence?—I did not give it any consideration; my mind was occupied with other things.

Just think?—My business——

Just think what you say. Your mind, according to what you have told us, was much agitated by her putting this money into the trunk in her room?—That was months before.

That was on 19th June, 1911?—Yes.

And you have told us that it disturbed you?—At the time, yes, but then she told me she knew what to do with it.

Did you make any further inquiry from her about it?—No, she said she knew what to do with it, and she walked out of the room, and she treated me with indifference for about a week after.

But so far as you were concerned?—I treated it like that. (The witness snapped his fingers.) I did not bother anything further about it.

You treated the £200 like that. (Snapping his fingers.) Is that your explanation?—Yes.

So far as you were concerned, then, you had no reason to doubt that she had taken the money up and done what she said she was going to do with it?—I did not know what she was going to do with it.

Do you mean that you did not know whether she had put the money into the box or not?—Yes, I believe she did that day.

And with this anxiety of yours as to what was to happen to the money in her trunk did you never inquire from her as to whether it was still there?—She did not give me any satisfaction on the occasion when I put it to her, and when she said she would know what to do with it, well, then I left it to her. You must remember she was a peculiar person to deal with.

As far as you were concerned, when you made this will this £200 odd might have been in her trunk?—I did not know; I never considered

Evidence for Defence.

Frederick H. Seddon

it; it never entered into my mind. I told you I did the thing hurriedly. I did not give sufficient consideration to it.

When you were making her will, and taking her instructions, as I understand you, it never occurred to you what had happened to that money that she had drawn from the bank?—Her instructions only amounted to that she wanted the boy and girl to have the things belonging to their parents; that was all; that was the whole sum and substance of the instructions. That was drafted up, and she read it for herself.

Did you not give some sort of thought of what was to happen in case she died and this will had to take effect?—I did not take that into consideration.

Did you hear the evidence of the boy Ernie Grant?—Yes.

Did you hear what he said about her counting out the money from the cash box?—About Miss Barrow?

On the bed?—Yes, I heard it. She would count out the £10 I gave her, you know, would she not? Whenever I paid her £10 she would count that.

By Mr. Justice Bucknill—If you thought that what she intended to do with the will was only that she wanted the children, and not the Hooks, to have the things she was possessed of—the jewellery, furniture, and so forth—and if you had thought about the money which had been taken out of the savings bank, you must have known, must you not, that that would go to her nearest relations?—Yes, if I had given that amount of consideration I should certainly.

And so you might have said to the Vonderahes, "Look here, she has only left the children these particular things, but there was a time in June when she had over £200 in a box, and it is not there now. That would have come to you"?—Yes.

So you were not surprised perhaps at not finding it there?—I did not mention that sum of money, because I had no way of accounting for that sum of money; I did not know what had become of it, you see.

Have I got this down right, and is this a fair way of putting it, "I did not mention the savings bank money to the Vonderahes after her death because I did not know what had become of it"?—That is not exactly the reason why I did not mention it; it never came to my mind at that time.

Would it be fair, then, to add, "And it did not enter my mind"?—That is an honest statement; it never entered my mind during the interview with the Vonderahes.

By the Attorney-General—You had had a good deal of time to think about what had happened before you saw Mr. Vonderahe?—I had a lot of things to think of. My mind is occupied at all times.

I want to give you this opportunity. Do you mean to tell my lord and the jury that from the time you made that will until after the death, on 9th October, when you saw Mr. Vonderahe, you never thought about that savings bank money or what had become of it?—It had puzzled me as to what had become of it, certainly.

Why did you not tell the relatives?—Because I was puzzled to know what had become of it.

187

Trial of the Seddons.

Frederick H. Seddon

Was not that a very good reason why you should tell the relatives?—At the time of the interview it never entered my head.

I do not think you are doing yourself justice by that answer. Just let me recall to you what you have said. You make the will on 11th September; she dies on the morning of the 14th; you have inquiries made by the Vonderahes on 20th September and 21st September. You have an appointment with Mr. Vonderahe, the male relative, the husband, to whom you are going to give an account, on 9th October. I have asked you whether it had occurred to you during the whole of this time as to what had become of this money which had been drawn on the 19th June?—It had certainly occurred to me as to what had become of it, but, as I have already given in evidence, I did not consider that the Vonderahes were entitled to the full details without he showed that he was the legal next-of-kin. Even now he proves he is not.

Let me point out the position to you. This woman dies in your house very suddenly, according to your view, on the morning of 14th September?—Yes.

You were very surprised at her death?—Yes.

You were shocked?—Yes.

You thought she was sleeping peacefully?—Yes.

She had been snoring an hour and a half or two hours before, according to you?—Yes.

And with your experience as a life insurance superintendent, you thought she was asleep?—I have no experience of deathbeds.

You thought she was sleeping?—Certainly, yes; she is only the second person I have ever seen die.

You know, I suppose, that a patient may collapse, and it is not always possible for a layman to tell whether a patient is dead or not?—I did not think so; she was snoring.

She was snoring according to you—she was sleeping?—Yes.

And you had no reason——?—And my wife was asleep in the chair by the bedstead.

And you were smoking your pipe?—I was at the door.

You stood by the door for some time?—I was standing at the door; it is only a step to the door.

This was the only night you stood at the door?—Certainly.

That night, from the 13th to the 14th, was the only night on which you had stood at the door of Miss Barrow's room?—That I had stood at the door?

I mean watched at the door; it was the only night on which you waited at the door smoking your pipe?—I never smoked my pipe at her door before.

That is what I am putting to you?—Yes.

And suddenly, according to your view, instead of sleeping peacefully, you think she is dead?—I raised her eyelid.

You and your wife were the only persons in the room with her that night?—Yes, my wife was dozing at the bedside in a basket chair.

You knew you were her executor and trustee?—I had not given that consideration.

Evidence for Defence.

Frederick H. Seddon

You had made the will only three days before?—Yes, but these things were not going through my mind all the time. I was not thinking of all that kind of thing.

You knew she had relatives living close by?—Yes, such as they were, according to her statement.

You knew that in ordinary prudence you ought to take care—to have some relatives there before you got the keys and looked in her cash box?—I did not think so. She had already spoken about what she thought of her relatives. I was sure she would not have it. I do not see why I should if she did not want her relatives. It was not my business to call them.

I will tell you why you do not think you should. You are an experienced man of business?—No, that is not the reason. They treated my daughter with indifference and slammed the door in her face.

Listen to what I am going to put to you. I said you are an experienced man of business?—In one direction, yes.

If you had nothing to conceal, what I suggest to you is that the first thing you would do would be to get some independent person into that house before you proceeded either to open her cash-box and before you had carried her out of the house to be buried?—There was an independent person in the room.

Who was that?—Mrs. Rutt, the charwoman, who laid the body out.

She dies on the morning of the 14th, at a quarter past six in the morning?—Or twenty minutes past.

Now, I understand from what you have told us you had not sent for any doctor during the whole of the night of the 13th?—I did not see the necessity of calling a doctor up.

During the whole of the night of the 13th?—During the whole of that night, because I understood it was only a repetition of what had been going on.

By Mr. Justice Bucknill—Forgive me for saying so, but when the boy called out and you went upstairs, she was sitting on the floor and the boy was supporting her body?—Yes, but she got out of bed for something.

But it was not the same; she had not done that before?—No, she had never done that before.

I only want to remind you?—I considered that was due to weakness.

"Getting out of bed I consider was due to weakness"?—Yes, naturally a person who had suffered so long from diarrhœa would be weak.

By the Attorney-General—And when you had come home that night your wife had told you that Miss Barrow said she was dying?—Yes.

Had she said that before?—She often had said she would not live long, and she often said she wished she was dead.

Those are two very different things to the question I am putting to you?—Well, she never said "I am dying" before; no, not to my knowledge.

Here was a woman who was very ill?—Yes. I quite realised that, but I did not realise that she was as bad as she proved to be.

The doctor had been on the morning of the 13th?—Some time during the day.

Trial of the Seddons.

Frederick H. Seddon

On the morning of the 13th?—I was not sure of the time he had been. I thought it was in the afternoon he had been.

I think you said he came in the morning, and your impression is that you were in bed at that time?—I thought that referred to when my father and sister went to the White City. Anyway, I did not see the doctor when he came on the 13th.

We know from the doctor that he did come on the morning of the 13th?—I know he had been.

And am I not right in this, that from the time when he came on the morning of the 13th, no doctor ever saw that woman again before she was put in her coffin and buried?—No, but I understood he was coming again that morning; he had been coming every day.

According to the story you have told us, death occurred suddenly on that morning. She stopped breathing suddenly; she died suddenly?—Yes, of course.

Do you wish my lord and the jury to understand that there was no indication to you that that woman was in danger of dying until you found she was dead?—I do not think so; I do not know the signs of death.

All the more reason, I suggest to you, why you should call in a doctor immediately you thought she was dead?—I did. I went for the doctor immediately. I was at his house before seven o'clock—from twenty minutes past six.

You went to the doctor and you came back with the certificate?—I did not know he was going to give me a certificate.

Never mind; you came back with a certificate?—Yes, certainly.

But the doctor had never seen her?—No; but I was not to know he was not going to see her. I naturally expected he would come and see her.

Did you ask him to come and see her?—No; it is not for me to teach a doctor his duty.

Did you not want, for your own satisfaction, to make sure the woman was dead?—I had no desire. I had no idea at all in the matter.

Or were you not certain in your own mind, although you had no experience of it, that the woman was dead?—She was dead.

You had no reason to doubt it?—No, because her mouth dropped. My wife put a handkerchief round her head, and I lifted her eyelid up and it did not go down.

How long after she had ceased snoring was that?—I had been down to see how the baby was, and I came up in the room, and she had stopped breathing. I said to my wife, "Good God, she's dead!" and I went for the doctor immediately. The doctor knew when he was there last; he knew what time she died. I told him what time she died.

Do you not realise the position. Let me put it to you once more in fairness to yourself. The doctor had been on the morning of the 13th?—Yes.

He did not consider she was then in a critical condition. That is what he has told us?—How was I to know?

She had been very ill during that night?—Yes.

Evidence for Defence.

Frederick H. Seddon

And your wife had told you when you came home after twelve o'clock that night that she said she was dying?—Yes.

You do not send for a doctor during the whole night when, undoubtedly, on your story, she is worse than she has been before—that is right, is it not?—I had never seen her on the other nights; I had only heard her calling.

When she is sufficiently ill for you to think it right to remain up all night?—This night?

Yes?—That is because my wife is remaining up. My opinion of Miss Barrow was that she wanted Mrs. Seddon to sit with her, and I thought these repeated calls were on that account.

You had never had such a night as this before with her?—I had not. My wife had been up two or three times on other nights.

You then remain outside the room smoking?—I was not exactly outside the room; I was at the door.

The door was open?—Yes.

So you could see into the room?—I had the door open—yes, the door was open, and I could see into the room—the door was wide open.

And you could see what was going on in the room?—I am not quite sure that the door does not open against the bed; I think it does. I was standing up against the wall by the side of the door.

Did you hear what was going on in the room?—I heard the snoring.

As I understand, you told us you heard the snoring for something like one and a half hours before she died?—Certainly.

During the whole of that time?—I did not time it, you know.

No, but you have told us that she was snoring for something like an hour and a half to two hours—you said that?—Yes.

During the whole of that time you were standing outside that door smoking your pipe, and your wife was inside?—During the whole of that time I was not standing outside the door; I went out occasionally.

To see the baby?—Yes.

And you came back again?—And went down for a drink, &c. I did not remain absolutely all the time; my wife was sitting beside the bedstead.

As I understand from what you have said, there was no thought in your mind of any danger of her dying during all this night?—I did not think she was dying.

Did you think she was in danger?—I did not think so, no; I did not think she was in danger of dying, no more than the ordinary danger.

No more than what?—The ordinary danger with anybody that is ill; I did not think she was going to expire then.

Do you mean the danger of a collapse from exhaustion?—I did not think of that.

Weakness?—Yes, but I did not think she would pass away like that.

You go to the undertakers at 11.30 on that morning the 14th?—I could not swear to the time.

How far is Evershot Road from your house?—Not very far.

Is it about 200 yards?—It might be; it is not far, anyway; it is a few minutes.

Trial of the Seddons.

Frederick H. Seddon

Is that where you thought the Vonderahes lived at that time?—Yes.

How far off did Dr. Paul live?—Ten minutes' walk or quarter of an hour.

Was there not a doctor almost opposite your house?—I think there is a doctor close to.

And was your daughter Maggie in the house?—In bed.

The servant?—In bed.

And at this time your father?—Yes, he was in bed; they were all in bed.

Your two sons?—They were in bed.

And another daughter?—A little girl, seven or eight, and the baby.

It never occurred to you between the death of this lady at a quarter-past six in the morning until you went to the undertakers to send some one round to Evershot Road to the Vonderahes?—I did not; but Miss Barrow had already got my daughter on a previous occasion to call at the Vonderahes at Evershot Road to see if there were any letters for her, and my daughter had the door slammed in her face, and was treated very abruptly, and I told my daughter not to go there any more, and I told Miss Barrow never to send her to that house any more.

Is that your explanation of why you did not send round to the Vonderahes on this morning?—No, it was my intention to write to them.

The letter which you thought was of such importance that you copied it?—I generally do copy letters; that is why I have got carbon paper; I used to keep a copy-press.

Why should not your father, or your wife, or your sons, or some one else have gone round to the Vonderahes between 6.15 and 11.30 in the morning when you went to the undertakers?—Because it was my intention for to write the letter, and I would not send one of my family round to their house to be insulted by them, and they had had enough trouble about Miss Barrow all the time she lived there, and she herself said she did not want any of the relatives called in.

Did you then see Mr. Nodes, and was the result of your interview with him that the burial was to be in a public grave?—At Finchley.

For which you were to be charged £4?—Yes.

And of this £4 you were to have 12s. 6d. commission?—He mentioned that on the way in the trap, as a business suggestion.

So you were to pay £3 7s. 6d.?—And he said his son would bring with him a receipt for £4.

So you could put it into your accounts as executor and trustee as a sum of £4 paid?—I do not think he had that idea in his head.

You had?—At the time, no I had not.

But you did it?—I know I did it.

You have given an account of how you have spent that £10 which was found on her death when you came to look for the cash?—I do not know whether I drew that account up for anybody especially.

There is an account?—There is an account I kept of the spendings of money, which came to over £11.

In that account you include the funeral, £4?—I put down the £4 funeral.

Which you had not, in fact, paid?—Well, I had had the allowance

Evidence for Defence.

Frederick H. Seddon

that he allowed me as a commission. If an agent for a Singer's sewing machine buys one himself he gets a commission.

Were you in the habit of getting a commission from Nodes?—I was under commission if I introduced him business, and I gave my agents his cards.

Their business would be to introduce him——?—I do not know that my agents introduced him.

Did you get any commission for the business that was introduced?—No.

Through your agents?—No, I had none.

Was this the first commission transaction you had done with him? A moment ago you said you were in the habit of getting commissions?—Did I? If I did, I withdraw it. I had no intention of saying that. I said if an agent was on commission for to sell sewing machines, and he bought one himself, he would have the commission on it, or a piano. What I did say was that I was under commission with Nodes if I introduced him business, or from my agents, and I gave them cards.

Did you not think it right before this lady was buried in a public grave that you should communicate with the relatives?—I did communicate with the relatives.

That you should get some communication from the relatives?—No, I considered that they treated the thing as indifferent as what they treated her throughout.

Did you realise that you had made this arrangement about the public grave, on your own showing, before you had written the letter at all?—Yes, a temporary arrangement, subject to any alteration they would like to make.

Let me put something else to you about that. In the letter that was written——?—I expected them to call and see me that night, Thursday, because they would get the letter posted by the 5 o'clock post before 9 or 9.30 at night.

The funeral was to be——?—I think Nodes said about 1 or 2 on Saturday. We waited a little time at home to see whether they turned up; I think we were late; we were half an hour later than he arranged by waiting.

Mr. Nodes has told us you said you had others to consult?—Yes.

There was somebody to consult in the matter?—Yes.

Did you mean by that, the Vonderahes?—I meant the wife and my father.

This is what he says, " Mr. Seddon said, ' I will let you know when I let you know about the funeral.' Q.—Did he say why he could not let you know the day of the funeral then? A.—He said he had others to consult; there was somebody else to consult on the matter "?—I did not say that in those words; it was something to that effect; I said I would see how the arrangement suited.

Was not that with the object of consulting the relatives?—No.

Did you not mean to consult the relatives about the funeral?—I did not intend to consult personally the relatives.

N

Trial of the Seddons.

Frederick H. Seddon

Whether you intended personally to go there or not, did you not intend to consult them before the funeral?—Personally, no.

What do you mean by "personally"? Do you mean going yourself?—I wrote to them. They could take what steps they liked on that, and, if they did not turn up——

Your house was within, as you thought, some 200 yards of theirs?—My house was just as near to them as theirs to mine if they wanted to come. They knew she was ill.

But you did not, as I understand, send round to that house or to their other house?—No, and they never came near me. It cuts both ways; they never came near. They said they met her at the end of August, and they knew she was ill.

Do you say they knew she was ill?—Yes.

Who knew she was ill?—Mr. and Mrs. Vonderahe; they told me at the interview; they said they had met her.

Met her in the street?—Yes.

When she was under Dr. Paul, do you mean?—I suppose so.

In the month of August, when she was being treated for a bilious attack, and later on for asthma?—The end of August.

Later on is the period when Dr. Paul has told us?—And the boy going to the same school as the two Vonderahe boys they would know that Miss Barrow was ill in bed; he could tell the Vonderahe boys. They are in the same school, the two boys and Ernie Grant, and I fail to see how they can say they had no knowledge.

The Court then adjourned.

Seventh Day—Monday, 11th March, 1912.

The Court met at 10.15 a.m.

The ATTORNEY-GENERAL—My lord, there is one matter I should like to mention before I go on with the examination. Your lordship will remember there was some cross-examination of a somewhat intricate scientific detail by my learned friend as to the effect on the distal ends of the hair, and Dr. Willcox made one statement as to which he said he was not quite clear. Your lordship will remember that he said that he thought that the soaking of the hair in the blood fluid would account for what he found in the distal ends of the hair. He has made an experiment with it in order to enable him to put this matter before the Court quite clearly, and what I desire to do is to let him tell the Court, at a time which would be convenient, the result of it, and I also propose, having now ascertained that that is the fact, to give my friend an opportunity and the gentleman who was present, and who is concerned in this matter, an opportunity of witnessing the experiment so that there can be no doubt about it. The whole point of the thing is this,

Evidence for Defence.

Frederick H. Seddon

that Dr. Willcox said, taking the blood fluid which belonged to the body, which he found, as he has already stated, and taking some hair which was free from arsenic, hair which of course did not belong to her, and soaking that hair in the blood fluid he found there in the distal ends that there was a slight quantity of arsenic such as he actually found in the hair of Miss Barrow which had been soaked in the blood fluid. That is the whole point.

Mr. MARSHALL HALL—My lord, without making any further comment, that cannot apply to the hair which was examined, which was cut off by the undertaker.

The ATTORNEY-GENERAL—I agree with my friend in that. Of course, he will remember the only point of that was that that hair which was examined was mixed hair.

Mr. JUSTICE BUCKNILL—Now that has been suggested I am sure you will agree with this, if you have a written proof of what Dr. Willcox is going to say, if you give that to your learned friend now, he can examine it, and this gentleman and Dr. Willcox can make the experiment together.

The ATTORNEY-GENERAL—I have already done that.

FREDERICK HENRY SEDDON (prisoner), further cross-examined by the ATTORNEY-GENERAL—I was asking you, when the Court rose on Saturday, about what had happened on the night of the 13th and early in the morning of the 14th. When you were called upstairs for the fourth time that night, it was because of Ernie Grant having cried out from the top of the stairs that Chickie was out of bed?—Yes.

And did you then go up and find the boy very terrified?—Certainly He was supporting her.

And in an expression of your own, you say he was supporting her?—She was sitting in an upright position, and he had his hands under her arms.

Did he tell you that she had said, "I am going"?—No.

Did you hear her say anything like that?—No, I could not hear—I was not there.

But you came up and found her on the floor?—She did not say it again.

I am asking whether she did?—No—she never spoke. I asked her what she was doing out of bed—she never answered.

You saw then that she was very ill, did you not?—Apparently. I thought she was exaggerating for to have Mrs. Seddon there, do you see. I thought she was exaggerating for the purpose of keeping Mrs. Seddon there. She wanted Mrs. Seddon all night, you see, the same as on former occasions.

This had never happened on a former occasion?—I had not been up on a former occasion.

Did you ever hear that this had happened on a former occasion; sitting on the floor and the boy calling out?—No, I heard on a former occasion she had got out of bed and gone into another room. I knew she used to get out of bed.

Was it after that that you remained upstairs outside the door?—Off and on, yes.

195

Trial of the Seddons.

Frederick H. Seddon

Reading the paper?—Occasionally; I could not see very well to read the paper.

Smoking your pipe?—Yes.

Occasionally going downstairs either to see the baby or to have a drink?—Yes.

Now, she was sleeping quite peacefully, as you have told us, for some time?—Yes, I should say for about an hour and a half, or perhaps two hours.

Why did you not go to bed then?—To keep Mrs. Seddon company; it was not very thoughtful of me to leave my wife alone. I could not sleep.

Had your wife been up with her on the previous night?—Not sitting up with her. She had gone up attending to her almost every night.

Why should you not leave your wife sitting in the room if Miss Barrow was sleeping peacefully?—It was early in the morning—it was about four o'clock in the morning. We had been up best part of the night, so I said, "Well, if you are going to sit up with her, I must arrange to-morrow for her to go to the hospital, for we cannot have another night like this," and I said, "I will sit up with you."

She was dozing in a chair herself?—Yes.

Why did you want to stay up outside the door when your wife was dozing and the patient was sleeping peacefully?—Because my sleep was broken.

Was it not because you were afraid the end was coming and you didn't want your wife to be alone?—Certainly not. My sleep was broken being up the best part of the night off and on, backwards and forwards.

I suggest to you that your object in waiting there was to be there with your wife when the end, which you were expecting, came?—I did not expect the end, and that was not my reason for remaining.

Did you yourself give her brandy twice that night?—No, once. I didn't know there was brandy in the house. She asked for brandy. I said, "You cannot get brandy at this time in the morning; everywhere is closed." My wife says, "There is a drop there in the bottle."

When your wife said there was a drop in the bottle, where was the bottle then?—It was on the top of the commode—it was a high commode, with steps to it.

In her room?—At the side of the bed, yes, between the door and her bed.

By Mr. JUSTICE BUCKNILL—How large was the bottle?—It was only a bottle that would hold an ordinary noggin. What would hold a shilling's worth of whisky, or something like that.

By the ATTORNEY-GENERAL—My friend will prove this plan of Miss Barrow's room directly. I see the way the door opens there?—I believe it opened to the bed.

Yes. Do you suggest that you did not see the bed? You would see the bed as the door opened?—I explained in my former evidence, or in cross-examination, that I thought the door opened towards the bed, because I did not see her when I was standing at the door smoking—I heard her snoring.

When you were standing at the door and the door was open, as you

Evidence for Defence.

Frederick H. Seddon

have told us, you could see the bed?—I could see half of it. I could not see her head.

Where was your wife sitting?—Just at the foot of the bed, opposite the door, facing me.

Could you see her?—Oh, yes, facing me.

And where was the commode that you are speaking of?—Behind the door.

Between the bed and the door?—Yes, if the door opens towards the bed; I am not quite clear on the point.

This plan shows it—there is no doubt about it?—Yes.

The door opens away from the bed. So that the commode would be quite clearly in view between the opening of the door and the bed.

By Mr. JUSTICE BUCKNILL—Does this plan show where your wife was sitting at the bottom of the bed?—No, the plan does not show where my wife was sitting.

By the ATTORNEY-GENERAL—It shows a chair?—Yes, but the chair was brought here to the foot of the bed. (Marks on plan.)

Now would you just follow what I am going to put to you? This is what Mrs. Vonderahe says you told her on the 21st September—this is Mrs. Vonderahe's deposition—"His wife was sent out, so he had to go to her himself"; this is what she says you said to her?—Yes.

"And he asked her what she wanted, and he gave her some brandy," that is, you, according to her statement, giving Miss Barrow some brandy?—Yes.

"And he said they would be retiring to rest, and he hoped that she would not trouble them again." Is that right?—Yes.

Did you go on to say that the boy came down again after that? That is true, is it not—after you had given her some brandy?—Yes.

This is what Mrs. Vonderahe says you told her?—Yes, the boy called again.

And did you then go up and give her some more brandy?—No, sir.

Listen. This is what Mrs. Vonderahe says—"The boy came down again after that, and he went up again and gave her some more brandy"?—Certainly not.

And that you had left some brandy in the bottle?—Yes. I divided what there was—there was very little.

And that had gone by the morning—by the next morning?—It had gone by the time we came up to lift her off the floor into the bed.

It is not quite the same thing, you know. This is what Mrs. Vonderahe says that you said to her?—But I did not say that. I did not say it had gone in the morning.

You see the significance of it, do you not?—Yes, but I never said that. I say it was gone when we went upstairs for to lift her into the bed.

Did you ever tell Mrs. Vonderahe that you had stood outside the door reading a paper and smoking your pipe for an hour and a half, or two hours, before this lady died?—No, I did not.

Why not?—I never thought of it. I said, "We have been up all night."

You saw Mr. Vonderahe on 9th October. Did you ever tell him

197

Trial of the Seddons.

that?—We did not go into the conversation, as far as I can recollect. He was dealing with her properties. He was not concerned with about how she died, or the night she died.

Now, in the morning, when you returned from the doctor's, which is somewhere between eight and half-past eight on the 14th according to what you have told us, had Mrs. Rutt been sent for?—I believe so; she was there. My wife said she had sent for her.

And had she arrived there just about the time that you came in, or was it afterwards?—I think she was already there.

Just a little before?—As far as my recollection serves me.

Did you then, according to your statement, set to work to search for money?—I opened the trunk.

Was it for the purpose of searching for money?—I opened the trunk to see what was in it.

You had got the keys from your wife?—Yes.

You then found the cash box in the trunk?—Yes.

The cash box was locked?—Yes.

You proceeded to open it with a key?—Yes, there was a bunch of keys.

And when it was opened, according to your statement, you found £4 10s. in it?—Yes.

That was a matter of great surprise to you, was it not?—Yes.

Quite a shock?—Well, it was a surprise, a considerable surprise.

Did you think anybody had taken her money out of her cash box when you found only £4 10s. there?—I did not know. She had workmen coming into the room off and on. She had a window-cleaner.

When was the last time she had had workmen in the room before she was taken ill?—I could not say.

Did you make any further search then?—I went right through the trunk.

How long did it take you?—I could not say. It might have taken a quarter of an hour or twenty minutes. I am referring to the trunk; going right through the trunk. Of course, I felt everything. We looked all through the drawers.

You mean the drawers of the chest?—The chest of drawers, of course.

You looked everywhere where you thought you could find money?— Yes; I believe the wife felt the bed all over.

And the bag?—No.

But the bag was hanging on the bed?—Yes.

As I understand you, you did not open that?—I did not open the bag.

But you opened the drawers and found nothing in them?—Yes.

The total result, then, of your search that morning was £4 10s.?— £4 10s.

Was it not perfectly plain to you that there must be more money, unless somebody had taken it, than £4 10s. when you were looking?—I did not understand it.

That is the full amount of money which you had found up to the time of your going to see Nodes at 11.30?—Yes.

Did you ever think any of her money had been stolen?—I don't know what she had done with her money; she was such a peculiar woman

Evidence for Defence.

Frederick H. Seddon

when you mentioned these matters to her that I did not go into details with her; she had a funny temper.

Her funny temper could not show itself after death?—No, but you are asking me what had become of her money during life.

No, I am not. I am asking you now what had become of her money after death?—It was not there.

That struck you, as you have told us, as a very remarkable thing, did it not?—Certainly, because I had paid her £10 on the 2nd of September.

And you know perfectly well that she could not have been out to spend it?—She had not been out to my knowledge.

So that, when you found £4 10s., at the very least you ought to have found the £10 which you had paid her in gold on 2nd September?—Of course I didn't know what amount had been spent during the twelve or fourteen days when she was ill, because she had been sending out.

Did you ask your wife that morning about the money?—Yes; she said she had been giving her money for what she required.

Why did you not ask your wife that?—I asked her if she had any idea what had become——

When?—The morning while we were searching for it.

Between 8 and 11.30?—I asked her where she had been keeping her money for to purchase what was required for her. She said she had it in a purse under her pillow.

Did you look for the purse?—We found the purse with 3d. in it.

Where?—Under her pillow.

You found the purse with 3d. in it, and except for the money that you had paid her on 2nd September you found nothing else?—3d. in copper in her purse.

Yes—except that 3d. in copper and the £10 which you paid her on the 2nd September you found nothing else?—No.

At any time?—No.

Did you think when you had made your very thorough search during the whole of that day that somebody had been stealing her money?—I didn't know what she had been doing with it.

Did it cross your mind that somebody may have stolen it?—No, I don't think evil of people like that; I am not so ready to think evil of people.

Not even of the workmen or the window-cleaners who came into her room?—I have nothing to support the idea that they had.

Did you not think that it was a matter in respect of which some inquiry must be made?—No.

Do you realise how much money, according to your statement, there must have been in gold of hers during the eight months of the year before her death?—Yes.

What do you make it?—£165, less anything she had spent.

That is to account for the notes?—Yes.

Notes are easily traceable, are they not?—Oh, yes.

Gold is not, is it?—I have not given that a thought.

When you say the gold, are you speaking of the £165 that was

Trial of the Seddons.

Frederick H. Seddon

changed from notes, according to your statement, into gold?—But you are suggesting I had her money.

Do you say that the £165 which had been traced into thirty-three notes——?—The notes that had been cashed?

Yes?—Well, I don't know what she had done with it.

But, according to the statement you have just given, that was turned into gold?—Yes, Mrs. Seddon said she gave them her to change; it might have been turned into silver and gold.

Do you know what has become of that money?—No.

Did it strike you as odd that none of that money was found?—I never thought of it.

Or the money which you yourself had given her in gold in change for £5 notes?—Yes, and of the £10 I had paid her.

Yes, I am not forgetting the £10. You yourself, according to your statement, had changed £5 notes which she had paid you with; you had given her back £4 8s. each time?—Yes, that would be before the January previous.

That is your statement?—Yes, that is all I knew about her notes, and one of the notes Mrs. Seddon had cashed for her, after she had been out herself, and nobody would change it for her.

During this period—I am dealing only with 1911—according to your statement, you paid her eight times £10 in gold?—Nine times—£91 I paid her.

Nine times if you include the 2nd September?—Yes.

Up to the 2nd September the amount you had paid was £91?—£91 I paid up to October.

£91 in gold. I will leave out altogether for the moment what happened in 1910, the three months of October, November, and December, and I will leave out the notes which you say you cashed for her in that year. I am going to deal only with 1911. Do you know that £105 in notes was dealt with by your wife?—I have not calculated how much had been dealt with by my wife.

That is proved already in this case?—Yes—twenty-seven.

Yes, but I am dealing only with 1911. It is twenty-one in 1911. Six of them were dealt with by her in 1910, and six by you?—Yes.

That leaves twenty-one which are proved to have been dealt with in each month of 1911, making £105. You follow that?—Yes.

Then there is £91 which you yourself had paid her in gold during that period?—Yes.

And there is £216 which she had drawn out in gold on the 19th June, 1911?—Yes.

Making £412?—Yes.

In gold, according to you?—I do not know whether it was in gold or not. What does she live on if she has all that money?

Now, we will take off the £10 that you paid her on the 2nd September, and that will leave £402 in gold according to the evidence which we have got?—Yes.

Traced to her in eight months, to the end of August, 1911?—Yes.

Now, of that £402, as I understand your statement, when you came

Evidence for Defence.

Frederick H. Seddon

to look for the money on the morning of her death you found 3d. in copper in her purse?—Yes.

And that is all?—Yes.

Did you make any inquiry about the money?—I hadn't any idea regarding it.

Then does that mean you made no inquiry?—I made the search. I thought if she had deposited it I ought to find a receipt. I didn't know whether she might have placed it in the hands of friends or relatives of hers, though.

What, with you in her house and in her confidence?—I had nothing to do with the property—I only dealt with the property twelve months before that. I had finished with the matter, and it was settled twelve months before with regard to the financial transactions. I never had her money, otherwise it would be in my banking account or invested by me. I have not concealed anything.

According to your view, you had nothing whatever to conceal from her relatives?—I couldn't explain what had become of that money.

Why did you not tell the relatives that you could not explain it?—I told him he had not shown me that he was the next-of-kin.

Is that your reason?—Yes, I did not go into details beyond what I had already given him.

Now, Mr. Seddon, just think for a minute. If you have any other explanation to give, give it?—I told you that I did not give a thought to the matter.

And is that your only explanation to my lord and the jury of your not having said anything to the relatives about that money being missed? —Yes.

That the man who asked you was not the legal next-of-kin?—And that I could not say where it was.

Was not that the very reason why you should have told him that you could not tell where it was?—It didn't enter my head for to go into all the details.

Did you ever tell the police?—No.

So that unless this inquiry had taken place no one would ever have known anything about it?—I don't know. I don't know what information the relatives are possessed of regarding this matter. She might have told them all about the financial transactions for all I know. She was meeting them. I did not know she was meeting them until they said in evidence—they said they were meeting her—they said they met her as late as the last week in August. I have been expecting all through this prosecution to see the documents come out.

What documents?—I concluded she had invested it somewhere or deposited it somewhere, or something like that. I thought all kinds of things about it.

And of all kinds of explanations?—No. I have not got any explanation regarding it. It has not been in my possession.

If you thought the relatives had it or anybody had it?—I did not know the relatives had it. I thought that.

Then, what I want to know is why you did not mention it to them when they came to you?—At the interview I didn't give it a thought.

Trial of the Seddons.

Frederick H. Seddon

Did you realise, Mr. Seddon——?—I don't think of everything.

You do not think of everything, but you think of several hundreds of pounds in gold, that is what I am suggesting to you?—Several hundreds?

Yes, that is what I am suggesting?—The only money I thought about was the money she had drawn out of the Finsbury Savings Bank in June.

That was £216?—I don't know what she did with it. She said that she knew what to do with it.

You knew when the appointment was made for 9th October with Mr. Vonderahe what the object of that meeting was?—He wanted to know about her investments.

Yes, and her property?—And her property.

This money had come into your house, the £216, and as you told us on Saturday was causing you anxiety?—But I did not know it remained in my house.

That would be one of the very reasons why you should make inquiry of them, would it not?—When I looked in the trunk it was not there, and I could not account for it. How do I know what the woman had done with it? She went out every day and met her relations and met friends. She used to be out the best part of the day. A person does not want much assistance with regard to pounds, shillings, and pence.

I will put this last question about it. I will give you an opportunity of making any explanation?—How can I explain something I do not know?

Listen. If you had nothing to conceal, what I am suggesting to you is that you would have made inquiry as to what had become of this money, and would have informed the relatives or the police?—We can all be wise after an event.

On the same day, the 14th, it is in the afternoon that you make another search in the bedroom, is it not?—About noon.

Did you commence when you found the £3 in the drawer—in the fold of the paper in the drawer—that is the drawer you had already turned out?—We had only lifted the things out. We did not take the paper lining out.

And the £2 10s. in the bag which all the time had been hanging on the post of the bed?—Yes, I believe Mrs. Seddon had looked inside that bag, but she did not feel in the outside pocket of it—the close-fitting pocket. She said she had looked in the bag.

Where was your family on the evening of the 14th September?—I don't know. I was in the office.

Do you not know where they went?—Yes; they went to a theatre.

Your wife?—Yes.

Your father?—I am not sure he went. I know my sister went and the wife went. The wife did not want to go.

That was the night, of course, that the body was taken away?—Yes, they went before the body was taken away.

You remained at home?—Yes.

While they were at the theatre and you were left at home the body was taken away?—Yes, the undertaker sent for it.

Evidence for Defence.

Frederick H. Seddon

Just let me ask you some further questions about the cash-box. You were in Court, of course, when Mr. Hook gave his evidence?—I have heard his statement from the beginning.

You know that he says there was £380 in gold and a large sum in notes?—I believe he always said there was £420 till he came into this Court.

This is in answer to my learned friend in cross-examination. " £380 she told me. *Q.*—£40 in gold had been got rid of since 1906? "—he says, " Yes, that is right. *Q.*—Then she had £380 in gold and a large sum in bank notes? *A.*—That is right." If this woman had this money in the house I don't think she would have gone away for four days' holiday to the seaside and leave all that money in the house.

You are speaking of August, 1911?—Yes. August Bank Holiday, when she went away for four days.

By August of 1911 the greater part of these bank notes had already been dealt with?—Yes, but still, according to the prosecution, there would be some money there in the box.

There would have been gold?—Yes.

You know about all these notes having been dealt with. I am putting to you that these notes came out of the cash box?—I don't know where they came from.

Have you any suggestions to make as to where they did come from, if they did not come from the cash-box?—No, I never queried the matter.

You know the statement has been made, not only by Mr. Hook but by Mr. Vonderahe about the notes in the cash-box?—Yes, they have seen more than I have seen.

I see Mr. Vonderahe says he saw this cash-box and that it had bags of money and a roll of bank notes in it. Do you remember that? —Yes.

The roll of bank notes at the bottom of the cash-box?—Yes.

Supposing that the gold and the notes were there, according to the sworn statement of these two witnesses, can you in any way account for the disappearance of it?—I cannot. I have got a perfectly clear conscience on that. I believe Mr. Vonderahe himself mentioned something to me at the interview that there was money in her trunk. I forget whether I told him how much I found there or not—I am not sure.

You know you have told us that when Mr. Hook was leaving she had asked you to take care of the cash-box?—Yes.

First of all, let me see what were your relations with Mr. Hook when he was being turned out. Do you remember saying this—" Miss Barrow has put all her affairs in my hands "?—No, I never said that.

Is that untrue?—Yes. All her affairs were not in my hands.

Did Mr. Hook ask you if she had put her money into your hands?— Certainly not. It was not mentioned.

Is that an invention of Mr. Hook's?—Yes, positively.

An untruth deliberately told by him?—It is an untruth.

Did he say to you, " I will defy you and a regiment like you to get her money in your hands "?—Certainly not; there was no mention of it.

Trial of the Seddons.

Frederick H. Seddon

Did you say that you did not want her money?—No, it was not mentioned.

That you were going to look after her interests?—No. I said, "I am looking after her interests as the landlord." I said, "You are not my tenant. I have told Miss Barrow to go, and she does not want to go, and she said she had given you notice and you will not go, and she has asked me to give you notice." He said if he went he would take the boy with him.

Do I understand you that all this conversation which I have just been putting to you which Mr. Hook has been deposing to in the box, and upon which he has been cross-examined, is all an invention of Mr. Hook?—Yes.

Now, on this occasion, when Mr. Hook was going, according to your statement, she asked you to take care of her cash-box, and said there was £30 or £35 in it?—Yes.

You know, do you not, that at least £165 in notes, dating 1901 to 1910, have been traced to Miss Barrow?—Yes, I have heard it.

And subsequently traced to your wife and yourself, and you have admitted it?—Yes—subsequently traced that she cashed them for Miss Barrow.

Yes?—There is no trace that they were in my possession.

Not traced to your possession because the notes have been dealt with?—Yes.

They have been in your possession?—But without having the money either.

Do you represent that when she asked you about this cash-box she said there was only £30 to £35 in it?—Yes.

After what you know?—Yes.

And what we know about the notes?—I do. That is what she told me. Perhaps that is why she did not come back again.

You were willing to take care of it if she counted it out in your presence?—So that I could give her a receipt for the correct amount and she could hold the key. I did not know the woman—she was a perfect stranger to me—I was not going to be let into a trap like that by taking possession of a box when I did not know how much it contained.

When you said that, instead of counting the money out and getting a receipt for it as you expected that you would do, she took the box upstairs?—She went upstairs again. She said she would go up and make sure.

Make sure of what?—How much she had got in it.

Why should not she go upstairs to do that?—Because she was not sure; she said £30 to £35.

She had got the box with her?—Yes, but she thought I was going to take the box just as it was and ask no questions how much it contained.

Why should she open the box there and then?—I am sure I could

Evidence for Defence.

Frederick H. Seddon

not enter into the woman's thoughts. I could not read the woman's mind.

There was no reason why she should not have opened it there and then, taken the money out and counted it?—I did not see any reason why she should not, if I was to be trusted.

The box was taken away upstairs by her?—And she locks herself in her bedroom.

And, as I understand your story, that is the last you see of the cash-box until after her death?—Yes, I waited some time and then went out. I had got my business to attend to, and it appears that Hook had gone when I came in. It was the day that Hook left.

I want to ask you one or two questions about what happened on the 14th at the interview with Mr. Smith and Mr. Taylor. You know what Mr. Taylor has said about this, " A little after nine o'clock on the 14th I saw some gold." You know what I am speaking of now?—Yes, and I am supposed to have had her money early in the morning.

" I think the last collector went out of the office certainly before seven o'clock." That is what Mr. Taylor says?—Yes, possibly.

Then he says this—" I heard the chink of money and I just turned my head, when I had a side view of Mr. Seddon's desk and I saw several piles of sovereigns and a good little heap besides. Q.—About how much money in gold? A.—Well, at the time I estimated it at over £200." Then he is asked what was done. " Can you say whether that was part of the collectors' money or not? A.—No, I should say not. Q.—What was done with the collectors' money when it was received? A.—The collectors' money was put in the till which Mr. Seddon kept in the cupboard. And he personally packed these sovereigns into four bags." I think it becomes quite clear from another question. " At the time you saw this quantity of gold that you estimated at £200, where was the till? A.—In the cupboard. Q.—Did you see what the prisoner did with this quantity of sovereigns? A.—Yes, he packed it into four bags. Q.—And what did he do with it then? A.—He took them up, and he held three under his arm. He took up the other one in his hand and turned round facing myself and Mr. Smith, my fellow assistant, put one bag in front of Mr. Smith and said, ' Here, Smith, here is your wages.' He picked it up again and he put it into the safe. He put the four bags into the safe." You heard that—you heard that evidence given?—Yes; the statement is absurd. In the first place, the chink of money takes place every Thursday, so there is nothing extraordinary in it. When a man who has got his back turned to me, when he hears the chink of money for him to turn round would be a most unusual thing for him to do. Then, further, for him to have observed so much actually having to turn in his chair and stand watching me doing this, if he had done that I should have told him to get on with his accounts.

Are you suggesting that this is an invention of Mr. Taylor?—I do not know what you like to call it, but the statement is exaggerated. There is no occasion for the man to turn round at the chink of money, to begin with.

You know what the point is. Nobody knows better than you, Mr.

Trial of the Seddons.

Frederick H. Seddon

Seddon, what the point of this conversation is. You understand the point of it, do you not?—Yes, but that is something that did not happen. He might have turned round and had a glance and then went on with his accounts.

The importance of the difference between your story and his story is this. He says that the collectors' money had been put into the till in the cupboard?—Certainly not.

That is his story?—He is guessing—he is absolutely guessing.

He says, further, that after nine o'clock at night, when he heard the chink of money, he turned round and saw what he says were sovereigns? —No.

You say that is untrue?—Yes, certainly. He has been reading the papers.

He says, further, that he saw you count the sovereigns and put them into four bags?—Well, how could he see with his back turned to me? Look at the plan and see the man's position. Smith might overlook me, but Taylor would have to turn round and look at me and neglect his duties, and it is getting very late at night and there is no time to lose. It is not likely that I should bring money from the top of the house down to the bottom—stolen money, as suggested by the prosecution— and count it in the presence of my assistants. I had all day if I wanted to count money, from early morning until nine o'clock at night.

Did you say, jokingly, " Here, Smith, here's your wages "?—Yes.

Then part of it is not an invention?—No, it is not the first time that I had done that either.

And did you take up the four bags and put them into the safe?— No, I had that sliding till—I kept that on the drawer, and I pulled another drawer out. I always have that till on this drawer when the men are paying in their cash, and I used to count up at the finish—I used to ask them what the total is by the superintendent's sheet, and then I would start counting the cash. The chink of money is a common thing on post days.

No doubt, but if the money had been put away in the till in the cupboard?—But it had not been put away in the till in the cupboard. The till was out on the drawer in the office.

If the money had been put away in the till in the cupboard the chink of money would naturally draw his attention, would it not?—It had been in the cupboard. I took it out of the cupboard to count it.

Had you worked long with Mr. Taylor and Mr. Smith?—No, they had both been latterly introduced into my office as assistants ; they were both practically new men to me. Mr. Taylor had been a superintendent and he had been reduced.

What do you call practically new—how long had they been working with you?—A month or two. Smith had been an agent under me.

How long had Smith been working with you? How long had you known him?—I cannot say exactly—about twelve months or something like that, but he had only been in my office a month or two—either of them. They were practically new men to me in that capacity as assistants. My other men had been promoted.

Do you know that Mr. Smith has said also that in the evening, he

Evidence for Defence.

Frederick H. Seddon

says about 8.30, as far as he can remember, he saw loose sovereigns and half-sovereigns?—That is right, there were loose sovereigns and half-sovereigns. There was £99 altogether in gold. These men never thought of this until they had seen that there was £200 missing in the paper. They never said a word of this at the inquest. They had all got £200 on the brain by reading it in the paper.

Do you know that Mr. Smith says definitely that there was neither silver nor copper on the table when he saw these sovereigns?—He must have seen both if he could overlook me.

What?—He was *this* side (describing) he could see me.

You know quite well the importance of it. Listen and answer the question?—Yes.

You see you have said in your evidence, in explanation of this incident, that the money that was being dealt with was one bag of gold and that the rest of it was silver?—Oh, the gold was in two bags. It was in one bag at the finish to go to the bank, and the balance was in another bag and put in the safe. There were three bags of silver—there were four bags altogether.

Your explanation of this incident is that it was the money that was being dealt with either from the bag or which you had taken out in order to put with the other money of the company?—It was the company's money and my own.

And that the rest, the silver and the copper, was all there, too?—No, there was very little or no copper.

Well, leave out the copper. The silver was there, too?—Yes, there was £15 17s. 6d.

So that the difference between you and Mr. Taylor and Mr. Smith is that you are putting this incident of the money as having taken place with regard to all the collectors' money that was brought in.?—Certainly.

What they are saying is that that had all been dealt with and disposed of?—It had not, no.

Listen. And that you were simply then dealing with heaps of gold and no silver and no copper?—No—absurd. It was the company's money and my own. It is not feasible a man is going to do a thing like that.

What do you mean?—The prosecution are suggesting that I am dealing with the deceased woman's gold; that I should bring it down from the top of the house to the bottom into the office in the presence of my assistants and count it up? Is it feasible?*

I do not want to argue with you, but you know that sometimes people do very foolish things?—Well, I am not a degenerate. That would make it out that I was a greedy, inhuman monster.

What?—That I am a greedy, inhuman monster, or something with a very degenerate mind, to commit a vile crime such as the prosecution suggest, and then bringing the dead woman's money down and counting it in the presence of my two assistants and flouting it like that. The suggestion is scandalous. I would have all day to count the money.

Now, let me ask you about what happened the next day. In point

---

* In this and the following two answers Seddon exhibited the first sign of indignation and heat that he had shown in his long cross-examination.—ED.

Trial of the Seddons.

Frederick H. Seddon

of fact you had paid in, on the 15th September, to your bank £35 more in gold?—Over and above the company's money I had paid in £35 to my own current account.

Did you, on the same day, pay £30 in gold to the savings bank?— I did—that is £65.

And did you, on the 18th September, pay £90 in gold for the three Building Society shares?—Yes, I took £100 down to put into the Building Society towards my mortgage.

All this time, of course, you had your banking account, the London and Provincial?—Yes, but there was a good balance there as it was.

And you had money on deposit with the bank?—Yes.

And had money on deposit in the Post Office Savings Bank?—Yes.

You had paid in so small a sum as £30 to get the interest on deposit? —Yes, I put a little in each.

And the £70 you had paid in which was the balance of the £116 you had drawn out of the London and Westminster Bank?—Yes.

In order to earn interest on the money on deposit?—Yes.

So that the money should not lie idle and unremunerative?—That is it.

On 15th September you went to the jeweller, Mr. Wright?—Yes, I had to pass there when I went to see my sister off to Wolverhampton.

How far was it from your house?—How far? A quarter of an hour or twenty minutes' walk.

There is no doubt that on 15th September, the day after this woman's death, you did go to the jeweller's and ask for the diamond ring that is exhibited to be made larger?—No doubt whatever.

To fit your middle finger?—To fit this finger.

So there can be no doubt about what I am putting to you. What I am suggesting is that you had taken this ring after her death, and were having it altered to fit your finger?—I had it on the little finger—I had got two diamond rings and a curb ring. I wore the two diamond rings on these two fingers because I did not want to interfere with the ring during Miss Barrow's—during the time Miss Barrow was with me. I did not want to hurt her feelings. I wore it on the little finger during the lifetime, and on the 15th September I had it enlarged to fit this finger.

As I understand, what you have told us was Miss Barrow had objected to pay any costs to the solicitors in respect of the annuity?—She said she had no money to spare.

That was in January of 1911?—I showed her the bill—I showed her the two bills—tremendous costs.

According to your story, you told us on Saturday she gave you the diamond ring?—Yes, she brought it down.

Instead of money?—Yes. The amount I paid on her behalf to Mr. Knight was £4 13s.

It is not till the day after her death, on the 15th, that you took the ring to the jeweller?—No, that is right.

For this purpose?—Right.

Did you take a watch there on the same day?—The same day.

You know that this ring that we have just been speaking of was found in your safe when you were arrested. You were not wearing it.

208

Evidence for Defence.

although it had been altered to fit your finger. You know that, do you not?—I had not had it on that day—the day I was arrested. I did not always wear the three rings.

Now, let me ask you about the watch. On the same day you went on a second occasion to the jeweller's?—Yes.

That was Friday, the day after the death?—Yes, that was the time I took the watch—on the evening of the same day.

Yes, with your wife?—Yes, we had been to see my sister off at the station—at Euston.

But you had been twice. You had not seen your sister off both times?—No, I am talking about the second time when I went to the jeweller's with the watch when I had been to see my sister off. I had called in before.

You had been to the jeweller's again?—I did not go especially to the jeweller's on that morning. I called in as I was passing.

When you went about the ring it was not because you had been seeing your sister off?—Oh, no, no. I was merely passing.

Then in the evening you went with your wife, when you had been to see your sister off?—I told her I was having the ring enlarged. She said, "What about my watch? I would like it to take on my holidays," and I said, "All right; we are passing to-night seeing Emma off. I will take it, and let Wright put a new dial on it, and perhaps he will get it done before we go away."

Is that what you went for, to have a new dial put on it?—A new dial and the name erased.

We have seen where the name was?—Yes.

It did not show?—No.

Nobody could see it?—But while I was having one job done I might as well have both done at the same time.

Why should you be in such a hurry to have the name taken off the watch, on the day after her death?—There was no hurry beyond this. We had decided to go for our holidays to Southend-on-sea. We had sent the children in advance, and Mrs. Seddon wanted to wear her jewellery at the seaside. So as I had called in to get the ring enlarged she said, "You might as well get my dial done, and get the watch done at the same time, and perhaps they could get it done in time for me to wear at the seaside."

Who suggested the taking of the name off the back plate of the watch?—I did.

When did you notice that the name of Eliza Jane Barrow was on the watch?—When she presented it to Mrs. Seddon.

Were you present?—Yes.

When was it?—On the 22nd or 27th of April, 1911. I am not sure. It was her birthday, anyway. It was a birthday present.

There was no reason why she should not have had the name taken off the back plate during the lifetime of Miss Barrow?—Oh, yes, certainly; it was her mother's watch—I would not hurt the woman's feelings like that.

But you did hurt them the day after her death?—But she was dead then. Had she removed from my house while she lived I would have

209

Trial of the Seddons.

done it, and I told my wife I would not have it done in consequence of that, and my wife would not wear the watch in consequence of that because the dial was discoloured and cracked, and she wanted to wear it here on a swivel. (Describing.) I said, "It is worth a gold dial," but I said I would not have it done while Miss Barrow was with us.

You know you told me that watch was found in the wardrobe, and she was not wearing it at the time of your arrest on the 4th of December?—That may be, I dare say; she did not have the rest of her jewellery on.

I still would like to know why did you want to take that name off at all. Why was it worth spending a penny on if that watch was honestly your wife's?—When I was having the dial put on I might as well have the name taken off at the same time. A watch is greatly depreciated in value by having a name engraved on it.

You were not thinking of selling it, were you?—No, certainly not, but still Eliza Jane Barrow was no relative of ours—it was the mother's watch. I should have had it done if Miss Barrow had removed into other lodgings, but I would not do it while she was living with us. It looks as if you did not appreciate the giver.

You did not think it would have been kind to do it?—No, it would not have been kind. Mrs. Seddon had often asked me to get it done for her.

Why had you not done it?—I have told you. I just explained why I would not do it. I said, "I will not do it while she is with us. Perhaps in the future she may leave here, and then you can have it done then." She said she would not wear it until she had got it done. The jeweller told me that he would have to send it to Switzerland to be done; to the makers of the watch to have it done.

That was to have the dial done?—That is what I mean. The erasing of the name was an easy matter.

Just look at that (a brooch, exhibit 33). Did that belong to Miss Barrow?—It did.

Was that included in the inventory which you had made of the jewellery left to the children?—It was not Miss Barrow's at the time of her death.

Then it was not included in the inventory?—No, it was presented to my daughter on her birthday. She had another one presented to her at Christmas.

Do you mean by Miss Barrow?—Yes.

That, exhibit 32, is the inventory of her total effects at £16 14s. 6d.?—That is the auctioneer's valuation.

How many watches had this lady?—Three.

Now, those are the other two?—They look like it.

Would you let me also see the watch (same handed to the Attorney-General)? Those are the three which she had?—Yes, this looks like it.

Now, that watch which you hold in your hand had the name of Miss Barrow's mother on it?—Yes.

And the date "1860"?—Yes.

She treasured it, did she not, very highly?—As her mother's watch, yes. She never wore it—she never wore any jewellery. Of course, that gold watch did not look as nice as that before it had the gold dial put on

Evidence for Defence.

Frederick H. Seddon

it, you know. It was very much discoloured and cracked; the dial looked more like the dial of the silver watch.

If your wife had it in her possession, then, during that time, from April to Miss Barrow's death, why did she not have the dial mended?—I told you I would not allow her to have the dial altered.

You told us you would not allow her to have the name taken out?— I would not allow the watch to be interfered with at all during the time Miss Barrow was with us. That is what I said—she said she would not wear it until it was done.

Now, I have asked you about these three pieces of jewellery. Were not those three the three most valuable pieces of jewellery she possessed? —I don't know.

The diamond ring, the gold watch which belonged to the mother?— Yes.

And the gold chain and pendant?—Yes, I should think that chain was invaluable attached to that lever watch—the gold-digging chain.

Why I am asking you is because you have got the inventory before you of what was, in fact, valued for the benefit of the two children, Hilda and Ernest Grant?—Yes.

Look at the inventory. You know what is valued in it, and it comes to £16 14s. 6d., the whole amount—jewellery, furniture, and clothing?— Yes. That does not represent what the stuff would cost, you know.

Have you any doubt that these three pieces of jewellery to which we have just been referring were the most valuable pieces of jewellery in her possession?—I have not considered it till now.

Then, will you consider it now. You know perfectly well they are not in the inventory, of course. But there is a lot more jewellery than that, is there not?—There is some more. I have not had all the jewellery put to me for to value it now. I cannot carry everything in my mind.

The three articles of jewellery we have just been dealing with, I am putting to you, were the three most valuable pieces of jewellery that Miss Barrow possessed?—Well, I think I would sooner have the lever watch and that chain.

I am asking you to look at what there is in the inventory. I will read it if you have any doubt about it, so that the jury may know what it was that forms the jewellery in that inventory. "Three seaside brooches, silver locket and chain, two small mourning brooches"?—They are gold; it is not stated gold here.

It is called here, "Two small mourning brooches, one pair of pince-nez, three pieces of Maundy money, a pair of gold solitaires, silver thimble, gent.'s silver lever watch," &c. That is the lot?—Yes, that gold-digger's Australian cable chain is composed of all the minerals that are found in the gold mines, I believe—a very valuable chain.

Then that is part of the value of the £16?—Yes, but I have not valued them.

You remember you wrote the letter on the 21st September, exhibit 3?—Yes.

It is 1911. It is dated by mistake 1910, "To the relatives of the

211

Trial of the Seddons.

Frederick H. Seddon

late Eliza Mary Barrow, who died on 14th September at the above address." You remember that?—Yes.

I am going to suggest to you that this letter concealed from the family what had really happened—concealed from them the annuity—this arrangement between you and her about the annuity—and suggested to them that the arrangements that had been made about the annuity had been done through stockbrokers and solicitors, and not a word in it to suggest that you had anything to do with it?—It does conceal it, yes, but not intentionally. As you put it I can see it.

As I put it to you, you see that it does conceal a very important fact?—Yes.

According to your view, is that an accident?—Certainly.

A pure accident?—Yes.

In a letter which you are drafting for the purpose of informing the relatives of what had become of her property—that is the object of the letter, is it not?—Yes.

And you do not tell them the important fact?—I am not informing them what has become of the property. I am telling them what she has done—that she has disposed of her property to purchase an annuity. That is what I had in my mind.

You are writing this, you know, as an executor under the will?—I am not an experienced man as an executor. I have never been executor under a will before.

No, but you were executor under this will, and in that capacity you purported to write to the relatives?—Yes.

You give them a formal notice?—Yes.

Writing a letter—I will read it now. "To the relatives of the late Miss Eliza Mary Barrow, who died on 14th September, 1911, at the above address, from epidemic diarrhœa, certified by Dr. Sworn. Duration of illness, ten days. As executor of the will of Miss Barrow, dated 11th September, 1911, I hereby certify that Miss Barrow has left all she died possessed of to Hilda and Ernest Grant, and appointed me as sole executor to hold in trust until they become of age. Her property and investments she disposed of through solicitors and stock exchange brokers, about October and December, 1910, last to purchase a life annuity which she received monthly up to the time of her death, and the annuity died with her. She stated in writing that she did not wish any of her relatives to receive any benefit on her death, and during her last illness declined to have any relatives called in to see her, stating that they had treated her badly, and had not considered her, and she would not consider them. She has merely left furniture, jewellery, clothing——"?—That is as far as I found.

Not only does this letter conceal the truth, as you have admitted, but I am suggesting to you that it is deliberately written by you to conceal the truth?—No.

You write the letter as executor of the will, and you certify that she left all she died possessed of to Hilda and Ernest Grant?—But I could not hope to conceal it; there was no hole and corner business about

Evidence for Defence.

Frederick H. Seddon

it. I could not hope to conceal it. I could not stop anybody from making the necessary inquiries.

You prevented Mr. Vonderahe making inquiries because he was not the legal next-of-kin?—It had gone through many hands, but they were free to do what they liked.

"Her property and investments she disposed of through solicitors and stock exchange brokers about October and December, 1910, last, to purchase a life annuity"?—That is true.

Do you consider that that is the whole truth that is to be told to the relations by the executors?—The letter does prove—it does not explain everything.

Do you consider that that was a true statement to put before them? Do you represent now, with that letter before you, that that was a true, honest statement?—At the time, yes.

What do you mean by "at the time"?—As you represent it to me now it is not, but at the time it was to my mind.

The facts have not changed from that time to this?—No, but I am not in the habit of writing this kind of letter.

Therefore, I suggest to you that unless you set to work to do it, you would not be in the habit of concealing anything?—Unless I set to work to do it?

If you sit down to write a letter and are honestly putting forward a plain businesslike statement to the relatives?—I gave them what I considered necessary information.

What you considered necessary, but not full information?—I could not, unless I wrote a big document, give them full information.

Do you not think you might have written in that letter, if you did not wish to conceal it, "I have purchased the property and granted her an annuity"?—This letter is not posted to them. They called personally and they received this by hand.

What do you mean?—I gave it to Mrs. Vonderahe to give to her husband.

You meant that as the formal document from you as executor of the estate?—Information.

To the relatives?—Information, yes.

And if they had not suspected you that would have been the end of the thing?—I don't see that.

Not even now?—I do now.

And when Mr. Vonderahe called afterwards on 9th October, did you not say to him that you had given him full information?—I said "I have given you information. I will give you a copy of the will, and I have explained to you what she did with her investments. If there are any further details that you require, if you show me you are the legal next-of-kin to Eliza Mary Barrow I will go into further details with you."

But you know he was not the legal next-of-kin?—How did I know that?

I thought you told us Miss Barrow had told you there was a brother? —Miss Barrow stated there was a brother. I understood her to say he was the black sheep of the family, or something like that.

Trial of the Seddons.

Frederick H. Seddon

And, of course, if you could maintain that contention that it was the elder brother who was entitled to ask, you knew he would be in a difficulty to produce that elder brother?—No, I did not.

Not after what Miss Barrow had told you?—He said, "Supposing he is dead?" "Well," I said, "you can get a certificate of death, or you can, if you like, go to a commissioner of oaths and swear that you are the next-of-kin of Eliza Mary Barrow." These were business transactions that had taken place fourteen months before.

If the Vonderahes had read that letter with that statement in it about her property and investments, was there anything in it which wou·d show them that you were the person who had granted the annuity?—No, but there was a letter in my handwriting that they could have taken to any solicitor they liked and caused an investigation to be made.

Which letter in your handwriting?—This. I told them I was prepared to stand by what I had given them in writing. I had given them a copy of the will. I had given them a letter. I had also shown them a letter that Miss Barrow had written to me. I did not consider my past business transactions with Miss Barrow had got anything to do with it.

And is that why you did not tell them about it?—I suppose so.

Is that why you did not tell them about it?—I did not give it the fullest consideration at the time.

You have just told us that you did not consider that your past transactions had anything to do with it?—Not these transactions—not the business transactions that had been closed.

And is that the reason why you did not give them any explanation of it?—I cannot say it was at the time. I cannot say that that is the thought that was passing through my mind at the time. It is a thought that occurs to me now.

That letter is not a very frank statement, is it?—That is the view you have taken of it, and I have agreed.

I understand you agree with that?—Well, I could have put more in the letter evidently.

It would have taken less words to have said that you had sold her the annuity and had got the property?—But what difference did that make?

Don't argue with me. Now, Mr. Seddon, you see that letter with the statements in it about having disposed of the property and investments—"Her property and investments she disposed of through her solicitors and Stock Exchange brokers." That would convey to the mind of any person reading it that the transactions had been by her with solicitors, or Stock Exchange brokers—meaning with strangers?—No, that it had been done in order. Stockbrokers deal with stock, and solicitors deal with deeds.

Do you understand the question I am putting to you?—Yes, that is my answer.

Let me read it to you again—"Her property and investments she disposed of through solicitors and Stock Exchange brokers about October and December, 1910, last, to purchase a life annuity." Would not that suggest that the transaction had been done with strangers in an ordinary,

Evidence for Defence.

Frederick H. Seddon

formal, and regular way?—No. What I meant to convey was it had been done in order.

What is the point of saying it has been done in order unless you had said that it had been done with you. Can you give any explanation? —I can only follow what you said, that that is something that should have been introduced that I have omitted.

You had that document already written out when Mrs. Vonderahe came to see you on the 21st?—I wrote it at midnight. I did not come in till midnight, and I was told that they were coming in the morning, and of course I drafted it out before I went to bed.

You had it all prepared?—For the interview next day, yes.

You knew they were coming, and you knew why they were coming? —Yes, I knew. I had not much time to interview them. I had my business to attend to, and they were coming at an awkward time for me. Really I did not intend to grant them as long an interview as I did, because I had to neglect my business to do so. I ought to have been at the office at nine o'clock, and I had the interview with them at half-past ten.

You did not want an interview?—I did not want to have an interview, but I did.

Did you tell Mr. Vonderahe when he came to you on 9th October that you had nothing to do with the annuity?—No, the question was not asked.

Do you know that he said you did?—I don't know what he says I did. I will tell you what he did say. He said, "What insurance company did she get this annuity from?" I said, "If you show to me that you are the legal next-of-kin to make investigations regarding Miss Barrow's affairs I will go into full details with you."

You did not tell him at that interview that it was you who had granted the annuity, did you?—No. He asked me who was the landlord of the Buck's Head and the barber's shop. I said, "I am." There is an admission.

And I put it to you, not only did you not tell him, but you told him that you had nothing to do with it?—No, I did not.

Listen to what he has said?—Well, I am speaking the truth. He had a friend with him, and the prosecution have not called that friend.

Listen?—All he said is not gospel.

He says, "I said to him 'Who is the owner of the Buck's Head now'"?—Yes. And I said, "I am."

Then, did you say this, "I am always open to buy property. This house I live in, fourteen rooms, is my own, and I have seventeen other properties. I am always open to buy property at a price"? Did you say that?—Yes, but I may tell you that I did not say that it was in the open market. He said I said that, but I did not say that.

Is that an invention of his?—It is a false statement.

When you said to him that you had seventeen other properties, were you not referring to the properties in the Coutts Road, which you had bought with the proceeds of the India stock?—Yes, fourteen houses.

Now, I want your careful attention to this. "I asked him how it was that my cousin was buried in a common grave when she had a

Trial of the Seddons.

Frederick H. Seddon

family vault at Highgate. He "—that is you—" said, ' I thought it was full up,' I "—that is Mr. Vonderahe—" said, ' Who bought the India stock ? ' He said, ' You will have to write to the Governor of the Bank of England and ask him whether everything has been done in a perfectly legal manner through solicitors and stockbrokers. I had nothing to do with it.' " ?—I said, " If you are the legal next-of-kin of Eliza Mary Barrow I am prepared to go into details with you, otherwise you can write to the Governor of the Bank of England."

Then, when he asked you who had bought the India stock did you not say to him, " You can write to the Governor of the Bank of England " ? —Yes.

And did you say to him, " Everything has been done in a perfectly legal manner through solicitors and stockbrokers " ?—I do not know whether I used the word " legal." I said, " I have told you in the letter that I have written to you that everything has been done in perfect order, and I am prepared to stand by it."

And then you did say this, " I had nothing to do with it " ?—No, I did not, because he would find me out in a lie, would he not ?

But you see it takes a great many inquiries to find out some lies ?— You would not have far to go to find that out, because already I have admitted that I am in possession of the Buck's Head.

Now listen, " Was anything said about why or how he had become possessed of the Buck's Head and the barber's shop ? A.—He said it was in the open market, and that he had bought it " ?—No. The open market was not mentioned.

That is the last communication you had with Mr. Vonderahe, was it not, on 9th October ?—Yes, I do not remember any other interview.

I want to put this last question to you. If you had nothing to conceal and these were perfectly honest transactions you were dealing with, why should you object to telling Mr. Vonderahe when he came to you as the representative of the relations ?—I did not like the man's demeanour for one thing. I did not like the way he put it to me. Another thing, the way they spoke about Miss Barrow did not show that they were kindly disposed people, and the way they treated my daughter, in having the door slammed in her face. Mrs. Vonderahe admitted in the box here that the door must have been blown to, but she slammed the door in my daughter's face. I stood by what I told him, that the position was this. I said, " If you show to me that you are the legal next-of-kin of Eliza Mary Barrow I will answer all your questions and give you details," and while he did not do that he was still trying to wheedle this information from me. If I had anything to conceal I would not have written these letters.

You have just told us about the writing of the letter of the 14th September. The copy has been produced. The typewritten letter has not been produced ?—That was sent to the Vonderahes. It would not go to the Evershot Road if they had altered their address in the post office, as they say they had ; it would go direct to Corbin Street.

If it was posted ?—It was posted, most decidedly it was posted.

You said that when Mrs Vonderahe came in and you spoke about that letter that she seemed very flushed and excited ?—Yes.

216

Evidence for Defence.

Frederick H. Seddon

Did you mean to suggest that she was not talking the truth?—I firmly believe, and have done all along, that they have actually received that letter.

And there are three of them?—I do not know about the one from Clapton. I am talking about Mrs. Frank Vonderahe.

Very well, you think that she had it, and was not telling the truth? —My opinion is that they have had that letter, and that they have torn it up after the funeral.

And that in what she said in the witness-box she has perjured herself?—Well, I am contradicting her.

As I understand, the letter was written on mourning paper just like the one on which the typewritten copy has been produced?—It was the exact same.

These happened to be the only two sheets of mourning paper you had in your possession at that date?—Yes. If you look at that paper again it might have been stained through age. It had been standing in the desk pocket for a considerable time.

Just two sheets?—Yes.

You have told us that that letter was posted at some time, or you gave it out to be posted at some time, in the afternoon?—It was very near 5 o'clock, because I told my daughter distinctly I wanted to catch the 5 o'clock post—I wanted them to get it that night as the funeral was so early on the Saturday.

There were plenty of members of your family able to go round to Evershot Road in the afternoon?—Yes, but I would not send one of my family round there after the way my daughter had been treated.

That is the slamming of the door against her?—Yes, certainly. Why should my daughter be treated like that? My daughter went round to ask if there were any letters for Miss Barrow, and they said "No," and slammed the door in her face. Miss Barrow cried about it. My daughter came in very much upset. I said, "Don't you go there under any circumstances again." I told Miss Barrow, and I asked her not to send my daughter round to that house again.

But there was your father?—I would not send any of my family round after that. I looked upon it as the more businesslike way to drop them a line for them to inform the rest of the relations; and if they felt disposed to come to the funeral they could do so, and if they did not they could stop away.

And you never thought of sending round the next day, or even the day of the funeral, to know whether they had the letter?—I expect they did not intend to come. I spoke to Smith the next morning about it, and said the relations had never come.

If you had posted that letter, according to you, you expected them round that night, and they did not come?—They did not come all the next day. I expected when I posted the letter that they would get the letter, and they were treating the matter with the same indifference all the time as they had treated things when Miss Barrow lived there.

You thought they were living at 200 yards distance away?—I thought they were living at Evershot Road. I could not say the distance, as I have never been there.

Trial of the Seddons.

Frederick H. Seddon

Do you not know how far it is?—I think it is the next street to me.

So although you had expected them to come and they did not come——?—I did not expect them to come; I did not know whether they would come or not.

I thought you said you expected them round that evening?—Yes, certainly, if they were coming—if they intended to come to the funeral. They did not come, and I thought they would come on the Friday, and they did not come on the Friday.

You found on the Saturday they did not come?—Then the arrangement stood good that was made temporarily.

Did it occur to you to send Ernie round before she died to tell them?—Ernie was going to the same school as the two boys. I did not know whether they were not in the same class. I do not know whether he told the boys or not.

Ernie on the morning of the 14th, as we know, was sent to Southend by you before he knew anything about the death?—Yes.

He was sent off there with your sons?—Yes. I only sent the one boy to look after them—Freddie, he was fifteen.

Have you a son seventeen?—Yes, but he is with the Daimler Motor Company.

Does he not live in the house with you?—Yes, but he is seldom in; I see very little of him. There is one other point I would like to put about the Vonderahes coming about—it is only that they said in evidence that they saw the windows wide open. That was only on the three days—Thursday, Friday, and Saturday—that our windows were open. Everybody in the neighbourhood knew about the death; the shopkeepers all knew about it; the undertaker drove up to my home in his trap; there was no secret about it. They only lived a few yards away. The windows were wide open, and the windows were not closed till we came back from the funeral, and the Vonderahes have said that they have seen the windows were open. That is why I think they got the letter.

Do you not think that is because they found out these facts and they came to make inquiries?—But they did not come till 23rd September. The windows would be closed on the 17th.

On 23rd November there was an inquest, and I want to ask you about this statement that you made on the 4th December to Inspector Ward. You remember when he arrested you you asked him if he was going to arrest your wife as well?—I was crossing over the Tollington Park towards my home when two gentlemen I saw talking together came up behind me. One got hold of each wrist. They said, "We are police officers; we arrest you." I said, "What for?" "Well," they said, "Chief Inspector Ward of Scotland Yard will be here in a moment or two; he will tell you. You know him, do you not?" I said "No." Just then Dectective-Inspector Ward came up. He said, "Come round the corner; I will let you know why you are arrested." I said, "I am only three doors from home; can you not take me home and let my wife and family know that I am arrested?" He said, "Oh, you need not worry about that. You will see your wife down at the station." I said, "Are you going to arrest her, too?" He said, "Yes." All that time we were round in Fonthill Road, just past the letter box, and

218

Evidence for Defence.

Frederick H. Seddon

Dectective-Inspector Ward said, "You are arrested for the murder—for the wilful murder of Eliza Mary Barrow by poison—by arsenic," or "by arsenic poisoning," or something like that. I said, "Wilful murder? Absurd! Why none of my family has ever been—it is the first of my family that has ever—that such a charge has been made against," or something to that effect, and we started to walk to the station.

Now, let me put to you what Chief Inspector Ward has said in the witness-box here. "Absurd! What a terrible charge. Wilful murder? It is the first of our family that has ever been accused of such a crime"?—That is right, those are the words.

That is what you did say?—Yes.

And then it goes on, "Are you going to arrest my wife as well"?—No, not then. I said, "Can you not take me home and let my wife and family know that I am arrested?" He said, "You need not worry about that, you will see your wife at the station; I am coming back for her." I said, "Are you going to arrest her as well?" That I swear before God is the words that took place, and I have been waiting the opportunity to get into this box for to relate the true words that were spoken on this occasion.

All the statements that you are making are statements before God?—Yes, sir, I recognise that. I want to emphasise that, because I do not look upon it as material—it does not make me innocent or guilty, but I want the truth, and I was very much upset at the North London Police Court when the evidence was given and the two detective-sergeants that arrested me were allowed to be in Court to hear it. If they had not been in Court they could have been cross-examined on this point.

I will read you the statement and you can tell me———?—There is nothing hurt me more than that since my arrest.*

Listen to the question?—Do you think a man with five children would want to see his wife arrested and a baby ill which had been to the doctor that day?

It is not suggested that you wanted to see your wife arrested?—Yes, it is suggested, "Are you going to arrest my wife, too?" That was my greatest concern. It has been the greatest trial of my life since she has been arrested, and we have neglected the five children.

Why did you think that your wife was going to be arrested?—Only by what he said.

Who?—Detective-Inspector Ward said he was going back for her. I said, "Are you going for her now?" He said, "I am not going to let you know what I am going to do." I said, "I am concerned to know."

He has been in the witness-box already?—Yes, well, I am in the witness-box, too. I sat up till 2 o'clock in the morning waiting for her in the cell—in the police cell.

Listen to what I am going to read to you, that no suggestion was ever made to you that your wife was going to be arrested?—What I have just told you now is the exact words that took place; and at the station, when I sent for Mr. Saint, the solicitor, I said, "You had better wait,

---

* Seddon again exhibited strong indignation here.—ED.

Trial of the Seddons.

Frederick H. Seddon

because he has gone to arrest my wife, too, and you had better wait to see her."

Did you go on to say this, " If not, I would like to give her a message from me "?—That was at the station when I asked him, " Are you going for her now?" He said, " I am not going to tell you what I am going to do." I said, " I am concerned to know, because I want a woman to look after my home," and a sergeant took the name and address of this woman—it was Mrs. Brumswich, in Tavistock Place, Holloway Road.

Did you say, " Have they found arsenic in her body "?—Yes, he said he had. I said, " Have you found arsenic in her body?" He said yes.

He had not said to you about arsenic in her body; what he told you was that you were arrested for arsenic poisoning?—Arsenic poisoning, yes —that is where it would be, in the body, would it not?

Did you not put the question, " Have they found arsenic in her body "?—Yes.

And then he said " Yes "?—Yes, I knew they had had a post-mortem —it had been taken.

" She has not done this herself?" That was put in the form of a question?—I do not know whether I said that or not.

" It was not carbolic acid, was it, as there was some in her room "?— Yes.

" And Sanitas is not poison "?—Yes, I said that.

That is mentioning the two things that were in her room?—Yes, I told him that there was carbolic in her room.

Did you say this to Detective-Sergeant Hayman when you were taken to Hornsey Road Police Station with Sergeant Cooper? Did you say, " Poisoning by arsenic—what a charge "?—Yes.

Did you say, " Of course, I have had all her money affairs through my hands, and this means Police Court proceedings and trial before a jury, but I think I can prove my innocence "?—I did not say it exactly in those words, but still that is the substance of it.

" I know Miss Barrow had carbolic in her room "?—Yes.

" But there is no arsenic in carbolic "?—I do not know whether I said, " But there is no arsenic in carbolic." I said, " I know she had carbolic in her room." I do not remember saying that there is no arsenic in carbolic.

You heard Detective-Sergeant Hayman say that at the Police Court, did you not?—Yes. What I considered the most unfair at the Police Court was that the two detective-sergeants would have been there while Chief Inspector Ward gave his evidence of arrest. That I consider was most unfair to me as a prisoner on a grave charge.

Is exhibit 39, a document headed " £10 cash found at Miss Barrow's death," in your handwriting?—Yes.

It is signed by you?—Yes.

Does it purport to account for what was done with the amount?— Yes.

The first item is, " Board for Ernest Grant, two weeks at 10s., £1 "? —That was during her illness; he boarded with us during the illness— principally that.

Evidence for Defence.

Frederick H. Seddon

" Fourteen days at 1s. a day due to Maggie, 14s."?—Yes.

" Seven shillings and sixpence, tips to bearers and gravediggers, and £4 funeral, £4 7s. 6d."?—Yes.

" Doctor's bill, £1 5s." That, I suppose, is Dr. Sworn?—Yes.

" Ernie's holiday, Southend-on-Sea, £1 2s. 6d. ; pocket money, 2s. ; fare, 1s. 9d. ; death probate certificate, 3s. 7d."?—That was for the probate.

What?—I took that to Somerset House for the probate.

Did you get probate?—No; this was the certificate for the applying for probate.

That means a death certificate, I suppose?—Well, it says, " Death probate certificate " here.

" Inventory, £1 1s."—that is the inventory for £16 14s. 6d.?—Yes.

" Woman for laying out and cleaning room, 5s."; is that Mrs. Rutt? —Yes.

" Suit of clothes and pants extra for Ernie, 13s."?—The total is £11 1s. 10½d., and the amount found was £10.

That included, as I have just pointed out, Ernie's holiday at Southend and a suit of clothes for him?—Yes.

When did you make that up?—I think it was about the time of the inquest, for Mr. Saint.

Had you made up no account till then?—I had a note; I had not drafted it out in this form.

Now, I want to ask you about the statement you made as to the cash you had. The whole of your statement accounting for the money that you had paid out on 15th September depends upon your statement that you had £220 in gold, does it not?—Yes.

Have you any document of any kind to show that you had £220 in gold?—No, but I think there is ample evidence.

How long was the wardrobe business carried on?—Just on twelve months.

Is it from February, 1909, until the beginning of 1910?—Yes, I suppose it would be.

When Mr. Naylor and Mr. Wilson were present did you ever make any statement to them about how much gold there was in the bag?—I do not think I told them how much there was. I told him that if he came across any wardrobe stocks for sale Mrs. Seddon was prepared to purchase up to any amount.

From whom?—From Mr. Naylor; he is an auctioneer and gets about a bit. I said that if he knew of anybody that had any ladies' wardrobes to dispose of she was prepared to buy for cash, and I showed him that we kept plenty of ready cash on hand for the purpose. It was necessary, because business people came into the shop to sell their wardrobes.

The amount you have told us was £100 or £130, or it might be £150?—I could not say for certain at that date. I know what I came out with, but I do not know exactly what there was at any particular date; it was accumulating.

It was not as much as Mr. Naylor said in the witness-box, about £200?—There was not that much.

Then, according to you, he must have been mistaken when he said

Trial of the Seddons.

you told him it was about £200?—I may have done so, I could not say for sure.

Your own statement about it on Saturday was that it might be £100 to £130, or perhaps £150, but not so much as they, that is Naylor and Wilson, said. That is your own statement?—It certainly was not £200. Even if I told him it was £200, it would not be true. I would not have so much as that; I may have said, in a jocular way, "There is a couple of hundred here at any time to buy stock," or something like that.

You sold the whole of the stock at the beginning of 1910?—Yes.

And gave up business?—That is it.

And you got £30 for it?—Yes.

Did you place that £30 in the Post Office Savings Bank on deposit?—Yes.

To carry interest?—Yes.

Why did you not put all the money you had into the Post Office Savings Bank to carry interest?—Because I wanted to keep it on hand for the purpose of paying off the mortgage when desired. Also Mr. Wainwright, the estate agent, who had acted in the sale of that property, had suggested to me the possibility of some more bargains coming along, as owing to the papers that Lloyd George had been sending out, I think, or something like that—something about land returns—property was down; it was cheap at the time.

There was no difficulty in drawing money out of the bank if you wanted it at any time, was there?—But my wife could not have the same facility if anything happened to me. She would have to wait to take out letters of administration, or wait for probate.

Had you made a will at the time?—No, it was not in existence then. I had made a will a long time before that, but I tore it up when my wife went away. You understand the business was one which a gentleman could not very well manage, it being a wardrobe business, but I used to keep the books for the wife at the week-end; on the Sunday I made them up for her. I also used to label the stock for her in lot numbers, so I could at any time go through the stock and see how the business stood. I had had differences with my wife regarding the lot numbers getting off the stock, so I could not recognise what had been paid for it. These differences in business caused a family quarrel between us, and I was going to throw the books behind the fire. As a matter of fact, I did mutilate them in consequence, and I never kept the books after.

What has become of those books?—Some of them are in existence.

Have you got them?—I believe my solicitor has got them. I believe Detective-Inspector Ward has seen them at home.

Will these books show in their present condition the amount of takings in the business?—Yes.

And the amounts spent in the stock?—Not all of it.

Will you produce the books, please?

Mr. MARSHALL HALL—I produce them just as they came to us. (Four books were handed to the witness.)

By the ATTORNEY-GENERAL—Would those books say what amount has been expended on the stock which was sold for the £30 at the beginning

Evidence for Defence.

Frederick H. Seddon

of 1910?—I do not think there is a summary of the stock sold. There is an account of the week's takings, week by week, from 6th March, 1909, to 20th November, 1909.

Would it also show the week's expenditure?—No; it would have to be taken on an average from the figures I have got here.

What average do you make the figures you have got there in expenditure; I do not want it accurately, but about?—I have here stock purchased, total £132 6s. 1d.

For how long is that?—This shows the date, 8th May, 1909.

Does that show what the sales were also?—Yes.

What were the sales up to 8th May, 1909?—From April, 1909, to 8th May, 1909, stock that had cost £43 15s. 4d. had sold for £85 18s. 7½d., yielding profit in eight weeks of—no, yielding a profit in four months, of £42 1s. 3½d.—no, not so long as that—no, from 20th March.

Is there any account in the books which will show how much money there was at the end of the business?—I give you this here. I have got it here now. Total, eight weeks, less forfeit, £43 15s. 3½d.; stock sold yielded £85 18s. 7½d., showing a profit of £42 1s. 3½d. for the eight weeks.

You have given an explanation about the purchase of 63 Tollington Park and as to your payments. Summarising what you have said, you paid £15 deposit by cheque to Mr. Wainwright, and you sold £100 Cardiff stock, as you have said, for about £84⅝?—£85 odd, I think, according to my bank book; that made up the £100 margin.

And you got a mortgage of £220?—Yes, and that paid for the house.

What rate of interest were you paying on the mortgage?—5 per cent.

What rate of interest were you getting on the money deposited in the Post Office?—2½ per cent.

According to that view you were paying 5 per cent. on the £220 mortgage, whilst you had £220 gold in the house?—Yes; I did the same with the Temperance Permanent Building Society eight years ago.

That £220 was idle money? It was not bringing in any income?—It was very valuable to my wife if anything happened to me.

What was the difficulty about this mortgage?—Supposing you had got your mortgage for £220 on the property, there would be notice before you had to pay off the mortgage? I don't think they would call upon you to pay off the mortgage you have got over a term of years—fifteen years.

How many years had you it over?—I forget whether it was fifteen or twenty years.

The mortgage had been given at the beginning of 1910?—Yes.

So that you could not be called upon by the society to pay off the mortgage for some period of fifteen or twenty years?—I could manage to pay off the mortgage and everything else while I was earning; but in the event of my decease my wife would not have the same income coming, and it was a good big house, and she would let off—that is what she had done in Isledon Road—to boarders, and she could make a living that way.

Trial of the Seddons.

Frederick H. Seddon

Do you not think that would be just as available to her if it had been in your bank?—No, I do not—not to her; it would be to me.

What date was it that you and your wife separated?—3rd January, 1910; the time that the shop was disposed of.

How long were you separated?—Four weeks; it might have been five.

I must ask you, what was the cause of the separation?—I did not know it was necessary for to introduce domestic affairs into this charge.

The stock we know was sold for £30. Now, how much money was there in the business. Is there any account which will show that?—Only up to that date; there is £132 6s. 1d. at this date, 8th May, 1909.

1909?—Yes.

I am asking when the business was sold?—No, I have only got an account of the takings up to 20th November, week by week.

You told us the books were mutilated?—Yes.

Was that at the beginning of 1910?—No, it was somewhere between this date that I stopped keeping the books and the time my wife went away.

The time your wife went away was the beginning of 1910, you have told us?—Yes, January, but then we had a quarrel over the business for two or three months.

Why did you mutilate the books?—I did it in a fit of temper. I have used the books since; when I have wanted any spare paper I have torn pages out. Another thing, it is over two years ago, and I did not think they would ever be further required any more; I had done with the business entirely; I had sold out, and it is over two years ago. I half thought of putting them behind the fire.

Now, I want you to tell me—never mind about the books for the moment——?—I have got over £300 takings here from 6th March to November.

Now, will you tell me about the £220 that you have spoken of? Did you represent that it was a mere coincidence that on 15th September and 18th September you were dealing with £155 in gold on your own admission?—Because I was going away on my holidays; it was not safe for me to go away for fourteen days on my holidays and leave it on hand.

You realise that you dealt on 15th September and 18th September with £155 in sovereigns?—Yes, what I kept on hand for the purpose of paying off the mortgage should occasion require; I took it down to the very same building society, and put it there in shares for the very same purpose.

And so you could have done at any time during the whole of 1910 or 1911?—Yes, I could have done.

But you only dealt with this gold in this way on 15th September and 18th September?—Because I was going away. It was perfectly safe in the house while I was about.

You had been away before?—I had only been away for four days, and there was somebody at home then; my father was there.

You were away in August of that year?—Only for the Bank Holiday, but all the family were going away on this occasion.

The safest place for it would have been in the bank?—I put it in the bank; I put some of it in the Post Office, some of it on current account,

Evidence for Defence.

Frederick H. Seddon

and the rest I invested in shares in the building society where I had the mortgage. I could have paid the mortgage when I got £1600 in my hands after selling the stock; I had £1519 in my hands after I had sold the stock; I could have paid the mortgage then.

Do you represent that this statement of yours about the £220 by a mere coincidence is so close to the £216 which Miss Barrow had drawn out?—But there is not, there is only £170. I have not got £220 on hand; I have only got £170.

You had had £220 on hand?—Oh, yes, I know I had, for the mortgage when I first went into the house.

You had begun to draw on that money although you wanted to keep it for the mortgage in case anything happened?—I had broken into it, but still I had got £170 in hand.

Are those receipts torn from a book?—Yes.

Have you got the counterfoils?—I believe they are in existence.

Did you fill up the counterfoils?—I cannot remember.

Is there any reason why you should not?—It is not necessary; I might have done; I am not sure.

These are the only two counterfoil books that have been found (handed)?—These are not them.

Those are the two books of counterfoils that have been found. Do you suggest there was another?—Yes, certainly.

Two others, then, according to you?—Yes. These are not the same size; these are not the same print.

Do you know what has become of them?—Yes, they are in the house they were when I was arrested.

I see there are a number of counterfoils here which are blank with receipts torn out?—Is that the rent book?

No, the cash receipt book. So far as I can see from the book there are seven?—Yes. I have no recollection of doing that.

Just look at the end of the book. Read it out aloud?—" Life annuity January 2nd, 1911. Received from Frederick Henry Seddon the sum of £10, being £6 monthly allowance as arranged in consideration for the transfer of £1600 India 3½ per cent. stock, and £4 monthly allowance as arranged in consideration for assignment of leases of properties situate 202 High Street, Camden Town, N., Buck's Head public-house and the barber's shop adjoining known as No. 1 Buck Street."

Do you know anything about that receipt?—I think that was kept as a copy.

Does it appear to have had a stamp upon it?—Yes, it looks as if it had a stamp on it. I know why this was done.

Tell us?—Because it required two separate receipts, and I was making this all up in one £10. This was the first receipt drafted out, and you will find for January on that date two separate ones—£4 and £6.

That is in that book which contains several counterfoils blank?—Yes, but this is not the book which was continued to be used for it.

Do you know what has become of it?—It is in the house. I had four of these.

It has not been found?—I had four of these. This was used for another purpose.

Trial of the Seddons.

Frederick H. Seddon

I notice that on that counterfoil the receipt is not filled in?—No.

But it appears to have been carried out and stamped?—No, it was not carried out.

It was stamped?—I put the stamp on it. Well, then, I decided that it required two separate receipts for £6 and £4.

When did you decide that?—After I had written it out and put the stamp on it when I was going to pay her the first £10. Very likely the same stamp that has come off this is on one of them. The only difference is that this is a combined receipt, and the others are separate. (Two counterfoil receipt books were put in.)

Was your daughter Maggie in London on 26th August, 1911?—Yes.

According to what we have heard, on the 6th December, 1911, she went to purchase fly-papers at Mr. Price's, the chemist?—I have heard so in evidence; I was under arrest.

Were you consulted about it at all?—Yes, Mr. Saint had mentioned it to me.

Was that before or after your arrest?—He consulted me the night of my arrest.

Did you then know these fly-papers contained arsenic?—I did not know for certain; Mr. Saint had suggested to me that they did.

Had you ever seen a packet of these fly-papers?—No.

Did you know they were called " arsenical fly-papers "?—No.

Did you know that they were poisonous?—I knew they were poisonous to insects.

And to children?—I did not know that.

You have said that you saw them in her room?—Yes.

When first?—The night that the will was signed.

How often did you see fly-papers in her room?—I saw them the night the will was signed, and I saw them the night she died.

Were you in the habit of using them?—No, I have never seen them in the house before—only the sticky ones that the flies stick to.

Had you been in the habit of using the sticky ones?—We had used the sticky ones.

You began to use the arsenic papers, according to you, about 11th September?—I did not begin to use any at all. I did not know they were there until I was told about them.

Was 11th September the first time that you had seen arsenic fly-papers used in the your house?—I have no recollection of ever having seen them before.

Have you ever heard of poisoning by arsenic taken from fly-papers? —Yes, since I have been arrested.

Do you know that two-thirds of a grain of arsenic, according to the evidence of Dr. Willcox, was found in the stomach and intestines of this lady when he examined her two months after her death?—I have heard that; I cannot remember the exact amount that he found, but something like that.

I am understating it, really it is ·63 in the stomach and ·11 in the intestines—that is the exact amount. It is ·74 grains, which is just upon three-quarters of a grain. Can you account for the arsenic having got into her stomach and intestines?—It's a Chinese puzzle to me.

Evidence for Defence.

Frederick H. Seddon

Re-examined by Mr. MARSHALL HALL—Did you know how it was that fly-papers came to be brought into Miss Barrow's room at all?—Yes. Mrs. Seddon told me that she had purchased fly-papers to satisfy Miss Barrow, as she complained of the heat in the room and the flies, and that is why she had got up out of bed and gone into this little room—that Miss Barrow had asked for them to be purchased, and, as she was leaving the room, she says, " Don't get the sticky ones, they are dirty; get those you put water on."

So far as you know, what we call fly-papers that had water put upon them had never been used in your house before?—I have no recollection.

You have been asked if you can account for the fact of arsenic having been found, as it has been found, in the body of Miss Barrow. Is there any knowledge of your own which will enable you to account for it—was there anything you ever did, or your wife ever did, to account for any arsenic being found in the body?—I do not know of anything.

What is the date of the letter that you have got which was written by Miss Barrow saying she did not wish her relatives to benefit by her death?—I believe it is 27th March, 1911.

The learned Attorney-General has made a point that when Miss Barrow came to you she had £1600 worth of East India stock and the Buck's Head property, and that when she died there was practically nothing left except £10. Were the Buck's Head property and the proceeds of the £1600 East India stock still intact, and are they still intact?—Yes, I have not touched them, only improved the investment.

You had got absolute possession of the £1519 in the month of October?—Yes, thirteen months before; I have been in possession all throughout the year, receiving the rents; I had full possession throughout the year from October and January.

At any rate, you had had possession of the money for nearly four months before you began to pay the annuity on it?—Yes.

Did you make any attempt of any sort or shape to part with that £1500?—No; I could have paid my mortgage off with the £200 I had.

The learned Attorney-General has asked you about the document, and I want to see if I understand it. There was a document prepared without the assistance of a lawyer purporting to carry out this arrangement?—Yes.

When it was drawn up as far as being signed and witnessed, you came to the conclusion that it was not valid and it was destroyed, and you went to the lawyer?—Yes, this was because she would not have solicitors, and then I said she would have to have solicitors, this was not satisfactory, and I destroyed it.

Under the legal effect of that will the next-of-kin would still have taken any property that she might have left other than the property which was described in the will?—That was not enclosed in the will.

Because there was intestacy as to any other property except the property comprised in the will?—Yes.

And the next-of-kin are, as we know, the Vonderahes?—I do not know that they are; they said they were.

Had you any expectation whatever that that will would ever become a

Trial of the Seddons.

Frederick H. Seddon

document to be acted upon?—I did not, or I would not have had anything to do with it.

Who is the person who is making the claim to be the next-of-kin in the Probate Court at the present time? Is that one of the Vonderahes or anybody else?—No, it is an absolutely different individual altogether named Barrow, and he is down in Bristol.

Dr. Sworn has told us that she could not hear what he said. Did you ever find any difficulty in making her hear?—None whatever. Why, she could hear the little boy.

Did she read this will herself?—Yes, I read it to her first, and then she read it.

Would the calling in of a solicitor on the 11th to make this will have affected your position in any way at all?—Oh, no, not at all.

If you had thought she was going to die you would have called in a solicitor for your own protection?—Certainly I would, because the will was not to benefit me at all, and it was no advantage to me to draw the will up or have anything to do with it; in fact, it would have protected my interests to have had a solicitor to do so.

As to this £216, you told my learned friend that, when you said something to her about it, she said she knew what to do with it?—She said she knew what to do with it. She never spoke to me for over a week.

Have you any idea what she has done with it?—I have not any knowledge. I have got ideas, but that is all.

Come to the night of the death. My learned friend has asked you if you expected her to die that night, and you said you did not. How long prior to actual death did Miss Barrow sleep peacefully?—I should say about a couple of hours.

How long did the ordinary sleeping take place before you heard this heavy breathing?—I could not tell for certain; I am judging by the last time I went upstairs, I reckoned it was about four o'clock in the morning when we put her back into bed.

Did she sleep peacefully after that?—Yes. We never left the room after that occasion.

She died about 6.30, did she not?—About 6.20 or 6.15.

By Mr. Justice Bucknill—You understand the difference between a peaceful sleep and a snoring sleep. A person may be asleep and not snore? —I mean she was in a good heavy sleep—a sound sleep; it was safe for the missus to leave her.

She first of all fell asleep quietly and afterwards began the heavy snore?—Yes; then I said to the wife, "It will be quite safe to leave her now; she is in a quiet sound sleep."

You say, as I understand from that, that you thought when she was snoring that she was in a sound sleep?—Yes, and that the wife could safely leave her now, and she would not be likely to waken, but she said, "What is the good of doing that? It only means going down and getting nicely settled and coming up again." Then we thought of the boy. We could not leave her without the boy was with her again, so we would have had to call the boy up if we wanted to leave her.

By Mr. Marshall Hall—Some little suggestion is made with regard to your smoking your pipe. You were smoking in the doorway?—Yes.

Evidence for Defence.

Frederick H. Seddon

I think you told us before that the smell in the room was very, very bad?—Oh, yes.

And you have said that on one occasion it made you feel very sick?—That is why I stayed outside the door and smoked my pipe on that night.

As regards this question of the £216, the Savings Bank people who paid that out would, of course, keep a record of any payment out?—Most decidedly; I knew it was on record.

In answer to my learned friend, you said you had expected during the case that some document might be found, or some document would turn up?—I have been expecting to see it turn up in the course of the proceedings.

Is there any important document that you know of missing in this case?—There are two important documents—the duplicate of the deed which I gave the coroner and the annuity certificate that I gave pinned to the deed.

The deed, as we know, was executed in counterpart?—In a counterpart which she had.

One part you had and the other part you handed to Miss Barrow?—I had the original and she had the other that I paid the 30s. for.

You are speaking of the assignment?—Yes.

The assignment that you have got is the one from her to you?—Yes.

And it was executed in duplicate, and the counterpart is charged for, as we know?—Yes, I paid for it for her.

Did you hand that counterpart to her?—Yes, I did.

Do you know what has become of that?—No, she had it.

In addition to that, you say you gave her a memorandum as to the annuity that was payable?—Yes, I gave it her typewritten, and signed it over a sixpenny stamp.

That has disappeared?—It is with that document wherever it is.

The document that was handed to the coroner was your copy of the assignment?—Yes.

But there was a copy given to Miss Barrow, and that has disappeared?—Yes.

By Mr. Justice Bucknill—Is that the typewritten document *re* the £1600?—Yes.

By Mr. Marshall Hall—The assignment itself shows the annuity of the £52 typewritten document over a sixpenny stamp acknowledging your liability in respect to the £1600?—Yes, and it had to be paid by my heirs, executors, administrators, and the charge on my estate.

By Mr. Justice Bucknill—That is what we call the £6 annuity?—Yes.

As distinguished from the £4 annuity, which was *re* the brewery and the shop?—Exactly.

By Mr. Marshall Hall—With regard to Hook, I think you told my learned friend you deny what he states—he is not telling the truth?—About that £420?

Yes?—It must be a lie.

And did you say to Hook, "You are not my tenants. Miss Barrow has given you notice, and you won't go, so I give you notice to go"?—Yes.

When you used the words, "I am looking after her interest," in what meaning were you using those words?—As my tenant, to protect her, because she had come there with what proved to be undesirable

229

Trial of the Seddons.

people, and she wanted to remain, and she wanted them to get out, and they would not get out, and naturally she looked to me, as the landlord, to protect her. You see, they had threatened to take the boy as well, and she appealed to me to save him for her.

There is one other question about another matter, with regard to the alteration of the ring and watch. You went to the jeweller's, Mr Wright?—Yes.

As he has told us, he knew you, and he had your name and address? —Yes, I took them to this man, who did know me.

You had dealt with him some time?—Yes.

So there was no possibility, or any idea, of concealing your identity? —No, and he did another ring for me previous to that.

This gold watch, the diamond ring, and the articles that were given to your girl, never belonged to the Grants as far as you know?—Miss Barrow said they did not. What she gave us she said was her own family's, but the rest in her trunk belonged to the Grants, excepting some brooches which she had, mourning brooches.

When did you suggest calling in a nurse?—The day that the will was signed.

Who did you suggest should be called in?—I said she ought to have a hospital nurse, or go to a hospital, but she would not have either. I said, "Would you like me to write to Mrs. Cugnoni?" She said, "No," she did not want to have any relations.

Was that a cousin who had written to her?—Offered her a home at Clapton.

When Mr. Vonderahe came to call upon you, on 9th October, was his attitude conciliatory or not?—No, it was the opposite.

And, so far as he was concerned, it made no difference who was paying the annuity so long as the property had been sold for an annuity? —Yes.

That is the attitude you took up?—He seemed very sarcastic.

And are you sure you never said about "the open market"?—No, he spoke with a kind of sneer all the time. That is why I said, "Well, you can go and get a solicitor."

You told my learned friend you have always believed that that letter did reach the Vonderahes?—I feel certain.

Just now you said, when talking about putting the money on deposit with the building society, you had done the same thing years before. Now, about the bundle of receipts. Are those receipts absolutely genuine receipts given to you by Miss Barrow, as they purport to be?—I swear they are. I will stake my life on that.

Are you willing that I should call Mrs. Seddon as a witness on your behalf?—Yes.

Mr. MARSHALL HALL—Your lordship will see that I put that question because of the decision in the House of Lords. I am going to call Mrs. Seddon as a witness for Mr. Seddon, by her consent, otherwise I should have to wait until the end of my case before she was called. In accordance with the decision of the House of Lords, I have got his consent and I have got her consent, and after calling two formal witnesses I shall call her as a witness for Mr. Seddon.

Evidence for Defence.

Frank Edward Whiting

FRANK EDWARD WHITING, examined by Mr. ORR—I am a member of the firm of Whiting & Ford, architects, 30 Bedford Road. On 2nd January, on the instructions of Mr. Saint, I drew the plan of Miss Barrow's bedroom which is now produced, and is correct.

ALBERT SIDNEY WAINWRIGHT, examined by Mr. MARSHALL HALL—I am a member of the firm of Ramsay, Wainwright & Co., auctioneers, 279 Seven Sisters Road. I have known the male prisoner for some years. On my return from my holidays at the end of August, 1909, I submitted particulars of the leasehold property at 63 Tollington Park to him, and eventually he offered £320, which the vendors accepted on 3rd September. In the evening of that day I called on the male prisoner at 200 Seven Sisters Road, and filled in a form of contract, which we discussed. I wanted £30 deposit, but he would only pay £15 because there was a forfeiture clause in it. To pay the £15 he brought out a bag of gold, which he emptied on to his desk. He counted out £15, and I said that as I was going out that night I would prefer to have a cheque. He said it would make no difference to him, and then he put all the gold back into his bag and we had a chat. He said that the repairs to the property were going to cost him about £50, and he tapped the bag and said, "With this money and other money I am possessed of I can pay for this house." I said, "Well, if that is the case I should not put all your eggs into one basket. Why not buy two or three houses, and put a small amount in each? Get mortgages and the houses will pay for themselves." He fell in with that idea, and from time to time I gave him particulars of other houses. He made an offer for one, but it was not accepted. It was my suggestion entirely that he should get a mortgage on this property. I thought it was a good time to speculate in house property, and by paying a deposit and a certain amount of the purchase price and borrowing the rest on mortgage from a building society he would be able to bu more property with the same amount of money. I got instructions to let the house, but I did not find a tenant, and so Mr. Seddon decided to inhabit the house himself. The matter of the mortgage cropped up once or twice. I might say that just before the completion Mr. Seddon was rather annoyed about the solicitors' charges. The law costs came to more than he thought they would be, and so he came to me and kicked up rather a row with me, as if it were my fault. I told him to go down to see the lawyers, and I believe he went and saw them, and as a matter of fact I know he carried the mortgage through. Not only did I originally suggest it, but I persuaded him to carry it through. I looked upon Mr. Seddon as a man of substance.

Cross-examined by the ATTORNEY-GENERAL—I knew afterwards that he held Cardiff stock, but I cannot say how much it was.

THOMAS CREEK, examined by Mr. MARSHALL HALL—I am a carman, and I reside at 11 Greenwood Place, Kentish Town. I have known the man Hook for some years. On 26th July, 1910, at his request I removed some goods belonging to Miss Barrow from 31 Evershot Road to 63 Tollington Park. The goods were in one room. I think the removing was done between twelve and three. Hook helped me to load and unload

231

Trial of the Seddons.

the van. He did not carry anything in his hand. I cannot remember anything left behind that he went back for. I did not see him carrying a bag. He and I stopped and had a drink in a public-house while Miss Barrow and the boy stood by the van. After we had done unloading I left Hook putting down the oilcloth. I was paid 4s.

Cross-examined by the ATTORNEY-GENERAL—I get my living doing these jobs. I do not keep any note of them; all I am concerned with is doing my work and getting my pay. There was nothing special about the moving that I have spoken about. I should know if any one was carrying a bag in his hand or if he was carrying nothing, although it was eighteen or nineteen months ago. It was some time this year when Mr. Saint came to me and asked if I could remember about this.

It is not a very unusual thing for you to have a drink?—It would be an unusual thing if we didn't.

Re-examined by Mr. MARSHALL HALL—Hook only engaged me on that one occasion to remove goods from Evershot Road to Tollington Park.

MARGARET ANN SEDDON (prisoner, on oath), examined by Mr. RENTOUL —I am the wife of the male prisoner. I am thirty-four years of age. I have been married for eighteen years, and I have five children, my youngest child being born on 3rd January of last year. In 1909 we lived at 200 Seven Sisters Road, where I carried on a wardrobe business under the name of "Madame Rowan." My husband found the money to start that business partly from the bank and partly from what he had in the Cardiff stock. He always used to keep money in hand, and I have seen it myself from time to time. He always kept the takings, first in the secretaire, and then later on in a safe that he bought. We did a splendid business. Books were kept, but they were mutilated. In February, 1910, we moved to 63 Tollington Park, where we occupied the basement and the first two floors and let the top part. My husband used the basement as an office for transacting his business. He had got another safe, which was placed in the office, the first safe being in our bedroom. We advertised for a tenant for the top floor, and in July, 1910, Miss Barrow called to see the rooms. I saw her myself, with the little boy Ernie. She did not decide to take the rooms then, as she said she had a friend. She called again with Mrs. Hook, and then decided to take the rooms, paying a week's deposit. She came to live in the rooms, along with Ernie Grant and the Hooks. The Hooks left our house through a quarrel with Miss Barrow, on a Saturday night, I think. They must have all had a little drop of drink, and they started quarrelling together. Then, on the Sunday, they took Ernest out and left Miss Barrow in bed sick all day. She had no one to attend to her but my daughter. When the Hooks returned at night Miss Barrow was still sick. They were quarrelling, and my husband wrote a note and pinned it on the door. Miss Barrow complained to my husband and me about the way that they carried on, and said that she could not have it. I remember Miss Barrow coming downstairs and speaking to my husband in the dining-room a day or two before the Hooks left the house. She said she was frightened of the Hooks, she could not trust them, and she wanted to put her cash

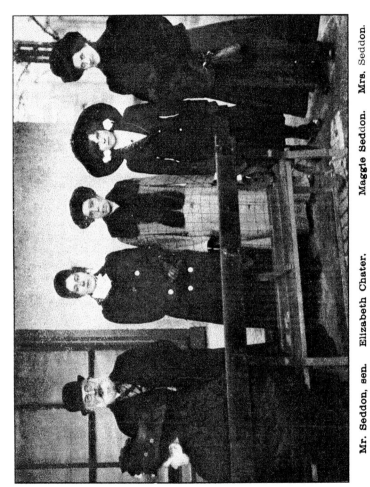

Mr. Seddon, sen.   Elizabeth Chater.   Maggie Seddon.   Mrs. Seddon.

Evidence for Defence.

Margaret A. Seddon

box in my husband's safe. She said there was between £30 and £35 in the cash box. My husband said that he would not have it unless Miss Barrow counted it out. She took her cash box upstairs again, and my husband thought she had taken it up to count it, but she did not come down again. The Hooks left a day or two later, on the Tuesday I think it was. After that my daughter Maggie looked after Miss Barrow right up to the time she took ill, and she used to get a shilling a day pocket money.

After the Hooks left, I noticed that Miss Barrow was always sitting crying; she told me it was about the compensation funds in regard to the public-house that she had, and she asked me to tell my husband that she wanted to see him. My husband saw her later on. I don't know whether I was present then or not, nor do I remember whether my husband went up or she came down. My husband told me something about Miss Barrow's properties, but I don't understand these financial affairs. I witnessed an annuity certificate, and later on the will. When Miss Barrow first came to the house she paid 12s. a week rent, which was entered up by my husband in her rent book every week. After the arrangement about the annuity I think my husband wrote in the rent book "Free as arranged," and signed it underneath "Clear" every week. I know about the diamond ring.

What happened with regard to that?—I was confined at the time. Miss Barrow brought it into the bedroom and made a present of it to my husband when the transaction was finished. I have seen my husband wear it on his little finger during Miss Barrow's life. She made me a present of a gold watch and chain with three charms upon it (exhibits 121 and 122) on my thirty-first birthday. My husband made me a present of a gold bangle at the same time. The charms are on my bracelet now. Miss Barrow also gave my daughter Maggie a gold necklet and locket (exhibit 123) on her birthday. I remember Miss Barrow giving me a letter she had written with regard to her relations in March of last year (exhibit 7).* My husband was out at the time, and I gave it to him when he came in.

When Miss Barrow was living at our house she asked me to cash bank notes for her. I think she had been out herself to get one cashed, and some one would not cash it for her, so she asked me if I would get it cashed. I took it to the Post Office, and they asked me for my name and address. I thought it was rather funny, as I never cashed a note in my life before, and so I gave the first name that came into my head. I did not give my own name and address. That would be about a month or so after Miss Barrow came to the house, I could not exactly say when. I gave the cash to Miss Barrow when I came back, five sovereigns, as far as I can remember. I have an idea that the name I gave at the Post Office was "M. Scott, 18 Evershot Road," or "12 Evershot Road," I am not sure which. After that day Miss Barrow from time to time asked me to change notes for her, and I had no difficulty whatever in changing them.

By Mr. JUSTICE BUCKNILL—I would go out to do some shopping, and

* Appendix F.

Trial of the Seddons.

Margaret A. Seddon

then I would change the note and make the balance up. I sometimes gave her all gold, and sometimes I gave her some silver. It depended if I had bought anything—if I bought and paid for anything, then I made it up. At the shops I went to where I was known I gave my right name and address, because they already knew it. When I went to the shops where I was not known I gave the name of "M. Scott."

Examination continued—I always gave the money to Miss Barrow. I remember going with Miss Barrow to draw some money from the savings bank. She asked my husband, would he allow me to go with her. You see, I had a young baby at the time. She wanted to draw out this money on account of the bank—the Birkbeck Bank, I think. She was paid in two bags containing £100 each, and £16 loose gold, and I think some coppers. She emptied it all out on the counter, and the cashier passed the remark that it was not necessary because it was just as it had come from the bank. I never touched the money at all, and I have never seen that money since. When she came in my husband said something to her about putting it away, that he did not like to have it all in gold, and she said she knew what to do with it. I do not think she spoke to my husband for a week after that.

Up to the time of her illness Miss Barrow used to go out every day. She used to take the little boy to school and stop out till perhaps 10 or 10.30, and then bring in her dinner with her, and sometimes she would see the boy start to school, and come back and go out and get her dinner. She used to say that she met a woman when she was out, but I could not tell who it was. She told me that her relations were not kind to her. With regard to her hearing, she could hear my baby crying, and she could hear quite plainly Ernie's voice or my voice just by putting her hand to her ear. I had no difficulty in making her hear, she got used to me.

As far as I know, she was out on the morning of 1st September, the day when she was taken ill, but I cannot say positively, because I did not get up till about 10.30. When I came down she was sitting in our kitchen. She complained about being sick, bilious, and I advised her to go upstairs and have a lie down. I helped her upstairs, and she lay down on the bed without undressing. I gave her a cup of tea, but she was sick after it. I had seen her like this before, off and on, with these sick bilious attacks every month. The next day she had sickness and diarrhœa, and I thought it better to send for a doctor. She asked me in the morning to tell my husband that she could sign for her annuity, and he went up to her, and she signed two receipts in my presence. After dinner she gradually seemed to have the diarrhœa and sickness, and we thought it safer—best—to call in a doctor, and I went for Dr. Paul, to whom I had previously taken her, but he could not come. We sent for him a second time, and he said finally he could not come, but to get the nearest doctor in the neighbourhood. My daughter telephoned for Dr. Sworn, who was our own family doctor. I saw Dr. Sworn when he came, and he told me that Miss Barrow was to have no solid food, that everything she ate was to be light. He sent her some medicine, but she would not take it, because it was a chalky, thick medicine. The doctor called again on Sunday, the 3rd, and gave her a dose himself, and said that she would have to take it. There was no mention made of her going to the hospital till Monday or Tuesday.

Evidence for Defence.

Margaret A. Seddon

She had been ill a few days then before the doctor suggested her going to the hospital. I complained about her not taking the fizzy medicine, and when the doctor said that she would have to go to the hospital, she said she would not go. I asked her myself in the doctor's presence, would she go to the hospital, and she said, "No," and she refused to have a nurse.

I remember Miss Barrow soon after the commencement of her illness leaving her own room and going into the boy's bedroom. I remonstrated with her for it, and told her that the doctor would blame me if anything happened to her. She complained of the flies in her bedroom; it was very hot, and we had to have all the windows open, and we were fanning her to keep the flies from coming on to her. The doctor said there were a great many flies—he had never seen so many. It was the smell that caused that. Miss Barrow asked me if I would get her some fly-papers; she said she did not want the sticky ones, she wanted those that you wet, and I got her some. I think this was either on Monday, the 4th, or Tuesday, the 5th, but I cannot swear to dates. I got these fly-papers at Meacher's, the chemist, in Stroud Green Road, just round the corner from our house. An old gentleman served me. I think I ordered at the same time a 9s. 6d. bottle of the baby's food, Horlick's malted milk, but they had not got it, and he said he would send it home when he had it in. I also bought a pennyworth of white precipitate powder, with which Miss Barrow used to wash her head. I have also seen her cleaning her teeth with it. When I bought the fly-papers I did not sign any book or anything. I never bought a packet; I have never seen packets. I asked first for two fly-papers, and I put down twopence, and then Mr. Meacher, or whatever his name is, said, "Why not have four? You can have four for threepence." I said "Very well, then, I might as well have the four." They were rolled up in a piece of white paper. When Miss Barrow saw the papers she said they were the ones she wanted. I put them in a plate to damp them, and wet them all over with water, and then I put them in four saucers, two of which I put on the mantelpiece and two on the chest of drawers in between her mirror.

By Mr. Justice Bucknill—When I put the damp papers in the saucers I also put water in the saucers.

Examination continued—Up to the time that Miss Barrow took ill Maggie did her cooking; but after that, when she was ill in bed, I did the cooking down in my kitchen. There was really no cooking to do, unless the Valentine's meat juice, which had to be prepared with cold water; the other things, of course, wanted boiling, such as barley water. Before she was taken ill the cooking was done in her own kitchen, except once or twice, when she asked me to cook her a pudding or sometimes some fish. She used to have a cup of tea in the morning; Mary always made that, but I did not see it made, as I was in bed. Maggie, I think, used to take it into the bedroom both before and after Miss Barrow was ill. At first I used to get up at six o'clock when I heard the milkman and get her a glass of cold milk. After that, when my boys were called up about seven o'clock, she used to have this cup of tea that the servant made. She continued to have the tea until four days before she died, when the doctor said she was to have no more, because she never kept it in her stomach.

During her illness no one waited upon her besides myself, except, if

Trial of the Seddons.

Margaret A. Seddon

I happened to be out of the road, when perhaps Maggie would go up, or any one who was knocking about. My husband gave Miss Barrow her medicine only on one occasion—that was when I complained to him that she would not take her medicine while it was fizzing, and the doctor had said that if she did not do so it would never do her any good.

On the Sunday or Monday Miss Barrow wanted to see my husband with reference to the will, but he did not go up at once. I think he went up on the Monday morning, or afternoon, but I could not say for certain. I was present when he went up, and I heard Miss Barrow say that she wanted to make it out for the boy and girl, what furniture and jewellery she had belonging to her—for Hilda and Ernie. She did not want Mr. Hook or any of the other relations to have what belonged to the boy's mother and father; she only wanted the boy and girl to have it. My husband suggested a solicitor to her, but she did not want a solicitor; she did not want the expense, and she asked him if he could not do it himself.

Did she say anything else?—I cannot remember. I think my husband went down into the office after that. The next thing I remember with regard to the will is going up to sign it. We had my sister-in-law with us at the time, and between six and seven o'clock, after we had all had dinner and everything, my husband called me and my father-in-law to come up and witness this will of Miss Barrow's. We propped her up in bed with pillows in a sitting position to get her to sign it, and then I signed it on a little table, and my father-in-law signed it. My husband read the will to Miss Barrow, and then she asked for her glasses to read it herself, which she did, and then she signed it. This was the day on which my sister-in-law came on a visit. I think her husband had written to Mr. Seddon asking whether she could come for a few days, and he answered back that she could take pot-luck. "We had an old lady ill in the house, but if she cared to come she could take pot-luck." The doctor came again on the Tuesday, and I saw him. On that day, I think it was, I had an accident with one of the saucers—I knocked one off the mantelpiece. I then went down and got a soup plate, and lifted the fly-paper up that had come out from the saucer that was broken and put the others together—the whole four—into the one soup plate, and put it on the little table between the two windows. I had to put fresh water into the soup plate. It remained there until the morning Miss Barrow died.

Adjourned.

Eighth Day—Tuesday, 12th March, 1912.

The Court met at 10.15 a.m.

MARGARET ANN SEDDON (prisoner), recalled, examination continued by Mr. RENTOUL—During Miss Barrow's illness she used to get out of bed. Dr. Sworn saw her on the morning of Wednesday, 13th September. My husband went to the theatre that evening. About twelve o'clock, while standing at the gate waiting for my husband with my sister-in-law—I

Evidence for Defence.

Margaret A. Seddon

think it was my sister-in-law or my daughter—I heard Miss Barrow calling out, "I'm dying." I said to my sister-in-law, Mrs. Longley, "Did you hear what Miss Barrow says?" So with that I rushed upstairs. I also asked my sister-in-law to come up with me. She did not like at first, but then she followed up afterwards. I asked Miss Barrow what was the matter with her, and she said she had violent pains in her stomach, and that her feet felt cold. I asked my sister-in-law what should I do, as I had no hot water bottles in the house. She replied, "Wrap a flannel petticoat round her feet," which I did. Then I done the same what I generally done with her stomach—put the hot flannels on and tried to make her as comfortable as I possibly could. I turned the gas down and went downstairs.

My husband came in about 12.30, and I told him what had happened. He did not go up immediately; he was talking to my sister-in-law about a man doing him out of sixpence or something at the theatre. I think in the meantime the boy came down, but I am not certain. My husband, my sister-in-law, and I went up—I think it was after the boy had been down, but I will not say for certain. My husband introduced Mrs. Longley to Miss Barrow, but Miss Barrow just looked at her, and I think my sister-in-law went downstairs—I am not quite sure. She said the boy had no right to be in bed with Miss Barrow; it was unhealthy, and then she went half-way down the stairs. I remained and attended to what Miss Barrow wanted. I do not know whether my husband gave Miss Barrow a drop of brandy at that time or not, but he told her that she must go to sleep and rest, that I would be knocked up, and she said she could not help it. We then went downstairs to bed—my husband leaving the room first, you must remember—and I attended to Miss Barrow while they went downstairs. I then went down and got into bed. We were not in bed long before the boy came downstairs again and said that "Chickie" wanted me. I went up and put hot flannels on her and attended to her properly—she was suffering from diarrhœa then.

Did you think she was dying?—No, I have never seen anybody dying. I went downstairs, and I had just got the baby on my arm when I was called upstairs again by the boy saying, "Chickie wants you." He knocked at our door and called from the bottom of the stairs. I went up again and attended to her just the same as I had done before. She did not seem sick—she was only once or twice sick during that night; she seemed to be retching, not proper vomiting, but a nasty froth came up. She had the diarrhœa bad. My husband did not go up with me on that occasion, but he did the next time when the boy called out that Miss Barrow was out of bed. My husband told me to stop in bed and he would go up and attend to her. I said, "It is no good of you going up," because I thought she wanted me the same as before, but my husband would go up, and so I followed after him.

By Mr. JUSTICE BUCKNILL—How long after?—Just at the same time. We were both on the staircase at the same time.

Examination continued—When we got up Miss Barrow was in a sitting position on the floor and the boy was holding her up; we lifted her into bed again. This must have been between three and four in the morning—I could not tell the time. I made her the same as I had done before, hot flannels, and made her comfortable.

Trial of the Seddons.

Margaret A. Seddon

By Mr. Justice Bucknill—Where did the hot water come from that you put on the flannels?—From her kitchen.

Was there plenty of hot water there?—No, there was not. I had to put a pan on the gas stove, put the flannel between two plates, and wait till they got hot, and then put it on.

Examination continued—Miss Barrow was not complaining then of anything to my knowledge, but generally she was always complaining. She asked me to stay with her, and my husband said to her, "If Mrs. Seddon sits up with you all night she will be knocked up. You must remember Mrs. Seddon has got a young baby, and she wants a rest." The little boy was in and out of her bed all this time. My husband told him to go to his bed every time that we went up and down stairs. The fourth time was the last time that I went up, and I stayed with her after that; I sat in a basket chair near the end of the bed. I put on more hot flannels. She seemed to go to sleep, and my husband, who was standing at the bedroom door smoking his pipe and reading, said to me, "Why don't you go down and go to bed?" I said, "What's the good of going to bed? She will only call me up again." So I made up my mind to sit in the chair. Then Miss Barrow seemed to be sleeping, and I was dozing in the chair. I was sleeping tired.

Was Miss Barrow snoring?—Yes.

By Mr. Justice Bucknill—She seemed to be sleeping peacefully for some time, then after a while she seemed to be snoring. It was getting on towards daylight then, and my husband drew attention that the snoring had stopped and her breathing had stopped. Then he lifted up her eyelid, and said—I can't say it—I don't like to say it.

Never mind, say it low?—He said, "Good God, she's dead!" So with that he hurried out and went for Dr. Sworn. This would be between 6 and 6.30, as far as I can reckon the time.

Examination continued—While your husband was gone for Dr. Sworn what did you do?—I came down with my husband the same time, locked the door so that the boy should not go in, and came downstairs into the kitchen. Mary was in the kitchen, and I told her Miss Barrow, I thought, had passed away. Then I had a cup of tea, I think. Then I went up and woke my daughter, and also the boys, and told them. I do not know whether my daughter or one of the boys went for Mrs. Rutt, the charwoman—I can't just remember. My husband came in from the doctor's about the same time, and then we all three went up to the bedroom. Perhaps Mrs. Rutt and I went up first. We attended to the body. I asked my husband to help us with the feather bed from under her so that she could lie flat. After that my husband asked me if I knew where Miss Barrow kept her keys, and I said I didn't know, and I started looking for them. I felt in Miss Barrow's bag that hung on the bed, but there was only the street door key in that. Then it was suggested, "Look in the chest of drawers," and I lifted out what was in one of the drawers, and in the first little drawer that I opened I found them hidden under the paper. I gave them to my husband—Mrs. Rutt was there—and he tried two or three keys before the trunk would unlock, and then he opened it. There were two or three articles of clothing on the top. I think

Evidence for Defence.

Margaret A. Seddon

there was a tray which he lifted out, and the cash box was underneath this tray. He tried two or three keys before the little box would open, and then he found £4 10s.

By Mr. Justice Bucknill—That was in gold in a little brown paper bag. My husband still went on searching the trunk. I don't know what he did with the cash box; I don't know whether he locked it up and put it back again, as Mrs. Rutt and I were washing Miss Barrow at the time. My husband continued searching the trunk and found a silver watch and chain, and another silver watch and chain, and some brooches, and I think there was a bracelet, and then some articles of clothing.

Examination continued—We didn't find any more money then in the trunk, but later on in the afternoon we found some more.

By Mr. Justice Bucknill—I was emptying the clothes out of Miss Barrow's drawers—every drawer—and in the little drawer where I found the keys I found three sovereigns wrapped up in tissue paper. They were in the folds of the paper which lay in the drawer, so that if the drawer paper was bent like that (indicating) to make it fit they were in the folds.

Examination continued—The inside of the handbag that I previously looked at in the morning was quite empty, but in the side pocket I found £2 10s. in gold wrapped up in white tissue paper. Between 9 and 10 o'clock on the morning Miss Barrow died the children went off to Southend. We did not tell the little boy Ernie anything about the death. I remember Mr. Nodes, the undertaker, coming to the house on the morning of this same day. My husband and he went upstairs first, and, of course, I naturally wanted to listen to what they were saying, and I followed up after them. I don't know whether I noticed Mr. Nodes taking the measurement of the body or not. He advised the body to be removed out of the house, and I said, "What a shame, when she died in the house." He said, "Remember, Mrs. Seddon, you have a young baby, and your health is not very good," and, with the bad smell that was coming from Miss Barrow, it was better for the body to go to his shop or mortuary. I don't know what he said exactly. The body was removed that evening, but I was not in the house then.

On the Friday morning I went out with my sister-in-law to do some shopping. We went to a florist and I ordered a wreath of my own design, and then asked them to send it to my address, 63 Tollington Park, and it was there when I got home. After dinner, about a quarter to two or two o'clock, my father-in-law, my sister-in-law, and I took the wreath to Mr. Nodes. As the door was locked I rang the bell. The servant who came said that Mrs. Nodes was resting, and that she would go and tell her, and then Mr. Nodes came down, and I said, "I have brought this wreath to put on Miss Barrow's coffin." My father-in-law asked for the lid to be opened, so I put the cross (it was a cross wreath) on her body, and I kissed Miss Barrow. Next day my husband, my father-in-law, and I went to the funeral. Our blinds were drawn from the moment Miss Barrow died. My sister-in-law interfered with them first, and pulled them up. I said, "What a shame. Let us show her a little respect"— you see her body had already gone out of the house then—" by keeping the blinds down until after she is buried," and then I pulled them down

Trial of the Seddons.

Margaret A. Seddon

myself.   The windows remained open until we came back from the
funeral.   My husband spoke to me about the letter that he sent to the
Vonderahes.

By Mr. Justice Bucknill—On the day of Miss Barrow's death I was
tired and went to bed.   I knew my husband was in the office with the
office men.   He came upstairs to me and said he was tired, and I asked
him, " Why don't you go to bed and have a rest? "   He said he had one
particular thing to do, and that was to write a letter to the relatives.
So he left me at that; I don't know what happened after that.

Examination continued—I remember the two Mrs. Vonderahes calling
on 21st September.   I was present at the interview, but I cannot tell
word for word what passed.   I remember my husband asked them if they
had not received the letter, and Mrs. Vonderahe seemed to be a little
excited, and she said, " No, what letter do you mean? "   So my husband
brought out of his pocket a copy that he kept and gave it to her to read, as
far as I can remember.   Then I think they went on talking about Miss
Barrow and about her being buried in a public grave, and she said she
had a family vault.   My husband then told them that if they liked they
could take the body out and have it buried in her own grave.   Then
Mrs. Vonderahe turned round and said it was quite good enough—the
public grave, I mean—for Miss Barrow, as she had been a bad, wicked
woman all her life.   Then she went on to describe how they fell out, and
that she had spat at them through the window—also about the boy's
mother and father throwing bottles and fire-irons at one another.   Then
my husband said that she was a woman that only required a little humouring,
and that we had got on all right with her.   Then I think they spoke about
the boy; they wanted to know what was going to happen to him.   My
husband said he had quite a good home with us unless any of his relatives
could give him a better one, and he said, " We have no claim upon
him."   Then they wanted to know about her public-house and the stock.
I think my husband said she had bought an annuity with it, but I am not
quite certain.   One of the Mrs. Vonderahes said something about
" It would have to be a clever person to get over her with her business
transactions."   They asked my husband if he could see the two Mr.
Vonderahes that evening or the next evening, but as we were going on our
holidays he said that he would see them when he came home.

We went away to Southend and stayed there nearly a fortnight.
When we got back the little boy was sent round to the Vonderahes to let
them know that my husband was at home.   On 9th October Mr. Vonderahe called with a friend.   I was present on that occasion.   I think
my husband asked Mr. Vonderahe if this was his brother, and he said,
" No, it is a friend."   So I think my husband said he did not like
to go into details, or he would not go into details (I don't remember
which), unless he could prove that he was the legal next-of-kin, or something of that sort.   I think Mr. Vonderahe replied, " How about if he is
dead? "   I do not remember what my husband replied.   I wasn't sufficiently interested to pay close attention to the conversation.

Have you ever administered or caused to be administered arsenic to Miss
Barrow in any shape or form?—None whatever, none whatever.

Cross-examined by the Attorney-General—Did you look after the

240

Evidence for Defence.

Margaret A. Seddon

house—housekeeping of the house?—You see I cannot go into all details, because it brings family matters into it.

I don't want all the details; I want to know who did the housekeeping of your part of the house?—My husband allowed me—he paid the bills at the end of the week, you see.

Who ordered the things?—I did.

They were sent in, and then were there the weekly bills from various tradespeople, which he paid?—Yes.

Did your daughter Maggie help in the house?—She looked after Miss Barrow.

Did she also at times do errands for you?—Yes.

Did she take the baby out in the perambulator?—Yes.

Used she to do that when Miss Barrow was ill?—I cannot just remember. I don't think Margaret went out much with the baby when Miss Barrow was ailing.

How old was the baby at the time Miss Barrow came to you?—I hadn't a baby when Miss Barrow came to me. It was born on 3rd January, 1911.

Were you on friendly terms with Miss Barrow?—Yes, very friendly terms.

And did you and your husband get on well with her?—I always got on well with her.

From the time that she came to you until 1st September she was never laid up, was she?—Not in bed.

She had small ailments, but nothing of any importance?—I used to take her to Dr. Paul.

You took her to Dr. Paul in August. You may have taken her before?—Well, I think, if Dr. Paul will remember, I took Miss Barrow to him before that date.

But Dr. Paul has told us——?—Well, I would like Dr. Paul to look at his books and see. I took Miss Barrow to Dr. Paul before my baby was born.

Now, about Miss Barrow's cash box; how often do you say you saw the cash box?—On the day that she brought it down for my husband to have the cash in the safe, and the next occasion was when she was dead.

That is just two or three days before the Hooks left. That is what you are speaking of?—Yes.

Where did the notes come from that, according to you, Miss Barrow gave you?—I couldn't tell you.

Where did she take them from?—I couldn't tell you where she took them from.

How did you get them?—She used to bring them down to me in the dining-room.

Did she go out with you sometimes?—Very seldom.

She went out every day by herself?—Yes, but she didn't go with me.

Or with the boy. Do you mean she came down with a note in her hand?—Yes.

Ever more than one note in her hand?—She has brought me two twice, I think.

Q

Trial of the Seddons.

Margaret A. Seddon

Did you ever say anything to your husband about her bringing notes to you to change like this?—Only on one occasion.

I mean before the arrest?—Only on one occasion.

When was that?—When I had been to the Post Office to get it cashed. My husband said, why did I not ask him to cash it.

Was that the first time, then?—Yes.

Did you tell him what you had done?—No, I don't remember telling him what I had done.

Did you tell him you had given a false name?—No.

Or a false address?—No.

Were you troubled about it at all?—No, not in any way.

Did you think it quite an ordinary thing to write your name at the back, or rather to write a false name at the back, when you were asked for your name?—No, it never struck me.

Never struck you as what?—Well, you see, I had never changed a note in my life before; this is the first note I had ever changed.

How long had you been in the wardrobe business—something like a year?—Yes, but I never had a note in the wardrobe business.

You had a good deal of money, according to what we have heard?—Yes, but I never had a note.

All gold?—Always gold.

By Mr. Justice Bucknill—Or silver?—Or silver or copper.

You do not pay a sovereign for every old piece of clothing, I am sure?—No.

By the Attorney-General—When you had the note given to you did you know what to do with it?—I went to the Post Office.

You knew that much?—Yes.

And you were asked to write your name and your address?—Yes.

Did you then take the note and write " M. Scott "?—Yes, I did; I put " M. Scott."

And the address, " 18 Evershot Road "?—Yes, that is quite right.

Had you ever lived at Evershot Road?—No.

Had " Scott " ever been your name?—No.

Did you know anybody called " Scott " in Evershot Road?—No.

Were you at all alarmed about putting the false name and address on the back of the £5 note for the first time in your life?—I never thought there was any harm in it whatever.

Why didn't you give your own name?—The note did not belong to me.

Then, why didn't you give Miss Barrow's name?—Because I have no right to sign her name.

So you put a false one—an invented one?—Yes.

And an invented address?—Yes.

How came you to use the name of " Scott "?—It was the first thing that came into my head.

You got more used to changing notes afterwards?—I only changed them at shops where I had always been used to going; I gave the same name, and shops where I dealt with they knew me, and they did not want my name and address.

But do you know you gave a false name and a false address at three shops?—Yes, I think that would be right.

Evidence for Defence.

Margaret A. Seddon

The first note, according to the evidence we have got, in which yo gave a false name and address, was changed on 12th October, 1910, a Noakes, the grocer, and Post Office. A few days afterwards did you change another note?—I could not tell you whether it was on 20th October.

That is eight days after?—Yes.

Did you change that at Garner & Somerfield's?—Yes.

What were they—drapers?—Yes, drapers.

Were you asked to sign your name there?—Yes, I believe I was aske to sign my name.

And your address?—Yes.

Did you then give a false name and a false address again?—I gave the same name and address as I gave at the last.

Not yours?—No.

The invented name and address?—Yes.

You had had eight days to think about it?—I never thought about it

Or to speak to your husband about it?—No, I did not speak to m husband about it, because he would never take any notice.

What?—He never used to take any notice when I said anything t him; he always had other things to think of.

I thought you told us just now that he told you why didn't you as him to change the note?—On this one occasion.

Then, you see, you had another note to change within a few days afterwards?—Yes.

Did you ask him to change it then?—No.

Why not?—Because I have already told you; perhaps he was not in; he may have been out.

According to what you are telling us, it was all so strange to you to change a £5 note that you gave a false name and address?—You see, this is it, when I once gave the false name and address I had to keep it up, I could not change it then back into my own name; if I could I would have done, quick.

You had never changed a note at Garner & Somerfield's before?—No, but I had changed it at the Post Office, hadn't I?

What would that have to do with changing the note at Garner & Somerfield's?—It was already another one, and I could not change my name after I had given the first name.

They would not know anything about your giving a false name to the Post Office?—I do not know what they do.

Let me suggest to you that if you had adopted the false name in order to prevent the notes being traced to you, it would be useful to go on in the same false name and address that you had given. You see that?—I don't quite understand what you say.

Supposing you wanted to conceal that you were passing these notes, it would be a useful thing to do to give a false name and address, wouldn't it?—Yes.

In point of fact, do you know, with this second note which you changed at Garner & Somerfield's, you gave another address, " 12 Evershot Road," not 18?—Well, that was not with any wrong intention of being 12 instead of 18; it was meant to be 18, not 12.

Trial of the Seddons.

Margaret A. Seddon

You wrote that yourself, with your own handwriting?—As far as I can remember, I did.

It has been proved; if you have any doubt about it you shall see it?—No, I will not doubt it, because I know I did write some.

Did you during October, November, and December change a number of notes?—If Miss Barrow gave them to me, then, of course, I would change them. She never liked having notes; she wanted gold.

Just think a little, Mrs. Seddon. Do you mean that?—Well, as far as I could understand Miss Barrow she always wanted to have gold; she did not want to have notes, and that is why she gave them to me to cash.

Where did you think she was getting the notes from?—I couldn't tell you; I had no idea. I never went into Miss Barrow's business.

Did you ever ask her?—No, I never asked her.

Did she ever tell you?—No, she never told me.

Did you say anything to your husband about this large number of notes that you were cashing for her?—No.

You knew that he was in confidential business relationship with her, did you not?—Yes, I had nothing to do with her business transactions whatever.

You knew that your husband——?—They were going on, yes.

Did you usually give her gold?—Not always.

You made up the £5 sometimes with a half-sovereign change in silver, I suppose?—Yes.

Did you know that during this same time your husband was getting £5 notes from her?—Yes.

At the same time?—It was for rent.

Every time the 12s. was due do you mean he got a £5 note from her?—Sometimes she would give him a £5 note.

Mr. MARSHALL HALL—I don't think my learned friend is putting it accurately.

Mr. JUSTICE BUCKNILL—That is what I have got down—" I knew that he was getting £5 notes from her sometimes when her rent was due."

The WITNESS—Yes, that is right.

By the ATTORNEY-GENERAL—Did he tell you that?—No.

How did you know it?—Only through what I heard here yesterday.

You mean you didn't know it until you heard it yesterday?—No.

Does it come to this, that you didn't know your husband was getting £5 notes from her, and he did not know you were getting £5 notes from her?—No; my husband didn't know that Miss Barrow was giving me £5 notes to cash.

In March, 1911, you signed another £5 note in the name of " M. Scott, 18 Evershott Road "?—I cannot swear to dates; I didn't dispute them.

Have you any reason to doubt it? You can have them produced to you. All this has been proved?—Yes, I know.

That is " M. Scott, 18 Evershott Road." Do you know that during the month of April, 1911—let me call your attention to this—by that time you had got pretty used to cashing £5 notes, hadn't you?—I suppose I had.

And during this month of April you cashed three £5 notes, which were

Evidence for Defence.

Margaret A. Seddon

endorsed by you with a false name and address; why was that?—Because as I have told you, when I first gave the wrong name and address I ha still to keep that name and address.

On 8th April, 1911, at Rackstraw's, that is a new one?—Yes.

You had never been there?—No, that was the first time I had change one there.

Why did you give them a false name and address?—You see I ha already given at the shops where I was not known my wrong name an address, and I gave at the shops which knew me my right name and address they didn't ask me, because they didn't want to, so I still had to keep u the same name and address.

You had not been to Rackstraw's with a £5 note before?—No, but still kept up that name. They didn't know me.

By that time—the occasion at Rackstraw's—you had changed a ver considerable number of £5 notes—something like eighteen?—I didn't kno how many I had changed.

When you go to Rackstraw's, and Rackstraw's ask you for your nam and address, why do you give a false one then?—Because what I hav already told you; when I first gave a false name and address I had to kee it up. I cannot give you any other explanation than that.

Do you know that there was no such person as "M. Scott" living a "18 Evershott Road" at the time?—By what I have heard in Court.

Did you ever inquire whether there was such a person?—No.

All the time you were passing this false name and address?—No, never inquired at all.

It would make it very difficult to trace those notes with the name o "Scott" at Evershott Road at the back, wouldn't it?—I didn't understan anything about it.

Now, altogether during this time you had cashed twenty-seven note for her. You are cashing notes during every month, beginning fro October up to the end? Do you know that?—I suppose I was if you hav got them there. They were only just as Miss Barrow gave them to me.

And during the whole of this time are we to understand that yo never said a word to your husband about it?—I never mentioned it to m husband at all; I didn't tell my husband everything I did.

You were living in the house with him?—Yes, but he never told m everything he did.

Why should not you have told him what you had done?—I don't know.

Here was this person living on the second floor with you, paying thi 12s. rent according to you, giving you bank notes every month in the year, and you bringing back gold to her?—Quite right.

You knew your husband was paying her gold?—Paying her gold?

Yes, paying her gold for her annuity?—Oh, yes, for her annuity.

So I mean, according to you, there was a considerable amount of gold coming into the house in exchange for notes as well as the gold he wa giving her?—Yes, that is quite right.

Were you anxious at all about this gold that was coming into the house?—No, I was not Miss Barrow's keeper.

You were not anxious at all as to what would happen to it?—Miss Barrow's affairs never concerned me, not whatever.

Trial of the Seddons.

Margaret A. Seddon

Did you know whether your husband was anxious?—No, I didn't know; he done her transactions, and that is all I know.

According to your story, at an early date he was anxious—from the time that the Hooks were going when she brought down this cash box?— My husband refused to take it until Miss Barrow counted the money that was in it.

But she never did?—No, I never seen it after she took it back upstairs again.

You remember the £216 which was drawn out on 19th June, 1911?— Yes, quite well.

Do you remember that gold being brought into the house?—Yes.

Was your husband anxious about that gold being brought into the house?—He didn't wish her to have it in the house.

Why not?—He said it was not safe, she had a right to put it in some other bank; there were plenty of good banks, such as the Bank of England and other banks.

Did you hear him say that?—Yes, I was coming out of the dining-room.

But did you say to him, " I know she must have a lot of gold, as I have constantly been changing notes into gold for her "?—No.

Why not?—I never thought about anything like that; it did not concern me at all—Miss Barrow's business.

Don't you see that your husband at this time, according to your story, is anxious about the gold which has been brought into the house?— I am not responsible for my husband.

No, but don't you see that he was fearful of its being stolen?—Yes.

You understood that?—Yes.

And you knew he was anxious, according to you, that there should not be gold in the house upstairs in her room?—Yes, I quite understand what you mean.

I want to know, if that is the case, and you had been changing notes for her up to that date into gold, why you didn't tell him that you had been changing these notes and giving her gold for the notes, and there must be other gold upstairs?—It had nothing to do with me at all.

You never troubled yourself about it?—No, I never troubled with Miss Barrow's business whatever.

Did you go on during that very month and the next month cashing more notes for her?—If you have got them here I must have done; I cannot tell you the dates.

In July you turned three into gold for her?—I cannot tell you the dates, or how often.

And four in August?—Yes. I cannot tell you the dates.

Did it strike you as curious that with all that gold that she had upstairs she should be changing notes into gold?—I never knew what Miss Barrow had.

You knew she had got the £216—you went with her?—Yes, I went with her to draw that.

You knew she had got that?—Yes.

You thought she had got that up to her death?—As far as I know of.

And more?—I couldn't tell you.

But you yourself had changed notes into gold for her?—Yes, but then

Evidence for Defence.

Margaret A. Seddon

you must remember Miss Barrow went out, and I was not responsible for what Miss Barrow did.

Nobody suggests you were, but there was a certain amount of gold had been given by you to her——?—Not given.

Given by you to her in exchange for notes; that is right?—Yes.

Besides that, you knew, of course, your husband was paying her money?—Yes, the annuity.

So that, according to that, when she died you would have expected to find a very substantial sum of gold there, wouldn't you?—Well, I suppose there should have been.

Do you remember witnessing Miss Barrow's signature to a document not very long after she came to live in the house with you?—I do remember one.

You have talked about it. You have said in chief that there were two documents—the annuity certificate and the will—which you had witnessed?—Yes, that is quite right.

Is the annuity certificate you are speaking of something that you witnessed shortly after she came to live there?—No, I think you are referring to the time that my brother signed a paper.

That is another document?—Yes; but I don't think I signed the one my brother signed.

Your husband has told us that you witnessed Miss Barrow's signature?—Yes, I believe I did witness Miss Barrow's signature, but not the one my brother did.

But about the same time?—I don't know whether it was the same day or the day after.

Either the same day or the day after; it does not matter. Was that her signature to a document about the annuity—the first one?—I couldn't tell you.

You knew, of course, that your husband was paying an annuity to Miss Barrow?—I don't know whether it was at that time or not when this transaction was finished with, as far as I know.

Will you tell us when you think the annuity was paid from?—It was when I was in bed confined; I cannot just tell you. You see, I am not acquainted with that business; I was not mixed up in it at all.

But you knew it was being paid?—Yes, I knew that my husband paid it, but I couldn't tell you what date or what day.

I don't want you to tell me the details of it, but you did know, in point of fact, that at some time, at any rate, in 1911, he was paying her an annuity?—Yes.

And that he had to pay her this sum of money so long as she lived?—Yes, that is right, and after, if anything happened to my husband, it was to come from his estate. You know I don't understand the transaction, but it was still to be paid.

Do you remember that document being torn up?—Yes, my husband tore it up.

The one that you witnessed Miss Barrow's signature to?—Yes.

It was very shortly after that that your first transaction with the £5 notes took place?—I couldn't tell you when it first took place, only by you going back to the dates.

Trial of the Seddons.

Margaret A. Seddon

It was soon after Miss Barrow came?—No, it was not.

Miss Barrow came at the end of July, 1910?—Yes, now I can remember.

You are speaking as to the time when your brother was there and witnessed a document; that was in September of 1910?—I cannot tell you the dates or months.

Was it, at any rate, about that time that you began to change £5 bank notes?—No, I think it was soon after Miss Barrow came to live with us.

That you did what?—That I started to change the bank notes.

How long after?—I don't know whether it was a month or two months; I cannot recollect.

We can tell. Where was it you changed the first one?—At Noakes.

That we know was on 12th October. Your daughter Maggie did the cooking for her right up to the 1st September, except on a few occasions?—Yes.

Were the other occasions when your daughter was out, or when there was something special to cook?—No, perhaps Miss Barrow would want a suet pudding cooked.

She had her meals upstairs?—Yes.

Maggie used to cook them in the kitchen next door?—Quite right.

And she and Ernie used to have them——?—In this little kitchen.

That was the sort of life she was leading?—Yes.

She didn't go out at night?—Yes, she did go out at night.

Did she go out much?—She used to take the boy out at night.

Now I want to ask you, were you in the habit of using fly-papers in your house?—Never.

Do you mean that you never had any at all?—I never bought fly-papers at all until I bought them for Miss Barrow.

Are you sure of that?—Positive—sure.

And when were the first ones you bought for Miss Barrow?—About 4th September; she had been in bed; it was on the Monday or Tuesday, I am not quite certain.

On Monday or Tuesday, that is 4th or 5th September?—The 4th it would be.

Those were the first fly-papers you had bought?—In my life.

Or used in your house?—Or used in our house.

That you are clear about?—Quite clear.

Of any sort or kind?—Of any sort or kind, yes.

Were they the first you had ever seen in your house?—Yes.

According to what you have told us, you bought these fly-papers at Mr. Meacher's?—Yes.

Is he here?—I couldn't tell you.

I understood you to say the shop was in Stroud Green Road?—Yes, round the corner.

Are there two shops of Meacher's in the Stroud Green Road?—I don't know; I only went to the first one round the corner.

Is that one you went to the one to the right—do you turn to the right when you go from your house?—This side (indicating).

Well, that is the right. Is that 61 Stroud Green Road?—I couldn't tell you the number.

Evidence for Defence.

Margaret A. Seddon

Have you been in the habit of dealing there?—Several things I have bought there.

Had you bought white precipitate powder there before?—Yes.

At that shop?—Yes; I bought white precipitate there.

I want to understand you; were these fly-papers the only fly-papers that were ever in Miss Barrow's room, according to you?—That is quite positive—the truth—the only fly-papers that were ever in Miss Barrow's room were the four that were bought.

They were not renewed at all?—Not at all, no.

Did you ever send Maggie for the fly-papers?—Never in my life.

Did Maggie ever go for fly-papers?—No, no, no.

Never in her life?—No, no.

By Mr. Justice Bucknill—One moment; be calm?—I never sent Maggie for fly-papers in my life—if this was the last day I had to live, I never sent my daughter for fly-papers.

By the Attorney-General—You never sent her, and she never went, according to you?—No, not to my knowledge at all—never went.

What?—Not to my knowledge, Maggie never bought fly-papers.

Or went for fly-papers?—No.

Didn't she on 6th December?—For Mr. Saint.

Mr. Saint is the solicitor for you and your husband?—Yes, that is right.

Did you read the directions on the fly-papers when you bought them? —No, the man in the chemist's told me to put water on them. I never read no directions on the paper at all.

Did he tell you to moisten them?—Yes, he told me to moisten them with a little water.

And that is what you did?—Yes.

And did I understand you to say that they were left from the 4th or 5th of September, the Monday or the Tuesday, until after Miss Barrow's death?—Until the morning of Miss Barrow's death.

Who moved them away then?—I did.

Were all four fly-papers in the one soup plate then?—In the soup plate, yes.

And you had begun by putting them single in saucers?—Yes, two on the mantelpiece and two on the chest of drawers.

Then you say you had an accident on the Tuesday?—Yes, Monday or Tuesday, I don't know which.

On the Tuesday is what you said; it was the 12th. I do not mind which it is?—Monday or Tuesday; I believe it was Tuesday.

That is what you have said. Then you put them all four together in one soup plate?—Yes.

Was the object of putting them singly in saucers to make them useful?—No, you see the water used to dry up off them, and then I used to put more water on them.

First of all, you put them in saucers separately, moistening them, and put them, as you have told us, two on the mantelpiece and two on the drawers?—Yes, that is quite right.

So that you could get the best use out of the four papers; that was

Trial of the Seddons.

Margaret A. Seddon

the object of it?—No, that is not the object of it at all. You see, I had an accident; I knocked one down.

I don't think you are following the question; I am not asking you about the soup plate; I am asking you about before that. When you first took them up into the room you put one fly-paper on to one saucer?—Yes.

You repeated that four times?—No; four different fly-papers.

Yes, four different fly-papers in four different saucers?—Yes, that's right.

And you moistened the fly-paper in each case?—Yes.

And I say the object of doing that was to make the four papers useful; that is what you did it for?—Yes, put it on the top of the——

Now, I want to know why did you take the four fly-papers and put them into one soup plate on the Tuesday?—Because, as I have told you, I had an accident. I knocked one off, and I felt I could not be bothered with them, and I emptied them all into one soup plate, and picked the one up that I dropped.

Just follow, you had got the two on the mantelpiece, according to you?—Yes.

You knocked one over?—Yes.

Did you put it into the saucer of the other one?—No, I put it into the soup plate.

But had you a soup plate there at the time?—I went downstairs and got a soup plate.

Had you been repeatedly moistening these fly-papers during this time?—Yes, because, you see, they dry up because of the heat of the room.

Was it you who moistened them?—Yes, I always moistened them.

Then on this date, the 12th, you take all four fly-papers, and, as I understand you, you put all four fly-papers into one soup plate?—Yes, that is right.

And moistened them?—Yes.

Was that to make the solution stronger?—I don't know what you mean.

Was that to make the water that was on the fly-papers stronger?—You see, when I put them in the soup plate there was not much water on them, and then I put more water on.

By Mr. JUSTICE BUCKNILL—What the learned Attorney means is this, four fly-papers in one saucer with the same amount of water would make it worse for the flies—they would die sooner?—Yes.

Did you do it for that purpose?—The flies were nearly all gone. I did it for convenience.

You said before that you were bothered with them, so you put them all four into one plate?—Yes.

By the ATTORNEY-GENERAL—Did you say that the flies were all gone? —There were not so many flies in the room.

A good many had died?—Yes.

I suggest to you, having the two on the mantelpiece and one having gone——?—That only left one on the mantelpiece.

It did not interfere with the two on the drawers?—No, it did not interfere with the two on the drawers.

Why did you interfere with the two on the drawers?—Because I put them altogether to save having so many saucers about.

Evidence for Defence.

Margaret A. Seddon

Do you know Thorley's shop in the Stroud Green Road?—No, I have never seen Thorley's shop.

Do you know Meacher's second shop in the Stroud Green Road?—No; I don't know Meacher's second shop.

Mr. MARSHALL HALL—Thorley's shop is in a different place altogether.

The ATTORNEY-GENERAL—Just round the corner.

Mr. MARSHALL HALL—Crouch Hill.

By the ATTORNEY-GENERAL—Now, I want to ask you about what happened during this illness. The 2nd September was the first day she was in bed during the whole time she was with you?—Except for her bilious attacks once a month—she was bad once a month.

She used to have sick headaches or something of that kind?—No, she used to be sick—a proper sick, bilious attack.

About once a month?—Every month, yes.

During the whole time from the 2nd September you had been in attendance?—Yes, that is quite right.

Had you been up all night with her at all?—I got up in the middle of the night.

Often?—Once or twice.

Do you mean once or twice during the night, or once or twice during the time?—No, during the night.

Was Ernie Grant sleeping with her during the whole time?—Yes, it was Ernie who used to call me.

Did she say anything about her personal belongings on the 11th, the day when the will was made?—It was on the Sunday that I think she first mentioned it.

What did she say?—She wanted to know if she could have a will made out as regards the furniture for the boy and for the girl—also some jewellery she had.

By Mr. JUSTICE BUCKNILL—That she could have a will made out?—For Ernest and Hilda Grant.

For furniture and——?—Jewellery. Of course, I told her I couldn't give her any information on it, so I said I would tell Mr. Seddon. So I went down and told Mr. Seddon what she had said, so he said he wouldn't be bothered just at that time; he was busy I think in his office; in fact, I don't think he went up at all on the Sunday, he went up on the Monday.

By the ATTORNEY-GENERAL—You heard the will read?—Yes.

Do you know anything more about it than what you have told us?—No, none whatever.

I am going to ask you about the 13th, that is the Thursday; you know the day I am speaking of?—The day Miss Barrow died.

The day before?—That is the Wednesday.

She died on the morning of the 14th?—Yes.

She was worse than she had been, wasn't she?—She seemed rather weaker—the diarrhœa—but she was not so sick. That is what I told the doctor.

Pains in the stomach?—Stomach, yes.

That had been going on then for a pretty long time?—On and off.

From 2nd September?—On and off during the time she was ill.

Trial of the Seddons.

Margaret A. Seddon

When the doctor left did you think there was any fear of her death within twenty-four hours?—None whatever.

Did she get worse after the doctor left?—I never noticed.

Did she continue to complain about pains in her stomach?—You see, I was not with Miss Barrow, you must remember, all day long.

You were with her in the evening?—No, not until twelve o'clock. At about nine or ten I gave her a dose of medicine—about ten o'clock—and I never seen her then till twelve o'clock.

Let us see what happened in the evening. Your husband went out to the theatre?—Yes, that is right.

You were at home?—Yes.

You were looking after her?—Yes, I was.

She complained a good deal, didn't she, before your husband came home?—No, not that I know of.

Didn't she say that night, "I am dying"?—Oh, yes, that was at twelve o'clock; I thought you were referring to earlier than that. That night at twelve o'clock she said, "I am dying."

Was she complaining a good deal——?—Well, I had been up on and off to see her, putting flannels on her stomach.

Before your husband came back?—Yes.

So she was complaining a good deal?—Yes.

Of bad pains in the stomach?—It was nothing unusual to hear Miss Barrow complaining all the time she was ill; in fact, she would always want you to sit and be fanning her all the time. Of course, I couldn't always be doing that.

But on this night of the 13th she was worse than she had been?—After twelve o'clock.

You knew from the time the doctor had come in the morning she was worse than she had been?—No, she did not seem any worse after the doctor had been up to midnight.

No, but when the doctor came in the morning of the 13th, I think you have already told me he found her rather worse on the morning of the 13th?—Rather worse, no. He did not find her rather worse—somewhere about the same.

Mr. MARSHALL HALL—"I found the diarrhœa worse—but no complaint of the sickness; the sickness was not worse, but only the diarrhœa."

The ATTORNEY-GENERAL—He said he found her rather worse.

Mr. MARSHALL HALL—The diarrhœa was worse.

Mr. JUSTICE BUCKNILL—Let me read my note. I am much obliged to you, but I think I would rather read my own note on this part. I will tell you what I have. "On the 13th the diarrhœa had come on again. She did not seem to be in much trouble. I gave her a mixture. She had a little return of the sickness. I gave her a chalky mixture—the strength was about the same. She was weaker on account of the diarrhœa. I saw Mrs. Seddon on that day, and I simply said Miss Barrow was worse and that I would send her a mixture to be taken after each motion. I gave no diet instructions on that day. She was in a little danger, but not in a critical condition." I think that is what he said.

The ATTORNEY-GENERAL—Those are the words as near as possible.

252

Evidence for Defence.

Margaret A. Seddon

The only words left out are immaterial, because your lordship has the actual words, "She was rather worse."

Mr. JUSTICE BUCKNILL—It is pretty accurate, is it not?

The ATTORNEY-GENERAL—Yes, "I simply told her that I thought the patient was worse, and I would send her up a diarrhœa mixture." (To the witness)—You remember that?—Yes, Dr. Sworn sent it for the diarrhœa, and not for the sickness.

Dr. Sworn told you that he thought the patient was worse. You have heard what the doctor says about it?—Well, you see, I don't remember. I cannot remember everything that happened.

You see, this lady had been ill in your house for a considerable time?—Yes, I know.

And the doctor, coming on the morning of the 13th, and saying that he found her rather worse, and the diarrhœa being rather worse, did that alarm you at all?—No, because, you know, Miss Barrow had been ill all the time—all the fourteen days.

But he told you——?—She had worse attacks than that.

But he told you when he came that morning that he found her worse?—I don't remember.

But he certainly did not find her better, did he?—Only for the sickness; that stopped. She had not the sickness. She had diarrhœa.

And did he tell you she was getting weaker, and that he found her weaker?—No, he said she was in a weak condition.

Then, she had the pains on and off during the whole time after he left?—During the day.

During the day he left?—Yes.

And diarrhœa, I suppose?—She had the diarrhœa and these pains in the bowels.

Did the diarrhœa get worse?—No, not as I noticed.

Before your husband came had she said to you, "I am dying"?—Not to me, no.

To whom did she say it?—You see, I was standing at the front door, waiting for my husband coming in. This would be about twelve o'clock. I heard her shout. The windows were open, and I heard her shout, "Come quick; I'm dying," so, of course, I went upstairs. I asked my sister-in-law to come with me, but she did not care to come at first. Then she did come; she followed me up after.

Then you went up and found her very ill?—No; she was just the same as she usually was, but she had bad pains in her stomach, and she wanted to be sick.

Had you ever heard her say before, "Come quick, I'm dying"?—No.

Rather an alarming statement for a patient who had been ill for a number of days, and was getting worse?—No; Miss Barrow would always be calling, and sometimes I would never answer to her calls, you see.

Did you tell your husband about it when he came in?—Yes, I did.

Did you smile at it?—Well, I have a usual way of smiling at almost everything, I think. I cannot help it. It is my ways. No matter how serious anything was I think I would smile; I cannot help it.

Do I understand that your smile was merely from your habit. You

Trial of the Seddons.

did not mean him to think there was no cause for anxiety?—No. It is always my way—always.

A way that he would understand?—He knows my ways.

Then when you told him that she had said she was dying, and that you had heard her calling this out, you didn't mean him to think lightly of it?—Of course, you must remember I had been up in the meantime and attended to Miss Barrow once—what she wanted—after hearing her call out that she was dying.

I want to understand what you meant your husband to understand?—Yes.

You told him when he came in that Miss Barrow had called out she was dying?—Yes.

He asked you whether she was?—And I said " No."

And smiled?—And smiled; it is my usual way; I cannot help it.

But you smiled at the idea of her dying?—No, I did not smile at the idea of her dying.

Listen to the question. You meant him to understand that in your opinion she was not dying?—She was not dying, certainly. I never wish anybody dead. I thought too much of Miss Barrow. I waited hand and foot on her. I did all I possibly could do to get her better.

Did you go to bed at all that night?—On and off.

How long was it after your husband had come in that you first went up to her?—You see, when Mr. Seddon came in from the theatre, he told my sister-in-law about the dispute over 6d. That a man had given him the wrong change, and two or three other words passed between them, and then I think Ernest called out that Chickie wanted me, and then, of course, my husband and all three of us went up together.

Was that immediately after he came in?—No, it was a few minutes after.

That is what I am putting to you. That is the first time?—I know he told me not to come up; he told me to lay down and rest.

Was there a doctor living almost opposite your house in Tollington Park?—Not opposite, I don't think.

Very near by?—Somewhere lower down.

Yes, but quite close?—Yes.

By Mr. JUSTICE BUCKNILL—In the same road?—There are two or three, I think.

By the ATTORNEY-GENERAL—There are certainly several?—Yes, there is, at the bottom end of Tollington Park.

I do not want to go through the story at length. You went up altogether four times that night?—Yes.

Four times, counting the first from the time your husband came in?—Yes.

They would not include the times you had gone up before?—No.

She certainly was worse that night than she had ever been?—Yes, she was worse that night than she had been before.

You say you do not remember, or you do not know whether your husband gave her brandy or not?—He gave her brandy, but I don't know whether it was that time he went up or the last time.

You did see him give her brandy?—Yes; there was not much in the

254

Evidence for Defence.

Margaret A. Seddon

bottle. I remember him saying to Miss Barrow that it would have to last her all the night, so he only gave her half of it.

And did he leave the rest there by her?—Yes, on the commode where her bottles are.

Was it gone in the morning?—It was gone, yes.

She had drunk it?—Yes; this must have been the time when she was out of bed.

Was it about 2 o'clock in the morning that Ernie was sent away for the last time from his bed to his room?—Not the last, I don't think—not 2 o'clock.

By Mr. Justice Bucknill—What time?—It could not have been, because we didn't go to bed until between half-past and 2.

Tell the jury when Ernie was sent away to his bed the last time?—It would be between 3 and 4—just before she went off into this sleep.

Just when she went off to sleep?—Yes.

Ernie was sent away to his bed?—It was after she was lifted up o the floor.

That follows. Ernie was there when she was lifted up?—Yes.

By the Attorney-General—Did you say at the inquest, "Miss Barrow died between 6 and 7 a.m. on 14th September; I and my husband were present; we were the only people in the room; both of us had been hanging on and off in the room. The boy did not sleep in the room after 2 o'clock"?—That must have been a mistake; that was not what was meant. We did not go to bed till after that took place, and that was the first time Mr. Seddon told Ernie to go to bed.

You did say it, because you signed the paper?—I must have said it, certainly.

Mr. Justice Bucknill—"I did say before the coroner that the boy did not sleep in the room."

Mr. Marshall Hall—It says in my copy "bed."

Mr. Justice Bucknill—Then the copy that is given me is wrong. My copy says "room."

The Attorney-General—It doesn't make any difference.

By Mr. Justice Bucknill—"I did say before the coroner that the boy did not sleep in the bed after 2 o'clock, but that is a mistake"?—That will be a mistake, because, you see, that would be the first time my husband told him to go to his own bed.

Because 2 o'clock was the first time?—Yes.

Not the last?—No, it would not be the last.

By the Attorney-General—You put it at between 3 and 4 o'clock when he left the room for the last time?—For the last time, yes.

And is it right that from that time until the death you were in the bedroom?—Yes.

In Miss Barrow's bedroom?—Yes. I sat in the chair.

And was your husband outside?—Standing by the door.

It was open, as we have heard?—Yes, that is quite right.

I think you have said that he was smoking and reading?—Yes.

You knew by that time, after you had been up four times during that night, that she was certainly worse than she had been; weaker?—Yes, she was weaker, certainly.

255

Trial of the Seddons.

Margaret A. Seddon

You had been called up the last time by Ernie telling you she was out of bed?—Yes.

And you came up and found her sitting there, as you described. I don't want to go through it again?—That is quite right, yes.

You had never seen that before?—Previous to that my husband stood outside the door before we lifted her into bed. She wanted the commode, and I helped her on to that, and I called my husband back into the room; and we got her into bed.

I thought you had found her sitting up when you went up?—Yes, that is quite right—in a sitting position.

And the boy trying to hold her up?—Yes.

And the boy was very frightened?

By Mr. JUSTICE BUCKNILL—When she was sitting on the floor did she appear to be in great pain?—I couldn't tell you. She wanted to use the commode, and I helped her.

By the ATTORNEY-GENERAL—She was complaining all that night of bad pains in her stomach?—Yes, in her stomach, which I attended to all the night through.

I want to understand how long it was after you were there in the room, sitting in the basket chair, before she began to do what you describe—snoring?—Well, I couldn't give you a stated time.

No, I do not want the stated time, but I want to get some idea of the time?—I couldn't; you see I was tired and sleepy myself; I kept on dozing, you know.

Was she sleeping peacefully for any length of time so far as you know?—She seemed to be in a nice—just a quiet sleep.

There was no reason why your husband should not go down to bed, was there?—My husband wanted me to go to bed, you see.

You were sitting dozing in the room?—Yes, he thought that she might sleep like that all night—for the rest of the morning.

The next day was his——?—Office day.

So far as I follow what you have told us there was no reason why he should not go to bed if you were going to sit up there and watch?—He said he would not leave me in the room alone.

That is the explanation?—And he kept going down and seeing if the baby was all right.

By Mr. JUSTICE BUCKNILL—You have heard people snore before, I dare say. Did you ever hear anybody snore like Miss Barrow?—It was an ordinary kind of snoring; it seemed to be coming from the throat.

It didn't frighten you?—No, I never dreamt anything was wrong like that.

By the ATTORNEY-GENERAL—As I understand you, there was nothing alarming about her snoring?—No.

An ordinary kind of snore?—She seemed to be snoring from her throat.

I want to understand it. Was it an ordinary kind of snoring or not?—I don't know what you would call it; it was snoring from her throat—ordinary snoring.

You have heard people snore?—Yes, but everybody don't snore alike.

Was it that kind of snoring that you heard?—Yes.

Nothing to alarm you?—Nothing whatever.

Evidence for Defence.

Margaret A. Seddon

Then you must have been very shocked when you found she was dead?—Yes, I was.

Were you sure she was dead?—I really could not believe it until my husband proved by the lifting of her eyelids that 'she was dead.

All that happened almost immediately, according to the story you have told us?—I think she stopped drawing her breath; she did not breathe.

Follow me. Was that the first thing that called your attention? The stopping of her breathing? Then your husband called attention to it?—Yes, and he lifted the eyelid.

Immediately?—Yes, and I told you the remark that he passed.

By Mr. JUSTICE BUCKNILL—" Good God, she's dead "?—Yes.

By the ATTORNEY-GENERAL—You couldn't believe it?—No, I didn't; I couldn't believe it.

Did you ask for a doctor?—My husband went straight away to Dr. Sworn.

How far off is he?—Highbury.

About half an hour, I think, we have been told?—Yes, I expect it is.

Now, I want to understand this from you. Do you mean that whilst you were sitting there, there was nothing to alarm you until you saw that she had stopped breathing?—Positively.

No indication of any kind before that?—No, it was the first sick room I had ever been in in my life.

I suggest to you that that was a very good reason why you should have wanted a doctor under the circumstances?—No.

Because you had so little experience?—I never gave the doctor a thought.

You never gave the doctor a thought?—No, because I knew Dr. Sworn would come in the next morning. I never knew Miss Barrow was dying.

According to what you said, you went down below and saw Mary Chater, and you said you thought she had passed away. You were not sure?—No; Mr. Seddon, you see, had gone to see Dr. Sworn.

What?—I expected Dr. Sworn to come back with Mr. Seddon.

To see whether she was really dead or not?—Yes, I suppose that would be it.

Had you touched her at all—had you felt her?—No; I don't know whether I put my handkerchief up to her or not.

You cannot remember?—Whether it was before or after Mr. Seddon came back.

According to what you told us, you know it could not have been before; if he said, " Good God, she's dead," and with that he hurried off to Dr. Sworn, and you were in doubt whether, or, at any rate, you were not certain that she was dead, you couldn't have tied up her jaw before that, could you?—No, I do not think so.

Do you think you tied it up after your husband came back?—I don't know whether it was when Mrs. Rutt came; I cannot remember.

Either when Mrs. Rutt came or when your husband came back you did it?—We went up together, you see.

Then the search for the money started?—Yes.

R

Trial of the Seddons.

Margaret A. Seddon

Did your husband say he was going to look for the money?—No, he never said what he was going to do.

Did he tell you what he wanted the keys of the trunk for?—No.

Was the key of the cash box on that same ring as the key of the trunk?—I believe so.

Whilst the keys are being looked for, let me ask you this. You told us that £4 10s. was found in the cash box?—Yes.

Did you see where in the cash box the money was found?—In the tray part.

Do you mean inside one of the little receptacles in the tray?—Yes.

And nothing on the top of the tray?—Not that I saw.

Were you standing looking at your husband?—No, we were by the bed; we were doing Miss Barrow.

Did you see him actually find the money?—Yes, he put the box on the bed.

Was the body on the other side of the bed?—The body was this side (indicating).

The body was the one side and he put the cash box on the other?—Yes.

Did you see how the money was found—did you see yourself whether it was found loose or wrapped up?—No, it was in the bag.

Did you see your husband take the bag out?—Yes.

So far as you know, up to the afternoon that was all the money that had been found?—Yes.

You knew that she had £10 on 2nd September?—Yes, that is right.

And she had not been out; I mean she had not been able to spend any money?—No, only what she gave me to spend.

How much was that?—I cannot count it up.

I mean it must have been some small amounts?—Yes; I think there was Valentine's beef juice.

Valentine's beef juice?—Yes, 2s. 10d.

And did she give you gold or silver?—Silver.

She did not give you any gold at all?—No.

Was she taking the Valentine's beef juice long?—No, she had only two bottles.

About how many days had she been taking it?—I could not say exactly; I couldn't say how many days.

Was it several days before she died?—Oh yes.

That, I understand from you, was given in cold water?—Yes.

It did not require any particular preparation, did it?—Yes, it had to be mixed.

It had to be mixed?—Yes, it had to be mixed.

You took a spoonful out of the bottle which we have seen produced?—Yes.

We know from what you have told us that this was given in cold water?—Yes, cold water, by the doctor's orders.

How often a day did she used to take this?—Only once.

When was it taken?—In the afternoon.

The kitchen next to Miss Barrow's room had a gas stove, and that was used for heating flannels?—Yes.

Evidence for Defence.

Margaret A. Seddon

Was it also used for boiling water?—No, I never boiled water—only just to heat the flannels.

It was a great surprise to you, was it not, that only £4 10s. was found in the cash box?—Yes.

You naturally thought there would be a great deal more there?—I thought there was certainly more.

As far as you knew, the £216 would still be there?—As far as I knew.

And, as far as you knew, at any rate, a good part of the gold that you had brought her in exchange for the notes, according to your statement, should have been there?—Yes, it should have been there.

And also the £10 in gold that was paid to her month by month by your husband?—Yes.

And I suppose I may take it that it was rather a shock to you to find there was not the money there?—Well, my husband told me to search the place to see if there was not more.

Did you know where she had put the gold which she got on 2nd September?—No; you see, I was not always in her room.

Did you tell your husband you were rather surprised at this small amount of money being found there?—No, I never mentioned it.

Did he say anything to you about it?—No, only he said it was funny what had become of it.

Did you tell him then that you had changed a number of notes into gold for her?—No.

Never said a word to him about it?—No, not a word.

Why not?—Because I didn't think it was necessary. My husband didn't tell me everything. I never dreamt to tell him anything at all about it.

But, you see, you expected to find a considerable sum of money in gold in that cash box, as you told me?—Yes, but I was not responsible for what Miss Barrow had done. She used to go out. I was not responsible; I was not her keeper. I never knew what she done with her money.

Do you mean to say you never had any conversation with your husband at this time about the money that ought to have been in the box?—No; I only said "It seems strange; whatever has she done with it?"

Did he say anything to you about the £216?—No, he only said he wondered whatever she had done with it.

Or about the £10 that had been paid her on the 2nd September?—No, I don't remember that being mentioned.

Can you tell us is that the bunch of keys (handed)?—I know them being on the ring. My husband has not got a ring like that.

You mean, I suppose, being on a ring like that, you think they are the keys, because your husband has not got a ring like that?—He has not got a ring like that.

Therefore, you mean they would not be his?—Yes.

Did you hear your husband saying anything to Mr. Nodes as to it being necessary for him to consult somebody before he fixed the funeral?—No.

Trial of the Seddons.

Margaret A. Seddon

Now, tell me about the afternoon when you had another search, and when you told us that the three sovereigns were found wrapped in tissue paper?—Yes.

Each coin, as I understand, was separately wrapped in tissue paper?—Yes, that is right.

Did they look as if they had been wrapped up any time?—No, I couldn't tell you.

And the £2 10s. in the bag; was that wrapped in tissue paper also?—Yes.

Could you tell whether that had been wrapped up any time?—No.

Did you ask any questions in the house on this day as to whether anybody knew what had become of the money?—There was nobody in the house but the children and the servant.

That means you did not?—No.

Are we to understand that until after you were arrested you never spoke to your husband about having changed these notes?—Certainly—never.

What?—I am positive I never did.

Didn't you talk together about the disappearance of this money?—No.

What?—We have said on several occasions it was funny where it went to.

Where "it" went to—what was the "it"?—Where the money—this £216 that she drew out of the bank—had gone to.

Didn't you say to your husband, "And besides that there was a lot of money that I changed for her into gold"?—No.

Not a word about it?—Not a word.

We have heard from him that you spoke about it after you had both been arrested?—After I was arrested.

You heard what he said?—Yes.

Was that right? In the Court?—I don't remember what he did say.

I will tell you what he said; that you said you had given the false name and address because you didn't want everybody to know your business?—No, I do not think that is exactly what I said.

And that you didn't want everybody to know who you were?—After giving my wrong name and address.

Did you say this, that if you went into a shop where you were not known to buy a small article you didn't want everybody to know who you were?—But, you see, I had already given my wrong name and address.

Did you say that to him?—I don't remember; you see, I cannot remember everything.

Can you give any reason why you should not have told him then?—No, no reason—only the reason what I have given you before.

That is the reason you did not give to him; the reason you give us is that when you were asked to change a note you had never done it before, and you gave the first name and address that came into your head?—That is quite right.

That is not the explanation that you gave to him?—No.

According to what he has said?—Well, I do not remember.

Evidence for Defence.

Margaret A. Seddon

You cannot give any other explanation?—No, no other explanation than I have already given.

On the night of 14th September, that is, the day of the death, you went to the music-hall or theatre, did you not?—Yes, I did.

Which was it?—The Grand, Islington.

What is that?—A music-hall.

What time did you go about?—About 8 o'clock.

What time did you come back?—Midnight.

You were away when the body was removed?—Yes.

Did you know the body was going to be removed that night?—Yes, I knew in the morning Mr. Nodes was going to take it away.

About what time was it when your husband came up to you on that day, and you asked him to lie down—to rest?—It would be getting on for 3 or 4 o'clock.

Do you remember on 15th September, that is, the day after, going with your husband to the jewellers?—Yes, that was the evening.

Did you know that he had gone earlier in the day?—No.

Did he tell you he had gone to have the ring enlarged?—I cannot tell you that. I cannot remember; it was a busy day for me that day.

Do you mean in the household?—Yes.

Then you went about the watch?—Yes, that was coming back after seeing my sister-in-law off.

Was it your idea to have the name taken out of the back plate?—Yes; I would never wear it.

You would never wear it?—No, I would not wear it with the name in.

Does that mean you had never worn it?—No, I had never worn it. I have never worn it yet.

Nobody would see the name?—Oh, well, I did not like Miss Barrow's name being on it—Miss Barrow's mother's name being on it.

What was your objection to wearing it with a name on the back plate which no one could see?—And then it had a cracked dial as well.

Yes, but I am asking you about the name. You said you would not wear it because it had her mother's name engraved on it?—I did not like to wear it with a name on it.

I want you to explain what difference it made. Nobody could see that on the back plate?—They could have opened it, couldn't they?

People do not take your watch out and open it if you are wearing it?—There is a good many people you come into contact with that would take it out and open it.

Why should that affect you?—It did not belong to me; it was Miss Barrow's mother's; it was not my mother's.

Given to you?—Yes. by Miss Barrow.

According to you?—Yes, that is quite right.

And, even after it was altered, you didn't wear it?—No, I never wore it.

This lady had not been buried then; she was not buried until the next day?—No.

You went to the jeweller's the day after her death and the day before her funeral?—Yes.

To have this name taken out?—Yes.

Trial of the Seddons.

Margaret A. Seddon

You told us a little while ago, very definitely, that there had never been any fly-papers of any kind in your house before you bought these four?—I made a mistake there; there has been sticky papers.

Oh, how did you know you had made a mistake?—I called it to mind after I went away.

I asked you a good many questions about it, and you were very definite?—Well, you see, I get mixed up between one thing and another.

Was your attention called to the fact that your husband had said you had sticky ones in the house?—I beg your pardon.

Was your attention called to your husband's statement that you had used sticky ones in the house?—No.

You know he had said so?—When?

Here, in Court?—That I do not remember.

Don't you?—No, I don't remember what he said.

How long had you used the sticky ones?—Oh, not very often.

Had you been using them during Miss Barrow's illness?—I don't think so.

Had you been using them during that hot summer?—No; I don't think we used them in that house.

By "that house" you mean 63 Tollington Park?—Yes.

What papers did you ask for when you went to the chemist?—I never asked for any particular papers; I just asked for fly-papers.

Is that all?—I asked for two.

Tell us exactly what you said, as near as you can remember?—Yes, I asked for two fly-papers—those that you put the water on—those that you wet.

Had you never seen them before?—Never.

Had you never seen fly-papers that you wet before?—No, no.

Never?—No.

Anywhere?—No.

Do you know whether or not your solicitor has been to this chemist, Mr. Meacher?—I could not tell you. I told Mr. Saint about it.

Would you know the man again, if you saw him, who served you?—Very likely.

Do you mean to say, Mrs. Seddon, that you do not know whether Mr. Saint has ever been to this chemist or not?—No.

That you do not know whether he had tried to get him to make any statement about them?—No, none whatever.

You do not know?—No.

He had never reported to you?—No.

He has been acting for you and your husband throughout these proceedings, has he not?—Yes.

From the time of the inquest?—Yes.

Did you tell your solicitor that you had bought some precipitate there?—Yes.

Did you tell him that very soon after your husband's arrest?—Yes.

Was that about the time that your daughter went to Price's to purchase Mather's fly-papers?—Yes, I believe it would be. I will not say for certain.

Evidence for Defence.

Margaret A. Seddon

That, we know, is 6th December, two days after your husband's arrest?—Yes.

You knew that?—Yes.

You knew your daughter was going there for that purpose?—Yes.

You know your solicitor's signature, I suppose?—No, I do not.

Have you ever seen it?—No; I see it, I think, on paper, but I could not recognise it.

Just look at that. (Document handed.) Look at the fifth line, and tell me whether you recognise that signature?—No, I couldn't tell you; you see, I have seen it in prison on the paper.

You cannot recognise whether that is his signature or not?—Not that, because it was a larger signature.

Is Mr. Meacher here? (Mr. Meacher stepped forward.) Is that the gentleman who served you?—Yes. (Mr. Meacher took a seat in the well of the Court.)

Did you sign any book?—No.

Were you asked to sign a book when you purchased the papers?—No.

Has your daughter ever been to Meacher's?—I could not tell you—Yes, I will tell you.

Yes?—As regards the baby's food.

Did you change any notes after the 1st September for Miss Barrow?—I don't think so.

Is your memory clear about it?—Well, if I did it was what I had on hand; I will not say for certain.

One you had on hand?—Yes.

Do you mean one she had left with you?—One I changed for her, and it was my own money, but I don't think it was after Miss Barrow's death.

I am asking you after the time she was ill, from 1st September?—No, I don't remember.

What do you mean by saying, " One you had on hand "?—You see I had some money of my own, and out of this I cashed Miss Barrow's note.

Sometimes you cashed notes for her which you did not take to shops?—No, only this one.

Which one?—This last one I had.

When was it?—I couldn't tell you the date.

Did you pay it into your bank?—I didn't pay her £5 note into the bank.

Just look at your book for a minute and tell me. (Post Office Savings Bank book handed.)?—Yes, I know the book.

Do you see the entry?—Yes.

That is 18th September, is it not?—Yes.

" £5 "?—Yes, I will account for that.

What was it?—I think Greigs cashed that £5 note; that was the last note that I cashed for Miss Barrow.

That was a note of Miss Barrow's?—Yes.

Apparently, so far as we have got, you paid £5 in gold on 18th September into your Post Office Savings Bank account?—Yes, that is right.

That £5 in gold was money which you had got for a £5 note?—Of Miss Barrow's.

Trial of the Seddons.

Margaret A. Seddon

And which, if Miss Barrow had lived, would have been paid to her; is that what you mean?—No, that is not correct.

When did you get the £5 note from Miss Barrow?—I could not tell you the date, but I wanted to pay Greigs their grocery bill. Miss Barrow had already had the note cashed.

When had she had the note cashed?—You see this £5 was my own £5.

It is Miss Barrow's note that I want to know about?—On this day that I went to Greigs.

18th September is the day you paid it in?—No, I had the money then.

How long had you the money before you paid it in?—It was my own money which I had saved.

How long had you it before you paid it in?—Oh, I had this money on and off—money I had saved.

When had you got the £5 note from Miss Barrow?—I couldn't tell you.

I must ask you to look at the book for a minute. I see the book starts from 8th April, 1911, with an entry of " £1 10s.," and then the total amount paid in previous to this entry is 14s. in three sums of 10s. in August, 2s. in August, 2s. in August, and then comes this entry of £5 on 18th September?—Yes, well, you see I had already paid Miss Barrow her £5.

You see that is right? (Book handed.)?—Yes, I cannot quite catch what you mean.

By Mr. Justice Bucknill—Never mind what he means. Try and answer the question. " I had already paid her her £5." Now, he asks you to look at the book. Now, look at the book?—Yes, that is the £5 I had put in.

Look at the book and wait for the question. You will see some entries there. Look at the entries before the £5?—Yes, there is 2s., 2s., 10s., and £1 10s.

By the Attorney-General—I am very anxious that you should under-stand what I mean?—I will try and understand as far as I can.

So that you may give your explanation of it. On this date, 18th September, you were paying in £5?—Yes.

You had never paid in any such sum before?—No, that is quite right.

The book which is there before you shows entries of £2 4s. altogether?—Yes.

During the whole time from April?—Yes.

This appears to be another account, an earlier one. I thought it was the same carried on, but it appears to be another one; it appears to be an account for 1910. (Post Office Savings Bank book handed)?—Yes.

There is no such sum as £5 in any of those payments in?—No.

There are some payments of a few shillings?—Yes.

Ten shillings, I think, is the most I have seen?—Yes.

I want you to explain to us how you came to pay that £5 in on 18th September?—You see, I was going away on my holiday for one week, and when I came back I wanted to buy a fur and fur hat and muff to match, and this was my money that I had already saved to do it with. I didn't buy it before I went away; I put it in the bank.

Now, will you tell us what that had to do with that £5 note of Miss

Evidence for Defence.

Margaret A. Seddon

Barrow's—this one that you know of?—The last note I changed for Miss Barrow was in October, as far as I remember.

You must be mistaken. She died in September?—October. We have got mixed up a bit now. I cannot follow you back to where I was before.

Just follow. Miss Barrow died on 14th September?—Yes.

What I want to know is about this note that you had from Miss Barrow before her death?—Yes.

I want you to tell us what that was—when did you get it?—Well, you see, if I have it, and I paid Miss Barrow with the money, that is still my money that I had; I paid it out of my money, and I had still got my £5.

Then do you mean you did change a £5 note for Miss Barow during the time that she was ill?—Not while she was ill, no.

When had you got it from her?—From the time previous.

Do you know how long previous?—No, I don't know.

Did you ever hold the notes over that you got from Miss Barrow?—One—this last one—I kept it back and paid Miss Barrow the money.

Let me see if I understand what you mean. She wanted to change a £5 note?—Yes.

And you had £5 of your own?—That is right.

And you gave her that £5 for the £5 note?—Yes.

And then it is your £5 note?—Yes, that is right.

And then, when you were going to pay in, you changed the £5 note into five sovereigns?—Not at the Post Office.

Did you pay in the note or the gold?—The gold.

Then you had changed the £5 note which you had got into gold before you paid it in?—I had been and paid Greigs their grocery bill, you see.

With that £5 note?—Yes.

Then you made up the balance, I suppose, of what you had spent, and paid in the five sovereigns?—Yes, that is right.

Is that right?—Yes, that is right.

The ATTORNEY-GENERAL—There is an observation I want to make to your lordship, and that is that that note is not one of the thirty-three.

Mr. JUSTICE BUCKNILL—I assumed that all the way through, because otherwise you would have told us so, I am sure.

Re-examined by Mr. MARSHALL HALL—My learned friend has asked you about changing some notes for Miss Barrow. Do you know in the least what Miss Barrow did with the money you gave her in change for those notes?—No, I couldn't tell you.

Or did you ever see Miss Barrow take the note which you changed for her from any particular place?—No.

Then as regards this £216 which she brought back in gold from the savings bank, you were with her?—Yes, I was with her.

You went to the bank with her?—Yes.

And came back with her?—Yes.

And, as you have told us, your husband objected to her having so much money in the house?—Yes.

What did she say?—My husband objected, and she was disagreeable over it; she fell out with him over it; she did not talk to him for a week. She said "She knew what to do with it"; these were her words.

When you were asked about the fly-papers you said that you had

Trial of the Seddons.

Margaret A. Seddon

never bought any fly-papers until you bought them on 4th September. How did you come to buy the fly-papers that had to be wetted on 4th September?—Because Miss Barrow asked me; she said, "Don't get the sticky ones; they are too dirty."

There are reels of sticky paper?—Yes, the other ones.

With things that hang?—Yes.

As a matter of fact, have you had any of these fly-papers that catch them alive at Tollington Park?—Not to my knowledge, I have not.

My learned friend asked you whether you had ever sent Maggie to buy any fly-papers?—Never.

You did know that Maggie went to a shop on 6th December to try and buy some, and that she did not get some; that was through Mr. Saint?—That was Mr. Saint's instructions.

It is suggested that Maggie had bought fly-papers from Thorley on 26th August. When did you first know that?—Not until I heard it in Court.

You heard it in Court before the magistrate?—Yes, before the magistrate.

Has Maggie ever brought any fly-papers to the house?—Never.

When I say "fly-papers" I mean Mather's fly-papers?—Never.

I just want to ask you one or two questions about this night that Miss Barrow died. If I understood your answer to the learned Attorney-General aright, you say that when you went upstairs and found her sitting on the floor in great pain, and the little boy trying to hold her up, your husband went out of the room for a few minutes?—I asked him to go outside the room.

Was that because you found that Miss Barrow wanted to use the commode?—Yes.

For decency's sake, he was outside the door while you helped her to use the commode?—Yes.

You sat down in the chair at the foot of the bed?—Yes.

Have you any idea how long it was, when you sat down in the chair at the foot of the bed, before the final end came?—I never took notice.

I think you said you were "sleeping tired"?—Yes.

That is a north country expression, which means that you were dog-tired?—Yes.

You were "sleeping tired," and you dozed and woke up?—Yes.

You cannot give us any idea of the exact time?—No, I cannot.

Did you notice any difference between the ordinary snoring you hear and any sound which took place immediately before your husband called out to you?—No, as I said before, it seemed a snoring that came from her throat.

Did she complain of asthma?—Before she took to bed?

Yes?—Yes.

Did she ever have bronchitis while she was in your house?—She was troubled on and off.

The bronchial tubes gave her trouble—there was trouble with her chest?—She couldn't get her breath.

Will you tell me if it was an ordinary habit of hers to snore?—I do not know.

Evidence for Defence.

Margaret A. Seddon

You would not be able to hear her from your room?—No.

My learned friend suggests that there was no reason why your husband should not have gone downstairs that last night?—He did not like to leave me alone.

You were up there all alone with Miss Barrow, and if you had gone down, instead of staying in the room, what would you expect?—I do not know.

Do you think you would have got a nice rest?—No, I could not sleep when I knew my husband was up.

Supposing both of you had gone away, would you have been left in peace?—No, Miss Barrow might have called out again.

You had been up several times before twelve?—Yes.

And you went up four times after twelve o'clock?—Yes.

In what sort of a glass was it that you gave her the Valentine's beef juice?—In a cup.

Do you remember how much beef juice you gave her?—I gave her two or three teaspoonfuls.

How much water did you put to it?—Nearly full.

That would be a white cup, would it not, or what?—Yes, an ordinary china cup.

What colour would two or three teaspoonfuls added to a cup of water be; would it be pale or dark when it was mixed up?—It was a browny colour.

Who ordered the Valentine's beef juice for her?—Dr. Sworn.

Do you remember how many bottles you bought of it?—Two.

At about 2s. 10d., or something like that?—2s. 10d. a bottle.

Now, I will go to another point. Whereabouts in the room did this big trunk stand?—Under the window.

The jury have seen that. It is right under the window. You do not know which is the key of the trunk?—No, I could not tell you.

There are two here which, to my unobservant eye, are like duplicates. Anyhow, I should like the jury to see these keys. I will tie this piece of red ribbon on to the key which I am told is the trunk key. (Bunch of keys handed to the jury.) This trunk was underneath the window in the bedroom?—Yes.

Have you any knowledge whatever as to what Miss Barrow used to do when she went out?—No, I could not tell you.

Now, about this music hall. How came you to go to the music hall on the Thursday night?—Well, when my eldest son came home from work he said he had booked four seats at the Empire. I said I felt too tired, and I would rather stay at home, but, anyway, my husband thought it would do me good, and he advised me to go, and I went.

All I want to get is that the seats had been taken. Mrs. Longley was staying with you?—Yes.

Who went—you, Mrs. Longley, your son, and——?—And a girl friend that came in.

The seats had been got without your being consulted?—Yes.

You did not want to go, but you did go?—Yes.

Mr. MARSHALL HALL—I think that is all I have to ask.

Mr. JUSTICE BUCKNILL—The jury have handed me this paper contain-

Trial of the Seddons.

ing some questions. The questions have not been put, so will you attend. "The jury would like Mrs. Seddon's evidence read over as to when she went to Meacher's the chemist, for fly-papers, and how much money was expended." Now, gentlemen, I will read my note, and it will be checked by others. The first reference to it is this. Yesterday afternoon the witness said "She" (that is Miss Barrow) "complained of the flies in her bedroom, we had to fan her to keep the flies from her. She asked me to get fly-papers—the wet ones, not the sticky ones. That was on the Monday or the Tuesday, the 4th or the 5th." (To witness) If I am not putting it right, just tell me?—That is right.

"I got them at Mr. Meacher's, the chemist, just round the corner close to us. An old gentleman served me. I may have bought the baby's food at the same time, Horlick's malted milk." I understand it was a bottle. "I believe I bought for Miss Barrow white precipitate powder, also to wash her head. Once I saw her clean her teeth with it. I signed no book when I bought the fly-papers. I never had a packet of them. I asked for two papers. I bought four for 3d. I showed them to Miss Barrow, and she said they were the sort she wanted. I put them on plates first"?—No, that is wrong. I put them on one plate first to moisten them.

I see you say that now I look at it. "I put them on a plate first to damp them all over"?—Yes, that is right.

"And then I put them in four saucers"?—Yes.

"Two on the mantelpiece and two on the chest of drawers. I put water in the saucers." That is all there is about that. I don't know that I have got anything else until I come to (to-day). "At the chemist's I asked for two fly-papers—those that you wet. I have never seen those before. I told Mr. Saint about it. I don't know if he had been to the chemist's about them," and so on.

The FOREMAN OF THE JURY—There is something left out, my lord.

Mr. JUSTICE BUCKNILL—What is it?

The FOREMAN OF THE JURY—There is a part where Mrs. Seddon said she remembered it because she took four fly-papers.

Mr. JUSTICE BUCKNILL—That is what I have already read.

The FOREMAN OF THE JURY—And it was brought back to her memory because she got them cheaper that way.

The ATTORNEY-GENERAL—I have the shorthand note. I know the exact words are not in your lordship's note, although the substance is. "Mr. Meacher, or whatever his name is, said, 'Why not have four? You can have four for 3d.' I said, 'Very well, then, I might as well have the four.'"

Mr. JUSTICE BUCKNILL—That is at length; my note in the abbreviated form is, "I asked for two papers, and I bought four for 3d."

The FOREMAN OF THE JURY—At the same time, my lord, she bought the white precipitate and Horlick's malted milk, so she must have paid more than 3d.

By Mr. JUSTICE BUCKNILL—What did you pay for the precipitate?—1d.

The next thing the jury want to know is this—"To ask Mrs. Seddon did her husband allow her any money weekly?"—Well, you see, when-

Evidence for Defence.

Margaret A. Seddon

ever I wanted anything my husband would give it me; if I wanted to buy anything, he would always give me money to buy it.

Then the rest, "If not," does not matter, because you have got what you want.

"If I wanted money, my husband would give me whatever I wanted"?—Yes.

Let me ask you one question so as to make it quite clear. There was what we call the last £5 note that you had from Miss Barrow?—Yes.

For that note I understand you gave her money?—Yes, that is right.

That money, I understand you to say, was your own savings?—My own money.

Listen. Say yes or no. Having done that you then had the £5 note still in your possession?—Yes.

You dealt with that in this way; you took it to your own grocer to pay your little grocery bill?—Yes.

And got change for the £5 note?—Yes.

And then wishing, as you say, to pay £5 into your Post Office Savings Bank, with the money you had you made up the £5, and so paid £5 into the bank, is that right?—Yes.

JOHN ARTHUR FRANCIS, examined by Mr. MARSHALL HALL—I am a member of the Royal College of Surgeons, and live at 108 Fortress Road, Tufnell Park. From October, 1904, to February, 1910, I attended the late Miss Barrow on and off. She was then living with the Grants at 52 Lady Somerset Road. On some occasions when I attended her she had gastritis, which was brought on by alcohol really. I have no doubt about it at all. I would say that she suffered from gastritis, brought on by alcohol, every three months or so, but I could not give the dates; there were two years that I did not see her at all.

By Mr. JUSTICE BUCKNILL—You say that every three months or so you saw her for alcoholism?—Not always alcoholism; she had gastritis, but not always. Sometimes she had bronchitis, but it was generally for gastritis that I saw her.

Examination continued—I have here extracts from my ledger showing the dates upon which I attended Miss Barrow. I find that from 19th October, 1904, to 20th September, 1905, is the time that I attended her at 52 Somerset Road. Mr. Grant died on 20th October, 1906. I attended Miss Barrow at 38 Woodsome Road on various occasions in 1909. Towards the end of that year and the beginning of 1910 she was suffering from general debility. The last time I attended her for gastric trouble would be in March, 1909. I understood she was a quarrelsome sort of woman, but I had not seen it myself. One day she would not come down to see me, and Mrs. Grant had to fetch her down. She behaved in a very sulky and queer sort of manner.

She was a businesslike woman, so far as you could judge, was she not?—I think she had all her wits about her. (It was arranged that this witness should come again to-morrow morning for cross-examination and bring his books with him.)

Trial of the Seddons.

Ernest B. Poole

ERNEST BURTON POOLE, examined by Mr. MARSHALL HALL—I am a clerk with the firm of Frere, Cholmeley & Co., solicitors, Lincoln's Inn Fields. The correspondence between Miss Barrow and my firm in reference to the compensation charges of the "Buck's Head" passed through my hands. I produce four letters to my firm from Miss Barrow and four from my firm to her which passed in 1910.

Do you find that a cheque for £9 8s. 4d. was paid for ground rent at the "Buck's Head" through a cheque of Mr. Seddon's in October?—I cannot say whose cheque it was. Miss Barrow always paid by money order, but I was asked to verify a cheque, and I looked it up. It was so unusual that I went to the bank to see that it was a cheque, and I found that it was. It was drawn on the London and Provincial Bank, Finsbury Park branch. I cannot say more than that.

Cross-examined by the ATTORNEY-GENERAL—That was the first time we were paid by cheque, and from that time onwards we were always paid by cheque. That was the last rent that we received from Miss Barrow. After that, from Lady Day, Mr. Seddon became the lessee. We had notice of the assignment.

MARY CHATER, recalled, further cross-examined by Mr. MARSHALL HALL—I asked you about a cup of tea being made for Miss Barrow. I want to ask you again who made the cup of tea in the morning for Miss Barrow?—Not me.

Did you not take a cup of tea up the stairs and give it to Margaret, and Margaret took it into Miss Barrow's room?—No.

Do you know that Margaret took a cup of tea into Miss Barrow's room each morning?—No.

I put it to you that every morning you used to make a cup of tea downstairs and give it to Miss Margaret, who gave it to Miss Barrow?—No, that is not so.

MARGARET SEDDON, examined by Mr. MARSHALL HALL—I was sixteen years of age on 17th January last. I remember Miss Barrow and Mr. and Mrs. Hook coming to live at our house. There was some quarrel, and Mr. and Mrs. Hook left.

Did you ever take a cup of tea to Miss Barrow in the morning?—Yes.

How often did you take it?—Well, every morning. The servant, Mary, used to bring it up to my bedroom at seven in the morning, and I used to take it from her up to Miss Barrow's room. I remember my mother sending me on 6th December, after my father had been arrested, to buy some fly-papers. I went with two other young ladies. I do not know Mr. Thorley, but I know his daughter, and I have been to Mr. Thorley's shop to see her at the side door. I remember on one occasion when I went to the side door Mr. Thorley opened the door, but I did not have any conversation with him. He opened the door twice to me when I went to see his daughter. I have never been to his shop to buy fly-papers. (Shown exhibit 126.) I have never bought a fly-paper like that.

We know that you did go to buy some fly-papers with the other

Evidence for Defence.

Margaret Seddon

young ladies, but they did not sell them to you?—No, I have never bought any fly-papers either at Mr. Thorley's or anywhere else at any time.

By Mr. JUSTICE BUCKNILL—The two other girls who went with me were two of Mr. Saint's daughters.

Cross-examined by the ATTORNEY-GENERAL—That was at Mr. Price's shop?—That was Mr. Price's shop.

Did you sometimes go out and take the baby in a perambulator?—Yes.

During the warm weather of July, August, and September?—Yes.

Do you know Crouch Hill?—I do.

Did you sometimes go up that way with the perambulator?—No.

Do you remember buying anything at all on the 26th August?—No.

Do you remember a shop called Wilson's?—Yes.

Do you know you bought something there on the 26th August?—No.

Do you say you did not?—No.

Are you quite sure?—Quite sure.

Have you ever been into the shop?—I have been.

Did you go in at all last year?—Yes.

Did you go in during the summer?—Yes.

Did you go in in August?—I could not say.

Do you remember buying a pair of shoes and a little writing case there?—I remember buying them.

But you do not remember the date?—No.

We have got the date, if you can remember it. It is the 26th August. You do not remember whether it was that date or any other?—No, I could not remember.

About how far is Wilson's shop from Thorley's?—Well, I should say about five minutes' walk.

Have you ever seen any fly-papers like that at all?—Do you mean at our place?

Ever, anywhere?—Yes.

Where?—In Miss Barrow's room.

When?—During her illness in September.

How often were you there?—Well, every day.

You were in the room every day?—Yes.

Had you ever seen any before?—No.

Have you ever heard of sticky fly-papers?—Yes.

You know what they are?—Yes, I do.

Have you ever seen a packet like that (handing an envelope)?—No.

Never?—No.

Have you ever been into Thorley's shop at all?—No.

You were within a very few minutes' walk from there on this day?—I couldn't say what day it was.

But I am trying to help you. We have got the evidence already that you were at Wilson's?—Yes, but I couldn't say I was, because I don't remember.

On the day that you were at Wilson's you were only a few minutes' walk from Thorley's shop?—Yes.

Trial of the Seddons.

Now, I must ask you, did you tell Mr. Thorley that you wanted four packets of fly-papers?—No, sir, I have never been in the shop.

Did he ask you what kind, and did you say that you did not want the sticky ones?—I have not been in the shop.

Never been in there at all?—No.

I will put to you the exact words. Did he say to you, " Do you want the sticky ones? " and did you say, " No, the arsenic ones "?—I have never been in conversation with him about fly-papers at all.

I understand you have never been into the shop?—Never.

You did know him, and he knew you by sight apparently?—Well, I couldn't recognise him again; I only knew him through calling at the side door for his daughter.

You used to see his daughter occasionally, I suppose?—Certainly, yes.

Did he tell you that he couldn't let you have four packets because he had not got them in the shop, or anything of that kind?—No, I never saw him about fly-papers.

I am putting to you what he says. You say you had no conversation with him at all?—No, I had not.

Were you asked by Chief Inspector Ward at the Police Court whether you had ever been to purchase fly-papers?—Yes, sir.

Did he ask you whether you had ever been to the chemist's shop at the corner of Tollington Park and Stroud Green Road to purchase Mather's fly-papers?—Yes.

And did you say " No "?—I said I had not been to Thorley's.

That is not the question I am putting to you. The corner of Tollington Park and Stroud Green Road is Price's shop, isn't it?—I see; yes, that is right.

Did you say to the police officer that you had never been to the chemist's shop at the corner of Tollington Park and Stroud Green Road to purchase Mather's fly-papers?—No, sir, I did not.

Did he ask you the question?—He did.

What did you say?—I told him I had been to try and get them, but Price would not give them to me when I mentioned my name owing to the trouble we had already got.

Just let me put the question to you. Is that your signature on each of the pages (handing depositions)?—Yes.

Look on the first page. Do you see the question there, " Have you ever been to the chemist's shop at the corner of Tollington Park and Stroud Green Road to purchase Mather's fly-papers," and the answer, " No." Do you see that?—Yes.

Is your signature immediately underneath that?—Yes, that is my signature.

Do you remember that paper being read over to you?—Yes, I do.

And your being asked whether it was correct?—Yes.

And if it was correct you signed it?—Yes.

And did you sign it?—I did.

Did you think it was correct? I am sorry to press you, but I must ask you?—Well, I did, because you see I did not purchase them because he wouldn't let me have them. That is the way I am looking at it.

Evidence for Defence.

Margaret Seddon

This is the question, "Have you ever been to the chemist's shop at the corner of Tollington Park and Stroud Green Road to purchase Mather's fly-papers," and the answer is, "No." Let me put to you, did he go on and put this further question to you," Did you, on the 6th December, 1911, go to this shop to purchase Mather's fly-papers," and you said, "Yes"?—Yes, that is right.

I will read the whole answer. "Yes. I went there, but I did not get any; the chemist was going to give them to me until I mentioned my name"?—That is right.

Were you asked who sent you for them?—Yes.

And you said you could not say whether it was your mother or Mr. Saint?—That is right.

By Mr. JUSTICE BUCKNILL—"Have you ever been to the chemist's shop at the corner of Tollington Park and Stroud Green Road to purchase Mather's fly-papers," answer "No." That is a simple enough question. Why did you say no?—Because I did not get them.

That was not the question. "Have you ever been there," that is the question?—That was put as a second question.

Do not get confused. This is the question—the learned counsel is pressing you quite fairly—this is the question in writing, "Have you ever been to the chemist's shop at the corner of Tollington Park and Stroud Green Road to purchase Mather's fly-papers," answer, "No." Why did you say you had never been there?—That was a misunderstanding.

By the ATTORNEY-GENERAL—You knew why you were being asked these questions. I am sorry to ask you, but I cannot help it. You knew very well that your father and mother were arrested at the time you were asked these questions?—Yes.

And that these questions had to do with the case against them?—Yes, I did know that.

And until the inspector put this question to you about the 6th December, you did not know that they had traced you to Price's shop, did you?—No, I didn't know.

When he put this question to you about the 6th December then it was clear to you that the police knew you had been to Price's shop, wasn't it?—I cannot say.

But it looked like it, didn't it, because they put the date. You knew you had been there on that day, didn't you?—Yes, I knew I had been there.

Of course, you knew you had gone with the two Misses Saint, who were the sisters of the solicitor who was acting for your father and mother. You knew that?—Yes.

And you knew that you had gone to Price's to purchase these papers in connection with the case against your father?—I did not know what I had gone there for.

Didn't you?—No.

Who sent you?—Mr. Saint sent me.

What did he tell you to do?—He simply told me to go in and ask for them.

To go in and ask for what?—A packet of Mather's fly-papers.

And you did?—Yes.

Trial of the Seddons.

Margaret Seddon

You were asked to sign the book, weren't you?—Yes.

Then you gave your name?—Yes.

And then, when you gave your name, he would not serve you?—No, sir.

That is right, isn't it?—Yes, sir.

You remember all that perfectly well when you were at the Police Court, didn't you?—I did, yes.

Re-examined by Mr. MARSHALL HALL—"Have you ever been to the chemist's shop at the corner of Tollington Park and Stroud Green Road to purchase Mather's fly-papers"; they do not say Price's. They only say, "The chemist's shop at the corner of Tollington Park and Stroud Green Road." Where did Inspector Ward see you?—I was in the Court waiting to get in.

In the Court where your father and mother were going to be taken to?—The North London Police Court.

Was it the day that the magistrate had a hearing?—Yes.

Where did Inspector Ward take you to?—Well, it was round to the gaoler's room.

Was anybody else in the room?—No—Inspector Cooper.

Inspector Ward and Inspector Cooper took you into this room and asked questions, and took them down in writing, and you signed it?—Yes.

Mrs. ALICE RUTT, examined by Mr. MARSHALL HALL—I live at 1 Blenheim Road, Holloway. My husband is a labourer. I was employed by Mrs. Seddon to help her in the house work and do some washing about two days a week for some years. While Miss Barrow was ill in September I went most days. I usually went about 9.30 or 10 in the morning, and I stayed till 5 or 5.30. I was once in Miss Barrow's room while she was alive, but there was no prohibition to my going into her room at any time. I remember the day I was sent for early in the morning, and came and found Miss Barrow dead. I should say it was about 7.30 when I arrived at the house. Mr. Seddon was not at home when I arrived. I went into the kitchen and had a cup of tea, and then I went upstairs into Miss Barrow's room with Mr. and Mrs. Seddon. On my way from the kitchen to Miss Barrow's room I saw Mr. Seddon in the dining-room; he had his overcoat and a muffler on, and, so far as I could see, he had just come in from the doctor's. I do not remember whether he took his coat and muffler off. Anyhow, he went upstairs with Mrs. Seddon and me. Mrs. Seddon and I washed the body and laid it out. After we laid the body out I saw Mr. Seddon open the trunk. I did not see him take anything out of the trunk. I saw him open the cash box, which is now produced; he had got it out of the trunk. When he opened the cash box there were four sovereigns and a half-sovereign in the box. Some time about April last year Mrs. Seddon told me that she had had a present of a watch and chain given to her by Miss Barrow for her birthday.

Cross-examined by Mr. MUIR—I had been working for the Seddons for seven or eight years.

Were you left in charge of the house in September last?—I don't think that I was left entirely in charge of the house; there was a servant.

274

Evidence for Defence.

Mrs. Alice Rutt

Were you left in the house?—I cannot say exactly. I have been in the house ever so many times myself. I was in the house in September last when the Seddons were away on a holiday.

Did you steal some of the things from the house?—No, I never did.

A quantity of bed linen?—No, I did not steal them.

What did you do with them?—Well, I will tell the truth. My husband was out of work. I used to wash those things at Mrs. Seddon's and take them home to iron them. I pledged these things. I intended to get them back again, but Mr. and Mrs Seddon came back from their holiday quicker than I thought they would, and I had not got them ready at home for them. They threatened to prosecute me, but I do not think they intended to do so. I rather think it was underneath the tray that I saw the £4 10s. in the cash box, but I really could not say exactly. The gold was loose, it was not in a bag.

It would be untrue to say that it was in the tray?—I could not say for certain, but I thought it was in the tray.

Re-examined by Mr. MARSHALL HALL—That is my recollection of it. Mrs. Seddon was very angry with me about these things; I had not stolen them, but my husband being out of work, I had pawned them with the intention of taking them out again.

By Mr. JUSTICE BUCKNILL—I am quite sure that the search of the trunk was made after the body was laid out. The trunk generally stood up under one of the windows, and it was not moved from there. The cash box was not taken more than a yard away from the trunk.

Nothing was put on the bed?—Well, I think it was on the bed where Mr. Seddon counted the money out—at least, it did not want much counting, because I could see what was in it as he opened it.

What was done on the bed?—Only the cash box just laid on the bed.

Mrs. LONGLEY, recalled, further cross-examined by Mr. MARSHALL HALL—My friend asked you as to whether the Seddons thought that Miss Barrow was going to die. You went upstairs, did you not?—Yes.

Were you standing outside with Mrs. Seddon?—Before Mr. Seddon came up.

Do you remember Mrs. Seddon saying something to you then?—Yes, when she brought the flannels down to warm.

Did you eventually go upstairs into the sick room where she was?—No, I did not go in; I stayed out on the landing.

But you saw Miss Barrow?—Only the leg part of her. The door opened on to the bed, and I could only see her up to her knees. I did not go into the room that time.

Did you see her at all that night?—Yes, I went in with my brother when he came home.

After Mr. Seddon came back you and Mrs. Seddon and your brother went up together?—No, Mrs. Seddon was already in the room.

You and Mr. Seddon went up?—Yes.

Looking at Miss Barrow, did you think that she was dying or anything of the kind?—Oh, dear, no; she did not look like it.

Further re-examined by the ATTORNEY-GENERAL—You were only there just a moment? You did not stop in the room?—No, only a second; the

Mrs. Longley

smell was too bad to remain in the room. I should not have gone up only through Mrs. Seddon telling me how she was. It was through a conversation whilst we were warming the flannels. She said to me, "She says she is dying." "Well," I said, "if she is dying she could not shout loud enough for you to hear her at the gate, and I do not believe it; I think she is making more of it than is necessary." Then when my brother came in, and she was telling him over the supper how troublesome she had been during the evening, he said, "What do you think of it?" and I said, "Well, what can I make of her? I think she is making more fuss than need be, because if she was a dying woman you could not possibly hear her from the top floor out at the front gate."

Then apparently there was some discussion as to whether it was probable that she was dying or not?—Well, Mrs. Seddon came and told us what she had heard, and then my brother said, "Will you come up with me and see what you think of her?" That is how I came to go into the room.

By Mr. Justice Bucknill—Did Mrs. Seddon, as far as you could see, appear genuinely anxious to know what your opinion was?—Yes, because she knew I had had a lot of sickness.

Never mind about that. Did she appear to you to be genuinely anxious about the woman's condition?—Yes.

Mr. Marshall Hall—That concludes our evidence.

The Attorney-General—That will be subject to Dr. Francis attending with his books to-morrow morning.

Mr. Marshall Hall—Certainly.

Further Proof for the Prosecution.

Dr. William Henry Willcox, recalled, further examined by the Attorney-General—There is no arsenic in white precipitate powder. I have made a further experiment with reference to the distal ends of the hair. I took some hair which was quite free from arsenic and soaked it for twenty-four hours in the blood-stained fluid from Miss Barrow's body.

By Mr. Marshall Hall—This blood-stained fluid is fluid that was in the body, and not in the coffin at all. It came from the chest. It was after the post-mortem; there was a lot of the same kind of fluid, from which I made the experiment on the second lot of hair.

Re-examination continued—There were two analyses that I made of hair; one of them was on the hair which had been soaked in the blood-stained fluid which was in the coffin, and the other was upon some mixed hair which I had obtained from the undertaker, and which had not been soaked in blood-stained fluid. The hair which is the subject of the present experiment was hair from a normal person, and was quite free from arsenic. I soaked this hair for twenty-four hours in this blood-stained fluid —the same fluid as the other hair had been soaked in. I thoroughly washed the hair that had been soaked in this experiment as completely as possible. I then broke it up to destroy the organic matter, and submitted the hair to the Marsh test. I found that the hair had absorbed an appreciable amount of arsenic. The mirror—which I have here—showed that the hair

Miss Barrow.

Further Proof for Prosecution.

Dr. William H. Willcox

had absorbed an appreciable amount of arsenic. The result of that experiment is that hair when soaked in a blood-stained fluid containing arsenic will absorb the arsenic from that fluid throughout its entire length. There is a constituent in hair which will absorb arsenic called keratine.

Will you tell us how this experiment bears upon the view which you have already expressed, that the distal ends of the hair obtained from the coffin at the second post-mortem examination must have absorbed arsenic from the blood-stained fluid?—I have no doubt that the presence of arsenic in the distal ends of the hair obtained from the coffin was due to absorption from the blood-stained fluid in which the hair lay, and which I know contained arsenic. This deposition of arsenic in the hair would occur after death, and not during life. Fourteen days elapsed between my first post-mortem and my second post-mortem. I heard Dr. Francis' evidence. From the post-mortem examination which I made I found no indication of chronic alcoholic indulgence. If chronic alcoholic indulgence had been continuing over a number of years, and up to the time of death, I should have expected to find signs of it.

Further cross-examined by Mr. MARSHALL HALL—I do not mean to say that Dr. Francis' evidence is not accurate. If there was a condition of gastritis due to abuse of alcohol in February, 1910, it is quite possible that there would be no traces of it in November, 1910, if in the interval the alcohol taking had ceased.

Cirrhosis of the liver would not be distinguishable in a post-mortem, the body having been buried all that time?—Cirrhosis of the liver would have been distinguishable; there was no cirrhosis. There were no signs of any advanced alcoholic indulgence at all.

The point I am suggesting to you is that a person who has once had gastritis brought on by abuse of alcohol, when she had an attack of diarrhœa later on the mucous membrane of the intestines is more liable to damage by the diarrhœa than would be if she had not been accustomed to drink; it would predispose her to cirrhosis of the liver?—It would depend entirely on the extent of the inflammation set up by the alcohol. There might have been one or two attacks of gastritis years ago from alcohol which would have made all the difference.

By Mr. JUSTICE BUCKNILL—This is merely common sense; it is not science. If any organ of the body is attacked by something which is not due to Nature there may be traces kept for an indefinitely long or short period, and so much must depend upon the strength of the constitution, the age of the person, and so forth, that neither you nor Solomon could give any firm opinion about it. Is that right?—Yes, the conditions vary so much.

By Mr. MARSHALL HALL—I showed Mr. Rosenheim all my results of the analysis of the distal ends of the hair. My analysis showed one-eighteenth part of arsenious acid per pound of hair in the tips.

Unless you explain that from some outside source you agree that is indicative of a course of arsenic taking over a period of time?—It might be.

But according to all the best reports, it probably is?—Well, practically no analyses of hair have been made in acute arsenical poisoning.

Do you not know that the result of the Royal Commission on the effect of arsenic on the hair was to lay it down, as far as they could lay

Trial of the Seddons.

it down, that the presence of arsenic in the distal ends of the hair was indicative of a prolonged course of arsenic taking?—Yes, that might be so.

So I understand that, as you do not think there was a prolonged course of arsenic taking in this case, you have made these further experiments to prove that a similar condition of hair can be arrived at by the soakage of the hair in blood-stained fluid containing arsenic?—Yes, I have made that experiment. That experiment would not apply to the hair which was cut off at the undertaker's shop. There was a similar amount of arsenic in the hair that was cut off at the undertaker's shop—one-twentieth of a grain per pound. The hair obtained from the undertaker's was fairly long hair, and it included, no doubt, some of the roots. My mirror here is a mirror of a 300th part of a milligramme of arsenic.

Your deduction from that is that there was one-third of a grain of arsenic per pound of hair which you soaked in this way?—Yes, there was one 300th part of a milligramme in the distal ends of the hair. It was the same size of mirror, but I took a little larger quantity of hair. There is no difference between the distal and the proximal ends except that the proximal ends might be thicker and might absorb more. It is only upon the question of what gets into the hair during life, or whilst metabolic changes are going on, that this becomes important.

Ninth Day—Wednesday, 13th March, 1912.

The Court met at 10.15 a.m.

JOHN ARTHUR FRANCIS, recalled, further cross-examined by the ATTORNEY-GENERAL—I now produce my book. In the copy which I produced in Court, which was taken from my books, there is nothing to indicate what Miss Barrow was suffering from, but the prescriptions might show a little. I have got the prescriptions in my book. What I have produced is a verbatim copy of the dates of my attendances. I never attended Miss Barrow for any alcoholic indulgence after March, 1909. In July, 1909, and December, 1909, I attended her for mere general debility; she asked me for a pick-me-up merely. She brought the boy with her at the same time, and also in February, 1910. There was nothing of any consequence the matter with her then; she wanted a tonic.

Mrs. MARGARET ANN SEDDON, prisoner, recalled, by Mr. JUSTICE BUCKNILL—The disagreements which afterwards led to my leaving my husband first began about October, 1909. At that time I was carrying on the wardrobe business. Those disputes were simply disputes about the business, the money taken by me, and that sort of thing, and the lot numbers getting off the clothes. We had a dispute, and I left him on 3rd January, I think it was, and came back five weeks afterwards.

Proof closed.

Closing Speech on behalf of F. H. Seddon.

Mr. Marshall Hall

Mr. MARSHALL HALL—May it please you, my lord. Gentlemen of th jury, it is in no spirit of affectation that I offer you my congratulations, at any rate, that we are nearing the end of this very long trial. Again, it is in no spirit of affectation that I tender you on behalf of the defence my grateful thanks for the care and attention which you have bestowed upon this case up to the present. I am sure that that care and attention will be bestowed upon it up to the end.

Gentlemen, nobody can attempt to deny that this is one of the most interesting cases that probably has ever been tried either in this building or the building of which it is a successor, and I presume you will not grudge the time that you have taken in dealing with a matter of such vital importance, because upon your verdict depends the life of one or two human beings.

The task that has been laid upon my learned friend for the Crown is no invidious task, I can assure you; and I think you will probably realise that I and my learned friends have had imposed upon us a very considerable burden, entailing a very large amount of work in order to do our duty. Fortunately, in this country it is the privilege of people who are accused of offences to avail themselves of the services of advocates to appear for them. It would be deplorable if that were not so; otherwise, with all the skill that the Crown, with its unlimited power, can command, and which is at the disposal of the prosecution, it would indeed be a very one-sided matter if the defence were not allowed to put their case before you in the way they thought best, and by the means which they thought best on behalf of the accused person.

Gentlemen, appearing as I do here with my two learned friends Mr. Dunstan and Mr. Orr on behalf of the man Seddon, it would be impossibl for me in dealing with the case to avoid making some reference to Mrs. Seddon, although technically I am not representing her; her interests are in the hands of my learned friend Mr. Rentoul. However, from time to time, it will be absolutely necessary in the course of what I have to say to you to refer to her in passing, but I am sure that you will not take anything I say as in any way attempting intentionally to injure her.

In this country the administration of criminal justice stands, I think, upon a platform which is unique. As far as I know, there is no other country in the world that has attained the perfection of criminal administration of justice that has been attained in this country. Our judicial system is above question, and fortunately we still hold in this country the doctrine, which I think has been departed from in all other countries, that every accused person is presumed to be innocent until proved guilty. The presumption in other countries, I am sorry to say, very often is, that the moment a prisoner is arrested by the police he or she is presumed to be guilty, and he is subjected to searching interrogatories, and every sort of presumption is raised against the accused person until it becomes very difficult to deal with the case on an equitable and fair basis. Now, nothing of the kind prevails in this country. I might start, and I shall probably finish, by telling you the same thing. In this case, as in every case, the presumption is that both of these people are innocent, and you should not find them guilty until that presumption is displaced by evidence. You hear people say that in Scotland, where the

Trial of the Seddons.

Mr. Marshall Hall

jurisdiction is in some way akin to our jurisdiction, there are three verdicts—there are the verdicts of "guilty," "not proven," and "not
guilty," and it is a pity we do not have three such verdicts here in this
country. We do not have them because—and I say this without fear of
contradiction; there is no possibility of argument—the two verdicts that
are known to the law here include the three verdicts which are dealt with
under the Scottish system of jurisprudence, because in this country we call
the verdict of "not proven," "not guilty." Therefore you have got
two verdicts, "guilty" and "not guilty," and unless you are satisfied
that the case is proved against the prisoner, your verdict must be a verdict
of "not guilty."

Gentlemen, what is the case for the Crown here? It has been
altered. Before the magistrates, when these prisoners were committed
for trial, there was a charge against them of murdering Miss Barrow by
administering one fatal dose of arsenic; the charge was merely the charge
of murdering Miss Barrow by the administration of one fatal dose of
arsenic, and the evidence that was given by the scientific expert who was
called for the Crown was this, "It is impossible to say what the dose
was in this case. It must have been considerably more than two grains.
I should call a moderately fatal dose something about five grains or more.
I could not form an estimate in this case. I think it would come within
my definition of a moderately large fatal dose. The death would probably
be within three days after the moderately large fatal dose. It would
probably kill within six hours—any time between six and twenty-four
hours. This would depend on the state of the patient. If there had
been gastro enteritis that would hasten the effects of the arsenic." In
opening this case, I think you will find that that was practically the theory
that was put forward by the learned Attorney-General. But the case for
the Crown consists of other matters besides strict evidence of the proof of
poisoning as against these two persons. There is a good deal of prejudice—
a great deal of prejudice, I might say—and a great deal of suspicion, and
a great deal of scientific evidence I shall have to deal with, but I submit
to you that there is not sufficient proof here that either of these two
prisoners administered a dose of arsenic to this woman with the intention
of causing her death. Originally, as I have already pointed out to you,
the charge was practically involved in the administration of one moderately
large fatal dose within three days of the death. Now, there is a shifting
of that proposition. It is suggested now that the process may have commenced upon 1st September, and continued during the whole thirteen days
that Miss Barrow was confined to her room. As I submit to you, it is
changed because of the difficulty of proving the administration
of ₜthis so-called "moderately large fatal dose." It is changed
because it is suggested that the poison was purchased on August the
26th, and was immediately begun to be used. It is also changed,
I submit to you, for another reason—because the scientific evidence in this
case as originally given was self-destructive. The presence of arsenic in
the hair of this dead woman, as far as the latest scientific knowledge (and
I submit that scientific knowledge is not infallible), so far as it goes,
shows that the administration of arsenic must have been before three days
of the death. It is in the hair which is cut off at the undertaker's shop

Closing Speech on behalf of F. H. Seddon.

Mr. Marshall Hall

on 15th September, and therefore it could not have been contaminated by any fluid exuding from the body. And the presence of that arsenic in that hair is, I submit to you, as far as any scientific evidence can be satisfactory upon the matter, conclusive evidence that there was arsenic taken by Miss Barrow independently of any dose that may have been administered or any quantity which may have been taken within a shor period of the death.

I should like to point out to you what absence of proof there is in this case. First of all, there is absolutely no proof that Mr. Seddon ever handled any arsenic. Secondly, there is no proof whatever that Mr. Seddon ever administered any arsenic. Thirdly, there is no proof tha Mr. Seddon ever knew that Mather's fly-papers contained arsenic. Fourthly there is no proof that, even if he did know it, he knew that they contained a quantity sufficient to be dangerous to human life, and that that quantity could be extracted by a simple process. I am going to submit to you tha there is not sufficient evidence before you to show that Miss Barrow did in fact die of arsenical poisoning. The evidence, in my submission to you is quite consistent with her having died of gastro-enteritis, accelerate possibly, as Dr. Willcox says, by the taking of some arsenic. Then further, there is no evidence, if she did die of arsenical poisoning, or if her death was hastened by arsenical poisoning, it was not self-administered or accidently administered, and there is no evidence of any purpose or inten tion in administering it. Lastly, I say there is not sufficient realisabl evidence which will enable you, as men of the world, to say affirmatively that you believe the quantity of arsenic calculated to be in this body— not found in the body, but calculated to be in the body—there is no sufficient evidence for you to say that those quantities are based upon sufficiently accurate basis to enable you to rely upon them absolutely Gentlemen, those are some of the points that I shall have to deal wit in this case, and I submit to you that every one of those points has be proved affirmatively to your reasonable satisfaction before you ca convict either of these prisoners of this charge of murder.

There is prejudice, gentlemen, any quantity of it. The whole thin has been overladen with prejudice. It is one of those curious cases where by reason of the fact that it is necessary in law to prove a motive for th poisoning, for the object of proving a motive, this man and this woman have been exposed to merciless cross-examination on the suggestion tha they were thieves. In no other circumstances would that have been possible. If this man had been charged with any other crime, he could never have been cross-examined, nor could the woman have been cross-examined, as my learned friend the Attorney-General frankly admitted, to carry out the suggestion that they had robbed this woman. We are not trying these people on a charge of robbery. You will have to take th greatest care in this case that you do not allow the prejudice which has been brought into it to influence you unduly. I do not say that it has been unnecessarily brought into it, because the learned Attorney-General, who is at the head of our profession, exercises a discretion which is almost judicial, and he decided that it was necessary in the interests of the cas that this prejudice should be imported into it; but I know this, and know that the learned judge will tell you also, that, whereas it may be

Trial of the Seddons.

necessary to deal with these prejudicial matters for the purpose of ascertaining whether the motive alleged is sufficient or insufficient, you cannot deal with these prejudicial matters on the question of deciding, ay or no, is this man or this woman guilty of murder? Gentlemen, on the question of motive and of opportunity, as the learned Attorney-General opened the case, I do not question it. If you are against these people, and if you think the evidence is against them, I do not say for one moment there is not sufficient evidence of opportunity, and sufficient evidence of motive, although the motive I submit to you is nothing like so strong as represented to you by the learned Attorney-General. Then I shall have to deal with the question of the cause of death. Of course, there is some evidence that I shall have to deal with having regard to the evidence of Mrs. Seddon, because that is the only evidence I am going to ask you to deal with, on the question of the purchase of fly-papers, and then, of course, I shall have to deal with the medical and scientific deductions.

Gentlemen, this is a joint charge. This is a charge against these two people. There has been no attempt from first to last to differentiate between these two. It is a charge against these two people that they practically conspired together to kill this woman, and that they killed her; and the weakness of the case against the one is the weakness against both. This is charged as a joint offence, and you cannot, under our system of criminal law, say on behalf of the Crown, " Here is some evidence. It is suspicious evidence. It points to one or two people. We cannot say which, so we will put them both in the dock, and let the jury take their choice." Of course, no man who occupies any position at the bar would ever put forward such a proposition. You are not to take your choice. You have got to deal with this case as it is launched—a charge of wilful murder against these two people—a charge that has been deliberately and advisedly made after protracted hearings, where the woman was arrested long after the arrest of the man, I presume upon some authority which was given to the police. Therefore, gentlemen, this is a joint charge, and my learned friend, I submit to you, has got to stand or fall upon this case as put forward.

I have already reminded you of what the charge is. It is a charge of murder—not a charge of larceny, or fraud, or getting the better of this woman—nothing of the sort. There is no suggestion of fraud so far as the transactions which I will compendiously call " the annuity transactions " are concerned. There is no evidence at all to suggest that those transactions were fraudulent, and there is no suggestion of fraud made on behalf of the Crown. The only possible thing in which the matter might be dangerous, so far as your honest deliberations are concerned, is that you might think that the proposition is, " We have cross-examined these people to show they are thieves. If you think they are thieves therefore you must think they are murderers." It is a fallacy. It is a proposition which will not hold water in a Court. It has nothing whatever to do with the question we have to deal with. You have heard the explanation of both these people. You have had the opportunity of judging for yourselves the demeanour of both in the witness-box, and you have heard their explanation in the matters with regard to which these suggestions have been made.

The verdict from you must be a unanimous verdict. You know that

Closing Speech on behalf of F. H. Seddon.

Mr. Marshall Hall

as well as I do. You know perfectly well in a case of this kind no man surrenders his individual opinion. There is no question of majority. Each one of you has to give a verdict upon the evidence that is brought forward, as you have sworn when you took the oath to try the case. And before you can convict this man of murder each one of you must be in this position; you must be prepared to make a statutory declaration on your oath that you believe to the best of your belief that the man has murdered Miss Barrow. If you have any reasonable doubt, such a reasonable doubt as would apply to you in business affairs, then, gentlemen, you are bound to give the accused person, not the " benefit " of that doubt, but to acquit him. As has been said by great judges over and over again, it is not a question of " the benefit of the doubt." If the result of the case is that the Crown has not removed all doubt from your minds, the prisoner is entitled, as of right, to be acquitted, and he is entitled to demand at your hands a verdict of acquittal, because the proof by the evidence has not amounted to such as would satisfy you beyond all reasonable doubt that he or she is guilty. If any one of you has any reasonable doubt upon this matter, you are entitled to give effect to it.

Gentlemen, do not sweep these two people off their feet by the waves of prejudice, and then drown them in the backwash of suspicion. Do not let this prejudice in this case as against these people—because that prejudice exists, and I will deal with it in a moment; I know the points that are prejudicing everybody's mind who has had anything to do with this case—do not let that prejudice warp your judgment and blind your eyes as to what the real issue you are now trying is. I say it again, and I say it advisedly, that the prejudice in this case overlays all the evidence until it has become a real danger to justice; it becomes a real danger that you may do an injustice, being misguided by the prejudice in which the case is involved.

I have no complaint to make whatever of the way in which the case has been put forward by the Crown, except for one thing which I have to deal with. In fact, if I may say so, without suggestion of fulsome flattery, the nature of the prosecution is always more deadly when it is conducted with the fairness with which this case has been conducted by the learned Attorney-General, and I hope it will be a model to those who practise in these Courts of the way in which prosecutions should be conducted by the Crown. But there is one incident about which I have a grievous complaint to make, and that is the incident with regard to Maggie Seddon.

Gentlemen, I submit to you it was a most unjustifiable thing on the part of Inspector Ward to subject that girl on 2nd February to the cross-examination which he subjected her to. I admit that it is perfectly proper that police officers should ask questions of witnesses for the purpose of obtaining information, but here they did not want to obtain information; they had the information; they knew the answers to both the questions they were asking. Their emissaries had watched this girl, and had seen her go to Price's shop, and they knew perfectly well that she had asked for fly-papers, and had been refused; and yet, when the police have made every effort to get Mr. Thorley to identify her, and he failed, on this day, when these two poor wretches are awaiting their trial on a charge of murder, Inspector Ward takes this child of fifteen years of age, with her

283

Trial of the Seddons.

father and mother locked up in different prisons, into the gaoler's room with another detective and asks her two questions. What for? Not to get truthful answers to them, because he knew perfectly well what the answers were; they had watched the girl, and he knew perfectly well that she had been to Price's. He does not even have the kindness to talk about Price's; he talks about "a chemist at the corner of the road." What does he ask the questions for, then? In order to get, if he possibly can, a denial, which he can use as a lie so as to discredit her when she is called into the witness-box, as she knows she will be called to contradict Thorley upon the question of purchasing the fly-papers on 26th August. Gentlemen, I say it is indefensible. There is absolutely no justification for it in our English methods. It never has been done before, and I trust it never will be done again. If Inspector Ward did not honestly want to know whether this little girl had been to Price's, what right had he to ask her these questions? He was getting up this case for the Crown, and what right had he to cross-examine this girl to get a statement from her merely for the purpose of endeavouring to get her to tell an untruth, in order to discredit her evidence, as it was discredited, when she was put into the box?

What is the result? It does injustice, gentlemen. I could not ask that girl any questions at all. I put the girl into the box, as I said, for cross-examination. It was almost immaterial, having regard to the evidence of Mrs. Seddon, whether she did in fact buy four fly-papers on 26th August, but I had cross-examined Mr. Thorley upon instructions, and I thought it was only fair, after the cross-examination of Thorley, to put the girl in the box. After my learned friend's cross-examination of Mrs. Seddon, I might have asked in re-examination whether the girl had ever told her she had bought fly-papers at Thorley's—by our rules of evidence. I refrained from doing so. I put the girl into the box for cross-examination. My learned friend never deigned to cross-examine her upon the two main issues upon which she could have been cross-examined. He merely contented himself with putting forward this bit of successful cross-examination of Ward's, whereby Ward, by his questions, had got her to say something that was not true, the first question being a carefully involved question, and the truth being told immediately afterwards in reply to the second. You are asked to disbelieve her upon that. My learned friend never asked her about the chain, and he never asked her one word about the posting of the letter, of which she knew perfectly well. It was no good my asking her. If the child had sworn right up to the hilt that the chain had been given to her, and if she had sworn that she had posted the letter, and if she had sworn that Smith had touched her on the shoulder and said "Good afternoon" at that time, when my learned friend came to cross-examine her she would have been subjected to the deadly cross-examination, "You told a lie to Inspector Ward, and you are not to be believed upon your oath."

The only thing in the case which I complain about of the conduct of my learned friend is when he turned round and said, "Why don't you call her?" It is no part of the defence to call witnesses to disprove what is not properly proved by the Crown. The proper way to prove that this girl bought fly-papers was to put the girl who is alleged to have

Closing Speech on behalf of F. H. Seddon.

Mr. Marshall Hall

bought them in the box, or, having regard to the flimsy identification that is put forward by Mr. Thorley, to have satisfied themselves that the evidence was not reliable, and therefore not have called Mr. Thorley upon it at all.

Gentlemen, I appeal to you with confidence so far as that part of this case is concerned, and I appeal to you on behalf of that child, as well as on behalf of her mother and father. It is not true that that child was ever sent to buy four packets of fly-papers on 26th August. Nor is it true that she ever went into Mr. Thorley's shop for the purpose of buying fly-papers at all. As I said before, and I say again, I am not suggesting that Mr. Thorley deliberately told you what he believes to be false—nothing of the kind. I would not make such an accusation against a perfectly independent witness of that kind. What I suggest to you is this—he could not identify the buyer of those fly-papers. He has told us when the police came to him he was unable to tell them he could identify her, and when at last on 2nd February he is taken down to the Police Court for the purpose of identifying the person, he does identify the girl he has seen on two occasions when she had been to the private door to see his daughter. He knows perfectly well that one of the people who is put up is Margaret Seddon, and having seen the picture of the girl in the illustrated papers before he went down— it almost might be a case of auto-suggestion—he identifies this girl because hers is the only face amongst the twenty people he knows. First of all, she is one of the only two children that are there, and, secondly, she is the only one of the whole lot that he has ever seen; and he has seen her upon occasions when she has been to call upon his daughter. I submit to you a more flimsy bit of evidence was never put forward in any case, leave alone in a capital case, than the suggested identification of Margaret Seddon by Mr. Thorley after an interval of something like five months. On 26th August, 1911, Mr. Thorley sells four fly-papers to a girl, as he says, and he has no entry of any sort or shape in his book of the transaction. Then on 2nd February, having in the interval told the police he cannot identify the girl, he is taken down to the Police Court where Margaret Seddon is, and then he professes to identify her, and asks you to rely upon his identification of the person who bought these four fly-papers on 26th August. Gentlemen, I say that is not evidence upon which you can rely, and there is no evidence whatever that you can rely upon that any fly-papers ever came into this house until they were purchased on the 4th or 5th September (probably Monday, the 4th) by the prisoner, Mrs. Seddon, herself.

Before we go any further, let us consider all the assumptions against Mr. Seddon. There is a strong mass of assumptions in this case which you are asked to make. First of all, you have got to assume that he had an intimate knowledge of arsenic as a poison and its effects; secondly, you have to assume that his knowledge was such that he knew that the symptoms of arsenical poisoning were identical with those of epidemic diarrhœa; thirdly, you have got to assume that he knew the quantity for a fatal dose, or the alternative theory, that he knew exactly how much to administer for a gradual dose which would ultimately terminate fatally and yet not excite suspicion during the interval of its administra--

Trial of the Seddons.

Mr. Marshall Hall

tion.   Next, you have got to assume against him that he knew that the fly-papers contained arsenic in sufficient quantity to kill an adult human being.   Next, you have got to assume that he knew how to extract the arsenic from the paper in a proper way, so as to get the maximum amount of arsenic out of each paper.   And yet (you have got to assume the negative against him now), knowing all this, you have got to assume that, having made this extract of arsenic for the purpose of poisoning this woman, he never discovered the one thing which is the characteristic of arsenic, which can be found in any book dealing with arsenic, that it has a preservative effect upon the body, and therefore from that point of view, and from the prisoner's point of view, it is one of the most dangerous poisons that can be used.   You have got to assume that he was entirely ignorant of that, or you must assume this, that he could have been such a madman as not to take advantage of the opportunity of cremating her, which would destroy all traces of his crime.   You have also to assume that he knew the symptoms of arsenical poisoning were so identical with those of epidemic diarrhœa that it was safe for a doctor to visit the patient from day to day as she was being poisoned, and that he knew that merely an inspection of the stools and vomit would not indicate the presence of poison in the patient.   Lastly, you must assume that he knew that the effect of arsenic was such that in the case of a person being poisoned by arsenic, the external appearance of the dead body was so indistinguishable from that of a person who had died from epidemic diarrhœa that it would be perfectly safe to call in a doctor in order to get a death certificate.   While I am on that, do not forget that he never asked for a death certificate.   He went to get Dr. Sworn to see the body.   Dr. Sworn said it was not necessary to see the body, and he tendered to him voluntarily the death certificate which he got.   Gentlemen, eight assumptions have to be made against these two people.   Am I not justified in saying that every one of them is a violent assumption?

Gentlemen, there is another comment.   If this man or this woman knew that arsenic was a poison, and they knew of its action, and they knew that it simulated the symptoms of epidemic diarrhœa, they must have known those symptoms could only have been simulated by the production of intense pain, intense suffering to the person to whom they were administering it; and is it conceivable that those two people could have calmly sat down together to administer poison in small doses to this woman, causing all this intense agony, from 1st September up to 13th September, when she died?   My learned friend is driven to it.   He cannot help himself by the exigencies of the case.   My learned friend asks the doctor—" It might have been that the poison had been administered from 1st September," and you are asked to find, not only that they are murderers, but murderers so cruel that they would have administered this poison in doses for a long period of time, causing this awful agony and suffering to this victim of their evil design.

All these assumptions are to be drawn against these two people because of two things.   First of all, because the male prisoner benefits by the death of the deceased in that the annuity ceases, and secondly, there is the suggestion—and here I submit that there is no evidence at all worthy of your consideration—that Miss Barrow was in possession of

286

Closing Speech on behalf of F. H. Seddon.

Mr. Marshall Hall

a large sum of money at the time of her death, and that they murdered her in order to obtain possession of it. I am not dealing with Mrs. Seddon in this case, but I cannot help commenting on that for a moment. I am not dealing with it one way or the other; I am merely dealing with the fact which is proved. It is suggested by the prosecution that Mrs. Seddon wrongfully got possession of these notes, amounting to something like £105, which she cashed, and the notes that were dealt with by the husband, £165 in all in notes, were wrongly dealt with by him. According to the prosecution, all those notes were obtained and dealt with in the lifetime of this woman. What need was there to kill her? Put it as a proposition on the very lowest possible level. What need was there to kill her if they had so successfully got from her in her lifetime, the Crown suggests wrongfully, this large sum of money? On the contrary, if it is so easy to get this money from her, there is no complaint. One of the last things we hear she said to the doctor when he suggested her going to the hospital was, " Oh, no; the Seddons will look after me better." The boy said that he was happier at the Seddons' than he ever was when he was at the Vonderahes'. It is suggested that these people murdered this woman for gold, or for notes, whatever it is alleged she had in her possession at the time of her death, and that they robbed her after death.

Let me deal with the annuity for a moment. It is not suggested even by the Crown that there was anything wrong or fraudulent in that annuity. We know that Miss Barrow was a keen woman of business: we know she was " a hard nut to crack," to use the colloquial expression that has been used. We know she fully understood and approved of the business transaction. To put the question whether she fully and entirely approved of this annuity transaction beyond all possible doubt, you have only to refer to the letters which are in existence written by Miss Barrow, which show conclusively that she not only knew of it, but that she approved of it, and thoroughly and entirely understood it. Although comment may be made that Mr. Seddon as an insurance agent has told you that he did not look upon her as a very good life, it may be you will not like a man striking what would be a good bargain for himself under the circumstances, but, after all, it does not follow that because a man thinks that it is a good investment to make from his point of view, because he does not think that the annuitant is going to live the number of years which upon the table is computed to be her expectation of life—you are not going to say that a man is a murderer because he makes a bargain which he thinks an advantageous bargain, and she wished him to make it, approved of and carried out by the formula required by the stockbrokers and the Bank of England. She is absolutely in one transaction represented by solicitors. I will only trouble you with one letter. Look at her letter of 4th January, 1911. I do want you to realise this. This letter of 4th January, 1911, was written when the whole matter has been through the solicitors' hands, and when she has disposed of her India stock.

I do not want to take up too much of your time; it will take hours if I detail all the points; and I do not want to detail them, because it is not necessary; but I will just take a summary of them, and my learned friend

Trial of the Seddons.

Mr. Marshall Hall

will correct me if I am wrong. You will remember all the formalities that had to be gone through with regard to the transfer of this stock. She wrote to the savings bank, where she was known. She asked for somebody to accompany her to identify her. She is introduced to the stockbrokers. She is taken by the stockbrokers to the Bank of England. She signs the transfer in the presence of the stockbroker, and the stock is transferred. Then comes the transaction with regard to the Buck's Head. First of all, some attempts are made to deal with it without solicitors, an inoperative document is drawn up which is destroyed, and that is raked up here, I do not know why—I do not know what it has got to do with the case. It is raked up in order to make some suggestion or other, I suppose; but still the document was absolutely inoperative, and was destroyed. Later on she was told she must consult a solicitor. A separate solicitor is instructed on her behalf, and a separate solicitor appears for her and advises her. After all this is done, the climax of it is on 4th January, 1911, when she writes this letter. I will read every word of it to you—" Re the Buck's Head public-house, 202 High Street, N.W., and the hairdresser's shop adjoining, No. 1 Buck Street, N.W.— Mr. Keeble, Messrs. Russell & Sons, solicitors, 59 Coleman Street, E.C.— Dear Sir,—I regret I was unable to call upon you to-day with Mr. Seddon as requested by your letter to him of the 3rd instant. However, I understand from him that you are preparing a deed of conveyance of these properties to Mr. Frederick Henry Seddon entitling him to receive rents and take over liabilities and responsibilities from Quarter Day, 25th December last, in consideration of a life annuity of £52 per annum payable to me by him. These arrangements I am quite agreeable to, and will arrange to be at home between 3 and 4 p.m. on Friday next to meet you to sign the deed of conveyance.—Yours faithfully, Eliza Mary Barrow.'' There is no suggestion that that letter is anything but a perfectly honest and straightforward letter, and that letter is written from beginning to end in her own handwriting. I think the address, " 63 Tollington Park,'' is a printed address, but with that exception the whole of that letter is a letter written by this woman. This woman was a shrewd woman, a business woman, and " a hard nut to crack,'' yet there she is by that letter of 4th January divesting herself of practically the biggest items of property she possesses. I do not know why we should not draw some assumption in the man's favour. Everything is presumed to be in favour of an accused person. It may be that she realised the great business capacity of that man; it may be she realised, " Here is a man who has made his way in his own profession, who has climbed up from the lowest beginning to one of the highest positions that an insurance company can offer him, and he is a shrewd man of business,'' and she trusts him absolutely, as demonstrated. Do not get away from this—do let us remember this. Let us go back to the time before any question of the taint of murder arose. On 4th January she trusts this man implicitly. She has handed over to him this stock without any security except a memorandum which he gave her, saying he was going to give her £72 per annum—a document which is lost. With the exception of that memorandum in the month of October, when she executed a transfer to him of the East India stock, by which he acknowledged to give her £72

288

Closing Speech on behalf ot F. H. Seddon.

Mr. Marshall Hall

per annum for her life, she had no sort of security of any sort or shape for this £1519, which was the net proceeds of this particular stock.

Gentlemen, do consider this for a moment. This man who is no called a thief, a perjurer, and a murderer, and everything else that th law can call him, or suggest that he is, in the month of October is gettin possession of this stock, which he could the next day if he so pleased (h has got the transfer, and it is absolutely in his own name) have sold an done whatever he liked with the money. He might have taken it an thrown it into the Thames for all the law could interfere with him. Ye what does he do? He never deals with the transfer at all. He neve begins to realise the money until after the whole arrangement is complete when the lawyers have completed the transfer of the Buck's Head, an the whole question of the annuity has been finally and definitely settled The annuity becomes payable in advance in the month of January, an he regularly paid it for every month of that year. His receipts prov that. It is only then that he deals with this stock. How does he dea with it? Does he deal with it like a thief or a dishonest man? Ho does he deal with it? He acts as a competent, shrewd, sharp man o business. He says, "Here is an investment which has depreciate largely." Miss Barrow was worried about it. She told him that i had cost—and we know it had cost—£1720, and it sold for £1519, and therefore £200 of her money absolutely ran away in the few years sh held that stock; £200 of her capital has gone. She is alarmed. Th whole world was alarmed about that time. Anybody holding stocks shares, and securities on land of any sort or shape was alarmed. I there a man in this country who has not been alarmed during the past tw years with regard to the security of his tenure and the price of Consols? Is there any man or woman who has not been properly alarmed as to the financial condition of this country? This woman is alarmed. She has seen £200 of her money run away. She has only got $3\frac{1}{2}$ per cent.; she bought for $108\frac{5}{8}$ths, and therefore she is only getting that. She has seen her capital running away, and therefore she is naturally anxious, and seeing that this man is a shrewd man she hands it over to him. What does he do with it? He absolutely invests it in the purchase of leasehold property bringing in a large yearly rental, so that out of that he can make perfectly certain of being able to pay Miss Barrow the annuity which he has covenanted to pay, and which will have to be paid if he dies and she survives him, and which will also provide the sinking fund whereby he can at the end of the time reinstate the value of those leaseholds when they have expired and run out. You cannot attack these transactions. They may have been foolish on the part of the lady. You may think it was foolish of her not to go to the Post Office or to an insurance company and buy Government annuities or insurance office annuities. If you go to an insurance office to-morrow and want to insure your life they would look at you, and say, "You are a very bad life, and we will put you into the fourth or fifth class, and charge you double or treble premiums." But if you go the next morning and say, "I want to buy an annuity," you have to buy the annuity at the biggest rate. It may be that this man did that with this woman, and thought that if he could get this investment it was a good investment.

Trial of the Seddons.

Mr. Marshall Hall

He is a north countryman, a thorough man of business, and not a man of sentiment. I am not asking for any sentimental pity, or anything of that kind. This man may have thought this was a good investment, and she may have thought the same for two reasons. First of all, the insurance office or the Post Office only pay after a period of six months, and she wanted her money at once; and, secondly, if she was paid it weekly she only got her first payment at the end of six months, and there would be six months without any interest at all. In addition to that, she got £26 more over and above what she would get from the Post Office or insurance office, because their rates are practically identical. Yet it is because of this transaction this prosecution must have been originally launched. The Crown says, "Here is a man who is granting an annuity to a woman in return for cash which she has paid him, and she dies within twelve months. The presumption is that he murdered her because he was interested in avoiding the payment of the annuity for the rest of her natural life. Upon her death this man benefits to the extent of £2000." He does nothing of the kind. Supposing this woman continued to live in this house. It is a large house, and it pleased her. She was to have had the rooms rent free. She would have had to pay some 7s. a week for the girl for her work. There would also have been the boy's keep, amounting to 13s. a week if she died—13s. for the boy and 7s. for Maggie makes 20s. All he had to pay her was £2 8s. a week; so the total benefit to this man upon her death was £1 8s. a week. People do not commit murders for £1 8s. a week. You have got to consider what this man is. Here is a man of unblemished character. If there is anything sure about this case it is the fact that he is a man of unblemished character. There is nothing whatever against him. He has been successful in his business. He has won the admiration of the people for whom he worked, and he is put into one of the finest positions which they have to offer. He has been twenty-one years in the same employ, and he is getting seven guineas a week by way of salary and commission. He is a man who for his class of life is well to do. He has got some money put by; he has got some Cardiff stock.

The ATTORNEY-GENERAL—£5 10s., not seven guineas.

Mr. JUSTICE BUCKNILL—£5 6s.

Mr. MARSHALL HALL—£5 15s., my lord, and then there were some other matters. He was drawing interest from his stock, and he has got other property. He is practically living rent free. He has made his will. From one interest and another we will say that he was getting over £6 a week—£300 a year. For a man in that position that is a very good and substantial income. There are instances on record where people have been murdered for coppers. It cannot be suggested that a man in that position is going to murder a woman with all the attendant risks for £1 8s. a week. That is the assumption. Is it a more violent assumption than all these eight assumptions against him, or the assumption I submit to you, that he did not murder her, and that he had no real and sufficient motive to murder her? Look at Miss Barrow. We know perfectly well that she was a difficult woman to deal with on the question of business. That is what we are told; yet we know perfectly well that she did deal with him, and she dealt with him in the way which

Closing Speech on behalf of F. H. Seddon.

Mr. Marshall Hall

her own letters indicate, and which the documents in existence corroborate up to the hilt.

Let us now take the facts in chronological order so far as they are material in this case. The first date that I refer to is a date towards the end of 1909. Mr. Seddon, who has on his wife's behalf financed a wardrobe business in Seven Sisters Road, is doing quite a good turnover, because, so far as they are available, the books corroborate it. The books are at your disposal, and you can see them for yourselves. Out of an investment of something like £40 he makes 100 per cent. in the course of eight weeks. He has some money which he has put into the business to finance it, and he has made this profit. Then comes this trouble. You have heard it again this morning; I was going to allude to it, of course. In the month of November there was some trouble with regard to business matters between himself and his wife, which, unfortunately, culminated in a quarrel, and eventually in a separation. On 6th January she leaves him for a period of five weeks, and, as he said, "I tore up the books; I was angry; I thought of putting them at the back of the fire; I did not put them at the back of the fire; I left them in the house." When Inspector Ward came to examine the house he saw them, and he could have made any comments on them, which he did not; therefore we are entitled to assume that those books, as far as they are not in any way impeached by the prosecution, are correct. Was that all? Are you going to entirely disregard the evidence here? I do not think, as far as I can judge from the cross-examination, that you are asked to disbelieve either Naylor, or Wilson, or Wainwright, but if Naylor, Wilson, and Wainwright are right in the month of November, or October, 1909——

The ATTORNEY-GENERAL—July, 1909.

Mr. MARSHALL HALL—It was in the middle of 1909—some time in 1909—he had in his possession a bag containing a very considerable amount of gold, put at something between £130 and £150—sworn to by one of these men, who is a man of business, another who is a man in trade, and another a Post Office employee—all people of position, presumed to be respectable men whose characters are unimpeachable. They swear positively to Mr. Seddon having possession of this money on the night they saw it. There is a slight discrepancy as to whether Seddon did or did not say he had £200, but Seddon said, "If I did, all I said was 'Here is a couple of hundred pounds. If you know of any wardrobe stock going, I have a couple of hundred pounds to buy it with.'" Mr. Seddon said, "If I did say it, it would not have been strictly true; I had not got a couple of hundred pounds, but I had £150." He sold the business for £30. That is not challenged. He "gave it away," to use his own expression. That brings it up to £180. Mr. Wainwright, who is obviously a respectable man, a man of position, a man who had got a business, and a man who it cannot be suggested had any motive or interest in this case, comes along and tells you a very substantial story indeed. What is it? He said, "I advised Seddon to buy some property, to buy this house at 63 Tollington Park. The price was rather more than he wanted to give, but I eventually got the vendor down to £320." There was a deposit to be paid. The deposit was £30, 10 per cent., but Seddon, who was no fool, pointed out the fact that there was a forfeiture clause, and he did not like the for-

Trial of the Seddons.

feiture clause in the lease, and therefore he said, "I will not pay you £30, I will only give you half that deposit." Then Mr. Wainwright properly observed, "I could not get over the forfeiture clause. There it was, and Mr. Seddon was perfectly right. I said, 'Very well, let us make it £15 instead of £30.' He agreed to take that, and he produced £15 in gold out of a bag containing a large sum of gold. I said, 'I do not want gold. . Give me a cheque.' I thought he was a man of substance and position, and I was perfectly prepared to take his cheque. He said, 'If you don't mind I don't,' and he gave me a cheque." Then this gentleman, who, I suppose, was not altogether disinterested (I do not believe many actions in this world are purely disinterested actions; they are very rare) gave him the advice which meant a little business to himself. Seddon said, "I have got enough money to pay for this house, £320"; but Mr. Wainwright said, "Do not pay for it; it is a very good time to buy house property; there is a great slump in house property at this time; the Budget has just come through, and people are frightened about house property. Now is the time. Do not get rid of your ready money." You cannot buy house property unless you put down some ready money, as you know. The more you leave on mortgage the more ready money you will have to distribute over a series of properties. He said, "Get a mortgage for the £220." "Well," says Seddon, "it is rather a good idea. If you have got any more property you might let me know, and I will find the money to buy it and get mortgages." If property is going up, he stands to win. I do not say it offensively, but I suggest to you that no doubt Mr. Wainwright would get some small fee or commission. It is his business to sell properties, and therefore he would get commission. I am told the date is 3rd September, 1909.

Mr. Justice Bucknill—"On 3rd September I called on Seddon."

Mr. Marshall Hall—Yes, 3rd September, 1909. On 3rd September we get this man with enough money in the house to pay in cash for this house, which has cost him £320, and we know also that he had at any rate £300 of Cardiff stock after he had taken out the actual £100 which he took out for the purpose of eventually paying the purchase price of the house, less the mortgage. You are not to strain points against this man. That is not what you are here for. We are none of us here to strain points against him. We have got to take everything in his favour. Here we have independent evidence, before any question of motive or shady transactions arises, the specific statements of three creditable witnesses, that this man was possessed of something like £200 in gold at the end of the year 1909. What does he tell you? I do want you to give your careful attention to this. He said, "I accepted the position; I agreed; and I thought of buying other property. Mr. Wainwright submitted other properties to me, but I did not care for them, and therefore I did not accept them, but I was eventually compelled to take possession of 63 Tollington Park. I had originally bought it to let it. I advertised for a tenant. I could not get a tenant, and, not having got a tenant, I could not afford to let that money lie idle and pay two rents, as I was paying rent in Seven Sisters Road, so I lived at 63 Tollington Park, and saved money by so doing." As you see, it is admitted he was allowed to charge a certain proportion of the rental value of 63 Tollington Park for the office premises in the

Closing Speech on behalf of F. H. Seddon.

Mr. Marshall Hall

basement which he used for the company, so that was a very advantageous business for him. The basement pays itself, because it goes *qua* rent, but he also lets the other part of the house, not to Miss Barrow, but some person before. The man is in a very good position. He is drawing money from the insurance company, he has got interest on the balance of the Cardiff stock, he has got money in the savings bank, and he has got this £200 in gold. We cannot judge of a man by the highly-trained intellects which some possess. We have got to deal with this man in his own way of looking at life, and the way he looked at his position was this, " I am earning £5 15s. a week. I have got a little money coming in from the Cardiff stock. I have got a certain amount of ready money in hand, some portion of which I am using for trading purposes in the wardrobe business, and if an opportunity turns up I can make a bargain with it; but that is all very well when I am alive. Suppose something happens to me, my wife has got five children, amongst whom is a little baby. She has to be considered. If I die my wife will be in this position. She will have this house mortgaged to the tune of £120, and she will either have to pay interest on that mortgage or there may be a clause that on the death of the mortgagor the mortgage could be called in." Apparently, so long as he lived, the mortgage could not be called in within a certain number of years, but we do not know whether in the event of his death the mortgage might not at once be called in, because every mortgage contains a personal covenant, and the personal covenant in this mortgage is of considerable value (the man is earning £5 15s. a week), which becomes valueless when the person dies. The legal personal representative of Mr. Seddon would, of course, have only had the house and the balance of the few hundreds. Therefore he says this, " I did not want my wife to be in that position, so I will put £200 in the house." He has got two safes; he has a second safe which he has brought there. He used the two. He puts £100 in one safe and £120 in the other safe, and he says, " I put that there as a provision against my death, and my wife suddenly being called upon either to pay off the mortgage or to part possession of the house." My learned friend, with that knowledge of finance which most of us possess in a minor or lesser degree, points out, why not put it into the savings bank and get 2½ per cent.? How long would it take the wife to get it as the legal personal representative? I do not know. There is no evidence of it. You can only use your own knowledge on the subject. Seddon says, " That was not good enough for me. I wanted it absolutely available for my wife." Do you disbelieve him? Why should you? You have had positive evidence that at the end of 1909 he had close upon £300 in the house. I suggest to you that you have indisputable evidence, which you cannot attack, that he certainly had £200 in the month of November, 1909, in gold, which was all available. Gentlemen, he has got this money in the house in gold. There is his position.

Now, he loses his tenant, and Miss Barrow comes along. We know very little about her. We do know that she was a woman of queer temper. One of the Vonderahes said that she spat in her face. Another one said that she was very irritable. Another one said she was " a ' hard nut ' to crack on the question of money." On the evidence of Dr. Francis we know that she was a woman of curious temperament. From any point of view she

Trial of the Seddons.

Mr. Marshall Hall

had curious habits with regard to money. We know she did have £165 in notes. That is in evidence. She also had a deposit account at the savings bank. When she on 19th June, 1911, goes to the savings bank she draws out £216 in gold, and will not take it in notes. We do know from Dr. Francis that up to some time in March, 1909, she had been over-indulging in strong alcohol, and had severe attacks of gastritis, from which, I suggest to you, she eventually died. She had attacks of gastritis, which is inflammation of the gastric region, brought on by the abuse of strong intoxicants, and that would predispose her to be more susceptible to an attack of gastro-enteritis when gastro-enteritis in fact came on; I do not put it higher than that.

There is a little more we know about her. She at first lived with some people named Grant, and Mr. and Mrs. Grant had both died, and had left two children entirely unprovided for. Mr. Hook was the brother of Mrs. Grant, and he admitted that Mrs. Grant was also an alcoholic subject who had drunk to excess, and, in fact, that was more or less the cause of her death. We know, as it very often happens, when the evil influence of Mrs. Grant was removed, possibly Miss Barrow resumed her normal condition. It is common knowledge, and everybody knows, that one person will often incite and encourage another person to drink. Anyhow, Miss Barrow came as tenant with the boy Ernie Grant. We can realise her taking a fancy to this child, because he was the child of these unfortunate people, the two Grants. She brought with her the two people named Hook. As to Hook, we know nothing except what he has told us. He was a man of no means at all, and he was entirely dependent upon Miss Barrow for his living, and it was a matter of vital importance that he should live rent free and be provided for at her expense. Anyhow, Miss Barrow does provide for them, and brings the husband and wife to the Seddon's house. The only return for this living rent and board free is that Mrs. Hook is to teach Miss Barrow how to cook. This is Hook's story. I am not putting him forward as a witness of credibility, and I should have thought that the same reason which operated upon the prosecution not calling Margaret Seddon would have also operated upon them not to call a man of Hook's class. The class of man Hook is does not depend upon hearsay evidence. You heard the class of man he was when he tried to quibble with me when I slipped out "Mrs. Barrow" instead of "Miss Barrow" in the question. He said, "No, obviously untrue," and when I said that I meant "Miss Barrow," he said, "Oh, yes, Miss Barrow." That is the sort of man you have got to deal with. You remember the avidity with which he recognised a watch which had been absolutely altered. This woman's watch had had a cracked white face, but he instantly recognised it with the gold face. Then he said he did not look at the face; he did not turn it over; and then he reluctantly told you he did look at the face. I submit to you that he is an absolutely unreliable witness. We have not got much to test him on. We have not got the Treasury funds at our back. We cannot employ all the scientists and analysts to come and give evidence upon scientific matters. We cannot employ detectives to watch who comes to buy fly-papers. We have got to do what we can under the conditions which exist, and therefore we have no opportunity of

Closing Speech on behalf of F. H. Seddon.

Mr. Marshall Hall

tracing Mr. Hook's career backwards to its early stage. It may be if we could we would find out something to Mr. Hook's discredit. Anyhow, we have not. There is nothing to know, but we have got to know that wherever he is met he has been contradicted. Upon his evidence depends this preposterous statement that this woman had £380, besides a bundle of notes, in a little tin cash box, when she came to this house in July, 1910. He is very positive in his evidence; he says, "I helped to move. Creek helped me. I carried that box in a bag in my hand at 5 o'clock when I delivered it to her. We never had a drink. We never stopped and had a drink. There was no public-house on the way. The cart was never stopped." I had him back, and asked him, "Did you have a drink before you started, or at the moment of starting?" and he said, "No, we never had a drink. Miss Barrow never held the horse's head." Creek is called. He is a perfectly respectable man. He may not be a rich man, and he may not have the position that some other people have, but he is an honest, hard-working man at his particular trade. He says that this was the only afternoon on which he ever remembers moving anybody from Evershot Road to Tollington Park, and that that took place between 12 and 3, and the moving was all over at 3. "I swear that Hook never had anything in his hand. He never carried a bag in his hand," and, more than that, he says, "I am perfectly positive that we did have a drink while Miss Barrow held the horse's head."

I submit to you, Hook is lying, and yet you are asked to believe Hook upon the vital question as to whether this lady had £400 in gold and a bundle of notes, which she took into that house. It is a very small matter, but on the point of time, you will remember Mrs. Vonderahe corroborated what Creek said. She said that it was all over at 3 o'clock at the latest, yet, when I put it to Hook, he persisted in 5 o'clock; I gave him 12 to 3, but he persisted in his 5 o'clock. He had come to tell one story, and he did not mean to alter it. Whether it was true or not was a matter, I submit to you, of absolute indifference to him. He told his story. He had not been heard of for some time, and he came upon the scene, and he was going to tell his story for what it was worth. It may be that his memory was entirely faulty, but if it were faulty upon one subject it would be faulty upon another, I suggest to you.

What happens when he gets into the house? It is to Hook's interest to stop; he admits that. What happens? Well, gentlemen, as I say, we have not got the actual letter that Miss Barrow wrote to him, but he admits that it was very much in this form—"Mr. Hook, as you and your wife have treated me so badly, I must now inform you of my intention to part with you. I wish you to leave my rooms at once, and I desire to remain here without you and your wife.—Yours, Eliza Mary Barrow." You would think that a man and his wife, who are entirely dependent upon this woman, and who are there as her guests would have, at any rate, recognised her right to say, "I do not want you any more— I want to terminate this arrangement; there is no arrangement for any definite time," and you would think that they would, at any rate, treat her with some courtesy. She was his old sweetheart, you know. He had known her for many, many years. What is his answer? Fortunately, we have got his answer; it is exhibit 24. "Miss Barrow, as

Trial of the Seddons.

Mr. Marshall Hall

you are so impudent to send the letter to hand, I wish to inform you that I shall require the return of my late mother's and sister's furniture, and the expense of my moving here and away.—Yours, D. B. Hook." What does that mean? He had got his sister's furniture, but he had no right to sell it, as he admits he sold it to her, as it did not belong to him. He would not be the next-of-kin, but he had sold her the furniture and taken a receipt for it. He is not a very creditable person to have anything to do with. What is he saying to her, "If you are going to get rid of me I am going to make myself disagreeable. I am going to have all the furniture, and you will be in a nice hole then—I am going to take away the furniture that belonged to my mother and sister." And then he goes on to add finally the postscript—just as a woman would do—the final threat—"I shall have to take Ernie with me, as it is not safe to leave him with you." Why was not it safe to leave him with her? What do we know of Miss Barrow? We do know that the boy said in his evidence that she once threatened to jump out of the window because he had done something that annoyed her, and that is probably true, but what had Miss Barrow done to Hook that Hook should dare to say, "It is not safe to leave Ernie with you?" Of course, it is a veiled threat. He knew he could get at the poor woman that way. He knew he could hurt her more by taking the child, and he says, "If you are going to get rid of me I shall take the furniture, and I shall take Ernie. Where will you be then?"

The threat is not efficacious, and Miss Barrow is not frightened by it. She persists in getting rid of him. She goes to Seddon, and she says to Seddon, "I cannot get rid of this man, you must get rid of him for me. I am your tenant. Get rid of him." Seddon thereupon writes him that letter, and gives him a notice on 9th August—"Dear Sir,—As due notice has been given you, and duly expired, I now find it necessary to inform you that you are no longer entitled to remain on my premises," &c. Hook says to Mr. Seddon he will not go in twenty-four hours, and there is an angry scene between them, and he insults him. He has only been there ten days at the outside. "I told him to his face, 'It is her money you are after.'" What ground had he for making such a monstrous suggestion? There was absolutely nothing, except that Mr. Seddon had backed up Miss Barrow in her desire to get rid of this man, who, according to the boy's evidence, had taken the boy and his own wife out on that Sunday, leaving her crying. What possible foundation was there for Hook making that suggestion, "I told him it's her money you are after. It would take a regiment like you to get her money out of her." He was grossly impudent to this man who, at any rate, was his landlord. This man was entirely dependent upon the charity of the woman with whom he was living.

Has it occurred to you—I know it has in this case—that Hook's conduct was absolutely inexcusable? If Hook was an honest and genuine man, and he meant what he said, and it was not mere vulgar abuse, and he thought Mr. Seddon was after her money, and it was not safe for the boy to be with her there, and Mr. Seddon was going to steal her money, and that she had in her possession £400 in gold, besides a large sum in notes, he knew where the Vonderahes lived, and he knew where the other

296

Closing Speech on behalf of F. H. Seddon.

Mr. Marshall Hall

relations were, and he could have given some information to them. Yet, when he is turned out of that house, as he is, because he will not go, in August, 1910, he never makes any sign of any sort or shape. So far as Miss Barrow is concerned, he might have been dead. He never turned up again upon the scene until 25th November, when, reading in a newspaper that there was an inquest upon Miss Barrow, and that she had drawn £216 in gold, he comes upon the scene and makes a statement to the police. Gentlemen, I say that evidence is absolutely unreliable, and it is absolutely unworthy of any credence of any sort or shape, and I ask you to disregard it entirely, because you cannot possibly rely upon it.

Gentlemen, as far as I know, nothing took place in August or September. Then we come to October, when the first negotiation took place with regard to the annuity. In October we get the negotiations with regard to the India stock. I think I have already dealt with them. I have already pointed out, and I am not going to repeat it, that she got what she herself wanted—an annuity. I will just go over the figures for one moment as to what annuity he granted for her own satisfaction. He granted her £72 and £52 per annum, and, in addition to that, there was £31 4s. made up of 12s. a week for the rent. So that you see the total amount that he had to pay under the annuity was £155 4s. Against that, what he received was this. He received £1519 16s., the proceeds of the East India stock, and he received a figure, which you must take as genuine in this case, because there has been no contradiction of it, £706, which was the then value of the Buck's Head property, according to the valuation which was put in in the case. Therefore he received £1519 16s. and £706. As against that he had to pay some £38 14s. for costs and incidental expenses, so the net amount he received was £2187 2s. Now, I have made a calculation, and I have no doubt it will be checked if it is not accurate. For that sum, in the Post Office, in the event of death no payment, and the first payment after six months, which is a very important consideration in dealing with the value of an annuity, she would be able to purchase an annuity of £128. So, you see, she benefits to the extent of £27 per annum by the purchase of an annuity in this way, assuming the annuity she is paid is secured. The question of security, with all deference to my learned friend the Attorney-General, is entirely immaterial so long as the annuity is paid. I quite agree that for the purpose of valuing an annuity for the purpose of sale it would make a great deal of difference as to who was the guarantor of the annuity; but, for the purpose of merely paying the value of the annuity to the annuitant, it makes no difference, because, so long as the instalments are duly and punctually paid, she has no claim or remedy against the person who has granted the annuity to her. Seddon, honestly and honourably, carried out his obligation, and she got £27 per annum more than she would have got under any other scheme of annuity through the Post Office or through a first-class insurance office. My learned friend Mr. Dunstan reminds me that as to £52 of an annuity she was absolutely secured upon the property. As to the £72, I agree she is entirely dependent upon the honour of Mr. Seddon. As a proof, however, of his honourable intentions, he does not invest this money in some "wild-cat" securities, or anything of that kind, with a view to making a large profit,

Trial of the Seddons.

but he bought substantial house property, which could not run away. I say that, although it may have been theoretically a bad security for this woman, he appears to have been behaving honourably, as far as he was concerned, and she benefited to the extent of £30.

One little item comes in here. It is a very small item, but sometimes the slightest straw shows the way the wind blows. He tells you he had paid £4 13s. for costs. She would not pay them, as she objected very much to solicitors—an objection which is shared by a great many people; nobody likes the law, whatever branch of the law one deals with; there is a great prejudice against it. I am not suggesting it is any insane view on her part, but she said, "I will not pay any costs," and he has to pay the costs. In addition to the costs which he had paid, which were the proper costs of the conveyance, he had to pay a sum of £4 13s. for the costs of the solicitor who represented her. He asked her to pay it, and she said, "No, she would not pay it," but she gave him a small diamond ring. I merely asked, in the dark, as to the value of it, when the jeweller was in the box, and he said, "I would give £4 for it myself"; therefore you may assume that it is worth something between £4 and £5 for the purpose of purchasing. That is merely a question of a diamond ring which she gave him for having paid her costs over and above the costs which she had properly incurred. As I say, that is a small amount, but it shows he was not robbing the woman. We are not experts or judges of what diamond rings are worth, and when we hear of a diamond ring we think it is worth a lot of money, whereas the jeweller, who is an expert, says that it is worth £4 or £5 to buy. That is the transaction, as far as we know, which took place in October. The stock was transferred, and then the annuity was deferred until the whole matter could be settled up with regard to the Buck's Head property. Upon the completion of the Buck's Head property transfer in January, 1911, the annuity was paid promptly from that time. I do not suppose for a moment that my learned friend will attempt to question those receipts, for the very simple reason that he has made use of them in his argument to show that Miss Barrow had more money in the house. My learned friend cannot have it both ways, and he cannot say they are bogus receipts. On the face of them they are all obviously genuine, and not to be questioned. Any way, they are not questioned, and therefore I am entitled to say that, so far as the bargain was concerned, it was honourably carried out until the month of September, when she died.

There is one tiny bit of evidence in this case which I want to deal with, now I think of it. You will remember the curious little bit of evidence that Ernie Grant gave, which, as far as I know, had not been given before; I may be wrong about that; I do not profess to have every minute detail of this case in my head at this minute. As far as I know, Ernie Grant for the first time said she used to go down and sometimes come up with gold. He said he thought she came up with about £3 in gold. That is a curious point. I am not suggesting that those were the annuity payments at all. I am suggesting that those were occasions when she paid her rent by a bank note, and came up with the change of a bank note, £4 8s., or whatever it was. Those four or five occasions——

Closing Speech on behalf of F. H. Seddon.

Mr. Marshall Hall

The ATTORNEY-GENERAL—He did not say four or five.

Mr. MARSHALL HALL—Well, three or four.

The ATTORNEY-GENERAL—He said "Sometimes three pieces of gold."

Mr. MARSHALL HALL—You cannot expect the boy to be exactly accurate. I suggest to you it is an absolute corroboration of the boy's story, having regard to Mr. Seddon's story about this £5 note. With regard to the other £5 note he is absolutely corroborated, because he has said, though the learned Attorney-General was not actually in the position to admit the justice of the statement, that he had made inquiries with regard to the other £5. I have dealt with one, and, with regard to the other £5 note, he admittedly received it, and he said, "That was given to me because I paid the Buck's Head rent." You heard the gentleman yesterday who told you that the rent was nearly always paid in postal orders. In this particular case it was paid by cheque. There is the entry in Seddon's bank book of a cheque having been paid upon that date. It is admitted that he did pay that, and he took a £5 note and £4 in gold from her. There are six notes altogether which have been dealt with by Mr. Seddon. Five of them were paid into his bank as part of a payment in which he made, and which he explained to you as money he had received which he had changed for gold, and the other, the sixth note, he paid in to make up the cheque for £9 8s. which he drew to pay for the ground rent of the Buck's Head.

There is just the little matter I want to mention in 1910, because I think it is material when you come to consider this case. You must remember that in the month of August, 1910, Miss Barrow was suffering from some complaint, which was congestion of the liver, or some stomach complaint which produced this gastric disturbance. She was taken by Mrs. Seddon to Dr. Paul, who is a strange doctor, and therefore in no way a person who was known to Mrs. Seddon. That is a matter I do not think ought to be lost sight of. When questions are put to Mrs. Seddon with regard to what took place towards the end of the year 1910 and the beginning of the year 1911, you have to remember that she was in an interesting condition, and that early in January a baby was born, and for some little time, at any rate, she would not know what was going on. That would account for her ignorance with regard to certain matters that have been dealt with in March, 1911, after Miss Barrow comes to the house.

In April that extraordinary lady, Miss Mary Chater comes. You have seen her in the box. You are the judges of the demeanour of people. You have seen this woman. There she is—a woman earning 5s. a week as a general servant, insisting upon dressing herself as a hospital nurse. When not expecting to be called on the second day, she certainly came without her uniform, but in case she might be called upon she appeared in uniform yesterday. She is a woman who had had I do not know how many situations, and I suggest to you she is absolutely of a very eccentric disposition. I put to her questions in cross-examination, and, as my lord pointed out, I was entirely bound by her answers, because they were questions as to her credit. I cannot call a witness to say that her brother has been twenty years in an asylum, and that her late employer stated she was off her head. She denies that, and I cannot call evidence to disprove it. You saw her face, and you saw her demeanour. You were nearer to

Trial of the Seddons.

her than I, and I venture to think you have probably no doubt whatever with regard to her true mental condition. I am only saying that for the moment; I am going to say something more presently.

About this time, it is admitted, Miss Barrow went to a funeral at the Vonderahe's house. There, again, there was a quibble. When I said to Mr. Vonderahe "funeral at your house?" he said, "Not at my house—from some other place." Miss Barrow complained of the way she had been treated by the Vonderahes, and, evidently burning under the feeling of the injustice which had been inflicted upon her on 27th March of that year, she writes this letter to Mr. Seddon:—"Dear Mr. Seddon, my only nearest relatives living are first cousins," &c., &c. (reading down to the words), "Yours sincerely, Eliza Mary Barrow."* So, again, there is no possibility of a question that that letter is a letter in the handwriting of Miss Barrow, and obviously from the way in which it is worded a perfectly voluntary document written by Miss Barrow, and obviously meant by Miss Barrow to be considered tantamount to a will. That is of some importance when we come to consider the subsequent events which took place on 11th September. Undoubtedly Miss Barrow, from the very phraseology of that document, considered that it had all the effect of a will, the fact being that she did not wish her relatives to receive anything whatever at her death, as they had treated her badly. The fact that she had been to this funeral started the subject of a will. No doubt death does make us realise our own possible death; and there is that suggestion which accounts for the writing of that letter at that otherwise isolated period. That document, as I say, is in existence, and there is no suggestion of any sort of shape made against Mr. Seddon in respect of that.

The next date of any importance is 30th May, 1911. On 30th May, 1911, beyond all question there was sent to the Surveyor of Income Tax by Miss Barrow a document which we have got. It is in Miss Barrow's handwriting again. Gentlemen, it is of the most vital importance to remember that fact. "This is to certify," &c., &c. (reading down to the words), "Eliza Mary Barrow." So you see she gave a notice to the Inland Revenue people that she was in receipt of this annuity, and this would be always valuable in the event of Seddon's death, or Seddon disputing it, as it created evidence of some sort in the hands of the Inland Revenue people to show that this annuity was in existence, and was a valid charge which was being carried out. Gentlemen, I think I may fairly say that at that point I can dismiss the annuity question; I need not argue or deal with the annuity question any more. First of all, it is not attacked here, and therefore I am entitled to say, as we lawyers say, "Everything is presumed to be rightly carried out," and therefore we must presume everything was rightly carried out, because the law does not inquire into a bargain where the adequacy of the consideration is shown; in a transaction of this kind you have got to accept a bargain, and, so far as Seddon is concerned, his part of the bargain was regularly carried out up to the time of the death.

On 19th June a very important thing takes place. On the 19th June Miss Barrow, who had become alarmed by reason of the Birkbeck

*See Appendix F.

Closing Speech on behalf of F. H. Seddon.

Mr. Marshall Hall

Bank scare, having given notice a week before, on the 12th, in pursuance of that notice goes to withdraw the sum of £216 9s. 7d., which she had invested in the savings bank. It is an interesting fact to notice that in that bank there was an investment account which was open to further sums of money had she been disposed to invest it. It is only available to depositors who must have £50 before they can use it, and I think $2\frac{3}{4}$ per cent. was paid. She had given notice that she wanted half in notes and half in gold, but she will not have it in notes. She is evidently alarmed by the Birkbeck Bank scare, and she does not think the Bank of England is good enough, so she asks for gold. It may be that you will take into consideration when you are considering the speech of my learned friend, Mr. Rentoul, that there is this obvious disinclination of this lady to hold notes. Anyhow, she insists on having gold. She comes back with Mrs. Seddon, who has gone with her, and they come to the house bringing back this £216 9s. 7d. in gold, silver, and copper. I do not think you can have any doubt upon this. Of course, there is no other evidence of it except Mrs. Seddon's, but please let me warn you of this. In this Court, when accused persons were enabled by Act of Parliament to give evidence, there is not the smallest presumption to be made against them that their evidence is untrue. You have got to remember that. On the face of it the evidence of an accused person is *prima facie* as true as the evidence on behalf of the Crown, otherwise it would be a cruel injustice. There is no presumption that anything an accused person says in his own favour should be regarded as false. We start with that; it is not challenged, and you may assume the evidence is true. Where it is challenged you have to judge for yourselves what effect you will give to the evidence as given, and the cross-examination as against it.

Upon this date, according to the evidence, Mr. Seddon said, "I do not like you to bring the money into the house. It is not safe to have this large amount of money in the house, but she got quite angry with me for saying that, and sulked for a week. She said to me, 'I know what to do with it.'" Now, as to what became of that money in your view may depend a good deal upon your decision as to whether Seddon is an honest or a dishonest man. I agree that on what you think became of the money—upon the view you take with regard to that money—will depend your decision in your own minds as to whether Mr. Seddon is an honest or a dishonest man, but whether Seddon is an honest or a dishonest man has nothing whatever to do with the question of whether Seddon has committed this murder. There is this £216. Let me say this—this woman was an eccentric person, about money from all points of view; she was not normal on the subject of money. Although she has an investment account she does not use it. Having a deposit account in a big savings bank she draws it all out in gold because she will not trust even the bank notes of the Bank of England. Seddon tells her that there are several banks where she can put the money, but she says, "I know what to do with it."

I want you to draw a mental picture of this woman up to this time. Up to 1st September this woman is a hale and hearty woman, out at all hours and late at night, as you have been told; coming back quite late.

Trial of the Seddons.

meeting relatives, and meeting people in the park. How do we know that this woman had not gone and hidden this money in some hole of her own? A woman who will not trust the Bank of England is the sort of person who will stuff this money in some place where it cannot be traced. Why is it such a violent assumption to assume that this woman, who is such an eccentric person, has dealt with this money in some such way? Why is it a more violent assumption to assume that than to assume that Seddon has not murdered her? Because you are asked to draw the assumption that Seddon has murdered Miss Barrow because of the £216 which was in her possession in June that year, and which has disappeared when her box is searched on 14th September of the same year. I know my lord will point out to you that it is not really absolutely relevant in this case of murder. Why should you draw the assumption that Seddon has murdered her and taken this money, as I say, against the assumption that she may have dealt with it in some eccentric manner? Here is a woman who will not trust the bank, who will not trust an investment account even in a big bank, and a peculiar woman to deal with on the subject of money. You know in your own experience of life what silly, foolish things are done by people who believe that by hiding their money in some stocking, or in some other extraordinary way, they have protected themselves against the dishonesty of banks and people of that class. How often has money been lost, and after a number of years discovered in an unexpected way? You are trying this man for his life. How do we know that she might not possibly have put it somewhere under an assumed name, so that people could not trace it in any sort of way? She might have absolutely hidden it in some hiding place. If the evidence for the prosecution is true, she was a woman who would leave £400 in gold in an ordinary common trunk. You have seen the keys. I hope you know something about keys. Look at them. I think if you went into any trunk shop in London and asked for twenty keys haphazard to fit that class of trunk you would find 25 per cent. fit this trunk. You see the class of key it is. Yet the evidence of the prosecution is that this woman goes away from 5th August to 8th August, to Southend, and leaves her cash-box behind her with £300, or more with the notes, with not a soul in the house except that poor unfortunate girl Chater. I do not suggest for a moment that she stole a farthing of it; I am only suggesting that she is not a competent watch dog to take care of £300 or £400 in gold. If that woman had that money at the time of her death, she must have had it between the 5th and 8th August, and yet all that time she goes away and leaves her trunk behind. No evidence is called to suggest that she took the cash-box with her, or anything of the kind, so she presumably left it behind. Which is the more violent assumption— that this eccentric woman would do something of that sort, or when she said she knew perfectly well what to do with it she had put it into some place which according to her own ideas was safe?

They all go away together, and they are all on the best of terms. They come back from Southend in that frightfully hot weather which you will all remember. Miss Barrow had the run of the house; she was allowed to go downstairs into the dining-room, or sit in the kitchen;

Closing Speech on behalf of F. H. Seddon.

Mr. Marshall Hall

she had the run of the place. I think the little chap said that he and Miss Barrow went downstairs whenever they liked. She was treated entirely as one of the family, and the little chap was treated as one of the family; and we know how successfully, because we have the little chap's admission that he was very happy indeed, as the Seddons were very kind to him. He calls Miss Barrow "Chickie," and was very fond of her.

And now I am approaching the critical dates of this case. On 1st September she has a bilious attack. I do want to know what the theory is, because the suggestion was certainly put to one of the medical men. Is it suggested she never had this epidemic diarrhœa at all? This is the question as put: that for some time she suffered from pains which were consistent with arsenical poisoning. If that is not merely put forward as something for you to clutch hold of, but if that is put forward as a really substantial suggestion in this case, I want to know where we begin? Is it suggested that on 1st September this woman was being poisoned? It looks like it, because they rely so much upon the purchase of the fly-papers on 26th August—a purchase which on behalf of the defence I most strenuously deny, and a purchase which on behalf of the defence I challenge you to use your own discretion as to whether you would hang a cat upon as regards the identification furnished by Thorley under the circumstances which have been given to this case. Gentlemen, on 1st September this woman has a bad bilious attack. She has had them before; she has had them several times before; she has had them in November; she has had them, according to Dr. Francis, in the form of gastritis, some time before; she has had them for years on and off, and Mrs. Seddon tells you in her evidence that she had been constantly, having this sort of illness all the time she was there, and she was always complaining. Do not forget this important bit of evidence —always making the most of her maladies. Why? Because she wanted the sympathy and the attention that she got from Mrs. Seddon. On 1st September she has a very bad bilious attack, and she was sick, "A real bilious attack," was Mrs. Seddon's explanation of it. She helps her upstairs, and all I can say is—and here I am trespassing rather on my learned friend Mr. Rentoul's province—if this woman is a murderess you will have to consider the extraordinary care, and the extraordinary kindness and devotion that she lavished upon the woman whom it is alleged she eventually murdered. There was no call upon her; she was not a relative of hers. A lot of sentiment envelopes the dead. You always speak with hushed breath of virtues which never existed in the living person. This woman was a bit of a nuisance. We have got to take the facts; we have not got to clothe our minds with sentimental expressions. She was a bit of a nuisance in that house. She was always complaining of something; and she was eccentric; when she was ill she was always wanting attention. My learned friend will deal with that very eloquently.

I am sure it has not escaped my lord, and it has not escaped my learned friend the Attorney-General, that every attention was lavished upon this woman by Mrs. Seddon. Is it conceivable that any woman of that temperament could have been such a Judas? This woman has

Trial of the Seddons.

Mr. Marshall Hall

nursed her night after night, putting hot flannels on her, and doing everything she could do for her, sitting in the room with all this fœtid stench, then murdering her with a corrosive poison, burning out her inside in agony, and then when she is dead remonstrates because the blinds were not pulled down—remonstrates because they wanted to take the body out of the house—goes and buys a wreath, and takes the wreath to the undertaker, and—the final climax of hypocrisy that is worthy of a Borgia—when the coffin lid is lifted kisses the brow of the woman she has murdered! I should have thought that a statement of those facts would have created such an irresistible presumption in her favour that it would be impossible to conceive such a fiend in human shape walking the earth if this woman has been guilty of this crime.

I have trespassed for the moment. This woman is the client of my learned friend. But she is the wife of my client. The first outbreak that he made in the box he made when it was suggested by my learned friend to him that what he had said on arrest was capable of the construction that he had suggested the arrest of his wife. Of course, he had never suggested anything of the kind. You remember this man had stood for hours and hours under the torture of examination and cross-examination in this case, and you remember how he kept his voice and manner level and never got excited, but when that suggestion came up he said, '' I have longed to get into this box to refute that. To suggest that I suggested that my wife should be arrested is an iniquitous thing. I never suggested anything of the kind.'' Is it likely that a man with five children at home should suggest that his wife should be arrested? I have been carried away by the necessity of saying something which had to be said, and which I know will be said with greater effect by my learned friend, but it came in at that moment, because upon that hypothesis these people are villains beyond imagination.

If it is suggested that the symptoms which occurred on 1st September were not the symptoms of a genuine bilious attack, but were the symptoms of the commencement of poisoning, which culminated upon the night of the 13th and 14th September, then I suggest to you that you would have to search the annals of the Italian poisoners to find anything so cruel and so dastardly. Let me make one comment in passing. Supposing the fly-papers were bought, as is suggested, on 26th August, supposing these people, such contemptible cowards, sent their little child to buy the poison to poison this woman, supposing they concocted this poison, and they began to administer this poison so as to create those symptoms from that date : is it credible they would have called in two doctors—first, Dr. Paul and then Dr. Sworn? It is too impossible to need argument. It is an insult to your intelligence to suggest it. It is an insult to the intelligence of any man to suggest that people who are going to poison a woman under circumstances like those, by gradual doses of an irritant poison, should call in one doctor, and then, when that doctor cannot come, to fetch another. I say that theory goes to the winds. There is no possible foundation for it. It was never suggested by that great expert, Dr. Willcox, at the coroner's inquest. His suggestion was that there was a moderately large fatal dose administered within twenty-four possibly, but not less than six hours probably, within three days of death, and

304

Closing Speech on behalf of F. H. Seddon.

Mr. Marshall Hall

that was the case that we came here to meet, until the suggestion is now seriously made by the Crown that the whole of the symptoms of this epidemic diarrhœa could not have been symptoms of epidemic diarrhœa at all, but were symptoms created and caused by the gradual administration of this irritant and corrosive poison.   Gentlemen, that is for you to consider.   And, do not forget this, that the adoption of the second theory is of itself a weakening of the first.   They themselves realise the weakness of their case upon the one fatal dose theory, and they are driven to adopt the suggestion that there may have been a continuous administration over a period of thirteen days.   One is mutually destructive of the other, and, so far as it is mutually destructive of the other, you are entitled to take it into consideration when you are considering the question of this man's guilt or innocence.

Anyhow, Mrs. Seddon does all she can all through August.   She had been to Dr. Paul; there were five visits, I think, in August.   I may not be quite accurate, but I think there were five or six visits in August for a· similar complaint.

Up to 29th August Dr. Paul had been visiting her.   What does this criminal woman do?   What does this murderess do?   When she has got the fly-papers it is alleged she is concocting them, and that he or she, or both of them, are administering this poison. , What does she do? She sends the girl for Dr. Paul the next morning when this woman gets worse.   Does she know that Dr. Paul cannot come when she sends for him?   When Dr. Paul will not come, because he is so busy, she says, " Then go and fetch Dr. Sworn, our own doctor, who has attended on me for ten years."   Dr. Sworn arrives, I think it was late at night.   The diarrhœa is worse, but she is well enough, curiously enough, to send for Seddon and sign for her annuity, and the money is fetched and paid her the next morning.   Then, as time goes on, Dr. Paul is sent for, and, as I pointed out to you, he could not come because he was too busy.   Then Dr. Sworn comes in.   May I say here at once that there is no suggestion here made by any one that Dr. Sworn is other than a thoroughly honest, competent, and reliable medical man.   There is no attempt of any sort or shape made to attack Dr. Sworn.   I know that my learned friend would not for a moment make an attack against him, unless he had ground for it.   Dr. Sworn is put into the witness-box by my learned friend as a witness of credibility, and as a thoroughly competent and reliable medical man, and I ask you therefore to accept that evidence as the evidence of a man competent to tell the truth, and who does tell the truth, and, consequently, a man who would not be a party to hiding anything he had seen.   He says she is suffering from epidemic diarrhœa, he has not got any poison idea in his mind, and he has got no doubt about it.   Curiously enough, epidemic diarrhœa is very prevalent about this time, and he instantly recognises it as a case of epidemic diarrhœa, and he says she must be well looked after, and Mrs. Seddon nurses her.   This woman is only her tenant; she has nothing else whatever to do with her, but Mrs. Seddon, with her own children and a tiny baby in her arms, goes up time after time to nurse her.   Is that the sort of thing a woman who is poisoning another does?   On 3rd September he comes again, and on 4th September he comes again.   She is a little better, but she is not so

Trial of the Seddons.

much better as Dr. Sworn expected she would be. Are the prosecution going to turn round upon us, and say, "No, of course, she was not better because you were giving her minute doses of poison?" That had been suggested in other cases—that has been suggested in every poisoning case. Are they going to suggest it here? They dare not, because their own witness gives them away. "I noticed she was making progress," says Dr. Sworn, "but the progress was not sufficient. I was making inquiries, and I was told she was not taking her medicine." Whether you believe it or not, medicine is sometimes efficacious in a case of diarrhœa, and everything that will soothe the mucous membrane of the intestines makes a very valuable adjunct to the skill of the doctor, and makes the chance of curing very much greater. She did not like this medicine, so he gave her a chalky mixture. Why has not the medicine done its work? She seems to be a little better, only a little better, and if the medicine had done its proper work she ought to have been very much better, but Mrs. Seddon says, "Oh, I cannot get her to take her medicine." What did the doctor say? "I told her you must take your medicine. If you don't take your medicine you must go to the hospital." Miss Barrow says, "Oh, not a hospital—the Seddons will look after me very well." What a testimony to the kindness of this woman! The doctor says, "Come, you must take it," and he gave her another medicine; he recognised, as a skilled medical man would recognise, that her first medicine might be nauseous and distasteful to a person who was suffering as this woman was suffering, so he changes this medicine and gets rid of the thick milky stuff, and, like a sensible man, he says, "I cannot get her to take that medicine, so I will get her to take something that is more palatable to her," and he gives her an alkali and an acid, which, when poured together, produce an effervescent effect. It is all important that it should be drunk during effervescence.

There is a curious little piece of corroboration here from the little boy, Ernie Grant. Nobody would suggest that that little chap would tell you anything except the absolute truth, as far as he knows. Such desperate straits are the prosecutors in to find some administration of this poison to this woman that they ask the boy, "Did Mr. Seddon give her any medicine," and he replied, "Oh, yes, I remember him giving it to her once." The prosecution at the Police Court, all on the *qui vive*, then say, "There is a valuable piece of evidence. It shows that he is giving her this concoction in her medicine." Unfortunately, that falls very flat when you come to cross-examine the boy. Not knowing the object of the questions, he says, "Oh, he took the medicine in two glasses; it was just like water, and when he poured one from the other it fizzed, and she drank it when it fizzed." You could not put Dr. Willcox's solution of fly-papers into that without attracting attention, so that falls down. The only other positive evidence is the brandy. That is the only other positive evidence of any sort or shape. Mrs. Vonderahe, I think, said that Seddon said he gave her brandy twice. Seddon says he cannot say whether he gave it her once or twice, and whenever he did it, as far as he remembers, it was the end of the bottle. It is a little difficult to see how that minute quantity of brandy, with the woman in that extreme state of exhaustion, could contain enough solution of fly-papers to

Closing Speech on behalf of F. H. Seddon.

Mr. Marshall Hall

make a large or moderately large dose. Those are the only two pieces of positive evidence in any sort or shape of any administration of anything by Mr. Seddon to this woman, and, as far as the second dose, the brandy, is concerned, if it was given it must have been given within an hour or two before the death, and therefore it can be absolutely eliminated from any consideration in this matter.

If you remember, I was dealing with the events of 4th September. Dr. Sworn said, " I told her if she did not take her medicine I should have to take her to the hospital, and I sent her a different medicine." Something happened on that afternoon—and here, again, I do want you to remember—it was quite a chance remark that came from Dr. Sworn. You are judges of a man's demeanour. You cannot think for a moment that Dr. Sworn was endeavouring to help these people in any sort of way. I will not insult you by thinking that any one of you believe that Dr. Sworn would go one inch from the path of truth to help these people. He said one of the most vital things that has been said in this case. I asked him whether there were any flies, and he said, " I never saw flies worse in any room in my life than were in that room." He said that they were probably brought there by the stench. Does not your common sense lead you to think so? These people are not well-to-do; they do not keep a servant; they have only a sort of half-witted girl down at the basement. They cannot empty things as cleanly as skilled nurses can, and particles of things undoubtedly remain—certain portions of these evacuations that are passing in this horrible vomiting. You have got the same thing happening every summer day. If there is anything particularly filthy or fœtid, there are the flies like eagles on a corpse. Dr. Sworn gave us an extremely valuable piece of evidence. " I never saw anything so bad as the flies in that room." Nobody knew that Dr. Sworn was going to give that evidence; there was no evidence of it before; it was entirely a chance answer of Dr. Sworn's. How does it come in? Mrs. Seddon has given her evidence that so bad were the flies on this Monday, the 4th, that is the day which Dr. Sworn was talking about, that she had to keep fanning Miss Barrow in order to keep the flies off, but at last she said she could bear them no longer, and she must have some fly-papers, and then she said, " I don't want those sticky ones; I want the ones you wet." I said this three or four days ago, and since then I have been thinking it over, and I should like to say it again with even more emphasis. I appeal to your own knowledge. In a sick room have you ever seen these sticky fly-papers, which are hung up in the form of a ribbon, or laid flat, for the purpose of catching flies? If you have, I ask you to take your mind back to them. Do you not remember the abominable, irritating noise of these unfortunate flies when their feet stick to these sticky fly-papers? If there is one thing, I submit to you, that a person in a state of exhaustion and nervous tension, which would naturally follow an attack of this kind, could not bear, it would be this. They would say, " I don't want those with the irritating buzz and the noise of these flies." To say nothing of another thing which you know perfectly well according to your experience, I suggest to you, that when these flies escape from these sticky fly-papers they will come

Trial of the Seddons.

towards the face of a person who is ill in bed, and stick there with their sticky feet.

I am not allowed to say anything about it myself; I can only suggest. Can you imagine any state of things more horrible, when these flies are saturated with this filthy stuff upon which they have been feeding, and as we all know are the source of every possible infection, to which fact the country is largely waking up? The medical officer of health is so awakened to the dangers of these flies from this point of view that he has sent a circular in which he says, " Kill the fly." That was only brought to your notice in case we could not get evidence as to the state of the flies; but after Dr. Sworn's evidence it did not become material. Nobody is suggesting that fly-papers were bought because of that circular; the fly-papers were bought by Mrs. Seddon on 4th September in consequence of the request by Miss Barrow that she should get some fly-papers to deal with the fly nuisance, and that she should not buy the sticky ones, but the ones that you wet. One of your body asked yesterday what I venture to think was a most pertinent and a most proper question. Evidently something was passing in your mind with regard to the alleged purchase of these fly-papers by Mrs. Seddon. Gentlemen, there was no need for Mrs. Seddon to say that she bought them if she were a lying and dishonest woman, and if she is the woman who committed this foul crime. I do want you to bear this in mind. I am sure my lord will bear it in mind when he comes to deal with it. There was no need whatever for her to say she bought these fly-papers. My learned friend who got Mr. Meacher, brought him here and called him——

The ATTORNEY-GENERAL—I did not call him.

Mr. MARSHALL HALL—You brought him here. I am entitled to assume that my learned friend must have thought that Mr. Meacher could not give them any assistance one way or the other, but any how, what we do know is this, that there was no evidence in the possession of the police that Mrs. Seddon had bought fly-papers anywhere. I venture to think it even came as a surprise to my learned friend when he heard me say when I opened the case that she was going to say she bought fly-papers. I do not think you realise the importance of this, although perhaps my lord does. I will tell you. At the end of the case for the Crown I submitted there was no evidence to go to the jury upon which they could properly rely. That is a question of law. As I told you the other day, I could, if I liked, have said, " I will not call any evidence, I rest upon my contention." That is what the Court of Appeal have said in civil cases ought to be done. They have held that if counsel contends that there is not sufficient evidence to go to the jury, they should not call evidence. If you do not call evidence, then the question as to whether there is evidence to go to the jury is to be taken upon the whole of the evidence that is called. My submission with regard to the unreliability was that the unreliability of the evidence of Maggie Seddon having bought these fly-papers was so great that you could not act upon it; but I myself supplied the necessary evidence of the purchase of fly-papers in that Mrs. Seddon has herself gone into the witness-box and has sworn that she bought the fly-papers at a time when they could be used for the purpose it is suggested they were used. We have nothing to gain by

Closing Speech on behalf of F. H. Seddon.

Mr. Marshall Hall

doing that, yet this woman of her own free will said that she bought these fly-papers at Meacher's, and she also bought a pennyworth of white precipitate powder and Horlick's malted mixture. Then she said, "I want the fly-papers that you wet—not the sticky ones. I want two." She put down the 2d., but she is told that she can have four for 3d., and with that she pays 3d. and takes the four. Is there anything more probable than that? Is it not the sort of thing a man would say? I am not saying it unkindly, but we have all got our business to attend to. He says "I can sell you four for 3d." He had no suspicion that they were wanted for poisoning purposes. She gets four for 3d., instead of paying a penny a piece for them. You asked a question upon that. There were other things she bought, and she paid for them. It is not suggested that she put down the 2d. only. She gave an order for a big quantity of Horlick's malted mixture, she gave an order for the white precipitate powder. So far as the fly-papers were concerned, she put the 2d. down, and she said, "Will you give me two?" He said, "You can have four for 3d.," and she takes the four. She goes home, and she first of all puts them on one plate and moistens them, and then she puts them into four saucers in Miss Barrow's room, two on the mantelpiece and two on the chest of drawers. For the moment I will leave the fly-papers there.

On 5th, 6th, 7th, 8th, and 9th September Dr. Sworn called. I do not suppose if you searched all the annals of poisoning cases you would find such a thing as that. On the 9th he gave her a blue pill, which, you will probably know, is a cleanser of the system, and will tend to get rid of any poisonous matter that may be in the system. On the 10th, for the first time, Dr. Sworn did not call. Now, on the 11th comes the incident of the will. We have no evidence except the evidence of the father to corroborate the story. We have evidence that Miss Barrow said something about making a will; she wanted to make a will so that the property which belonged to Mrs Grant should go to the Grant boy and the Grant girl. It had nothing to do with her own property—she wanted, if possible, having bought it from Hook, to leave it to these children, so that they should have their father's and their mother's property. She makes that will. Some criticism is made of the way in which the will is drawn. My learned friend is asking you to assume, not only that this man is an expert poisoner, but that he is an expert lawyer, knowing the meaning of all the terms that a lawyer would know, and that the mere substitution, or the putting in of a wrong word, would not pass the whole of her personal effects. There it is. The will is made. As Mr. Seddon says, "It was nothing to do with me. I never took any benefit under the will." She had already said, a long while ago, that she did not want her relations to benefit under the will at all. She is making a will dealing only with the things she had bought from Hook, and which belonged to the Grants originally. "Well," says Seddon, "I made the will to the best of my ability. I never thought it would be operative; I had not the smallest suspicion that this woman would be likely to die, and that the will would be acted upon. I intended to take it to a solicitor's and have it properly drawn up."

There it is. The wife and the father are present. Against the father, I suppose, no suggestion of any sort or shape is made. The father

Trial of the Seddons.

Mr. Marshall Hall

witnessed it; he says that it was read over to her and she seemed to understand it, but she asked for her glasses, and she read it and said, "Thank God, that will do." At that time Mrs. Longley is expected, and she did arrive. Here, again, there is a point which may be small as compared with some others; but I submit to you it is a point that you cannot disregard when you are considering the guilt of these people. Mrs. Longley is Mr. Seddon's sister. This is not challenged, and therefore I can take it as accepted. My learned friend most courteously said we can accept this statement of Mrs. Longley with regard to it. She is their witness. Mrs. Longley said, "My husband had written up a few days before to know whether we might come up and stay at Tollington Park." That letter had arrived upon the 10th. Then Seddon had written back and said, "We are very sorry we are full up, but still, if you do not mind coming and taking pot luck, we shall be glad to have you." Is it conceivable, is it credible that a man and woman who are going to commit this appalling murder, and who are going to commit it with diabolical skill by never exceeding the dose so as to avoid a rash coming out, or any objective symptoms which would be recognised by a medical man, should invite another woman and child into the house, and turn out of their own bedroom in order to accommodate these people? I submit that it is incredible that any man could have done that, and have been intending to murder at the time. The Seddons gave up their room to them. Now, Dr. Sworn says—"I do not think she was in a fit state to make a will on that day. I never thought highly of her mental condition at all." He did not call on the 12th.

Now, I come to the crucial day. As far as the evidence goes, they all went to bed at midnight on Tuesday, the 12th, and on the morning of the 13th the first thing we know of any importance is that Dr. Sworn came at 11 o'clock. He found her weaker on account of the diarrhoea, but the sickness was not worse. He told us that he had given her some other medicine, and you find that he has given her fresh medicine that day, and apparently the medicine has done what it was calculated to do—relieved the nausea. The diarrhoea was much the same, and he said, "I thought she was in a serious condition." My learned friend cross-examined him, I think, a little unduly—I will not say unfairly, because nothing my learned friend would do would be unfair—because I do not think he appreciated quite what Dr. Sworn meant. What he said was, "Anybody who is ill is in danger, but the question of immediate danger and danger is a question of degree which you cannot possibly decide." In most cases the actual proximate cause of death is heart failure; it is brought on by circumstances which tend to cause that, but the absolute cause is heart failure. Now, if a person is in bed some days with epidemic diarrhoea and her constitution has been rapidly weakening, and she is in a gastric condition brought about by intemperance, the question as to the immediate moment at which the danger becomes imminent is impossible for any medical man to tell, because it depends upon things you cannot see. It depends upon the power of the heart to resist the pressure which the abnormal condition of the body puts upon it. If the heart responds, and responds properly the heart goes on, and it will beat itself through that particular crisis, but if the circulation and the vitality have been

Closing Speech on behalf of F. H. Seddon.

Mr. Marshall Hall

enfeebled by a long illness the heart is enfeebled relatively with the rest of the constitution, and therefore the heart is less able to repel an insidious attack of this kind than it would at the commencement of the illness. So Dr. Sworn says, "I could not say what the condition of the heart was. There was no excessive temperature. As far as I know, her pulse was certainly thin and flabby. The diarrhœa had weakened her. The vomiting had stopped to a certain extent. I thought she was in danger, but I did not think she was going to die. I thought she would recover." That recovery depended upon whether, if a crisis supervened, the heart was sufficiently strong to resist it. Here the crisis does come on within thirty-two hours of the time the doctor saw her. The constitution was so enfeebled by the long period of diarrhœa from which she had been suffering that the heart which is attacked has not got the strength to repel the attack; and failure of the heart was brought on from that very reason, and death ensues. You get death ensuing from heart failure the heart failure being in consequence of its having been weakened by the long course of diarrhœa and sickness which this woman had gone through He said, "I thought the woman was in danger, but not imminent danger. did not think she was going to die; I thought she was going to recover." can see nothing in that to quarrel with. He said that it all depends upon her condition inside, which he could not diagnose. I think we are justified in assuming that any person looking at this particular woman on this particular day would assume that she was not going to die; Dr. Sworn said that he did not think she was going to die before he saw her again when he was coming to see her next morning. She is not very strong either mentally or physically on this day, and Dr. Sworn sends her do a new medicine first. He sends down another chalky mixture, which is of course, to deal with diarrhœa. It is of no good for the sickness; is to do with the diarrhœa.

On this day something happened which was not thought much of at the time, but Mrs. Seddon, going in and out of the sick room, getting flannels for this woman, upset one of these fly-papers on the mantelpiece and my lord put to her by way of examination, not cross-examination perfectly fairly, certain questions, and it is an answer which she gave to my lord to which I wish to direct your attention—"I broke this saucer and I could not be bothered with having all these things about—two or one plate and two on the other—so I took the whole four and put the whole four in a soup plate and poured on some more fresh water. I put the soup plate on the little table between the two windows." That was within three feet of Miss Barrow. Nobody has ever thought anything of it, and, although, technically we are not on behalf of the defence driven to explain, or to deal with the evidence for the prosecution, unless it is evidence that presses against us, any human being who has considered this case will probably consider for himself—how does this arsenic, which undoubtedly was in the body come to be there? I will deal with the question of quantity presently, but the question will be, how did it get there? That will be the question which I must elaborate upon presently. I am sorry to take up your time about the mass of matter I have to deal with; I would gladly spare myself and you, but I must do what I have got to do

Trial of the Seddons.

on behalf of the client for whom I am appearing, and I am afraid I shall have to take some little more of your time.

Mr. JUSTICE BUCKNILL—I do not want to be disclosing at the last moment, so to speak, what the object of those questions was, so I will tell you now, so that each of you may deal with the object I had in view. The evidence is that Mrs. Seddon bought those four fly-papers on 4th September, and, as I understand, took them to the house to use forthwith. From the moment when they first began to soak in water they had begun, as fly-papers, to lose their arsenical powers by being in the water, and each time the water was renewed, or the old water was thrown away, as the case may be, the distillation of the water would become weaker and weaker. Then, finally, when the four fly-papers were taken, and if the water in the three saucers had not been put in the soup plate (there is no evidence that it was) you would get those long-used papers put into the soup plate with clean water, and it would be for the jury to say whether they think, under those circumstances, that anyhow that stuff would have been strong enough to produce poisonous effects if it had ever got down the throat of Miss Barrow.

Mr. MARSHALL HALL—I follow, my lord.

Mr. JUSTICE BUCKNILL—I shall not read it any other way than to suggest certain facts, and to tell them why I put certain questions. That is all.

Mr. MARSHALL HALL—It is for you, gentlemen, to interpret the evidence. You heard it. I am merely suggesting to you what that evidence comes to. I submit to you that it comes to this, that Mrs. Seddon did pour such of the liquid contents as there was in the three saucers which were not broken on to the soup plate, and then added some further water as well. If what I have stated is challenged in any way by my learned friend, I do not know whether my lord would permit it, but whether he did or not, I should raise no objection to a medical man being called to deal with the point at any stage of the case.

I will tell you what I suggest is the real truth in regard to the arsenic in this case. The arsenic in this case is not in the form of ordinary crude arsenic; it is arsenic with sodium, which is very soluble. Assuming that there are four or five grains in each paper—it is for you to form your opinion as to that; it is more or less guesswork—this would be partly dissolved by a small addition of water; but, if you add more water, as the water evaporates, the arsenic would not evaporate with it. You would get the return of the arsenic; it would reprecipitate into the paper, and if the water remained on that, the water would operate more readily on the arsenic which had already been extracted by the first operation, and then would also again reoperate upon the paper as it stood and extract more. Assuming that there were four papers, although some portion of the arsenic may have been extracted, taking the average at three or four grains, taking fourteen grains of arsenic in the papers, a very small quantity of fluid would have accounted for, at any rate, two or three grains, which is allowing for a certain amount of evaporation. I put that before you. Dr. Willcox has heard what I have said, and I think he will accept that as being accurate.

Now, gentlemen, I am coming to the night of the 13th. Gentlemen, I cannot help saying to you that it is impossible to overestimate the im-

Closing Speech on behalf of F. H. Seddon.

Mr. Marshall Hall

portance of the events of that night when you come to make up your minds affirmatively one way or the other upon the question of the guilt of these two people. I do not think it is controverted, because I understood it was not going to be controverted, and that there was no necessity to call corroborating witnesses from the Marlborough Theatre—that the statement made by the prisoner that he was that night at the theatre is correct. I do not think that is seriously contested.

The ATTORNEY-GENERAL—No.

Mr. MARSHALL HALL—I understand from my friend that it is not contested. Therefore we can leave Seddon out of the question altogether as far as that night is concerned until 12.30 at night, or, rather, in the early morning of the 14th. Now, what happened? It was a very hot night, we are told. Mrs. Seddon and her sister-in-law, Mrs. Longley, were standing at the gate looking for her husband to return. They were more or less in and out, the window of Miss Barrow's room being open. Miss Barrow had been complaining of pain, and I think some flannels had been got ready for her even before this time, but about midnight Mrs. Seddon suddenly was startled by a voice crying out, "I am dying, I am dying," proceeding from Miss Barrow's room. Mrs. Seddon goes up into the room, and in the room she finds Miss Barrow in bed with considerable pain; she promptly gets her some hot flannels for the purpose of relieving this intense gastric pain. That takes place, as far as she can say, about midnight.

About 12.30 Seddon returns. They go into the house, and some discussion takes place between Mr. and Mrs. Seddon and Mrs. Longley as to what the real condition of Miss Barrow is. Apparently Mrs. Seddon tells Mr. Seddon what has happened, that she heard this woman crying out, "I am dying, I am dying," and Mrs Longley is appealed to and asked whether, as she told you in re-examination, she really thought that Miss Barrow was so very ill. She said, "No, I do not think so, because anybody so ill as that could not call out as loud as that, and I think she is making herself out worse than she is." The rest of that conversation was that there was some delay, but apparently at about one o'clock these people go to bed. Mrs. Longley goes to bed, and, as far as I know, on the way up Mr. and Mrs. Seddon and Mrs. Longley look in to see Miss Barrow. Mrs. Longley tells you, if I recollect the evidence rightly, that she did not see Miss Barrow's face—she was then in bed—and therefore she could form no opinion from the personal appearance of Miss Barrow; she only formed her opinion from the loudness of the voice which she had heard described by Mrs. Seddon when the woman called out, "I am dying, I am dying." Now, gentlemen, undoubtedly Mr. Seddon and Mrs. Seddon and, as I say, Mrs. Longley do go up before they go to bed, and Seddon remonstrates with Miss Barrow and says, "Do, for goodness sake, leave us in decent quiet. My wife is very tired. She has been looking after you for a long time. Let us get some sleep." I do not think there is the smallest suggestion about Mrs. Longley being present when this poisonous dose was administered. Anyhow, Mr. and Mrs. Seddon then retired to bed, and upon the events of the night after that I do not think there is any dispute at all between

Trial of the Seddons.

the prosecution and the defence. As I gather they went to bed about one o'clock.

About 1.30 the boy calls out, "Chickie wants you." Mrs. Seddon went up alone, as I gather it, and attended to Miss Barrow and went to bed. I suppose she attended her as far as the commode was concerned, and so forth. It is important to remember that on the 4th September she had got out of her own bed and complained of the flies and gone to the boy's room at the other end of the passage.

Of course, the woman would have to be going in and out of bed; there was no question of passing motions in the bed; the commode was at the side of the bed. I do not know whether she got out one side of the bed or the other. It is a big bed. It is shown to have been more used on the opposite side than that. There is very little point in that, but we must take it, knowing what we do of her condition, that she must have been getting out and in of bed during this period for the purpose of using the commode, because there is no suggestion of anybody attending upon her with bed pans or anything of that kind. A commode is being used for the purpose. That being so, you have got to remember that when Mrs. Seddon goes up the first time after they had been called she goes up and attends to her, puts some flannels under her, and possibly, as I say, helps her in the other matter. She then returned to bed.

About three o'clock—I do not think it matters exactly—but within an hour or an hour and a half, the boy calls down. Mrs. Seddon goes up again, and again returns to bed, having put some more flannels on. Then, about four o'clock, the boy calls again, and this time they both got up. You remember the conversation. Mr. Seddon said, " Let me go." She said, " Oh, no, I must go, too ; it is no good your going, you cannot do what is necessary," and they both go, and they find Miss Barrow on the floor and the boy holding her up. Then what happened was this. Miss Barrow told Mrs. Seddon that she wanted to make use of the commode, and for decency's sake Mr. Seddon went outside the door, whilst Mrs. Seddon assisted Miss Barrow to the commode. Then, afterwards, both got her back to bed. Miss Barrow was anxious for Mrs. Seddon to stop. Mr. Seddon did not want her to stop, but eventually Mrs. Seddon sat down in the cane chair which stood at the foot of the bed, and she used an expression which may be familiar to some of you ; she said. " I dozed. I was sleeping tired." If any of you have been in the north you know what that expression means. It means, " I cannot keep awake, I am dozing off." She said very fairly to the Attorney-General, when he asked her the question, " I really cannot say how long I was in that condition, because I was dozing off." As you know, it is very difficult to think of the time when you are in that condition ; you do not know how the time goes. What she does say is this, " As near as I remember she passed into a sound, peaceful sleep, and I remember her beginning to snore ; she always did snore more or less. I did not take any notice of it ; it was a natural snoring." My learned friend asked Mr. Seddon what was the necessity for him to stay. He said, " I was not going to leave my wife all alone. I stayed there, and as the smell was very bad I stood at the door and put on a pipe in order to kill the smell ;

Closing Speech on behalf of F. H. Seddon.

Mr. Marshall Hall

and, as far as I could in the very faintish light I endeavoured to rea
something while my wife dozed in the chair." As far as we know, thi
must have taken an hour and a half, or even more. As far as Mrs.
Seddon is concerned, she does not seem to have heard the rapid transition
to the final state of stertorous breathing which you have heard described.
but she may have been awakened by something, very likely this very
noise itself, not appreciating what the noise was, and Seddon himself says
that he distinctly heard it, and he reproduced that noise which anybody
who has been in a death-room knows immediately precedes death—heavy
breathing in the throat. Then he goes and looks at her. Breathing
has stopped altogether, and he does what I venture to think is a very
proper thing to do, having a doubt as to what had happened, not bein
ᵕa doctor, he raises her eyelids. As you all know, that is where you get th
first indication of death. And he says—" Good God, she's dead." That
is the story of that night.

Now, to put into it the most you can put into it, Mrs. Seddon says
that certainly once on that night—she does not remember which time it
was—he gave her some brandy. Seddon says he thinks it was only once
but he is not very clear about it. But whether it was once or twice does
not much matter. Except for the administration of brandy, there i
no vehicle suggested by which any poison could have been given.

Now, gentlemen, this woman is then dead. It is then about a quarter
or half-past six in the morning, and here is this man left there. If he is
a guilty man, there he is, having succeeded in accomplishing this terrible
murder. He has murdered this woman. Of course, I know that there is
no bound to the marvellous histrionic powers of certain persons. But
I suggest it is an incredible thing—the actor is not born who
would have the marvellous control that it is supposed this man had—wher
he suddenly sees the pulse of life cease—the lifting of the eyelids to find
that the woman he has murdered is in fact dead—this marvellous actor to
turn round and shout, " Good God, she's dead! "

There it is for your consideration. If you believe the story, there
never was a more consummate piece of acting than this man ejaculating
in this way, " Good God, she's dead "—the real truth being that he has
himself killed her by administering a fatal dose of poison.

Now, gentlemen, after the death really I do not understand that any
serious suggestion is made so far as regards Mr. Seddon's immediate
conduct. Obviously the first thing he ought to do is to go for a doctor.
Obviously the proper doctor to fetch, all other things being equal, is the
doctor who has attended the patient. My friend with great force has
already made the comment, because he has the information, that there
were three or four doctors in the street who were available—but Mr. and
Mrs. Seddon have both told you that they never for any one moment during
that night thought that this woman was going to die. They only thought
that she was in the same condition as she had been in, and not in any
immediate danger of dying. They never thought that for a moment.
Otherwise it is obvious that if they were so immune from detection as is
obviously the case, for their own protection they would have fetched the
first doctor they came to, and he would never have been able to detect
that there was anything wrong. All that he could have done was to have

Trial of the Seddons.

given some palliative—some soothing draught—and probably ordered her hot flannels to soothe the pain. If these people realised that she was dying it was their duty to bring the nearest doctor they could. Mr. Seddon said, in answer to a question, "Of course, I knew the doctor was coming in the morning, and, therefore, not thinking that she was dying, there was no need for me to be alarmed about it at all." You have heard about the woman's heavy breathing and snoring. We know she was asthmatic, and we were told by one of the doctors that she suffered from bronchitis. That would probably suggest some congestion in the bronchial organs; therefore, you might expect more snoring from her than from a person in a normal condition. All these things are perfectly consistent with death from epidemic diarrhœa or syncope—heart failure—in no way to be distinguished from death by arsenical poisoning. According to the scientific evidence, death from arsenical poisoning is produced in the same way except that it is the arsenical poison which induces the attack. The attack is the same whether it come from gastro-enteritis or arsenical poisoning. The only point is the strength of the heart. If the heart does not resist the attack you have death. Gentlemen, I need not trouble to labour that point, but as far as the actual death is concerned, even if a doctor was called in, nothing could have indicated that this death was otherwise than what I suggest it was—a death from epidemic diarrhœa.

Now, gentlemen, there is another point. The moment this poor woman is dead the first thing Seddon does is to go off to Dr. Sworn. His place is fifteen or twenty minutes' walk. He goes off for Dr. Sworn, and asks Dr. Sworn to come at once. He tells him he believes that she is dead—a very important piece of evidence. Dr. Sworn says—and it is here that he was rather pressed by my learned friend—"I was not surprised to hear she was dead—I did not expect she was going to die, but having regard to her condition when I had seen her the previous day, I was not surprised to hear that she was dead—and dead of epidemic diarrhœa—and, without being asked for it, I handed him a certificate of death."

Now, consider for a moment. This is in the north of London—Tollington Park. No one can live in that part of the world without the knowledge of the enormous stride that has been made in the hygienic disposition of the dead by the introduction of the Golder's Green Crematorium, which rears its chimney within the view of anybody—within a drive of this place, ready to meet the needs of the poor as well as the rich. Gentlemen, I put this to you as the strongest point in this case, because you cannot get away from this. If this was a murder, it was not only a cruel murder, but a highly skilful and deliberate murder, compassed by a highly skilful man of great knowledge—a man who knew the way in which arsenic acted, who knew the effect of arsenic, who knew that the symptoms produced by arsenic were the same as the symptoms produced by epidemic diarrhœa, and who took advantage of an attack of epidemic diarrhœa to produce by administering arsenic symptoms which might be mistaken for those of epidemic diarrhœa. Gentlemen, it is incredible that this man would not have known that one of the effects of arsenic is the preservative

Closing Speech on behalf of F. H. Seddon.

Mr. Marshall Hall

effect upon the body. What I am going to suggest to you is probabl known to every man who knows that the symptoms of the one an the other are identical. What has he to do? He has only to ge another death certificate, and he can at once have that body cremated and all evidence of the arsenic practically destroyed. I do not kno that some small portion might not possibly remain in the ashes, bu you may take it for all practical purposes the evidence of arsenic woul be entirely destroyed. This man must have known two things, if h was the skilful person that is suggested—that arsenic remains in th body, and, remaining in the body, preserves it from decomposition eve if it is buried.

There is one point here which is of most vital importance in thi case. It is admitted in the course of the cross-examination by all th doctors that, so far as the objective symptoms—you know what I mea by objective symptoms—the symptoms which appear upon the outside— so far as the objective symptoms are concerned, not only are the symp toms of arsenical poisoning and symptoms of epidemic diarrhœa identica during the course of the illness, but after death on the body as it lies Unless the arsenic has been administered for a long period so as t produce a rash, watery eyes, or something of that kind, there is n objective symptom on the face of the corpse which would enable anybod to say whether that person had died of epidemic diarrhœa or had die of arsenical poisoning. Gentlemen, if you are going to assume th intimate and minute knowledge as against these two people for the pur pose of convicting them, you must accept the corrollary that they als knew the other great facts, which are well known facts with regar to arsenical poisoning. This man, if he is guilty, has committed most skilful crime, a crime so skilful that, whatever the verdict of thi Court will be, there must always, to all eternity, be some differenc of opinion about it. Of course, that has nothing to do with you; you have to make up your minds solely upon the evidence in the case; bu we all know that, whatever the result of a case of this kind, there ar always people who hold different opinions afterwards. I say if this crime has been carried out so skilfully as has been alleged, it is incred- ible that this man should not have taken the opportunity to have the body cremated. Immediately he sees Dr. Sworn he is given a certifi- cate; all he has to do is to go to Dr. Paul or any other doctor and say, " I want to cremate this body; I have the certificate signed by the doctor who attended the woman; will you give me a second certificate? " The doctor would come and see the body which had to all intents and pur- poses died of epidemic diarrhœa; and is there any doctor who would have hesitated, having regard to the certificate of Dr. Sworn that the woman had died of epidemic diarrhœa, to give the necessary second certificate?

Mr. JUSTICE BUCKNILL—You are saying what another person would have done.

Mr. MARSHALL—I say, is there any doubt about it? Is there any doubt, gentlemen, that any medical man called in would have been able quite honestly to have given that second certificate? I put it entirely for your consideration, or, at any rate, I will put it as I am absolutely

Trial of the Seddons.

Mr. Marshall Hall

entitled to put it. I may have been led away just now into putting it too high, but this I am entitled to put to you, have you any doubt that Seddon would be justified in thinking that that would have been the course taken by any second medical man? I put it in a round about way just now, but that is the way I intended to put it.

Now, gentlemen, he comes back armed with a certificate. He meets Mrs. Rutt. Gentlemen, you have heard the cross-examination of Mrs. Rutt by my learned friend, Mr. Muir. I do regret that my learned friend should have thought it necessary to cross-examine as he did. I do not know why he should have suggested that Mrs. Rutt was a thief. It seemed to me a little far-fetched to suggest that because she had been accused of dealing improperly with some linen, therefore she should come and commit perjury. She gave her explanation of the circumstances. You will remember she said, "We were very poor; my husband was out of work; I was washing some linen; I had taken some linen home to wash. I was very pressed, and I pawned the linen to get something temporarily until my husband was able to get a job. The moment my husband came back I would have taken it out. Unfortunately, the Seddons came back before I got it out, and I was charged with it. I have never denied it; they threatened to prosecute me, but they did not prosecute me." Gentlemen, I hardly think that that is suggestive of any favour on the part of Mrs. Rutt towards these people. I think it is a little far-fetched to suggest that because of that this charwoman would come and commit perjury. What is her evidence? I quite agree her evidence is not altogether parallel with the evidence of the others. Would you expect it to be? I know what would have been said if identically the same story had been told. But it is a curious incident. After my friend had done with her, my lord asked her a question. I noticed—everybody noticed—she did not notice because she had been out of Court—but it was obvious to anybody who had been in Court what was the purport of the last few questions that he asked her. She is asked whether the £4 10s. was in a bag or not, and she said it was not. She may have been talking of the time when Seddon pulled it out on to the bed. To clear that up she was asked the question, and she says, "Oh, yes, the cash box was on the bed; he put it on the bed to count the money." Therefore you see that on this most important point we have her corroboration that although the box was taken out of the trunk it was put on the bed for the purpose of counting. The other discrepancy as to whether the counting took place after the body was, in fact, laid out or before, is a matter into which we need not investigate. There is that small discrepancy, such as it is, between Mrs. Rutt's story and the story told you by the two Seddons. After all, it is a matter of small importance. If you are going to make up your minds that this man had stolen £216 and any other money that might have been in the house, or that his wife stole it, they would have ample opportunity of stealing it before this period. Therefore, the question of whether £4 10s. was, in fact, found that day is really taken very little further by the evidence of Mrs. Rutt. However, that is their case—that they found £4 10s., and £4 10s. only.

Closing Speech on behalf of F. H. Seddon.

Mr. Marshall Hall

Now, gentleman, I come to this point, which, of course, I do not disguise for a moment the importance of, from the point of view of prejudice. The prejudice is absolutely overwhelming. There is not a man in this Court who, assuming these people to be absolutely innocent of the charge you are investigating against them—there is not a man in this Court who will not condemn the monstrous meanness and covetousness of Seddon in regard to this unfortunate woman's funeral. I do not care a bit about the suggestion of his having stolen money, or the suggestion of his having murdered her to the tune, as it is said, of the annuity—in common decency he ought to have buried her properly and well. Gentlemen, you have to judge everybody by himself; you have to judge the individual as you see him. I am not going in any way to palliate what I call the meanness and covetousness of this man; even if she had never had a farthing piece, the halo of sentiment immediately the breath was out of the body ought to have impelled this man to have given her a decent funeral; there is no question about that. The real danger is that you should allow it to have too much effect upon your minds. The natural feeling is one of repugnance and hostility. The danger is that you should allow it to warp your minds too much. The whole of that business with regard to the funeral and taking 12s. 6d. commission, is too petty, too mean, to be justified in any way; and I am indeed sorry to think that there could have been any man so mean-spirited as to have taken advantage of that opportunity for the purpose of making 12s. 6d. on the funeral. The body being buried in a public grave, he is not responsible for the number of bodies being buried in the same grave. You know the way these undertakers talk; we know the flippant way in which they deal with death; they get so accustomed to it. You will remember this undertaker's expression about the " old lady " and the " good turn-out," and so on. Do not let that warp your minds; it has nothing to do with the case one way or the other, except so far, that if this man is a guilty man it makes it even more incredible that he should have called attention to it by doing these things. However, she was on the Saturday buried in this public grave. I have one little comment to make. Do not let this sentiment weigh upon you too much. His explanation is that he knew that Miss Barrow had a vault at Highgate, but that he believed, from what the deceased had told him, that that vault was full up. Anyhow, the Government, having had this body exhumed, did not see fit to bury her anywhere else; they buried her again in another public grave, so that any question of sentiment, however it reflected upon Seddon, would seem to reflect upon His Majesty's Government, who, having had the body exhumed, re-buried it in a public grave. I will not argue it further. I wish to say this at once. I tender my grateful thanks to my learned friend for the way in which he put this point. He did his best to eliminate prejudice from it, and for that I am thankful.

I have said all I have to say about that unfortunate funeral. I have nothing more to say. I have not shirked it. I know the weight of it from the point of view of prejudice. As I say, it is one of those great big storm waves of prejudice, but you must not, because of that, drown this man in that wave of suspicion and prejudice.

Trial of the Seddons.

Mr. Marshall Hall

Now, gentlemen, I should like to pause for one moment to consider this position. Either this man is guilty or he is innocent. Let us for one moment take the hypothesis that this man is guilty. He has murdered this woman; she is dead; he has got a death certificate. He has arranged with the undertaker, and the body is to be removed at a time suggested by the undertaker, not by him, which, I venture to say, with a child in the house a few months old, was a perfectly proper suggestion. There is no suggestion of friendship between Seddon and the undertaker; it was a perfectly proper suggestion, and no inference must be drawn against this man for allowing the body to go out of the house that evening as suggested by the undertaker, especially having regard to the fact that Mrs. Seddon had a baby a few months old, and therefore the liability to toxic poison, or anything of that kind, would be very serious. As I say, at the suggestion of the undertaker, the body is out of the house and the funeral is arranged for. What would you expect a man to do if, according to the theory of the prosecution, he had first of all murdered the woman and then robbed her of a large sum of ready money, most of it in gold? Gentlemen, you know, anybody knows, that the payment of a large sum in gold, any sum over £10 or £15 in gold, instantly excites the suspicion of the person to whom the payment is made. If you want to attract attention to the payment of any large amount, pay it in gold and the person you pay it to will probably never forget it. Therefore, if you are anxious to concentrate attention on the way in which you are making payments you will make them in gold, and the person you make them to will never forget it, especially if you happen to pay a sum like £90. Gentlemen, that is the first thing that strikes one as a curious thing to do, if this man has stolen £200 in gold, and he knows perfectly well that there is a record of the fact that this woman had taken this money in gold, because he knows that it comes out of the savings bank and he knows, as everybody must know, that the savings bank make an entry in their waste book of the exact form in which the payments are made. What is it really that it is suggested that he should do? He has got over the first difficulty; he has got over the death certificate. He could easily, as I have pointed out, have got the body cremated and out of the way. He could have done all those things; but not only does he not do them—this skilful, clever poisoner—but what does he do? According to the evidence of the prosecution, if you believe it, he goes and gets this £200 in gold that he had stolen from this woman, he takes it downstairs past the safe in his bedroom where he could lock it up, on the Thursday, the busiest day of the week for him, when he knows that his assistants are coming in, and he parades it before all those people, swaggering about with this stolen property. Gentlemen, he knows perfectly well that the fact that the £216 had been paid out of the savings bank to Miss Barrow must, at some time or another, be known to somebody, because somebody would have a record of it, and the moment this woman's death is known they, knowing that she had this little money within a short period of time in all probability—at least they would be entitled to assume it—some inquiry would be made with regard to it. The suggestion that he should go and get this money in gold and parade it about on the table and show it to these

Closing Speech on behalf of F. H. Seddon.

Mr. Marshall Hall

men, I submit, is so incredible that it is really hardly worth serious con-sideration.

There is one little point on which I must touch; it is not a very big point; I do not think much turns upon it—the point with regard to the letter. He says he wrote a letter to the relations. If you look at the local directory for that period you will find the address of the Vonderahes is 31 Evershot Road. You will find in the letter which Miss Barrow had written to him about her relations there is given that address. This man says, "I did write a letter; I kept a copy of it." A carbon copy of it is produced; it is obviously a carbon copy, there is no question about that. "I kept the carbon copy; I sent Maggie to go and post it; I would not allow her to deliver it herself because the door had been slammed in her face." That is the evidence upon that. It is not quite complete, be-cause Mr. Smith admits in cross-examination that when the coroner first began the inquest he did call upon Mr. Seddon, and he remembered per-fectly well what Seddon said, "Why didn't one of the relatives come?" Seddon has sworn that he did write that letter; and he had produced the copy.

Now, we come to deal with the question about the money. Gentle-men, I want you here for a moment to consider this evidence, because I venture to say to you the criticism that has already been passed upon it by Mr. Seddon in the course of his cross-examination is a perfectly sound criticism. You heard the outburst he made when, in answer to a question put to him by the Attorney-General, the Attorney-General suggesting that this was Miss Barrow's money, he said, "At any rate, I am not a brutal, inhuman degenerate; I should not be capable of doing anything of that kind." Now, gentlemen, I want you particularly to follow this plan. Here is the table where the gas jet is; this is where the man sits to count his money; he brings it from there to there. Mr. Taylor sitting at his desk is half-face towards the back of that table, and Mr. Taylor could no more see what was going on on that table without turning round than he could see what was going on there. It is true that Mr. Smith, as Seddon remarks, could see it; he was sitting there; there is his chair looking in that direction. Now, what Mr. Smith says is really very different to what Mr. Taylor says. Mr. Taylor said, "I saw at least £200 worth of gold loose being put into bags by Seddon." Although he said it was £200 before the coroner, he says now it must have been at least £400. Before the coroner he fixed £200—why? Because when I saw what his evidence had been before the coroner I asked him, and he admitted that he knew that £200 was missed, and from that he drew his own conclusion, and fixed it at £200. Mr. Smith's evidence is not quite so complete. He says that three bags were filled; he says, "I did not see what was in them; I saw it was gold, but I saw outside the three bags about £100 of gold."

The ATTORNEY-GENERAL—He did not say three bags. He said he saw £200.

Mr. MARSHALL HALL—I understood him to say he never saw what was put into the bags; he assumed they were full of gold; but he never saw it. All the gold he saw was about £100. Mr. Smith may very well have seen £100 of gold; there was more than £100 at that moment,

Trial of the Seddons.

because there was the gold that had been taken in from the collectors, and there was the gold that this man had in the safe. You will remember the evidence that was given with regard to that, and perhaps this would be a convenient moment just to deal with the evidence dealing with the money. Gentlemen, I do not really know that it is necessary to deal with it; I think I can save your time and my learned friend's time, and everybody else's time over this, and I should be very glad to save it if I can. Perhaps the learned Attorney-General will indicate that he disagrees with me if I am not making a proper and fair statement. As I gather from the Attorney-General's cross-examination, if you admit that this man had £200 in gold, or a little over £200—£210 or £220—in the house, and if you admit that he had that amount in gold, all the payments in gold are accounted for. If you do not admit that, it is a question for you, and it does not matter; if it is not admitted, it is no use attempting to account for it. I will let my learned friend go into it if he likes in detail; I do not think it is necessary. I submit that it really comes back to this. That evidence is absolutely valueless if he had not got the £200 in gold. If he had £200 in gold, the only effect of it is that it will account for the payments in gold made at or about that period; I do not want to deal with it in minute detail, because, after all, however minutely I dealt with it in detail, with the exception of £10 which Mr. Seddon corrected—he said he did not quite know as to the £10; I am sure you will not hold him down to the £10 at this distance of time—if he had £200, at any rate, in the house at that time, at the death, legally belonging to him, you can account for all the payments both to the savings bank, to the building society, and anybody else.

The ATTORNEY-GENERAL—I agree.

Mr. MARSHALL HALL—That will save a lot of detail. My learned friend agrees that this is a perfectly sound proposition to put before you. Now, do you believe that he had £200 in gold? Upon that you have only his evidence and the evidence of the three men who deposed that in the latter part of 1909 he had a sum varying from £250 to £300 in gold. I leave that, only asking you not to forget when you come to consider the evidence of these men, that they made no comment at the time on the fact of this man having this amount of gold in his possession; they did not think anything of this man having so much money in gold; and it was not till the inquest was opened and they heard that sum of money was missing that they come forward to give the testimony which they eventually gave.

The next thing we have to do with is the letter which I have already dealt with. As I say, it is no good my dealing with the question of Maggie, because if Maggie comes into the box and says that she did post the letter, and she remembers Smith tapping her on the shoulder, you would only be told not to believe her—that she is a liar—that as she did not tell the truth to Inspector Ward she is a liar. What is the good of putting a child in the terrible position of having to give evidence in a case where her own father and mother are charged with murder? I put her into the witness-box; it was open to my learned friend to cross-examine her upon this point; he did not do so; it may be because he thought that he had no necessity to cross-examine a child on a matter of

Closing Speech on behalf of F. H. Seddon.

Mr. Marshall Hall

that kind; and, after all, anything she said you could be invited to disbelieve, because she is interested to tell a lie having regard to the relationship with the prisoners.

The ATTORNEY-GENERAL—I shall have something to say about it to the jury. I should say it is an extraordinary position that when my friend puts the witness into the box he does not ask a single question about this point.

Mr. MARSHALL HALL—I quite expected my learned friend would say that, and I reply in this way. I say that under the extraordinary relations that exist between that child and the people in the dock it was not advisable to ask her more than was absolutely necessary. I put her into the box for cross-examination. I said so at the end of my examination. I said, "I ask you no more; I leave you for cross-examination." Therefore my friend was entitled to put any questions, but he did not put any question upon this point, and he cannot go any further; he cannot comment upon the fact that I did not question her, because, as I say, if I had, you would have been called upon at once to say she is a liar, because Inspector Ward got from her two statements, one of which is true and one of which is false.

Now, I come to another matter—although I do not think the prejudice is very great as far as the ring is concerned. He took the ring to have it altered. He says, "I did not want to have it altered during her life, for fear that she would see it, and I might have hurt her feelings." Gentlemen, that does not prove that he is a murderer nor anything of the sort. What he says about the watch does not prove that he is a murderer. The wife says she did not want to wear a watch with a cracked dial and somebody else's name at the back. There it is, and that does not strike one as an unreasonable explanation. However, she says that is so; we cannot deal with what was in her mind. Anyhow, it does not prove that she was a murderess, because she wanted to have this name of somebody else, the mother of the donor, erased from it. The only thing about it is, I quite agree, that she might have waited a little longer, and that it was rather indecent to deal with this matter so soon after the woman's death. That is prejudice again, and prejudice which I do not think you will attach much weight to.

Now, gentlemen, we come to the other matters to which I have alluded somewhat vaguely already, the buying of the wreath and the lifting of the coffin lid and kissing the dead woman. I will leave all that for my friend to deal with afterwards. Then the blinds were pulled down, the windows are wide open; every opportunity is given—even if the Vonderahes did not receive a letter—letters do not always go straight if they are re-directed or directed by the Post Office—there may be such an accident; the Post Office does occasionally make a mistake; anyhow, we do know this, and Mr. Vonderahe would not deny it in cross-examination, that his boys went to the same school as the boy Ernie Grant, and he might have known at least a week before that Miss Barrow was dead. I think Mr. Seddon was perfectly entitled to assume that the relations would get to know of the illness having regard to the fact that the Vonderahes' two children went to the same school with Ernie Grant.

I pass over the funeral on the 17th. Then on the 18th comes the

Trial of the Seddons.

application for shares, which were paid for in gold. As I say, it is the work of a madman if he is a murderer and has robbed this woman of £200 in gold. He goes to a building society, where record is kept of the money paid in, and he is manufacturing evidence against himself in the event of any accusation being made against him. You know the explanation that he has given to you. My learned friend says, "Why did you get rid of your £200?" The explanation is perfectly obvious, I should think; first of all, owing to the death of Miss Barrow, the necessity of providing for his wife's immediate income was not so paramount; he had not to pay this annuity to Miss Barrow, and therefore the money would be available to maintain his wife, and there would be no pressing need for money in the house as there was before. So that, instead of her having to take possession under a will, or something of that kind, if anything happened to him, he could make her a safe provision. Further than that, he says, "I am going away for a fortnight's holiday, and I am not going to leave £200 in the house." It is for your consideration. He is answering the Attorney-General, who thought it very strange that £200 had disappeared; it may have crossed his mind that it was not safe to leave £200 even in a safe in the house, and that therefore it was better for him to deal with it as he does—manufacturing evidence against himself if he is guilty. It is incredible that he would have paid this money in gold, if it was stolen, that he had got from Miss Barrow's possession.

Now, gentlemen, I need not trouble you with the further lot of three shares. He paid for them with no incriminated money at all; the money is completely traced to his possession. No suggestion is even made about it. The Attorney-General did not even comment on it. The effect of his buying those shares is, as he told you, practically equivalent to levelling up the mortgage in the same building society upon the house; so that instead of keeping £200 in the house he buys £180 worth of shares in the building society, which, of course, would be set off as against the mortgage held by the building society over this particular house.

On the 20th Vonderahe called, and he only sees the servant. On the 21st and 22nd the Mrs. Vonderahes called. So far as they are concerned nobody can say that their attitude was very friendly either to Miss Barrow or to the Seddons. It is perfectly clear that there was some discussion about Miss Barrow's manners and character, because Mrs. Vonderahe admits that she told Mr. Seddon that Miss Barrow once spat in her face. She said she never did say that she was a bad wicked woman, and that a public grave was good enough for her. Mr. Seddon says she did. They ask for an interval so that Mr. Vonderahe can see her husband. Mr. Seddon says, "I am going away for my holiday; there is a copy of the will; you can take that to your husband."

He goes away a day or two afterwards for a fortnight to Southend. He comes back from Southend. Then the boy Ernie is sent round to the Vonderahes' house to tell them Mr. Seddon is back, and, he thinks, the two Vonderahes turned up on the 8th October. It appears that there is only one Mr. Vonderahe. Then Mr. Seddon, with that peculiar mind which he seems to have, rather traded upon his own legal position. He is in a very difficult position; assuming that he is an absolutely innocent man, he is in a very difficult position. Here he has granted an annuity calculated on

Closing Speech on behalf of F. H. Seddon.

Mr. Marshall Hall

something like twenty years' expectation of life, and the life has genuinely and naturally fallen in within twelve months. The man is in a very awkward position. It might be suggested that he had used undue influence. It might be suggested that he had got the better of this woman. They do not know of the letters and documents which were found there. Mr. Vonderahe, bringing a friend with him as a witness, goes for the purpose of cross-examining Seddon about Miss Barrow's property, and Seddon retires into his legal position. He says, "If you are the next-of-kin I will give you any information you want, but you are not the next-of-kin"; he adds, "There is an elder one than you. All I will tell you is that she sold her property in order to get an annuity, and an annuity has been granted to her." He did not say that he had granted it; he says he never said anything about purchasing it in the open market; but even if he had, he would have been so far telling the truth, because he might have meant that he had given far more than she would have got in case of a sale in the open market.

You know the hostility that had been shown by the Vonderahes. It was suggested that he made too much of it by standing at the door when Mrs. Vonderahe was leaving, and so on; anyhow, he did not want to have anything more to do with them. I suggest to you that the attitude of the two Vonderahes, their attitude of attacking Seddon if they could find any opportunity, justified him in taking up that position. True, he conceals the truth by not disclosing that he was not the person who granted the annuity; but when the particular question is asked, "Who is the landlord of the Buck's Head?" he says, "I am, and of the barber's shop adjoining"; so that he does not tell a direct falsehood; all he does is to conceal the true facts as to the person who had granted the annuity. It is incredible that if this man was guilty of the murder of this woman, he should not have done everything he could to pacify these people; incredible that he should have held them at arm's length and said, "Everything has been done through the stockbrokers and lawyers in a perfectly legal manner."

On 11th October Vonderahe or somebody communicated with Scotland Yard. On 15th November the body was exhumed. During this time Seddon had plenty of money, and there was plenty of time for him to have got away and gone anywhere he liked; there was no evidence against him at all; they do not arrest him until 4th December. On 15th November there is the exhumation of the body and the post-mortem, and Dr. Spilsbury very frankly says he found at that time no signs inconsistent with the death on the medical certificate from epidemic diarrhœa. On the 23rd there is the inquest; Mr. and Mrs. Seddon attend; they both give evidence; their evidence has been read in this case. On 29th November there is a further examination by Dr. Willcox, and we got the evidence which I have already read to you in the beginning of my observations in this case—the evidence of Dr. Willcox of the absorption of the moderately large fatal dose which had been given to this woman probably within three days and certainly not less than six hours before her death. That is what it comes to; that was the material of the prosecution at that time. Upon that, on 4th December, Mr. Seddon was arrested. When he is arrested he is told at once that he is being charged with murdering Miss Barrow by administra-

Trial of the Seddons.

Mr. Marshall Hall

tion of arsenic; and he asks at once, "Has any arsenic been found in the body?" Of course, he is very indignant, because he says they told him they were going to arrest his wife. You heard Inspector Ward's evidence as to the conversation between him and Seddon, and you heard Seddon's account of it. I venture to think that the outbreak of anger on the part of Seddon was quite justified, because it is impossible that any man should be such a cur as to suggest that his wife should be arrested. Up to this time Ernie Grant had been in the house, clothed, fed, and looked after, and now the boy had been taken away by the police. There was no inquiry and no evidence of any sort or kind brought against him. This man had carried out his bargain which he said he had made with Miss Barrow, and kept the boy in comfort as one of his own children, and provided for him decently in every way.

Now, on 4th December this man is arrested, and on 6th December, in consequence of exhaustive inquiries which are made by Mr. Saint, he gets to know this: (of course, the moment a man is charged with poisoning, and you hear from the medical evidence that arsenic has been found in the body, anybody with any sense would make inquiries) that four fly-papers had been used in the room; and Mr. Saint—I do not think wisely, but that makes no difference—suggests that the girl should go and buy fly-papers from Price's. She takes with her two young friends that she knows at school, and these fly-papers are refused; there was no concealment about it; the police knew it; they were watching her; and immediately after she comes out the police officer goes in and buys some papers, either there or at the adjoining shop.

The ATTORNEY-GENERAL—You must not say that the police watched her when she went there. There is no evidence of it, and it is not the fact. The police had ascertained from Price, from the inquiries they were making, that she had been there on 6th December, and she admitted the purchase of fly-papers, and that Price had refused them.

Mr. MARSHALL HALL—And so expeditious are their methods that the same day one of the policemen admitted that he bought fly-papers at Price's shop—the same day—so that they knew within a very short time of the attempted purchase of those fly-papers. Anyhow, on the next day the papers are purchased by Mr. Saint at another chemist's, and there is no question about that; the book was produced where the signature had been made. You may take it that there is no evidence offered against the evidence of Dr. Willcox upon this point; you may take it that those papers do contain various quantities, 6 to 3 grains of arsenic, and that the arsenic can be extracted in the way indicated by Dr. Willcox. On 11th December Dr. Willcox makes the examination of the hair. On the 14th December there is the adjourned inquest; then on the 5th, 19th, and 22nd December, the 2nd, 19th, and 22nd January, and 26th February there are examinations before the magistrate.

Now, gentlemen, will you please follow that for a minute. There are ten examinations before the magistrate, two inquiries on the inquest, and up to the 2nd February, the last day, there is not one tittle of evidence brought forward by anybody as to the purchase of arsenic or

Closing Speech on behalf of F. H. Seddon.

Mr. Marshall Hall

arsenical fly-papers by either the prisoner or his wife or anybody in his household. We know now from Mr. Thorley's evidence that the police had been up to Thorley's to ask him if he could identify somebody who bought some fly-papers from him. Thorley said that the police came to him several times; he told them that he could not identify Maggie Seddon.

The ATTORNEY-GENERAL—No; the exact words were that he did not know whether he could identify her or not.

Mr. MARSHALL HALL—It is the same thing; he did not know whether he could identify her or not. Anyhow, he has not identified her, and up to 2nd February nobody has identified her. I have already said something about the means of identification. I say that our means of identification in this country are deplorable. Taking down a number of people to the police station, a number of people drawn haphazard and put together—I do not know whether that is a proper way of identification or not. Suppose you go into a room where there are twenty women and you are asked to identify one of them—I mean to identify a girl; on looking at these twenty people you see a girl you have seen before on two occasions. Is it possible for the human mind to carry differences so accurately as to remember that one girl—who according to his own evidence he has only seen once in his shop—is the girl that he there and then picks out on 2nd February? Anyhow, on that evidence it is suggested for the first time that on 26th August fly-papers were bought. Apparently if they were bought they were not used unless in the manner alternatively suggested on the part of the Crown. On 15th January Mrs. Seddon was arrested. On 2nd February Maggie is taken into a room and cross-examined by Inspector Ward, and as a result of that and the identification by Thorley the case is committed for trial on the charge of wilful murder as against these prisoners.

Now, gentlemen, the only matter that I have to deal with of any importance is the medical evidence. I want to make it perfectly clear to you how I put it. Gentlemen, I am not attacking in any way either the genuineness or honesty, or the ability of Dr. Willcox. Nobody who has anything to do with Dr. Willcox will doubt that he is not only probably the ablest man in his profession, or in that particular line, but one of the fairest. He would not withhold one particle of evidence which he thought to be in favour of the prisoner merely because he was called as a witness on behalf of the Crown. I should like to pay in public that tribute to Dr. Willcox because it is most thoroughly deserved. But what I do complain of is this. We are dealing with highly scientific evidence. My friend says, why did you not call scientists to put forward counter theories? Gentlemen, it is the base root of the science upon which the deductions are founded that I complain of. I just want you to follow me for a moment in dealing with this so-called Marsh test. It is not disputed on behalf of the defence that there was some arsenic in the body; that is not disputed. What is submitted is that the calculation by which Dr. Willcox arrives at the amount of two grains of arsenic in the body is based upon an erroneous factor, and that the error is due, not to any want

Trial of the Seddons.

Mr. Marshall Hall

of science, but to the very base root of the method by which arsenic is estimated. Gentlemen, I want you to follow me. I have no doubt that presently you will be allowed to see these mirrors. Here is a question of the human eye, trained to a nicety which is almost beyond comprehension, as I submit to you. Here are a range of mirrors ranged from one-fifth of a millegramme of arsenic to one five-hundredth of a millegramme. You all know that a millegramme is a thousandth part of a gramme, and a gramme contains 15 grains; so that you can have some idea what five-hundredths of a millegramme would be. It is something so infinitesimally small that the human mind cannot possibly conceive it. I suggested to Dr. Willcox, would it be practically impossible to weigh it out? He says it is not impossible; because theoretically nothing is impossible, but practically it would be impossible, because you would not be able to calculate it with sufficient nicety. Now, gentlemen, all this depends upon two things. It depends upon the skill of the scientists to be able to compare one of these tubes, the tube that is made from the incriminated matter, with one of these tubes which are made upon a fixed scale. I want you, if you can, to follow it; I will put it to the best of my ability. What are called these test mirrors are made by a highly scientific process which I will try to describe. An incriminated portion of something, it does not matter what, is weighed out, and it is known to contain a certain quantity of arsenic. That incriminated stuff is mixed with the hydrogen apparatus, the hydrogen apparatus is passed into one of these tubes which is brought up at the end with an opening—of course, lying laterally at that time—and as the gas passes through it the tube is heated by a Bunsen burner, and as the result of that, if there is arsenic in the incriminated substance it is deposited in these tiny films upon the mirror. For the sake of argument, take the one three-hundredth of a millegramme of arsenic; it is put into a known substance, and is passed through this process. I have eliminated any question of contagion from outside. It is put into water; it is then mixed with the hydrogen apparatus, and the result of that is that the minute quantity of arsenic converts a certain amount of the hydrogen into arsenical hydrogen, and that is deposited in the form of a mirror. Now, where the fallacy of the test arises is this; it is said that that always makes the same mirror; that if you put one three-hundredth of a millegramme of arsenic and then pass it through the Marsh test you will always get a mirror absolutely identical. I am not disputing, scientifically, that for the purpose of ascertaining whether there is arsenic in the incriminated solution or not, this test is infallible in showing that arsenic does in fact exist; but where I join issue with the test is this. There is no evidence whatever that the whole of the one three-hundredth of a millegramme is deposited on the mirror. Some portion of the arsenic may escape by the end of the tube, and therefore there is no evidence that the whole one three-hundredth part is deposited; and when you are making a calculation which involves a multiple of 2000 in order to arrive at a result, the difference between 300, 400, or 500 is something enormous. I know scientists will tell you that I am wrong. They will tell you that their method is infallible. They will tell you these mirrors are so absolutely exact that they can take any mirror, and at a

Closing Speech on behalf of F. H. Seddon.

Mr. Marshall Hall

glance of the eye they can tell what it shows to the three-hundredth or five-hundredth of a millegramme. They cannot go any higher.

There is a reason why they are obliged to employ these infinitesimal quantities of arsenic; because if you employ a large quantity you get a mirror so black as to be useless for your purpose. Originally the Marsh test was a qualitative, not a quantitative test; originally the Marsh test was used for the purpose of detecting the presence of arsenic, but detecting the presence of arsenic and measuring the quantity of arsenic are two totally distinct things. This is common to all the calculations. I agree that in certain cases the multiplying factor is very small, and therefore the margin of error is not so important; but in some cases the multiplying factor is as much as 2000, and by the minutest margin of error you get an error which is of enormous value in a calculation of these small amounts. "What I say is this," Dr. Willcox says—and, of course, it is his honest belief—"in this mirror if I put a sixtieth of a millegramme of arsenic in the solution, the result of that is that it shows that the whole of that sixtieth of a millegramme of arsenic is deposited in that so-called mirror." That mirror is open at the end; the gas must escape; you may put a porcelain or any similar cover you like over it; if it is on the porcelain cover it gets out. Therefore, I say that when you are dealing with these minute quantities it becomes of most enormous interest to ascertain that these things are, not relatively, but absolutely and unmistakably correct. Gentlemen, you will presently see one or two of these mirrors, and you will see for yourselves, you will be able to compare them. Of course, Dr. Willcox's trained eye has already told you—and, gentlemen, do not misunderstand me, Dr. Willcox honestly believes that he has got on the mirrors a sixtieth of a millegramme of arsenic, but he cannot prove it to me by ocular demonstration. It is theory, that is all. It is scientific theory of the highest possible character, but it is not the sort of theory upon which a man's life ought to be put in peril. So far as this body is concerned I am not contending that there is no arsenic in the body at all. Mind you, of the two grains of arsenic, one grain is made up by a calculation of what is called muscle fibre, and Dr. Willcox admits that that is purely a matter of calculation. You cannot get at that for this reason, that you cannot get at the weight of muscle tissue, and therefore you have to estimate it. It has never been estimated on a dead body, and therefore you have to deal with it with a live body, and with a live body it is calculated that muscle tissue accounts for 44 per cent.—three-fifths of the total weight of the body; that is, the total weight of the *live* body. This body had shrunk from something like 10 stones to under 5 stones, so that there was a wastage of half. Now, the muscle contains 77 per cent., and the bone only contains 56 per cent.; therefore, suppose they are all losing moisture proportionately, and at the same rate, you would get a much greater loss of weight in the muscle than in the bone. Therefore, in calculating the weight, if you take it at two-fifths, you are taking it much too high. If you multiply by that factor the amount that is shown in the minute quantity of muscle, you are multiplying it by a factor which is absolutely wrong. Of course, in the case of the liver, the multiplying factor is only something like four or five, and therefore the margin of error is not so great. What I say is this, and what I ask

Trial of the Seddons.

Mr. Marshall Hall

you to find as a fact in this case is this, that there is arsenic in this body, that it did not cause the death, that she died of gastro-enteritis— that is, that she died of epidemic diarrhœa. Possibly the condition may have been aggravated, but that there is no evidence upon which you can satisfactorily rely that the arsenic in the body was of itself sufficient to cause death, because you cannot rely scientifically on the quantity alleged to have been found.

Gentlemen, I am not dealing with the question of the hair. I do not care a bit about the further experiments of Dr. Willcox. I might just say, without for a moment claiming any kind of triumph for myself, that at any rate we shook him so successfully that he had to shelter himself in order to get out of the difficulty with regard to the distal ends of the hair by making further experiments. Those he made with hair taken from the body after death. I think it is quite possible that any arsenic found in that may have come in from external contact with the blood-stained body, and it would be consistent with the taking of arsenic over a long period of time. I drop that, but, gentlemen, this point does remain, and for what it is worth I am entitled to the benefit of it. Dr. Willcox has frankly admitted that in the whole length of hair, some 12 inches and some 3 inches long, it was cut from the dead body in the coffin; and he does find, I think, that there is one-twenty-first of a grain per pound weight of hair. Gentlemen, as you know, there has been a most exhaustive Royal Commission with regard to the poisoning that took place in Manchester some little time ago from arsenic in beer, and most exhaustive reports were made upon that question; and the balance of scientific opinion at the moment is that if you find arsenic in the hair in all probability there has been an administering of arsenic for a period of over ten weeks. That, I admit, shows to you that there has been at some time some arsenic taken by this lady; but it becomes immaterial—I do not care a bit about it— because I come down to this, that somehow or another within a reasonable time of this woman's death some arsenic found its way into her body. Gentlemen, how did that arsenic get there? It is for the prosecution to prove affirmatively that it got in through the instrumentality of these people. If the prosecution fail to prove that they fail to prove their case. I have not got to discuss it. I have not got to put before you any theory, or suggestion which will explain it, until the prosecution have proved it. And the prosecution in this case, as in every case, must prove affirmatively to your satisfaction that this arsenic was administered by both of these persons, and that that arsenic caused the death of Miss Barrow. Other-wise, the case for the Crown falls. It is the weakest part of their case that is the strength in this case. If you take the opportunities that have been proved against Mr. and Mrs. Seddon, I say you cannot possibly say that you are satisfied that it is proved to your satisfaction that either or both of these people administered this arsenic with intent to kill. It is not for me to offer any explanation, or to present any theory to you. I do not suggest that that poor, half-witted girl ever administered arsenic to this woman, not for a moment; but here is arsenic in the house, there are those fly-papers in the house, containing, let us say, sixteen grains of arsenic, and the less water the more concentrated the solution. You

Closing Speech on behalf of F. H. Seddon.

Mr. Marshall Hall

have to remember that. I suggest to you in some way or other some portion of that, not sufficient to cause her death, but sufficient in the state in which she was to aggravate the symptoms from which she was suffering —some portion by some means or other got into this unfortunate woman's stomach, and so into her body. Gentlemen, that possibility has not been eliminated successfully. The prosecution have never called any sufficiently reliable evidence to prove that that opportunity was not taken advantage of, and that the arsenic was not, in fact, administered in that way. As I say here, gentlemen, the benefit of every doubt must be given to the prisoner when he is accused of an offence, when anything short of complete, satisfactory proof is tendered by the Crown. It is not only the benefit of the doubt that this man is entitled to, but he is entitled as of right to demand at your hands a verdict of acquittal, because the prosecution have failed to prove their case.

Gentlemen, I have practically done. I have attempted no high flights of forensic eloquence. I have attempted to deal with this as a business proposition, addressing twelve business men. I have only dealt with the evidence before you—the evidence against my client. I submit that that evidence is entirely unsatisfactory. The presumption of innocence has never been removed; the prisoner is entitled as of right to your verdict of acquittal, and you must say he is not guilty because he has not been proved to be guilty.

Gentlemen, I often think, when I look at the great figure of Justice which towers over all our judicial proceedings, when I see the blind figure holding the scales—I often think that possibly the bandage over the eyes of Justice has a twofold meaning. Not only is it put there so that the course of Justice should not be warped by prejudice or undue influence one way or the other; but sometimes I think it is put there so that those who gaze should not see the look of infinite pity which is in the eyes of Justice behind that bandage, the look of infinite mercy which must always temper justice in a just man. Gentlemen, in that hand of Justice are held two scales, and you are the people to watch and decide, as the inanimate hand of Justice holds those scales aloft—it is you who decide what is the result of the weighing. The one scale is the scale of the prosecution, the other is the scale of the prisoner. The prosecution come, under your careful and acute observation, and they begin to put into the scale of the Crown the bits of evidence which are to weigh and to count to make that scale go downwards to a lower level than the other and convict the prisoner of the crime of which he is charged. That scale is empty when they begin. You must take away from your eyes any faulty vision that you may have, caused by prejudice or suspicion. You are sworn to do your duty according to the evidence, and upon your oaths you must give your verdict, and you must let no faculty lie dormant in the most minute examination of the line, the balance of those two scales. But remember this. The other scale is not empty. The prisoner's scale has something in it invisible to the naked eye, invisible to anybody who examines it however skilfully, however scientifically; because in that prisoner's scale is a thing called the Presumption of Innocence, which, if the scales go level, is to bump the prisoner's scale down and outweigh the scale on the other side. You cannot see that presumption of innocence. If in your judgment the balance of those two scales is so fine and so minute

331

Trial of the Seddons.

that you cannot in your mind's eye and in your mental vision say to yourselves in which of those sides the span is going to fall, remember that in the one scale, the prisoner's scale, is the invisible weight—the presumption of innocence, which, when the scales are level, must inevitably bump that span to the ground.

Gentlemen, the great scientists who have been here have told us much of the marvels of science, and of the deductions that can be made from science. There is one thing the scientists have never yet been able to find, never yet been able to discover, with all their research, and with all their study, and that is, how to replace the little vital spark that we call life. Upon your verdict here depends, so far as I am concerned, the life of this man. If your verdict is against him, that vital spark will be extinguished, and no science known to the world can ever replace it. As far as I am concerned, my responsibility is ended. To the best of such abilities as I possess I have put this man's case fairly and strongly before you. I have endeavoured to put it in the fairest light that I can put it from his point of view; but yours is the responsibility. Not that you are to be afraid of it. If your oaths constrain you to find a verdict of guilty, let no consideration of the consequences hinder you—in the name of Society, find that verdict if you are constrained to find it. But, gentlemen, regarding the consequences of your verdict, I may remind you that they are irrevocable. I invite you to say, on all this evidence, having heard it all, and listened to it all, and weighed it all, you are constrained to come to one verdict, and one verdict only—that the Crown have not proved the case against Frederick Henry Seddon, and that, therefore, your verdict must be a verdict of Not Guilty.

Closing Speech on behalf of Mrs. Seddon.

Mr. RENTOUL—May it please you, my lord—Gentlemen of the jury, it is now my duty to address you on behalf of Mrs. Seddon, and I need hardly say that I rise to do so with a very heavy feeling of responsibility. For even the ablest and most experienced advocate could not discharge a duty of this kind without experiencing considerable anxiety, without the fear being ever present in his mind lest he should leave unsaid something that ought to be said, or should use some argument that ought to be omitted. Nevertheless, I for one, am deeply thankful that the time has now come when, having all the evidence before you, I can deal with it on behalf of Mrs. Seddon, and can claim from you on her behalf a verdict of Not Guilty. It may be thought that in using that expression I am speaking somewhat too confidently, that, were my experience of the uncertainties of criminal administration greater than it is, I should hesitate before using an expression which only the strongest confidence can justify. But, gentlemen, I venture to hope that you will not think that confidence unjustified when you come to examine the evidence for yourselves, and look at the case of mere suspicion that has been raised against her, and ask yourselves whether on that evidence you dare to accept the conclusions of the prosecution.

I do not think, fortunately, that it will be necessary for me to detain you more than a very short space of time. I only want to deal with this case now as it stands against Mrs. Seddon, and against her alone, as if there were no question of any one else being charged along with her.

Gervais Rentoul, Esq.

Closing Speech on behalf of Mrs. Seddon.

Mr. Rentoul

My learned friend, Mr. Marshall Hall, in his address on behalf of her husband has dealt, and dealt exhaustively, with many matters affecting the wife about which I should have otherwise been called upon to say a word. He has urged upon you many considerations in favour of Mrs. Seddon, and in favour of the assumption of her evidence which I now ask you confidently to accept. I am, of course, perfectly satisfied to leave all those matters in the exact position in which they have been left in the observations of my learned friend, and I trust therefore that you will not think that I am trying to evade any point in this case if I abstain from repeating, and possibly weakening by repetition, whatever Mr. Marshall Hall has so clearly and forcibly said. Therefore I leave out of consideration altogether any criticism of the medical evidence that was given by Dr. Willcox under cross-examination, which might go far, I suggest to you, to raise a doubt in your minds as to whether Miss Barrow did really die from the effects of arsenic or not. I am willing to assume for the purpose of my argument to-day that she did. Even on that assumption, let us consider the case for a moment against Mrs. Seddon, and see exactly what it amounts to. You will no doubt have noticed that to the vast majority of the witnesses called on behalf of the Crown it was not necessary for me to put any questions whatever in cross-examination. That was because the vast proportion of these witnesses never even mentioned the name of Mrs. Seddon, much less made any suggestion against her of any kind whatsoever. The learned Attorney-General told you in opening that this case was one that rested upon evidence purely circumstantial. That men and women have been found guilty upon evidence purely circumstantial is true, but it was only when the chain was so complete as not only to make the guilt possible or even extremely probable, but when the chain in every link, in every single part, was so complete and strong as to make a verdict of guilty the only one that any single juror could possibly arrive at. You, gentlemen, now hold the life of this woman in your hands. Perhaps no one of you was ever placed in such a position before, and doubtless you hope and pray that you may never be similarly placed again.

Now, what are the circumstances as affecting Mrs. Seddon? She lived in the house where Miss Barrow died. She did much of the house work and practically all the cooking; she had free access to Miss Barrow's room at all times. Miss Barrow died, if you will, of poison, how administered no one can possibly tell; Mrs. Seddon could have helped to commit this crime; but is there anything in all that on which you could find a person guilty of petty larceny, much less murder? Thought out and planned for weeks or months, and you will not fail to recollect that wilful murder, carefully planned and horribly executed, is the charge, and the only charge, against her.

Now, what is it that you are asked to believe with regard to this woman? That Mrs. Seddon, thirty-four years of age, who all her life has lived blameless, honoured, faithful as a wife, as a mother, and as a friend, respected by all who knew her, is suddenly transferred into one of the most inhuman monsters that ever stood in a criminal dock; that she watched over the dying agonies of her victim without one spark of pity, without one quiver of remorse; nay, more, that she actually prolonged those agonies by the application of remedies in order to relieve the pain for the

Trial of the Seddons.

time being; that she was ever ready with hot flannels and other means of affording temporary relief to the agony that she herself, according to the case for the prosecution, had brought on by the poison she had administered. And then, after the death, without any need to do so, that she had gone and kissed her victim as she lay in her shroud, and finally placed a wreath of flowers on her coffin. Was ever a jury asked for a more incredible verdict than a verdict of guilty in this case would be? You, gentlemen, had the opportunity of seeing Mrs. Seddon giving her evidence in the box. You no doubt will have formed your own conclusions with regard to her. You have heard the frank and open way in which she answered every question that was put to her. You heard the evidence of other witnesses such as Mrs. Longley and others, who spoke of the tireless and devoted manner in which she nursed Miss Barrow all through her fatal illness, and that in their opinion she was absolutely wearing herself out by the kindness and devotion that she was showing to this poor lady. Is it on facts like these that you are going to find this woman guilty of murder? Are acts of kindness and watchful solicitude of a nurse to be turned into evidence of murder? Surely, gentlemen, to effect such a transformation as this it would need a motive that should be absolutely overwhelming. Now, what is the motive in the case of Mrs. Seddon? The only motive that can be alleged by the prosecution is an indirect one. I took down some words that the learned Attorney-General used in the course of this case, so suggestive did they strike me. When speaking of the motive that Mrs. Seddon might have had in Miss Barrow's death, he described it as "the interest, whatever it was, that she had in Miss Barrow's death." That was as high as he could put it, an indirect motive; that, presumably, as the wife of the male prisoner, she would share, to some extent, in the money that he might gain by Miss Barrow's death; that is the sole motive that could be alleged against her. Now, where is the evidence by which this motive is supported? The evidence that is produced is that on certain occasions she cashed bank notes that were traced once into the hands of Miss Barrow. On twenty-seven occasions in all—and you will not forget, gentlemen, that there has never been any denial of this on the part of Mrs. Seddon; the instant the point was raised she has admitted it in the frankest manner from the very outset—on twenty-seven occasions she cashed bank notes that once belonged to Miss Barrow. Now, the suggestion that the prosecution makes with regard to these notes is that they were notes that she or her husband had stolen from Miss Barrow, and that Mrs. Seddon was cashing them with a guilty knowledge, and that that was the reason why on a few occasions she gave a false name and address. But if she had a guilty knowledge she must have had a guilty knowledge with regard to the whole of the notes. It is not open to the prosecution in this case to pick out any particular note here and there and say she had a guilty knowledge with regard to that and not with regard to the other. She must have had a guilty knowledge with regard to the whole of them. Then, if that is so, do you think it credible that in eighteen of the instances, two-thirds of the whole, she should go and cash them at shops where she was perfectly well known as a customer for years, where there was no need for her to give any name and address whatever? Then, with regard to the other instances when

Closing Speech on behalf of Mrs. Seddon.

Mr. Rentoul

she cashed nine notes and gave a false name and address, you have heard her explanation in the box, and I suggest to you that it is a perfectly reasonable and credible one. If she wanted to cash these notes, and they were stolen notes, is not it more likely that she would have taken them to some place miles away from where she lived, perhaps to the West End, and cash them in some of the big shops there, where she might naturally have though there would be no difficulty in tracing them? But, no, even on the occasions that she gave a false name and address, she took them to the shops tha she would naturally be patronising in the neighbourhood where she lives And what is the explanation she gives you with regard to these notes? Tha Miss Barrow from time to time gave her a note and asked her to cash it That at the first place she took it to they asked her for name and address As you know, gentlemen, it is not necessary at all to give a name an address when you are cashing a Bank of England note; it passes as lega tender. I know that some business houses do make a practice for thei own convenience of asking for the name and address. It was not her note she gives the first name that comes to her head, the common name of Scott choosing a number at random in the road in which she lately lived, 1 Evershot Road. Is not that a perfectly reasonable explanation? Th Attorney-General cross-examined her at great length, but he was not abl to shake her on that point. And also you will not forget that these note were cashed over a period of eleven months, and that the last note wa cashed some time before Miss Barrow's death.

Do you imagine it possible that Mrs. Seddon could have stolen these notes, or that these notes could have been stolen, and that Miss Barro for nearly a year would never have detected it—so careful a woman as sh was? We know the way in which she was always counting her money. Is i conceivable that these notes could have been stolen, and she never to have missed them or know that they were gone? There was no conceal ment, as I say, about the notes from the very first; but, assuming it as high as you like against this woman, if it is evidence of anything, assum all the guilty knowledge you like, if it is evidence of anything it is evidence of larceny, and certainly not of murder, but I suggest to you that it is evidence of larceny on which no jury in the world would convict her even of that offence.

Then passing on from that there is the question of the purchase of the fly-papers. There has never been any concealment with regard to that from the very start. Mr. Saint, the solicitor acting on behalf o both these prisoners, was told of the incident from the very start. N attempt has ever been made to conceal it. And surely the story—I need not deal with it further; it has already been dealt with at considerable length—the story that Mrs. Seddon told to us with regard to the purchase of the fly-papers is a perfectly reasonable and probable one. It is, o course, immaterial who actually purchased the fly-papers, if they were in the house; it is immaterial even from the point of view of the prosecution; but Mrs. Seddon comes forward and says, "I bought them at the request of Miss Barrow." Another point is that Mrs. Seddon accompanied Miss Barrow to the Finsbury and City of London Savings Bank to draw out the money. You have heard her explanation with regard to it, and I need not deal with it further now. Then we come to the time of the illness.

Trial of the Seddons.

Mr. Rentoul

Now, the suggestion of the prosecution is that these people, owing to a deeply-laid scheme, were poisoning Miss Barrow during the time of her illness. If you think it is so, is it credible that they would have allowed Mrs. Longley and her daughter to come up on a visit to their house? If that is so, surely they would have invented every excuse to put her off, when to their knowledge they were poisoning with arsenic, a poison which causes most terrible internal pain, and when the victim would probably scream aloud in her agony. Do you suppose that that would be the time these people would choose to have visitors in the house? Would not they rather invent any excuse to put her off and prevent her coming? Instead of that, they say, " Oh, yes, we have got an old lady in the house, but come along and take pot luck if you like." Then we know that after the death the blinds were pulled down and the windows opened. No concealment of any sort or kind. We know that the Vonderahes lived 200 yards away. Could they imagine for one moment that the Vonderahes would not be passing the house time and again, and notice the blinds down, and make inquiries as to who had died in the house? You know, of course, I need not emphasise it, that before you can convict this woman the prosecution has to banish every reasonable doubt from your minds. My submission to you has been, and still is, that so far as this woman is concerned, on the evidence that has been called, there should be no doubt whatever, and that you should unhesitatingly acquit her. But we know that sometimes juries, in their anxiety to do complete justice, do hesitate, do have doubts, and therefore one wants to be prepared to meet them.

If you have a doubt it is your duty unhesitatingly to acquit her, and I will tell you why you should have a doubt, and where there is a great and irresistible doubt in this case, and that is in the minds of the prosecution. I rely on the presence of the Attorney-General in this case as a fact more important than any other that could be adduced in favour of the prisoner; because, remember these prisoners are no great or celebrated people. It is not a question of some great conspiracy or some great revolutionary movement; it is, according to the prosecution, a sordid murder, committed for gain and gain alone, alleged to have been committed by a small insurance agent and his wife. And yet we have here for the prosecution an array of counsel such as I believe has not been seen together in a murder case since these Courts were built. So great was the doubt in the minds of the prosecution that it was deemed absolutely necessary to bring down the Attorney-General in order that he might lend to the prosecution of these prisoners not only the weight of his great ability, but, vastly more important still, the weight of his position as chief law officer of the Crown. Who will venture to say in face of facts such as these that the prosecution have not doubts amounting almost to fear in proceeding with this trial? And, if they have doubts after sifting every atom of evidence, after having behind them the whole detective forces of the Crown, are not you, the jury, entitled to doubt—nay, bound to doubt? Why, of course you are, and, if bound to doubt, or even able to doubt, then bound to acquit without a shadow of hesitation.

I do not want to deal in any detail with the evidence, because that has already been done by my learned friend Mr. Marshall Hall. There are, however, two points on which I would like to say a word, two incidents

Closing Speech on behalf of Mrs. Seddon.

Mr. Rentoul

that happened yesterday afternoon; perhaps the most suggestive incidents in the whole history of this prosecution. You will remember the last two witnesses who were called for the defence. Will you ever forget that little girl, Maggie Seddon, going into the witness-box, looking across the Court at her parents, on trial for their lives? Is there a man amongst you who did not have the feeling then, God help her! You know how she was cross-examined on a written statement that had been obtained from her under circumstances which have been dealt with to-day already. I do wish to emphasise them further. We know that in France, unless the law has been altered, officials are allowed to examine and cross-examine prisoners in their cells, and then use what they say against them; but such a system has always been abhorrent to English ideas of fairplay, justice, and mercy. And there is really not much difference between cross-examining the prisoners themselves and questioning their little daughter of fifteen in order that she may help to twine the rope to hang her father and her mother. Do you remember the questions asked? First of all, " Did you not go to the chemist's at the corner to purchase fly-papers?" To that she answers that she did not remember. There may have been a misunderstanding. It only means the alteration of one little word to make her answer a perfectly truthful one. If she thought the question was, " Did you not go to the chemist's at the corner and purchase fly-papers?" because we know that the chemist did not give them to her; she was refused them; but, take it which ever way you like, it was a misunderstanding, a mistake that even an educated person might have made; and yet she is cross-examined on that discrepancy, in order to discredit, if possible, the whole of her testimony. Does that not show to what straits the prosecution are reduced? We know that the Attorney-General himself felt the pain of the position as acutely as any one. Not once but several times he said, " I am sorry to press you, but I must." Does that not show the weakness of the case for the prosecution? Would they not, if they had had a strong case, rather have let that little girl go uncross-examined than attempt to discredit her on a statement that would be a pain for her in so unusual, I may say, so un-English a fashion? Then the last witness that was called was Mrs. Rutt, the charwoman. You will not forget my friend Mr. Muir's first question to her, "Are you not a thief; did you not steal from the Seddon's house?" and I need not relate to you again the facts. You know her explanation; what she did might be technically a theft, but certainly it was not morally one. And yet that again is used in order to discredit her and make you disbelieve her testimony in this terrible struggle of life and death. The very last thing that counsel ever like to do is to attempt to discredit a witness for some fault, even for some crime, that has nothing to do with veracity, and I am sure that Mr. Muir would have been the last to do such a thing if he had not known that he was before a jury who would never convict in this case unless every material witness that could be called for the defence was discredited. And from those facts, gentlemen, I suggest to you that the doubts for the prosecution have not disappeared as this case has proceeded.

I am not making any appeal for mercy to you on behalf of this woman; I am only asking you for justice, and to say that on the evidence the case has not been made out against her. When I have finished the

Trial of the Seddons.

Attorney-General will address you in a final speech on behalf of the Crown. Suppose, for the sake of argument, that his speech were to banish all your doubts and make them disappear; we know what effect a powerful speaker can produce, and what a vital effect the last word in a case often has. Might it not well happen that after the effects of that speech had grown dim, doubt might come creeping back, and you might begin to ask yourselves later on, when you thought over this case, whether a murder really had been committed by the prisoners in the dock, or whether a judicial murder had not been committed from the jury box? But, on the other hand, it might be said that, suppose you were to acquit her, and hereafter the conviction were to come out that these prisoners were guilty, what would be your feelings then? Why, merely that you had let guilty prisoners escape, and left to them that most terrible of punishments, a guilty conscience, and to that other tribunal where the secrets of all hearts shall be known. But I trust, gentlemen, that you will have no such doubts in this case, and that you will answer the question that will be put to you later on with two words that I know will give relief to every man in this Court, from my lord on the bench to the least important person connected with this trial, or to the least interested spectator. I know full well that you are not going to decide this case on the speeches of counsel. It is on the evidence, and the evidence alone, that you will decide. The inquiry has been an exhaustive one, and the decision rests with you. It is a burden so heavy that I do not suppose any man in this Court would desire to share it with you, even if he could. It is, indeed, a grave responsibility for men to be called away, as you have been, from your ordinary everyday affairs, to be kept apart, and asked to decide upon matters of life and death. That you will only do so after the most careful and most anxious consideration, that you will decide each and every doubtful point in favour of the prisoners, as it is your duty to do, I know full well. And it is just because I am convinced of that, and because I know that there exists deep in your hearts a desire to do justice in this case, that I ask you on behalf of Mrs. Seddon to return the only verdict that you can return, without fear or hesitation, and that is, an emphatic verdict of Not Guilty.

The Attorney-General's Closing Speech for the Crown.

The ATTORNEY-GENERAL—May it please you, my lord—Gentlemen of the jury, after what has undoubtedly been a long trial, we are now approaching the closing stages of this case. Much has been said to you by both my learned friends of the responsibilities which rest upon you in deciding this case, and I agree with every word that has been said so far as it deals with the responsibilities cast upon you. I am glad that during this case both the prisoners have had the advantage of being defended by counsel who have put their case with all the ability that can be commanded. It is fortunate that during this long inquiry you have had, principally at the hands of my friend, Mr. Marshall Hall, cross-examination of the various witnesses who have been called before you, and examination of the witnesses called for the defence. Gentlemen, there are some persons who think that the march of Justice is

Closing Speech for the Crown.

Attorney-General.

too slow. For my part I am sure you will agree with me when I say that no moment spent in inquiring into the truth of a case of this kind has been wasted. At least, you will have heard everything that can possibly be said for the defence. My learned friend, Mr. Marshall Hall, during the course of what I would call (particularly as he is not present) an admirable speech for the defence, in which every point that possibly could be made was made by him with all the force, and with all the eloquence possible to be exerted, referred to the fairness with which he said the prosecution had been conducted. I only wish to say one word about that. It is this; that in my view no credit is due to any advocate who on behalf of the Crown presents his case with fairness and with that impartiality which ought to be expected of him; and I am glad at any rate for the administration of justice in this country that that reputation for fairness is always preserved, and invariably maintained by those who appear for the Crown when the law officers do not come to this Court.

Gentlemen, the presence of a law officer of the Crown adds nothing to this case. All that it means is that in the course of my duty as the senior law officer of the Crown I have come to this Court to present the case to my lord and to you. In the course of the administration of the criminal law which devolves upon me in my position as Attorney-General, it is an obligation upon me in certain cases to come here to prosecute. I only make that reference—which otherwise certainly would never have been made by me—in consequence of the observations which were made by my learned friend.

Now, gentlemen, he said, perfectly rightly—he was quite justified in the statement—that the case was of importance. It would be of extreme importance if it was the smallest and meanest case that ever existed, when a man is on trial and a woman is on trial for life. This case is of importance, and of more importance, perhaps, than most, because in all cases that depend upon circumstantial evidence there is the necessity, as I indicated to you in opening the case, of scrutinising carefully the evidence that has been given. You will remember that in opening this case I pointed out to you, what I will only now venture to repeat in a few words, that the mere fact of these persons having committed theft or meanness, or been guilty of—well, I will say only, of deplorable conduct—is not of itself sufficient to convict any person of murder. Of course not. You will remember that I pointed out carefully that in considering the various pieces of evidence which I had to put before you, you must not allow your minds to be prejudiced against the prisoners by thinking, because they had committed some other crime, that therefore they could be convicted of murder. What I did point out, and what I will again point out to you is that, when you are considering a case which depends, as this does, upon indirect evidence, it is of vital importance to consider the conduct of the prisoners, both before and after the death; more especially in relation to the person whose death has led to this inquiry.

Gentlemen, my learned friend, Mr. Marshall Hall, has said a good deal about the introduction of what he designated as prejudice into the case. He quite properly made no complaint of it, because he realised,

Trial of the Seddons.

as everyone must who had ever dealt with trials of this character, that evidence which is given of motive, of interest, in the prisoners charged, and their subsequent conduct, such as is invariably, almost invariably, given in these cases, must, if it is to be of any value at all, be evidence which will prejudice the defendant—in the proper sense of the word, that is; that when this evidence is given and accepted, it shows that there was a motive or interest in getting rid of the dead person, and also, inasmuch as it shows that the conduct both before and after of the persons charged was bad, undoubtedly it acts to the prejudice of the prisoners. That, as I have indicated to you, is used by the prosecution for this purpose only—of bringing your minds to bear upon the cause of death of this woman, and it is only in that relation that I intend to make any reference to it.

I propose now to address you, and I hope to be able to do it at not too great a length, upon this whole case, reminding you of the case that I opened now some few days ago. The case I put to you then was this —that I relied upon the evidence of the interest of these parties, of both of them, the motive that they had in desiring the death of this woman, the opportunities which they had had of compassing her death, and the conduct of both of them after the death; and I am going to call your attention to the evidence as it stands now; because my submission to you will be that the case I opened to you and presented to you then is a case which has not been shaken by the evidence for the defence. I shall call your special attention to points which have been made and dwelt upon by my learned friends, and refer, as far as is necessary, though it shall be very briefly, to the evidence of both sides, that is to say, both of the Crown and of the defence, as affecting the particular point. My duty, gentlemen, is to put this case to you, with such ability as I can command, to enable you to come to a just conclusion. There my duty begins and ends.

The first question which you have to consider—but upon which I do not propose to say very much, because I cannot help thinking that there has been no very serious contest with regard to it—is, whether this woman died of arsenical poisoning. That is the first thing which it is incumbent upon the prosecution to establish, and I submit to you that that, at any rate, has been established beyond all reasonable doubt. I am not quite sure that even at this moment I understand exactly the view that my learned friend, Mr. Marshall Hall, puts before you with regard to it. He says that he does not dispute that there was arsenic in her body after death, but what he says is that what was found was not sufficient to cause her death, and that she died of gastro-enteritis, perhaps assisted by arsenical poisoning. My learned friend, of course, would never make that admission if he could have escaped from it in any way upon the evidence, but there is no escaping from it. Whatever else may be said of science, whatever criticism may be directed to medical testimony, this is at least established in this case—that the evidence of Dr. Willcox and of Dr. Spilsbury, examined, closely scrutinised as it was, and quite properly by my learned friend, stands quite uncontradicted and unchallenged. My learned friend paid a very high compliment to Dr. Willcox, and I would only like myself in passing to say this,

Closing Speech for the Crown.

Attorney-General

that in the course of what is now a very long experience at the bar I never remember hearing witnesses give their evidence as Dr. Willcox and Dr. Spilsbury did, as I submit to you—of course, it is for you to judge—with more impartiality, more honesty in every word they uttered. This, however, is not in controversy in this case; I am not uttering a word with which my learned friend would disagree. On the contrary, my friend, Mr. Marshall Hall, has emphatically stated that he is in complete agreement with the view which I have just stated to you.

Now, both Dr. Willcox and Dr. Spilsbury have proved by scientific testimony—which if it has any merit at all has this merit, that it proves a thing beyond any doubt—Dr. Willcox has established to you that beyond all doubt, in his opinion, acute arsenical poisoning was the cause of death, and Dr. Spilsbury has stated the same thing. My learned friend, Mr. Marshall Hall, with great ease in dealing with these medical and scientific matters, and with undoubtedly great knowledge, has only ventured to make one criticism, and that was, that the Marsh test, according to the view that he puts forward, because it deals with such very minute quantities, is not reliable. He had before him standard mirrors which were made for this case; you have seen them; Dr. Willcox had them in the box. Mr. Rosenheim, my friend's expert witness, the physiologist, the chemist, who was going into the box to contradict, has not been called in this case by my learned friend. He was here, and rightly here, of course, during the whole of the evidence given by Dr. Spilsbury and Dr. Willcox. He is here assisting my learned friends, and imparting to them the knowledge which he possesses; and the result of it all has been this, that he has not been called; and he has not been called for the simple reason that he could not contradict anything that Dr. Willcox and Dr. Spilsbury had said. And what is the whole value of the cross-examination of my learned friend? He says that these minute calculations are not to be relied on. Really, we have only my learned friend's word for that, and that only a forensic word; he states it in argument. The witnesses have told you that that is not so, that the test is quite absolute, except in one respect, with which I will deal in a moment; and Mr. Rosenheim, who is himself a gentleman of expert knowledge, agrees with that, because he has not been called.

My learned friend's criticism has been directed to one or two of the most minute items which he selected from the table, which has been before you, but he omitted to deal with what is the most important part of this analysis; and he omitted it because he could not say anything in criticism of it, not because attention had not been drawn to it. Both my lord and you during the course of the case drew attention to this, that the Marsh test, which is the calculation by these mirrors, these standards, comparing the standard mirror with the mirror got by the test described by Dr. Willcox, is not the test which is of value in this case at all. My learned friend has given the go-bye to the real point in this case, and has not ventured to deal with it. I put it only yesterday to Dr. Willcox. When it was found that the liver and the intestines showed, as I said yesterday, $\frac{3}{4}$ of a grain—not by the Marsh test; that was not the point; that is taken by weight; the proportions of the liver and intestines and the stomach, if taken together, show just upon

Trial of the Seddons.

a grain. If you take what is taken by weight only, that is the liver and the intestines, you get, as you may have noticed from the table when it was before you, over ¾ of a grain, that is ·8· The liver is ·17; the intestines ·63; so you get ·8 of a grain. Four-fifths of a grain is actually found in the organs of the body which would contain the arsenic, if arsenic had only been recently administered, and which even then only contains one portion of it, part of it having been ejected by means of vomiting, or by means of the excreta, or it may be by the passing of urine. Then, gentlemen, just take into account that ·8 of a grain which is found by the weight on a very small particle; in one case it is a quarter of the weight of the organ which gives the result; in the other it is a fifth of the weight of the organ which gives the result. If you take that into account, that, according to Dr. Willcox, would be sufficient to kill a person. He has told you that if you find two grains in the body you would expect to find that there must have been taken, according to his view, 5 grains of arsenic, and 2 grains is a fatal dose. Then if you had, as has been established here beyond all doubt, four-fifths of a grain in the stomach and intestines, and had nothing more at all, you would have sufficient to account for the death of this woman.

But I do not want to stop quite at that, because it is right that you should clearly be convinced of this point before we go into what I think is more controversial evidence. I asked Dr. Willcox—you will remember it—in the presence of Mr. Rosenheim, who was sitting in front of my learned friend, whether he had not had a visit from Mr. Rosenheim. My learned friend, Mr. Marshall Hall, quite rightly referred to it just now; and Dr. Willcox had had all the materials, had all the apparatus ready for the test. Any further test could have been made if Mr. Rosenheim had required them. As he has told you, he always keeps, so that any further tests can be made if desired, a portion of the organs still. So that all this could be tested, and could be, right up to this very minute, if my friend had desired it. That is in existence now. There is the opportunity, and there has been the opportunity throughout this case. As Dr. Willcox told you, " I could boil up the intestines and get the exact weight, instead of taking the weight that I find in a quarter of the intestines, but for the fact if I did, and if there is any subsequent challenge, how on earth are you to ascertain whether the analysis is right or not? " Therefore, in order to give the defence the fair opportunity of making tests or of asking for tests, portions of the organs are kept in this way, so that if they are dissatisfied with the result they may say, " Let me make a test before you, or you make a test before me, so that I may prove which of us is right." The standard mirrors were all exhibited to Mr. Rosenheim; the mirrors found as the result of the analyses were all exhibited to Mr. Rosenheim; the tables with the results were placed in front of Mr. Rosenheim. Not a criticism, not a fault, can be found by Mr. Rosenheim; and for that reason he has not been put into the witness-box to contradict Dr. Willcox.

Now, gentlemen, upon that state of facts I will only make one further observation. My learned friend cross-examined a great deal about the relative quantities of arsenic that had been found as the result of experiment in the proximal and the distal ends of the hair;

Closing Speech for the Crown.

Attorney-General

but it is quite immaterial for the purpose of the point as we now have it, because you will remember, I think, what was pointed out when you had the table before you. What was found in the hair has never been calculated in the 2·01, which is the result of the calculations as found in the body. It has never entered into it at all—neither the hair, nor the skin, nor the bones. Whatever was found in the hair, skin, and bone, has not been counted at all; and the only point of Dr. Willcox telling you what he did was because in fairness he had to say exactly what arsenic he had found, and what traces there were throughout the whole of that body. The value of the Marsh test is to show this; that the arsenic was widely distributed throughout the body. That is the point. It is not in order to arrive at all these minute quantities; there are infinitesimal portions, of course; but the value of it is that there were traces of arsenic in this organ as in the others.

The only other criticism, I think, that has been made with reference to it was my friend's point about the muscle. He said that two-fifths of the muscle had been taken, and he compared the weight of the body alive with the weight of the body dead. The weight of the woman's body alive may have been 10 stone or more, and the weight when dead was 4 stone 11 lbs. The result is this. What Dr. Willcox has done is to take the two-fifths of the weight of the body, which is the proper method of calculation, and, as he has told you, a method of calculation which gives a less result in arsenic than if he had adopted the usual method of calculating these quantities. He pointed out that it was in favour of the accused that he had taken this view. And again, even if you say that 1·03 is too much, even if you leave out the whole of it, you still get enough. If you take half of it you have got enough, and it does not affect the calculation in the slightest degree.

The only other criticism was one of my learned friend's, which, so far as I understood him, was based upon his own results, and certainly was not the effect of anything that Dr. Willcox said, and I confess it surprised me. Because, as I understand, he says, "Oh, well, but if you take these Marsh tests they cannot be reliable, because there is the opening at the end, and some of the arsenic must escape and did escape." The evidence upon it is that none of it escapes—that the whole value of the Marsh test is that whatever arsenic there is is precipitated on to the glass of the tube and forms the mirror. If my friend is right in his contention that some of it escapes, then the inevitable conclusion is that there must have been more arsenic than Dr. Willcox shows by his tests and by his calculations. I do not say that that is right. All I say is that it shows the danger of an advocate attempting to deal with things of which he may have some knowledge, but which he cannot possibly understand as the experts can who give their lives to the study of these matters, and who alone have a right to testify when they are in the witness-box giving their evidence on oath.*

Gentlemen, my submission to you with reference to this case is that it is established beyond all possible doubt that this woman died from acute

---

* Mr. Marshall Hall's remarks referred to possible inaccuracy in the standard or measuring mirror, which, as he suggested, might lead to the amounts found in the body being inaccurately estimated.—ED.

Trial of the Seddons.

arsenical poisoning. Quite true that it is not discovered till some more than two months after her death. You know the story of that. You know why it is, and what led to the exhumation, and I am not going to repeat that to you. You have given such attention to this case, and really have listened to it with such diligence that I want to spare you, if I can, the recital of either immaterial details or details which have been sufficiently established beforehand.

Then, gentlemen, that being established, comes the next point, upon which, of course, I shall have more to say. The second question which you will have to determine is—did these prisoners, or did one of them, administer this arsenic? As I pointed out to you in the opening of the case, the case made by the prosecution is that the administering of the arsenic was the result of a common purpose. I shall have something more to say about that before I conclude, so that you may follow exactly what my view, as presented to you, of the legal position is, always remembering, of course, that I speak subject to my lord's direction, and any view which my lord may take. But this question, whether this poison was administered by the prisoners, is one which does involve an examination, and a somewhat close examination, into the facts of this case. You have had the opportunity of seeing the male prisoner and the female prisoner in the box. I shall not say too much, and I am quite certain that I shall not be saying one word which can operate unfairly against the male prisoner, if I put him forward before you as a shrewd, acute, keen person, and I will add also that, so far, I am in direct agreement with what my learned friend Mr. Marshall Hall said in speaking of him. But I will add this—and I shall submit to you the facts upon which I base this view which I am submitting for your consideration and your judgment—that he is a man full of cunning and craft; according to what my learned friend has been compelled to say, a man also actuated by greed and covetousness. Upon admitted facts in this case—I am not dealing with the facts that are in controversy—those qualities are displayed over and over again, and, as I shall show you, at every turn, at every fresh movement in the history of this case, you will find the same qualities of mind operating as the case proceeds from day to day.

Now, let me call your attention, gentlemen, to some of the facts which are not now and which have not been from the beginning of the trial in dispute. You will remember that when I opened the case I told you that there was an agreement for an annuity which had been made by Seddon. That was one of the points to which I drew special attention. The case made by Seddon until I cross-examined him was this—this was the case made by my learned friend Mr. Marshall Hall over and over again, referring to the document—that this agreement about the annuity was an agreement which had been entered into and made with stock-brokers, solicitors, all skilled persons, who watched over her interests. When we got to what were the real facts of the case, it was established that the original bargain was made by Seddon with Miss Barrow alone; neither solicitor, nor stockbroker, nor any skilled adviser entered into this transaction. He made the contract. He drew up the document. My learned friend said that I was suggesting that he was a lawyer.

344

Closing Speech for the Crown.

Attorney-General

No; I never suggested that. What I have suggested is that he had got a certain smattering of legal knowledge, and, as I shall show you, as very often happens in such cases, it has proved a very dangerous thing to him. He has used it. He used it first of all to draw up this document which we have never seen, because, as he tells us, he destroyed it; it is the document which you may remember—in fact, to speak quite accurately, according to the evidence, there were two. One was the document which had his signature upon it, and which was witnessed by his brother-in-law and another person, a Mr. Robert, whom we have not seen, but whose name was given. That was the document which was first drawn up. It must have been, according to the evidence, some time in September, 1910. There was another document contemporaneous with it. I said it was signed a day or so afterwards, but I treat them as contemporaneous documents which were signed by Miss Barrow, and witnessed by Mrs. Seddon; that was the bargain, the original transaction. We know now that that was destroyed, and that subsequently solicitors were called in to carry out the assignment of the public-house and the barber's shop. Seddon's story of it was not quite clear, but I do not desire to make any special point of how it was that he came to the conclusion that it was void. At one time he said that it was in his own opinion void, and then he subsequently says that he was advised that it was void; but it does not matter. He came to the conclusion, whether upon advice or his own view, that it was void, and thereupon it was destroyed, and recourse was made to the solicitors, Messrs. Russell & Sons, who came upon the scene, and, as you will remember, Messrs. Russell & Sons, as respectable solicitors, realising that this man was doing a transaction with this lady, living in his house, that she was unprotected, and had nobody to advise her, said, "You ought to have somebody in to advise you"; and so another solicitor, Mr. Knight, the brother-in-law of Mr. Keeble, is introduced for that purpose. The point that I want to make to you, and that is established upon Seddon's own evidence, is that all this parade of stockbrokers and solicitors acting in the matter is only a parade, and that the bargain was a bargain which had been struck between him and her. All this information about this original bargain and the drawing up of these documents was suppressed; we never heard a word about it.

The full significance of it becomes even more apparent when you remember what happened when he came to see the relatives after the death. You may remember the sentence that I read to him out of a letter which he had himself written, the letter of 21st September, which he had to admit concealed the truth. It is a letter which would have led anybody to believe that the whole transaction had been done with stockbrokers and solicitors, and that he had nothing to do with it. Gentlemen, that is the first comment that I desire to make upon this annuity transaction.

The second is this, that the India stock, the £1600 India 3½ per cent. nominal value, was transferred to him under date 14th October, 1910, without a single scrap of writing, or any agreement between him and Miss Barrow. He had got possession of the whole of it. He could sell it that day; he could sell it the next day. According to his statement he got possession of it on a verbal agreement, to use his own words from his

345

Trial of the Seddons.

evidence given at the inquest. He says (to do him justice) that subsequently, in January, there was an annuity certificate. What he means by an annuity certificate is something which he drew up, in which he stated that he had to pay her an annuity; that does not come into existence till January. We have not seen it. I make no point of it. I make no challenge of it; I leave it at that, but what I do ask you to infer is that what happened in September and October, when apparently the transfer was made of this stock, which was as good as money to Seddon, shows that she had given him, to use my learned friend's words in his speech, her implicit confidence; she trusted him absolutely. Gentlemen, need I dwell upon that? You have seen Mr. Seddon; you have seen him in the box—under circumstances of great stress, I agree, in which every allowance that is possible should be made for him. Having seen him there, and watched him, can you have any doubt but that he had secured the "implicit confidence" of Miss Barrow? And I will tell you what I am submitting to you followed from that. Not only had he got her £1600 India $3\frac{1}{2}$ per cent. stock, but, either then or at some later time, she trusted him with her gold, and she trusted him with her notes. For it is no good these two people going into the box and giving the accounts that they have given to you about that part of the transaction. How it affects the question of guilt on the charge for which they are now prosecuted is another matter; but upon the facts of the case, I submit to you it is idle for them to suggest that they know nothing at all about this money—either the gold or the notes. Just conceive the position. Here was this woman. She has been talked of as an old maid; she was forty-eight or forty-nine years of age; she was in the habit of going out every day with the boy—the boy to whom, according to the evidence, her whole heart seems to have been given. Whatever her failings may have been, whatever her faults may have been (and I have no doubt that in the lives of all of us, when examined, some will be found when we are gone), whatever they may have been, she seems to have been devotedly attached to this boy. I am going to suggest to you—of course, for your consideration—that she had no notion during the whole of this time that she was parting with her property, with her gold, or with her notes, and had never intended to get rid of gold or notes in the ordinary course of things—allowing that she did not intend to give it to her relatives—that she meant to retain it for her boy, whom, in the maternal instinct, no doubt, of the spinster heart, she was cherishing, and to whom she had become devoted.

Now, just let me ask you to think for a moment of what the evidence is as regards the money. When you come to put this case together and see what was happening, my submission to you is that it is absolutely impossible to explain what had become of this woman's money, except upon the view that these two persons had got hold of it, and had got hold of it before her death—at any rate, a large quantity of it. That it was in Miss Barrow's mind to entrust her money to him is shown by an incident which took place a day or two before Hook leaves. The incident to which I want to refer for a moment is this, because, according to the view that I present to you, it shows that the statements that they are making with reference to this money are absolutely untrue. According to Hook's testimony—I shall have something to say about him a little

346

Closing Speech for the Crown.

Attorney-General

later on—but, according to Hook's testimony, which is corroborated, as I shall show you in a moment, by Mr. Vonderahe, in the cash box there was a considerable sum of notes. According to him, he saw £380; it had been £420 in 1906; he saw it counted out again when it went to the house in Tollington Park, and it was 380 sovereigns and a lot of notes in that cash box. The notes are gone. The gold is gone. More gold is added to the store, and that is gone. Some money was withdrawn from the savings bank, and that has disappeared—all disappeared whilst she was in the house living with these two persons. As I indicated to you in opening the case, actual sovereigns are difficult to trace; current coin passes from hand to hand, and you cannot identify particular sovereigns; but you can identify particular bank notes. My learned friend Mr. Rentoul (no doubt in his enthusiastic advocacy for his client, for which, I am sure, he will not think I am blaming him, but on the contrary I will, if I may, commend him) said that she admitted it directly the question of the notes was brought forward. I have looked in vain for the admission. To whom did she admit it? Where did she admit it? If my friend means, under that phrase, that she admitted it when her husband asked her when they were both being charged together, yes, then I follow what he means; but what the value of that admission is I fail to grasp. This question of tracing the notes had been a most difficult and laborious process. Possibly it is only in the hands of the authorities that you can get a thorough tracing of notes. It is only when the Director of Public Prosecutions or the Commissioner of Police takes up a case of this kind, in all probability that you can get such a tracing of notes as has taken place in this case. Why, gentlemen, the number of witnesses called in order to establish this dealing with the notes is—I will not pledge myself to the exact number, but it is between forty and fifty persons—persons who have been called at the Police Court and called here before you. Of course, as my learned friend rightly pointed out, all the evidence that has been given at the Police Court and the evidence that has been given here in regard to that is not challenged. It is not challenged for what reason? Why, the elementary lesson that an advocate learns is never to challenge evidence which he will not be able to dispute. Of course, all this is undisputed, necessarily undisputed—and the class of evidence does not admit of dispute. It proved this. It proved the dealing with £165 in £5 notes, to which must be added another note of which we had an admission yesterday from Mrs. Seddon. But leave that out of the calculation; after all, it adds little to it. Where did those notes come from? The money found its way into the pockets of Mr. Seddon and Mrs. Seddon. How did they get them? You have heard a remarkable story of how Mrs. Seddon got the money. She says Miss Barrow was in the habit of coming down and handing a £5 note to change; that was continued right up to the end of August, 1911. Mind you, after she had actually got the £216 in sovereigns in her box on the 19th June, July, and August, and even in September, to bring down notes for the purpose of having them changed into gold.

Mr. Justice Bucknill—I do not think Mrs. Seddon got anything in September; I think her last was in August.

The Attorney-General—Thirty-three notes are traced on the table to

Trial of the Seddons.

the end of August, 1911; they form the £165. There was one note which she admitted yesterday——

Mr. JUSTICE BUCKNILL—I thought you were going to leave that out.

The ATTORNEY-GENERAL—I am. I was only referring to the fact that she admitted that one yesterday.

Mr. JUSTICE BUCKNILL—The 23rd August was the last date.

The ATTORNEY-GENERAL—I was only going to observe this, that on the 19th June the £216 is withdrawn in actual gold, and it is taken home to the house. On the 26th June, the 5th July, the 15th July, then 4th August, the 8th August, the 10th August, and the 23rd August notes are being passed by Mrs. Seddon. And, gentlemen, let me further observe this. During the month of August, 1911, when the changing of notes has become as familiar to her as eating bread and butter, even in that month of August she gives a false name and false address. Mrs. Seddon, when pressed with this, gave you what I submit is a very extraordinary explanation. Of course, these matters are for you to judge. It is a very difficult situation, no doubt, for her to explain. Again, it is a matter partly for her, and no doubt a matter upon which you may judge, whether under the circumstances, in view of what has happened, it was any good making the pretence that these notes had been given by Miss Barrow to her to cash. But when she is asked whether she could give any reason for Miss Barrow doing this, she gave what is perhaps one of the most extraordinary answers in this case. She said, because Miss Barrow did not like notes; she did not like having notes. Upon the evidence, which is beyond all dispute, and is not disputed, Miss Barrow had hoarded notes from the year 1901 until the time when she went to live at Tollington Park; and some of these very notes with which we are now dealing which have been traced are notes which Miss Barrow had hoarded up in the years 1901, 1902, 1903, 1904, 1905, and so on, till the year 1910, because she had this fancy for keeping the notes in her cash box. Those are the admitted facts. No explanation, no suggestion has been given why all of a sudden she went to change these notes into gold.

Then Mrs. Seddon goes to the Post Office to change the notes. Well, gentlemen, you heard her. She was asked to give her name and address; she said she had never handled a £5 note. It is a little difficult to accept in view of this that she had been carrying on a business for some twelve months, and, according to them, if you accept their statement, a business in which hundreds of pounds passed. I will assume that she had never changed a £5 note in her life. She goes to the Post Office. Gentlemen, can you conceive the state of mind of the woman who is honestly there with a £5 note which she is asked to cash for some one who is a friend of hers, and who is asked by the postmaster to give her name and address, and immediately gives a false name and a false number of the street in which she had lived? She says she did that because she was unused to it. Well, if it had been a solitary occasion—difficult as it might seem—one might in mercy have accepted the explanation, but how can you? She goes on in March—months afterwards—when she has been dealing with some of these £5 notes in shops where she is known, spending money, and having to change the note; of course, there she could not give a false name and address, because she spends the money, and they

348

Closing Speech for the Crown.

Attorney-General

know her there; but at these other places that she goes to on other occasions she changes notes and gives false names and addresses. Gentlemen, she is bound to admit that she did not know anybody of the name of Scott; she did not know anybody living at 18 Evershot Road; and equally is it not perfectly clear that, of course, notes with false names and addresses endorsed upon them are very much more difficult to trace than notes with a right name and address upon them.

Gentlemen, the conclusion which I ask you to draw when you consider the evidence upon this part of the case is that she had improperly made use of these £5 notes. That the £5 notes were in existence when she went into the house there is no doubt; that is proved beyond all contradiction; it is indeed admitted. Yes, in August of 1910, according to the story as told, when this incident occurred with the Hooks—there is some small controversy which I will not pause for a second to deal with—some squalid dispute between him and Hook—Miss Barrow brings the cash box to Mr. Seddon and asks him to take care of it. That is very likely true. That is in accordance with the agreement that had been made by which she had placed herself in his hands entirely with regard to the annuity. It will accord with the transfer by her of £1600 worth of stock into his name without even a scrap of document to show that she had an interest in an annuity at all. It will accord with everything that had taken place. It would be, as my friend says, an example of the implicit confidence that she was placing in him. She brings in the box, and he says she said to him, "There is £30 to £35." Why does he say that? If he were to tell you the truth, which was that she told him what money there was really in it, of course, it adds a great deal to the money which has got to be accounted for somehow or other on his own showing, or which, at any rate, would have been in her possession. But he says she told him there was £30 to £35. Now, Miss Barrow could not possibly have said that. That is the point I want to make clear to you; because, on their own showing, there was, at the very least, £170 in notes in that cash box. This story about the £30 to £35 is absolutely untrue. I am not unmindful of the fact which, in fairness to them, perhaps ought to be mentioned, that they say they do not know, or did not know, that the £5 notes were kept in the cash box; they both say that; because they say they never saw it opened until after her death. They have failed to give the faintest explanation of where these £5 notes came from, and you had the most definite evidence, both of Hook and of Mr. Vonderahe, about it. It is quite clear, in my submission, that it is an absolute impossibility that Miss Barrow could have said to him that there was £30 to £35 there. They tell me the same story, of course; their evidence to a certain extent—except as to some points to which I will call your attention—is an echo the one of the other. £30 to £35 she brings to him to take care of, their story is, because she is afraid of Hook. Mr. Seddon is absolutely precise about it. He says he will not accept that cash box for safe custody unless she counts out the money then and there to him, and he would give a receipt for it to her. His story is that she said there was £30 to £35; he says, "Count it out," and, for some reason utterly unexplained, she goes up to her room with the cash box and never comes down, and nothing more is heard of it. Of course, to a great extent, you have to reconstruct what happened during

Trial of the Seddons.

this time; because we have only the evidence of Mr. and Mrs. Seddon as to what happened at the particular moment; but, fortunately, there is the evidence to which I have called your attention, which makes that statement of theirs absolutely untrue.

Now, gentlemen, just let me remind you of the money that passes into this woman's hands, according to the story told by the defendants themselves. There is—I will leave out the £8 which was discussed yesterday; it only complicates matters—there is £165 cashed by the changing of notes into gold. There is £91 which was received by this lady for the annuity, according to the Seddons' own statement. There is £216 which was drawn out on the 19th June. That is £472. But you will observe, gentlemen, I have not taken into account at all in that £472 the amount of gold that she had when she came into the house. Now, there is no doubt that there was a considerable quantity of gold. There are three persons who have spoken to it—Hook, Mr. Vonderahe, and Ernie Grant—they all saw it; the exact amount is not very material, but, so far as we are able to get the figures, there is, upon the evidence, £380. If there was £380, as has been deposed to in such definite terms, that would give £850 as the total sum of money which was in her hands, subject, of course, to this—you must put on the other side of it what she was spending. We have got a very great light upon the kind of life she was living and the amount she was spending. She was living up in this one bedroom with a small kitchen in which she used to have her meals with Ernie Grant. We know what Ernie Grant cost to keep according to the Seddons, and I will assume that Ernie Grant was kept by them during the two weeks as he was kept by Miss Barrow; that comes to 10s. a week—the cost of keeping the boy. I say I know that, because we have got the account which I put in, where he accounts for the £10 which he found, and he puts down the keep of Ernie Grant for two weeks at 10s. a week. It really is not very material; there is 12s. a week which only for a few months she was paying as rent, because from the 1st January she does not pay any rent at all; that is included in the annuity; she had not got to pay that; leave that out of account. Apparently she was a very shabbily dressed woman, and spent very little upon herself. Let us put down that she spent £1 a week upon herself for mere food and clothing, or 30s.; it does not matter, it is not worth spending a moment over. The utmost you can get out of it is that she spent about £2 a week at the very highest, and spending that for a short time from the 1st January, we will say, until the 14th September, you have got the total amount of money that she could have spent; say she spent £100 during that time. According to the way in which she was living, she could not have spent it very well without spending some money outside; but, say, £100. Then you have got £750 to account for; that is assuming that there were no other notes than those we have traced. You may leave out the £10 which had been given her on the 2nd September. Then, gentlemen, the total amount of money found in this woman's possession on the day she died was 3d. in coppers.

Now, gentlemen, if they had possession of the money out of the cash box; if, just in the same way he had complete custody of her bank notes and her gold, at some time or other the day of reckoning would come, and that money would have to be paid over. My submission to you

Closing Speech for the Crown.

is that this is a material factor to take into account in this case, because if you come to the conclusion that they had dishonestly used the notes and had got the gold, with the greed and covetousness, unfortunately, of some men, dreading the arrival of the day when they might be called upon to account for the money, you get motive, overwhelming motive, for desiring this woman's death. If you add to that that there was the payment of the annuity which had to be made, the payment of which rested upon him as long as this woman was alive, then you again get a further reason why it would have been to his interest beyond all dispute that this woman's life should cease.*

Adjourned.

Tenth Day—Thursday, 14th March, 1912.

The Court met at 10.30 a.m.

The ATTORNEY-GENERAL, resuming—When the Court adjourned yesterday I was asking you to bear in mind the story told by both prisoners as to the dealings with the cash box, in order to put before you what I suggest is the true explanation of how these prisoners came to be passing these notes when dealing with Miss Barrow's money. In this connection it is not unimportant to refer for a moment to what has been said by the female prisoner, in addition to what I mentioned yesterday. She apparently gave the explanation to her husband when he asked her about it, according to the story we have heard in the witness-box, that she did not want everybody to know her business, and that is why she had given the false name and address. That is an explanation which one understands if she was improperly passing these notes, the property of Miss Barrow, but an absolutely impossible explanation to accept if the story she is now giving is true. It was very remarkable how the story shifted. The male prisoner in the box gave this explanation when I pressed him about the passing of these notes, and he said that was her story. You may remember that I put some very simple and easy questions to him, which showed perfectly plainly that that was a theory which no reasonable man could ever accept in explanation. When she came into the witness-box she never said a word about that story. There was an entirely different suggestion about never having passed a note before.

I am not going to delay by dwelling at any greater length upon those incidents, except to say a word or two in passing about the male prisoner's dealing with the notes. According to his story, he received one £5 note in payment for a cheque for £9 8s. 4d., which he says he sent to Frere, Cholmeley & Co. in October, 1910, for the ground rent which was due on the Buck's Head. The other £5 note, which got into his banking account at the beginning of January, 1911, he says came into his possession by her giving him a £5 note on five different occasions in payment of the 12s. rent, and for which he returned her £4 8s. change. With regard to the first £5 note as to the cheque, it is of very little importance in this case, but when we once know, as we do know, that he had already made

---

*See note by Seddon, Appendix K.

Trial of the Seddons.

the bargain in September of 1910, by which the India stock was to be transferred and the Buck's Head property was to be his, and he was to pay an annuity, and when we know that on the 14th October he had already got her India stock, and that on the 5th October, from the letters produced, the solicitors were already upon the scene to make out the assignment of the Buck's Head, it is not very difficult to understand that as part of that bargain it would have been his duty to pay the ground rent then, as he did on subsequent occasions from the moment the assignment was completed. It is not a very important matter. But, as regards the other £5 notes, it is very difficult to follow from his point of view. During that time a considerable number of notes are also getting into the possession of his wife, and, if you can understand the story as told by them, it would seem that she was always giving out £5 notes and getting gold in change; that year, I think during October, November, and December, she received at least £25, which she passes and deals with in notes, and he gets £30. The explanation as to his five £5 notes, I submit to you, is quite impossible to accept in the circumstances of her story and of his story. Apparently she must have been getting all the gold she could possibly want. She is getting gold changed from these notes of the wife. She is getting all the gold she could possibly want from him, if only to change one, and in addition to this she must be having, according to this story, in her possession, a considerable amount of gold, even on their statement. There it is. I do not mean to go into it in more detail. It shows us this, that both of them are dealing with this money, both of them are dealing with these notes, and I submit to you both of them are unable to give any reasonable explanation of why they are dealing with it.

Now, that brings me up to the month of August. I do not mean to repeat either what was said yesterday in the history of the case by my learned friends, or what I may have referred to myself. That brings us to the month of August, 1911, when apparently she consults Dr. Paul. You have heard Dr. Paul's evidence; he says that she was suffering from a slight ailment, congestion of the liver, or a bilious attack, but it was not bad enough to keep her in the house. That was for the first two or three times that she goes to see him, and during the last twice she is suffering from a slight attack of asthma, and not congestion of the liver at all—asthma which, he said, was not sufficient to keep her indoors for a moment; she was walking about in her usual health, meeting her relatives, as we know, during this month of August, and taking the boy to school, fetching him from school, and living her ordinary life.

Then we get to the month of September, and I want to direct your attention to what appears to me to be the most important point in this case, and that is the purchase of arsenic on 26th August, 1911. The theory of the prosecution, as I opened, supported by evidence, as I will show you directly, is this, that Margaret Seddon had gone to Thorley's shop at Crouch Hill on 26th August, 1911, and had purchased there a packet of arsenical fly-papers. The answer that is made to that case by the defence is that she never did go there, and that Mr. Thorley had made a mistake in identifying Margaret Seddon as the person who bought those papers. If the view put forward by the prosecution is

Closing Speech for the Crown.

Attorney-General

right; if, on examination of the evidence that has been given, you come to the conclusion that she did go to Thorley's on 26th August and purchase these fly-papers, then the whole theory of the defence, all the views put forward by the defence, break down, and the case for the defence crumbles away. I will tell you why I say that—because no attempted explanation has been given as to why it was that those fly-papers should have been asked for on 26th August. What is far more important even than the purchase is that when this girl went to Thorley's, as we know she did, she asked for *four* packets of fly-papers, which would contain twenty-four papers, each one of which, as we know, contains more than sufficient to kill an adult human being. Of course, it may be very well that any person who was going to use these fly-papers to poison a human being would not know exactly how much there was in a fly-paper. But if the girl went to buy four packets of Mather's arsenical fly-papers according to Thorley, whose evidence I will read to you directly, then I do say that there is absolutely no explanation that could possibly be given by the defence which is consistent with innocence, and, indeed, none has been attempted.

The case for the defence is based upon this, that the girl never did buy these fly-papers. Let us see what happened. Let me just recall to your minds what took place in this Court. Mr. Thorley was called, and his evidence amounted to this. You may remember as I opened the case all that I said in reference to it was that Margaret Seddon had purchased a packet of these fly-papers on 26th August; and Mr. Thorley came into the box and stated that a girl had come into his shop to purchase them; he did not know her name was Margaret Seddon; all that he knew was that on a particular day, which was a Saturday, a girl came and he sold her a packet of fly-papers. He was cross-examined, and, of course, tested, as he had to be by my learned friend, and he was asked why it was that he had any special recollection of that particular sale, and he gave evidence which hitherto could not have been admitted, but which became admissible evidence, whatever doubts there might be about it before, the moment his memory was challenged upon it, and he said that he remembered it distinctly because on that date the girl came in and asked for four packets of fly-papers, and that he had not got four packets to sell her, he had only one, that that was the last of his stock, and that he made a note in his order book to order more because she had wanted more, and he said that he would have them in the next week. That is how the evidence stood with regard to it. He said, further, that he had seen the girl before, because once he had opened the door for her, and he had seen her on another occasion with his daughter. He did not know her name, and he did not know who she was, but what he did know was that she had been to his house—to the door, at any rate, to speak to his daughter, on two occasions. He remembered her face, that was all; he never knew her name. Then inquiries are made by the police—necessarily made—in the neighbourhood to ascertain whether any fly-papers had been sold to the Seddon household during this period; and he is asked whether he can identify the girl or not. He says he does not know whether he can identify her or not. Then he goes into a room where there are some twenty people,

Trial of the Seddons.

and he picks her out for a very good reason—because he has known her—he has seen her on two occasions before, and he remembers that the girl who came in to purchase the arsenical papers was the girl he had seen twice when she had called for or been with his daughter. Mr. Thorley was sharply cross-examined by my learned friend necessarily, and he was asked whether this was not the result of some conversation with Mr. Price, another chemist. He explained that it had nothing whatever to do with it, and he didn't have any such conversation. Mr. Price was the person who was supposed to have put it into his mind. You remember why that was. Mr. Price is the chemist from whom Maggie Seddon, on the 6th December—that is two days after his arrest—sought to purchase fly-papers. He refused to sell them to her, no doubt because of what he had heard in connection with the case. But Mr. Price, according to the view that was put by my learned friend in cross-examination, was supposed in some way to have suggested to Mr. Thorley the material from which Mr. Thorley came to the conclusion that Maggie Seddon was the girl to whom he had sold fly-papers in August. Mr. Thorley says he had no conversation with him about it; and in order that there should be no doubt, and that the matter should be at least thoroughly questioned and sifted, I put Mr. Price into the box at once, so that my learned friend could cross-examine him upon this point. He never ventured to ask him a question upon it.

Mr. MARSHALL HALL—Thorley's evidence was that he identified her in the morning before he had seen Mr. Price, so it was useless to ask him questions about it.

The ATTORNEY-GENERAL—I agree with my learned friend that it was useless to ask the question of Mr. Price, but the reason why I put Mr. Price into the witness-box was, if any suggestion of that kind were made, it could be put to him; but if my learned friend says it was useless to put it, I am quite in accord with him about it. Therefore Mr. Price had not suggested it in any way to Thorley. How was it Thorley identified the girl? He told us. He went there in the morning, and I will just call your attention to what he actually said about it, because of its extreme importance. Gentlemen, may I make this further reference to Mr. Thorley. It is not suggested, and, indeed, on the material before you it could not be suggested, that Mr. Thorley is anything but an honest, straightforward tradesman, carrying on his business in this locality. There is no ground for any aspersion upon his character, and none is made. Mr. Thorley's anxiety must be, not to be a witness in a murder case in connection with fly-papers which he sold to a girl, but his anxiety must be to keep out of the case if he possibly can. He is not a man who wants to put himself forward in the witness-box to come before you to tell his story. One knows quite well, first of all, in the case of a tradesman selling goods such as these, that he is by no means desirous to explain and tell you what happened. There is always the question for consideration as to whether he was not bound to make an entry of it, and whether he ought not to have made an entry of it in a poison book. That, of course, is not material for the purpose of this case, and I pass from it; but a chemist knows that, and he does not want to come into the witness-box and tell his story. And above that, as we know, no man who is carrying on his business

Closing Speech for the Crown.

Attorney-General

is desirous of attending either the Police Court or this Court and giving up a good deal of his time in order that he may give his testimony. But Mr. Thorley is an honest man; he is unable to tell a lie about it, and the consequence of it is that when Mr. Thorley is asked to come to the station and see if he can identify that girl, and he does identify the girl, he is bound to say that he does as an honourable man, and he goes into the box and tells you without the faintest doubt that the girl to whom he sold those fly-papers on 26th August was Margaret Seddon. I only desire to read to you some short passages from his evidence in order to recall to you what happened, because they are so important. You will recollect that my learned friend raised the point that the evidence of Margaret Seddon's purchase was not admissible evidence, and then the girl Chater was recalled to prove that Margaret Seddon slept in the house and attended to the household. Then the examination was continued. The material passage begins thus—

Q. Can you fix the date when you gave evidence at the Police Court? What I want is, how long it was before that day on which you gave the evidence at the Police Court that you were asked about this sale of the Mather's fly-papers?—A. About week.

About a week before he gave evidence, and he gave evidence, we are agreed, on 2nd February, 1912.

Q. Then you were asked to go to the Court on that particular day on which you gave evidence, that is 2nd February, 1912, do you remember that?—A. Yes. Q. And you were asked to go into a room where there were a number of women and girls? A. Yes. Q. About how many, do you know?—A. About twenty. Q. Did anybody go in with you?—A. No. Q. What did you go there for?—A. To identify a girl that I had sold some fly-papers to.

Then he picks her out, and he knows her now as Margaret Seddon because he saw her in Court.

Mr. MARSHALL HALL—He said "Margaret Ann Seddon."

The ATTORNEY-GENERAL—Yes, that is quite true, but I do not think there is any point in that. He did say first that he thought her name was Margaret Ann Seddon; he explained that he had got the name "Margaret Ann Seddon" in his mind, but the girl he identified was beyond all question Margaret Seddon, the daughter. You have seen the girl. I suggest to you that it is not very likely that he has made a mistake about it, particularly if he has seen her three times. Here was a girl who was in the habit of coming up, or had been twice to see the daughter, and then she comes and buys these fly-papers. I will not read to you about what happened as regards the purchase, because there is no doubt, if Mr. Thorley is right, that this girl came in there and he sold a packet of Mather's fly-papers on that 26th August, 1911, and that it was the last packet that he had in stock. Indeed, that is not challenged. What is challenged is that he sold it to this girl. Then my learned friend puts this question in cross-examination—

Q. Will you tell the jury how you profess to remember the date of 26th August. You have no note, have you—no memorandum of any sort or shape?—A. I have got my invoices. She had the last packet of a dozen that was ordered in on one day. Q. The last packet?—A. She had the last packet. Q. Do you keep a record of the sale of the last packet?—A. No. Q. How do you know when the last packet was sold?—A. She asked for four packets. Q. For four packets?—A. Yes. Q. Four packets of six

Trial of the Seddons.

papers?—*A.* Four packets, twenty-four papers. *Q.* The girl who came in on the 26th asked for four packets?—*A.* Yes. *Q.* 3d. a packet?—*A.* 3d. a packet. That was the last one I had. I put them down to order in the book, and told her we should have some more on Monday. *Q.* Then you fix the date from the fact that you did sell your last packet on 26th August?—*A.* Yes.

Now, so far Mr. Thorley cannot be making a mistake. He has got his invoices and he has got his memorandum in his order book, which, if challenged, of course, could be produced; but it was not challenged. He had got the note there that they had to be ordered, and he told Margaret Seddon that he would get them in during the next week.

Mr. MARSHALL HALL—I wish you would read the next piece.

The ATTORNEY-GENERAL—It goes to another point.

Mr. MARSHALL HALL—I know my learned friend wants to be perfectly fair, but there is one point he has not touched upon at all; I made a great point that this gentleman admitted that he had seen a picture of Margaret Seddon.

The ATTORNEY-GENERAL—I quite agree that point was made about it, but I want to read first of all the part that deals with this, and then I will come back to any passage my learned friend wants. He was re-examined. Your lordship will remember what happened upon that. I asked the question, "Now, tell us what happened when the girl came into the shop." There was some discussion as to whether that particular part of the evidence was admissible. It became admissible, as your lordship thought quite clearly, in consequence of the question necessarily put by my learned friend, and I put the question then, as I suggest, in a different form, so as to remove all possibility of doubt. I asked the same question as my learned friend; I asked him to tell us his special reason for remembering the sale to the girl, and his identifying her as Margaret Seddon, and he tells us the special reason was this—

A. She asked for four packets and I had only one in stock. *Q.* Four packets of what?—*A.* Fly-papers. *Q.* Was any particular kind of fly-paper referred to?—*A.* Arsenical fly-papers. *Q.* Who used those words?—*A.* Margaret Seddon. *Q.* Then what did you say?—*A.* I said, "Will you take a packet?" She said, "I will take four." She took the papers and left the shop. *Q.* Do you mean the packet.—*A.* The packet. *Q.* I want to know what happened then. If you do not remember say so. You said, "Will you take a packet," and she said, "I will take four." Now was anything said after that?—*A.* Yes, I said, "That is the only one I have. I shall have some more on Monday." *Q.* Had you any more Mather's fly-papers in stock than that one packet when the girl came in.—*A.* No. *Q.* Did you make any note or entry in a book on that date?—*A.* Yes. *Q.* Did you order any more Mather's fly-papers?—*A.* Yes.

That evidence shows clearly that she purchased one packet and that she wanted four packets. I will read you now the passages to which my learned friend is calling attention with reference to the identity. He is asked at page 54, "Do you know the girl, Margaret Seddon at all?"

A. Yes. *Q.* She is a friend of your daughter's, is she not?—*A.* She is known to her; I do not know her as Margaret Seddon. *Q.* Your daughter Mabel?—*A.* Yes, I did not know this girl as Margaret Seddon until I saw her in the Police Court, although I have seen her. *Q.* When you identified——
The Attorney General—Would you mind letting him finish his answer.
The Witness—Although I have seen her about the neighbourhood.
Mr. MARSHALL HALL—*Q.* The girl you identified in the Police Court as the person who came to your shop to buy these fly-papers is somebody who has been to your house to see your daughter Mabel?—*A.* Yes. *Q.* On two occasions she called to see

356

Closing Speech for the Crown.

Attorney-General

Mabel?—*A.* Yes, she did not come in. *Q.* No, that is just what I put to you. You opened the door and said Mabel was not at home, and she went away?—*A.* Well, could not identify anybody I did that to; I did that to many other girls. *Q.* That i the point I am on. The person you identified as having bought the papers after thi lapse of time is the identification of somebody whom you had seen on your premise having come to see your daughter. That is the suggestion I make to you?—*A.* I hav seen her in the shop. *Q.* I suggest to you that you have made a mistake. I am no suggesting that it is a wilful mistake, but I am suggesting to you you have made a mis take, and that the girl you identified on the 2nd February as the girl who had bought fly-papers at your establishment on 26th August, 1911, is not that girl but the girl who had twice called at your place to see your daughter Mabel. Do you still say that she is the girl who bought the fly-papers?—*A.* Yes. *Q.* Let us come to the identity. Yo are fetched in a motor car on 2nd February, that is so, is it not?—*A.* Yes. *Q.* Yo are brought down to the Police Court with Mr. Price and somebody else in th car. Were you and Mr. Price taken in together to a room where there wer about twenty people?—*A.* No, that was in the morning. *Q.* In the morning? *A.* I came down by myself in the morning. *Q.* You have been down to th Police Court before you came down in the motor car?—*A.* Yes.

So, you see, up to that point the suggestion was quite wrong. H had not been with Mr. Price at all to identify the girl. He went alone he did not see Mr. Price until the afternoon, when he is sent for to giv evidence. Then, my learned friend puts this question—

Q. Had you seen the photograph of Margaret Seddon in the papers—a picture mean, not a photograph?—*A.* Yes. *Q.* Before you went to identify her?—*A.* Not tha day. *Q.* No, I know.—*A.* Before it. *Q.* You were taken down by the police to identif a girl whose picture had been published in the illustrated papers, and which you had seen?—*A.* I refused to identify the girl from the pictures I had seen. *Q.* Of cours naturally you would, but the picture was shown to you for the purpose of identification —*A.* It was not shown to me by the police. *Q.* Anyhow, you tell me you had see it?—*A.* Yes. *Q.* You had seen the picture of a girl whom you knew to be Margare Seddon, the daughter of the man who is charged with this murder, and you are take down by the police to identify that particular girl among twenty others. That is so, i it not?—(No answer). *Q.* Is that so?—*A.* I do not know whether they knew I ha seen the picture. *Q.* Did not they happen to ask you?—*A.* No. *Q.* You knew yo had seen the picture, did you not?—*A.* Yes. *Q.* Until I asked you, would you hav told anybody that you had seen that picture?—*A.* Yes.

It is quite right that you should have that present to your mind, a that is the reason why my learned friend says you should not rely upor Mr. Thorley's evidence of identification.

Mr. JUSTICE BUCKNILL—There is a better reason still, if you wil remember, why he did not go on the picture—because the picture was but picture in the illustrated papers, and they sometimes are very bad.

Mr. MARSHALL HALL—If there is any point made on that I will produce the actual picture.

The ATTORNEY-GENERAL—Of course, I quite follow my learned friend's point with regard to it, and, although I should not put it with the same force as he would for his client, still I will put his point with reference to it, and if I am wrong he will correct me. What he means is, you must not rely on the evidence of Mr. Thorley, because Mr. Thorley had, before he went to the Police Court, seen a picture in the paper of a girl called "Margaret Seddon," and that therefore he had in his mind what he had seen in the paper, and that that was Margaret Seddon, and jumped to the conclusion that the girl to whom he had sold the papers was Margaret Seddon. In my submission to you exactly the opposite would have happened, that if Mr. Thorley saw the picture there he would not jump

Trial of the Seddons.

to any conclusion that that was Margaret Seddon, unless he said to himself, " Well, that is very like the girl whom I have seen twice come in for my daughter, and whom I saw in the shop." He had no interest in this case except to keep out of it, and he was particularly careful, as any honourable man would be. Of course, he said he could not identify the girl, and would not jump to any conclusion, and he would not identify the girl from what he saw in the paper. Then he is brought into the room where there are these twenty women and girls, and he picks out the girl unhesitatingly as the girl whom he had known as visiting his daughter and as the girl who had come into his shop, and to whom he had sold the fly-papers. That is the evidence upon it with regard to Thorley. At one time, I will not say it was suggested, because, of course, my learned friend was quite entitled to try and shake the evidence, but there was some doubt thrown upon Margaret Seddon's presence in London on 26th August.

Mr. MARSHALL HALL—I could not press that.

The ATTORNEY-GENERAL—I am not suggesting that there is anything wrong in it. Whether it was a mistaken date given to my learned friend or not is quite immaterial. The only reason I am referring to it is that in consequence of the suggestion that was made at one time during the cross-examination we called Miss Mavis Wilson who kept a shop. She came into the box and told you definitely and clearly—and her evidence is uncontradicted; it is admitted by Margaret Seddon—that on 26th August, 1911, this very day, Margaret Seddon, the girl, did go to Miss Wilson's shop and bought, if I remember aright, some shoes and a writing case at Miss Wilson's shop. The most significant feature of all is that on that day she goes to Miss Wilson's shop, and from her shop to Mr. Thorley's shop is only two minutes' walk. Margaret Seddon says she thinks it is five minutes, but it does not matter; people's opinion differ as to time; that her shop is a very little way from Mr. Thorley's is made manifest by the evidence. So that you have got there Margaret Seddon going to Wilson's shop and going to Thorley's shop. It is a singular coincidence that Mr. Thorley, without any knowledge of that, without the remotest notion that she had been to Miss Wilson's shop upon that day, should come forward and say, as he does, that upon that date she came into his shop, and that she purchased these fly-papers. Gentlemen, you see how significant that statement is. It is not possible to exaggerate it, so it strikes me, and so I submit to you, because once it is clear, as I submit to you it is clear, that Thorley is right when he says that the girl Margaret Seddon came to his shop, then you have got the fact of this large number of arsenical fly-papers being purchased on 26th August, and all the story told about their not knowing anything about arsenic, and not knowing anything about these fly-papers, and not having obtained any arsenical fly-papers on this date, has to be rejected, and is all proved to be absolutely untrue.

Now, I want to deal with the last feature of that part of the story which is Margaret Seddon's evidence. Margaret Seddon is called. Gentlemen, I am not going to say a single harsh word in criticism of Margaret Seddon. The girl is placed in a most trying and difficult position. She has to come forward as a girl of sixteen years of age to give evidence. She goes into the witness-box, and she says that she never was there, and she never purchased them. Then she is confronted with the statement which she

Closing Speech for the Crown.

Attorney-General

made, to which I must refer and say something directly in answer to the criticisms made by my learned friend. That statement upon the face of it made by her at the time was untrue. She was asked whether she had ever been to any other chemist in that neighbourhood to purchase poison, including poisonous fly-papers. She says "No." She knew perfectly well that she had. No girl could forget it, and I will tell you why. Two days after her father's arrest she went to purchase these arsenical fly-papers from Mr. Price, the chemist, and he refused to sell them to her. She knew why she went. She went with the sister of the solicitor who was acting for her father, and she knew what the object of purchasing them was. She knew her father had been arrested for having murdered this woman by administering arsenic. She knew quite well that she was to purchase these fly-papers, as they were purchased immediately after, for analysis purposes. You will remember what we have heard about this. You will remember the male prisoner was arrested on 4th December. That very same day that he is arrested, having been informed, as he was, by Chief Inspector Ward that he was arrested for having murdered this woman by administering arsenic and poisoning her, he sees his solicitor, the gentleman instructing my learned friend. Immediately he sees him this question of the arsenical fly-papers comes into consideration; we know from the evidence it is on that day that the question of the purchase of the arsenical fly-papers comes into consideration. According to the story as told by the defence, what is done then? Instructions are given. I do not pause to inquire whether it is Mr. Saint, or whether it is Mrs. Seddon; it does not matter. The girl says she does not remember whether it was Mrs. Seddon or Mr. Saint. Instructions are given for the purchase of fly-papers at Mr. Price's on 6th December, and the girl does go and try to purchase them on that date. Can you imagine a girl who had done that with the knowledge that her father had been arrested for murder forgetting that she had been to that shop on the 6th December to buy these arsenical fly-papers?

The girl is asked a question by Chief Inspector Ward on 2nd February, 1913, and he put a question to her which admits of no doubt—" Have you been to any other chemist in that neighbourhood to purchase poison, including poisonous fly-papers?" She says, "No." She must have known she was telling an untruth at that time. She said it, no doubt, because she thought it served the interest of her father. Chief Inspector Ward then goes on and puts another question to her—"Have you ever been to the chemist's shop at the corner of Tollington Park and Stroud Green Road to purchase fly-papers?"—that is Mr. Price's shop. She says, "No." How could that girl truthfully have made that answer? She makes that answer because she thinks it is in the interest of her father that she should. Then Chief Inspector Ward says to her—"Did you, on 6th December, 1911, go to this shop to purchase Mather's fly-papers?" Then she says, "Yes." She knows by that time that the police know the date; they have put to her, "On 6th December, 1911, did you go there to purchase Mather's fly-papers?" and she says, "Yes, I went there, but I did not get any. The chemist was going to give them to me until I mentioned my name." You have seen this paper which was signed by her. No suggestion was made, so far as I follow, until my

Trial of the Seddons.

learned friend came to sum up the case, about any impropriety on Chief Inspector Ward's part in putting the questions to her in the way in which he had asked her the questions and taken the answers. The girl says quite plainly—"The questions were read over to me after they were taken down and I had given the answers, and I signed them." And you saw that each paper was signed by her; and it so happens that the first paper is signed at exactly where the very material question is that was asked her about the purchase of poison.

Now, in a word, my submission with regard to it is that Margaret Seddon is not telling the truth. My learned friend referred to what Chief Inspector Ward had done. Well, gentlemen, Chief Inspector Ward, so far as can be seen from this, I submit, was acting quite properly. He had to get information for the purpose of this case, and he asked this girl whether or not this had taken place. You have seen Chief Inspector Ward, and certainly if my learned friend had any question that he desired to put to him, or to cross-examine him any further about this, he could have asked for him and re-cross-examined him. You have got to judge of these matters as men of the world, applying to these facts as proved the same test that you would apply to your own affairs in order to arrive at the truth. There is no magic in applying these tests in a case of this kind more than there is in any other case, except that I agree with my learned friend you have to do it with scrupulous care. The test, however, is always the same. You judge of actions as they are proved to you, testing them according to your knowledge of the world as you understand human affairs. You have to apply that test in this case to this most important feature of it, and that is whether or not Mr. Thorley is right in his identification of Margaret Seddon. Of course, if Mr. Thorley is right, then you have an ample explanation of how this arsenic got into the house, and how this arsenic, from the introduction into the house, gets into the body. Of course, you must proceed further with reference to that proposition.

The point I make about it is that the real reason why the defence has set up this untrue story about the purchase at Thorley's shop on 26th August is that if it took place they are quite unable to explain it; there is no theory which can be put forward by them which can explain their going into that shop and asking for those four packets on 26th August. Of course, it was known, and known during the course of this investigation, that the girl Margaret had been to Price's shop on 6th December to purchase fly-papers; and, of course, it was equally seen that the question would arise, why did she go on 6th December to buy these fly-papers? It was not hot; there was no need for them; it is not suggested that they were wanted for any other purpose than analysis; they were wanted because of the case which was being made against him of poisoning by arsenic. The sending of Margaret Seddon on 6th December to Price's shop to buy these fly-papers required explanation. The true explanation, as I submit, the purchase at Thorley's, could not be given, and another explanation was given which is that Mrs. Seddon bought fly-papers on the 4th or 5th September at Meacher's, the chemist.

Now, gentlemen, there are two views with regard to that. It is introduced at a very late stage of this case; it is introduced for the first

Closing Speech for the Crown.

Attorney-General

time at the end of the case. In my submission to you you should consider, scrutinise, and examine that with care. Mrs. Seddon, and those responsible for her defence, have been given every opportunity to prove that that statement about the purchase of fly-papers at Meacher's is true. They knew it was challenged; they knew that I challenged Mr. Saint by asking the question whether Mr. Saint, the solicitor, had been to Mr. Meacher's to get him to make a statement with regard to the matter. Mr. Meacher was produced in Court so that there would be no question about it, but the statement rests absolutely and entirely on the uncorroborated testimony of Mrs. Seddon; not a person is called who could have thrown any light upon it. Let me observe further. It is a very remarkable fact, you know, in this case that that story told by Mrs. Seddon about the use of fly-papers, and the putting of the four into the soup plate on the little table between the windows comes in at such a late stage in this case. Throughout the whole of the cross-examination by both my learned friends from beginning to end of this case there has never been a suggestion of that having happened. The first we ever heard of it was the story told by Mrs. Seddon. My learned friend, Mr. Marshall Hall, in opening the case frankly and rightly said it was not for him to explain what had happened, but suggested it was possible that somehow or other the water from all the four fly-papers had been poured into something, and he suggested that was done by Chater, the servant. That was the suggestion then put forward—that it was Chater who had done it.

Then Mrs. Seddon tells you the story about this purchase, and the putting of the four fly-papers into the soup plate. I shall examine that carefully, of course, as I quite agree it deserves careful examination. What I am now directing your attention to is this, that not only is no question ever put about it, but every witness who has been asked about the fly-papers called by the Crown, every one of whom having been cross-examined about seeing fly-papers in that room, with one exception, the father, whose evidence I will call attention to in a moment, denied having seen them. Who would be the people who would see the fly-papers in that room? Remember what is said according to Mrs. Seddon's story now—there were fly-papers in the room from the 4th or 5th of September.

Mr. MARSHALL HALL—Bought on the 4th.

The ATTORNEY-GENERAL—I will take it whichever day my learned friend likes. I thought she said she was not sure whether it was the 4th or the 5th.

Mr. MARSHALL HALL—You are quite right, they were not used until the 5th.

The ATTORNEY-GENERAL—Very well, bought on the 4th and used on the 5th, as my learned friend says. I will accept that. They were used from the 5th. The story is now put forward, advisedly I say, for the first time in the defence, when Mr. and Mrs. Seddon go into the box, that these four fly-papers were put into four separate saucers in the room and remained there until after 14th September, after the death of Miss Barrow. That is the case. Now, who were the people who would have seen them if they were there? They say the four fly-papers were there until the 14th, but the papers on the 12th, as you remember, had been changed from the four saucers and put into a soup plate. I am going

361

Trial of the Seddons.

to refer to that more in detail in a moment. Now, who were the people who would have seen those fly-papers? Who has been asked about them? The boy Ernest Grant, I should have thought, could not possibly have missed them. According to their story there are fly-papers in the room in which he is sleeping, from 5th September right up to the night of the 13th, when, as you know, he goes into his own room somewhere about three o'clock in the morning. This boy is asked whether he had ever seen them in his life, and his answer is that he had never seen these papers. He had once in his life seen fly-papers, and that was at Southend. They were not arsenical fly-papers, they were sticky fly-papers. You remember a Mather's fly-paper was handed to him, and he said he had never seen a fly-paper of that kind before in his life. Now, if there was the boy living in that room, living there from 5th September to 14th September, my submission to you is that he would have been the first to have noticed anything new, attracted by wondering what it was, as children are. Who else ought to have noticed them? Chater, the girl, who has been the subject of so much attack in this case, has given her evidence before you. You will judge whether or not she was telling the truth in her story that she never saw fly-papers—she never saw arsenical fly-papers, or fly-papers, at any time there. All that was asked her was whether she had seen them. Dr. Sworn—it is most important that he should have seen them. Dr. Sworn has given his evidence, and he says when he came to the house he never saw so many flies about. It is a remarkable thing if that is the case he never noticed the fly-papers. Then, of course, I quite appreciate, and I think it right to make the observation, that he may have been there and may not have noticed in any way that there were fly-papers once, if you like, or twice; but it is an odd thing that if his attention was directed to the large number of flies that were there —and as he naturally would be looking to the comfort of his patient—that he never sees them. The only person who says anything about them is Mr. Seddon, senior, who is asked about them. I do not know whether you remember his evidence, but it was very halting on the point. It is on the second day.

Mr. JUSTICE BUCKNILL—He thought he saw some in August.

The ATTORNEY-GENERAL—In point of fact, nobody suggests that there were ever any there in August in the room—the case for the defence is that they were not there. That is what he told us. He was pressed by my learned friend to say that he had seen a fly-paper upon the mantelpiece, but he would not go so far.

Mr. MARSHALL HALL—I put it to him later.

The ATTORNEY-GENERAL—Yes, you were cross-examining him, and you put it to him later. He is asked about it, and he says, oh, no, he cannot say at all, he will not go so far as that. He does, very haltingly, as I suggest to you, in a very difficult position here for a father, say he thinks he did see some, as my lord says, in August. Well, he is wrong in that. When the specific thing is put to him as to whether he ever saw any on the mantelpiece, he cannot say he did; he cannot even go so far as that. Therefore you have got this remarkable state of things, that according to the story told now with these four saucers containing fly-papers from 5th September to 12th September not a single one of these witnesses whom

Closing Speech for the Crown.

Attorney-General

we have called have seen them. Why is it that that story, as I suggest to you, is invented about the purchase of these fly-papers on 5th September?

Something has to be put forward to account for Margaret Seddon having gone to Price's shop on the 6th December, two days after the arrest of the father. Something evidently must be put forward to explain why that girl should have gone to the shop to purchase these arsenical fly-papers. Some explanation must be attempted, otherwise it stands as the clearest possible corroboration of the story that she had been buying arsenical fly-papers in August, 1911, and the moment Mr. Seddon was arrested he knew quite well where the arsenic had come from. He knew his danger; he knew his difficulty; and he sees his solicitor that day, and as the result of that the arsenical fly-papers are purchased. Of course, if that remained unexplained, nobody could suggest why Margaret should have been sent into the shop on 6th December.

You get the story put forward now, and, as I am going to submit to you, it is put forward with a twofold purpose. I have dealt up to now with the reason why you should disbelieve the story that Margaret Seddon did not buy these fly-papers on 26th August, and why you should believe Thorley's story, that she did. Now, let me deal with the other part of Mrs. Seddon's story about it. She gives you an account which I suggest to you is a very, very difficult one to accept, except upon one theory, that the putting of the fly-papers into that soup plate was done with a very definite purpose. Her story, as told to us for the first time in the witness-box when she was called—a story that no human being in this Court had heard suggested before—was, that having had these four fly-papers in the four saucers on Tuesday, 12th September, she comes into the room, and for some reason, having broken one of the saucers, she says then she was not going to be bothered with them any more, and for convenience she puts them into a soup plate. She goes downstairs to fetch the soup plate, on her own story. A most remarkable thing to have done if all that she wanted was, for convenience sake, to change the one into the other. However, she gets the soup plate, having gone down for the express purpose of fetching it, as she has told us, and then, having got that soup plate into that room, she takes the four papers, the one that had been in the saucer that was broken and the other three, and she puts the whole four of them on to the soup plate. It is very difficult to follow. Every fly-paper that is on that soup plate will substantially cover it. As you put them on the soup plate you very nearly cover the whole of the plate, except part of the rim no doubt. What is the point of putting four on it? It is not because the flies had not been killed. I could understand if that could be suggested, but her own story is that when she was doing that the flies had already been nearly all killed, or at any rate, to use the exact expression that she used, not to do her any injustice, "The flies had nearly all disappeared." Then why was the solution to be made stronger? What was the point of putting four on to that one soup plate and pouring the water on? I have no doubt it has occurred to you what the suggestion is, and why that is put forward—a very skilful and a very ingenious theory, and, of course, used with all the power which my learned friend possesses, in suggesting to you that what had happened was that by putting this soup plate with the four arsenical papers on to the table between the two

Trial of the Seddons.

windows, this woman had got out of bed, and had, somehow or other, drunk the water which was on the top of the fly-papers; that is the suggestion to account for this woman's death by arsenic. That is what the case means. That is why it is that, of course, great importance is attached to the four arsenical fly-papers on the table between the two windows.

My learned friend's case about it, and I have followed it very carefully, is that either this was the result of an accident, or it may have been something else; he did not use those words, but that was suggested also during the course of the case. The view put forward is that this was self-administered by her or at one time (I do not pause to dwell much upon this in view of the evidence), that it was accidentally administered by Chater. Those are the views which are put forward to you to explain the undoubted fact that we know, if nothing else, from the state of preservation of the body according to the medical evidence that I referred to yesterday, that this woman died from acute arsenical poisoning. You are face to face with that fact. We cannot get away from it, gentlemen. We cannot shrink from it. We are face to face with the fact that that woman died not from epidemic diarrhœa, but from acute arsenical poisoning, from arsenic which was administered to her in that house, because from what was found in that house she could have only taken the last dose—the fatal dose—within some forty-eight ·hours of the death; it cannot have been longer than that. Therefore during the time that she is lying upstairs in her bed with this illness upon her, this arsenic had got into her body, and it killed her. The suggestion that is made to you is she had taken it herself by drinking the water which was in the soup plate.

I want to say one word about that. According to the evidence which has been given, it is not a question of putting water on the top of these fly-papers. There seems to have been a complete misapprehension. What happens is, these fly-papers are moistened; that is what she says. She was told what had to be done with them—they had to be moistened, and, of course, it appears on the printed directions on the fly-paper which have been read to you. They are moistened; a little water is poured on them, and there is an end of it. From time to time during the hot weather fresh water is put on them to moisten them. During the whole course of this case so far, what seems to have been forgotten is that there is plenty of water in her room. No one has suggested that she had not any water in her room. According to the evidence, there were two jugs on the wash-stand with water in them, there was the water bottle with water in it and the glass, and there was, according to Mr. Seddon's evidence, a syphon of soda which stood there. For what reason this woman got up and licked —because that is what it must come to—the water off these fly-papers, it is impossible to understand. There was brandy by the side of her, and there was soda water by the side of her—everything she could want.

That is the only explanation and the only suggestion that could be put forward, and which is put forward by the defence, with the addition, as I have already stated, of the suggestion that Chater may have accidentally administered it. Now, we know this about Chater, and this appears to be now absolutely contradicted—Chater had nothing whatever to do with waiting upon this woman during her illness, and she had nothing whatever to do with the cooking of her food. There is a conflict of testimony as

Closing Speech for the Crown.

Attorney-General

to whether she prepared the tea for her. Chater emphatically says that she did not, but it is a statement in this case which is beyond dispute that this woman was not allowed to take tea for at least the last four days before her death, and, as the fatal dose of arsenic was administered within at least forty-eight hours of the death, and tea was never given to her during the last four days, the suggestion comes to nothing. The suggestion is that Chater had prepared tea for her in the earliest days, but it is proved to demonstration that Chater had nothing whatever to do with the administration of arsenic to this woman. I have gone into this in a little detail, because it is due to this girl Chater that it should be done. It is not right that the suggestion should remain, however much my friend may strive to moderate it. He cannot get away from this, that the suggestion is, or was at one time, that she did do it. I think as the case proceeded that suggestion was dropped, and certainly you have heard very little of it at the end of the case; but, for the reasons I have just given to you, if you accept the whole of the evidence against Chater, it is not anything that Chater did that could have been the cause of the administration of this arsenic. What it comes to, and what my submission to you upon it is, is this, that on the 26th August you have got the purchase by Margaret Seddon, and you have got the introduction of the fly-papers into the house.

My learned friend says, " How could Mr. Seddon have got to know what arsenic there was in the fly-papers, and what effect it would have? " I should not have thought that was very difficult; I should not have thought that any man who was capable, as Seddon undoubtedly was, of drawing up legal documents, who has studied, as he told us, would have found any difficulty in understanding that, more particularly as on the fly-papers themselves it says they have to be kept out of the reach of children. It is known, of course, that they are poisonous, but if they are introduced into the house at the end of August, 1911, it becomes much more easy to understand why it is that this woman was taken ill at the beginning of September.

I notice my learned friend has made some observations about the case for the prosecution having shifted, that at first it was only said it was this last dose that had been administered, and not the suggestion it was more. Well, my learned friend is wrong with regard to that. The great stress of the case has been laid on what has been called the fatal dose administered within the last forty-eight hours. Of course, that is so, because it is that which necessarily, according to the case as put forward, killed her, and it is the administration of that dose which is the murder. Everything has been laid upon that. The evidence of Dr. Willcox, a gentleman whose honesty is vouched for by everybody who has to do with the case, including my learned friend as well as myself, is that from the distribution of arsenic in the body, in all probability arsenic must have been administered within a few days before the last fatal dose. He says that the symptoms of gastro-enteritis are exactly the same which you would find in a case of arsenical poisoning, and he says all that he found is consistent with an earlier dose having been administered which had not proved fatal. In this case what we are concerned with, of course, and very materially, is the fatal dose. As the evidence stands, and with the purchase on 26th August, it does look, as I suggest for your consideration, without

Trial of the Seddons.

scientific knowledge of the amount of arsenic which there was in the fly-papers, or which it would take to kill, that a dose had been administered (that is consistent with the whole of the scientific testimony upon this case which is undisputed), but that it had not proved fatal, and that she was recovering. A doctor was called in. He had to be called in, because it would not have been safe for him not to have been called in. He finds the patient suffering from pains in the stomach, vomiting, and diarrhœa, and he diagnoses it, as I have no doubt a vast number of doctors, if not all, would do at first sight, as a plain case of gastro-enteritis or epidemic diarrhœa. There are no means for his discovering arsenic. He does not suspect that there is any arsenic poisoning. Why should he? The result is that he goes on attending the patient. The patient seems to be recovering. Then comes this fatal dose, given at some time within the forty-eight hours. Gentlemen, of course my learned friends have both made, as they are entitled to, all the capital they can out of the fact that we were not able to give direct evidence of the administration of the dose. That is quite true. That is why it is that this case has necessarily occupied more time than cases of this kind usually do, because it does depend upon indirect evidence—upon circumstantial evidence. What we have shown you is at least this. It is not disputed, and cannot be disputed, that there was every opportunity for doing it, and, moreover, we have shown you that the arsenic was brought into the house—we have shown you that it was there.

Mr. Marshall Hall—My learned friend ought not to say that. He says that it was proved the arsenic was brought into the house. He will not accept our proof. He says our evidence is not true. I do not think there is any proof that Margaret ever brought any papers into the house, even if she did purchase them. My learned friend will not accept that because he says Seddon destroyed them.

The Attorney-General—Gentlemen, let us understand what that interruption means. My learned friend says that there is no proof that Margaret Seddon brought fly-papers into the house. What did he think Margaret Seddon was buying them for on 26th August? Was it to throw them into the street? Was it to give away? Did she go into that shop to ask for four packets of fly-papers at 3d. each to tear them up when she came out? What is the fair and reasonable inference that every man would draw? This girl is employed in the house—to run errands for Mrs. Seddon, eating, drinking, and sleeping in the house, and attending to the household duties in the house. Is not it a fair inference if she buys fly-papers that they would be brought back to the house? Gentlemen, I will not say more with reference to my learned friend's interruption—and I do not complain of it—than this. If all the interruption means, as I followed it, that he objects to my saying that it is proved that arsenic was introduced into the house, because I have proved that Margaret Seddon bought arsenic papers, well, I will not waste another word about it, because I should have thought that it was the only possible inference that, if she did buy them, they must have been introduced into the house. My learned friend says I do not accept his story. That is perfectly true; I do not. But the story which is told by Mrs. Seddon, if accepted as true, does not in the slightest degree destroy the story that

366

Closing Speech for the Crown.

Attorney-General

I am putting to you. If her story is true, that she bought these fly-papers on the date that she says, and had used them as she says, it does not in the slightest degree get rid of the fact that four packets of fly-papers had been asked for on 26th August of Mr. Thorley, and it is not explained why that should have happened.

You have heard how this could have been administered. I am not in a position to state exactly how it was done. My learned friends are entitled to make the most of that, but I am in the position of saying how it could have been done, and I have shown you that it could have been administered either in Valentine's meat juice or in brandy, particularly in the condition in which she was. You have seen the two bottles produced, and you can judge for yourselves. You have seen how much one is like the other—how the Valentine's meat juice or brandy would look with water, and how it would look with a solution of arsenical fly-papers. But I do think there is one piece of evidence which my learned friend has called, which, at any rate, assists one somewhat to a conclusion in this case. Apparently he says that Miss Barrow had at one time, certainly up to March, 1906, been addicted to alcohol. Apparently the brandy in this case was ordered for her. Dr. Sworn, you will remember, says that when he came on the 11th he ordered her brandy, and so from that time she must have had that. We know that when Mrs. Vonderahe saw Mr. Seddon that Mr. Seddon himself said that he did give her brandy. I agree that the brandy was given on the night of the 13th, but the fair view is that she must have been taking brandy from an earlier date, because you remember the explanation that was given of the bottle; there was only a very little left in it on the night of the 13th, and that little was gone by the morning of the 14th, when she died. You had the bottle described to you. I do not know whether you caught more fully than I did the description of it; I am not sure that I heard it. We cannot deny that there was at one time plenty of brandy. Mrs. Seddon was constantly in attendance there, and Mr. Seddon could come up at any time and at any moment. He did come there on various occasions. And, of course, the fatal dose could have been given at any time within, as we know now, the last forty-eight hours from what was found in the stomach and in the intestines.

Just let us see what happens on this night of the 13th. Just before I do that I want to say one or two words about what happens on the 11th. The 11th is the day of the will. That is a curious story. Here is this old lady, propped up with pillows in her bed in order to be able to sign this will. According to the doctor's evidence, he heard nothing about making a will either then or after. Her mental condition was not very satisfactory; that is the view which Dr. Sworn has given. I think my learned friend, both at the Police Court and here, said that Dr. Sworn had said he did not think that she was in a mental condition to make a will, and he went on to explain that, unless it was very carefully explained to her, she would not be able to take it in. I am not going to dwell at any length upon what happened on that date, except just to say something to you about the will itself. It is drawn up by Mr. Seddon. It is a very useful document if it means to dispose of all the property that this woman had, and you see all that it does dispose of is her personal

367

Trial of the Seddons.

belongings and the furniture and jewellery. It is said that that was the property of Mr. and Mrs. Grant, and she was intending to give it to Hilda and Ernest Grant, but it clearly was not, because it deals with all the property and all the effects which she had; we know on the evidence that it included some things which had not belonged to the Grants at all, and certainly the clothing and things of that kind had nothing whatever to do with the Grants. What it indicates is the intention of this woman to give what she had to Hilda and Ernest Grant. Of course, if there had not been all this inquiry the will made on the 11th September would appear to be in order. It would look, if you came to examine into it, as if she knew perfectly well that she had nothing but personal belongings to leave, which she had left with Mr. Seddon as executor and trustee for these two children. I have been unable to follow from the evidence what is the explanation of making this will on the 11th. If this woman was very ill on the 11th, and was in fear of death, and wanted a will made hurriedly one follows it, but that is not the view which is put forward. The view presented by the defence is, "Oh, no, there was nothing the matter with her on that day; she was quite all right, but she wanted to make her will, and she wanted Mr. Seddon to do it, and Mr. Seddon did it."

I pass now to the 13th, of which you have heard so much, that I am going to say very little about it. You remember the incidents as they arise on this most awful, horrible night, which we have heard described in this Court necessarily so many times. You have got the history of that night, and nobody but Miss Barrow and Mr. and Mrs. Seddon could give us the true story, but we know something of what happened. The first thing is this, that on the night of the 13th she is ill. I should go a little earlier, as it is important; in the morning she is worse; that is Dr. Sworn's evidence. That is the condition then from that time onward. She is having pains, she is having this diarrhœa, and that continues. I think some one said that the sickness was not as bad. It goes on, and in the evening of the 13th she is evidently worse. Mr. Seddon comes in; he has been out to some theatre. When he comes in he hears that this woman, who, upon the evidence before you, has only made her will two days before, and who was worse on the morning of the 13th, had said, "I am dying." Upon that there is some discussion. He says that his wife did not believe it, and smiled. She says it was a nervous smile. I do not know which it was, and he does not know. At any rate, the effect upon him, who must have known his wife's smile, was, according to his own statement, that she treated it as of no account. That is his view, that Miss Barrow was exaggerating.

Then you get this series of incidents of going up three times and finding this woman worse, in awful pain, with all the symptoms which have been described to you so often, until it culminates in this little boy shouting out "Chickie is out of bed," or words to that effect, and she said, "I am going." Picture to yourself this unfortunate woman in agony getting weaker, and no doubt the poison working its full effect. This poor, unfortunate woman is sitting on the ground holding herself in agony, and the boy terrified, as we know he was from the evidence that has been given, doing his best to hold her up. According to the evidence Mr. and Mrs. Seddon came up. I am not sure whether it was on that

Closing Speech for the Crown.

Attorney-General

occasion that she put some hot flannels on or not. For the purpose of my case it does not make any difference; I will deal with the incidents. Later she is helped into bed. No explanation of any sort or kind from Miss Barrow to Mr. and Mrs. Seddon, on their own statement. Then the boy is sent to his own room and they remain there.

Then you have heard about the one and a half to two hours' snoring. It is not quite easy to get at the true effect of the evidence on that night, but I have looked at it very carefully, and, of course, my lord has his notes. If I may say so, with respect, I observe he followed it with very close attention, and if he thinks what I am saying is wrong he will correct it. The prisoner Seddon emphatically stated at the start that she snored; his words were, "Sleeping peacefully; snoring for an hour and a half to two hours." That was the beginning of it. He was cross-examined about that, and he was pressed. I asked what sort of snoring it was, and you remember he gave an illustration. He was asked why he did not fetch a doctor in those circumstances, or why he did not do something on hearing a snore like that? My learned friend had described the snoring as "stertorous breathing"; that is a phrase introduced by him, and I have no doubt correctly—it was stertorous breathing—"snoring," as they call it. I would ask you to picture to yourself what happened on that night when they are up there listening to this. If it is true that the woman was sleeping peacefully, it is difficult to understand why the man did not go down to bed. He had got a busy day the next day, Thursday, as it was his office day—the day on which he had most to do. The only explanation which has been given to me is that he wanted to stop up with his wife. Of course, you will consider that explanation in conjunction with the rest, and consider it in the light of all the circumstances. He stays outside that door with the door open so that he can see what is going on in that room. He is smoking and he is reading a paper, and at times, as he tells us, he is going down to look after the baby and to get a drink. My submission to you, which I ask you to take into consideration, is that he was waiting up that night with his wife because he knew the end could not be far off; he knew that the end was approaching, and he could not leave his wife, and probably she would not stay alone to see it. Somebody must be there. The wife sits up through it. The husband stays outside the door. That, I submit to you, is an explanation of why he does not go down to bed.

Then the end comes. Do let us examine the story with regard to it. There are really three stories that have been given of that end. It is a gruesome story, and one upon which I do not want to dwell at any length, but this is the story, according to Mr. Seddon; he was standing outside, and he heard the snoring going on, and all of a sudden it ceases. He hears nothing more, and he says, "Good God, she is dead," and then he lifts an eyelid and sees that she is dead. He is pressed about that, and he says that before that his wife had tied up the jaw. The wife gives a different story. That was a night upon which I should have thought there could be no doubt. The wife's story is that she sat dozing; she does not seem to know very much about what did happen; she was, as my learned friend said, sleeping tired. According to her account the breathing stopped suddenly, and her husband lifted an eyelid and said, "Good God, she is dead"; but she said she was uncertain as to whether she was dead or not.

Trial of the Seddons.

Now, gentlemen, just imagine that state of things. She had not tied up the jaw. Seddon's story is wrong with regard to that. There cannot be any mistake; he cannot say that he was uncertain she was dead, and therefore he did not want to know anything more at all about it, or any medical man to know. Then I have said she may be mistaken about it, as she admitted that if she had tied up the jaw she would have known perfectly well the woman was dead. She did not know that, because, according to her story, she went down and said that she thought the woman was dead. Do see what happens when her husband went away. Here is this woman, who is not expected to die, according to the story she is now putting forward to-day (the doctor did not expect her to die, because, according to him, she was not in a critical condition), all of a sudden dies, and the husband then goes to the doctor. The story he tells to the doctor, according to the doctor, is worthy of your consideration. It has passed no doubt from your recollection, as it is a considerable time ago since it was said, but this is his account of it—"The husband came to me about seven o'clock. I asked him how she was; he said she was taken in a lot of pain—seemed to have a lot of pain in her inside, and then she went off a sort of insensible. They had been up all night with her. She had been in a considerable amount of pain, and then went off in a sort of unconscious insensible." A very different story from what he has told here. According to their story, she is sleeping peacefully, and then suddenly dies.

Then, gentlemen, you have the account of what happens with Dr. Sworn. I am not going to make any reflection upon Dr. Sworn, but I do say this, that it makes one pause a little when you hear from a medical man who had left his patient on the morning of the 13th not in a critical condition, and whom he did not expect to die, but who gets a message the next morning at seven o'clock that the patient has become "unconscious insensible," and then died, that he gives a certificate without anything further. If he did anything which is to be made a subject of criticism, that, of course, must not reflect upon the Seddons. I only make that observation in passing, because I cross-examined about it. Quite understand what I am saying. If there is some criticism to be visited upon him—*if* there is—it must not be visited upon them.

What happened after that? There is the search. Again, you have heard so much about that. It is such a wretched squalid story, and I am not going to take up your time by going through it. The search for gold is recommenced as soon as he comes back, before anything else is thought of, to find out how much money there was. Mr. Seddon was cross-examined as to why he did not do what any honest man would have done under the circumstances—what I submit to you any man who had nothing to conceal would have done, even if he was a wise, shrewd, and astute man, as we know Mr. Seddon was. He sets to work to examine the room before he sends a word to the relatives. When he is pressed about that, he says he has an independent witness. The independent witness was Mrs. Rutt, who pawned his sheets and pillow cases, and things of that kind, when they were away on their holiday. That is the independent witness whom he had sent for.

Mr. MARSHALL HALL—They did not go for their holiday until the middle of September.

Closing Speech for the Crown.

The ATTORNEY-GENERAL—Quite right.

Mr. MARSHALL HALL—22nd September.

The ATTORNEY-GENERAL—I do not think it really affects the point I am making, although my learned friend is quite right in his date; I do not pay any attention to it, and I do not think it matters for the purpose of what I am putting before you whether it was before or after. What I am upon is that Mrs. Rutt is put forward as an independent witness, and what I am saying is that this independent witness was the witness whom you heard had pawned his things. Some criticism was directed upon the cross-examination of my learned friend Mr. Muir. Was he to allow Mrs. Rutt to be put forward to you as an independent witness, a person who was vouched for by Mr. Seddon, without asking her a question which at least throws a considerable light upon the amount of independence which she exhibited under the circumstances? So the result of the search you know. It is stated that none of the gold except this £4 10s. was found. You know also the visit to the undertaker's.

I want to direct your attention now to what I call the third stage of the circumstantial evidence which I am putting before you. I have called attention to the motive and to the opportunity, and I am now going to deal with the third stage, which is the subsequent conduct. If you will observe what has taken place in the case, as I know you have already, you will see how material it is that you should take it into consideration when you come to determine whether or not this woman was murdered as we say. Nothing whatever is done during the whole of that morning to get the relatives to appear or to give them any notice. Now, I agree that apparently the relatives do not seem to have been on the most friendly terms. Quite a justifiable observation on that was made by my learned friend, but it does not in the slightest degree get rid of this fact, the only relatives of whom he knows and to whom he should have sent he did not communicate with. The only explanation that I have been able to get you have heard. You have heard the whole case, and you will be able to judge why he did not send round to the house to tell the Vonderahes. His case is that some time after the Vonderahes had ceased to lodge and board Miss Barrow Miss Margaret Seddon had gone round to the door, and the door had been slammed in her face, or rather rudely. That is the whole explanation you have had. I pressed him and asked him, " With all the people in your house, why did not you send somebody else? You could have got the father, you could have got the two sons. You could have gone yourself." The only explanation was that they had shut the door rudely in Margaret's face. Then it is said that he wrote a letter. You will remember the incident about the funeral. Gentlemen, I am not going to say anything more about it. I told you about it in opening the case, and I explained to you how I used it. I pointed out to you that its bearing in this case was only as an indication of the man we are dealing with. That now stands so revealed during the course of this case that I will not waste time to comment further upon it. But Mr. Seddon says he wrote a letter upon 14th September. I submit to you that that incident helps to show that he is concealing the facts, because he does not want any inquiry, and he does not want any examination, because he knows his own guilt. He says that on the 14th he wrote; by some extraordinary coincidence he

Trial of the Seddons.

happened to have two mourning sheets of paper, and he wrote a letter, which has never been discovered, and which no one has ever received, and which has never been returned. He says he wrote a letter on the afternoon of 14th September to acquaint the Vonderahes of the death of Miss Barrow. It is very curious that nobody has ever heard of it. Mr. Smith was cross-examined about it. I noticed my learned friend yesterday made a very extraordinary observation about my not having asked Margaret Seddon the question as to whether she had posted the letter. I had opened the case; I had proved the case; I had made perfectly plain what the suggestion was—that no such letter ever was sent, and my learned friend called her, and he did not put the question to her. I do not quite understand the reason that he gave yesterday, or why he did not. If I followed him correctly, his suggestion was, what was the good of asking her any question when we had got a statement from her which had been given to the police, and we would say from that that she was not to be believed? I do not know whether that is his view; if it is, it would be an extraordinary one, because he is putting her forward as a witness of truth. But, gentlemen, do not let me make any capital out of it. It may be—I do not know—that it was passed over, as sometimes such things are, by omission. Whether it was that or whether it was designedly done I do not want to make any capital out of the fact that my learned friends did not ask Miss Margaret Seddon to say more than was absolutely vital. She is the daughter of this man, and I should not have made any criticism upon my learned friend not having asked her to go into the details and history of this case, but that letter remains in great doubt. In my submission to you he never sent it, and he only wrote it when the Vonderahes were coming to him on 21st September, when the two ladies appeared and wanted to know something about it. As far as he was concerned, he did not know whether they had received the letter or not, but there he is armed with this copy which he produced from his pocket, and he says, " Why, here is the copy of the letter I wrote to you." The suggestion he made to you was that Mrs. Vonderahe knew quite well she had had it, but would not admit it. I will not dwell upon that at all. You have seen Mrs. Vonderahe, and you have heard her story about it.

The incidents of 14th September, however, are important in another aspect. On that date discussions arise about the money. Now, it is a most extraordinary thing that 14th September is the first day on which, according to the evidence, you find him dealing with a lot of gold. I know what has been said about Mr. Naylor and Mr. Wilson, who were called, but they really, as I submit to you, do not help at all in this case. Their evidence does not agree, but it shows this, that at that time he had some money, possibly £100—it may have been a little more—in gold. He was then carrying on a wardrobe business, and he had got purchases to make, and therefore had to keep gold in the house very likely. But they were speaking of June, 1909. On 14th September, 1911, you find him dealing with a considerable amount of gold.

In opening the case I submitted to you, and I submit to you now, that gold that he was dealing with was Miss Barrow's gold, and nobody else's, and that it was there for him to deal with on that day, because she was dead, and the jubilation at the possession of this money, and not having

Closing Speech for the Crown.

Attorney-General

to account to her either for the notes or for the gold, or to pay her annuity, made him a little incautious. My learned friends both made criticisms and comments upon his conduct, and said that if this man had been the criminal that is suggested, he would have had the body cremated; one of my learned friends said that, and the other said that the last thing he would have done would have been to show the gold. That is the kind of argument you hear in every criminal case that ever comes before a Court. If every criminal knew when he was committing the crime of all the various steps that he might take in order to prevent the detection of the crime, and had the advantage of very able lawyers to tell him how to cover up his tracks (which, of course, they would not do), no doubt there would be a great many more undetected crimes than at present—there are enough. That kind of argument about what he might have done is of very little use, as I submit to you, in this kind of case. But how is it that it just happens to be this day, 14th September, when the body is still lying upstairs in the room, that you find him dealing with this amount of gold which hitherto apparently he had possessed, but you never find him dealing with? You have heard the explanation about the £200 or the £220.

As my learned friend said, and I quite agree, all this shuffling to and fro of sovereigns out of one bag into another is quite immaterial, and throws no light upon it. We have had a long story about it. I make no complaint, but I say it does not help us at all, because there still remains the fact that the money was there, and the whole question is whether that money which was there was the money he had got from Miss Barrow, or whether it was his own. My learned friend says he had this money, because he had £220 which he had been using for a mortgage. Do you remember the evidence with regard to that? I do ask you to take that into account. This acute man of business, who knows how to turn every penny to account, who pays in a small sum of £30 in order that he should get the 2½ per cent. interest on it, who pays in a sum of £70 into a deposit account as soon as he has got the money, who never allows the money to remain unremunerative, according to his case which he now has to set up, has £220 in gold which he is keeping there idle. For what purpose does he do it, considering he has got a banking account at the London and Provincial Bank, that he had laid money out in deposit at the London County and Westminster Bank, and that he had a savings bank account? For what purpose was he keeping this £220 in gold? The only explanation he has been able to give you is that the £220 was used for the purpose of a mortgage, and that it was there in case anything should happen to him, so that the money should be taken to the building society to pay off the mortgage. Naturally, you ask what difference would it make if he died? Whether the mortgage, according to his own statement, is a mortgage for fifteen to twenty years, it could not be called in. He did not require the money for that purpose. It is an invention, as I submit to you, to account for his having this gold in his possession on that date in order that he may explain what he was doing on 14th September with the gold.

Now, see again, on this very date, according to all the evidence we have had before us, how does he deal with this money? My learned friend says he pays it into three or four places. So he does, but you will observe that he distributes it over as wide an area as he can. If you have got

Trial of the Seddons.

gold which you do not want traced in a lump, it is very convenient no doubt to use it in three or four different ways. What happened in this case? He pays in £35 of the money on 14th September in addition to the money which he has to pay in which had been received on account of the insurance company. The collectors' money is brought there, and it is dealt with before seven o'clock, on the evidence. On the morning of the 15th he pays in the collectors' money, to which, according to his own story, he has added £35 in gold. His story is that he did it the night before, but it does not matter. The £35 is paid in in gold, and, as I suggest to you, in the gold which had belonged to Miss Barrow. That is one way of dealing with it. £35 goes into that bank, then £30 goes into the Post Office Savings Bank, and three days after ninety sovereigns are used for the purpose of paying for three shares in the building society. Now, is it not an extraordinary thing that you should, so immediately after the death of this woman who was known to be possessed of a considerable sum of money, have a dealing with a large sum of gold like that in that way by this man who had a banking account and a Post Office Savings Bank account also? If, of course, he was not free, as he thought, to deal with the money, and he was afraid of detection, you would understand why it is he was dealing with it in that way; but, if that was not the case, what a marvellous coincidence it is that he should just on that day have chosen to pay away all those sums of gold when the body lay cold upstairs before it was taken away that night to the undertakers.

We do not stop at that, because on that very same day come two incidents upon which I rely strongly. My submission to you is that those two incidents are consistent with guilt, fairly, properly, and carefully scrutinised. The first is the incident with the ring. Now, the story about that is, that the ring had been given to him by her as a present because he had incurred some costs to the lawyer in connection with the assignment. The evidence upon it is this, that the moment he was told, as he was, by Messrs. Russell & Son that some lawyer ought to go through the agreement for her, and he told her about that, she objected to paying any lawyer's costs. He said that she would not pay a single penny, so he agreed to pay those costs, and they came to £4 13s., and he had given a cheque for it. His explanation of the ring is—you will consider whether or not it is a true explanation, or whether it is untrue and invented for the occasion— his explanation is that he told her that he had had to incur solicitors' costs, and that she had said to him she would not pay any money, but she would give him a ring instead; the substance of the words were that "She had not any money to spare," and she gave him a ring. On his own story, he himself had to pay those solicitors' costs, and he had to pay with his own cheque, and the ring is given to him.

Now, the ring is taken on 15th September, between the death and the burial, by this man to the jeweller. What for? Because it was too small for him to wear, and he had to have it enlarged so that he could wear the ring, which this lady had worn, upon his finger; therefore the jeweller had the commission to make it larger—he said that he wore it on his little finger. It is a most remarkable fact which you ought to take into consideration that this point which I made against him in the opening of the case about the ring has never been explained except upon this view—that no

Closing Speech for the Crown.

Attorney-General

single person who has been called, and who knew him, has been able to say that he saw him wearing that ring upon his little finger. It is a most vital point, and, as you will remember, I made use of it in opening, as I did of all these points, so that my learned friends should know the points on which I was resting my case, and every opportunity should be given them for explanation. Not a single person has been able to say he ever saw that man with that ring on his little finger. Even after he had it altered he did not wear it. The ring was found in his safe; he did not wear it. What an extraordinary story it is that he puts forward to you upon this! He asks you to believe that the day after her death it occurred to him, as a coincidence apparently, that he should go to a jeweller's and ask the jeweller to enlarge it. Put to yourself the other side of the story. Suppose this ring did not belong to him at all, but had been amongst the jewellery, which was left to Hilda and Ernest Grant and the watch also, and that he had taken possession in his greed and coveteousness of that ring and of that watch. Something must be done with them, so that if there is any inquiry hereafter, at any rate it would be shown that the ring is not the one that Miss Barrow had been in the habit of wearing, and the watch cannot be identified. Then you get that incident of the alteration of the ring on the day after the death, which I submit is only explicable, applying the ordinary test which you would apply to your own affairs in this case, on the theory that this man had taken the ring, and that he wanted to alter it so that nobody would know. What about the watch? There, again, that matter stands before you. It is clearly demonstrated in evidence, and the point is so plain that I will only make this one observation to you— if that watch had been honestly obtained by Mrs. Seddon, what reason was there that she should go hot-foot with her husband before the woman is even buried, for whom she confessed to have had so much regard, and have the name of Eliza Jane Barrow taken out of the back plate of the watch, where nobody in life could ever see it, unless he came to examine it for the purpose of identifying it? Gentlemen, we do not open the back plates of the watches of our friends to see whether there are the names there when you examine a watch to see what kind of a watch it is, but it is a most serious thing if you want to identify the watch that the name should be erased from it; and that is the reason of the incident on the 15th of September of the going to this jeweller's for the purpose of having it rubbed out.

.Now I proceed to the next material date, 21st September; I am passing over intermediate dates. On that date there is the interview with the Mrs. Vonderahe, and there is the remarkable story given by him about the letter of 21st September. When you have got documents to deal with it is a very difficult thing even for a shrewd man like Seddon to escape from the consequences of what he has written. It is easy to give explanations when the only person who can contradict them is dead, but it is not easy when you are confronted with a letter, and in this letter of 21st September he makes an undoubted false suggestion, in my submission to you, with the purpose and with the intention of concealing really what had happened, and trying to cover up that he had had the dealings with this woman's property and that he would benefit by the

Trial of the Seddons.

death, because he did not want any inquiry into how this woman had met her death.

Just imagine this for yourselves. Suppose you had been a relative of this woman, and you had come to inquire and find out what had really happened, and you saw that this man, in whose house she had been lodging, was benefiting so greatly on his own showing, when you got the real facts about her death you would want to know a little more about the cause of death, and you would want to inquire a little more closely into what had happened. So he wants to put them off the scent. The authorities, the police or the Director of Public Prosecutions can, when they start inquiry, find out a lot. His object is to prevent inquiry, and he writes this letter to the relatives as executor to the will—" I hereby notify "—he has drawn it up carefully; it is not a mere letter which he has sat down to write, and which is done in great haste or hurry; it is a letter which he has carefully prepared and which he hands over to them for them to give to their husbands, who would want to know something about what has happened—" As executor under the will of Miss Barrow, dated 11th September, 1911, I hereby certify that Miss Barrow has left all she died possessed of to Hilda and Ernest Grant, and appointed me as sole executor to hold in trust until they become of age." What would you have imagined if you, a relative, had seen that statement— that all that there had gone to Ernest and Hilda Grant? I daresay they may have expected that Miss Barrow would leave it all to Ernest and Hilda Grant. " Her property and investments she disposed of through solicitors and stockbrokers."* etc. If you had received that letter would you ever have expected that he was the man who had got all her property, and that it was he who had granted the annuity. Gentlemen, I will not labour that. Seddon, in the box, was quite unable to deal with that letter. He had to admit that it concealed the facts; he had to admit that it was untrue; all he could say about it was that it was unintentionally untrue. You will judge whether Seddon, who was carefully preparing a letter which he was going to give as executor to the relatives, wrote something which was unintentionally untrue when you come to consider the whole of his conduct.

Then, on 9th October, he sees Mr. Vonderahe, and a most serious conversation took place, because at that interview, according to Mr. Vonderahe's statement, Seddon tells him deliberate untruths, and Seddon has had to admit again in the witness-box that he did not tell the truth to Mr. Vonderahe. He did not tell Mr. Vonderahe that it was he who had sold the annuity and got all the property. What did he say when he is asked, " Who is the owner of the Buck's Head and the barber's shop?" he says, " I am," but he adds, according to Vonderahe's evidence, " I purchased it in the open market." He has told you that he did not tell them that he had granted an annuity for it. One thing further. He is asked then, " What about the India stock—who bought that?" and the answer which he gave is, " You will have to write to the Governor of the Bank of England and ask him, but everything has been done in a perfectly legal manner through solicitors and stockbrokers. I have nothing to do with it." Gentlemen, for what reason should Mr.

---

* See Appendix C.

376

Closing Speech for the Crown.

Seddon tell these untruths to Mr. Vonderahe? For the simple reason that he did not dare tell him the truth in case Mr. Vonderahe wanted an inquiry. He knew quite correctly that Mr. Vonderahe, as he had stated, was not satisfied and wanted to know more about it, and the one thing he was anxious about was that Mr. Vonderahe should not take any further trouble, and should not pursue his inquiry. You have had the story told by him about the legal next of kin. I can only say with reference to that that it is very difficult to understand why a man who is in a position of executor and trustee, as he was in this case, who had nothing to conceal, who had acted honestly, and who wanted to satisfy the relatives, and whose duty it was to satisfy the relatives, who was only desirous of doing what an honest man should do in reference to the woman who is dead—why he should not have told the whole of the story truthfully, honestly, and straightforwardly when he was asked questions, and even before he was asked questions, to the relatives.

That series of incidents to which I have called your attention after the death of Miss Barrow, as I suggest to you, show that his conduct after the death was inconsistent with innocence, but was quite consistent with the guilt of a man who, in consequence of his crime, was most anxious to cover everything up and to prevent inquiry. My learned friend said, " Well, he called in a doctor." Do you imagine that Mr. Seddon, who apparently was so fond of study, and who has told us in his own words, " One thought led to another," and who had his encyclopædia——

Mr. MARSHALL HALL—He never said that he had an encyclopædia.

The ATTORNEY-GENERAL—I think he did distinctly say so, but my learned friend thinks that is putting it too high.* I think he did most distinctly say so, but I will leave it out—who had opportunities of consulting books—do you think Mr. Seddon did not know if he did not have a doctor there would have to be a coroner's inquest? Gentlemen, all this parade about the doctor falls to the ground when you bear that in mind. If there were an inquest it would be much more serious than calling in a doctor. My learned friends have also, during the course of this case, commented upon the conduct of this woman—particularly my learned friend Mr. Marshall Hall, if he will permit me to say so, in a passage of remarkable eloquence, dwelt upon what Mrs. Seddon had done in attending to this woman. Both he and my learned friend Mr. Rentoul, with all the force which they addressed you, said, " Oh, but look at Mrs. Seddon's conduct. Why, she had put hot flannels upon Miss Barrow, and even kissed the corpse!" Gentlemen, that leads me to make one comment upon it, which otherwise I should not have made. All this suggestion of her affection and care of Miss Barrow, and the shock to her of Miss Barrow's death, falls a little flat if you remember that on the very night of the woman's death, and before even the body was carried out, she goes off to the music-hall somewhere about eight o'clock at night, staying till twelve o'clock. I am bound to call attention to that when my learned friends are suggesting that she was so fond of Miss Barrow that these various things happened.

---

* He said "There may have been something of the kind in the office."—ED.

Trial of the Seddons.

Attorney-General

I have dealt really now with all the material aspects of this case. There is one other suggestion which, perhaps, I ought not to pass unnoticed —that is the suggestion that my learned friend Mr. Marshall Hall made, "That her money might have been hidden in a hole which nobody has ever yet been able to discover." His suggestion was that this £216, and the gold, and the notes, might be somewhere in a hole dug by Miss Barrow for the purpose of hiding it. The awkwardness of that suggestion, far-fetched as it is, is that Ernie Grant has told us that he actually saw her counting out something which she had taken out on the bed—gold— just before they went to Southend, and that was in the month of August, 1911. So it was there then, and there is no question that it was in existence.

Now, gentlemen, I have gone through this story to you, I hope, in all fairness to these prisoners, and I have called your attention to the strong features against them, and my learned friends have quite rightly called your attention to what should be said in their favour. Certainly no jury could have been more attentive to all the details of this case, and have been more watchful than you have been during the many days that this case has now occupied, and I do not think I should be serving any useful purpose if I went at any great length into the various incidents in connection with this case. You see now how the matter stands. You understand, as you have done from the first when I opened the case, that this case rests upon circumstantial evidence. It is right, when you are dealing with circumstantial evidence, that you should scrutinise, examine, and investigate it most carefully. It is utterly wrong to suggest, as has been suggested during the course of the speeches in this case, that you should not convict on circumstantial evidence. If criminals can only be convicted upon direct evidence of the crime, well, the result would be that a vast number of crimes which are detected, inquired into, and punished in these Courts, never would be discovered; but I agree entirely with this observation, made by my learned friend many times—I am not saying that it was made too often; it is quite natural that they should dwell upon it and emphasise it—that you must be very slow to convict upon circumstantial evidence. I agree entirely with that, and indeed, as I am saying it, I am not at all certain that I am not going to repeat almost his exact words.

If, as the result of the whole of that evidence, you come to the conclusion that these prisoners, either both or one of them, did commit this murder, then it will be your duty to say so notwithstanding that the evidence is circumstantial. Upon that I do not think it is necessary to dilate, because the proposition is well known. We have been brought up to study the law, and I have no doubt you are well aware of it, and certainly my lord will tell you so. But if you have any doubt—any reasonable doubt—after you have considered all the circumstances of this case, then it is your duty to acquit. If, on the other hand, you come to the conclusion beyond reasonable doubt—if you come to the conclusion that you are satisfied beyond all reasonable doubt—that either one or both of the prisoners did the act, you must not fear the consequences. You must not shrink from your duty, you must not fail to perform the obligations you have undertaken on oath.

Closing Speech for the Crown.

Attorney-General

It is right that I should at least put before you my view as I indicated to you when I began the address to you, subject, of course, to anything which my lord may say, from whom you will take your direction in law. The case that I put before you is that both these defendants were engaged in the common purpose of administering the arsenic to this woman an thereby bringing about her death. If any acts were done by either o them, or by both of them, in furtherance of the common purpose, or by on of them with the knowledge and acquiescence of the other that these act are being done in furtherance of the common purpose, both are guilty If, for example, one brewed the solution and the other administered it, i those acts were done with a common purpose, both are guilty. It ma be when you come to take the whole of this case into your consideratior you may think that the evidence shows beyond all reasonable doubt that one of these prisoners is guilty, but that you have some element of reasonabl doubt with regard to the other. Supposing you come to the conclusior that you have no reasonable doubt with regard to the male prisoner, bu that you have some doubt—you are not quite satisfied beyond all reason able doubt—that the woman is guilty, then it would be your duty to acquit her. You will only find them both guilty if the conviction i forced upon your minds from the consideration of the circumstances o this case that they are both guilty. I agree with my learned friend Mr Marshall Hall that in these cases it is not right to speak about "th benefit of the doubt." If there is a reasonable doubt it means the Crowr has failed to prove its case. If we have not established it to you satisfaction beyond all reasonable doubt in this case when you have brough to bear upon the examination of the facts and circumstances the wisdom you possess, and which you would supply to ordinary human affairs, why, then, of course, my learned friends are entitled to say, and I say with them, that both prisoners would be entitled to be acquitted.

I am not going now to consider the differences that may be made with regard to the evidence, but I will only say this, that the evidence of subsequent conduct to which I have adverted during the course of m observations to you during the last half hour, are mostly matters of evidence against the male prisoner, and not so much against the woman, but you must bear in mind in seeking to do justice in this case that she is present at, I think, all, at any rate, most of the conversations to which I have referred with the Vonderahes. You must bear in mind what her position is with regard to her husband. You will also bear in mind this. Our law is very merciful, and very merciful particularly to a wife, but not in a case of murder. The presumption which the law would other-wise make is not made in favour of the wife in a case of murder. I mean by that, that suppose a wife is present when an act of larceny, or an act of stealing, is committed by her husband, the law presumes that she is acting under the coercion of her husband, and the law presumes there-fore that she is innocent of the crime, but the law says also that there is no possible duty upon her to obey her husband if he tells her to do an act in furtherance of murder. According to the law of this country there is no such presumption in favour of the wife that she did murder because her husband coerced her into it. I mention those matters to you because they may have occurred to you during the course of the hearing of this case. Those are the considerations of law which should apply, and I only venture to make them in the hearing of my lord, so that my lord if he differs from anything I say would put to you what he thinks is his view, and, in any event, as I have no doubt my lord will in charging you tell you what the legal position is as regards both the defendants. Now, gentlemen, the matter will rest, after the summing up, entirely with you. To you is entrusted the ultimate duty of deciding upon the facts of this case. References have been made to the responsibility which devolves upon those who are trying this case, or taking part in the trial of this case. Gentlemen, of course, that is quite true. There is a responsibility no doubt upon my lord, and a responsibility, of course, upon us as counsel, but the ultimate responsibility rests with you. You have to weigh the circumstances, take them into consideration, and determine them for yourselves with such assistance as my learned friends and I have been able to give you in arriving at a conclusion, subject, of course, always to the main assistance, no doubt, which you will get from the summing up of my lord. It rests entirely with you. All I ask you is, when you have made up your minds, not to shrink from the conclusions to which you think you are forced by the evidence that has been given. If you are satisfied, say so, whatever the consequences. If you are not satisfied, do not hesitate to acquit either the one or both. Give effect to the results of your deliberations and the conclusions you come to, and, if you have done that, you will have done your duty, and justice, I am satisfied, will have been done.

Mr. Justice Bucknill's Summing Up.

Mr. JUSTICE BUCKNILL—Gentlemen of the jury, after nine days of an anxious trial, during which time I have observed that you have paid a most intelligent interest and taken the greatest possible care to understand everything that has been said, either by way of evidence or by way of speeches, we are now drawing to the close of this painful inquiry, and my observations only stand between you and your final deliberation. I hope you have not yet made up your minds—not that I am going to argue for or against the accused people, far from it (I never do such a thing), yet I may be able to point out to you and to help you to appreciate some of the difficulties of the position; that is my duty. If I should be of assistance to you, how glad I should be. Therefore I hope that you have not yet made up your minds.

I also hope fervently that you will be able to come to a conclusion. I am certain of one thing, that, whatever judgment you may pronounce by your verdict, your country will say that you did it as honest and as intelligent men. You must not be frightened at the consequences if you find yourselves driven to give a verdict hostile to either both or one of these people. Verdicts given by timidity are always quite wrong, because they are not verdicts which are given according to the evidence. Nor are you going to give a verdict one way or the other moved by any feelings of prejudice or sympathy, although I know full well that you must have

April 2/12.

J. Walter Saint Esq.,
Dear Sir

I feel it is a very strong point in my favour that I had to draw on my own bank for the sums of £90 Sept 19/11, £100, Oct 6/11, also from my post office a/c "Nov" £43, Total £233. How is this consistent with the suggestions of the Prosecution that I was possessed of the £892 alleged to have been in the possession of Miss Barrow? I must not need to be drawing on my own banking a/c if I had had the money. Kindly put this to Counsel. Yours Faithfully, F. H. Seddon.

Note written by Seddon during the luncheon interval on the second day of the hearing of his Appeal.

Justice Bucknill's Summing Up.

Mr. Justice Bucknill.

a sympathetic feeling for a female who stands charged with the wilful murder of another female; I feel it, and every honest man must feel it.

You must forgive me for repeating this, but what I am saying will stand recorded, and may be criticised, and therefore I have to repeat to you what will not be recorded, the speeches of learned counsel, so that you may have it from me as if they had not said it. I must tell you again what your especial duties are in the consideration of the facts which have been laid before you. The Crown has to prove its case. You have heard that many times, for the reasons I have given you, but I will tell you again. The Crown has to prove its case, and the reason is that unless the Crown has proved to your satisfaction beyond reasonable doubt—not all possible doubt, but beyond reasonable doubt—these people are entitled to your acquittal. I have had to consider this matter very carefully, and I shall just read this passage to you so that I may be quite sure that the language I use may be what I wish it to be—"It is not necessary that a crime should be established beyond the possibility of a doubt, for there are doubts, more or less, involved in every human transaction. There are crimes committed in darkness and secrecy which can only be traced and brought to light by a comparison of circumstances which press upon the mind more and more as they are increased in number. Your duty is calmly and carefully to investigate the case and see what is the conclusion impressed upon your mind as men of the world, as men of sense, and as men of solid justice. If the conclusion to which you are conducted be that there is that degree of certainty in the case that you would act upon it in your own grave and important concerns, that is the degree of certainty that the law requires." So, of course, if you see a reasonable doubt, you must, as you will be very glad, not to give them the "benefit" of it, but to acquit them. I do not like those words "benefit of the doubt," because, where the Crown has to prove a case, if it has not proved it, there is a doubt; you do not give the accused person the "benefit" of it; you simply acquit him, because the Crown has not proved its case.

Now, this case, as you may gather from what I have read, is a case founded upon circumstantial evidence. The learned Attorney-General, in his very careful argument and very fair speech just now, called it "indirect evidence." I disagree a little about it. Circumstantial evidence is not indirect evidence, except that it is indirect in this way, that it is not as direct as the evidence of an eye-seer—the person who sees the thing done. Circumstantial evidence is made up of a series of circumstances or facts or events, each of which is direct necessarily, because, if it were not, you would not perceive it; each circumstance is direct until at last the sum of those circumstances may very rightly and properly impel you to find a verdict of guilty. Therefore circumstantial evidence is very often absolutely as strong as the most direct evidence that could possibly be adduced. Now, this is a poison case; these people are charged with having poisoned Miss Barrow. Needless to say (because I am sure you have thought it already, and you will accept it), if they, or either of them, are guilty of this crime, it was a crime which had been carefully thought out and was carefully committed in secrecy. The history of those great poisoning cases of which most of us know, and which many of us have had to study, shows (of course, again it is common sense) that the poisoner

Trial of the Seddons.

Mr. Justice Bucknill

does not poison in open daylight, that is to say, in the presence of other persons; it is one of those secret crimes which is done in the dark. And, if this case is made out against these people, there can•be no doubt that it was a very abominable crime. That is sufficient on that part of the case.

Now, I am going to ask you, if you will allow me, to bear in mind for a few minutes only the three people in this case—the deceased woman and the male and female defendants. Just consider for a moment or two the sort of people they were. Miss Barrow was a lady said to be forty-five years old or thereabout, and a spinster. She was deaf in the sense that she did not hear as other people did, and she perhaps had that same suspicious nature that deaf people have sometimes; they do not hear what people say, and they naturally get suspicious; one has experience of that. She was quick to like, and quick to dislike. She was a woman of good means; she had quite enough to support herself very nicely and properly. She was very keen to have her own way, I dare say, in money matters, and a good woman of business. So far as we know, she was very fond of Ernie Grant and his sister Hilda. Perhaps Ernie Grant was the one living person of whom she was really fond. She was very fond of the boy. She used to take him to school in the morning, bring him back to dinner, take him back after dinner, fetch him in the afternoon, and take him in the evening for a walk; she was as fond as a mother of him, and she was a respectable lady. She lived with the Grants until Mrs. Grant died; Mr. Grant was alive when she went; he died in 1906, and Mrs. Grant died in 1908. Then Miss Barrow went and lived with somebody else for a short time. Then she went to the Vonderahes, where she was several months, and there she took offence at something that they did or did not do; it may be they did not cook well; there is some evidence of that. However, they did not please her, and she went, as she was entitled to. Seeing an advertisement in the paper, inserted as we are told by the male prisoner, she answered it, and eventually took the upper floor of the house, and what she intended to do, according to Hook's evidence, was to live there with Ernie and have the Hooks with her, and Mrs. Hook was to teach her housekeeping and how to cook, so it would be a little family on the top floor. It was unfurnished; she took the furniture with her. It does not very much matter whether the furniture was hers or whether it was Hook's; that is a matter which is of no importance in this case at all. So she intended to live there, and she remained there until her death. Now, as regards these two people, the husband and the wife, so far as we know, up to the time of this alleged crime they were very respectable people. He was a man of considerable ability, who had worked his way up in the insurance company until he became a local superintendent in the north of London; he possessed the confidence of his employers; sums of money were entrusted to his care every week, and they were so satisfied with him that they allowed him to pay their money into his own bank and send a cheque on to them for it; so that he possessed their full confidence; nothing in the world is known against him. But I think one must say this, that, even on the evidence given by himself and given by his wife, he was fond of money. The only dispute of any importance that they appear to have had together arose on a matter of money. For some reason he was angry

Justice Bucknill's Summing Up.

Mr. Justice Bucknill

with her, as I understand it, with regard to some accounts in the wardrobe business she was carrying on with so much success, and he got into a passion apparently (we need not inquire into whether it was rightly or wrongly), and threatened to throw the books into the fire. He offended his wife, and to the extent that she left him; she would not have it. It was money that brought about that comparatively trivial matter. She came back again, and they lived happily together so far as we know. Now, only a few words about her, and we pass on. There was not a word to be said against her so far as we know; we must certainly assume there was not. She was a hard-working woman, who, although her husband was getting as much as £6 a week, did what many a woman would not do, most of the work in the house. She cooked and helped to keep the house in order; she was not only a wife, but a servant; they kept one servant, Chater, whose duties, I suppose, were comparatively light. So she is entitled to be introduced to you as a good wife and hard-working woman, and a woman of good reputation.

Now, these two people are charged with the murder of Miss Barrow, and there can be no doubt about it that if this crime were committed by one or the other, or both of these people—by the man if it were done by him, and if he only is responsible there is the love of gold that made him do it; and if the wife helped him, acted with him with one purpose, if the two acted together with one purpose, although she may not have done it for love of gold, and only have done it to serve her husband, if he compassed the death of this woman for her gold and the wife helped him either, as the learned Attorney-General has said, by cooking the food into which the poison was put with her knowledge—if that can be supported—or by doing anything else which would lead you to the conclusion that she was helping to bring about the death of this woman by poison, why, of course, she is equally as guilty as he is. But you may say there is a great difference between the two. It is the case put forward by the Crown that it was the cupidity (I think that was the very word used by the learned Attorney-General) of the man that brought about this unfortunate woman's death. There is a difference between his cupidity and the position of the wife, as you may think. And any point that can be taken in her favour you must take as also with regard to him. Although motive here has been made so much of, and although motive, if it exist, is such an important factor in this case, do not think motive is proof of crime; it is a matter brought into the case for the purpose of assisting the tribunal, that is yourselves, to come to the conclusion that, from the Crown's point of view, this murder was the act of the Seddons, or one of them, and that it was a murder, not of passion, not of hatred, not done in a moment of heat or anger, but a murder which was designed for the purpose of getting this woman's money, or, if it had been got before by illegal means, of getting her out of the way so that they should not be punished for that which they had done, if they had done it.

I think I have said enough on the general part of the case, except this one other observation, and that is, if there was motive, there certainly was opportunity. Up to the time of this woman's death from 1st September to 14th September she was living in this house alone, except for Ernie

Trial of the Seddons.

Grant, and the only people in the house were the Seddons, or their friends or relations. Therefore there was the opportunity.

Now, the first question that I want to draw your attention to is the first question you will ask yourselves. You have probably asked it yourselves already, because you have been discussing it; I am sure you have not been confined all these days without having discussed it more or less. What was the cause of Miss Barrow's death? The Crown says that the direct and approximate cause of her death was a fatal dose of arsenic given to her, although previous doses may have been administered, within three days of the death, or within four or five hours—three days being the greatest limit and four or five hours the shortest limit. That is the evidence of Dr. Willcox, to which I am now going to call your attention. Dr. Willcox's evidence is that of expressed certainty. You will remember he has told you, "I am sure that she died of acute arsenical poisoning; I have no doubt about it." I will read the words to you in a few minutes. I am sure you will forgive me if I take up some little time, because you know my address to you is not the address of counsel; it is the address of a judge who is trying to help you to remember some of the evidence which you might not otherwise have keenly in your recollection.

> I say it [says Dr. Willcox] because of the amount of arsenic that I found in the stomach and intestines; from that amount I feel satisfied that she [Miss Barrow] must have had administered to her, or must have taken, arsenic more than that amount which was found in the stomach or intestines, or in the body, which altogether amounted to 2·01 grains, and I should judge she had had a strong dose; the fatal dose would not have been less than 4 to 5 grains, and 2 grains is a fatal dose.

Now, gentlemen, you know it has been said very often that, however high the authority of a scientific witness may be, the jury are to be distinctly independent, because the evidence is the evidence of opinion only. Well, that has its limitations. In this particular case Dr. Willcox stands at the very top of his profession in regard to scientific analyses. That is admitted; I am not going to say anything which is not admitted; Mr. Marshall Hall has said that. Mr. Marshall Hall has also said of Dr. Willcox what, of course, he is entitled to say from all who know him as a public man, that he is an absolutely honest, straightforward man, and he would not go one hair's breadth out of his way to hurt anybody. He has a reputation which entitles him to have that said of him, and I should think you would agree with that from the way he gave his evidence—the modest and quiet, but at the same time the clear and firm manner in which he gave his evidence. He says that he is certain, so far as he can be certain of anything, so far as his scientific researches have taken him, that this woman died in the way I have just told you. And yet it is said that you might say that it is possible that a mistake has been made.

The way in which it is suggested the mistake may have been made is this, as I understand it. There is a calculation always necessary. You take a bit, and you leave a bit, and you analyse a bit, and you argue from that that the bit which is left, together with the bit you have analysed, gives a certain result. You take the different organs of the body; you make an analysis and test with regard to each. In each case there were two tests, the Marsh test and another. Those tests—the "mirror tests," as we will call them—were used with regard to all the organs except two,

Justice Bucknill's Summing Up.

Mr. Justice Bucknill

and with regard to those two another well-known test was used. As the result you get 2·01 grains found in the body of the deceased person. But the reason why Dr. Willcox says he is certain the fatal dose was administered either within three days or four or five hours, taking each as the limit, is because of the amount of arsenic which he found in the stomach and intestines. He has described all that to you. In the stomach he found ·11 grains and in the intestines he found ·63 grains, but the tests were different, for in the stomach the Marsh test was applied, and in the intestines and in the liver another test was applied. Gentlemen, when you get a man of this position standing absolutely uncontradicted with another well-known doctor who has not been called, to whom an offer has been made—in effect, "come and test yourself. Here is what I have done. Here is the hydrogen apparatus. Here are the parts of the different organs of the body which have not been tested. I invite you to test, and I invite you to do what you like"—is it not almost impossible to come to any other conclusion than that Dr. Willcox is right as to the amount of arsenic found in the body? It is entirely for you, but I do not know what could guide you to come to a contrary conclusion. If you see your way, of course, you will act on it, because of a certainty you would be entitled to take a view not in agreement with Dr. Willcox, if you saw some reason for doing it.

One point has been made with regard to the hair. Dr. Willcox was extremely fair with regard to that. He was pressed, and the answer comes to this, that if you find arsenic in the distal ends of the hair—the ends farthest from the roots—one would expect that the arsenic had been administered some time before. I do not think he has given any exact time for that. That would tend to show that that particular arsenic— some particular arsenic—eventually found its way into the distal ends of the hair more than three days before the death, as I understand it. Well, that is a fact, and there it is for what it is worth. But, the amount found in her hair has not been taken into calculation it seems; it has been left out. I cannot give you further assistance, except to remind you of the fact that Dr. Willcox was called back, and he told you that certain hair had been soaked in the fluid from the body, and how it had been tested after that, and it was found that the hair had absorbed a certain amount of arsenic. I cannot give you any more assistance about it; it is not my duty to try. You have heard counsel on both sides, and I myself am unable to do it.

Now, I assume that you come to the conclusion that Dr. Willcox is right, for which purpose I had better read you a few paragraphs of his evidence. I will read my note. I have taken it word for word from the transcript. He said, "There might have been an amount of, say, about 5 grains—up to about 5 grains, taken within three hours of death." Then, "The arsenic is conveyed all over the body by the blood stream rapidly." Do not forget that extreme rapidity. I offer this suggestion —probably more rapidly in one case than another. No two people are made exactly the same. The receptivity of one is not the receptivity of another. I mean by that that the absorption of arsenic into the blood and the passage into the different organs may be quicker in the case of one person than another, because the constitutions are different; it is possible. You cannot, therefore, be certain on these matters. You must

Trial of the Seddons.

make an allowance for any difference in the idiosyncrasies of individual people. "The fatal dose was taken within two or three days of death, probably within two days"—but I am going to give you further evidence on that. Then he gives the reason why he said that, "The relatively large amount of arsenic found in the stomach and intestines leads me to that opinion." You see my notes make the story consecutive by leaving out a great deal which is unnecessary. "Miss Barrow had certainly taken arsenic during the last two days, and it is likely that it might have been taken for some days before." Then he tells you how he tested these different papers, how he found papers which were bought at Price's, Thorley's, Needham's, Dodd's, and Spink's, all seemed to contain different amounts of arsenic; the lowest was 3·8 grains and the highest 6 grains. Then he tells you how a paper boiled for five minutes in a quarter of a pint of water gave the result to him, Dr. Willcox, of 6·6 grains; that would be what would happen in that particular case. Another paper was boiled, for the same time I suppose, and that gave 3·8 grains. Then we find this observation, "2·01 grains (which is the amount found in the body altogether) might kill a person, and that was probably part of 5 grains, the fatal dose," or words to that effect. Then he is cross-examined by Mr. Marshall Hall. He speaks of the individual idiosyncrasies of people. Then he says this, "In acute arsenical poisoning burning in the throat might occur, also cramp." There is no evidence that there was any burning of the throat, or any cramp in this particular case. You observe he uses the word "acute." In answer to Mr. Marshall Hall, he says, "A dose of four or five grains would produce abdominal pains in half an hour probably." Then he gives the answer I was referring to before, "The extreme period that would elapse between the fatal dose and death was three days, and the minimum period of a few hours—five or six hours, or less." Then he is cross-examined with regard to the multiplying factor, as we call it. You will understand what the multiplying factor is. This is a point which Mr. Marshall Hall is fully entitled to ask you to consider when you are considering the exact accuracy with regard to the 2·01 grains being found in the body. The multiplying factor is sometimes so high, Mr. Marshall Hall says, that error is possible —that error is probable. Therefore, without charging or suggesting that Dr. Willcox has not done the matter carefully and skilfully the argument adduced by Mr. Marshall Hall on behalf of his client is this: skilful as you may be, with all the science you can bring to bear with regard to the accuracy of the test, you have got to make a calculation which may make your ultimate figures wrong. Whether it would make them less or make them more I do not know, but, of course, if error is possible, that is the observation on it. The amount found may have been less, or the amount found may have been more, but using the best means that Dr. Willcox had, the results were those which he has given us. Then Mr. Marshall Hall made another very good point, if I may say so, with regard to the weight of the body. This woman, we will suppose, had a weight, we will say, of about 10 stone, but when the post-mortem took place it had reduced to 4 stone and something pounds, so it became much more difficult at that time to tell with accuracy what was the correct amount of muscle which you were to take as the supposed weight when you are calculating

Justice Bucknill's Summing Up.

Mr. Justice Bucknill

so as to get the amount of the arsenic found in the muscle. Dr. Willcox admitted it freely. There it is. You come to the same thing again, "I have done all that science enables me to do, and I tell you that that science gives me certain results with regard to the muscle." I think there was a grain found in the muscle, was there not? Then comes the answer which Dr. Willcox gave, "This was a case of acute arsenical poisoning. I have no doubt about it." Then he is cross-examined about the hair. I need not trouble you about that; it is unnecessary. Then he admits that the symptoms of arsenical poisoning and of chronic diarrhœa are identical. Then Dr. Willcox says, "Miss Barrow may have had some arsenic after Dr. Sworn saw her (I think Dr. Sworn saw her the last time). The fatal dose may have been given within a few hours of death." Then he repeats that the arsenic in the stomach, the intestines, and the liver must have got there within two days. Finally, "There cannot be the slightest doubt as to this being a case of acute arsenical poisoning."

That evidence has been very fairly dealt with by learned counsel on both sides. If I may say so, throughout this case that has been the case. I do not know what your answer may be which you have to give to this question, but I should not be surprised if you said that you are satisfied beyond reasonable doubt that this lady died of acute arsenical poisoning as distinguished from "chronic," which, from the Greek word "time," means that she had been taking arsenic for a period of time as distinguished from a few days.

The next question is, if she died of acute arsenical poisoning, was it taken by her accidentally, was it administered by some person medicinally, had it got into the medicine which she was given, or was it given to her by the accused persons, or by one of them? In consideration of this part of the case, I think I will begin with the woman's evidence. I will tell you why. She saw most of her during her illness. She was with her from day to day. She had taken her to Dr. Paul. Dr. Paul, I think, saw her six or seven days. "I yesterday looked up the last time, and I found the 29th was not the last day, it was the 30th of August." Then, having got better under Dr. Paul—Dr. Paul telling you that there was nothing the matter with her of so grievous a nature as to have even kept her indoors if she had chosen to go out—he is called in again on 1st September. Then Dr. Paul said, in effect, "Too busy, can't come." It is not my duty, and I am not going to criticise the duties of medical men, but I had an idea when you had a patient under your control, or under your care, you ought to give a better reason than "I can't come," if you are asked to come and see her two days after a visit. I do not know what the profession thinks about it. This woman had been seen by him on several occasions; she saw him last on 30th August. She wants to see him on 2nd September, and Dr. Pau says, "Too busy; can't come." Dr. Sworn is called in, he being the medical adviser of the male prisoner. Dr. Sworn comes in and sees her, and there was nothing that Dr. Sworn saw, according to his evidence (and there is no dispute about it) that led him to believe that she was suffering from anything else than epidemic diarrhœa. He treated her for it. I am going to read you his evidence, because I think it is important. I will not read it all, of course.

Trial of the Seddons.

Mr. Justice Bucknill

I was telephoned for. I went and saw Miss Barrow in bed. Mrs. Seddon was in the room. Miss Barrow and Mrs. Seddon gave me history of case. That day, before she had diarrhœa and sickness, she appeared to be very ill. Miss Barrow said she had been ailing on and off for a long time. Mrs. Seddon said she had had liver attacks and asthma. I asked if she had been attended to by another doctor. They said she had been attended by another doctor, and that they had sent for him at noon and at 8 p.m. Miss Barrow had pains, sickness, and diarrhœa, pain in the abdomen. She had been vomiting before, not whilst I was there. I prescribed bismuth [and so forth] and morphia, both in the same mixture, a dose every four hours. I saw her next day, 3rd, in the morning, 11 to 12 noon, she was no better, and that sickness and diarrhœa continued. I prescribed some medicine. On Monday the 4th I saw her again. About the same. I understood that sickness and diarrhœa had not ceased. She had not yielded to my treatment. She was no weaker. I was not satisfied with her condition on that day. Mrs. Seddon said she would not take her medicine.

Now, you see Mrs Seddon is there on each occasion apparently looking after the woman, according to that statement of Dr. Sworn, and apparently waiting on her in a friendly, kind manner, and was solicitous about the health of the patient. Now it is said she was poisoning her.

That was before I went into the room. And also before Miss Barrow. She was deaf. She could not hear what was said in an ordinary tone of voice. That day I prescribed an effervescent mixture, potash and bicarbonate of soda in two bottles. On that day diarrhœa was not so bad, so I gave her nothing for it. I spoke to Miss Barrow and said if she did not take her medicine I should send her to a hospital, and she said she would not go. On the 5th I went again. She was slightly better. Mrs. Seddon was present. She said her sickness was not so bad, and diarrhœa not so bad as yesterday. I did not alter the treatment. On the 6th she was improving and I continued same medicine. On the 7th she was slowly improving, same medicine. On the 8th the same medicine. Slowly improving. On the 4th I stopped morphia because the pain was less. On 9th she was about the same. Mrs. Seddon said motions very offensive, so I gave Miss Barrow a blue pill. On 10th, Sunday, I did not call. I said on 9th if patient no worse I should not call. On Monday 11th [This is the day the will was made] I saw her between 10 and 12 noon. She was about same as on Saturday. I saw Mrs. Seddon on 11th. Miss Barrow was then suffering from weakness caused by diarrhœa and sickness. She had no pain on 11th. I ordered Valentine's Meat Juice and brandy for the weakness.

Do not forget that date, because the Crown suggests that that is the day which would be one of the limitations—one of the limited periods —for the administration of the fatal dose; they suggest that the 11th, when the Valentine's Meat Juice was given, was the first opportunity for mixing this concoction got from poisonous fly-papers, which we have heard would also be of a brown colour.

I told Mrs Seddon to give her soda water and milk if sickness came on, and gruel, and later on some milk pudding. On 11th her condition was not very good. It was not very good any time that I saw her. On 11th a will was not mentioned by anyone.

The ATTORNEY-GENERAL—Is not that the mental condition, my lord? Mr. JUSTICE BUCKNILL—What did I say? I have here—

Her mental condition was not very good. It was not very good at any time that I saw her. On 11th a will was not mentioned by anyone. A will would have to be explained to her.

Do not forget that, because it is charged against these people that one of the suspicious circumstances, at all events against the man, is making the will for her when she was in the condition in which the doctor describes her to be. It is said that that is a very suspicious matter.

Justice Bucknill's Summing Up.

Mr. Justice Bucknill

A will would have to be explained to her. She would not grasp all the facts, but she was quite capable of making a will if it was properly explained to her.

The man says it was properly explained to her.

I did not want to make the will for her, not being a lawyer. I did not know very well how to put it together. I knew something about the expressions in a will and had a fair idea, and I did the best I could. I never expected her to die, so I was not very particular about it; I did what she told me to do. It was signed and witnessed. All I know about it is I did it because she asked me to.

On the other hand, you know what the learned Attorney-General has said, and I shall have to refer to the will again before I have finished.

Her mental condition from 1st to 11th did not improve. It was about the same. I first ordered Valentine's Meat Juice some time after the 4th I think. On 12th I did not see her. On 13th I saw her about noon, I think; not sure. On 13th diarrhœa had come on again. She did not seem in much pain. I gave her a mixture. She had a little return of the sickness. I gave her a chalk mixture, bismuth and chalk; strength about same. She was weaker on account of the diarrhœa. I saw Mrs. Seddon on that day. I simply said Miss Barrow was worse, and that I would send her a mixture to be taken after each motion. I gave no diet instructions on that day. She was in a little danger but not in a critical condition. I did not expect her to die that night any more than any patient who with an attack of that sort might die from heart failure or anything like that. Her pulse was weaker on 13th than the day before, not intermittent, simply weak. I did not see her alive again. I took her temperature twice; one day 101 on 7th [101, you know, is not dangerous] some days it was 99. I never found it subnormal. I did not take it every day. On 13th I did not take her temperature.

Then he tells you what happened afterwards when he saw Mr. Seddon. That is the evidence of the doctor during the time that he saw her. I have no observation to make about it except to remind you that Mrs. Seddon was there every time. You may take that from two points of view, and you will not take the hostile point of view, I am sure, unless you find yourself bound to. According to the evidence of the doctor, Mrs. Seddon was there every day looking after the woman, taking his orders, and, so far as we know (of course, it is suggested quite to the contrary), carrying them out. At all events nothing peculiar was found in Mrs. Seddon's conduct. She was there each time the doctor came; and the doctor gave her orders, and at one time the woman answered to the treatment positively. Now, the fact that she answered to the treatment and got better on three consecutive days, I think you may say is pretty good proof that Mrs. Seddon had carried out the doctor's instructions, because, if she was slowly poisoning this woman, the probability is she would not have answered to the medicine. Do I make myself clear? On the other hand the suggestion is that she was doing one of the most wicked and abominable things that any woman in the world could do—pretending to be the nurse and acting as the poisoner. So much with regard to Dr. Sworn's evidence.

Now, we will take Mrs. Seddon's evidence, if you please, because that follows on after Dr. Sworn's evidence. I will only take her evidence with regard to the illness; I shall have to come back to the other evidence when I come to the motive. On 1st September she tells you—I need not go through that. She introduced her to Dr. Paul, and took her there—

On the 1st September I did not get up till 10·30. She was in our kitchen then. She complained of being sick. I advised her to go upstairs and lay down. I helped her upstairs. She did not undress. [This is 1st September.] I gave her a cup of tea.

Trial of the Seddons.

She was sick after the tea. She lay down on the bed all that day. I had seen her like it before. Every month she would have sick bilious attacks. On 2nd September she had diarrhœa and sickness. In the morning she said she could not sign for her annuity. [That was the day it was due] and my husband went up to her and gave her the money, and she signed the receipt. I was present. After dinner I sent for Dr. Paul. He attended her before and I had gone with her. We sent for him at once, and he said he could not come, and he told us to get the nearest doctor in the neighbourhood. My daughter telephoned for Dr. Sworn, our own doctor. I saw him when he came, and he gave directions—everything she had was to be light—no solid food. He sent her medicine, chalky and thick, and she did not like it. On 3rd September doctor came again. I told him, and he said she must take it. Afterwards I asked her if she would go to a hospital and she refused. One day she went into Ernie's bedroom. I remonstrated with her and said the doctor would blame me. She complained of the flies in her own bedroom. We had to fan her to keep the flies from her. She asked me to get fly-papers—the wet ones, not the sticky ones. That was on the Monday or Tuesday, 4th or 5th. I got them at Meacher's the chemist, just round the corner, close to us. An old gentleman served me. I may have bought the baby's food at the same time also, Horlick's Malted Milk 9/6 a bottle. I believe I bought for Miss Barrow a white precipitate powder to wash her head, and once I saw her clean her teeth with it. I signed no book when I bought the fly-paper. I never had a packet. I asked for two papers. I bought four for 3d. I showed them to Miss Barrow and she said they were the sort she wanted. I put them on a plate first to damp them all over, and then in four saucers, two on mantelpiece, two on chest of drawers. I put water in the saucers. When she was ill I did her cooking in my kitchen—only Valentine's Meat Juice upstairs —barley water &c., downstairs. Before she was ill her cooking was always done in her kitchen, except when I cooked fish for her or made her a pudding. Mary always made her a morning cup of tea. I was in bed. Maggie used to take it up to her before and whilst she was ill. [There is a dispute about that between Maggie and Mary.] At 6 I would get her a cup of milk, and at 7 tea. During her illness I waited on her, but, if I had to go out, Maggie would. My husband only gave her medicine on one occasion when I complained that she would not take it. That was the fizzy medicine which she would not take fizzing. Whilst she was ill she wanted to see my husband about making a will. He did not go up immediately. He went up later. I was present when he went up. She wanted to make it out for the boy and the girl. What furniture and jewellery there was for Ernie and Hilda—what belonged to their father and mother—she wanted them to have it and not the Hooks. Husband suggested a solicitor to her. She did not want one—because of the expense—and asked if he could not do it himself. Then I went down and then I went up to sign it. Husband called me and my father-in-law up and we saw her sign it.

So there was a time when the wife left the husband with the deceased woman;* she went downstairs while the will was being prepared on the 11th, and she was called up, and she signed it—

The will was read over to her first, then she asked for her glasses, and then she read it and signed it. Sister-in-law arrived that day. Next day the doctor came and I was present. [Now we are coming to the 12th.] On Tuesday the 12th I knocked a fly-paper off the mantelpiece by accident. I went down and got a soup-plate and put the whole four into the soup-plate and put it on the little table between the windows. I put fresh water in the soup-plate as well. It remained there until the morning of her death.

You know what the learned Attorney-General says with regard to that. He says all that story is not to be believed—the soup plate story is not true and the buying of the papers is not true. I am not going to refer you again to the argument of the learned counsel; I give you credit for remembering that. I am now drawing your attention to the evidence. You will give weight to the arguments adduced by learned counsel on one

---

* This is not according to the evidence.—ED.

Justice Bucknill's Summing Up.

Mr. Justice Bucknill

side or the other; it is not my duty to repeat the arguments to you again but to read the evidence—

During her illness she used to get out of bed. On 13th September Dr. Sworn sa her in morning. Husband was not at home that evening; he was at the theatre. Abou midnight Miss Barrow called out, "I am dying." I could hear her from the front where I was standing awaiting my husband. My sister-in-law was with me, Mrs. Longley. I said to her "Did you hear what Miss Barrow said." With that I rushed upstairs. I also asked Mrs. Longley to come up with me. She did not like at first, then she followed up after. I asked Miss Barrow what was the matter with her. She said she had violent pains in her stomach and that her feet felt cold. I asked my sister-in-law what should I do, as I had no hot water bottles in the house. She replied "Wrap a flannel petticoat round her feet," which I did. Then I did as I usually did with her stomach. I put the hot flannels—[then she told you how she did that]. Then I went down the stairs again. Husband returned about half-past 12. I told Mr. Seddon what had happened. He did not go up immediately, you know; he was talking to my sister-in-law about the theatre. I think in the meantime the boy came down. I think that husband and my sister-in-law and I went up to her room afterwards, but I am not certain. My husband introduced Mrs. Longley to Miss Barrow. She just looked at her, and I think Mrs Longley went downstairs. She said the boy had no right to be in bed with Miss Barrow—so unhealthy. My sister-in-law went half way down the stairs I did not go then. I attended to what Miss Barrow wanted. I do not know i Mr. Seddon gave Miss Barrow a drop of brandy then or not, but he told her she must g to sleep and rest—that I would be knocked up. She said she could not help it. The we went downstairs to bed. My husband left the room first, you must remember. had to attend to her first. We were not in bed long before the boy came down agai and said "Chickie" wanted me. I went up then. I put hot flannels on her, an attended to her as she wanted. She had diarrhœa then. I did not think she wa dying. I never saw anyone die. I went back to bed again, and I had just got baby o my arm and was called up again by the boy—"Chickie wants you." He knocked a our door. I went up again and it was just the same as it was before. During tha night she was not properly sick, but nasty froth came up and she retched.

You can understand the position. I do not suppose there was much to bring up, poor soul, after all the vomiting she had gone through an the diarrhœa—

She had the diarrhœa bad. That time husband did not go up. He did next time Next time boy called out Miss Barrow was out of bed. My husband told me to stop i bed and he would go up and attend to her. I said, "It is no good your going up, because I thought she wanted me for the same as before, but he would go up, and followed up at the same time. Miss Barrow was in a sitting position on the floor, an the boy was holding her up, so we lifted her into bed again. It must have bee between 3 and 4 a.m. then. I could not tell the time. Hot flannels as before, an made her comfortable. She was not complaining then to my knowledge, but generall she was always complaining. She asked me to stay with her. Husband said to her "If Mrs. Seddon sits up with you all night she will be knocked up. You mus remember she has a young baby and she [Mrs. Seddon] wants her rest." Ernie was ir and out of her bed all the time. Husband sent him to his own room each time we wen up and down the stairs. That was the last time we went up—the fourth time. stayed with her and sat in the chair—a basket chair—at the end of the bed. Husban was standing by bedroom door. I did not put any more hot flannels on. She seemed to go to sleep, and my husband was standing by the bedroom door smoking and reading He said, "Why did not I go down and go to bed." I said, "What is the good o going to bed. She will only call me up again," so I made up my mind to sit in th chair. Miss Barrow seemed to be sleeping and I was dozing—sleeping tired. Mis Barrow seemed to be sleeping peacefully for some minutes, and then after a while sh seemed to be snoring. It was getting on towards daylight then, and my husband dre my attention that this snoring had stopped and her breathing had stopped. Then h lifted her eyelids and said, "Good God, she's dead!" So with that he hurried out an went for Dr. Sworn. It would be between 6 and 6.30 so far as I can reckon it. Whils he was away I locked the bedroom door so that the boy could not go in, and went dow to the kitchen.

Trial of the Seddons.

Mr. Justice Bucknill

That ends that. Death had taken place. Now, I want to refer you for a moment to the boy's evidence. We will see what the boy says about that night. He describes how he lived with the Seddons, how Miss Barrow was taken ill, and how he slept in his own bed, first of all, and when she got worse she asked him to sleep in her bed, and he did—

I remember the last night I slept with her. She kept waking up and it awoke me. I went downstairs to call Mrs Seddon. Miss Barrow asked me to. They slept on the floor below. Mrs. Seddon came upstairs, and so did Mr. Seddon, and I got into bed again with Miss Barrow. Mr. Seddon wanted me to go to my own bed in the small room to get some sleep. Then Miss Barrow called me again and I went. Mr. and Mrs. Seddon were there then. I had left them in the room and found them there when I returned. Miss Barrow called me back directly. I got into her bed. Mr Seddon told me to go back to my room and I went and remained there.

Mr. Seddon told him to go back and so forth, and you will remember how he went backwards and forwards. At all events, the point of his evidence is that he saw these two people up there, and apparently he saw this woman put flannels on, apparently doing her best to make the poor creature comfortable.

Now, Mrs. Seddon is cross-examined, and you will remember the cross-examination on this part of the case; I do not want to give you the evidence about the cash box or anything of that sort yet—

On 2nd September Miss Barrow was in bed. Once a month she had had bilious sick headaches. From 2nd to 13th September I was in constant attendance on her. I had got up in the middle of the night once or twice. Ernie slept with her all the time. He used to call me. On Sunday she wanted to know if she could have a will made out for furniture and jewellery for Ernie and Hilda. I said I could not give her any information but would speak to my husband, so I did. He said he could not be bothered just then as he was busy. I do not think he went up at all on Sunday, but he did on Monday, and I heard it read. I know nothing more about it. [Then she is cross-examined about 13th September.] Doctor had been in the morning. She seemed rather weaker—pains and diarrhœa. When doctor left I did not think there was any fear of death. I did not notice that she got worse. I was not with her all day. I saw her at 10 p.m. and gave her a dose of medicine. My husband had gone to the theatre. I was at home. I had been putting hot flannels on her before husband returned. She wanted me to fan her all the time but I could not do that. Up to midnight she did not appear to be any worse. In the morning Dr. Sworn had left her about the same as the day before. If he said she was worse I don't remember it. I was not alarmed. She had been worse than she was on the 13th. He said she was in a weak condition. During the day she had pains and diarrhœa. Diarrhœa did not get worse, not that I know of. Before husband returned she had not said to me "I am dying"—[She had only heard her saying it from downstairs]—When at the front door I heard her say "Come quick! I am dying!" She was the same, bad pains and wanted to be sick. She was always calling on us and sometimes we did not answer. I do not know if I smiled when I told husband she had said she was dying. I have a habit of smiling.

Let us stop there for a moment. You saw the woman. Some people have that manner of smiling. On the one hand it is suggested, I suppose, that it is not natural, and on the other hand the woman says herself that it was her habit. You noticed yourselves that the more difficult the question she had to answer, and the more necessary it was that she should be careful, the more she smiled. If so, it is a trick, and if it is a trick there is nothing in it—

He asked if she was dying, I said, "No," and smiled. I meant him to understand that she was not dying. I waited hand and foot on her and did all I could to get her better. A few minutes after husband returned from theatre he went up to her room. Two or three doctors live at bottom end of Tollington Park. I went up four times that

Justice Bucknill's Summing Up.

night from husband's return. She was worse that night than she had been before. [Now comes the brandy.]

I saw my husband give her brandy, and he said it would have to last her the night, and he gave her some and left some, and it had gone in the morning. She must have drunk it when she was out of bed. Ernie was sent away to his bed the last time between 3 and 4 just when she went off to sleep. I did say before the Coroner that the boy did not sleep in the bed after 2 o'clock, but that must be a mistake because 2 o'clock was the first time my husband told him to go to bed, not the last. The last time he was there was between 3 and 4 in the morning.

That is practically the cross-examination on that part of the case. Now, it may be put in two ways, and you must consider the two ways. If this woman was right, and she thought there was no danger of her dying, and she was no worse than she was when the doctor left her in the morning, you may think there was nothing wrong in not sending for the doctor, but, on the other hand, if the woman was worse, had called out she was dying, had said she was dying, and was found sitting on the floor in that position in an agony of pain with the boy holding her up—in an agony of pain as she doubtless was, exhausted and very ill, in the middle of the night—with doctors close to, you may think it is a strange thing that a doctor was not sent for. But on the other hand there are two ways of looking at it. If it was anticipated that Dr. Sworn would come next morning, and it was then already between 2 and 3 in the morning, you may think there is nothing extraordinary in not sending for Dr. Sworn. There it is. Look at it from both points of view. Make a fair consideration of it from all the views of the facts. That is with regard to that.

Is this story with regard to the fly-papers and her buying them a falsehood for the purpose of misleading you? Is it a point got up at the last moment really—for the purpose of making a defence either for the husband or a defence of her own conduct? Against that you have seen the wife in the box. You twelve men ought to be able to say if she is lying or not. That is why you are there. You are the constitutional tribunal to judge, amongst other things, of the manner in which witnesses give their evidence. You are much better than a single judge or any other tribunal; you are a constitutional tribunal for the purpose of seeing whether the witnesses are lying or whether they are speaking the truth. You have seen the woman. Do you think she is lying? Well, if she was lying she was lying very cleverly. If you think she was telling the truth with regard to what took place on the night of the 13th to the 14th, and with regard to the last illness, I should not be astonished if you found her not guilty.

Then it is said there is a motive. Before coming to the evidence of the motive I want to deal with the woman's case first. What is a motive? There is always a motive. Now, what is a motive? I do not know that I can define "motive" offhand, but a motive, I suppose from the very derivation of the word, is a condition of things, it may be a mental condition of things, which impels, or incites, or tends to impel, or tends to incite, a person to do, or refrain from doing, something, whether that something is good or is bad. There are motives of charity, kindness, brotherly love, and that sort of thing, and there are, of course, on the other hand, motives of selfishness, greed, passion, and anger, each

Trial of the Seddons.

man or woman being impelled to do, or refrain from doing, something that he or she ought to do. A person from an evil motive may stand by and see another person drowning and not help him because he hates him; he is impelled to stand still. Another man may be impelled to kill a person if he has a chance. Another person, if he has a strong motive (and in this case it is suggested the motive is love of money, greed, cupidity) may destroy the person who has the money, or who has been robbed, either to put an end to a monetary liability or to shut the door upon detection if there had been robbery.

Now, that is all very well with regard to a great part of this case; nobody can deny that if the man Seddon is a wicked man, loving gold better than anything else in the world, there was a motive—a possible motive—in wishing to cease to have to pay the annuity. But that was not the wife's. What did it matter to her whether he paid this £124 or £150; I forget for the moment the exact amount. What did it matter to the wife whether he paid this £10 a month, £4 and £6 re the public-house and barber's shop, and the India 3½ per cent. stock, or not? He had got plenty of money apart from that. He kept her in comfort. It is rather hard to say what her motive would be. He had a motive to kill this woman, because he had a motive to put an end to the annuity, and the direct motive that she is said to have arises from these, it must be admitted, rather strange and mysterious transactions with regard to the changing of these notes.

It stands in this way; it is said that when Miss Barrow went to live with these people she had a cash box. I will refer to the evidence shortly. The cash box which has been produced, and is in Court now, is one in which she had notes and in which she had gold. Never mind how many notes, and never mind how much gold; but she was a person who, when she went to live with the Seddons, had this cash box with the gold and notes in it. Now, Miss Barrow had in her possession certain notes which were the cashment of certain cheques which she received from the brewers for rent of the public-house for a period extending from October, 1901, to the time when they paid the last amount. These cheques were certainly cashed and ultimately paid into a bank and notes were given. Those notes passed into Miss Barrow's possession clearly. Equally clearly Miss Barrow gave* some of those notes, twenty-six or twenty-seven of them, to Mrs. Seddon to cash (that is not denied), and these notes were cashed by Mrs. Seddon, some in her own name and some in the name of "M. Scott," the address being given either "12 Evershot Road" or "18 Evershot Road." Of course, it is a matter of suspicion that Mrs. Seddon did what she did in giving a false name, but she explained it, and if you believe the explanation there is an end of it. What she said was this—

When I went to a shop where I was known I gave my own name; when I went to a shop where I was not known I did not give my own name; I did not care to and I gave a false name; I gave the name "M. Scott" and I intended to give the address in each case "12 Evershot Road" when I gave the name of "M. Scott."

Of course, the suggestion made on behalf of the Crown is, "You did it because you did not want these notes traced." She said, "No, that is

---

* There was no evidence of how the notes came into Mrs. Seddon's possession.—ED.

Justice Bucknill's Summing Up.

Mr. Justice Bucknill

not the reason I did it "—for the reasons that I have given you. When asked what she did with the money she said, " I paid it to Miss Barrow."

Then the next peculiarity about the case is this, Miss Barrow, to Mrs. Seddon's own knowledge, had taken her money out of the savings bank on 19th June, 1911; forgive me if I do not remember exact dates, as I am speaking from memory. Mrs. Seddon saw her paid in gold, and therefore there is every reason to suppose that Miss Barrow had that amount of gold in her cash box. What was the reason for Mrs. Seddon continuing to cash notes—I will call them the " brewers' " notes—after June? It was put this way by the Crown—Miss Barrow did not want the notes cashed, because she had got gold in her cash box; the story is untrue; she had been robbed of these notes; but whether she was robbed of them or whether she was not, Mrs. Seddon's or Mr. Seddon's possession of these notes (for he had possession of them as well) was illegal possession, and the transaction was altogether wrong, and would not stand the light of day; there was a fear of detection by Miss Barrow, and because there was a fear of detection by Miss Barrow there was the motive to kill. That is the way it is put most strongly against Mrs. Seddon. Mr. Seddon says, " I did not know that Mrs. Seddon had done this until after she was arrested." Answer—" I do not believe it; the story will not hold water; it is too suspicious, and you will not believe it." On the other hand, as I have said before, you have seen the woman, and you have heard her story given in her own words. If you believe her she ought to be acquitted, and, of course, if you disbelieve her the position then remains, has the Crown proved beyond a reasonable doubt that she is guilty?

With regard to what happened after the death, of course, the motive ceases. If there was a robbery of the box after death, that, of course, could not be the motive for the death; death had already taken place. If I were you, if you will allow me to suggest it, I should ask yourselves, first of all, do you find yourselves impelled as reasonable and honest men, apart from sympathy altogether—you must have no sympathy for her because she is a woman; your judgment must be that of cold-blooded men for the moment—are you satisfied beyond reasonable doubt that she is guilty? Are you satisfied that the Crown has made it out, that is to say, that she co-operated with, assisted, and actively helped her husband to kill this woman by poison administered within the limits which it is alleged that poison was administered? Her case, I think I may say, without a doubt, is not on altogether parallel lines with his. I will say nothing more with regard to Mrs. Seddon, because, indeed, I do not think I have anything more to say about it. It is not necessary to read you all about the notes and the cross-examination upon it. I do not suppose you want me to read you all about the notes.

The FOREMAN OF THE JURY—No, my lord.

Mr. JUSTICE BUCKNILL—The learned Attorney-General in cross-examining her, very fairly, if I may say so, put the questions in this way, and I wish to thank him for it—" Now, I am going to ask you a question. The object of that question is," so and so, " so there can be no catch in it." It was very gratifying indeed to the Court that the Attorney-General should tell the witness, as he went from step to step, what the point was,

Trial of the Seddons.

so that they could not possibly misunderstand what the questions were being put for.

As I went through Mrs. Seddon's evidence, so I must go through Mr. Seddon's evidence with regard to the last week, or the last night at all events after the death. You know, they do not stand at all in the same way, because Mr. Seddon was very much more active in what might be called " suspicious conduct " than she was. He begins by telling you about Dr. Paul, and how she went to see him, and then he says this—

On 1st September my wife told me Miss Barrow had a bilious attack. The annuity was due on September 1st and I paid it on the 2nd as she was unwell on the 1st. I very rarely visited her room. She said she thought she could sign for her annuity. I paid her £10, as I always did, although the receipt says only £6. [You understand that.] That was generally paid about noon. I probably drew it from the Bank the day before. I always paid her in gold, and she signed both receipts. I cannot say if she got better or worse. I went up on one occasion [September 4th] to remonstrate with her for leaving her room and going into the back room, the boy's room. [He goes up apparently alone.] My wife was upset about it and told me. 2nd September, Maggie was sent for Dr. Paul. He did not come, so I said "Send for Dr. Sworn," although Dr. Paul was much nearer, and Dr. Sworn called. On Sunday the 3rd and Monday 4th when I went to her room there were many flies, and wife said the reason for going into the other room was on account of the heat and the flies. My wife told me she had got fly-papers. From first to last I never handled a fly-paper. [I am not on this particular point, but I am mentioning it because I am going through this particular time.] I never heard of Mather's fly-papers before the Police Court. On Sunday, 10th, Dr. Sworn did not call. On Monday, 11th, wife told me Miss Barrow was worrying about her jewellery and furniture, and wanted to see me. I went to her and she said she did not feel well and she would like, if anything, at any rate to be sure that Ernest and Hilda got what belonged to their father and mother. [Then he speaks about the will; I am not upon that. She makes the will. Then we come to this.]

When my wife told me Miss Barrow wanted to make a will she said she had given her an effervescent mixture and that Miss Barrow would not take it fizzing, and asked me to speak to her, so I said to Miss Barrow, "Aren't you aware that your medicine is no good to you without you drink it effervescing." I said to wife "Give me a dose and let us see if I can get her to take it so." I did not know how it was mixed. Wife gave me two glasses. [Then he described how he did it; he took a dose himself, and then he gave it to her.] She did not drink it fizzing. I said "That is not a bit of good," and told wife to tell doctor, and I said "She ought to go to the hospital." The last night I gave her a drop of brandy. I had gone upstairs. Day before will was executed Mr. Longley had asked if his wife and girl might come up, and I said 'Yes,' and they arrived the day the will was made. We gave up our best bedroom. [Then he talks about the boy. Then he says this.]

On 13th September at 9.30 a.m. the Longleys, father, Frederick and Ada Seddon, spent the day at the White City. I was not very well that day. I believe I was in bed when the doctor called. I went out in the afternoon about 2, and returned to tea 6 to 7. Hurried tea and then I went to the theatre 7.30 to 8. I had a dispute about a 2/- piece or half a crown. I came in about 12.30 at night. I cannot say whether it was hot. My wife told me Miss Barrow had called out she was dying. I said, "Is she?" She said, "No," and smiled. I did not go upstairs for half an hour. It was 1 o'clock. Dr. Sworn is half an hour's walk distant. I can do it in a quarter. I had been in the house half an hour when Ernie called out from upstairs, "Chickie wants you." Wife said, "She has been calling like that," and she had done all she could for her, and had put hot flannels on her, and had been up several nights with her till early hours. Not unusual for Ernie to call out in the early hours of the morning. Wife was resting on couch. I said, "Never mind, I will go." I asked my sister to go up with me. We both went up together, and my wife followed immediately. We three went there together. I said, "Now, Miss Barrow, this is my sister from Wolverhampton. You know Mrs. Seddon is tired out, and I would like you to try and let her have a little sleep. It would do you more good to rest." She said, "Oh, but I have had such pain." I said, "Mrs. Seddon says she has given you flannels and done all she can for you." Miss Barrow did not take much notice of my sister so she left the room. Miss

Justice Bucknill's Summing Up.

Barrow asked for more hot flannels and asked for a drop of brandy. I said, "My dear woman, don't you know that it is after 1 a.m. and we cannot get brandy now?" Wife said, "There is a drop there in the bottle." I said, "Give her a drop then." Wife passed me the bottle, and I gave her a drop. There was very little in it. I gave her half what there was, and left the rest. I put a drop of soda in it from a syphon. I had no idea she was dangerously ill. She had been the same the other nights that week. I left wife preparing hot flannels. I was in the room only four or five minutes. My sister had only just gone downstairs and waited for me. I went to bed 2 to 2.30 a.m. A shocking smell in the room. I had a delicate stomach. I said if we did not let boy be in her room we should get no rest at all. In a few minutes boy called Mrs. Seddon again, and she went. That was twice in half an hour. She went up twice alone. The third time I went up with her. Then I spoke to her to see if I could get her to try to sleep, and I said we should have to get a nurse, or she would have to go to the hospital. Wife said she would stay with her, and I sent boy to his bed. Miss Barrow called for Ernie and he went to her, and then I sent him to his own bed again. Mrs. Seddon got hot water from Miss Barrow's kitchen for flannels. Then she recalled him, and wife and I went down again. In a quarter of an hour boy called us and we went up again. She was on the floor and the boy was supporting her. We lifted her into bed. Boy was much upset. Miss Barrow lay quiet and did not speak when I asked her why she was out of bed. She gave no explanation. Wife agreed to stay with her, and I told boy to go to his room. About 4 a.m. then, I did not go to bed. I stood at door smoking. Miss Barrow seemed to be sleeping. We decided to send Miss Barrow to the hospital next morning. For about an hour and a half she breathed heavily through her mouth, like that [and he described it]. I read a paper and smoked, wife dozed in a chair. I went down to see our baby. All of a sudden snoring stopped, and I said, "Good God, she has stopped breathing!" She died 6.20 by her clock. I was in a terrible state, and hurried off for the doctor.

There is one point which one cannot help mentioning, and which is one which everybody must think is important—why on earth did he not send for the doctor when he saw her upstairs sitting in an agony of pain? Do not be too prejudiced against a man like that. He may be a man of cold feelings, and a man of a hard heart, but it does not make him out to be a murderer. It certainly is an extraordinary thing, as I think; it is not for me to say. Why on earth did not he send for a doctor? Do not be prejudiced too much. It is not because he did not send for a doctor that he murdered the woman, but it is a fact to be taken into your consideration. Do not make too much of it, but do not forget it.*

Then, that is what happens on that night. He was cross-examined, of course, on that. He was asked about the will. I need not worry you about that. I do not think he is asked many questions about the night itself. He is asked about what he did immediately after, and he was asked why he did not send for a doctor, and so forth.

Now, the case against him is this, that either within a few hours before she died, that is to say, after he returned from the theatre, or before that, but within three days of the death, he administered arsenic. It is suggested that he had the opportunity of putting it into the brandy, although I think the evidence only goes to show his having given brandy on the 13th. But the Valentine's Meat Juice was recommended and got on the 11th, and it is suggested that the wife prepared it downstairs, and that he had an opportunity of putting this concoction from the poisonous fly-papers, this brown liquid, into the food, or into the brandy, or administering it himself, or with his wife, so bringing about the death. Of course,

---

*This passage, and the repetition of the words "Do not be too much prejudiced" (see p. 401), have been the subject of considerable comment and criticism.—Ed.

Trial of the Seddons.

there is no direct evidence that he did it. No one saw him do it. There is no direct evidence that he was ever seen to handle a fly-paper. There is no direct evidence that he was ever seen to handle the meat juice. The only thing he has ever been seen to handle was the brandy. To that extent it is important in his favour. But, then, if she died of acute arsenical poisoning, it is said, yes, there was a strong motive to do it, and the circumstances of the 13th, shortly before she died—not calling in the doctor, and that which he did immediately before her death—are very, very strong to lead you to the conclusion that he is the man whom either alone or with his wife directly caused this woman's death by feloniously administering this fly-paper liquid in something, and so bringing about her death.

Now, with regard to the fly-papers, how does it stand? As the learned Attorney-General has pointed out to you, his case stands or falls on the evidence of Mr. Thorley and Miss Wilson. You have seen Mr. Thorley, the chemist, cross-examined, and you have heard his story, and there is no doubt about it that one of the most important matters in this important trial is this, did Maggie Seddon buy Mather's fly-papers of Mr. Thorley on 26th August, 1911? I think I ought to say Mr. Thorley came into the witness-box and went out of it without any attack being made upon his character. Sometimes witnesses are attacked; they are challenged as to their credibility. There was no ground for attacking Mr. Thorley except as to memory. Now, memory does play the fool with us very often, and if Mr. Thorley had simply said, " I sold the fly-papers to that girl on 26th August, because I know it," you might very well say, " You are very likely wrong." But if he gives you a reason, which you think is a good reason, and explains how it was, apart from identification, he remembers he sold these papers, why, then, of course, to that extent you will ask yourselves whether that is a good reason for his recollecting what he swears he does recollect. He says he was short of these fly-papers. I do not suppose anybody denies that. He says he had not got as many as this young girl, Maggie—according to him—asked for. She wanted twenty-four fly-papers, or four packets, there being six in the packet. She was the girl whom he had seen at the side door of his shop in company with his daughter or daughters, I forget which. Her face was therefore not unfamiliar to him, and he is positive that on 26th August she came and asked for fly-papers, and asked for four packets of fly-papers, and he told her that he could not give her four, but could give her one, and she took one, and paid for it, and there was an end of it. That reason given by him for recollecting it may be a good reason. Anyhow, he says, " It is a fact, because I looked at my invoice book, and that confirms me." Of course, that does not make it any more positive, because he would make the entry himself. He says, " I was out, and I could not give her four packets, but I gave her one, and she took one, but she asked for four." That was on 26th August. He did not recognise her until some time afterwards; I think it was in the month of September.

Mr. MARSHALL HALL—February, my lord.

Mr. JUSTICE BUCKNILL—I am much obliged to you. He did not recognise her until February. Therefore, you know, memory which does play

Justice Bucknill's Summing Up.

Mr. Justice Bucknill

false, may have played false with him. Ask yourselves this question, do you think he sold fly-papers to Maggie Seddon? He has given you the reason why he remembers it. He did not make an entry in that book of the person to whom he sold them, because he did not know the girl as Maggie Seddon. From August to February is a long time, and therefore it is suggested to you that, as honest as he is, yet, and wishing to tell the truth, as he is, he is mistaken, and mistaken because Maggie says he is mistaken. Then he is asked to identify her, and, if you recollect the evidence, he says, " I refused to identify her by the picture." Now, if he was shown that picture by the police, and the question was put to him " Is that the girl who bought fly-papers? " I should feel it my duty to say that I thought that that was not the right way to have gone to work. am making no complaint; I do not know how it was done, but I do not think it would have been right for the police to have gone to him and said, knowing how important it was to identify this girl or not, as the case may be, shown him a picture and said, " Look here, did that girl come and buy fly-papers? " The proper way would be the way in which it was done. " Go into that room. You will find plenty of people there. Come back and tell me if you can see the girl who came in and bought fly-papers from you." Mr. Thorley has stated very positively, " I did not identify her by the picture." You will remember that Mr. Marshall Hall first mentioned the photograph, and then he said a picture. I should not like to be identified always by pictures which appear in the illustrated papers sometimes, and which are more or less hurriedly taken, and which not being photographs, may be inaccurate, although at the same time very cleverly done. That is all I meant to say when I mentioned that before. He positively swears he did not identify her by her picture. Mr. Marshall Hall asked him whether among the girls in that room it was not the fact that she was the only one who had her hair down, and he said, " Oh, I don't know, but I am perfectly certain it was Maggie."

You get this fact for what it is worth—I do not know whether it is worth very much, but at the same time it is a fact—and it is for you to say what weight you give to it. Mr. Thorley's shop is very near Miss Wilson's shop, and it is now an admitted fact—admitted, I think I may say, by Maggie; at all events, Miss Wilson swears to it, and I think Maggie has admitted it herself*—she did, on the 26th August, go to Miss Wilson's shop and make a purchase. To that extent it is a coincidence. although not enough to hang a man or a woman either. Perhaps by itself it is of very little value, but when you are asking yourselves whether Mr. Thorley's recollection is correct or not, it is a matter for your consideration. Do not give too much weight to it, because to do so, I think, would be wrong. Rather ask yourselves whether you are satisfied that Mr. Thorley is right.

Now, on the other hand, there is the girl's evidence. Of course, her position is an immensely painful one. The learned Attorney-General has found it his duty to say, and he said it as well as it can be said, " I do not want to attack the girl's character, but seeing that she stood in that box, and as the effect of her evidence in a certain event, that is to

---

* This was not admitted by Maggie Seddon.—ED.

399

Trial of the Seddons.

say, if she told the truth, she would be giving very, very painful evidence against her father and mother, one can hardly be surprised that she has said what she has, and what she has said is not true." Well, there is a good deal in that, but then, again, false evidence is perjury, and honest people do not perjure themselves on any account. I cannot say. I do not intend to say more. She is not an independent witness. Mr. Thorley is an independent witness. The girl may be truthful for all that. If you think she is from the way in which she gave her evidence, why, say so, and that part of the case falls to the ground—and a very important part of the case it is, too.

Now comes her examination by Ward. She was at the Police Court, and Ward wanted to get some information from her. Now, Chief Inspector Ward is a man of great experience, and, from what I know of him, I should venture to say a fair-minded man; anyhow, he is a man of great experience, and knows as well as anybody does what his duties are and his limitations. He saw this girl at the Police Court, and he was minded to ask a question of her. I am not going to express an opinion about that. It is very easy to express opinions which may or may not be right. I am just going to tell you the facts. On the one hand it is said by Mr. Marshall Hall, in very strong language, which may have been justified (I will not say what opinion I have got; I will not express my view) that Ward went much further than he ought to have done, and that he ought not to have put the questions that he did; therefore his examination of the girl was an impropriety on his part. The learned Attorney-General did, as I am doing, refrain from expressing any opinion. If you think Mr. Marshall Hall's view of the matter is right there is a severe criticism concerning Ward's conduct, but that does not affect the answers which were given; that is the point. Now, let us see what the answers were. I will read you the questions and answers—

Statement of Miss Margaret Seddon who says : I am 16 years of age and a daughter of Mr. F. H. Seddon of 63 Tollington Park. [Of course he knew she was the daughter of the accused persons.] By Chief Inspector Ward : I am going to take a statement from you respecting your dealings with the chemist whose shop is situated at the corner of Crouch Hill and Sparsholt Road. The name of the chemist is Mr. Thorley. Answer by Margaret Seddon : I know the shop, but I have never been in it or bought anything there.

You will observe there that there has been no question put to bring such an answer. The answer has been given without the question; only the introduction having been given.

Have you ever been to any other chemist's in the neighbourhood to purchase poison including poisonous fly-papers? Answer : No. [That is signed by Margaret Seddon.] Have you ever been to the chemist's shop at the corner of Tollington Park and Stroud Green Road to purchase Mather's fly-papers? [That is Price's shop you know.] Answer : No. Did you on December 6th, go to that shop to purchase Mather's fly-papers? Answer : Yes, I went, but I did not get any. The chemist was going to give them to me until I mentioned my name. Question : Who sent you for them?

I think that was not put. Anyhow those are the important questions. Now, it is said that the girl said what she knew to be untrue. She had been to Price's, but she first said she had not. She said she had not

Justice Bucknill's Summing Up.

been to any other chemist's shops in the neighbourhood, and then when the further question is put to her she said, " Yes."

Gentlemen, I should think on the whole it would, perhaps, be better not to place too much importance upon this particular part of the case. I will tell you why. If she is telling the truth in the box that she did not buy fly-papers of Mr. Thorley, what does it matter? If she did buy fly-papers and is telling you a wilful lie, what does it matter? It is only supposed to be a corroboration of the suggestion of the Crown that she is not telling the truth. But you have seen the girl. That is why I tell you so often you are there to exercise your power of discrimination as to the falsehood or wickedness of the evidence so often judged by the demeanour of the witness in the box. That is how that part of the case stands. If these fly-papers were bought at Thorley's and were taken back to her parents' house on 26th August, it is a point of the most serious and the greatest importance, because the man says it is not so and he never saw any, and the woman says it is not so and that the only fly-papers she saw she bought herself. The Crown suggests that is all false, and that the fly-papers that the man sent for, or the woman sent for, were not put into the room, but were used for the purpose of being boiled, or water put on them, for the purpose of obtaining the liquid for the purpose of mixing with some food or medicine for the purpose of giving to this woman—done feloniously with intention, and the most wicked, abominable act was carried out in cold blood.

Let us go for a moment to the acts of the husband after the death. Of course, you understand that is not evidence of motive; it is evidence which is laid before you as evidence of a wicked mind—the knowledge of a crime committed—of a course of conduct for the purpose of putting people off the scent. Now, Mr. Marshall Hall spoke—and everybody will agree with him—in very strong language of the improper conduct of his client with regard to this funeral—hurrying out of the house to make a bargain for a public grave, and to take 12s. 6d. discount. It may be a matter of business or commission, whatever you like to call it, but to get her buried in the way in which she was buried when she might have been buried in a really proper manner befitting her position, befitting her fortune, of course, indicates that Seddon was not a man of generous habits, and Mr. Marshall Hall denounced him strongly, but said, " You must be careful "—and I tell you the same—" not to condemn him of this because he was guilty of that." He may be an unfeeling creature, he may be so careless of the decencies in such a matter as to make him a person with whom you would not care to associate, but it is only a matter of prejudice; it is a long, long way off proof that he did this murder. It was bad—it was about as bad as it could be. Pass that over, and do not be too much prejudiced* against him.

Then, with regard to the subsequent conduct, first of all it has been said, Why did he not send, or why might not he have sent, Ernie to tell the Vonderahes? I think I put the question myself. They did not live far off. If he had sent him round to Evershot Road they would have told him there where they were. Why was he not sent round to say, " Chickie is dead "? It was not done. The answer given to me was, " Because he wanted the body out of the house; the baby was in the

---

* See note, p. 397.—ED.

Trial of the Seddons.

house, and it was not right." That might apply very well to the baby, because the baby was very young; but the body was moved out that very day. It stayed there twelve hours, and it was taken away the same afternoon. Anyhow, Ernie Grant was not sent, nobody was sent; but a letter was said to have been written, which it is said never arrived. And about that part of the case there must be some doubt. It was addressed to "31 Evershot Road," when the Vonderahes, as we now know, were not there. We will assume Seddon thought they were there. He says, "We did not send round because we were not going to have anything to do with people who slammed the door in Maggie's face." There, again, you must take the temperament of the man. I do not suppose there is a man in your box who would look with such miserable spitefulness on such a small transaction as that as he did. What did it matter if the girl had the door slammed in her face compared with the importance of the relatives knowing of the death of their kinswoman? She might have just stood out in the street and shouted it out, or asked a passer-by, or given a boy 2d. to go round, or even have sent a telegram, or done something. Nothing was done except the letter, and it is said the letter was not written. This is the alleged letter, of which he kept a copy—

Mr. Frank E. Vonderahe, Dear Sir, I regret to have to inform you of the death of your cousin Miss Eliza Mary Barrow at 6 a.m. this morning from epidemic diarrhœa. The funeral will take place on Saturday next between 1 to 2 p.m. Please inform Albert Edward and Emma Marian Vonderahe of her decease, and let me know if you or they wish to attend the funeral. I must also inform you that she made a will on the 11th instant leaving what she died possessed of to Hilda and Ernest Grant and appointed myself as sole executor under the will, Yours respectfully, F. H. Seddon. Frank Ernest Vonderahe, 31 Evershot Road.

They say that letter was never received. He kept a copy of it. What do you think of the letter? "I must also inform you that she made a will on the 11th instant leaving everything she died possessed of to Hilda and Ernest Grant, and appointed myself as sole executor." According to him, this will only disposed of the jewellery, furniture, and effects which belonged to Mr. and Mrs. Grant, the father and mother of Ernie and Hilda. It was only intended to apply to that, and the letter says she died leaving "what she died possessed of"—all she died possessed of it means, I suppose—"to Hilda and Ernest Grant."

What I do not understand for the moment is this (if there is an explanation, I should very much like to know it), at that time when he was writing that letter he had made a search in the trunk and in the cash box for money which he believed to be there; he believed £216 at least to be there, or part of that money, which she withdrew from the savings bank. The wife had seen her withdraw it, and the wife had said she believed she put it into the cash box. When he came to look for the money he must have expected to find the money. He was greatly astonished not to find more than £4 10s.; he believed she was possessed of a great deal more on 11th September, before she died, when she made this will. Therefore, it seems to me there is no answer to it in this respect (I do not know what importance you will give to it), that then he was saying to himself, "The jewellery and furniture and the goods which belonged to Mrs. Grant, let them go to the two children, but that

Justice Bucknill's Summing Up.

is not all she had got; the will does not pass all that she is possessed of, because she has got a lot of gold in the cash box." He never told the Vonderahes that. It is not suggested that he did. He did not say it in the letter, and he did not tell them one single word about having opened this cash box, and opened this trunk, to look for the gold that he thought was there, and to his great surprise was not. That part is left out from the letter. And when we go to the next document it is also apparently left out. The will says—

> This is the last Will of Mary Barrow. I revoke all other wills . . . I give and bequeath all my household furniture, jewellery and other personal effects to Hilda Grant and Ernest Grant . . . to hold all my personal belongings, furniture, clothing and jewellery in trust until the aforesaid Hilda Grant and Ernest Grant become of age, then for him to distribute as equally as possible all my personal belongings comprising jewellery, furniture and clothing to them, [and so forth, and so forth].

That is the will. When he made the will there was nothing there about the gold or cash, or anything else. That may be an accident, and much less important, because the man was not accustomed to making a will, and he may very often draw very silly documents which will not hold water afterwards. Therefore I should not give the same importance to that as I think you might think it necessary to give to the letter. The letter seems to be one which is worth your most serious consideration. And, then, consider the mode of looking for this gold when the body was being attended to by the independent witness and the wife. It was he who made the search in the first instance, not the wife; you will remember he said, "My wife gave me the keys, and I looked in the cash box, and I looked in the trunk, and afterwards we looked together in the drawers." He admits himself that he was the person who looked while the wife, according to him, is looking after the body. Considering the indecent hurry in opening that cash box and opening the trunk to see what this poor woman who, according to the letter, was only possessed at that time of furniture, jewellery, and apparently nothing else, although he expected to find gold in the cash box—that letter is a very, very serious document for your consideration. That is the conduct after the death. It is said that that conduct on the 14th points only one way—to guilt. That is for you.

Now, for one moment, let us consider the conduct before the death. I must take you to a much earlier date, because I want to say this in his favour; I want to say it in both ways if I can. A great deal has been said about that public-house and barber's shop transaction, and really (it is for you, not for me) everything seems to have been done in order. The woman was a woman of sound mind and understanding. Whatever her reasons were, she was willing to assign to him her interest in the barber's shop and public-house. It was done by a solicitor who represented her, and a solicitor who represented him. The figures were properly worked out, and the deeds were properly drawn up. It is a perfectly simple deed by which he binds himself in consideration of an assignment to pay her so much a year for life. So much has been said about it one way or the other, but I think where you get independent witnesses like Mr. Russell, a gentleman in a high position as a solicitor, saying that that transaction was perfectly fairly carried out, it is rather difficult to say that it was not.

403

Trial of the Seddons.

Therefore she was a free agent to do what she liked with this property, and she freely and voluntarily (and her letters show it) assigned to him, and he bound himself to pay her this annuity. You recollect that this public-house business was only concluded in January; in the October previous the negotiations began about the public-house affair, but were not concluded until January. And about the same time, August, or September, or October, there was the question of £1600 3½ per cent. India stock, but here he has not got the good fortune to be able to produce a document. He has told us it was in the nature of an annuity certificate given by him to her. That may be quite true; it has not been found, but still it is not proved that it did not exist. He says, " I gave it to her." At all events, he acted upon it; he paid her regularly £10 a month made up of £4 *re* the public-house and barber's shop, and £6 *re* the India 3½ per cent. stock. She got it; there is no suggestion that can be made that she did not get it. He was punctual in his payments, and many receipts have been put in. But then, of course, there was always, if a man had got a wicked and murderous mind, as it is alleged he had, the motive, " Well, if I could only get her out of the way I shall not have to pay her annuity any more, and I shall have the capital to do as I like with, and the property to do as I like with." Gentlemen, it is a far cry off murder, but still that is the allegation against him—he is a murderous creature who did these things for the purpose of getting back his money and freeing himself of the obligation. It is entirely for you to say. A more important point I should suggest for you to consider was the gold in the cash box. He thought there was gold in the cash box. He said so. He does not say how much he thought was there. He said when Miss Barrow offered him the custody of the cash box, she said there was only £30 to £35 there, but, anyhow, he thought there was gold in the house. Of course, if this woman was robbed of these notes and of this gold, of which there is no direct evidence, it would be the thing for wicked, criminal people to get her out of the way, but, at all events, it is put in this way; taking all these facts into consideration, the public-house property, the India 3½ per cent. stock transaction, the possession of the notes by the wife which were cashed by her, it is suggested it was a joint affair between them—all those circumstances coupled with the conduct of the man immediately after the funeral, coupled with the letter and the will—all those matters make up such a case against him that you can have no reasonable doubt that he is the man who administered the poison which killed this woman.

Gentlemen, there is very little more to be said, except about the question of the money which had been seen in this cash box from time to time. Hook has told you he saw a lot in bags. That is the beginning of the history. Ernie Grant has said he saw the bags at a very late period of her life; she put them on the bed, and she was counting money—money, not notes. There is the suggestion that this deceased person was in the habit of keeping money in the cash box; that she was in the habit of hoarding the money; she hoarded gold; she liked it; the money which came from the savings bank was put there. It is suggested that to this money which she could not have spent (or there is no evidence that she spent it) was added the money from the annuity. As you

Justice Bucknill's Summing Up.

Mr. Justice Bucknill

have been told so often in this case by Mr. Marshall Hall, there is no direct evidence of it all. No single witness comes forward and says, "She showed me so much money," or "Told me she had so much money," except the Vonderahes and Hook, which was a long time before this. In passing, you must remember this, that Hook's testimony has been somewhat discounted by a quarrel he had had with her; she would not have him; she did not want him; she turned him out. So it may be said with some justice that you should be careful how you accept Hook's evidence, because Hook is a man who had no good feeling for her really, because he thought it was a rare good thing for him to live with her, and she had turned him out either because of his neglect or of his troublesome conduct. To that extent you may think it necessary to discount Hook's evidence. But there were the Vonderahes. I do not know what attack could be made against them. I do not know what can be said against them. I do not suppose you want me to read their evidence to you about it.

Now, I come really to the concluding sentence or two which I wish to utter. Did she die of acute arsenical poisoning? In all probability you will say yes because Dr. Willcox says so, and Dr. Spilsbury says so, and they are uncontradicted. That is not enough, however, to justify a verdict of guilty against either of these people. Was that arsenic which so caused her death a fatal dose, administered within either three days or four or five hours by the prisoners or either of them? I have nothing more to say upon that subject now except to implore you to remember that the Crown has to make out the guilt. It is not for the accused persons to do it. The burden of proof is upon the Crown, and they have to satisfy you beyond the reasonable doubt of honest men on an important matter, as in the statement I read to you, just now of the guilt. If you are not satisfied, you will say, "Not guilty" as against both. If you think that the woman is not guilty, why, of course, you will only be too glad to say so.

The law in the matter with regard to husband and wife is very simple. In olden days it was considered more than it can be said now—I am not speaking jokingly—that wives were more under the subjection of the husbands. To-day women are more civilised, and they are on a different basis, so to speak, in husband and wife relationship than they ever used to be. The old law still stands—if any wife in the presence of the husband does a criminal act, murder and treason excepted, it is supposed if she does it in the presence of her husband she is acting under his marital coercion. But that does not apply to murder; a woman cannot plead or ask the Court to direct a jury to say there is that presumption in her favour in a case of alleged murder; she stands exactly as any other person would do. It is too heinous an offence for the rule ever to be applied to such a case. But you must be satisfied beyond all reasonable doubt that this woman did act in the way in which it is alleged she did, either by putting the poison into the food herself, or by giving it herself, or by helping the husband to give it himself, so that she did something of such importance in the matter that you are satisfied that she was acting with him in one common object, one common murderous design of taking this woman's life away. I asked one witness whether she thought that the

Trial of the Seddons.

wife seemed honestly solicitous about the woman's health. She said, "Quite." Are you satisfied that you can find a verdict of guilty of wilful murder against her? If you are driven to do it, do it, and I will tell you why—because even although she is a woman, she comes under the same laws as anybody else; she is one member of a society in a civilised country. If she is guilty of murder she has got to pay the penalty of it just the same as if it were a man. Do not be moved by sympathy. Do not be moved by fear. You have nothing to do with the consequences. We are not here to think of consequences. Believe me we are not. I am sure there must be men in your body who would have given anything not to have been in this case. I can only tell you, as far as I am concerned, I have the same feelings. But we have got to do it. We are both bound under our oaths—the oath that I took and the oath that you took—to do justice. Justice means to acquit them if you have a doubt. Justice directs you shall convict if they are guilty.

With regard to the man, it is said that this is designed cold-blooded murder, done for the purpose of getting the woman's money, or avoiding the result of obtaining money which he had got from her, it may be, illegally. That is more or less speculation; I mean to say there has been no direct proof given of one single dishonest act on his part; he is not proved to have robbed her; it has not been proved that he obtained these notes from her which his wife, it is alleged, cashed, no more than his wife did. His wife came into possession of them. It is not altogether inconsistent with the dead woman having given them to the wife, as she says she did. His obligations have been faithfully carried out in the two matters in which he had bound himself—the India 3½ per cent. stock and the public-house. But his conduct has been very suspicious. However, you cannot convict on suspicion. Take all these circumstances into your consideration. Take all the circumstances which you know are material to the point, not irrelevant circumstances—guard yourself from that—not circumstances which would arise from prejudice or gossip. I am sure you will not think about what you have heard about the case. That would be wicked. If you find yourself compelled to give a verdict hostile to him you will do it. It matters not what religion a man belongs to, what nationality he is, what sect or brotherhood or anything else he may belong to, he who lives under the protection of the laws of the country in which he abides must keep them, and if he breaks them he must pay the penalty, even although the penalty be his life.

Gentlemen, may you have strength given to you to come to the true conclusion. These people cannot be tried again. May you have strength given you to do that which is and will be justice if you do it on the lines which I have indicated to you. Then, whatever the result may be (which has nothing to do with you), you will have at all events the gratifying testimony of a clear conscience.

The jury retired at 3.58, and returned into Court at 4.58 p.m.

The DEPUTY-CLERK OF THE COURT—Are you agreed upon your verdict? The FOREMAN OF THE JURY—We are.

Justice Bucknill's Summing Up.

Mr. Justice Bucknil

The DEPUTY-CLERK OF THE COURT—Do you find Frederick Henry Seddon guilty or not guilty of wilful murder?

The FOREMAN OF THE JURY—Guilty.

The DEPUTY-CLERK OF THE COURT—Do you find Margaret Ann Seddon guilty or not guilty of wilful murder?

The FOREMAN OF THE JURY—Not guilty.

[At this point Seddon turned and kissed his wife, who became hysterical.]

The DEPUTY-CLERK OF THE COURT—You say that Frederick Henry Seddon is guilty and Margaret Ann Seddon is not guilty, and that is the verdict of you all?

The FOREMAN OF THE JURY—That is.

Mr. JUSTICE BUCKNILL—Tell her she is discharged, will you?

[Mrs. Seddon was then removed.]

The DEPUTY-CLERK OF THE COURT—Frederick Henry Seddon, you stand convicted of wilful murder. Have you anything to say for yourself why the Court should not give you judgment of death according to law?

The PRISONER (F. H. SEDDON)—I have, sir. I do not know whether anything I have to say can in any way affect the judgment that is about to be passed upon me, but there is one thing that is quite patent to me, and that is, that these moneys which it is suggested by the prosecution was in Miss Barrow's possession have not been in any way traced to my account, either during the life of Miss Barrow or since her death. There is the sum of £165 suggested in notes turned into gold. There is the sum of £216 which was stated to have been drawn out in June. There is the sum of £91 which has been paid to Miss Barrow in the shape of annuities by me. If Hook's evidence is accepted, there was the sum of £420 in the house. I think, my lord, that that sum comes to something like £890 odd. The prosecution, as far as I can learn, has traced my banking accounts back to the year 1907 or 1908. I have had submitted to me documents at Brixton Prison which I have gone through from that date, and I am in a position to explain every item on my banking accounts during that period. All that the prosecution has brought up against me in th shape of money is the sum of £155, which is since Miss Barrow's decease. It has been stated during the evidence just yesterday and to-day that the sum of £200 was stated that I had in my possession. I clearly pointed out from the witness-box when it was stated there that it was not £200 which the Attorney-General stated (it was very near the sum of £216 which Miss Barrow drew in June). I clearly stated then that it was £170 which I claimed to have in my possession, which was testified to by three independent witnesses. There were other witnesses in my home that I could have brought forward proving that I had that money in my possession, who have not been called in this case. I clearly show that the money I put in the Post Office Savings Bank, £30, that the £35 I put into my current account, say, £65, and £90 that I invested in the building society shares, say, £155, and £15 which I reserved for my holidays, was the sum of £170, and yet since I have stated that in the box it has been stated over £200, or £200 thereabouts.

There is one other point that I would like to put, and that is regarding Thorley's evidence regarding the alleged purchase of arsenical poison

Trial of the Seddons.

packets. If it was true that my daughter went to Thorley's for the purchase of arsenical fly-papers on 26th August, and he informed her that he had only got one packet of arsenical fly-papers in his possession, and that he would have more in on Monday, I have not heard one word said as to whether my daughter went back on the Monday for the other three packets of arsenical fly-papers. I have not heard any evidence adduced that if my daughter required the four packets of fly-papers she called at any other chemist on the way back again. If she was sent either by me or her mother for four packets, that is twenty-four fly-papers; naturally the girl would get the four packets of fly-papers either at the chemist's shop she went to, or she would call on some other chemist's shop on the way coming back, as there are plenty on the way. Another point I want to put forward in respect to the alleged purchase of this packet of fly-papers from Thorley's. It has been brought forward by the prosecution that my daughter called at Miss Wilson's on the way. It is not stated what the distance is, but, as far as I can judge, if Thorley's shop is anywhere in the vicinity of Crouch End station it is a much further distance than what has been stated as two minutes' walk from there.

I should also like to mention, my lord, that in your summing up—I do not know whether I am quite clear upon it or not—you said there was a time when the wife left me in the room when the will was being prepared. I have no recollection that my wife stated that she left the room at any time. As a matter of fact, I have never been in Miss Barrow's room alone from the 1st September until the date of death. On 4th September it is stated that I went up to speak to Miss Barrow, to remonstrate with Miss Barrow about leaving her room. I did go up on that occasion to remonstrate with Miss Barrow about leaving her room, but I was not alone; my wife was with me. I do not know when my wife stated she was not. It is not true. She did not state it. I do not know she stated it; I do not believe she was ever questioned upon the point.

I should also like to state that there has been no witnesses called respecting my possession of the jewellery previous to the death of Miss Barrow. There are witnesses respecting my being in possession of this jewellery. There is an independent witness.

It has been stated by the prosecution that Miss Barrow was devotedly attached to the boy, Ernest Grant. It has been pressed home to the jury by the prosecution that Miss Barrow was very devotedly attached to the boy—that she intended to make him her heir. There has been no witnesses brought forward by the defence to contradict that assertion. I contradict it, for Miss Barrow had repeatedly shaken the boy in the street, and she has from time to time in the home shaken him and shouted at him, and woke us up in the morning shouting at him when she has been getting him ready for school. It has been stated on one occasion, and one occasion only, did she threaten to throw herself out of the window in consequence of the annoyance that the boy gave her. There is witnesses to prove that this kind of thing went on between Miss Barrow and the boy, and even to the extent that she said it was getting [inaudible]. That was Robert Hook that gave evidence.

I venture to say that my position in this case is this: I am surrounded by a set of circumstances from which there seems no way of extricating

Justice Bucknill's Summing Up.

F. H. Seddon.

myself if I am condemned on circumstantial evidence. It seems to me that various points that might be in my favour perhaps have not been given sufficient consideration to. I say in this way, that had Miss Barrow thrown herself out through the bedroom window, this set of circumstances would be just the same. I would have been believed to have thrown her out or pushed her out through the window. Had Miss Barrow fallen downstairs the same thing would have applied. If she had been killed, Mr. Seddon had such interest in the matter he would have thrown her downstairs. When she went to Southend-on-Sea, had she have fallen into the sea Mr. Seddon would have pushed her into the sea. The same set of circumstances would have operated against me. I can see through it.

There is another point I would like to mention. My wife found a bottle of gin in her bedroom after her death. That has never been mentioned in the evidence. We do not know where Miss Barrow got that bottle of gin from. It was half-full of gin. We do not know what was in the gin. We know that it was only half-full. This inquiry did not take place for fully two months after the woman was buried; therefore we do not know what she was possessed of. Evidence has not been given that all the bottles that were in Miss Barrow's room were taken away—made a present of to the charwoman, so she " could get a few ha'pence," as she called it, to get a bit of food for her children. We do not know what bottles Miss Barrow had or what they contained. We have not the slightest idea as to whether Miss Barrow committed suicide or not.

I should like to put at this point that you referred in your summing up, my lord, to the jury, that Dr. Willcox has stated that a dose would produce violent pains in half an hour, or something like half an hour, after it had been taken or administered. You have heard in evidence that while I am at the theatre Miss Barrow has called out, " I am dying "—that is supposed to have been at twelve o'clock. If that statement is true (I made a note of it when it was mentioned) that violent pains would ensue half an hour after the dose being taken, there is that possibility that the woman had taken a dose of arsenic, and it had begun to operate with these violent pains, and she calls out " I am dying." Otherwise why should she say " I am dying " when she had the same pain off and on from the 1st or 2nd September to the 14th? Then earlier in the morning she states again, " I am going." All this is quite clear to me when I come to look at the evidence. As I stated before, it was a puzzle to me how she could get arsenic, but when I come to look at it, and think it over, it seems to me that that woman knew she was dying, she knew she was going, and therefore she must have had a reason for saying she was going.

Regarding what Maggie, my daughter, said in her evidence in the box that she was pressed by Detective Ward for her explanation of her purchase of fly-papers. I understand her clearly to say that from the way the question was put to her she said, " I did not buy fly-papers," and she meant, as she explained there, that she did not " get them." That was her explanation—she did not get them. She may have gone to purchase them at Price's, on the instructions of Mr. Saint, the solicitor, which I am not concerned about; it is after I am arrested. But my daughter has been terrorised evidently by Inspector Ward into the state-ment. She has already contradicted that she ever bought them at

Trial of the Seddons.

Thorley's. Then he comes round to the question of whether she bought them at Price's, and so he gets her in a moment of thoughtlessness—misunderstanding his question—to say "No." He takes advantage of that opportunity for to get her signature to it.

It has not been stated in the evidence, my lord, that Detective-Inspector Ward after arresting me went to my home and tried to terrorise my wife into making statements. I have only my wife's word for it; I was not there as a witness, but she stated that Detective Ward tried in every possible way to terrorise her into making statements, and telling her what trouble she would get into if she did not admit this and did not admit that. If he can be capable of doing a thing like that—and, further, he said, when he found he could not get her to agree to the statement he suggested to her, he said, "I have not done with you yet."

You have also referred, my lord, to the letter that I sent to the Vonderahes after her death wherein I omit to state anything at all regarding money. I thought I pointed out in the witness-box that at that moment when I wrote that letter, the search having been made in the box, there was no money to mention. I had not had the money. The prosecution has never traced the money to me. The prosecution has not traced anything to me in the shape of money, which is the great motive suggested by the prosecution in this case for my committing the diabolical crime of which I declare before the Great Architect of the Universe I am not guilty, my lord. Anything more I might have to say I do not suppose will be of any account, but, still, if it is the last words that I speak, I am not guilty of the crime for which I stand committed.

Sentence.

The judge having assumed the black cap, and the chaplain having been summoned,

AN USHER OF THE COURT—Oyez! Oyez! Oyez! My lords the King's Justices do strictly charge and command all persons to keep silence while sentence of death is passing upon the prisoner at the bar, upon pain of imprisonment. God save the King!

Mr. JUSTICE BUCKNILL—Frederick Henry Seddon, you have been found guilty of the wilful murder of Eliza Mary Barrow. With that verdict I am bound to say I agree. I should be more than terribly pained if I thought that I, in my charge to the jury, had stated anything against you that was not supported by the evidence. But even if what you say is strictly correct, that there is no evidence that you ever were left at a material time alone in the room with the deceased person, there is still in my opinion ample evidence to show that you had the opportunity of putting poison into her food or into her medicine. You have a motive for this crime; that motive was the greed of gold. Whether it was that you wanted to put an end to the annuities or not, I know not—you only can know. Whether it was to get the gold that was or was not, but which you thought was, in the cash box, I do not know. But I think I do know this, that you wanted to make a great pecuniary profit by felonious means. This murder has been described by yourself in the box as one

Sentence.

which, if made out against you, was a barbarous one—a murder of design, a cruel murder. It is not for me to harrow your feelings.

The PRISONER (F. H. SEDDON)—It does not affect me. I have a clear conscience.

Mr. JUSTICE BUCKNILL—I have very little more to say, except to remind you that you have had a very fair and patient trial. Your learned counsel, who has given his undivided time to this case, has done everything that a counsel at the English bar could do. The Attorney-General has conducted this case with remarkable fairness, and the jury have shown a patience and intelligence I have never seen exceeded by any jury with which I have had to do. I, as minister of the law, have now to pass upon you that sentence which the law demands has to be passed, which is that you have forfeited your life in consequence of your great crime. Try to make peace with your Maker.

The PRISONER (F. H. SEDDON)—I am at peace.

Mr. JUSTICE BUCKNILL—From what you have said, you and I know we both belong to one brotherhood, and it is all the more painful to me to have to say what I am saying. But our brotherhood does not encourage crime; on the contrary, it condemns it. I pray you again to make your peace with the Great Architect of the Universe. Mercy—pray for it, ask for it. It may be some consolation to you to know that I agree with the verdict that the jury has passed with regard to your wife. But that does not make it better for you. Whatever she has done that was blame-worthy in this case, short of any criminal offence, if there was anything I feel that she did to help you, not to murder, but, it may be, at some time to deal improperly with these notes——

The PRISONER (F. H. SEDDON)—She done nothing wrong, sir.

Mr. JUSTICE BUCKNILL—I am satisfied that the jury have done well and rightly in acquitting her. I am satisfied that they have done justice to you. And now I have to pass sentence.

The sentence of the Court is that you be taken from hence to a lawful prison, and from thence to a place of execution, and that you be there hanged by the neck until you are dead; and that your body be buried within the precincts of the prison in which you shall have been confined after your conviction; and may the Lord have mercy on your soul!

The CHAPLAIN—Amen.

The prisoner having been removed—

Mr. JUSTICE BUCKNILL—Gentlemen of the jury, in consideration of the time which has been occupied in this case, you are excused from serving on a jury for a period of ten years.

[END OF THE TRIAL.]

APPENDICES.

APPENDIX A.

(Exhibit 24.)

63 Tollington Park,
August 8th, 1910.

Miss Barrow,—As you are so impudent to send the letter to hand, I wish to inform you that I shall require the return of my late Mother's and Sister's furniture, and the expense of my moving here and away.—Yours,

R. D. HOOK.

P.S.—I shall have to take Erny with me as it's not safe to leave him with you and he not to go out again to-night.   R. D. HOOK.

APPENDIX AI.

31 Evershot Road, Tollington Park, N.,
24th March, 1910.

Messrs. Frere & Co.

Dear Sirs,

Re BUCK'S HEAD.

I beg to acknowledge receipt of your letter of 14 March, 1910.
My relative who advises me has referred to sub-section 3 of section 3 of the Licensing Act, 1904, of which you speak, and he informs me that as my lease is of the same term within a few days as that of my tenant, I am entitled to deduct as follows:—

For 1905, 11 per cent. of £50, -	-	-	-	£5 10 0	
1906, 12 per cent. of £30, -	-	-	-	3 12 0	
1907, 13 per cent. of £40, -	-	-	-	5 4 0	
1908, 14 per cent. of £40, -	-	-	-	5 12 0	
1909, 15 per cent. of £40,			-	6 0 0	
				£25 18 0	

This will more than balance any rent due for more than 12 months.

Yours truly,
E. M. BARROW.

Appendices.

APPENDIX B.

(Exhibit 1.)

63 Tollington Park, London, N.
14th Septr., 1911.

Mr. Frank E. Vonderahe.

Dear Sir,—I sincerely regret to have to inform you of the death of your Cousin, Miss Eliza Mary Barrow, at 6 a.m. this morning, from epidemic diarrhœa. The funeral will take place on Saturday next about 1 to 2 p.m.

Please inform Albert Edward and Emma Marion Vonderahe of her decease, and let me know if you or they wish to attend the funeral.

I must also inform you that she made a " will " on the 11th instant leaving what she died possessed of to Hilda and Ernest Grant, and appointed myself as sole Executor under the " will."—Yours respectfully,

F. H. Seddon.

Mr. Frank Ernest Vonderahe,
   31 Evershot Road,
      Finsbury Park, N.

APPENDIX C.

(Exhibit 3.)

63 Tollington Park, London, N.,
21st Septr., 1911.

To the relatives of the late (Miss) Eliza Mary Barrow, who died Sept. 14th instant at the above address, from epidemic diarrhœa, certified by Dr. Sworn, 5 Highbury Crescent, Highbury, N. (Duration of illness, 10 days.)

As Executor under the " will " of Miss Barrow, dated Septr. 11th, 1911, I hereby certify that Miss Barrow has left all she died possessed of to Hilda and Ernest Grant, and appointed me as sole executor to hold in trust until they become of age. Her properties and investments she disposed of through Solicitors and Stock Exchange Brokers about October and December 1910 last to purchase a life annuity (which she has received monthly up to the time of her death), and the annuity died with her. She stated in writing that she did not wish any of her relatives to receive any benefit at her death, and during her last illness declined to have any relations called in to see her, stating they had treated her badly and had not considered her, and she would not consider them She has simply left furniture, jewellery and clothing.

(Sd.)   F. H. Seddon.
(Executor.)

APPENDIX D.

(Exhibit 4.)

This is the Last Will and Testament of Me, Eliza Mary Barrow, of 63 Tollington Park, Finsbury Park, in the County of London, N. I Hereby Revoke all former wills and codicils, and in the event of my decease I Give and Bequeath all my household furniture, jewellery, and other personal effects to Hilda Grant and Ernest Grant and appoint Frederick Henry Seddon of

Trial of the Seddons.

63 Tollington Park, London, N., SOLE EXECUTOR of this my Will to hold all my personal belongings, furniture, clothing and jewellery in trust until the aforesaid Hilda Grant and Ernest Grant become of age (as they are at this date Minors). Then for him to distribute as equally as possible all my personal belongings comprising jewellery, furniture and clothing, to them or to sell for cash any article of furniture or clothing either of them do not desire and equally distribute the cash so realized, but no article of jewellery must be sold.

SIGNED this *eleventh* day of *September*, One thousand nine hundred and eleven.   ELIZA MARY BARROW.

Witness: Margaret Ann Seddon (Mrs.).
Witness: William Seddon (Senior).

APPENDIX E.

(Exhibit 5.)

(Memorial Card.)

In ever Loving memory

of

Eliza Mary Barrow,

who departed this life Sept. 14th, 1911,

Aged 49 years.

Interred in Islington Cemetery, East Finchley.
Grave No. 19453, sec. 2.

A dear one is missing and with us no more,
    That voice so much loved we hear not again,
Yet we think of you now the same as of yore,
    And know you are free from trouble and pain.

---- .

APPENDIX F.

(Exhibit 7.)

63 Tollington Park, N.,
27th March, 1911.

To Mr. F. H. Seddon.

Dear Mr. Seddon,—My only nearest living relatives are first cousins; their names and addresses are Frank Ernest Vonderahe, 31 Evershot Road, N.; Albert Edward Vonderahe, 82a Geldiston Road, Upper Clapton; Emma Marion Vonderahe, Gorringe Park Hotel, Clapton (or Clapham) Common, and it is not my will or wish that they, or any other relation of mine, should receive anything belonging to me at my death, or receive any benefit whatever at my decease, they have not been kind to me, or considered me.—Yours sincerely,
ELIZA MARY BARROW.

Appendices.

APPENDIX G.

(Exhibit 39.)

(Copy Mem. in prisoner's handwriting, found among papers taken from his house by police.)

£10 Cash found at Miss Barrow's death.

STATEMENT OF HOW UTILISED

Board for Ernest Grant—2 weeks at 10s.,	£1 0	0
Milk Bill, - - - - - -	6	6½
14 days at 1s. per day due to Maggie, -	14	0
7s. 6d. tips to bearers & grave-diggers & £4 funeral,	7	6
Doctor's bill, - - - - - -	5	0
Ernie's Holiday Southend on Sea, - - - -	2	6
,, Pocket Money, - - - - - -	2	0
,, Fare, - - - - - - - -	1	9
Death "Probate" Certificate, - - - -	3	7
Inventory, - - - - -	1	0
Woman for laying out, &c., cleaning rooms, -	5	0
Suit of clothes, &c. (Pants extra), for Ernie, -	13	0
	£11 1	10½

APPENDIX H.

LETTER WRITTEN BY SEDDON TO HIS WIFE ON THE EVE OF HIS EXECUTION.

H.M. Prison, Pentonville, 16 April, 1912.

My Dear Wife Margaret x x x x x x
  Love and kisses to all my Children x x x x x x x x
  Special for Ada and Baby Lily x x x x x x

I have just received your most welcome letter, though it is undated and I cannot tell when you wrote it, and you did not put the number of the house.* I am surprised to hear of the early arrival of Sister Agnes and Uncle Fred and Aunt Annie, and note they will be here to see me to-day. I heard from the Governor that I was to have visitors from Liverpool to-day, but I did not know who. What a great and alarming surprise for you to be knocked up at 1 a.m. midnight. I suppose you thought it was the King's Messenger with a free pardon, or myself suddenly released; however I am glad to know you have visitors to relieve your mind of the great strain and break the monotony. Many a good time I have had with Uncle Fred, and my mind goes back to the happy few days we spent together in the Isle of Man with him. It does not do to think of the past with such a future before you, and I have to dismiss all such thoughts from my mind, and I now await the interview with them, and I will strive to make it as pleasant as possible to them; it only causes pain and anguish if they found I was down in the dumps, and that is not so. I am still cheerful, and will be till the last, thanks to a clear conscience which sustains me, and this brings me to another important matter I wish to prepare you against. You remember in Crippen's case how false reports went about, and how he was supposed to have made a confession of his guilt; all kinds of tales and rumours, and false statements do get about, and if you should see anything in the papers which you know is not true,

---

*Mrs. Seddon had removed from Tollington Park.—ED

Trial of the Seddons.

instantly deny it. Believe nothing unless you first see it in my very own hand-writing, and signed by me, and believe nothing whatever that may be told to you by anyone, no matter who it is. I have nothing to confess, and the following will be my "final" statement, and believe nothing to the contrary, and instantly deny anything to the contrary.

THIS IS MY "FINAL" STATEMENT, I SWEAR BEFORE GOD IT IS THE TRUTH.

I am Not Guilty of the Murder of Eliza Mary Barrow. I swear that I have never purchased arsenic in my life in any shape or form, neither have I at any time instructed, directed, or influenced the purchase of arsenic. I did not administer arsenic to her in any shape or form, or any other poison, neither did I advise, direct, instruct, or influence the administration of arsenic, or any other form of poison to the deceased. And I further swear that I had no knowledge that she died from arsenical poisoning; I believed she died from epidemic diarrhœa—as per Dr. Sworn's certificate. I solemnly swear before my Creator, to Whom all secrets are revealed, that this is a true statement, and the Law, in its seeming blindness and misguided justice, has condemned an Innocent Man.

F. H. SEDDON.

This you may let all my children, all my family, and relatives read that they may know, if they see anything to the contrary, that no reliance may be placed upon it. If I cannot prove my innocence, no more than the prosecution could establish my guilt, still, while I have breath, I shall protest it in the sight of God.

I will now surprise you by a chapter of incidents since my arrest that will make you all wonder whether

THE NUMBER 13 IS UNLUCKY.

In my case it certainly appears so!

Miss Barrow came to my house August, 1910. Died Sept. 1911.	Months 13
Took ill Sept. 1st. Died Sept. 14th.	Days 13
I arrested Dec. 4th. Old Bailey trial, March 4th.	Weeks 13
Attended Inquest twice. Police Court 11 times.	Total 13
Appeal heard April 1st (13th week in New Year).	13
Grounds of appeal. 13 points of law on appeal paper made by Solicitor.	13
Reprieve papers to be sent in to Solicitor as arranged by him.	April 13
Left Brixton Prison in Van (several times) with 13 Prisoners.	13
Returned to Brixton Prison with 13 Prisoners.	13
Been with 19 Prisoners and position changed, placing me 13th in line.	13
Exercised several occasions at Brixton with 13 prisoners.	13
Sat at meal table in Hospital Ward, Brixton Prison. 13 at table.	13
Repeatedly found myself with the number 13 prisoners in Hospital Ward.	13
Official Number given to me on arrival at Pentonville, 13,990.	13
Cash in hand at Pentonville belonging to me 6s. 6d. (Sixpences 13).	13
Sent Wife a letter, and inadvertently placed a number of crosses as kisses. Counted	13
Sent Young Daughter Ada a note with 7 kisses. She replied with 6.	
	Total 13
I made this out on Good Friday, April 5th, and found, on reflection, that it was just 13 days to date fixed for execution, 18 April.	13

This will be considered by many people as a mere chapter of coincidences, and I would add that the set of circumstances that has surrounded my case, which has been the means of my conviction, are just as strange, and are a mere chapter of coincidences on which a perfectly innocent or business interpretation could have been placed, but on which the prosecution placed the worst possible construction, and thus secured my conviction.

There it is. Strange but true. Now I must close with Sincere Love and Best Wishes. God Bless You All. Love to Father.

Your Affectionate and Innocent Husband,

FRED.

[The foregoing occupies all the space allotted for writing on the prison paper, but inter-written between two of the pages, and underlined, are the words, "Bring Baby to-morrow."]

Appendices.

APPENDIX J.

COURT OF CRIMINAL APPEAL.

1-2 April, 1912.

(Before Mr. Justice Darling, Mr. Justice Channel, and Mr. Justice Coleridge.)

The prisoner, Frederick Henry Seddon, who was represented by Mr. E. Marshall Hall, K.C., M.P., appealed from his sentence.

GROUNDS OF APPEAL.

1. There was not sufficient evidence that Miss Barrow died of acute arsenical poisoning.
2. There was no evidence that I ever was in possession of arsenic.
3. There was no evidence that I ever administered arsenic to Miss Barrow.
4. The evidence of Walter Thorley as to purchase of fly-papers on the 26th day of August, 1911, by my daughter Margaret was inadmissible.
5. The evidence of identification of my daughter Margaret by Walter Thorley was insufficient and untrustworthy.
6. The statement of my daughter Margaret, dated the 2nd day of February, 1912, was improperly obtained by Chief Inspector Ward.
7. The evidence as to my wife having cashed bank notes was inadmissible as against me, but the learned judge omitted to point this out to the jury.
8. My wife and I were jointly charged with murder; the evidence was directed equally against both of us, and there was no evidence upon which the jury could discriminate between us. The verdict is therefore unreasonable and cannot be supported having regard to the evidence.
9. The learned judge misdirected the jury when he said, "So there was a time when the wife left the husband with the deceased woman."
10. The learned judge omitted to point out to the jury that my wife was called as a witness for me, and that her evidence, if they believed it, went to establish my innocence no less than her own.
11. The learned judge omitted to point out to the jury that the presence of Mrs. Longley in my house was an important matter in my favour.
12. The learned judge omitted to caution the jury that my conduct after the death of Miss Barrow pointed to guilt of larceny only, and not to guilt of murder.
13. The learned judge was wrong in ruling that there was evidence of murder to go to the jury.

After hearing arguments by Mr. Marshall Hall, their lordships retired for a short time, and on their return into Court the following judgment was delivered by Mr. Justice Darling:—

JUDGMENT.

In this case the appellant was indicted jointly with his wife for the murder of Miss Barrow, and after a ten days' trial, and the giving of a large amount of evidence, the wife was found not guilty and the prisoner was found guilty and sentenced to death. Against this verdict he appeals.

We think that before dealing with the points raised it is necessary that we should state what are the powers of this Court under the Act. The powers of the Court do not amount to a re-hearing of the case; we interfere only if there has been a wrong judgment on a point of law, or if the verdict of the jury, having regard to all the evidence in a case, is unreasonable in point of fact, or if on a general view of the case in law and fact it appears that there has been a mis-carriage of justice.

Various points have been taken for the appellant in this case; the first is that there was not sufficient evidence that Miss Barrow died of acute arsenical poisoning. In the opinion of the Court there was ample, and in fact, conclusive, evidence that she did die from that cause. Secondly, that there was no evidence that the appellant was ever in possession of arsenic or ever administered arsenic to Miss Barrow. That is true, but such evidence as that was not essential; had evidence been forthcoming that he was seen to give her arsenic with his own

Trial of the Seddons.

hand, and that she died within a short time thereafter, it would not have been a case of circumstantial, but of direct, evidence. The next point is that the evidence of identification of Maggie Seddon by Thorley was insufficient and untrustworthy; but that was evidence which was fairly left to jury, and the question was decided by them; their decision was not unreasonable, and the Court cannot interfere on this ground. The next point made was that the evidence of Mrs. Seddon having cashed bank notes was inadmissible as against the appellant, but that the judge omitted to point out this to the jury; it is enough to say that sufficient connection between the wife and husband as to the affairs of Miss Barrow was shown to make the evidence admissible. A great point has been made here that the wife was called as a witness for the appellant, so she could be asked anything that could be asked of any other witness for the defence; the questions were perfectly legitimate.

Then it was said that the wife and the appellant were jointly charged with murder; that the evidence was directed equally against both, and there was no evidence on which the jury could discriminate between them, and that the verdict was therefore unreasonable; it was further said that the judge omitted to point out to the jury that if they believed Mrs. Seddon's evidence it went to establish the appellant's innocence no less than her own. It is necessary that we should make clear the logical effect of the verdict. Both prisoners were given in charge of the jury, Mrs. Seddon was found not guilty and the appellant guilty; that meant as to the appellant that he did, either by his own hand, or by the hand of another, administer arsenic fatally to Miss Barrow with the intent that she should die, and as to Mrs. Seddon that it was not proved that she administered the poison, or that, if she did, it was not proved that she did so knowing it was poison and intending to kill. It is a mistake to say that it means she had nothing to do with the affair; in this country there are no means of expressing in a verdict the difference between "innocent" and "not proved guilty." The fallacy is shown in this case by this; it was insisted over and over again that the onus was on the Crown to prove the case; if so, the verdict as to the wife necessarily means that the case has not been proved, though it may mean more. When that is considered it is apparent that there is nothing illogical in acquitting the wife for want of proof and convicting the husband. There may be evidence against him which did not bear against her. Again, with regard to her being called as a witness on his behalf. She gave evidence, but we cannot say how much of it the jury believed; it does not follow that they believed it all; it is seldom that a witness with a strong interest tells the whole truth and nothing but the truth. So there is no logical dilemma in acquitting the wife and not the husband.

The next point is that the judge omitted to point out to the jury that the appellant's conduct after the death of Miss Barrow pointed to guilt of larceny only, and not to guilt of murder. If the judge had told the jury so it would have been a misdirection. It is untrue to say it only pointed to larceny; it was for the jury to say from all his actions what it was that the appellant wished to conceal; his omission to notify Miss Barrow's decease to the Vonderahes (for it is incredible that he really sent them a letter; the production of a copy is almost enough to make the jury disbelieve this); the fact that he did not publish the death in the papers; the hurried way in which the funeral was arranged, were all evidence that he desired to conceal the fact that Miss Barrow died of arsenic, and that he thought the sooner she was put out of the way the better.

There was no point of law here on which any wrong decision was given, so it only remains for us to deal with the main point raised, that the judge was wrong in ruling that there was evidence of murder to go to the jury. In our opinion there was ample evidence at that point. It is true that as the case proceeded the case for the prosecution was much strengthened by the cross-examination of the appellant, but the judge was right to leave the case to the jury. The case having been left fairly to them, the jury found him guilty. It must never be supposed that, because a particular point is not referred to by a judge, that point is not in the minds of the jury. It is true that there are points which it is desirable should have been within the consideration of the jury, and to which allusions cannot be found in the summing up, but we are satisfied that these points were not absent from the consideration of the jury. The jury must have had it in mind when Mrs. Seddon gave evidence that it was evidence to which they must have regard in deciding on their verdict in Seddon's case. She

Appendices.

was called on behalf of Seddon, so this must have been impressed on the minds of the jury.[1] If the judge did not mention it, it was because it was unnecessary to do so. The Court has no reason to think that the jury were wrong in coming to the conclusion they did come to. Then is there any ground for saying that the verdict was unreasonable? The Court cannot say so. The main point differentiating this case from certain other circumstantial cases of poisoning is that no poison was traced to the physical, manual possession of the appellant; it was traced to the house, but there is no evidence that it was put by Seddon into anything that Miss Barrow took. But the absence of that evidence does not justify us in saying that the jury were unreasonable in giving the verdict they did.

Beyond doubt Miss Barrow died of arsenical poisoning, and the appellant had a strong motive for killing her, as he had, by means which could not be described as commendable, become possessed of all her property, and had given her nothing of any value in return but the promise of an annuity at the rate of £1 a week.[2] If this sum was above the market rate the motive was stronger than if it had been a purely business transaction. On these grounds, and on the grounds that his conduct on the night of her death was that of a man anticipating her death; that he did not do the natural thing, namely, go to fetch the doctor, and that immediately after the death he was found[3] looking for what money was left in her room; that three days before her death he made a will constituting himself executor, and therefore in control of her property; that he never notified the relatives of the death, and that he arranged the burial with extreme haste, and not in the natural way—for although he had in his possession a document which showed that she had a right to be buried in a vault, yet he handed her over to a common grave and invited no one to the funeral; on all these grounds it may be said that the verdict was not unreasonable. There was no one of whom it was suggested by the defence that they might have poisoned Miss Barrow, and the suggestion that she committed suicide either purposely or accidentally has not been seriously contended, and is a hypothesis no jury would be likely to adopt. In all these circumstances, although no manual possession of the poison by appellant was shown, the jury came to the conclusion that the case was proved. There was evidence on which they could legally and reasonably so find, and the Court does not desire to indicate that it would have come to any other conclusion. There is therefore no power for this Court to interfere with the verdict, and the appeal is dismissed.

APPENDIX K.

NOTE ON THE CASE BY FREDERICK HENRY SEDDON.

It has dawned upon me that after I took those notes (£25 out of Bedroom safe to Bank) that I replaced the £25 by taking £20 gold from Office Safe and £5 I had loose cash, thus bringing up the amount in bedroom safe to £100 again, and leaving only £80 in office safe. Later £10 was taken from Bedroom safe to pay annuity to deceased and I had not replaced it at time of her death so that left £90 in Bedroom safe.

I complied with the wishes of the deceased, carried out my obligations and kept boy 10 weeks after death till Police took him away.

Had cash £1520 & did not pay off mortgage £200 on my house.

Purchased 14 houses with cash as greater security for her & thus bound myself to London so I could not get away readily if I had wanted to.

At Inquest learned body was exhumed and yet attended same & freely gave evidence *re* my financial transactions with deceased, inquest adjourned for 21 days for Home Office expert to analyse intestines, yet as *innocent man* knowing this I went about business as usual expecting nothing to happen & surprised at

---

[1] It was in fact pointed out by Mr. Marshall Hall.—ED.
[2] The annuity amounted to £4 a week.—ED.
[3] He went for the doctor first, and searched for the money afterwards.—ED.

result of analysis & arrest. Did not attempt in any way to avoid arrest, did not attempt to dispose of properties transferred to me by deceased, *improved the investments & all is still intact* & not depreciated, but greatly improved in value, returning double what the deceased previously received from it.

I do not benefit under "Will" that is left to two children, no relatives of deceased. I only intended it to be a temporary "Will" & intended to take it to a Solicitor & have a proper one drawn up from it for her signature but her death took place unexpectedly. I intended to go & visit Mr. Keeble with it & see him some time about £5 he owed me.

Deceased died about 6 to 6.30 a.m. & my assistants stated I counted £100 or £200 in gold about 9 p.m. *same night,* my *bedroom* safe is in room just below hers, therefore I would not be likely to take *her* money so far down to my office *in basement* & then wait all day till late at night to count "Stolen" (?) money in the presence of my assistants. (If Notes were stolen, deceased would have missed them, especially so many over a period of 11 months.) The deceased only kept the boy "Grant" for her own selfish ends & convenience.

There was no motive for me to commit such a crime, I would have to be a greedy inhuman monster, or be suffering from a degenerate or deranged mind, as I was in good financial circumstances, 21 years in one employ, a good position, a good home with every comfort, a wife, 5 children & aged Father (73) depending on me, my income just on £15 per week to pay the deceased the small annuity of £2 8s. 0. weekly & out of this my daughter received 7s. weekly and on death of the deceased I to keep & clothe the boy which is equal to 13s. weekly. So I should only gain 28s. weekly by the death of the deceased. Surely an insufficient motive for one in my circumstances in life, & to take such a risk as to administer poison under the nose of Doctor attending every day & he even testing the vomit & motion of deceased. It was in every way to my advantage for the deceased to have lived at least several years.

Printed by BoD`in Norderstedt, Germany